MURDER·ON·THE

ORIENT

EXPRESS

AND OTHER

HERCULE·POIROT

MYSTERIES

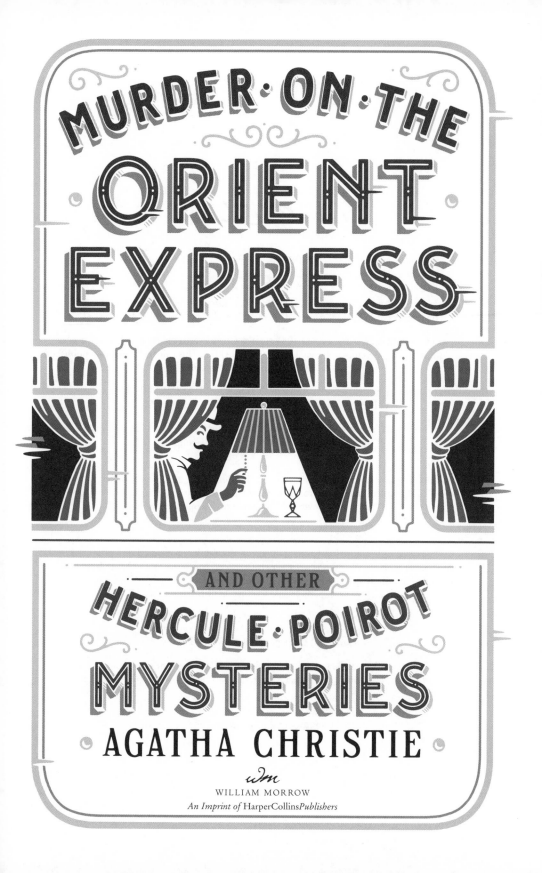

MURDER·ON·THE ORIENT EXPRESS

AND OTHER

HERCULE·POIROT MYSTERIES

AGATHA CHRISTIE

WILLIAM MORROW
An Imprint of HarperCollins*Publishers*

Agatha Christie

www.agathachristie.com

Cover and endpaper designs by Jim Tierney.

HarperCollins books may be purchased for educational, business, or sales promotional use. For information please email the Special Markets Department at SPsales@harpercollins.com.

ISBN: 978-0-06-267805-8

17 18 19 20 21 DIX/SC 10 9 8 7 6 5 4 3 2 1

CONTENTS

MURDER ON THE ORIENT EXPRESS

1

THE MURDER OF ROGER ACKROYD

217

CURTAIN: POIROT'S LAST CASE

443

MURDER ON THE ORIENT EXPRESS

To M.E.L.M. Arpachiya, 1933

Contents

Part One

The Facts

1 An Important Passenger on the Taurus Express   9

2 The Tokatlian Hotel   17

3 Poirot Refuses a Case   24

4 A Cry in the Night   31

5 The Crime   35

6 A Woman?   45

7 The Body   52

8 The Armstrong Kidnapping Case   61

Part Two

The Evidence

1 The Evidence of the Wagon Lit Conductor   67

2 The Evidence of the Secretary   73

3 The Evidence of the Valet   78

4 The Evidence of the American Lady   83

5 The Evidence of the Swedish Lady   90

6 The Evidence of the Russian Princess   95

7 The Evidence of Count and Countess Andrenyi   101

8 The Evidence of Colonel Arbuthnot   106

9 The Evidence of Mr. Hardman   113

10 The Evidence of the Italian   119

11 The Evidence of Miss Debenham   123

12 The Evidence of the German Lady's Maid   128

13 Summary of the Passengers' Evidence   134

14 The Evidence of the Weapon   141

15 The Evidence of the Passengers' Luggage   148

Part Three

Hercule Poirot Sits Back and Thinks

1 Which of Them?   163

2 Ten Questions   169

3 Certain Suggestive Points   174

4 The Grease Spot on a Hungarian Passport   181

5 The Christian Name of Princess Dragomiroff   187

6 A Second Interview with Colonel Arbuthnot   191

7 The Identity of Mary Debenham   194

8 Further Surprising Revelations   198

9 Poirot Propounds Two Solutions   204

PART ONE
THE FACTS

One

An Important Passenger on the Taurus Express

It was five o'clock on a winter's morning in Syria. Alongside the platform at Aleppo stood the train grandly designated in railway guides as the Taurus Express. It consisted of a kitchen and dining car, a sleeping car and two local coaches.

By the step leading up into the sleeping car stood a young French lieutenant, resplendent in uniform, conversing with a small lean man, muffled up to the ears, of whom nothing was visible but a pink-tipped nose and the two points of an upward curled moustache.

It was freezingly cold, and this job of seeing off a distinguished stranger was not one to be envied, but Lieutenant Dubosc performed his part manfully. Graceful phrases fell from his lips in polished French. Not that he knew what it was all about. There had been rumours, of course, as there always were in such cases. The General—*his* General's—temper had grown worse and worse. And then there had come this Belgian stranger—all the way from England, it seemed. There had been a week—a week of curious tensity. And then certain things had happened. A very distinguished officer had committed suicide, another had resigned—anxious faces had suddenly lost their anxiety, certain military precautions were relaxed. And the General—Lieutenant Dubosc's own particular General—had suddenly looked ten years younger.

Dubosc had overheard part of a conversation between him and the stranger.

"You have saved us, *mon cher*," said the General emotionally, his great white moustache trembling as he spoke. "You have saved the honour of the French Army—you have averted much bloodshed! How can I thank you for acceding to my request? To have come so far—"

To which the stranger (by name M. Hercule Poirot) had made a fitting reply including the phrase, "But indeed do I not remember that once you saved my life?" And then the General had made another fitting reply to that disclaiming any merit for that past service, and with more mention of France, of Belgium, of glory, of honour and of such kindred things they had embraced each other heartily and the conversation had ended.

As to what it had all been about, Lieutenant Dubosc was still in the dark, but to him had been delegated the duty of seeing off M. Poirot by the Taurus Express, and he was carrying it out with all the zeal and ardour befitting a young officer with a promising career ahead of him.

"Today is Sunday," said Lieutenant Dubosc. "Tomorrow, Monday evening, you will be in Stamboul."

It was not the first time he had made this observation. Conversations on the platform, before the departure of a train, are apt to be somewhat repetitive in character.

"That is so," agreed M. Poirot.

"And you intend to remain there a few days, I think?"

"*Mais oui.* Stamboul, it is a city I have never visited. It would be a pity to pass through—*comme ça.*" He snapped his fingers descriptively. "Nothing presses—I shall remain there as a tourist for a few days."

"La Sainte Sophie, it is very fine," said Lieutenant Dubosc, who had never seen it.

A cold wind came whistling down the platform. Both men shivered. Lieutenant Dubosc managed to cast a surreptitious glance at his watch. Five minutes to five—only five minutes more!

Fancying that the other man had noticed his surreptitious glance, he hastened once more into speech.

"There are few people travelling this time of year," he said, glancing up at the windows of the sleeping car above them.

"That is so," agreed M. Poirot.

"Let us hope you will not be snowed up in the Taurus!"

"That happens?"

"It has occurred, yes. Not this year, as yet."

"Let us hope, then," said M. Poirot. "The weather reports from Europe, they are bad."

"Very bad. In the Balkans there is much snow."

"In Germany too, I have heard."

"Eh bien," said Lieutenant Dubosc hastily as another pause seemed to be about to occur. "Tomorrow evening at seven-forty you will be in Constantinople."

"Yes," said M. Poirot, and went on desperately, "La Sainte Sophie, I have heard it is very fine."

"Magnificent, I believe."

Above their heads the blind of one of the sleeping car compartments was pushed aside and a young woman looked out.

Mary Debenham had had little sleep since she left Baghdad on the preceding Thursday. Neither in the train to Kirkuk, nor in the Rest House at Mosul, nor last night on the train had she slept properly. Now, weary of lying wakeful in the hot stuffiness of her overheated compartment, she got up and peered out.

This must be Aleppo. Nothing to see, of course. Just a long, poor-lighted platform with loud furious altercations in Arabic going on somewhere. Two men below her window were talking French. One was a French officer, the other was a little man with enormous moustaches. She smiled faintly. She had never seen anyone quite so heavily muffled up. It must be very cold outside. That was why they heated the train so terribly. She tried to force the window down lower, but it would not go.

The Wagon Lit conductor had come up to the two men. The train was about to depart, he said. Monsieur had better mount. The little man removed his hat. What an egg-shaped head he had. In spite of her preoccupations Mary Debenham smiled. A ridiculous-looking little man. The sort of little man one could never take seriously.

Lieutenant Dubosc was saying his parting speech. He had thought it out beforehand and had kept it till the last minute. It was a very beautiful, polished speech.

Not to be outdone, M. Poirot replied in kind.

"*En voiture, Monsieur,*" said the Wagon Lit conductor.

With an air of infinite reluctance M. Poirot climbed aboard the train. The conductor climbed after him. M. Poirot waved his hand. Lieutenant Dubosc came to the salute. The train, with a terrific jerk, moved slowly forward.

"*Enfin!*" murmured M. Hercule Poirot.

"Brrrrr," said Lieutenant Dubosc, realizing to the full how cold he was. . . .

II

"*Voilà, Monsieur.*" The conductor displayed to Poirot with a dramatic gesture the beauty of his sleeping compartment and the neat arrangement of his luggage. "The little valise of Monsieur, I have placed it *here*."

His outstretched hand was suggestive. Hercule Poirot placed in it a folded note.

"*Merci, Monsieur.*" The conductor became brisk and businesslike. "I have the tickets of Monsieur. I will also take the passport, please. Monsieur breaks his journey in Stamboul, I understand?"

M. Poirot assented.

"There are not many people travelling, I imagine?" he said.

"No, Monsieur. I have only two other passengers—both English. A Colonel from India, and a young English lady from Baghdad. Monsieur requires anything?"

Monsieur demanded a small bottle of Perrier.

Five o'clock in the morning is an awkward time to board a train. There was still two hours before dawn. Conscious of an inadequate night's sleep, and of a delicate mission successfully accomplished, M. Poirot curled up in a corner and fell asleep.

When he awoke it was half-past nine, and he sallied forth to the restaurant car in search of hot coffee.

There was only one occupant at the moment, obviously the young English lady referred to by the conductor. She was tall, slim and dark—perhaps twenty-eight years of age. There was a kind of cool efficiency in the way she was eating her breakfast and in the way she called to the attendant to bring her more coffee, which bespoke a knowledge of the world and of travelling. She wore a dark-coloured travelling dress of some thin material eminently suitable for the heated atmosphere of the train.

M. Hercule Poirot, having nothing better to do, amused himself by studying her without appearing to do so.

She was, he judged, the kind of young woman who could take care of herself with perfect ease wherever she went. She had poise and efficiency. He rather liked the severe regularity of her features and the delicate pallor of her skin. He liked the burnished black head with its neat waves of hair, and her eyes, cool, impersonal and grey. But she was, he decided, just a little too efficient to be what he called *"jolie femme."*

Presently another person entered the restaurant car. This was a tall man of between forty and fifty, lean of figure, brown of skin, with hair slightly grizzled round the temples.

"The colonel from India," said Poirot to himself.

The newcomer gave a little bow to the girl.

"Morning, Miss Debenham."

"Good morning, Colonel Arbuthnot."

The Colonel was standing with a hand on the chair opposite her.

"Any objection?" he asked.

"Of course not. Sit down."

"Well, you know, breakfast isn't always a chatty meal."

"I should hope not. But I don't bite."

The Colonel sat down.

"Boy," he called in peremptory fashion.

He gave an order for eggs and coffee.

His eyes rested for a moment on Hercule Poirot, but they passed on indifferently. Poirot, reading the English mind correctly, knew that he had said to himself, "Only some damned foreigner."

True to their nationality, the two English people were not chatty. They exchanged a few brief remarks, and presently the girl rose and went back to her compartment.

At lunch time the other two again shared a table and again they both completely ignored the third passenger. Their conversation was more animated than at breakfast. Colonel Arbuthnot talked of the Punjab, and occasionally asked the girl a few questions about Baghdad where it became clear that she had been in a post as governess. In the course of conversation they discovered some mutual friends which had the immediate effect of making them more friendly and less stiff. They discussed old Tommy Somebody and Jerry Someone Else. The Colonel inquired whether she was going straight through to England or whether she was stopping in Stamboul.

"No, I'm going straight on."

"Isn't that rather a pity?"

"I came out this way two years ago and spent three days in Stamboul then."

"Oh, I see. Well, I may say I'm very glad you are going right through, because I am."

He made a kind of clumsy little bow, flushing a little as he did so.

"He is susceptible, our Colonel," thought Hercule Poirot to himself with some amusement. "The train, it is as dangerous as a sea voyage!"

Miss Debenham said evenly that that would be very nice. Her manner was slightly repressive.

The Colonel, Hercule Poirot noticed, accompanied her back to her compartment. Later they passed through the magnificent scenery of the Taurus. As they looked down towards the Cilician Gates, standing in the corridor side by side, a sigh came suddenly from the girl. Poirot was standing near them and heard her murmur:

"It's so beautiful! I wish—I wish—"

"Yes?"

"I wish, I could enjoy it!"

Arbuthnot did not answer. The square line of his jaw seemed a little sterner and grimmer.

"I wish to Heaven you were out of all this," he said.

"Hush, please. Hush."

"Oh! it's all right." He shot a slightly annoyed glance in Poirot's direction. Then he went on: "But I don't like the idea of your being a governess—at the beck and call of tyrannical mothers and their tiresome brats."

She laughed with just a hint of uncontrol in the sound.

"Oh! you mustn't think that. The downtrodden governess is quite an exploded myth. I can assure you that it's the parents who are afraid of being bullied by *me*."

They said no more. Arbuthnot was, perhaps, ashamed of his outburst.

"Rather an odd little comedy that I watch here," said Poirot to himself thoughtfully.

He was to remember that thought of his later.

They arrived at Konya that night about half-past eleven. The two English travellers got out to stretch their legs, pacing up and down the snowy platform.

M. Poirot was content to watch the teeming activity of the station through a window pane. After about ten minutes, however, he decided that a breath of air would not perhaps be a bad thing, after all. He made careful preparations, wrapping himself in several coats and mufflers and encasing his neat boots in goloshes. Thus attired he descended gingerly to the platform and began to pace its length. He walked out beyond the engine.

It was the voices which gave him the clue to the two indistinct figures standing in the shadow of a traffic van. Arbuthnot was speaking.

"Mary—"

The girl interrupted him.

"Not now. Not now. When it's all over. When it's behind us—*then*—"

Discreetly M. Poirot turned away. He wondered.

He would hardly have recognized the cool, efficient voice of Miss Debenham. . . .

"Curious," he said to himself.

The next day he wondered whether, perhaps, they had quarrelled. They spoke little to each other. The girl, he thought, looked anxious. There were dark circles under her eyes.

It was about half-past two in the afternoon when the train came to a halt. Heads were poked out of windows. A little knot of men were clustered by the side of the line looking and pointing at something under the dining car.

Poirot leaned out and spoke to the Wagon Lit conductor who was hurrying past. The man answered and Poirot drew back his head and, turning, almost collided with Mary Debenham who was standing just behind him.

"What is the matter?" she asked rather breathlessly in French. "Why are we stopping?"

"It is nothing, Mademoiselle. It is something that has caught fire under the dining car. Nothing serious. It is put out. They are now repairing the damage. There is no danger, I assure you."

She made a little abrupt gesture, as though she were waving the idea of danger aside as something completely unimportant.

"Yes, yes, I understand that. But the *time!*"

"The time?"

"Yes, this will delay us."

"It is possible—yes," agreed Poirot.

"But we can't afford delay! The train is due in at 6:55 and one has to cross the Bosphorus and catch the Simplon Orient Express the other side at nine o'clock. If there is an hour or two of delay we shall miss the connection."

"It is possible, yes," he admitted.

He looked at her curiously. The hand that held the window bar was not quite steady, her lips too were trembling.

"Does it matter to you very much, Mademoiselle?" he asked.

"Yes. Yes, it does. I—I must catch that train."

She turned away from him and went down the corridor to join Colonel Arbuthnot.

Her anxiety, however, was needless. Ten minutes later the train started again. It arrived at Haydapassar only five minutes late, having made up time on the journey.

The Bosphorus was rough and M. Poirot did not enjoy the crossing. He was separated from his travelling companions on the boat, and did not see them again.

On arrival at the Galata Bridge he drove straight to the Tokatlian Hotel.

Two

The Tokatlian Hotel

At the Tokatlian, Hercule Poirot asked for a room with bath. Then he stepped over to the concierge's desk and inquired for letters.

There were three waiting for him and a telegram. His eyebrows rose a little at the sight of the telegram. It was unexpected.

He opened it in his usual neat, unhurried fashion. The printed words stood out clearly.

"Development you predicted in Kassner Case has come unexpectedly please return immediately."

"Voilà ce qui est embêtant," murmured Poirot vexedly. He glanced up at the clock.

"I shall have to go on tonight," he said to the concierge. "At what time does the Simplon Orient leave?"

"At nine o'clock, Monsieur."

"Can you get me a sleeper?"

"Assuredly, Monsieur. There is no difficulty this time of year. The trains are almost empty. First-class or second?"

"First."

"Très bien, Monsieur. How far are you going?"

"To London."

"Bien, Monsieur. I will get you a ticket to London and reserve your sleeping car accommodation in the Stamboul-Calais coach."

Poirot glanced at the clock again. It was ten minutes to eight.

"I have time to dine?"

"But assuredly, Monsieur."

The little Belgian nodded. He went over and cancelled his room order and crossed the hall to the restaurant.

As he was giving his order to the waiter a hand was placed on his shoulder.

"Ah! *mon vieux,* but this is an unexpected pleasure," said a voice behind him.

The speaker was a short, stout elderly man, his hair cut *en brosse.* He was smiling delightedly.

Poirot sprang up.

"M. Bouc."

"M. Poirot."

M. Bouc was a Belgian, a director of the Compagnie Internationale des Wagons Lits, and his acquaintance with the former star of the Belgian Police Force dated back many years.

"You find yourself far from home, *mon cher,*" said M. Bouc.

"A little affair in Syria."

"Ah! And you return home—when?"

"Tonight."

"Splendid! I, too. That is to say, I go as far as Lausanne, where I have affairs. You travel on the Simplon-Orient, I presume?"

"Yes. I have just asked them to get me a sleeper. It was my intention to remain here some days, but I have received a telegram recalling me to England on important business."

"Ah!" sighed M. Bouc. "*Les affaires—les affaires!* But you—you are at the top of the tree nowadays, *mon vieux!*"

"Some little success I have had, perhaps." Hercule Poirot tried to look modest but failed signally.

Bouc laughed.

"We will meet later," he said.

Hercule Poirot addressed himself to the task of keeping his moustaches out of the soup.

That difficult task accomplished, he glanced round him whilst waiting for the next course. There were only about half a dozen people in the restaurant, and of those half-dozen there were only two that interested Hercule Poirot.

These two sat at a table not far away. The younger was a likeable-looking man of thirty, clearly an American. It was, however, not he but his companion who had attracted the little detective's attention.

He was a man of between sixty and seventy. From a little distance he had the bland aspect of a philanthropist. His slightly bald head, his domed forehead, the smiling mouth that displayed a very white set of false teeth, all seemed to speak of a benevolent personality. Only the eyes belied this assumption. They were small, deep set and crafty. Not only that. As the man, making some remark to his young companion, glanced across the room, his gaze stopped on Poirot for a moment, and just for that second there was a strange malevolence, and unnatural tensity in the glance.

Then he rose.

"Pay the bill, Hector," he said.

His voice was slightly husky in tone. It had a queer, soft, dangerous quality.

When Poirot rejoined his friend in the lounge, the other two men were just leaving the hotel. Their luggage was being brought down. The younger was supervising the process. Presently he opened the glass door and said:

"Quite ready now, Mr. Ratchett."

The elder man grunted an assent and passed out.

"*Eh bien,*" said Poirot. "What do you think of those two?"

"They are Americans," said M. Bouc.

"Assuredly they are Americans. I meant what did you think of their personalities?"

"The young man seemed quite agreeable."

"And the other?"

"To tell you the truth, my friend, I did not care for him. He produced on me an unpleasant impression. And you?"

Hercule Poirot was a moment before replying.

"When he passed me in the restaurant," he said at last, "I had a curious impression. It was as though a wild animal—an animal savage, but savage! you understand—had passed me by."

"And yet he looked altogether of the most respectable."

"*Précisément!* The body—the cage—is everything of the most respectable—but through the bars, the wild animal looks out."

"You are fanciful, *mon vieux*," said M. Bouc.

"It may be so. But I could not rid myself of the impression that evil had passed me by very close."

"That respectable American gentleman?"

"That respectable American gentleman."

"Well," said M. Bouc cheerfully. "It may be so. There is much evil in the world."

At that moment the door opened and the concierge came towards them. He looked concerned and apologetic.

"It is extraordinary, Monsieur," he said to Poirot. "There is not one first-class sleeping berth to be had on the train."

"*Comment?*" cried M. Bouc. "At this time of year? Ah, without doubt there is some party of journalists—of politicians—?"

"I don't know, sir," said the concierge, turning to him respectfully. "But that's how it is."

"Well, well," M. Bouc turned to Poirot. "Have no fear, my friend. We will arrange something. There is always one compartment—the No. 16, which is not engaged. The conductor sees to that!" He smiled, then glanced up at the clock. "Come," he said, "it is time we started."

At the station M. Bouc was greeted with respectful empressement by the brown-uniformed Wagon Lit conductor.

"Good evening, Monsieur. Your compartment is the No. 1."

He called to the porters and they wheeled their load half-way along the carriage on which the tin plates proclaimed its destination:

ISTANBUL TRIESTE CALAIS

"You are full up tonight, I hear?"

"It is incredible, Monsieur. All the world elects to travel tonight!"

"All the same, you must find room for this gentleman here. He is a friend of mine. He can have the No. 16."

"It is taken, Monsieur."

"What? The No. 16?"

A glance of understanding passed between them, and the conductor smiled. He was a tall, sallow man of middle age.

"But yes, Monsieur. As I told you, we are full—full—everywhere."

"But what passes itself?" demanded M. Bouc angrily. "There is a conference somewhere? It is a party?"

"No, Monsieur. It is only chance. It just happens that many people have elected to travel tonight."

M. Bouc made a clicking sound of annoyance.

"At Belgrade," he said, "there will be the slip coach from Athens. There will also be the Bucharest-Paris coach—but we do not reach Belgrade until tomorrow evening. The problem is for tonight. There is no second-class berth free?"

"There *is* a second-class berth, Monsieur—"

"Well, then—"

"But it is a lady's berth. There is already a German woman in the compartment—a lady's maid."

"*Là, là,* that is awkward," said M. Bouc.

"Do not distress yourself, my friend," said Poirot. "I must travel in an ordinary carriage."

"Not at all. Not at all." He turned once more to the conductor. "Everyone has arrived?"

"It is true," said the man, "that there is one passenger who has not yet arrived."

He spoke slowly with hesitation.

"But speak then?"

"No. 7 berth—a second-class. The gentleman has not yet come, and it is four minutes to nine."

"Who is it?"

"An Englishman," the conductor consulted his list. "A M. Harris."

"A name of good omen," said Poirot. "I read my Dickens. M. Harris, he will not arrive."

"Put Monsieur's luggage in No. 7," said M. Bouc. "If this M. Harris arrives we will tell him that he is too late—that berths cannot be retained so long—we will arrange the matter one way or another. What do I care for a M. Harris?"

"As Monsieur pleases," said the conductor.

He spoke to Poirot's porter, directing him where to go.

Then he stood aside the steps to let Poirot enter the train. *"Tout à fait au bout, Monsieur,"* he called. "The end compartment but one."

Poirot passed along the corridor, a somewhat slow progress, as most of the people travelling were standing outside their carriages.

His polite *"Pardons"* were uttered with the regularity of clockwork. At last he reached the compartment indicated. Inside it, reaching up to a suitcase, was the tall young American of the Tokatlian.

He frowned as Poirot entered.

"Excuse me," he said. "I think you've made a mistake." Then, laboriously in French, *"Je crois que vous avez un erreur."*

Poirot replied in English.

"You are Mr. Harris?"

"No, my name is MacQueen. I—"

But at that moment the voice of the Wagon Lit conductor spoke from over Poirot's shoulder. An apologetic, rather breathless voice.

"There is no other berth on the train, Monsieur. The gentleman has to come in here."

He was hauling up the corridor window as he spoke and began to lift in Poirot's luggage.

Poirot noticed the apology in his tone with some amusement. Doubtless the man had been promised a good tip if he could keep the compartment for the sole use of the other traveller. However, even the most munificent of tips lose their effect when a director of the company is on board and issues his orders.

The conductor emerged from the compartment, having swung the suitcases up on to the racks.

"Voilà Monsieur," he said. "All is arranged. Yours is the upper berth, the number 7. We start in one minute."

He hurried off down the corridor. Poirot reentered the compartment.

"A phenomenon I have seldom seen," he said cheerfully. "A Wagon Lit conductor himself puts up the luggage! It is unheard of!"

His fellow traveller smiled. He had evidently got over his annoyance—had probably decided that it was no good to take the matter other than philosophically.

"The train's remarkably full," he said.

A whistle blew, there was a long, melancholy cry from the engine. Both men stepped out into the corridor.

Outside a voice shouted.

"En voiture."

"We're off," said MacQueen.

But they were not quite off. The whistle blew again.

"I say, sir," said the young man suddenly, "if you'd rather have the lower berth—easier, and all that—well, that's all right by me."

"No, no," protested Poirot. "I would not deprive you—"

"That's all right—"

"You are too amiable—"

Polite protests on both sides.

"It is for one night only," explained Poirot. "At Belgrade—"

"Oh, I see. You're getting out at Belgrade—"

"Not exactly. You see—"

There was a sudden jerk. Both men swung round to the window, looking out at the long, lighted platform as it slid slowly past them.

The Orient Express had started on its three-days' journey across Europe.

Three

Poirot Refuses a Case

M. Hercule Poirot was a little late in entering the luncheon-car on the following day. He had risen early, breakfasted almost alone, and had spent the morning going over the notes of the case that was recalling him to London. He had seen little of his travelling companion.

M. Bouc, who was already seated, gesticulated a greeting and summoned his friend to the empty place opposite him. Poirot sat down and soon found himself in the favoured position of the table which was served first and with the choicest morsels. The food, too, was unusually good.

It was not till they were eating a delicate cream cheese that M. Bouc allowed his attention to wander to matters other than nourishment. He was at the stage of a meal when one becomes philosophic.

"Ah!" he sighed. "If I had but the pen of a Balzac! I would depict this scene." He waved his hand.

"It is an idea, that," said Poirot.

"Ah, you agree? It has not been done, I think? And yet—it lends itself to romance, my friend. All around us are people, of all classes, of all nationalities, of all ages. For three days these people, these strangers to one another, are brought together. They sleep and eat under one roof, they cannot get away from each other. At the end of three days they part, they go their several ways, never, perhaps, to see each other again."

"And yet," said Poirot, "suppose an accident—"

"Ah no, my friend—"

"From your point of view it would be regrettable, I agree. But nevertheless let us just for one moment suppose it. Then, perhaps, all these here are linked together—by death."

"Some more wine," said M. Bouc, hastily pouring it out. "You are morbid, *mon cher*. It is, perhaps, the digestion."

"It is true," agreed Poirot, "that the food in Syria was not, perhaps, quite suited to my stomach."

He sipped his wine. Then, leaning back, he ran his eye thoughtfully round the dining car. There were thirteen people seated there and, as M. Bouc had said, of all classes and nationalities. He began to study them.

At the table opposite them were three men. They were, he guessed, single travellers graded and placed there by the unerring judgment of the restaurant attendants. A big, swarthy Italian was picking his teeth with gusto. Opposite him a spare, neat Englishman had the expressionless disapproving face of the well-trained servant. Next to the Englishman was a big American in a loud suit—possibly a commercial traveller.

"You've got to put it over *big*," he was saying in a loud nasal voice.

The Italian removed his toothpick to gesticulate with it freely.

"Sure," he said. "That whatta I say alla de time."

The Englishman looked out of the window and coughed.

Poirot's eye passed on.

At a small table, sitting very upright, was one of the ugliest old ladies he had ever seen. It was an ugliness of distinction—it fascinated rather than repelled. She sat very upright. Round her neck was a collar of very large pearls which, improbable though it seemed, were real. Her hands were covered with rings. Her sable coat was pushed back on her shoulders. A very small expensive black toque was hideously unbecoming to the yellow, toad-like face beneath it.

She was speaking now to the restaurant attendant in a clear, courteous but completely autocratic tone.

"You will be sufficiently amiable to place in my compartment a bottle of mineral water and a large glass of orange juice. You will arrange that I shall have chicken cooked without sauces for dinner this evening—also some boiled fish."

The attendant replied respectfully that it should be done.

She gave a slight gracious nod of the head and rose. Her glance caught Poirot's and swept over him with the nonchalance of the uninterested aristocrat.

"That is Princess Dragomiroff," said M. Bouc in a low tone. "She is a Russian. Her husband realized all this money before the Revolution and invested it abroad. She is extremely rich. A cosmopolitan."

Poirot nodded. He had heard of Princess Dragomiroff.

"She is a personality," said M. Bouc. "Ugly as sin, but she makes herself felt. You agree?"

Poirot agreed.

At another of the large tables Mary Debenham was sitting with two other women. One of them was a tall middle-aged woman in a plaid blouse and tweed skirt. She had a mass of faded yellow hair unbecomingly arranged in a large bun, wore glasses, and had a long, mild, amiable face rather like a sheep. She was listening to the third woman, a stout, pleasant-faced, elderly woman who was talking in a slow clear monotone which showed no signs of pausing for breath or coming to a stop.

". . . And so my daughter said, 'Why,' she said 'you just can't apply Amurrican methods in this country. It's just natural to the folks here to be indolent,' she said. 'They just haven't got any hustle in them.' But all the same you'd be surprised to know what our college there is doing. They've gotten a fine staff of teachers. I guess there's nothing like education. We've got to apply our Western ideals and teach the East to recognize them. My daughter says—"

The train plunged into a tunnel. The calm monotonous voice was drowned.

At the next table, a small one, sat Colonel Arbuthnot—alone. His gaze was fixed upon the back of Mary Debenham's head. They were not sitting together. Yet it could easily have been managed. Why?

Perhaps, Poirot thought, Mary Debenham had demurred. A governess learns to be careful. Appearances are important. A girl with her living to get has to be discreet.

His glance shifted to the other side of the carriage. At the far end, against the wall, was a middle-aged woman dressed in black with a broad expressionless face. German or Scandinavian, he thought. Probably a German lady's maid.

After her came a couple leaning forward and talking animatedly together. The man wore English clothes of loose tweed—but he was not English. Though only the back of his head was visible to Poirot, the shape of it and the set of the shoulders betrayed him. A big man, well made. He turned his head suddenly and Poirot saw his profile. A very handsome man of thirty odd with a big fair moustache.

The woman opposite him was a mere girl—twenty at a guess. A tight-fitting little black coat and skirt, white satin blouse, small chic black toque perched at the fashionable outrageous angle. She had a beautiful foreign-looking face, dead white skin, large brown eyes, jet-black hair. She was smoking a cigarette in a long holder. Her manicured hands had deep red nails. She wore one large emerald set in platinum. There was coquetry in her glance and voice.

"Elle est jolie—et chic," murmured Poirot. "Husband and wife—eh?"

M. Bouc nodded.

"Hungarian Embassy, I believe," he said. "A handsome couple."

There were only two more lunchers—Poirot's fellow traveller MacQueen and his employer Mr. Ratchett. The latter sat facing Poirot, and for the second time Poirot studied that unprepossessing face, noting the false benevolence of the brow and the small, cruel eyes.

Doubtless M. Bouc saw a change in his friend's expression.

"It is at your wild animal you look?" he asked.

Poirot nodded.

As his coffee was brought to him, M. Bouc rose to his feet. Having started before Poirot, he had finished some time ago.

"I return to my compartment," he said. "Come along presently and converse with me."

"With pleasure."

Poirot sipped his coffee and ordered a liqueur. The attendant was passing from table to table with his box of money, accepting payment for bills. The elderly American lady's voice rose shrill and plaintive.

"My daughter said, 'Take a book of food tickets and you'll have no trouble—

no trouble at all.' Now, that isn't so. Seems they have to have a ten per cent tip, and then there's that bottle of mineral water—and a queer sort of water too. They hadn't got any Evian or Vichy, which seems queer to me."

"It is—they must—how you say—serve the water of the country," explained the sheep-faced lady.

"Well, it seems queer to me." She looked distastefully at the heap of small change on the table in front of her. "Look at all this peculiar stuff he's given me. Dinars or something. Just a lot of rubbish, it looks. My daughter said—"

Mary Debenham pushed back her chair and left with a slight bow to the other two. Colonel Arbuthnot got up and followed her. Gathering up her despised money, the American lady followed suit, followed by the lady like a sheep. The Hungarians had already departed. The restaurant car was empty save for Poirot and Ratchett and MacQueen.

Ratchett spoke to his companion, who got up and left the car. Then he rose himself, but instead of following MacQueen he dropped unexpectedly into the seat opposite Poirot.

"Can you oblige me with a light?" he said. His voice was soft—faintly nasal. "My name is Ratchett."

Poirot bowed slightly. He slipped his hand into his pocket and produced a matchbox which he handed to the other man, who took it but did not strike a light.

"I think," he went on, "that I have the pleasure of speaking to M. Hercule Poirot. Is that so?"

Poirot bowed again.

"You have been correctly informed, Monsieur."

The detective was conscious of those strange shrewd eyes summing him up before the other spoke again.

"In my country," he said, "we come to the point quickly. Mr. Poirot, I want you to take on a job for me."

Hercule Poirot's eyebrows went up a trifle.

"My *clientèle*, Monsieur, is limited nowadays. I undertake very few cases."

"Why, naturally, I understand that. But this, Mr. Poirot, means big money." He repeated again in his soft, persuasive voice, "Big money."

Hercule Poirot was silent a minute or two, then he said:

"What is it you wish me to do for you, M.—er—Ratchett?"

"Mr. Poirot, I am a rich man—a very rich man. Men in that position have enemies. I have an enemy."

"Only one enemy?"

"Just what do you mean by that question?" asked Ratchett sharply.

"Monsieur, in my experience when a man is in a position to have, as you say, enemies, then it does not usually resolve itself into one enemy only."

Ratchett seemed relieved by Poirot's answer. He said quickly:

"Why, yes, I appreciate that point. Enemy or enemies—it doesn't matter. What does matter is my safety."

"Safety?"

"My life has been threatened, Mr. Poirot. Now, I'm a man who can take pretty good care of himself." From the pocket of his coat his hand brought a small automatic into sight for a moment. He continued grimly. "I don't think I'm the kind of man to be caught napping. But as I look at it I might as well make assurance doubly sure. I fancy you're the man for my money, Mr. Poirot. And remember—*big* money."

Poirot looked at him thoughtfully for some minutes. His face was completely expressionless. The other could have had no clue as to what thoughts were passing in that mind.

"I regret, Monsieur," he said at length. "I cannot oblige you."

The other looked at him shrewdly.

"Name your figure, then," he said.

Poirot shook his head.

"You do not understand, Monsieur. I have been very fortunate in my profession. I have made enough money to satisfy both my needs and my caprices. I take now only such cases as—interest me."

"You've got a pretty good nerve," said Ratchett. "Will twenty thousand dollars tempt you?"

"It will not."

"If you're holding out for more, you won't get it. I know what a thing's worth to me."

"I also—M. Ratchett."

"What's wrong with my proposition?"

Poirot rose.

"If you will forgive me for being personal—I do not like your face, M. Ratchett," he said.

And with that he left the restaurant car.

Four

A CRY IN THE NIGHT

The Simplon Orient Express arrived at Belgrade at a quarter to nine that evening. It was not due to depart again until 9:15, so Poirot descended to the platform. He did not, however, remain there long. The cold was bitter and though the platform itself was protected, heavy snow was falling outside. He returned to his compartment. The conductor, who was on the platform stamping his feet and waving his arms to keep warm, spoke to him.

"Your valises have been moved, Monsieur, to the compartment No. 1, the compartment of M. Bouc."

"But where is M. Bouc, then?"

"He has moved into the coach from Athens which has just been put on."

Poirot went in search of his friend. M. Bouc waved his protestations aside.

"It is nothing. It is nothing. It is more convenient like this. You are going through to England, so it is better that you should stay in the through coach to Calais. Me, I am very well here. It is most peaceful. This coach is empty save for myself and one little Greek doctor. Ah! my friend, what a night! They say there has not been so much snow for years. Let us hope we shall not be held up. I am not too happy about it, I can tell you."

At 9:15 punctually the train pulled out of the station, and shortly afterwards Poirot got up, said good night to his friend and made his way along the corridor back into his own coach which was in front next to the dining car.

On this, the second day of the journey, barriers were breaking down.

Colonel Arbuthnot was standing at the door of his compartment talking to MacQueen.

MacQueen broke off something he was saying when he saw Poirot. He looked very surprised.

"Why," he cried, "I thought you'd left us. You said you were getting off at Belgrade."

"You misunderstood me," said Poirot, smiling. "I remember now, the train started from Stamboul just as we were talking about it."

"But, man, your baggage—it's gone."

"It has been moved into another compartment—that is all."

"Oh, I see."

He resumed his conversation with Arbuthnot and Poirot passed on down the corridor.

Two doors from his own compartment, the elderly American lady, Mrs. Hubbard, was standing talking to the sheep-like lady who was a Swede. Mrs. Hubbard was pressing a magazine on the other.

"No, do take it, my dear," she said. "I've got plenty other things to read. My, isn't the cold something frightful?" She nodded amicably to Poirot.

"You are most kind," said the Swedish lady.

"Not at all. I hope you'll sleep well and that your head will be better in the morning."

"It is the cold only. I make now myself a cup of tea."

"Have you got some aspirin? Are you sure, now? I've got plenty. Well, good night, my dear."

She turned to Poirot conversationally as the other woman departed.

"Poor creature, she's a Swede. As far as I can make out, she's a kind of missionary—a teaching one. A nice creature, but doesn't talk much English. She was *most* interested in what I told her about my daughter."

Poirot, by now, knew all about Mrs. Hubbard's daughter. Everyone on the train who could understand English did! How she and her husband were on the staff of a big American college in Smyrna and how this was Mrs. Hubbard's first journey to the East, and what she thought of the Turks and their slipshod ways and the condition of their roads.

The door next to them opened and the thin, pale manservant stepped out. Inside Poirot caught a glimpse of Mr. Ratchett sitting up in bed. He saw Poirot and his face changed, darkening with anger. Then the door was shut.

Mrs. Hubbard drew Poirot a little aside.

"You know, I'm dead scared of that man. Oh, not the valet—the other—his master. Master, indeed! There's something *wrong* about that man. My daughter always says I'm very intuitive. 'When Momma gets a hunch, she's dead right,' that's what my daughter says. And I've got a hunch about that man. He's next door to me, and I don't like it. I put my grips against the communicating door last night. I thought I heard him trying the handle. Do you know, I shouldn't be surprised if that man turns out to be a murderer—one of these train robbers you read about. I dare say I'm foolish, but there it is. I'm downright scared of the man! My daughter said I'd have an easy journey, but somehow I don't feel happy about it. It may be foolish, but I feel anything might happen. Anything at all. And how that nice young fellow can bear to be his secretary I can't think."

Colonel Arbuthnot and MacQueen were coming towards them down the corridor.

"Come into my carriage," MacQueen was saying. "It isn't made up for the night yet. Now what I want to get right about your policy in India is this—"

The men passed and went on down the corridor to MacQueen's carriage.

Mrs. Hubbard said good night to Poirot.

"I guess I'll go right to bed and read," she said. "Good night."

"Good night, Madame."

Poirot passed into his own compartment, which was the next one beyond Ratchett's. He undressed and got into bed, read for about half an hour and then turned out the light.

He awoke some hours later, and awoke with a start. He knew what it was that had wakened him—a loud groan, almost a cry, somewhere close at hand. At the same moment the ting of a bell sounded sharply.

Poirot sat up and switched on the light. He noticed that the train was at a standstill—presumably at a station.

That cry had startled him. He remembered that it was Ratchett who had the next compartment. He got out of bed and opened the door just as the Wagon

Lit conductor came hurrying along the corridor and knocked on Ratchett's door. Poirot kept his door open a crack and watched. The conductor tapped a second time. A bell rang and a light showed over another door farther down. The conductor glanced over his shoulder.

At the same moment a voice from within the next-door compartment called out:

"Ce n'est rien. Je me suis trompé."

"Bien, Monsieur." The conductor scurried off again, to knock at the door where the light was showing.

Poirot returned to bed, his mind relieved, and switched off the light. He glanced at his watch. It was just twenty-three minutes to one.

Five

THE CRIME

H e found it difficult to go to sleep again at once. For one thing, he missed the motion of the train. If it *was* a station outside it was curiously quiet. By contrast, the noises on the train seemed unusually loud. He could hear Ratchett moving about next door—a click as he pulled down the washbasin, the sound of the tap running, a splashing noise, then another click as the basin shut to again. Footsteps passed up the corridor outside, the shuffling footsteps of someone in bedroom slippers.

Hercule Poirot lay awake staring at the ceiling. Why was the station outside so silent? His throat felt dry. He had forgotten to ask for his usual bottle of mineral water. He looked at his watch again. Just after a quarter past one. He would ring for the conductor and ask him for some mineral water. His finger went out to the bell, but he paused as in the stillness he heard a ting. The man couldn't answer every bell at once.

Ting . . . ting . . . ting . . .

It sounded again and again. Where was the man? Somebody was getting impatient.

Ting . . .

Whoever it was was keeping their finger solidly on the push.

Suddenly with a rush, his footsteps echoing up the aisle, the man came. He knocked at a door not far from Poirot's own.

Then came voices—the conductor's, deferential, apologetic, and a woman's—insistent and voluble.

Mrs. Hubbard.

Poirot smiled to himself.

The altercation—if it was one—went on for some time. It's proportions were ninety per cent of Mrs. Hubbard's to a soothing ten per cent of the conductor's. Finally the matter seemed to be adjusted. Poirot heard distinctly:

"*Bonne nuit,* Madame," and a closing door.

He pressed his own finger on the bell.

The conductor arrived promptly. He looked hot and worried.

"*De l'eau minerale, s'il vous plait.*"

"*Bien, Monsieur.*" Perhaps a twinkle in Poirot's eye led him to unburden himself.

"*La Dame Americaine—*"

"Yes?"

He wiped his forehead.

"Imagine to yourself the time I have had with her! She insists—but *insists*—that there is a man in her compartment! Figure to yourself, Monsieur. In a space of this size." He swept a hand round. "Where would he conceal himself? I argue with her. I point out that it is impossible. She insists. She woke up and there was a man there. And how, I ask, did he get out and leave the door bolted behind him? But she will not listen to reason. As though, there were not enough to worry us already. This snow—"

"Snow?"

"But yes, Monsieur. Monsieur has not noticed? The train has stopped. We have run into a snowdrift. Heaven knows how long we shall be here. I remember once being snowed up for seven days."

"Where are we?"

"Between Vincovi and Brod."

"*Là là,*" said Poirot vexedly.

The man withdrew and returned with the water.

"*Bon soir, Monsieur.*"

Poirot drank a glass of water and composed himself to sleep.

He was just dropping off when something again woke him. This time it was as though something heavy had fallen with a thud against the door.

He sprang up, opened it and looked out. Nothing. But to his right some way down the corridor a woman wrapped in a scarlet kimono was retreating from him. At the other end, sitting on his little seat, the conductor was entering up figures on large sheets of paper. Everything was deathly quiet.

"Decidedly I suffer from the nerves," said Poirot and retired to bed again. This time he slept till morning.

When he awoke the train was still at a standstill. He raised a blind and looked out. Heavy banks of snow surrounded the train.

He glanced at his watch and saw that it was past nine o'clock.

At a quarter to ten, neat, spruce, and dandified as ever, he made his way to the restaurant car, where a chorus of woe was going on.

Any barriers there might have been between the passengers had now quite broken down. All were united by a common misfortune. Mrs. Hubbard was loudest in her lamentations.

"My daughter said it would be the easiest way in the world. Just sit in the train until I got to Parrus. And now we may be here for days and days," she wailed. "And my boat sails the day after tomorrow. How am I going to catch it now? Why, I can't even wire to cancel my passage. I feel too mad to talk about it."

The Italian said that he had urgent business himself in Milan. The large American said that that was "too bad, Ma'am," and soothingly expressed a hope that the train might make up time.

"My sister—her children wait me," said the Swedish lady and wept. "I get no word to them. What they think? They will say bad things have happen to me."

"How long shall we be here?" demanded Mary Debenham. "Doesn't anybody *know*?"

Her voice sounded impatient, but Poirot noted that there were no signs of that almost feverish anxiety which she had displayed during the check to the Taurus Express.

Mrs. Hubbard was off again.

"There isn't anybody knows a thing on this train. And nobody's trying to do anything. Just a pack of useless foreigners. Why, if this were at home, there'd be someone at least *trying* to do something."

Arbuthnot turned to Poirot and spoke in careful British French.

"Vous êtes un directeur de la ligne, je crois, Monsieur. Vous pouvez nous dire—"

Smiling Poirot corrected him.

"No, no," he said in English. "It is not I. You confound me with my friend M. Bouc."

"Oh! I'm sorry."

"Not at all. It is most natural. I am now in the compartment that he had formerly."

M. Bouc was not present in the restaurant car. Poirot looked about to notice who else was absent.

Princess Dragomiroff was missing and the Hungarian couple. Also Ratchett, his valet, and the German lady's maid.

The Swedish lady wiped her eyes.

"I am foolish," she said. "I am baby to cry. All for the best, whatever happen."

This Christian spirit, however, was far from being shared.

"That's all very well," said MacQueen restlessly. "We may be here for days."

"What is this country anyway?" demanded Mrs. Hubbard tearfully.

On being told it was Yugo-Slavia she said:

"Oh! one of these Balkan things. What can you expect?"

"You are the only patient one, Mademoiselle," said Poirot to Miss Debenham. She shrugged her shoulders slightly.

"What can one do?"

"You are a philosopher, Mademoiselle."

"That implies a detached attitude. I think my attitude is more selfish. I have learned to save myself useless emotion."

She was not even looking at him. Her gaze went past him, out of the window to where the snow lay in heavy masses.

"You are a strong character, Mademoiselle," said Poirot gently. "You are, I think, the strongest character amongst us."

"Oh, no. No, indeed. I know one far far stronger than I am."

"And that is—?"

She seemed suddenly to come to herself, to realize that she was talking to a stranger and a foreigner with whom, until this morning, she had only exchanged half a dozen sentences.

She laughed a polite but estranging laugh.

"Well—that old lady, for instance. You have probably noticed her. A very ugly old lady, but rather fascinating. She has only to lift a little finger and ask for something in a polite voice—and the whole train runs."

"It runs also for my friend M. Bouc," said Poirot. "But that is because he is a director of the line, not because he has a masterful character."

Mary Debenham smiled.

The morning wore away. Several people, Poirot amongst them, remained in the dining car. The communal life was felt, at the moment, to pass the time better. He heard a good deal more about Mrs. Hubbard's daughter and he heard the lifelong habits of Mr. Hubbard, deceased, from his rising in the morning and commencing breakfast with a cereal to his final rest at night in the bedsocks that Mrs. Hubbard herself had been in the habit of knitting for him.

It was when he was listening to a confused account of the missionary aims of the Swedish lady that one of the Wagon Lit conductors came into the car and stood at his elbow.

"Pardon, Monsieur."

"Yes?"

"The compliments of M. Bouc, and he would be glad if you would be so kind as to come to him for a few minutes."

Poirot rose, uttered excuses to the Swedish lady and followed the man out of the dining car.

It was not his own conductor, but a big fair man.

He followed his guide down the corridor of his own carriage and along the corridor of the next one. The man tapped at a door, then stood aside to let Poirot enter.

The compartment was not M. Bouc's own. It was a second-class one— chosen presumably because of its slightly larger size. It certainly gave the impression of being crowded.

M. Bouc himself was sitting on the small seat in the opposite corner. In the corner next to the window facing him was a small, dark man looking out at the snow. Standing up and quite preventing Poirot from advancing any farther was a big man in blue uniform (the *chef de train*) and his own Wagon Lit conductor.

"Ah, my good friend," cried M. Bouc. "Come in. We have need of you."

The little man in the window shifted along the seat, Poirot squeezed past the other two men and sat down facing his friend.

The expression on M. Bouc's face gave him, as he would have expressed it, furiously to think. It was clear that something out of the common had happened.

"What has occurred?" he asked.

"You may well ask that. First this snow—this stoppage. And now—"

He paused—and a sort of strangled gasp came from the Wagon Lit conductor.

"And now what?"

"And now a passenger lies dead in his berth—stabbed."

M. Bouc spoke with a kind of calm desperation.

"A passenger? Which passenger?"

"An American. A man called—called—" he consulted some notes in front of him. "Ratchett—that is right—Ratchett?"

"Yes, Monsieur," the Wagon Lit man gulped.

Poirot looked at him. He was as white as chalk.

"You had better let that man sit down," he said. "He may faint otherwise."

The *chef de train* moved slightly and the Wagon Lit man sank down in the corner and buried his face in his hands.

"Brr!" said Poirot. "This is serious!"

"Certainly it is serious. To begin with, a murder—that by itself is a calamity of the first water. But not only that, the circumstances are unusual. Here we are, brought to a standstill. We may be here for hours—and not only hours—days! Another circumstance. Passing through most countries we have the police of that country on the train. But in Yugoslavia—no. You comprehend?"

"It is a position of great difficulty," said Poirot.

"There is worse to come. Dr. Constantine—I forgot, I have not introduced you—Dr. Constantine, M. Poirot."

The little dark man bowed and Poirot returned it.

"Dr. Constantine is of the opinion that death occurred at about 1 a.m."

"It is difficult to say exactly in these matters," said the doctor, "but I think I can say definitely that death occurred between midnight and two in the morning."

"When was this M. Ratchett last seen alive?" asked Poirot.

"He is known to have been alive at about twenty minutes to one, when he spoke to the conductor," said M. Bouc.

"That is quite correct," said Poirot. "I myself heard what passed. That is the last thing known?"

"Yes."

Poirot turned toward the doctor, who continued:

"The window of M. Ratchett's compartment was found wide open, leading one to suppose that the murderer escaped that way. But in my opinion that open window is a blind. Anyone departing that way would have left distinct traces in the snow. There were none."

"The crime was discovered—when?" asked Poirot.

"Michel!"

The Wagon Lit conductor sat up. His face still looked pale and frightened.

"Tell this gentleman exactly what occurred," ordered M. Bouc.

The man spoke somewhat jerkily.

"The valet of this M. Ratchett, he tapped several times at the door this morning. There was no answer. Then, half an hour ago, the restaurant car attendant came. He wanted to know if Monsieur was taking *déjeuner*. It was eleven o'clock, you comprehend.

"I open the door for him with my key. But there is a chain, too, and that is fastened. There is no answer and it is very still in there, and cold—but cold. With the window open and snow drifting in. I thought the gentleman had had a fit, perhaps. I got the *chef de train*. We broke the chain and went in. He was—*Ah! c'était terrible!*"

He buried his face in his hands again.

"The door was locked and chained on the inside," said Poirot thoughtfully. "It was not suicide—eh?"

The Greek doctor gave a sardonic laugh.

"Does a man who commits suicide stab himself in ten—twelve—fifteen places?" he asked.

Poirot's eyes opened.

"That is great ferocity," he said.

"It is a woman," said the *chef de train,* speaking for the first time. "Depend upon it, it was a woman. Only a woman would stab like that."

Dr. Constantine screwed up his face thoughtfully.

"She must have been a very strong woman," he said. "It is not my desire to speak technically—that is only confusing—but I can assure you that one or two of the blows were delivered with such force as to drive them through hard belts of bone and muscle."

"It was not, clearly, a scientific crime," said Poirot.

"It was most unscientific," said Dr. Constantine. "The blows seem to have been delivered haphazard and at random. Some have glanced off, doing hardly any damage. It is as though somebody had shut their eyes and then in a frenzy struck blindly again and again."

"*C'est une femme,*" said the *chef de train* again. "Women are like that. When they are enraged they have great strength." He nodded so sagely that everyone suspected a personal experience of his own.

"I have, perhaps, something to contribute to your store of knowledge," said Poirot. "M. Ratchett spoke to me yesterday. He told me, as far as I was able to understand him, that he was in danger of his life."

" 'Bumped off'—that is the American expression, is it not?" said M. Bouc. "Then it is not a woman. It is a 'Gangster' or a 'gunman.' "

The *chef de train* looked pained at his theory having come to naught.

"If so," said Poirot, "it seems to have been done very amateurishly."

His tone expressed professional disapproval.

"There is a large American on the train," said M. Bouc, pursuing his idea—"a common-looking man with terrible clothes. He chews the gum which I believe is not done in good circles. You know whom I mean?"

The Wagon Lit conductor to whom he had appealed nodded.

"*Oui,* Monsieur, the No. 16. But it cannot have been he. I should have seen him enter or leave the compartment."

"You might not. You might not. But we will go into that presently. The question is, what to do?" He looked at Poirot.

Poirot looked back at him.

"Come, my friend," said M. Bouc. "You comprehend what I am about to ask of you. I know your powers. Take command of this investigation! No, no, do not refuse. See, to us it is serious—I speak for the Compagnie Internationale des Wagons Lits. By the time the Yugo-Slavian police arrive, how simple if we can present them with the solution! Otherwise delays, annoyances, a million and one inconveniences. Perhaps, who knows, serious annoyance to innocent persons. Instead—*you* solve the mystery! We say, 'A murder has occurred—*this* is the criminal!' "

"And suppose I do not solve it?"

"Ah! *mon cher.*" M. Bouc's voice became positively caressing. "I know your reputation. I know something of your methods. This is the ideal case for you. To look up the antecedents of all these people, to discover their *bona fides*—all that takes time and endless inconvenience. But have I not heard you say often that to solve a case a man has only to lie back in his chair and think? Do that. Interview the passengers on the train, view the body, examine what clues there are and then—well, I have faith in you! I am assured that it is no idle boast of yours. Lie back and think—use (as I have heard you say so often) the little grey cells of the mind—and you will *know!*"

He leaned forward, looking affectionately at his friend.

"Your faith touches me, my friend," said Poirot emotionally. "As you say, this cannot be a difficult case. I myself, last night—but we will not speak of that now. In truth, this problem intrigues me. I was reflecting, not half an hour ago, that many hours of boredom lay ahead whilst we are stuck here. And now—a problem lies ready to my hand."

"You accept then?" said M. Bouc eagerly.

"*C'est entendu.* You place the matter in my hands."

"Good—we are all at your service."

"To begin with, I should like a plan of the Istanbul-Calais coach, with a note of the people who occupied the several compartments, and I should also like to see their passports and their tickets."

"Michel will get you those."

The Wagon Lit conductor left the compartment.

"What other passengers are there on the train?" asked Poirot.

"In this coach Dr. Constantine and I are the only travellers. In the coach from Bucharest is an old gentleman with a lame leg. He is well known to the conductor. Beyond that are the ordinary carriages, but these do not concern us, since they were locked after dinner had been served last night. Forward of the Istanbul-Calais coach there is only the dining car."

"Then it seems," said Poirot slowly, "as though we must look for our murderer in the Istanbul-Calais coach." He turned to the doctor. "That is what you were hinting, I think?"

The Greek nodded.

"At half an hour after midnight we ran into the snowdrift. No one can have left the train since then."

M. Bouc said solemnly.

"The murderer is with us—on the train now. . . ."

Six

A Woman?

First of all," said Poirot, "I should like a word or two with young M. Mac-Queen. He may be able to give us valuable information."

"Certainly," said M. Bouc.

He turned to the *chef de train*.

"Get M. MacQueen to come here."

The *chef de train* left the carriage.

The conductor returned with a bundle of passports and tickets. M. Bouc took them from him.

"Thank you, Michel. It would be best now, I think, if you were to go back to your post. We will take your evidence formally later."

"Very good, Monsieur."

Michel in his turn left the carriage.

"After we have seen young MacQueen," said Poirot, "perhaps M. le docteur will come with me to the dead man's carriage."

"Certainly."

"After we have finished there—"

But at this moment the *chef de train* returned with Hector MacQueen.

M. Bouc rose.

"We are a little cramped here," he said pleasantly. "Take my seat, M. Mac-Queen. M. Poirot will sit opposite you—so."

He turned to the *chef de train*.

"Clear all the people out of the restaurant car," he said, "and let it be left free for M. Poirot. You will conduct your interviews there, *mon cher?*"

"It would be the most convenient, yes," agreed Poirot.

MacQueen had stood looking from one to the other, not quite following the rapid flow of French.

"*Qu'est ce qu'il y a?*" he began laboriously. "*Pourquoi—?*"

With a vigorous gesture Poirot motioned him to the seat in the corner. He took it and began once more.

"*Pourquoi—?*" then, checking himself and relapsing into his own tongue, "What's up on the train? Has anything happened?"

He looked from one man to another.

Poirot nodded.

"Exactly. Something has happened. Prepare yourself for a shock. *Your employer, M. Ratchett, is dead!*"

MacQueen's mouth pursed itself in a whistle. Except that his eyes grew a shade brighter, he showed no signs of shock or distress.

"So they got him after all," he said.

"What exactly do you mean by that phrase, M. MacQueen?" MacQueen hesitated.

"You are assuming," said Poirot, "that M. Ratchett was murdered?"

"Wasn't he?" This time MacQueen did show surprise. "Why, yes," he said slowly. "That's just what I did think. Do you mean he just died in his sleep? Why, the old man was as tough as—as tough—"

He stopped, at a loss for a simile.

"No, no," said Poirot. "Your assumption was quite right. Mr. Ratchett was murdered. Stabbed. But I should like to know why you were so sure it *was* murder, and not just—death."

MacQueen hesitated.

"I must get this clear," he said. "Who exactly are you? And where do you come in?"

"I represent the Compagnie Internationale des Wagons Lits." He paused, then added, "I am a detective. My name is Hercule Poirot."

If he expected an effect he did not get one. MacQueen said merely, "Oh, yes?" and waited for him to go on.

"You know the name, perhaps."

"Why, it does seem kind of familiar—only I always thought it was a woman's dressmaker."

Hercule Poirot looked at him with distaste.

"It is incredible!" he said.

"What's incredible?"

"Nothing. Let us advance with the matter in hand. I want you to tell me, M. MacQueen, all that you know about the dead man. You were not related to him?"

"No. I am—was—his secretary."

"For how long have you held that post?"

"Just over a year."

"Please give me all the information you can."

"Well, I met Mr. Ratchett just over a year ago when I was in Persia—"

Poirot interrupted.

"What were you doing there?"

"I had come over from New York to look into an oil concession. I don't suppose you want to hear all about that. My friends and I had been let in rather badly over it. Mr. Ratchett was in the same hotel. He had just had a row with his secretary. He offered me the job and I took it. I was at a loose end, and glad to find a well-paid job ready made, as it were."

"And since then?"

"We've travelled about. Mr. Ratchett wanted to see the world. He was hampered by knowing no languages. I acted more as a courier than as a secretary. It was a pleasant life."

"Now tell me as much as you can about your employer."

The young man shrugged his shoulders. A perplexed expression passed over his face.

"That's not so easy."

"What was his full name?"

"Samuel Edward Ratchett."

"He was an American citizen?"

"Yes."

"What part of America did he come from?"

"I don't know."

"Well, tell me what you do know."

"The actual truth is, Mr. Poirot, that I know nothing at all! Mr. Ratchett never spoke of himself, or of his life in America."

"Why do you think that was?"

"I don't know. I imagined that he might have been ashamed of his beginnings. Some men are."

"Does that strike you as a satisfactory solution?"

"Frankly, it doesn't."

"Has he any relations?"

"He never mentioned any."

Poirot pressed the point.

"You must have formed *some* theory, M. MacQueen."

"Well, yes, I did. For one thing, I don't believe Ratchett was his real name. I think he left America definitely in order to escape someone or something. I think he was successful—until a few weeks ago."

"And then?"

"He began to get letters—threatening letters."

"Did you see them?"

"Yes. It was my business to attend to his correspondence. The first letter came a fortnight ago."

"Were these letters destroyed?"

"No, I think I've got a couple still in my files—one I know Ratchett tore up in a rage. Shall I get them for you?"

"If you would be so good."

MacQueen left the compartment. He returned a few minutes later and laid down two sheets of rather dirty notepaper before Poirot.

The first letter ran as follows:

"Thought you'd doublecross us and get away with it, did you? Not on your life. We're out to GET you, Ratchett, and we WILL get you!"

There was no signature.

With no comment beyond raised eyebrows, Poirot picked up the second letter.

"We're going to take you for a ride, Ratchett. Some time soon. We're going to GET you, see?"

Poirot laid the letter down.

"The style is monotonous!" he said. "More so than the handwriting."

MacQueen stared at him.

"You would not observe," said Poirot pleasantly. "It requires the eye of one used to such things. This letter was not written by one person, M. MacQueen. Two or more persons wrote it—each writing a letter of a word at a time. Also, the letters are printed. That makes the task of identifying the handwriting much more difficult."

He paused, then said:

"Did you know that M. Ratchett had applied for help to me?"

"To *you?*"

MacQueen's astonished tone told Poirot quite certainly that the young man had not known of it. He nodded.

"Yes. He was alarmed. Tell me, how did he act when he received the first letter?"

MacQueen hesitated.

"It's difficult to say. He—he—passed it off with a laugh in that quiet way of his. But somehow"—he gave a slight shiver—"I felt that there was a good deal going on underneath the quietness."

Poirot nodded. Then he asked an unexpected question.

"Mr. MacQueen, will you tell me, quite honestly, exactly how you regarded your employer? Did you like him?"

Hector MacQueen took a moment or two before replying.

"No," he said at last. "I did not."

"Why?"

"I can't exactly say. He was always quite pleasant in his manner." He paused, then said, "I'll tell you the truth, Mr. Poirot. I disliked and distrusted him. He was, I am sure, a cruel and a dangerous man. I must admit, though, that I have no reasons to advance for my opinion."

"Thank you, M. MacQueen. One further question—when did you last see M. Ratchett alive?"

"Last evening about"—he thought for a minute—"ten o'clock, I should say. I went into his compartment to take down some memoranda from him."

"On what subject?"

"Some tiles and antique pottery that he bought in Persia. What was delivered was not what he had purchased. There has been a long, vexatious correspondence on the subject."

"And that was the last time M. Ratchett was seen alive?"

"Yes, I suppose so."

"Do you know when M. Ratchett received the last threatening letter?"

"On the morning of the day we left Constantinople."

"There is one more question I must ask you, M. MacQueen: were you on good terms with your employer?"

The young man's eyes twinkled suddenly.

"This is where I'm supposed to go all goosefleshy down the back. In the words of a best seller, 'You've nothing on me.' Ratchett and I were on perfectly good terms."

"Perhaps, M. MacQueen, you will give me your full name and your address in America."

MacQueen gave his name—Hector Willard MacQueen, and an address in New York.

Poirot leaned back against the cushions.

"That is all for the present, M. MacQueen," he said. "I should be obliged if you would keep the matter of M. Ratchett's death to yourself for a little time."

"His valet, Masterman, will have to know."

"He probably knows already," said Poirot dryly. "If so try to get him to hold his tongue."

"That oughtn't to be difficult. He's a Britisher, and does what he calls 'Keeps himself to himself.' He's a low opinion of Americans and no opinion at all of any other nationality."

"Thank you, M. MacQueen."

The American left the carriage.

"Well?" demanded M. Bouc. "You believe what he says, this young man?"

"He seems honest and straightforward. He did not pretend to any affection for his employer as he probably would have done had he been involved in any way. It is true M. Ratchett did not tell him that he had tried to enlist my services and failed, but I do not think that is really a suspicious circumstance. I fancy M. Ratchett was a gentleman who kept his own counsel on every possible occasion."

"So you pronounce one person at least innocent of the crime," said M. Bouc jovially.

Poirot cast on him a look of reproach.

"Me, I suspect everybody till the last minute," he said. "All the same, I must admit that I cannot see this sober, long-headed MacQueen losing his head and stabbing his victim twelve or fourteen times. It is not in accord with his psychology—not at all."

"No," said Mr. Bouc thoughtfully. "That is the act of a man driven almost crazy with a frenzied hate—it suggests more the Latin temperament. Or else it suggests, as our friend the *chef de train* insisted, a woman."

Seven

THE BODY

Followed by Dr. Constantine, Poirot made his way to the next coach and the compartment occupied by the murdered man. The conductor came and unlocked the door for them with his key.

The two men passed inside. Poirot turned inquiringly to his companion.

"How much has been disarranged in this compartment?"

"Nothing has been touched. I was careful not to move the body in making my examination."

Poirot nodded. He looked round him.

The first thing that struck the senses was the intense cold. The window was pushed down as far as it would go and the blind was drawn up.

"Brrr," observed Poirot.

The other smiled appreciatively.

"I did not like to close it," he said.

Poirot examined the window carefully.

"You are right," he announced. "Nobody left the carriage this way. Possibly the open window was intended to suggest the fact, but, if so, the snow has defeated the murderer's object."

He examined the frame of the window carefully. Taking a small case from his pocket he blew a little powder over it.

"No fingerprints at all," he said. "That means it has been wiped. Well, if there had been fingerprints it would have told us very little. They would have been those of M. Ratchett or his valet or the conductor. Criminals do not make mistakes of that kind nowadays.

"And that being so," he added cheerfully, "we might as well shut the window. Positively it is the cold storage in here!"

He suited the action to the word and then turned his attention for the first time to the motionless figure lying in the bunk.

Ratchett lay on his back. His pyjama jacket, stained with rusty patches, had been unbuttoned and thrown back.

"I had to see the nature of the wounds, you see," explained the doctor.

Poirot nodded. He bent over the body. Finally he straightened himself with a slight grimace.

"It is not pretty," he said. "Someone must have stood there and stabbed him again and again. How many wounds are there exactly?"

"I make it twelve. One or two are so slight as to be practically scratches. On the other hand, at least three would be capable of causing death."

Something in the doctor's tone caught Poirot's attention. He looked at him sharply. The little Greek was standing staring down at the body with a puzzled frown.

"Something strikes you as odd, does it not?" he asked gently. "Speak, my friend. There is something here that puzzles you?"

"You are right," acknowledged the other.

"What is it?"

"You see, these two wounds—here and here"—he pointed. "They are deep, each cut must have severed blood vessels—and yet—the edges do not gape. They have not bled as one would have expected."

"Which suggests?"

"That the man was already dead—some little time dead—when they were delivered. But that is surely absurd."

"It would seem so," said Poirot thoughtfully. "Unless our murderer figured to himself that he had not accomplished his job properly and came back to make quite sure; but that is manifestly absurd! Anything else?"

"Well, just one thing."

"And that?"

"You see this wound here—under the right arm—near the right shoulder. Take this pencil of mine. Could you deliver such a blow?"

Poirot raised his hand.

"*Précisément,*" he said. "I see. With the *right* hand it is exceedingly difficult— almost impossible. One would have to strike backhanded, as it were. But if the blow were struck with the *left* hand—"

"Exactly, M. Poirot. That blow was almost certainly struck with the *left* hand."

"So that our murderer is left-handed? No, it is more difficult than that, is it not?"

"As you say, M. Poirot. Some of these other blows are just as obviously right-handed."

"Two people. We are back at two people again," murmured the detective. He asked abruptly:

"Was the electric light on?"

"It is difficult to say. You see it is turned off by the conductor every morning about ten o'clock."

"The switches will tell us," said Poirot.

He examined the switch of the top light and also the roll back bed-head light. The former was turned off. The latter was closed.

"*Eh bien,*" he said thoughtfully. "We have here a hypothesis of the First and Second Murderer, as the great Shakespeare would put it. The First Murderer stabbed his victim and left the compartment, turning off the light. The Second Murderer came in in the dark, did not see that his or her work had been done and stabbed at least twice at a dead body. *Que pensez vous de ça?*"

"Magnificent," said the little doctor with enthusiasm.

The other's eyes twinkled.

"You think so? I am glad. It sounded to me a little like the nonsense."

"What other explanation can there be?"

"That is just what I am asking myself. Have we here a coincidence or what? Are there any other inconsistencies, such as would point to two people being concerned?"

"I think I can say yes. Some of these blows, as I have already said, point to a weakness—a lack of strength or a lack of determination. They are feeble glancing blows. But this one here—and this one—" Again he pointed. "Great strength was needed for those blows. They have penetrated the muscle."

"They were, in your opinion, delivered by a man?"

"Most certainly."

"They could not have been delivered by a woman?"

"A young, vigorous, athletic woman might have struck them, especially if she were in the grip of a strong emotion, but it is in my opinion highly unlikely."

Poirot was silent a moment or two.

The other said anxiously.

"You understand my point?"

"Perfectly," said Poirot. "The matter begins to clear itself up wonderfully! The murderer was a man of great strength, he was feeble, it was a woman, it was a right-handed person, it was a left-handed person—*Ah! c'est rigolo, tout ça!*"

He spoke with sudden anger.

"And the victim—what does he do in all this? Does he cry out? Does he struggle? Does he defend himself?"

He slipped his hand under the pillow and drew out the automatic pistol which Ratchett had shown him the day before.

"Fully loaded, you see," he said.

They looked round them. Ratchett's day clothing was hanging from the hooks on the wall. On the small table formed by the lid of the washing basin were various objects—false teeth in a glass of water; another glass, empty; a bottle of mineral water, a large flask and an ashtray containing the butt of a cigar and some charred fragments of paper; also two burnt matches.

The doctor picked up the empty glass and sniffed it.

"Here is the explanation of the victim's inertia," he said quietly.

"Drugged?"

"Yes."

Poirot nodded. He picked up the two matches and scrutinized them carefully.

"You have a clue then?" demanded the little doctor eagerly.

"Those two matches are of a different shape," said Poirot. "One is flatter than the other. You see?"

"It is the kind you get on a train," said the doctor, "in paper covers."

Poirot was feeling in the pockets of Ratchett's clothing. Presently he pulled out a box of matches. He compared them carefully.

"The rounder one is a match struck by Mr. Ratchett," he said. "Let us see if he had also the flatter kind."

But a further search showed no other matches.

Poirot's eyes were darting about the compartment. They were bright and sharp like a bird's. One felt that nothing could escape their scrutiny.

With a little exclamation he bent and picked up something from the floor.

It was a small square of cambric, very dainty. "Our friend the *chef de train* was right. There is a woman concerned in this."

"And most conveniently she leaves her handkerchief behind!" said Poirot. "Exactly as it happens in the books and on the films—and to make things even easier for us it is marked with an initial."

"What a stroke of luck for us!" exclaimed the doctor.

"Is it not?" said Poirot.

Something in his tone surprised the doctor.

But before he could ask for elucidation, Poirot had made another dive on to the floor.

This time he held out on the palm of his hand—a pipe cleaner.

"It is perhaps the property of M. Ratchett?" suggested the doctor.

"There was no pipe in any of his pockets, and no tobacco or tobacco pouch."

"Then it is a clue."

"Oh! decidedly. And again dropped most conveniently. A masculine clue this time, you note! One cannot complain of having no clues in this case. There are clues here in abundance. By the way, what have you done with the weapon?"

"There was no sign of any weapon. The murderer must have taken it away with him."

"I wonder why," mused Poirot.

"Ah!" The doctor had been delicately exploring the pyjama pockets of the dead man.

"I overlooked this," he said. "I unbuttoned the jacket and threw it straight back."

From the breast pocket he brought out a gold watch. The case was dented savagely, and the hands pointed to a quarter past one.

"You see?" cried Constantine eagerly. "This gives us the hour of the crime. It agrees with my calculations. Between midnight and two in the morning is what I said, and probably about one o'clock, though it is difficult to be exact in these matters. *Eh bien,* here is confirmation. A quarter past one. That was the hour of the crime."

"It is possible, yes. It is certainly possible."

The doctor looked at him curiously.

"You will pardon me, M. Poirot, but I do not quite understand you."

"I do not understand myself," said Poirot. "I understand nothing at all, and, as you perceive, it worries me."

He sighed and bent over the little table, examining the charred fragment of paper. He murmured to himself.

"What I need at this moment is an old-fashioned woman's hatbox."

Dr. Constantine was at a loss to know what to make of this singular remark. In any case, Poirot gave him no time for questions. Opening the door into the corridor, he called for the conductor.

The man arrived at a run.

"How many women are there in this coach?"

The conductor counted on his fingers.

"One, two, three—six, Monsieur. The old American lady, a Swedish lady, the young English lady, the Countess Andrenyi and Madame la Princess Drago-miroff and her maid."

Poirot considered.

"They all have hatboxes, yes?"

"Yes, Monsieur."

"Then bring me—let me see—yes, the Swedish lady's and that of the lady's maid. Those two are the only hope. You will tell them it is a customs regulation—something—anything that occurs to you."

"That will be all right Monsieur. Neither lady is in her compartment at the moment."

"Then be quick."

The conductor departed. He returned with the two hatboxes. Poirot opened that of the lady's maid and tossed it aside. Then he opened the Swedish lady's and uttered an exclamation of satisfaction. Removing the hats carefully, he disclosed round humps of wire netting.

"Ah, here is what we need. About fifteen years ago hatboxes were made like this. You skewered through the hat with a hatpin on to this hump of wire netting."

As he spoke he was skilfully removing two of the attachments. Then he repacked the hatbox and told the conductor to return them both where they belonged.

When the door was shut once more he turned to his companion.

"See you, my dear doctor, me, I am not one to rely upon the expert procedure. It is the psychology I seek, not the fingerprint or the cigarette ash. But in this case I would welcome a little scientific assistance. This compartment is full of clues, but can I be sure that those clues are really what they seem to be?"

"I do not quite understand you, M. Poirot."

"Well, to give you an example—we find a woman's handkerchief. Did a woman drop it? Or did a man, committing the crime, say to himself 'I will make this look like a woman's crime. I will stab my enemy an unnecessary number of times, making some of the blows feeble and ineffective, and I will drop this handkerchief where no one can miss it.' That is one possibility. Then there is another. Did a woman kill him and did she deliberately drop a pipe cleaner to make it look like a man's work? Or are we seriously to suppose that two people—a man and a woman—were separately concerned, and that each was so careless as to drop a clue to their identity? It is a little too much of a coincidence, that!"

"But where does the hatbox come in?" asked the doctor, still puzzled.

"Ah! I'm coming to that. As I say, these clues, the watch stopped at a quarter past one, the handkerchief, the pipe cleaner, they may be genuine, or they may be fake. As to that I cannot yet tell. But there is *one* clue here which I believe—though again I may be wrong—has *not* been faked. I mean this flat match, M. le docteur. I *believe that that match was used by the murderer, not by M. Ratchett.* It was used to burn an incriminating paper of some kind. Possibly a note. If so, there was something in that note, some mistake, some error, that left a possible clue to the assailant. I am going to endeavour to resurrect what that something was."

He went out of the compartment and returned a few moments later with a small spirit stove and a pair of curling tongs.

"I use them for the moustaches," he said, referring to the latter.

The doctor watched him with great interest. He flattened out the two humps of wire, and with great care wriggled the charred scrap of paper on to one of them. He clapped the other on top of it and then, holding both pieces together with the tongs, held the whole thing over the flame of the spirit lamp.

"It is a very makeshift affair, this," he said over his shoulder. "Let us hope that it will answer its purpose."

The doctor watched the proceedings attentively. The metal began to glow. Suddenly he saw faint indications of letters. Words formed themselves slowly— words of fire.

It was a very tiny scrap. Only three words and a part of another showed.

"—*member little Daisy Armstrong.*"

"Ah!" Poirot gave a sharp exclamation.

"It tells you something?" asked the doctor.

Poirot's eyes were shining. He laid down the tongs carefully.

"Yes," he said. "*I know the dead man's real name. I know why he had to leave America.*"

"What was his name?"

"Cassetti."

"Cassetti." Constantine knitted his brows. "It brings back to me something. Some years ago. I cannot remember . . . It was a case in America, was it not?"

"Yes," said Poirot. "A case in America."

Further than that Poirot was not disposed to be communicative. He looked round him as he went on:

"We will go into all that presently. Let us first make sure that we have seen all there is to be seen here."

Quickly and deftly he went once more through the pockets of the dead man's clothes but found nothing there of interest. He tried the communicating door which led through to the next compartment, but it was bolted on the other side.

"There is one thing that I do not understand," said Dr. Constantine. "If the murderer did not escape through the window, and if this communicating door was bolted on the other side, and if the door into the corridor was not only locked on the inside but chained, how then did the murderer leave the compartment?"

"That is what the audience says when a person bound hand and foot is shut into a cabinet—and disappears."

"You mean—"

"I mean," explained Poirot, "that if the murderer intended us to believe that he had escaped by way of the window he would naturally make it appear that the other two exits were impossible. Like the 'disappearing person' in the cabinet—it is a trick. It is our business to find out how the trick is done."

He locked the communicating door on their side.

"In case," he said, "the excellent Mrs. Hubbard should take it into her head to acquire first-hand details of the crime to write to her daughter."

He looked round once more.

"There is nothing more to do here, I think. Let us rejoin M. Bouc."

Eight

The Armstrong Kidnapping Case

They found M. Bouc finishing an omelet.

"I thought it best to have lunch served immediately in the restaurant car," he said. "Afterwards it will be cleared and M. Poirot can conduct his examination of the passengers there. In the meantime I have ordered them to bring us three some food here."

"An excellent idea," said Poirot.

Neither of the other two men was hungry, and the meal was soon eaten, but not till they were sipping their coffee did M. Bouc mention the subject that was occupying all their minds.

"*Eh bien?*" he asked.

"*Eh bien,* I have discovered the identity of the victim. I know why it was imperative he should leave America."

"Who was he?"

"Do you remember reading of the Armstrong baby? This is the man who murdered little Daisy Armstrong—Cassetti."

"I recall it now. A shocking affair—though I cannot remember the details."

"Colonel Armstrong was an Englishman—a V.C. He was half American, as his mother was a daughter of W. K. Van der Halt, the Wall Street millionaire. He married the daughter of Linda Arden, the most famous tragic American actress of her day. They lived in America and had one child—a girl—whom they idolized. When she was three years old she was kidnapped, and an impossibly high sum

demanded as the price of her return. I will not weary you with all the intrica-
cies that followed. I will come to the moment, when, after having paid over the
enormous sum of two hundred thousand dollars, the child's dead body was discovered, it having been dead at least a fortnight. Public indignation rose to fever
point. And there was worse to follow. Mrs. Armstrong was expecting another
child. Following the shock of the discovery, she gave birth to a dead child born
prematurely, and herself died. Her brokenhearted husband shot himself."

"*Mon Dieu,* what a tragedy. I remember now," said M. Bouc. "There was
also another death, if I remember rightly?"

"Yes—an unfortunate French or Swiss nursemaid. The police were convinced that she had some knowledge of the crime. They refused to believe her
hysterical denials. Finally, in a fit of despair, the poor girl threw herself from a
window and was killed. It was proved afterwards that she was absolutely innocent of any complicity in the crime."

"It is not good to think of," said M. Bouc.

"About six months later, this man Cassetti was arrested as the head of the
gang who had kidnapped the child. They had used the same methods in the past.
If the police seemed likely to get on their trail, they had killed their prisoner,
hidden the body, and continued to extract as much money as possible before the
crime was discovered.

"Now, I will make clear to you this, my friend. Cassetti was the man!
But by means of the enormous wealth he had piled up and by the secret hold
he had over various persons, he was acquitted on some technical inaccuracy.
Notwithstanding that, he would have been lynched by the populace had he not
been clever enough to give them the slip. It is now clear to me what happened.
He changed his name and left America. Since then he has been a gentleman of
leisure, travelling abroad and living on his *rentes.*"

"*Ah! quel animal!*" M. Bouc's tone was redolent of heartfelt disgust. "I cannot
regret that he is dead—not at all!"

"I agree with you."

"*Tout de même,* it is not necessary that he should be killed on the Orient
Express. There are other places."

Poirot smiled a little. He realized that M. Bouc was biased in the matter.

"The question we have now to ask ourselves is this," he said. "Is this murder the work of some rival gang whom Cassetti had double-crossed in the past, or is it an act of private vengeance?"

He explained his discovery of the few words on the charred fragment of paper.

"If I am right in my assumption, then the letter was burnt by the murderer. Why? Because it mentioned the word 'Armstrong,' which is the clue to the mystery."

"Are there any members of the Armstrong family living?"

"That, unfortunately, I do not know. I think I remember reading of a younger sister of Mrs. Armstrong's."

Poirot went on to relate the joint conclusions of himself and Dr. Constantine. M. Bouc brightened at the mention of the broken watch.

"That seems to give us the time of the crime very exactly."

"Yes," said Poirot. "It is very convenient."

There was an indescribable something in his tone that made both the other two look at him curiously.

"You say that you yourself heard Ratchett speak to the conductor at twenty minutes to one?"

Poirot related just what had occurred.

"Well," said M. Bouc, "that proves at least that Cassetti—or Ratchett, as I shall continue to call him—was certainly alive at twenty minutes to one."

"Twenty-three minutes to one, to be precise."

"Then at twelve thirty-seven, to put it formally, M. Ratchett was alive. That is *one* fact, at least."

Poirot did not reply. He sat looking thoughtfully in front of him.

There was a tap on the door, and the restaurant attendant entered.

"The restaurant car is free now, Monsieur," he said.

"We will go there," said M. Bouc, rising.

"I may accompany you?" asked Constantine.

"Certainly, my dear doctor. Unless M. Poirot has any objection?"

"Not at all. Not at all," said Poirot.

After a little politeness in the matter of procedure, *"Après vous, Monsieur."* *"Mais non, après vous,"* they left the compartment.

PART TWO
THE EVIDENCE

One

The Evidence of the Wagon Lit Conductor

In the restaurant car all was in readiness.

Poirot and M. Bouc sat together on one side of a table. The doctor sat across the aisle.

On the table in front of Poirot was a plan of the Istanbul-Calais coach with the names of the passengers marked in in red ink.

The passports and tickets were in a pile at one side. There was writing paper, ink, pen and pencils.

"Excellent," said Poirot. "We can open our Court of Inquiry without more ado. First, I think, we should take the evidence of the Wagon Lit conductor. You probably know something about the man. What character has he? Is he a man in whose word you would place reliance?"

"I should say so most assuredly. Pierre Michel has been employed by the company for over fifteen years. He is a Frenchman—lives near Calais. Thoroughly respectable and honest. Not, perhaps, remarkable for brains."

Poirot nodded comprehendingly.

"Good," he said. "Let us see him."

Pierre Michel had recovered some of his assurance, but he was still extremely nervous.

"I hope Monsieur will not think that there has been any negligence on my part," he said anxiously, his eyes going from Poirot to M. Bouc. "It is a terrible thing that has happened. I hope Monsieur does not think that it reflects on me in any way?"

Having soothed the man's fears, Poirot began his questions. He first elicited Michel's name and address, his length of service, and the length of time he had been on this particular route. These particulars he already knew, but the routine questions served to put the man at his ease.

"And now," went on Poirot, "let us come to the events of last night. M. Ratchett retired to bed—when?"

"Almost immediately after dinner, Monsieur. Actually before we left Belgrade. So he did on the previous night. He had directed me to make up the bed while he was at dinner, and I did so."

"Did anybody go into his compartment afterwards?"

"His valet, Monsieur, and the young American gentleman his secretary."

"Anyone else?"

"No, Monsieur, not that I know of."

"Good. And that is the last you saw or heard of him?"

"No, Monsieur. You forget, he rang his bell about twenty to one—soon after we had stopped."

"What happened exactly?"

"I knocked at the door, but he called out and said he had made a mistake."

"In English or in French?"

"In French."

"What were his words exactly?"

"*Ce n'est rien. Je me suis trompé.*"

"Quite right," said Poirot. "That is what I heard. And then you went away?"

"Yes, Monsieur."

"Did you go back to your seat?"

"No, Monsieur, I went first to answer another bell that had just rung."

"Now, Michel, I am going to ask you an important question. Where were you at a quarter past one?"

"I, Monsieur? I was at my little seat at the end—facing up the corridor."

"You are sure?"

"*Mais oui*—at least—"

WAGON RESTAURANT

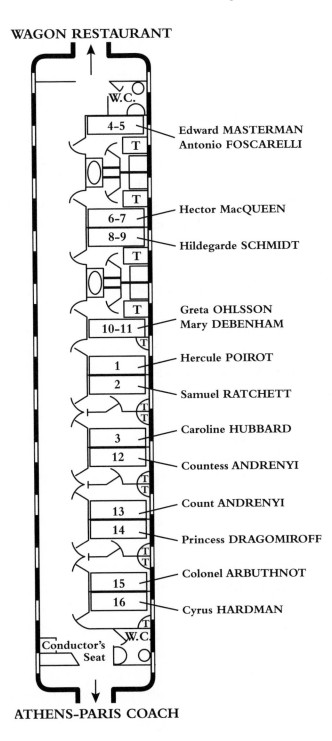

ATHENS-PARIS COACH

"Yes?"

"I went into the next coach, the Athens coach, to speak to my colleague there. We spoke about the snow. That was at some time soon after one o'clock. I cannot say exactly."

"And you returned—when?"

"One of my bells rang, Monsieur—I remember—I told you. It was the American lady. She had rung several times."

"I recollect," said Poirot. "And after that?"

"After that, Monsieur? I answered your bell and brought you some mineral water. Then, about half an hour later, I made up the bed in one of the other compartments—that of the young American gentleman, M. Ratchett's secretary."

"Was M. MacQueen alone in his compartment when you went to make up his bed?"

"The English Colonel from No. 15 was with him. They had been sitting talking."

"What did the Colonel do when he left M. MacQueen?"

"He went back to his own compartment."

"No. 15—that is quite close to your seat, is it not?"

"Yes, Monsieur, it is the second compartment from that end of the corridor."

"His bed was already made up?"

"Yes, Monsieur. I had made it up while he was at dinner."

"What time was all this?"

"I could not say exactly, Monsieur. Not later than two o'clock, certainly."

"And after that?"

"After that, Monsieur, I sat in my seat till morning."

"You did not go again into the Athens coach?"

"No, Monsieur."

"Perhaps you slept?"

"I do not think so, Monsieur. The train being at a standstill prevented me from dozing off as I usually do."

"Did you see any of the passengers moving up or down the corridor?"

The man reflected.

"One of the ladies went to the toilet at the far end, I think."

"Which lady?"

"I do not know, Monsieur. It was far down the corridor, and she had her back to me. She had on a kimono of scarlet with dragons on it."

Poirot nodded.

"And after that?"

"Nothing, Monsieur, until the morning."

"You are sure?"

"Ah, pardon, you yourself, Monsieur, opened your door and looked out for a second."

"Good, my friend," said Poirot. "I wondered whether you would remember that. By the way, I was awakened by what sounded like something heavy falling against my door. Have you any idea what that could have been?"

The man stared at him.

"There was nothing, Monsieur. Nothing, I am positive of it."

"Then I must have had the *cauchemar,*" said Poirot philosophically.

"Unless," said M. Bouc, "it was something in the compartment next door that you heard."

Poirot took no notice of the suggestion. Perhaps he did not wish to before the Wagon Lit conductor.

"Let us pass to another point," he said. "Supposing that last night an assassin joined the train. It is quite certain that he could not have left it after committing the crime?"

Pierre Michael shook his head.

"Nor that he can be concealed on it somewhere?"

"It has been well searched," said M. Bouc. "Abandon that idea, my friend."

"Besides," said Michel, "no one could get on to the sleeping car without my seeing them."

"When was the last stop?"

"Vincovci."

"What time was that?"

"We should have left there at 11:58. But owing to the weather we were twenty minutes late."

"Someone might have come along from the ordinary part of the train?"

"No, Monsieur. After the service of dinner the door between the ordinary carriages and the sleeping cars is locked."

"Did you yourself descend from the train at Vincovci?"

"Yes, Monsieur. I got down on to the platform as usual and stood by the step up into the train. The other conductors did the same."

"What about the forward door? The one near the restaurant car?"

"It is always fastened on the inside."

"It is not so fastened now."

The man looked surprised, then his face cleared.

"Doubtless one of the passengers has opened it to look out on the snow."

"Probably," said Poirot.

He tapped thoughtfully on the table for a minute or two.

"Monsieur does not blame me?" said the man timidly.

Poirot smiled on him kindly.

"You have had the evil chance, my friend," he said. "Ah! One other point while I remember it. You said that another bell rang just as you were knocking at M. Ratchett's door. In fact, I heard it myself. Whose was it?"

"It was the bell of Madame la Princesse Dragomiroff. She desired me to summon her maid."

"And you did so?"

"Yes, Monsieur."

Poirot studied the plan in front of him thoughtfully. Then he inclined his head.

"That is all," he said, "for the moment."

"Thank you, Monsieur."

The man rose. He looked at M. Bouc.

"Do not distress yourself," said the latter kindly. "I cannot see that there has been any negligence on your part."

Gratified, Pierre Michel left the compartment.

Two

The Evidence of the Secretary

For a minute or two Poirot remained lost in thought.

"I think," he said at last, "that it would be well to have a further word with M. MacQueen, in view of what we now know."

The young American appeared promptly.

"Well," he said, "how are things going?"

"Not too badly. Since our last conversation I have learnt something—the identity of M. Ratchett."

Hector MacQueen leaned forward interestedly.

"Yes?" he said.

"Ratchett, as you suspected, was merely an alias. Ratchett was Cassetti, the man who ran the celebrated kidnapping stunts—including the famous affair of little Daisy Armstrong."

An expression of utter astonishment appeared on MacQueen's face; then it darkened.

"The damned skunk!" he exclaimed.

"You had no idea of this, M. MacQueen?"

"No, sir," said the young American decidedly. "If I had I'd have cut off my right hand before it had a chance to do secretarial work for him!"

"You feel strongly about the matter, M. MacQueen?"

"I have a particular reason for doing so. My father was the district attorney who handled the case, M. Poirot. I saw Mrs. Armstrong more than once—she was a lovely woman. So gentle and heartbroken." His face darkened. "If ever a man deserved what he got, Ratchett or Cassetti is the man. I'm rejoiced at his end. Such a man wasn't fit to live!"

"You almost feel as though you would have been willing to do the good deed yourself?"

"I do. I——" He paused, then flushed rather guiltily. "Seems I'm kind of incriminating myself."

"I should be more inclined to suspect you, M. MacQueen, if you displayed an inordinate sorrow at your employer's decease."

"I don't think I could do that, even to save myself from the chair," said MacQueen grimly.

Then he added:

"If I'm not being unduly curious, just how did you figure this out? Cassetti's identity, I mean."

"By a fragment of a letter found in his compartment."

"But surely—I mean—that was rather careless of the old man?"

"That depends," said Poirot, "on the point of view."

The young man seemed to find this remark rather baffling. He stared at Poirot as though trying to make him out.

"The task before me," said Poirot, "is to make sure of the movements of everyone on the train. No offence need be taken, you understand? It is only a matter of routine."

"Sure. Get right on with it and let me clear my character if I can."

"I need hardly ask you the number of your compartment," said Poirot, smiling, "since I shared it with you for a night. It is the second-class compartment Nos. 6 and 7, and after my departure you had it to yourself."

"That's right."

"Now, M. MacQueen, I want you to describe your movements last night from the time of leaving the dining car."

"That's quite easy. I went back to my compartment, read a bit, got out on the platform at Belgrade, decided it was too cold, and got in again. I talked for a while to a young English lady who is in the compartment next to mine.

Then I fell into conversation with that Englishman, Colonel Arbuthnot—as a matter of fact I think you passed us as we were talking. Then I went in to Mr. Ratchett and, as I told you, took down some memoranda of letters he wanted written. I said good night to him and left him. Colonel Arbuthnot was still standing in the corridor. His compartment was already made up for the night, so I suggested that he should come along to mine. I ordered a couple of drinks and we got right down to it. Discussed world politics and the Government of India and our own troubles with the financial situation and the Wall Street crisis. I don't as a rule cotton to Britishers—they're a stiff-necked lot—but I liked this one."

"Do you know what time it was when he left you?"

"Pretty late. Getting on for two o'clock, I should say."

"You noticed that the train had stopped?"

"Oh, yes. We wondered a bit. Looked out and saw the snow lying very thick, but we didn't think it was serious."

"What happened when Colonel Arbuthnot finally said good night?"

"He went along to his compartment and I called to the conductor to make up my bed."

"Where were you whilst he was making it?"

"Standing just outside the door in the corridor smoking a cigarette."

"And then?"

"And then I went to bed and slept till morning."

"During the evening did you leave the train at all?"

"Arbuthnot and I thought we'd get out at—what was the name of the place?—Vincovci to stretch our legs a bit. But it was bitterly cold—a blizzard on. We soon hopped back again."

"By which door did you leave the train?"

"By the one nearest to our compartment."

"The one next to the dining car?"

"Yes."

"Do you remember if it was bolted?"

MacQueen considered.

"Why, yes, I seem to remember it was. At least there was a kind of bar that fitted across the handle. Is that what you mean?"

"Yes. On getting back into the train did you replace that bar?"

"Why, no—I don't think I did. I got in last. No, I don't seem to remember doing so."

He added suddenly:

"Is that an important point?"

"It may be. Now, I presume, Monsieur, that while you and Colonel Arbuthnot were sitting talking the door of your compartment into the corridor was open?"

Hector MacQueen nodded.

"I want you, if you can, to tell me if anyone passed along that corridor *after* the train left Vincovci until the time you parted company for the night."

MacQueen drew his brows together.

"I think the conductor passed along once," he said, "coming from the direction of the dining car. And a woman passed the other way, going towards it."

"Which woman?"

"I couldn't say. I didn't really notice. You see, I was just arguing a point with Arbuthnot. I just seem to remember a glimpse of some scarlet silk affair passing the door. I didn't look, and anyway I wouldn't have seen the person's face. As you know, my carriage faces the dining car end of the train, so a woman going along the corridor in that direction would have her back to me as soon as she passed."

Poirot nodded.

"She was going to the toilet, I presume?"

"I suppose so."

"And you saw her return?"

"Well, no, now that you mention it, I didn't notice her returning, but I suppose she must have done so."

"One more question. Do you smoke a pipe, M. MacQueen?"

"No, sir, I do not."

Poirot paused a moment.

"I think that is all at present. I should now like to see the valet of M. Ratchett. By the way, did both you and he always travel second-class?"

"He did. But I usually went first—if possible in the adjoining compartment to Mr. Ratchett. Then he had most of his baggage put in my compartment and yet could get at both it and me easily whenever he chose. But on this occasion all the first-class berths were booked except the one which he took."

"I comprehend. Thank you, M. MacQueen."

Three

The Evidence of the Valet

The American was succeeded by the pale Englishman with the inexpressive face whom Poirot had already noticed on the day before. He stood waiting very correctly. Poirot motioned to him to sit down.

"You are, I understand, the valet of M. Ratchett?"

"Yes, sir."

"Your name?"

"Edward Henry Masterman."

"Your age?"

"Thirty-nine."

"And your home address?"

"21 Friar Street, Clerkenwell."

"You have heard that your master has been murdered?"

"Yes, sir. A very shocking occurrence."

"Will you now tell me, please, at what hour you last saw M. Ratchett?"

The valet considered.

"It must have been about nine o'clock, sir, last night. That or a little after."

"Tell me in your own words exactly what happened."

"I went in to Mr. Ratchett as usual, sir, and attended to his wants."

"What were your duties exactly?"

"To fold or hang up his clothes, sir. Put his dental plate in water and see that he had everything he wanted for the night."

"Was his manner much the same as usual?"

The valet considered a moment.

"Well, sir, I think he was upset."

"In what way—upset?"

"Over a letter he'd been reading. He asked me if it was I who had put it in his compartment. Of course I told him I hadn't done any such thing, but he swore at me and found fault with everything I did."

"Was that unusual?"

"Oh, no, sir, he lost his temper easily—as I say, it just depended what had happened to upset him."

"Did your master ever take a sleeping draught?"

Dr. Constantine leaned forward a little.

"Always when travelling by train, sir. He said he couldn't sleep otherwise."

"Do you know what drug he was in the habit of taking?"

"I couldn't say, I'm sure, sir. There was no name on the bottle. Just '*The Sleeping Draught to be taken at bedtime.*'"

"Did he take it last night?"

"Yes, sir. I poured it into a glass and put it on top of the toilet table ready for him."

"You didn't actually see him drink it?"

"No, sir."

"What happened next?"

"I asked if there was anything further, and asked what time M. Ratchett would like to be called in the morning. He said he didn't want to be disturbed till he rang."

"Was that usual?"

"Quite usual, sir. He used to ring the bell for the conductor and then send him for me when he was ready to get up."

"Was he usually an early or a late riser?"

"It depended, sir, on his mood. Sometimes he'd get up for breakfast, sometimes he wouldn't get up till just on lunch time."

"So that you weren't alarmed when the morning wore on and no summons came?"

"No, sir."

"Did you know that your master had enemies?"

"Yes, sir."

The man spoke quite unemotionally.

"How did you know?"

"I had heard him discussing some letters, sir, with Mr. MacQueen."

"Had you an affection for your employer, Masterman?"

Masterman's face became, if possible, even more inexpressive than it was normally.

"I should hardly like to say that, sir. He was a generous employer."

"But you didn't like him?"

"Shall we put it that I don't care very much for Americans, sir."

"Have you ever been in America?"

"No, sir."

"Do you remember reading in the paper of the Armstrong kidnapping case?"

A little colour came into the man's cheeks.

"Yes, indeed, sir. A little baby girl, wasn't it? A very shocking affair."

"Did you know that your employer, M. Ratchett, was the principal instigator in that affair?"

"No, indeed, sir." The valet's tone held positive warmth and feeling for the first time. "I can hardly believe it, sir."

"Nevertheless, it is true. Now, to pass to your own movements last night. A matter of routine, you understand. What did you do after leaving your master?"

"I told Mr. MacQueen, sir, that the master wanted him. Then I went to my own compartment and read."

"Your compartment was—?"

"The end second-class one, sir. Next to the dining car."

Poirot was looking at his plan.

"I see—and you had which berth?"

"The lower one, sir."

"That is No. 4?"

"Yes, sir."

"Is there anyone in with you?"

"Yes, sir. A big Italian fellow."

"Does he speak English?"

"Well, a kind of English, sir." The valet's tone was deprecating. "He's been in America—Chicago—I understand."

"Do you and he talk together much?"

"No, sir. I prefer to read."

Poirot smiled. He could visualize the scene—the large voluble Italian, and the snub direct administered by the gentleman's gentleman.

"And what, may I ask, are you reading?" he inquired.

"At present, sir, I am reading *Love's Captive,* by Mrs. Arabella Richardson."

"A good story?"

"I find it highly enjoyable, sir."

"Well, let us continue. You returned to your compartment and read *Love's Captive* till—when?"

"At about ten-thirty, sir, this Italian wanted to go to bed. So the conductor came and made the beds up."

"And then you went to bed and to sleep?"

"I went to bed, sir, but I didn't sleep."

"Why didn't you sleep?"

"I had the toothache, sir."

"Oh, *là là*—that is painful."

"Most painful, sir."

"Did you do anything for it?"

"I applied a little oil of cloves, sir, which relieved the pain a little, but I was still not able to get to sleep. I turned the light on above my head and continued to read—to take my mind off it, as it were."

"And did you not go to sleep at all?"

"Yes, sir, I dropped off about four in the morning."

"And your companion?"

"The Italian fellow? Oh, he just snored."

"He did not leave the compartment at all during the night?"

"No, sir."

"Did you?"

"No, sir."

"Did you hear anything during the night?"

"I don't think so, sir. Nothing unusual, I mean. The train being at a standstill made it all very quiet."

Poirot was silent a moment or two, then he said:

"Well, I think there is very little more to be said. You cannot throw any light upon the tragedy?"

"I'm afraid not. I'm sorry, sir."

"As far as you know, was there any quarrel or bad blood between your master and M. MacQueen?"

"Oh, no, sir. Mr. MacQueen was a very pleasant gentleman."

"Where were you in service before you came to M. Ratchett?"

"With Sir Henry Tomlinson, sir, in Grosvenor Square."

"Why did you leave him?"

"He was going to East Africa, sir, and did not require my services any longer. But I am sure he will speak for me, sir. I was with him some years."

"And you have been with M. Ratchett—how long?"

"Just over nine months, sir."

"Thank you, Masterman. By the way, are you a pipe smoker?"

"No, sir. I only smoke cigarettes—gaspers, sir."

"Thank you. That will do."

The valet hesitated a moment.

"You'll excuse me, sir, but the elderly American lady is in what I might describe as a state, sir. She's saying she knows all about the murderer. She's in a very excitable condition, sir."

"In that case," said Poirot, smiling, "we had better see her next."

"Shall I tell her, sir? She's been demanding to see someone in authority for a long time. The conductor's been trying to pacify her."

"Send her to us, my friend," said Poirot. "We will listen to her story now."

Four

THE EVIDENCE OF THE AMERICAN LADY

Mrs. Hubbard arrived in the dining car in such a state of breathless excitement that she was hardly able to articulate her words.

"Now just tell me this. Who's in authority here? I've got some vurry important information, *vurry* important, indeed, and I just want to tell it to someone in authority as soon as may be. If you gentlemen—"

Her wavering glance fluctuated between the three men. Poirot leaned forward.

"Tell it to me, Madame," he said. "But, first, pray be seated."

Mrs. Hubbard plumped heavily down on to the seat opposite to him.

"What I've got to tell you is just this. There was a murder on the train last night, and the murderer was *right there in my compartment!*"

She paused to give dramatic emphasis to her words.

"You are sure of this, Madame?"

"Of course I'm sure! The idea! I know what I'm talking about. I'll tell you just everything there is to tell. I'd gotten into bed and gone to sleep, and suddenly I woke up—all in the dark, it was—and I knew there was a man in my compartment. I was just so scared I couldn't scream, if you know what I mean. I just lay there and thought, 'Mercy, I'm going to be killed.' I just can't describe to you how I felt. These nasty trains, I thought, and all the outrages I'd read of. And I thought, 'Well, anyway, he won't get my jewellery.' Because, you see, I'd put that in a stocking and hidden it under my pillow—which isn't so mighty comfortable, by the way, kinder bumpy, if you know what I mean. But that's neither here nor there. Where was I?"

"You realized, Madame, that there was a man in your compartment."

"Yes, well, I just lay there with my eyes closed, and I thought whatever should I do, and I thought, 'Well, I'm just thankful that my daughter doesn't know the plight I'm in.' And then, somehow, I got my wits about me and I felt about with my hand and I pressed the bell for the conductor. I pressed it and I pressed it, but nothing happened, and I can tell you I thought my heart was going to stop beating. 'Mercy,' I said to myself, 'maybe they've murdered every single soul on the train.' It was at a standstill, anyhow, and a nasty quiet feel in the air. But I just went on pressing that bell, and oh! the relief when I heard footsteps coming running down the corridor and a knock on the door. 'Come in,' I screamed, and I switched on the lights at the same time. And, would you believe it, there wasn't a soul there."

This seemed to Mrs. Hubbard to be a dramatic climax rather than an anti-climax.

"And what happened next, Madame?"

"Why, I told the man what had happened, and he didn't seem to believe me. Seemed to imagine I'd dreamt the whole thing. I made him look under the seat, though he said there wasn't room for a man to squeeze himself in there. It was plain enough the man had got away, but there *had* been a man there and it just made me mad the way the conductor tried to soothe me down! I'm not one to imagine things, Mr.—I don't think I know your name?"

"Poirot, Madame, and this is M. Bouc, a director of the company, and Dr. Constantine."

Mrs. Hubbard murmured:

"Pleased to meet you, I'm sure," to all three of them in an abstracted manner, and then plunged once more into her recital.

"Now I'm just not going to pretend I was as bright as I might have been. I got it into my head that it was the man from next door—the poor fellow who's been killed. I told the conductor to look at the door between the compartments, and sure enough it wasn't bolted. Well, I soon saw to that, I told him to bolt it then and there, and after he'd gone out I got up and put a suitcase against it to make sure."

"What time was this, Mrs. Hubbard?"

"Well, I'm sure I can't tell you. I never looked to see. I was so upset."

"And what is your theory now?"

"Why, I should say it was just as plain as plain could be. The man in my compartment was the murderer. Who else could he be?"

"And you think he went back into the adjoining compartment?"

"How do I know where he went? I had my eyes tight shut."

"He must have slipped out through the door into the corridor."

"Well, I couldn't say. You see, I had my eyes tight shut."

Mrs. Hubbard sighed convulsively.

"Mercy, I was scared! If my daughter only knew—"

"You do not think, Madame, that what you heard was the noise of someone moving about next door—in the murdered man's compartment?"

"No, I do not, Mr.—what is it?—Poirot. The man was *right there in the same compartment with me*. And, what's more, I've got proof of it."

Triumphantly she hauled a large handbag into view and proceeded to burrow in its interior.

She took out in turn two large clean handkerchiefs, a pair of horn-rimmed glasses, a bottle of aspirin, a packet of Glauber's salts, a celluloid tube of bright green peppermints, a bunch of keys, a pair of scissors, a book of American Express cheques, a snapshot of an extraordinarily plain-looking child, some letters, five strings of pseudo Oriental beads and a small metal object—a button.

"You see this button? Well, it's not one of *my* buttons. It's not off anything I've got. I found it this morning when I got up."

As she placed it on the table, M. Bouc leaned forward and gave an exclamation.

"But this is a button from the tunic of a Wagon Lit attendant!"

"There may be a natural explanation for that," said Poirot.

He turned gently to the lady.

"This button, Madame, may have dropped from the conductor's uniform, either when he searched your cabin, or when he was making the bed up last night."

"I just don't know what's the matter with all you people. Seems as though you don't do anything but make objections. Now listen here. I was reading a magazine last night before I went to sleep. Before I turned the light out I placed that magazine on a little case that was standing on the floor near the window. Have you got that?"

They assured her that they had.

"Very well, then. The conductor looked under the seat from near the door and then he came in and bolted the door between me and the next compartment, but he never went up near the window. Well, this morning that button was lying right on top of the magazine. What do you call that, I should like to know?"

"That, Madame, I call evidence," said Poirot.

The answer seemed to appease the lady.

"It makes me madder than a hornet to be disbelieved," she explained.

"You have given us most interesting and valuable evidence," said Poirot soothingly. "Now, may I ask you a few questions?"

"Why, willingly."

"How was it, since you were nervous of this man Ratchett, that you hadn't already bolted the door between the compartments?"

"I had," returned Mrs. Hubbard promptly.

"Oh, you had?"

"Well, as a matter of fact, I asked that Swedish creature—a pleasant soul—if it was bolted, and she said it was."

"How was it you couldn't see for yourself?"

"Because I was in bed and my sponge bag was hanging on the door handle."

"What time was it when you asked her to do this for you?"

"Now let me think. It must have been round about half-past ten or a quarter to eleven. She'd come along to see if I'd got an aspirin. I told her where to find it, and she got it out of my grip."

"You yourself were in bed?"

"Yes."

Suddenly she laughed.

"Poor soul—she was in quite a taking. You see, she'd opened the door of the next compartment by mistake."

"M. Ratchett's?"

"Yes. You know how difficult it is as you come along the train and all the doors are shut. She opened his by mistake. She was very distressed about it. He'd laughed, it seemed, and I fancy he may have said something not quite nice. Poor thing, she was all in a flutter. 'Oh! I make mistake,' she said. 'I ashamed make mistake. Not nice man,' she said. 'He say, "You too old." '"

Dr. Constantine sniggered and Mrs. Hubbard immediately froze him with a glance.

"He wasn't a nice kind of man," she said, "to say a thing like that to a lady. It's not right to laugh at such things."

Dr. Constantine hastily apologized.

"Did you hear any noise from M. Ratchett's compartment after that?" asked Poirot.

"Well—not exactly."

"What do you mean by that, Madame?"

"Well—" she paused. "He snored."

"Ah! he snored, did he?"

"Terribly. The night before it quite kept me awake."

"You didn't hear him snore after you had had the scare about a man being in your compartment?"

"Why, Mr. Poirot, how could I? He was dead."

"Ah, yes, truly," said Poirot. He appeared confused.

"Do you remember the affair of the Armstrong kidnapping, Mrs. Hubbard?" he asked.

"Yes, indeed I do. And how the wretch that did it escaped scot free! My, I'd have liked to get my hands on him."

"He has not escaped. He is dead. He died last night."

"You don't mean—?" Mrs. Hubbard half rose from her chair in excitement.

"But yes, I do. Ratchett was the man."

"*Well!* Well, to think of that! I must write and tell my daughter. Now, didn't

I tell you last night that that man had an evil face? I was right, you see. My daughter always says: 'When Momma's got a hunch, you can bet your bottom dollar it's O.K.' "

"Were you acquainted with any of the Armstrong family, Mrs. Hubbard?"

"No. They moved in a very exclusive circle. But I've always heard that Mrs. Armstrong was a perfectly lovely woman and that her husband worshipped her."

"Well, Mrs. Hubbard, you have helped us very much—very much indeed. Perhaps you will give me your full name?"

"Why, certainly. Caroline Martha Hubbard."

"Will you write your address down here?"

Mrs. Hubbard did so, without ceasing to speak.

"I just can't get over it. Cassetti—on this train. I had a hunch about that man, didn't I, Mr. Poirot?"

"Yes, indeed, Madame. By the way, have you a scarlet silk dressing gown?"

"Mercy, what an odd question! Why, no. I've got two dressing gowns with me—a pink flannel one that's kind of cosy for on board ship, and one my daughter gave me as a present—a kind of local affair in purple silk. But what in creation do you want to know about my dressing gowns for?"

"Well, you see, Madame, someone in a scarlet kimono entered either your or Mr. Ratchett's compartment last night. It is, as you said just now, very difficult when all the doors are shut to know which compartment is which."

"Well, no one in a scarlet dressing gown came into my compartment."

"Then she must have gone into M. Ratchett's."

Mrs. Hubbard pursed her lips together and said grimly:

"That wouldn't surprise me any."

Poirot leaned forward.

"So you heard a woman's voice next door?"

"I don't know how you guessed that, Mr. Poirot. I don't really. But—well—as a matter of fact, I *did*."

"But when I asked you just now if you heard anything next door, you only said you heard Mr. Ratchett snoring."

"Well that was true enough. He *did* snore part of the time. As for the other—" Mrs. Hubbard got rather pink. "It isn't a very nice thing to speak about."

"What time was it when you heard a woman's voice?"

"I can't tell you. I just woke up for a minute and heard a woman talking, and it was plain enough where she was. So I just thought, 'Well that's the kind of man he is. Well, I'm not surprised,' and then I went to sleep again, and I'm sure I should never have mentioned anything of the kind to three strange gentlemen if you hadn't dragged it out of me."

"Was it before the scare about the man in your compartment, or after?"

"Why, that's like what you said just now! He wouldn't have had a woman talking to him if he were dead, would he?"

"*Pardon.* You must think me very stupid, Madame."

"I guess even you get kinder muddled now and then. I just can't get over it being that monster Cassetti. What my daughter will say—"

Poirot managed adroitly to help the good lady to restore the contents of her handbag and he then shepherded her towards the door.

At the last moment he said:

"You have dropped your handkerchief, Madame."

Mrs. Hubbard looked at the little scrap of cambric he held out to her.

"That's not mine, Mr. Poirot. I've got mine right here."

"*Pardon.* I thought as it had the initial H on it—"

"Well, now, that's curious, but it's certainly not mine. Mine are marked C.M.H., and they're sensible things—not expensive Paris fallals. What good is a handkerchief like that to anybody's nose?"

Neither of the three men seemed to have an answer to this question, and Mrs. Hubbard sailed out triumphantly.

Five

THE EVIDENCE OF THE SWEDISH LADY

M. Bouc was handling the button Mrs. Hubbard had left behind her.

"This button. I cannot understand it. Does it mean that, after all, Pierre Michel is involved in some way?" he said. He paused, then continued, as Poirot did not reply. "What have you to say, my friend?"

"That button, it suggests possibilities," said Poirot thoughtfully. "Let us interview next the Swedish lady before we discuss the evidence we have heard."

He sorted through the pile of passports in front of him.

"Ah! here we are. Greta Ohlsson, age forty-nine."

M. Bouc gave directions to the restaurant attendant, and presently the lady with the yellowish-grey bun of hair and the long mild sheep-like face was ushered in. She peered shortsightedly at Poirot through her glasses, but was quite calm.

It transpired that she understood and spoke French, so that the conversation took place in that language. Poirot first asked her the questions to which he already knew the answers—her name, age, and address. He then asked her her occupation.

She was, she told him, matron in a missionary school near Stamboul. She was a trained nurse.

"You know, of course, of what took place last night, Mademoiselle?"

"Naturally. It is very dreadful. And the American lady tells me that the murderer was actually in her compartment."

"I hear, Mademoiselle, that you were the last person to see the murdered man alive?"

"I do not know. It may be so. I opened the door of his compartment by mistake. I was much ashamed. It was a most awkward mistake."

"You actually saw him?"

"Yes. He was reading a book. I apologized quickly and withdrew."

"Did he say anything to you?"

A slight flush showed on the worthy lady's cheek.

"He laughed and said a few words. I—I did not quite catch them."

"And what did you do after that, Mademoiselle?" asked Poirot, passing from the subject tactfully.

"I went in to the American lady, Mrs. Hubbard. I asked her for some aspirin and she gave it to me."

"Did she ask you whether the communicating door between her compartment and that of M. Ratchett was bolted?"

"Yes."

"And was it?"

"Yes."

"And after that?"

"After that I go back to my own compartment, I take the aspirin and lie down."

"What time was all this?"

"When I got into bed it was five minutes to eleven, because I look at my watch before I wind it up."

"Did you go to sleep quickly?"

"Not very quickly. My head got better, but I lay awake some time."

"Had the train come to a stop before you went to sleep?"

"I do not think so. We stopped, I think, at a station, just as I was getting drowsy."

"That would be Vincovci. Now your compartment, Mademoiselle, is this one?" he indicated it on the plan.

"That is so, yes."

"You had the upper or the lower berth?"

"The lower berth, No. 10."

"And you had a companion?"

"Yes, a young English lady. Very nice, very amiable. She had travelled from Baghdad."

"After the train left Vincovci, did she leave the compartment?"

"No, I am sure she did not."

"Why are you sure if you were asleep?"

"I sleep very lightly. I am used to waking at a sound. I am sure if she had come down from the berth above I would have awakened."

"Did you yourself leave the compartment?"

"Not until this morning."

"Have you a scarlet silk kimono, Mademoiselle?"

"No, indeed. I have a good comfortable dressing gown of Jaeger material."

"And the lady with you, Miss Debenham? What colour is her dressing-gown?"

"A pale mauve abba such as you buy in the East."

Poirot nodded. Then he said in a friendly tone:

"Why are you taking this journey? A holiday?"

"Yes, I am going home for a holiday. But first I go to Lausanne to stay with a sister for a week or so."

"Perhaps you will be so amiable as to write me down the name and address of your sister?"

"With pleasure."

She took the paper and pencil he gave her and wrote down the name and address as requested.

"Have you ever been in America, Mademoiselle?"

"No. Very nearly once. I was to go with an invalid lady, but it was cancelled at the last moment. I much regretted. They are very good, the Americans. They give much money to found schools and hospitals. They are very practical."

"Do you remember hearing of the Armstrong kidnapping case?"

"No, what was that?"

Poirot explained.

Greta Ohlsson was indignant. Her yellow bun of hair quivered with her emotion.

"That there are in the world such evil men! It tries one's faith. The poor mother. My heart aches for her."

The amiable Swede departed, her kindly face flushed, her eyes suffused with tears.

Poirot was writing busily on a sheet of paper.

"What is it you write there, my friend?" asked M. Bouc.

"*Mon cher,* it is my habit to be neat and orderly. I make here a little table of chronological events."

He finished writing and passed the paper to M. Bouc.

9:15   Train leaves Belgrade.

about 9:40   Valet leaves Ratchett with sleeping draught beside him.

about 10:00   MacQueen leaves Ratchett.

about 10:40   Greta Ohlsson sees Ratchett (last seen alive). N.B.—He was awake reading a book.

0:10   Train leaves Vincovci (late).

0:30   Train runs into a snowdrift.

0:37   Ratchett's bell rings. Conductor answers it. Ratchett says, *"Ce n'est rien. Je me suis trompé."*

about 1:17   Mrs. Hubbard thinks man is in her carriage. Rings for conductor.

M. Bouc nodded approval.

"That is very clear," he said.

"There is nothing there that strikes you as at all odd?"

"No, it seems all quite clear and above board. It seems quite plain that the crime was committed at 1:15. The evidence of the watch shows us that, and Mrs. Hubbard's story fits in. For my mind, I will make a guess at the identity of the murderer. I say, my friend, that it is the big Italian. He comes from America—from Chicago—and remember an Italian's weapon is the knife, and he stabs not once but several times."

"That is true."

"Without a doubt, that is the solution of the mystery. Doubtless he and this Ratchett were in this kidnapping business together. Cassetti is an Italian name. In some way Ratchett did on him what they call the double-cross. The Italian tracks him down, sends him warning letters first, and finally revenges himself upon him in a brutal way. It is all quite simple."

Poirot shook his head doubtfully.

"It is hardly as simple as that, I fear," he murmured.

"Me, I am convinced it is the truth," said M. Bouc, becoming more and more enamoured of his theory.

"And what about the valet with the toothache who swears that the Italian never left the compartment?"

"That is the difficulty."

Poirot twinkled.

"Yes, it is annoying, that. Unlucky for your theory, and extremely lucky for our Italian friend that M. Ratchett's valet should have had the toothache."

"It will be explained," said M. Bouc with magnificent certainty.

Poirot shook his head again.

"No, it is hardly so simple as that," he murmured again.

Six

THE EVIDENCE OF THE RUSSIAN PRINCESS

"Let us hear what Pierre Michel has to say about this button," he said.

The Wagon Lit conductor was recalled. He looked at them inquiringly.

M. Bouc cleared his throat.

"Michel," he said. "Here is a button from your tunic. It was found in the American lady's compartment. What have you to say for yourself about it?"

The conductor's hand went automatically to his tunic.

"I have lost no button, Monsieur," he said. "There must be some mistake."

"That is very odd."

"I cannot account for it, Monsieur."

The man seemed astonished, but not in any way guilty or confused.

M. Bouc said meaningly:

"Owing to the circumstances in which it was found, it seems fairly certain that this button was dropped by the man who was in Mrs. Hubbard's compartment last night when she rang the bell."

"But, Monsieur, there was no one there. The lady must have imagined it."

"She did not imagine it, Michael. The assassin of M. Ratchett passed that way—*and dropped that button*."

As the significance of M. Bouc's word became plain to him, Pierre Michel flew into a violent state of agitation.

"It is not true, Monsieur, it is not true!" he cried. "You are accusing me of the crime. Me? I am innocent. I am absolutely innocent. Why should I want to kill a Monsieur whom I have never seen before?"

"Where were you when Mrs. Hubbard's bell rang?"

"I told you, Monsieur, in the next coach, talking to my colleague."

"We will send for him."

"Do so, Monsieur, I implore you, do so."

The conductor of the next coach was summoned. He immediately confirmed Pierre Michel's statement. He added that the conductor from the Bucharest coach had also been there. The three of them had been discussing the situation caused by the snow. They had been talking some ten minutes when Michel fancied he heard a bell. As he opened the doors connecting the two coaches, they had all heard it plainly. A bell ringing repeatedly. Michel had run posthaste to answer it.

"So you see, Monsieur, I am not guilty," cried Michel anxiously.

"And this button from a Wagon Lit tunic—how do you explain it?"

"I cannot, Monsieur. It is a mystery to me. All my buttons are intact."

Both of the other conductors also declared that they had not lost a button. Also that they had not been inside Mrs. Hubbard's compartment at any time.

"Calm yourself, Michel," said M. Bouc, "and cast your mind back to the moment when you ran to answer Mrs. Hubbard's bell. Did you meet anyone at all in the corridor?"

"No, Monsieur."

"Did you see anyone going away from you down the corridor in the other direction?"

"Again, no. Monsieur."

"Odd," said M. Bouc.

"Not so very," said Poirot. "It is a question of time. Mrs. Hubbard wakes to find someone in her compartment. For a minute or two she lies paralysed, her eyes shut. Probably it was then that the man slipped out into the corridor. Then she starts ringing the bell. But the conductor does not come at once. It is only the third or fourth peal that he hears. I should say myself that there was ample time—"

"For what? For what, *mon cher?* Remember that there are thick drifts of snow all round the train."

"There are two courses open to our mysterious assassin," said Poirot slowly. "He could retreat into either of the toilets or he could disappear into one of the compartments."

"But they were all occupied."

"Yes."

"You mean that he could retreat into his *own* compartment?"

Poirot nodded.

"It fits, it fits," murmured M. Bouc. "During that ten minutes' absence of the conductor, the murderer comes from his own compartment, goes into Ratchett's, kills him, locks and chains the door on the inside, goes out through Mrs. Hubbard's compartment and is back safely in his own compartment by the time the conductor arrives."

Poirot murmured:

"It is not quite so simple as that, my friend. Our friend the doctor here will tell you so."

With a gesture M. Bouc signified that the three conductors might depart.

"We have still to see eight passengers," said Poirot. "Five first-class passengers—Princess Dragomiroff, Count and Countess Andrenyi, Colonel Arbuthnot and Mr. Hardman. Three second-class passengers—Miss Debenham, Antonio Foscarelli and the lady's maid, Fräulein Schmidt."

"Who will you see first—the Italian?"

"How you harp on your Italian! No, we will start at the top of the tree. Perhaps Madame la Princesse will be so good as to spare us a few moments of her time. Convey that message to her, Michel."

"*Oui, Monsieur,*" said the conductor, who was just leaving the car.

"Tell her we can wait on her in her compartment if she does not wish to put herself to the trouble of coming here," called M. Bouc.

But Princess Dragomiroff declined to take this course. She appeared in the dining car, inclined her head slightly and sat down opposite Poirot.

Her small toad-like face looked even yellower than the day before. She was certainly ugly, and yet, like the toad, she had eyes like jewels, dark and imperious, revealing latent energy and an intellectual force that could be felt at once.

Her voice was deep, very distinct, with a slight grating quality in it.

She cut short a flowery phrase of apology from M. Bouc.

"You need not offer apologies, Messieurs. I understand a murder has taken place. Naturally, you must interview all the passengers. I shall be glad to give all the assistance in my power."

"You are most amiable, Madame," said Poirot.

"Not at all. It is a duty. What do you wish to know?"

"Your full Christian names and address, Madame. Perhaps you would prefer to write them yourself?"

Poirot proffered a sheet of paper and pencil, but the Princess waved them aside.

"You can write it," she said. "There is nothing difficult—Natalia Dragomiroff, 17 Avenue Kleber, Paris."

"You are travelling home from Constantinople, Madame?"

"Yes, I have been staying at the Austrian Embassy. My maid is with me."

"Would you be so good as to give me a brief account of your movements last night from dinner onwards?"

"Willingly. I directed the conductor to make up my bed whilst I was in the dining car. I retired to bed immediately after dinner. I read until the hour of eleven, when I turned out my light. I was unable to sleep owing to certain rheumatic pains from which I suffer. At about a quarter to one I rang for my maid. She massaged me and then read aloud till I felt sleepy. I cannot say exactly when she left me. It may have been half an hour, it may have been later."

"The train had stopped then?"

"The train had stopped."

"You heard nothing—nothing unusual during the time, Madame?"

"I heard nothing unusual."

"What is your maid's name?"

"Hildegarde Schmidt."

"She has been with you long?"

"Fifteen years."

"You consider her trustworthy?"

"Absolutely. Her people come from an estate of my late husband's in Germany."

"You have been in America, I presume, Madame?"

The abrupt change of subject made the old lady raise her eyebrows.

"Many times."

"Were you at any time acquainted with a family of the name of Armstrong—a family in which a tragedy occurred?"

With some emotion in her voice the old lady said:

"You speak of friends of mine, Monsieur."

"You knew Colonel Armstrong well, then?"

"I knew him slightly; but his wife, Sonia Armstrong, was my god-daughter. I was on terms of friendship with her mother, the actress, Linda Arden. Linda Arden was a great genius, one of the greatest tragic actresses in the world. As Lady Macbeth, as Magda, there was no one to touch her. I was not only an ad-mirer of her art, I was a personal friend."

"She is dead?"

"No, no, she is alive, but she lives in complete retirement. Her health is very delicate, she has to lie on a sofa most of the time."

"There was, I think, a second daughter?"

"Yes, much younger than Mrs. Armstrong."

"And she is alive?"

"Certainly."

"Where is she?"

The old woman bent an acute glance at him.

"I must ask you the reason of these questions. What have they to do with the matter in hand—the murder on this train?"

"They are connected in this way, Madame, the man who was murdered was the man responsible for the kidnapping and murder of Mrs. Armstrong's child."

"Ah!"

The straight brows drew together. Princess Dragomiroff drew herself a little more erect.

"In my view, then, this murder is an entirely admirable happening! You will pardon my slightly biased point of view."

"It is most natural, Madame. And now to return to the question you did not answer. Where is the younger daughter of Linda Arden, the sister of Mrs. Arm-strong?"

"I honestly cannot tell you, Monsieur. I have lost touch with the younger generation. I believe she married an Englishman some years ago and went to England, but at the moment I cannot recollect the name."

She paused a minute and then said:

"Is there anything further you want to ask me, gentlemen?"

"Only one thing, Madame, a somewhat personal question. The colour of your dressing gown."

She raised her eyebrows slightly.

"I must suppose you have a reason for such a question. My dressing gown is of blue satin."

"There is nothing more, Madame. I am much obliged to you for answering my questions so promptly."

She made a slight gesture with her heavily-beringed hand.

Then, as she rose, and the others rose with her, she stopped.

"You will excuse me, Monsieur," she said, "but may I ask your name? Your face is somehow familiar to me."

"My name, Madame, is Hercule Poirot—at your service."

She was silent a minute, then:

"Hercule Poirot," she said. "Yes. I remember now. This is Destiny."

She walked away, very erect, a little stiff in her movements.

"*Voilà une grande dame,*" said M. Bouc. "What do you think of her, my friend?"

But Hercule Poirot merely shook his head.

"I am wondering," he said, "what she meant by Destiny."

Seven

The Evidence of Count and Countess Andrenyi

Count and Countess Andrenyi were next summoned. The Count, however, entered the dining car alone.

There was no doubt that he was a fine-looking man seen face to face. He was at least six feet in height, with broad shoulders and slender hips. He was dressed in very well-cut English tweeds, and might have been taken for an Englishman had it not been for the length of his moustache and something in the line of the cheek-bone.

"Well, Messieurs," he said, "what can I do for you?"

"You understand, Monsieur," said Poirot, "that in view of what has occurred I am obliged to put certain questions to all the passengers."

"Perfectly, perfectly," said the Count easily. "I quite understand your position. Not, I fear, that my wife and I can do much to assist you. We were asleep and heard nothing at all."

"Are you aware of the identity of the deceased, Monsieur?"

"I understand it was the big American—a man with a decidedly unpleasant face. He sat at the table at meal times."

He indicated with a nod of his head the table at which Ratchett and MacQueen had sat.

"Yes, yes, Monsieur, you are perfectly correct. I meant did you know the name of the man?"

"No." The Count looked thoroughly puzzled by Poirot's queries.

"If you want to know his name," he said, "surely it is on his passport?"

"The name on his passport is Ratchett," said Poirot. "But that, Monsieur, is not his real name. He is the man Cassetti, who was responsible for a celebrated kidnapping outrage in America."

He watched the Count closely as he spoke, but the latter seemed quite unaffected by the piece of news. He merely opened his eyes a little.

"Ah!" he said. "That certainly should throw light upon the matter. An extraordinary country America."

"You have been there, perhaps, Monsieur le Comte?"

"I was in Washington for a year."

"You knew, perhaps, the Armstrong family?"

"Armstrong—Armstrong—it is difficult to recall—one met so many."

He smiled, shrugged his shoulders.

"But to come back to the matter in hand, gentlemen," he said. "What more can I do to assist you?"

"You retired to rest—when, Monsieur le Comte?"

Hercule Poirot's eyes stole to his plan. Count and Countess Andrenyi occupied compartments No. 12 and 13 adjoining.

"We had one compartment made up for the night whilst we were in the dining car. On returning we sat in the other for a while—"

"What number would that be?"

"No. 13. We played picquet together. About eleven o'clock my wife retired for the night. The conductor made up my compartment and I also went to bed. I slept soundly until morning."

"Did you notice the stopping of the train?"

"I was not aware of it till this morning."

"And your wife?"

The Count smiled.

"My wife always takes a sleeping draught when travelling by train. She took her usual dose of trional."

He paused.

"I am sorry I am not able to assist you in any way."

Poirot passed him a sheet of paper and a pen.

"Thank you, Monsieur le Comte. It is a formality, but will you just let me have your name and address?"

The Count wrote slowly and carefully.

"It is just as well I should write this for you," he said pleasantly. "The spelling of my country estate is a little difficult for those unacquainted with the language."

He passed the paper across to Poirot and rose.

"It will be quite unnecessary for my wife to come here," he said. "She can tell you nothing more than I have."

A little gleam came into Poirot's eye.

"Doubtless, doubtless," he said. "But all the same I think I should like to have just one little word with Madame la Comtesse."

"I assure you it is quite unnecessary."

His voice rang out authoritatively.

Poirot blinked gently at him.

"It will be a mere formality," he said. "But you understand, it is necessary for my report."

"As you please."

The Count gave way grudgingly. He made a short, foreign bow and left the dining car.

Poirot reached out a hand to a passport. It set out the Count's name and titles. He passed on to the further information—*accompanied by wife.* Christian name Elena Maria; maiden name Goldenberg; age twenty. A spot of grease had been dropped some time by a careless official on it.

"A diplomatic passport," said M. Bouc. "We must be careful, my friend, to give no offence. These people can have nothing to do with the murder."

"Be easy, *mon vieux,* I will be most tactful. A mere formality."

His voice dropped as the Countess Andrenyi entered the dining car. She looked timid and extremely charming.

"You wish to see me, Messieurs?"

"A mere formality, Madame la Comtesse." Poirot rose gallantly, bowed her into the seat opposite him. "It is only to ask you if you saw or heard anything last night that may throw light upon this matter."

"Nothing at all, Monsieur. I was asleep."

"You did not hear, for instance, a commotion going on in the compartment next to yours? The American lady who occupies it had quite an attack of hysterics and rang for the conductor."

"I heard nothing, Monsieur. You see, I had taken a sleeping draught."

"Ah! I comprehend. Well, I need not detain you further." Then, as she rose swiftly, "Just one little minute—these particulars, your maiden name, age and so on, they are correct?"

"Quite correct, Monsieur."

"Perhaps you will sign this memorandum to that effect, then."

She signed quickly, a graceful slanting handwriting.

Elena Andrenyi.

"Did you accompany your husband to America, Madame?"

"No, Monsieur." She smiled, flushed a little. "We were not married then; we have only been married a year."

"Ah yes, thank you, Madame. By the way, does your husband smoke?"

She stared at him as she stood poised for departure.

"Yes."

"A pipe?"

"No. Cigarettes and cigars."

"Ah! Thank you."

She lingered; her eyes watched him curiously. Lovely eyes they were, dark and almond shaped, with very long black lashes that swept the exquisite pallor of her cheeks. Her lips, very scarlet, in the foreign fashion, were parted just a little. She looked exotic and beautiful.

"Why did you ask me that?"

"Madame," Poirot waved an airy hand, "detectives have to ask all sorts of questions. For instance, perhaps you will tell me the colour of your dressing gown?"

She stared at him. Then she laughed.

"It is corn-coloured chiffon. Is that really important?"

"Very important, Madame."

She asked curiously:

"Are you really a detective, then?"

"At your service, Madame."

"I thought there were no detectives on the train when it passed through Yugo-Slavia—not until one got to Italy."

"I am not a Yugo-Slavian detective, Madame. I am an international detective."

"You belong to the League of Nations?"

"I belong to the world, Madame," said Poirot dramatically. He went on, "I work mainly in London. You speak English?" he added in that language.

"I speak a leetle, yes."

Her accent was charming.

Poirot bowed once more.

"We will not detain you further, Madame. You see, it was not so very terrible."

She smiled, inclined her head and departed.

"Elle est jolie femme," said M. Bouc appreciatively.

He sighed.

"Well, that did not advance us much."

"No," said Poirot. "Two people who saw nothing and heard nothing."

"Shall we now see the Italian?"

Poirot did not reply for a moment. He was studying a grease spot on a Hungarian diplomatic passport.

Eight

The Evidence of Colonel Arbuthnot

Poirot roused himself with a slight start. His eyes twinkled a little as they met the eager ones of M. Bouc.

"Ah! my dear old friend," he said. "You see, I have become what they call the snob! The first-class, I feel it should be attended to before the second-class. Next, I think, we will interview the good looking Colonel Arbuthnot."

Finding the Colonel's French to be of a severely limited description, Poirot conducted his interrogation in English.

Arbuthnot's name, age, home address and exact military standing were all ascertained. Poirot proceeded:

"It is that you come home from India on what is called the leave—what we call *en permission?*"

Colonel Arbuthnot, uninterested in what a pack of foreigners called anything, replied with true British brevity:

"Yes."

"But you do not come home on the P. & O. boat?"

"No."

"Why not?"

"I chose to come by the overland route for reasons of my own."

"And that," his manner seemed to say, "is one for you, you interfering little jackanapes."

"You came straight through from India?"

The Colonel replied dryly:

"I stopped for one night to see Ur of the Chaldees and for three days in Baghdad with the A.O.C., who happens to be an old friend of mine."

"You stopped three days in Baghdad. I understand that the young English lady, Miss Debenham, also comes from Baghdad. Perhaps you met her there?"

"No, I did not. I first met Miss Debenham when she and I shared the railway convoy car from Kirkuk to Nissibin."

Poirot leaned forward. He became persuasive and a little more foreign than he need have been.

"Monsieur, I am about to appeal to you. You and Miss Debenham are the only two English people on the train. It is necessary that I should ask you each your opinion of the other."

"Highly irregular," said Colonel Arbuthnot coldly.

"Not so. You see, this crime, it was most probably committed by a woman. The man was stabbed no less than twelve times. Even the *chef de train* said at once, 'It is a woman.' Well, then, what is my first task? To give all the women travelling on the Stamboul-Calais coach what Americans call the 'once over.' But to judge of an Englishwoman is difficult. They are very reserved, the English. So I appeal to you, Monsieur, in the interests of justice. What sort of a person is this Miss Debenham? What do you know about her?"

"Miss Debenham," said the Colonel with some warmth, "is a lady."

"Ah!" said Poirot with every appearance of being much gratified. "So you do not think that she is likely to be implicated in this crime?"

"The idea is absurd," said Arbuthnot. "The man was a perfect stranger—she had never seen him before."

"Did she tell you so?"

"She did. She commented at once upon his somewhat unpleasant appearance. If a woman *is* concerned, as you seem to think (to my mind without any evidence but mere assumption), I can assure you that Miss Debenham could not possibly be indicated."

"You feel warmly in the matter," said Poirot with a smile.

Colonel Arbuthnot gave him a cold stare.

"I really don't know what you mean," he said.

The stare seemed to abash Poirot. He dropped his eyes and began fiddling with the papers in front of him.

"All this is by the way," he said. "Let us be practical and come to facts. This crime, we have reason to believe, took place at a quarter past one last night. It is part of the necessary routine to ask everyone on the train what he or she was doing at that time."

"Quite so. At a quarter past one, to the best of my belief, I was talking to the young American fellow—secretary to the dead man."

"Ah! Were you in his compartment, or was he in yours?"

"I was in his."

"That is the young man of the name of MacQueen?"

"Yes."

"He was a friend or acquaintance of yours?"

"No, I never saw him before this journey. We fell into casual conversation yesterday and both became interested. I don't as a rule like Americans—haven't any use for 'em—"

Poirot smiled, remembering MacQueen's strictures on "Britishers."

"—But I liked this young fellow. He'd got hold of some tomfool idiotic ideas about the situation in India; that's the worst of Americans—they're so sentimental and idealistic. Well, he was interested in what I had to tell him. I've had nearly thirty years experience of the country. And I was interested in what he had to tell me about the financial situation in America. Then we got down to world politics in general. I was quite surprised to look at my watch and find it was a quarter to two."

"That is the time you broke up this conversation?"

"Yes."

"What did you do then?"

"Walked along to my own compartment and turned in."

"Your bed was made up ready?"

"Yes."

"That is the compartment—let me see—No. 15—the one next but one to the end away from the dining car?"

"Yes."

"Where was the conductor when you went to your compartment?"

"Sitting at the end at a little table. As a matter of fact, MacQueen called him just as I went to my own compartment."

"Why did he call him?"

"To make up his bed, I suppose. The compartment hadn't been made up for the night."

"Now, Colonel Arbuthnot, I want you to think carefully. During the time you were talking to Mr. MacQueen did anyone pass along the corridor outside the door?"

"A good many people, I should think. I wasn't paying attention."

"Ah! but I am referring to—let us say the last hour and a half of your conversation. You got out at Vincovci, didn't you?"

"Yes, but only for about a minute. There was a blizzard on. The cold was something frightful. Made one quite thankful to get back to the fug, though as a rule I think the way these trains are overheated is something scandalous."

M. Bouc sighed.

"It is very difficult to please everybody," he said. "The English, they open everything—then others, they come along and shut everything. It is very difficult."

Neither Poirot nor Colonel Arbuthnot paid any attention to him.

"Now, Monsieur, cast your mind back," said Poirot encouragingly. "It was cold outside. You have returned to the train. You sit down again, you smoke—perhaps a cigarette, perhaps a pipe—"

He paused for the fraction of a second.

"A pipe for me. MacQueen smoked cigarettes."

"The train starts again. You smoke your pipe. You discuss the state of Europe—of the world. It is late now. Most people have retired for the night. Does anyone pass the door—think?"

Arbuthnot frowned in the effort of remembrance.

"Difficult to say," he said. "You see, I wasn't paying any attention."

"But you have the soldier's observation for detail. You notice without noticing, so to speak."

The Colonel thought again, but shook his head.

"I couldn't say. I don't remember anyone passing except the conductor. Wait a minute—and there was a woman, I think."

"You saw her? Was she old—young?"

"Didn't see her. Wasn't looking that way. Just a rustle and a sort of smell of scent."

"Scent? A *good* scent?"

"Well, rather fruity, if you know what I mean. I mean you'd smell it a hundred yards away. But mind you," the Colonel went on hastily, "this may have been earlier in the evening. You see, as you said just now, it was just one of those things you notice without noticing, so to speak. Some time that evening I said to myself, 'Woman—scent—got it on pretty thick.' But *when* it was I can't be sure, except that—why, yes, it must have been after Vincovci."

"Why?"

"Because I remember—sniffing, you know—just when I was talking about the utter washout Stalin's Five Year Plan was turning out. I know the idea—woman—brought the idea of the position of women in Russia into my mind. And I know we hadn't got on to Russia until pretty near the end of our talk."

"You can't pin it down more definitely than that?"

"N-no. It must have been roughly within the last half hour."

"It was after the train had stopped?"

The other nodded.

"Yes, I'm almost sure it was."

"Well, we will pass from that. Have you ever been in America, Colonel Arbuthnot?"

"Never. Don't want to go."

"Did you ever know a Colonel Armstrong?"

"Armstrong—Armstrong—I've known two or three Armstrongs. There was Tommy Armstrong in the 60th—you don't mean him? And Selby Armstrong—he was killed on the Somme."

"I mean the Colonel Armstrong who married an American wife and whose only child was kidnapped and killed."

"Ah, yes, I remember reading about that—shocking affair. I don't think I actually ever came across the fellow, though, of course, I knew of him. Toby

Armstrong. Nice fellow. Everybody liked him. He had a very distinguished career. Got the V.C."

"The man who was killed last night was the man responsible for the murder of Colonel Armstrong's child."

Arbuthnot's face grew rather grim.

"Then in my opinion the swine deserved what he got. Though I would have preferred to have seen him properly hanged—or electrocuted, I suppose, over there."

"In fact, Colonel Arbuthnot, you prefer law and order to private vengeance?"

"Well, you can't go about having blood feuds and stabbing each other like Corsicans or the Mafia," said the Colonel. "Say what you like, trial by jury is a sound system."

Poirot looked at him thoughtfully for a minute or two.

"Yes," he said. "I am sure that would be your view. Well, Colonel Arbuthnot, I do not think there is anything more I have to ask you. There is nothing you yourself can recall last night that in any way struck you—or shall we say strikes you now looking back—as suspicious?"

Arbuthnot considered for a moment or two.

"No," he said. "Nothing at all. Unless—" he hesitated.

"But yes, continue, I pray of you."

"Well, it's nothing really," said the Colonel slowly. "But you said *anything*."

"Yes, yes. Go on."

"Oh, it's nothing. A mere detail. But as I got back to my compartment I noticed that the door of the one beyond mine—the end one, you know—"

"Yes, No. 16."

"Well, the door of it was not quite closed. And the fellow inside peered out in a furtive sort of way. Then he pulled the door to quickly. Of course, I know there's nothing in that—but it just struck me as a bit odd. I mean, it's quite usual to open a door and stick your head out if you want to see anything. But it was the furtive way he did it that caught my attention."

"Ye-es," said Poirot doubtfully.

"I told you there was nothing to it," said Arbuthnot apologetically. "But you know what it is—early hours of the morning—everything very still—the thing had a sinister look—like a detective story. All nonsense, really."

He rose.

"Well, if you don't want me any more—"

"Thank you, Colonel Arbuthnot, there is nothing else."

The soldier hesitated for a minute. His first natural distaste for being questioned by "foreigners" had evaporated.

"About Miss Debenham," he said rather awkwardly. "You can take it from me that she's all right. She's a *pukka sahib*."

Flushing a little, he withdrew.

"What," asked Dr. Constantine with interest, "does a *pukka sahib* mean?"

"It means," said Poirot, "that Miss Debenham's father and brothers were at the same kind of school as Colonel Arbuthnot."

"Oh!" said Dr. Constantine, disappointed. "Then it has nothing to do with the crime at all."

"Exactly," said Poirot.

He fell into a reverie, beating a light tattoo on the table. Then he looked up.

"Colonel Arbuthnot smokes a pipe," he said. "In the compartment of Mr. Ratchett I found a pipe cleaner. M. Ratchett smoked only cigars."

"You think—?"

"He is the only man so far who admits to smoking a pipe. And he knew of Colonel Armstrong—perhaps actually did know him though he won't admit it."

"So you think it possible—"

Poirot shook his head violently.

"That is just it—it is *im*possible—quite impossible—that an honourable, slightly stupid, upright Englishman should stab an enemy twelve times with a knife! Do you not feel, my friends, how impossible it is?"

"That is the psychology," said M. Bouc.

"And one must respect the psychology. This crime has a signature and it is certainly not the signature of Colonel Arbuthnot. But now to our next interview."

This time M. Bouc did not mention the Italian. But he thought of him.

Nine

THE EVIDENCE OF MR. HARDMAN

The last of the first-class passengers to be interviewed—Mr. Hardman—was the big flamboyant American who had shared a table with the Italian and the valet.

He wore a somewhat loud check suit, a pink shirt, a flashy tiepin, and was rolling something round his tongue as he entered the dining car. He had a big, fleshy, coarse-featured face, with a good-humoured expression.

"Morning, gentlemen," he said. "What can I do for you?"

"You have heard of this murder, Mr.—er—Hardman?"

"Sure."

He shifted the chewing gum deftly.

"We are of necessity interviewing all the passengers on the train."

"That's all right by me. Guess that's the only way to tackle the job."

Poirot consulted the passport lying in front of him.

"You are Cyrus Bethman Hardman, United States subject, forty-one years of age, travelling salesman for typewriting ribbons?"

"O.K., that's me."

"You are travelling from Stamboul to Paris?"

"That's so."

"Reason?"

"Business."

"Do you always travel first-class, Mr. Hardman?"

"Yes, sir. The firm pays my travelling expenses."

He winked.

"Now, Mr. Hardman, we come to the events of last night."

The American nodded.

"What can you tell us about the matter?"

"Exactly nothing at all."

"Ah, that is a pity. Perhaps, Mr. Hardman, you will tell us exactly what you did last night, from dinner onwards?"

For the first time the American did not seem ready with his reply. At last he said:

"Excuse me, gentlemen, but just who are you? Put me wise."

"This is M. Bouc, a director of the Compagnie des Wagons Lits. This gentleman is the doctor who examined the body."

"And you yourself?"

"I am Hercule Poirot. I am engaged by the company to investigate this matter."

"I've heard of you," said Mr. Hardman. He reflected a minute or two longer. "Guess I'd better come clean."

"It will certainly be advisable for you to tell us all you know," said Poirot dryly.

"You'd have said a mouthful if there was anything I *did* know. But I don't. I know nothing at all—just as I said. But I *ought* to know something. That's what makes me sore. I *ought* to."

"Please explain, Mr. Hardman."

Mr. Hardman sighed, removed the chewing gum, and dived into a pocket. At the same time his whole personality seemed to undergo a change. He became less of a stage character and more of a real person. The resonant nasal tones of his voice became modified.

"That passport's a bit of bluff," he said. "That's who I really am."

Poirot scrutinized the card flipped across to him. M. Bouc peered over his shoulder.

Mr. Cyrus B. Hardman
McNeil's Detective Agency,
New York.

Poirot knew the name. It was one of the best known and most reputable private detective agencies in New York.

"Now, Mr. Hardman," he said. "Let us hear the meaning of this."

"Sure. Things came about this way. I'd come over to Europe trailing a couple of crooks—nothing to do with this business. The chase ended in Stamboul. I wired the Chief and got his instructions to return, and I would have been making my tracks back to little old New York when I got this."

He pushed across a letter.

The heading at the top was the Tokatlian Hotel.

Dear Sir,—You have been pointed out to me as an operative of the McNeil Detective Agency. Kindly report to my suite at four o'clock this afternoon.

It was signed "S.E. Ratchett."

"Eh bien?"

"I reported at the time stated and Mr. Ratchett put me wise to the situation. He showed me a couple of letters he'd got."

"He was alarmed?"

"Pretended not to be, but he was rattled all right. He put up a proposition to me. I was to travel by the same train as he did to Parrus and see that nobody got him. Well, gentlemen, I *did* travel by the same train and, in spite of me, somebody *did* get him. I certainly feel sore about it. It doesn't look any too good for me."

"Did he give you any indication of the line you were to take?"

"Sure. He had it all taped out. It was his idea that I should travel in the compartment alongside his—well, that was blown upon straight away. The only place I could get was berth No. 16, and I had a bit of a job getting that. I guess the conductor likes to keep that compartment up his sleeve. But that's neither here nor there. When I looked all round the situation, it seemed to me that No. 16 was a pretty good strategic position. There was only the dining car in front of the Stamboul sleeping car, the door on to the platform at the front end was barred at night. The only way a thug could come was through the rear end door to the platform or along the train from the rear—in either case he'd have to pass right by my compartment."

"You had no idea, I suppose, of the identity of the possible assailant."

"Well, I knew what he looked like. Mr. Ratchett described him to me."

"What?"

All three men leaned forward eagerly.

Hardman went on:

"A small man, dark, with a womanish kind of voice—that's what the old man said. Said, too, that he didn't think it would be the first night out. More likely the second or third."

"He knew something," said M. Bouc.

"He certainly knew more than he told his secretary," said Poirot thoughtfully. "Did he tell you anything about this enemy of his? Did he, for instance, say *why* his life was threatened?"

"No, he was kinder reticent about that part of it. Just said the fellow was out for his blood and meant to get it."

"A small man—dark—with a womanish voice," said Poirot thoughtfully.

Then, fixing a sharp glance on Hardman, he said:

"You knew who he really was, of course?"

"Which, mister?"

"Ratchett. You recognized him?"

"I don't get you."

"Ratchett was Cassetti, the Armstrong murderer."

Mr. Hardman gave way to a prolonged whistle.

"That certainly is some surprise!" he said. "Yes, *sir!* No, I didn't recognize him. I was away out West when that case came on. I suppose I saw photos of him in the papers, but I wouldn't recognize my own mother when a press photographer had done with her. Well, I don't doubt that a few people had it in for Cassetti all right."

"Do you know of anyone connected with the Armstrong case who answers to that description—small, dark, womanish voice?"

Hardman reflected a minute or two.

"It's hard to say. Pretty nearly everyone to do with that case is dead."

"There was the girl who threw herself out of the window, remember."

"Sure. That's a good point, that. She was a foreigner of some kind. Maybe she had some wop relations. But you've got to remember that there were other cases besides the Armstrong case. Cassetti had been running this kidnapping stunt some time. You can't concentrate on that only."

"Ah, but we have reason to believe that this crime is connected with the Armstrong case."

Mr. Hardman cocked an inquiring eye. Poirot did not respond. The American shook his head.

"I can't call to mind anybody answering that description in the Armstrong case," he said slowly. "But of course I wasn't in it and didn't know much about it."

"Well, continue your narrative, M. Hardman."

"There's very little to tell. I got my sleep in the daytime and stayed awake on the watch at night. Nothing suspicious happened the first night. Last night was the same, as far as I was concerned. I had my door a little ajar and watched. No stranger passed."

"You are sure of that, M. Hardman?"

"I'm plumb certain. Nobody got on that train from outside and nobody came along the train from the rear carriages. I'll take my oath on that."

"Could you see the conductor from your position?"

"Sure. He sits on that little seat almost flush with my door."

"Did he leave that seat at all after the train stopped at Vincovci?"

"That was the last station? Why, yes, he answered a couple of bells—that would be just after the train came to a halt for good. Then, after that, he went past me into the rear coach—was there about a quarter of an hour. There was a bell ringing like mad and he came back running. I stepped out into the corridor to see what it was all about—felt a mite nervous, you understand—but it was only the American dame. She was raising hell about something or other. I grinned. Then he went on to another compartment and came back and got a bottle of mineral water for someone. After that he settled down in his seat till he went up to the far end to make somebody's bed up. I don't think he stirred after that until about five o'clock this morning."

"Did he doze off at all?"

"That I can't say. He may have done."

Poirot nodded. Automatically his hands straightened the papers on the table. He picked up the official card once more.

"Be so good as just to initial this," he said.

The other complied.

"There is no one, I suppose, who can confirm your story of your identity, M. Hardman?"

"On this train? Well, not exactly. Unless it might be young MacQueen. I know him well enough—seen him in his father's office in New York—but that's not to say he'll remember me from a crowd of other operatives. No, Mr. Poirot, you'll have to wait and cable New York when the snow lets up. But it's O.K. I'm not telling the tale. Well, so long, gentlemen. Pleased to have met you, Mr. Poirot."

Poirot proffered his cigarette case.

"But perhaps you prefer a pipe?"

"Not me."

He helped himself, then strode briskly off.

The three men looked at each other.

"You think he is genuine?" asked Dr. Constantine.

"Yes, yes. I know the type. Besides, it is a story that would be very easily disproved."

"He has given us a piece of very interesting evidence," said M. Bouc.

"Yes, indeed."

"A small man, dark, with a high-pitched voice," said M. Bouc thoughtfully.

"A description which applies to no one on the train," said Poirot.

Ten

The Evidence of the Italian

"And now," said Poirot with a twinkle in his eye, "we will delight the heart of M. Bouc and see the Italian."

Antonio Foscarelli came into the dining car with a swift, cat-like tread. His face beamed. It was a typical Italian face, sunny looking and swarthy.

He spoke French well and fluently, with only a slight accent.

"Your name is Antonio Foscarelli?"

"Yes, Monsieur."

"You are, I see, a naturalized American subject?"

The American grinned.

"Yes, Monsieur. It is better for my business."

"You are an agent for Ford motor cars?"

"Yes, you see—"

A voluble exposition followed. At the end of it, anything that the three men did not know about Foscarelli's business methods, his journeys, his income, and his opinion of the United States and most European countries seemed a negligible factor. This was not a man who had to have information dragged from him. It gushed out.

His good-natured childish face beamed with satisfaction as with a last eloquent gesture, he paused and wiped his forehead with a handkerchief.

"So you see," he said, "I do big business. I am up to date. I understand salesmanship!"

"You have been in the United States, then, for the last ten years on and off?"

"Yes, Monsieur. Ah! well do I remember the day I first took the boat—to go to America, so far away! My mother, my little sister—"

Poirot cut short the flood of reminiscence.

"During your sojourn in the United States did you ever come across the deceased?"

"Never. But I know the type. Oh, yes." He snapped his fingers expressively. "It is very respectable, very well dressed, but underneath it is all wrong. Out of my experience, I should say he was the big crook. I give you my opinion for what it is worth."

"Your opinion is quite right," said Poirot dryly. "Ratchett was Cassetti, the kidnapper."

"What did I tell you? I have learned to be very acute—to read the face. It is necessary. Only in America do they teach you the proper way to sell."

"You remember the Armstrong case?

"I do not quite remember. The name, yes? It was a little girl—a baby—was it not?"

"Yes, a very tragic affair."

The Italian seemed the first person to demur to this view.

"Ah, well, these things they happen," he said philosophically, "in a great civilization such as America—"

Poirot cut him short.

"Did you ever come across any members of the Armstrong family?"

"No, I do not think so. It is difficult to say. I will give you some figures. Last year alone I sold—"

"Monsieur, pray confine yourself to the point."

The Italian's hands flung themselves out in a gesture of apology.

"A thousand pardons."

"Tell me, if you please, your exact movements last night from dinner onwards."

"With pleasure. I stay here as long as I can. It is more amusing. I talk to the American gentleman at my table. He sells typewriter ribbons. Then I go back to my compartment. It is empty. The miserable John Bull who shares it with me is away attending to his master. At last he comes back—very long face as usual. He will not talk—says yes and no. A miserable race, the English—not sympathetic. He sits in the corner, very stiff, reading a book. Then the conductor comes and makes our beds."

"Nos. 4 and 5," murmured Poirot.

"Exactly—the end compartment. Mine is the upper berth. I get up there. I smoke and read. The little Englishman has, I think, the toothache. He gets out a little bottle of stuff that smells very strong. He lies in bed and groans. Presently I sleep. Whenever I wake I hear him groaning."

"Do you know if he left the carriage at all during the night?"

"I do not think so. That, I should hear. The light from the corridor— one wakes up automatically thinking it is the Customs examination at some frontier."

"Did he ever speak of his master? Ever express any animus against him?"

"I tell you he did not speak. He was not sympathetic. A fish."

"You smoke, you say—a pipe, cigarettes, cigars?"

"Cigarettes only."

Poirot proffered him one which he accepted.

"Have you ever been in Chicago?" inquired M. Bouc.

"Oh, yes—a fine city—but I know best New York, Washington, Detroit. You have been to the States? No? You should go, it—"

Poirot pushed a sheet of paper across to him.

"If you will sign this, and put your permanent address, please."

The Italian wrote with a flourish. Then he rose—his smile was as engaging as ever.

"That is all? You do not require me further? Good day to you, Messieurs. I wish we could get out of the snow. I have an appointment in Milan—" He shook his head sadly. "I shall lose the business."

He departed.

Poirot looked at his friend.

"He has been a long time in America," said M. Bouc, "and he is an Italian, and Italians use the knife! And they are great liars! I do not like Italians."

"Ça se voit," said Poirot with a smile. "Well, it may be that you are right, but

I will point out to you, my friend, that there is absolutely no evidence against the man."

"And what about the psychology? Do not Italians stab?"

"Assuredly," said Poirot. "Especially in the heat of a quarrel. But this—this is a different kind of crime. I have the little idea, my friend, that this is a crime very carefully planned and staged. It is a far-sighted, long-headed crime. It is not—how shall I express it?—a *Latin* crime. It is a crime that shows traces of a cool, resourceful, deliberate brain—I think an Anglo-Saxon brain."

He picked up the last two passports.

"Let us now," he said, "see Miss Mary Debenham."

Eleven

The Evidence of Miss Debenham

When Mary Debenham entered the dining car she confirmed Poirot's previous estimate of her.

Very neatly dressed in a little black suit with a French grey shirt, the smooth waves of her dark head were neat and unruffled. Her manner was as calm and unruffled as her hair.

She sat down opposite Poirot and M. Bouc and looked at them inquiringly.

"Your name is Mary Hermione Debenham, and you are twenty-six years of age?" began Poirot.

"Yes."

"English?"

"Yes."

"Will you be so kind, Mademoiselle, as to write down your permanent address on this piece of paper?"

She complied. Her writing was clear and legible.

"And now, Mademoiselle, what have you to tell us of the affair last night?"

"I am afraid I have nothing to tell you. I went to bed and slept."

"Does it distress you very much, Mademoiselle, that a crime has been committed on this train?"

The question was clearly unexpected. Her grey eyes widened a little.

"I don't quite understand you."

"It was a perfectly simple question that I asked you, Mademoiselle. I will repeat it. Are you very much distressed that a crime should have been committed on this train?"

"I have not really thought about it from that point of view. No, I cannot say that I am at all distressed."

"A crime—it is all in the day's work to you, eh?"

"It is naturally an unpleasant thing to have happen," said Mary Debenham quietly.

"You are very Anglo-Saxon. Mademoiselle. *Vous n'éprouvez pas d'émotion.*"

She smiled a little.

"I am afraid I cannot have hysterics to prove my sensibility. After all, people die every day."

"They die, yes. But murder is a little more rare."

"Oh, certainly."

"You were not acquainted with the dead man?"

"I saw him for the first time when lunching here yesterday."

"And how did he strike you?"

"I hardly noticed him."

"He did not strike you as an evil personality."

She shrugged her shoulders slightly.

"Really, I cannot say I thought about it."

Poirot looked at her keenly.

"You are, I think, a little bit contemptuous of the way I prosecute my inquiries," he said with a twinkle. "Not so, you think, would an English inquiry be conducted. There everything would be cut and dried—it would be all kept to the facts—a well-ordered business. But I, Mademoiselle, have my little originalities. I look first at my witness, I sum up his or her character, and I frame my questions accordingly. Just a little minute ago I am asking questions of a gentleman who wants to tell me all his ideas on every subject. Well, him I keep strictly to the point. I want him to answer yes or no, this or that. And then you come. I see at once that you will be orderly and methodical. You will confine yourself to the matter in hand. Your answers will be brief and to the point. And because, Mademoiselle, human nature is perverse, I ask of you quite different questions. I ask what you *feel,* what you *thought.* It does not please you this method?"

"If you will forgive my saying so, it seems somewhat of a waste of time. Whether or not I liked Mr. Ratchett's face does not seem likely to be helpful in finding out who killed him."

"Do you know who the man Ratchett really was, Mademoiselle?"

She nodded.

"Mrs. Hubbard has been telling everyone."

"And what do you think of the Armstrong affair?"

"It was quite abominable," said the girl crisply.

Poirot looked at her thoughtfully.

"You are travelling from Baghdad, I believe, Miss Debenham?"

"Yes."

"To London?"

"Yes."

"What have you been doing in Baghdad?"

"I have been acting as governess to two children."

"Are you returning to your post after your holiday?"

"I am not sure."

"Why is that?"

"Baghdad is rather out of things. I think I should prefer a post in London if I can hear of a suitable one."

"I see. I thought, perhaps, you might be going to be married."

Miss Debenham did not reply. She raised her eyes and looked Poirot full in the face. The glance said plainly, "You are impertinent."

"What is your opinion of the lady who shares your compartment—Miss Ohlsson?"

"She seems a pleasant, simple creature."

"What colour is her dressing gown?"

Mary Debenham stared.

"A kind of brownish colour—natural wool."

"Ah! I may mention without indiscretion, I hope, that I noticed the colour of your dressing gown on the way from Aleppo to Stamboul. A pale mauve, I believe."

"Yes, that is right."

"Have you any other dressing gown, Mademoiselle? A scarlet dressing gown, for example?"

"No, that is not mine."

Poirot leaned forward. He was like a cat pouncing on a mouse.

"Whose, then?"

The girl drew back a little, startled.

"I don't know. What do you mean?"

"You do not say, 'No, I have no such thing.' You say, 'That is not mine'—meaning that such a thing *does* belong to someone else."

She nodded.

"Somebody else on this train?"

"Yes."

"Whose is it?"

"I told you just now. I don't know. I woke up this morning about five o'clock with the feeling that the train had been standing still for a long time. I opened the door and looked out into the corridor, thinking we might be at a station. I saw someone in a scarlet kimono some way down the corridor."

"And you don't know who it was? Was she fair or dark or grey-haired?"

"I can't say. She had on a shingle cap and I only saw the back of her head."

"And in build?"

"Tallish and slim, I should judge, but it's difficult to say. The kimono was embroidered with dragons."

"Yes, yes that is right, dragons."

He was silent a minute. He murmured to himself:

"I cannot understand. I cannot understand. None of this makes sense."

Then, looking up, he said:

"I need not keep you further, Mademoiselle."

"Oh!" she seemed rather taken aback, but rose promptly. In the doorway, however, she hesitated a minute and then came back.

"The Swedish lady—Miss Ohlsson, is it?—seems rather worried. She says you told her she was the last person to see this man alive. She thinks, I believe, that you suspect her on that account. Can't I tell her that she has made a mistake? Really, you know, she is the kind of creature who wouldn't hurt a fly."

She smiled a little as she spoke.

"What time was it that she went to fetch the aspirin from Mrs. Hubbard?"

"Just after half-past ten."

"She was away—how long?"

"About five minutes."

"Did she leave the compartment again during the night?"

"No."

Poirot turned to the doctor.

"Could Ratchett have been killed as early as that?"

The doctor shook his head.

"Then I think you can reassure your friend, Mademoiselle."

"Thank you." She smiled suddenly at him, a smile that invited sympathy. "She's like a sheep, you know. She gets anxious and bleats."

She turned and went out.

Twelve

THE EVIDENCE OF THE GERMAN LADY'S MAID

M. Bouc was looking at his friend curiously.

"I do not quite understand you, *mon vieux*. You were trying to do—what?"

"I was searching for a flaw, my friend."

"A flaw?"

"Yes—in the armour of a young lady's self-possession. I wished to shake her *sangfroid*. Did I succeed? I do not know. But I know this—she did not expect me to tackle the matter as I did."

"You suspect her," said M. Bouc slowly. "But why? She seems a very charming young lady—the last person in the world to be mixed up in a crime of this kind."

"I agree," said Constantine. "She is cold. She has not emotions. She would not stab a man; she would sue him in the law courts."

Poirot sighed.

"You must, both of you, get rid of your obsession that this is an unpremeditated and sudden crime. As for the reason why I suspect Miss Debenham, there are two. One is because of something that I overheard, and that you do not as yet know."

He retailed to them the curious interchange of phrases he had overheard on the journey from Aleppo.

"That is curious, certainly," said M. Bouc when he had finished. "It needs explaining. If it means what you suspect it means, then they are both of them in it together—she and the stiff Englishman."

Poirot nodded.

"And that is just what is not borne out by the facts," he said. "See you, if they were both in this together, what should we expect to find—that each of them would provide an alibi for the other. Is not that so? But no—that does not happen. Miss Debenham's alibi is provided by a Swedish woman whom she has never seen before, and Colonel Arbuthnot's alibi is vouched for by MacQueen, the dead man's secretary. No, that solution of the puzzle is too easy."

"You said there was another reason for your suspicions of her," M. Bouc reminded him.

Poirot smiled.

"Ah! but that is only psychological. I ask myself, is it possible for Miss Debenham to have planned this crime? Behind this business, I am convinced, there is a cool, intelligent, resourceful brain. Miss Debenham answers to that description."

M. Bouc shook his head.

"I think you are wrong, my friend. I do not see that young English girl as a criminal."

"Ah, well," said Poirot, picking up the last passport, "to the final name on our list. Hildegarde Schmidt, lady's maid."

Summoned by the attendant, Hildegarde Schmidt came into the restaurant car and stood waiting respectfully.

Poirot motioned her to sit down.

She did so, folding her hands and waiting placidly till he questioned her. She seemed a placid creature altogether—eminently respectable—perhaps not over intelligent.

Poirot's methods with Hildegarde Schmidt were a complete contrast to his handling of Mary Debenham.

He was at his kindest and most genial, setting the woman at her ease. Then, having got her to write down her name and address, he slid gently into his questions.

The interview took place in German.

"We want to know as much as possible about what happened last night," he said. "We know that you cannot give us much information bearing on the crime itself, but you may have seen or heard something that, while conveying nothing to you, may be valuable to us. You understand?"

She did not seem to. Her broad, kindly face remained set in its expression of placid stupidity as she answered:

"I do not know anything, Monsieur."

"Well, for instance, you know that your mistress sent for you last night?"

"That, yes."

"Do you remember the time?"

"I do not, Monsieur. I was asleep, you see, when the attendant came and told me."

"Yes, yes. Was it usual for you to be sent for in this way?"

"It was not unusual, Monsieur. The gracious lady often required attention at night. She did not sleep well."

"*Eh bien,* then, you received the summons and you got up. Did you put on a dressing gown?"

"No, Monsieur, I put on a few clothes. I would not like to go in to her Excellency in my dressing gown."

"And yet it is a very nice dressing gown—scarlet, is it not?"

She stared at him.

"It is a dark-blue flannel dressing gown, Monsieur."

"Ah! continue. A little pleasantry on my part, that is all. So you went along to Madame la Princesse. And what did you do when you got there?"

"I gave her massage, Monsieur, and then I read aloud. I do not read aloud very well, but her Excellency says that is all the better. So it sends her better to sleep. When she became sleepy, Monsieur, she told me to go, so I closed the book and I returned to my own compartment."

"Do you know what time that was?"

"No, Monsieur."

"Well, how long had you been with Madame la Princesse?"

"About half an hour, Monsieur."

"Good, continue."

"First, I fetched her Excellency an extra rug from my compartment. It was very cold in spite of the heating. I arranged the rug over her and she wished me good night. I poured her out some mineral water. Then I turned out the light and left her."

"And then?"

"There is nothing more, Monsieur. I returned to my carriage and went to sleep."

"And you met no one in the corridor?"

"No, Monsieur."

"You did not, for instance, see a lady in a scarlet kimono with dragons on it?"

Her mild eyes bulged at him.

"No, indeed, Monsieur. There was nobody about except the attendant. Everyone was asleep."

"But you did see the conductor?"

"Yes, Monsieur."

"What was he doing?"

"He came out of one of the compartments, Monsieur."

"What?" M. Bouc leaned forward. "Which one?"

Hildegarde Schmidt looked frightened again and Poirot cast a reproachful glance at his friend.

"Naturally," he said. "The conductor often has to answer bells at night. Do you remember which compartment it was?"

"It was about the middle of the coach, Monsieur. Two or three doors from Madame la Princesse."

"Ah! tell us, if you please, exactly where this was and what happened."

"He nearly ran into me, Monsieur. It was when I was returning from my compartment to that of the Princess with the rug."

"And he came out of a compartment and almost collided with you? In which direction was he going?"

"Towards me, Monsieur. He apologized and passed on down the corridor towards the dining car. A bell began ringing, but I do not think he answered it."

She paused and then said:

"I do not understand. How is it—?"

Poirot spoke reassuringly.

"It is just a question of times," he said. "All a matter of routine. This poor conductor, he seems to have had a busy night—first waking you and then answering bells."

"It was not the same conductor who woke me, Monsieur. It was another one."

"Ah, another one! Had you seen him before?"

"No. Monsieur."

"Ah! Do you think you would recognize him if you saw him?"

"I think so, Monsieur."

Poirot murmured something in M. Bouc's ear. The latter got up and went to the door to give an order.

Poirot was continuing his questions in an easy friendly manner.

"Have you ever been to America, Frau Schmidt?"

"Never, Monsieur. It must be a fine country."

"You have heard, perhaps, of who this man who was killed really was—that he was responsible for the death of a little child."

"Yes, I have heard, Monsieur. It was abominable—wicked. The good God should not allow such things. We are not so wicked as that in Germany."

Tears had come into the woman's eyes. Her strong motherly soul was moved.

"It was an abominable crime," said Poirot gravely.

He drew a scrap of cambric from his pocket and handed it to her.

"Is this your handkerchief, Frau Schmidt?"

There was a moment's silence as the woman examined it. She looked up after a minute. The colour had mounted a little in her face.

"Ah! no, indeed. It is not mine, Monsieur."

"It has the initial H, you see. That is why I thought it was yours."

"Ah! Monsieur, it is a lady's handkerchief, that. A very expensive handkerchief. Embroidered by hand. It comes from Paris, I should say."

"It is not yours and you do not know whose it is?"

"I? Oh, no, Monsieur."

Of the three listening, only Poirot caught the nuance of hesitation in the reply.

M. Bouc whispered in his ear. Poirot nodded and said to the woman:

"The three sleeping car attendants are coming in. Will you be so kind as to tell me which is the one you met last night as you were going with the rug to the Princess?"

The three men entered. Pierre Michel, the big blond conductor of the Athens-Paris coach, and the stout burly conductor of the Bucharest one.

Hildegarde Schmidt looked at them and immediately shook her head.

"No, Monsieur," she said. "None of these is the man I saw last night."

"But these are the only conductors on the train. You must be mistaken."

"I am quite sure, Monsieur. These are all tall, big men. The one I saw was small and dark. He had a little moustache. His voice when he said *'Pardon'* was weak like a woman's. Indeed, I remember him very well, Monsieur."

Thirteen

Summary of the Passengers' Evidence

"A small dark man with a womanish voice," said M. Bouc.

The three conductors and Hildegarde Schmidt had been dismissed.

"But I understand nothing—but nothing of all this! The enemy that this Ratchett spoke of, he was then on the train after all? But where is he now? How can he have vanished into thin air? My head, it whirls. Say something, then, my friend, I implore you. Show me how the impossible can be possible!"

"It is a good phrase that," said Poirot. "The impossible cannot have happened, therefore the impossible must be possible in spite of appearances."

"Explain to me then, quickly, what actually happened on the train last night."

"I am not a magician, *mon cher.* I am, like you, a very puzzled man. This affair advances in a very strange manner."

"It does not advance at all. It stays where it was."

Poirot shook his head.

"No, that is not true. We are more advanced. We know certain things. We have heard the evidence of the passengers."

"And what has that told us? Nothing at all."

"I would not say that, my friend."

"I exaggerate, perhaps. The American, Hardman, and the German maid—yes, they have added something to our knowledge. That is to say, they have made the whole business more unintelligible than it was."

"No, no, no," said Poirot soothingly.

M. Bouc turned upon him.

"Speak, then, let us hear the wisdom of Hercule Poirot."

"Did I not tell you that I was, like you, a very puzzled man? But at least we can face our problem. We can arrange such facts as we have with order and method."

"Pray continue, Monsieur," said Dr. Constantine.

Poirot cleared his throat and straightened a piece of blotting-paper.

"Let us review the case as it stands at this moment. First, there are certain indisputable facts. This man Ratchett, or Cassetti, was stabbed in twelve places and died last night. That is fact one."

"I grant it to you—I grant it, *mon vieux*," said M. Bouc with a gesture of irony.

Hercule Poirot was not at all put out. He continued calmly.

"I will pass over for the moment certain rather peculiar appearances which Dr. Constantine and I have already discussed together. I will come to them presently. The next fact of importance, to my mind, is the *time* of the crime."

"That, again, is one of the few things we do know," said M. Bouc. "The crime was committed at a quarter past one this morning. Everything goes to show that was so."

"Not *everything*. You exaggerate. There is, certainly, a fair amount of evidence to support that view."

"I am glad you admit that at least."

Poirot went on calmly, unperturbed by the interruption.

"We have before us three possibilities:

"One: That the crime was committed, as you say, at a quarter past one. This is supported by the evidence of the German woman, Hildegarde Schmidt. It agrees with the evidence of Dr. Constantine.

"Possibility two: The crime was committed later and the evidence of the watch was deliberately faked.

"Possibility three: The crime was committed earlier and the evidence faked for the same reason as above.

"Now, if we accept possibility one as the most likely to have occurred and the one supported by most evidence, we must also accept certain facts arising from it. To begin with, if the crime was committed at a quarter past one, the murderer cannot have left the train, and the question arises: Where is he? And *who* is he?

"To begin with, let us examine the evidence carefully. We first hear of the existence of this man—the small dark man with a womanish voice—from the man Hardman. He says that Ratchett told him of this person and employed him to watch out for the man. There is no *evidence* to support this—we have only Hardman's word for it. Let us next examine the question: Is Hardman the person he pretends to be—an operative of a New York Detective Agency?

"What to my mind is so interesting in this case is that we have none of the facilities afforded to the police. We cannot investigate the bona fides of any of these people. We have to rely solely on deduction. That, to me, makes the matter very much more interesting. There is no routine work. It is a matter of the intellect. I ask myself, 'Can we accept Hardman's account of himself?' I make my decision and I answer, 'Yes.' I am of the opinion that we *can* accept Hardman's account of himself."

"You rely on the intuition—what the Americans call the hunch?" said Dr. Constantine.

"Not at all. I regard the probabilities. Hardman is travelling with a false passport—that will at once make him an object of suspicion. The first thing that the police will do when they do arrive upon the scene is to detain Hardman and cable as to whether his account of himself is true. In the case of many of the passengers, to establish their bona fides will be difficult; in most cases it will probably not be attempted, especially since there seems nothing in the way of suspicion attaching to them. But in Hardman's case it is simple. Either he is the person he represents himself to be or he is not. Therefore I say that all will prove to be in order."

"You acquit him of suspicion?"

"Not at all. You misunderstand me. For all I know, any American detective might have his own private reasons for wishing to murder Ratchett. No, what I am saying is that I think we *can* accept Hardman's own account of *himself*. This story, then, that he tells of Ratchett's seeking him out and employing him, is not unlikely and is most probably, though not of course certainly, true. If we are going to accept it as true, we must see if there is any confirmation of it. We find it in rather an unlikely place—in the evidence of Hildegarde Schmidt. Her description of the man she saw in Wagon Lit uniform tallies exactly. Is there any further confirmation of these two stories? There is. There is the button found in her compartment by Mrs. Hubbard. And there is also another corroborating statement which you may not have noticed."

"What is that?"

"The fact that both Colonel Arbuthnot and Hector MacQueen mention that the conductor passed their carriage. They attached no importance to the fact, but Messieurs, *Pierre Michel has declared that he did not leave his seat except on certain specified occasions,* none of which would take him down to the far end of the coach past the compartment in which Arbuthnot and MacQueen were sitting.

"Therefore this story, the story of a small dark man with a womanish voice dressed in Wagon Lit uniform, rests on the testimony—direct or indirect—of four witnesses."

"One small point," said Dr. Constantine. "If Hildegarde Schmidt's story is true, how is it that the real conductor did not mention having seen her when he came to answer Mrs. Hubbard's bell?"

"That is explained, I think. When he arrived to answer Mrs. Hubbard, the maid was in with her mistress. When she finally returned to her own compartment, the conductor was in with Mrs. Hubbard."

M. Bouc had been waiting with difficulty until they had finished.

"Yes, yes, my friend," he said impatiently to Poirot. "But whilst I admire your caution, your method of advancing a step at a time, I submit that you have not yet touched the point at issue. We are all agreed that this person exists. The point is—*where did he go?*"

Poirot shook his head reprovingly.

"You are in error. You are inclined to put the cart before the horse. Before I ask myself, *'Where did this man vanish to?'* I ask myself, *'Did such a man really exist?'* Because, you see, if the man were an invention—a fabrication—how much easier to make him disappear! So I try to establish first that there really *is* such a flesh and blood person."

"And having arrived at the fact that there is—*eh bien*—where is he now?"

"There are only two answers to that, *mon cher.* Either he is still hidden on the train in a place of such extraordinary ingenuity that we cannot even think of it, or else he is, as one might say, *two persons.* That is, he is both himself—the man feared by M. Ratchett—and a passenger on the train so well disguised that M. Ratchett did not recognize him."

"It is an idea, that," said M. Bouc, his face lighting up. Then it clouded over again. "But there is one objection—"

Poirot took the words out of his mouth.

"The height of the man. It is that you would say? With the exception of M. Ratchett's valet, all the passengers are big men—the Italian, Colonel Arbuthnot, Hector MacQueen, Count Andrenyi. Well, that leaves us the valet—not a very likely supposition. But there is another possibility. Remember the 'womanish' voice. That gives us a choice of alternatives. The man may be disguised as a woman, or, alternatively, he may actually *be* a woman. A tall woman dressed in man's clothes would look small."

"But surely Ratchett would have known—"

"Perhaps he *did* know. Perhaps, already this woman had attempted his life wearing men's clothes the better to accomplish her purpose. Ratchett may have guessed that she would use the same trick again, so he tells Hardman to look for a man. But he mentions, however, a womanish voice."

"It is a possibility," said M. Bouc. "But—"

"Listen, my friend, I think that I should now tell you of certain inconsistencies noticed by Dr. Constantine."

He retailed at length the conclusions that he and the doctor had arrived at together from the nature of the dead man's wounds. M. Bouc groaned and held his head again.

"I know," said Poirot sympathetically. "I know exactly how you feel. The head spins, does it not?"

"The whole thing is a fantasy," cried M. Bouc.

"Exactly. It is absurd—improbable—it cannot be. So I myself have said. And yet, my friend, *there it is!* One cannot escape from the facts."

"It is madness!"

"Is it not? It is so mad, my friend, that sometimes I am haunted by the sensation that really it must be very simple . . .

"But that is only one of my 'little ideas.' . . ."

"Two murderers," groaned M. Bouc. "And on the Orient Express."

The thought almost made him weep.

"And now let us make the fantasy more fantastic," said Poirot cheerfully. "Last night on the train there are two mysterious strangers. There is the Wagon Lit attendant answering to the description given us by M. Hardman, and seen by Hildegarde Schmidt, Colonel Arbuthnot and M. MacQueen. There is also a woman in a red kimono—a tall, slim woman—seen by Pierre Michel, by Miss Debenham, by M. MacQueen and by myself—and smelt, I may say, by Colonel Arbuthnot! Who was she? No one on the train admits to having a scarlet kimono. She, too, has vanished. Was she one and the same with the spurious Wagon Lit attendant? Or was she some quite distinct personality? Where are they, these two? And, incidentally, where is the Wagon Lit uniform and the scarlet kimono?"

"Ah! that is something definite." M. Bouc sprang up eagerly. "We must search all the passengers' luggage. Yes, that will be something."

Poirot rose also.

"I will make a prophecy," he said.

"You know where they are?"

"I have a little idea."

"Where, then?"

"You will find the scarlet kimono in the baggage of one of the men and you will find the uniform of the Wagon Lit conductor in the baggage of Hildegarde Schmidt."

"Hildegarde Schmidt? You think—"

"Not what you are thinking. I will put it like this. If Hildegarde Schmidt is guilty, the uniform *might* be found in her baggage—but if she is innocent it *certainly* will be."

"But how—" began M. Bouc and stopped.

"What is this noise that approaches?" he cried. "It resembles a locomotive in motion."

The noise drew nearer. It consisted of shrill cries and protests in a woman's voice. The door at the end of the dining car flew open. Mrs. Hubbard burst in.

"It's too horrible," she cried. "It's just too horrible. In my sponge bag. My sponge bag. A great knife—all over blood."

And, suddenly toppling forward, she fainted heavily on M. Bouc's shoulder.

Fourteen

The Evidence of the Weapon

With more vigour than chivalry, M. Bouc deposited the fainting lady with her head on the table. Dr. Constantine yelled for one of the restaurant attendants, who came at a run.

"Keep her head so," said the doctor. "If she revives give her a little cognac. You understand?"

Then he hurried off after the other two. His interest lay wholly in the crime—swooning middle-aged ladies did not interest him at all.

It is possible that Mrs. Hubbard revived rather quicker with these methods than she might otherwise have done. A few minutes later she was sitting up, sipping cognac from a glass proffered by the attendant, and talking once more.

"I just can't say how terrible it was. I don't suppose anybody on this train can understand my feelings. I've always been vurry, vurry sensitive ever since a child. The mere sight of blood—ugh—why even now I come over queer when I think about it."

The attendant proffered the glass again.

"Encore un peu, Madame."

"D'you think I'd better? I'm a lifelong teetotaller. I just never touch spirits or wine at any time. All my family are abstainers. Still perhaps as this is only medical—"

She sipped once more.

In the meantime Poirot and M. Bouc, closely followed by Dr. Constantine, had hurried out of the restaurant car and along the corridor of the Stamboul coach towards Mrs. Hubbard's compartment.

Every traveller on the train seemed to be congregated outside the door. The conductor, a harrassed look on his face, was keeping them back.

"Mais il n'y a rien à voir," he said, and repeated the sentiment in several other languages.

"Let me pass, if you please," said M. Bouc.

Squeezing his rotundity past the obstructing passengers, he entered the compartment, Poirot close behind him.

"I am glad you have come Monsieur," said the conductor with a sigh of relief. "Everyone has been trying to enter. The American lady—such screams as she gave—*ma foi!* I thought she too had been murdered! I came at a run and there she was screaming like a mad woman, and she cried out that she must fetch you and she departed, screeching at the top of her voice and telling everybody whose carriage she passed what had occurred."

He added, with a gesture of the hand:

"*It* is in there, Monsieur. I have not touched it."

Hanging on the handle of the door that gave access to the next compartment was a large-size checked rubber sponge bag. Below it on the floor, just where it had fallen from Mrs. Hubbard's hand, was a straightbladed dagger—a cheap affair, sham Oriental, with an embossed hilt and a tapering blade. The blade was stained with patches of what looked like rust.

Poirot picked it up delicately.

"Yes," he murmured. "There is no mistake. Here is our missing weapon all right—eh, *docteur?*"

The doctor examined it.

"You need not be so careful," said Poirot. "There will be no fingerprints on it save those of Mrs. Hubbard."

Constantine's examination did not take long.

"It is the weapon all right," he said. "It would account for any of the wounds."

"I implore you, my friend, do not say that."

The doctor looked astonished.

"Already we are heavily overburdened by coincidence. Two people decide to stab M. Ratchett last night. It is too much of a good thing that each of them should select an identical weapon."

"As to that, the coincidence is not, perhaps, so great as it seems," said the doctor. "Thousands of these sham Eastern daggers are made and shipped to the bazaars of Constantinople."

"You console me a little, but only a little," said Poirot. He looked thoughtfully at the door in front of him, then, lifting off the sponge bag, he tried the handle. The door did not budge. About a foot above the handle was the door bolt, Poirot drew it back and tried again, but still the door remained fast.

"We locked it from the other side, you remember," said the doctor.

"That is true," said Poirot absently. He seemed to be thinking about something else. His brow was furrowed as though in perplexity.

"It agrees, does it not?" said M. Bouc. "The man passes through this carriage. As he shuts the communicating door behind him he feels the sponge bag. A thought comes to him and he quickly slips the bloodstained knife inside. Then, all unwitting that he has awakened Mrs. Hubbard, he slips out through the other door into the corridor."

"As you say," murmured Poirot. "That is how it must have happened."

But the puzzled look did not leave his face.

"But what is it?" demanded M. Bouc. "There is something, is there not, that does not satisfy you?"

Poirot darted a quick look at him.

"The same point does not strike you? No, evidently not. Well, it is a small matter."

The conductor looked into the carriage.

"The American lady is coming back."

Dr. Constantine looked rather guilty. He had, he felt, treated Mrs. Hubbard rather cavalierly. But she had no reproaches for him. Her energies were concentrated on another matter.

"I'm just going to say one thing right out," she said breathlessly as she arrived in the doorway. "I'm not going on any longer in this compartment! Why, I wouldn't sleep in it tonight if you paid me a million dollars."

"But, Madame—"

"I know what you are going to say, and I'm telling you right now that I won't do any such thing! Why, I'd rather sit up all night in the corridor."

She began to cry.

"Oh! if my daughter could only know—if she could see me now, why—"

Poirot interrupted firmly.

"You misunderstand, Madame. Your demand is most reasonable. Your baggage shall be changed at once to another compartment."

Mrs. Hubbard lowered her handkerchief.

"Is that so? Oh, I feel better right away. But surely it's all full up, unless one of the gentlemen—"

M. Bouc spoke.

"Your baggage, Madame, shall be moved out of this coach altogether. You shall have a compartment in the next coach which was put on at Belgrade."

"Why, that's splendid. I'm not an out of the way nervous woman, but to sleep in that compartment next door to a dead man—" She shivered. "It would drive me plumb crazy."

"Michel," called M. Bouc. "Move this baggage into a vacant compartment in the Athens-Paris coach."

"Yes, Monsieur—the same one as this—the No. 3?"

"No," said Poirot before his friend could reply. "I think it would be better for Madame to have a different number altogether. The No. 12, for instance."

"*Bien, Monsieur.*"

The conductor seized the luggage. Mrs. Hubbard turned gratefully to Poirot.

"That's vurry kind and delicate of you. I appreciate it, I assure you."

"Do not mention it, Madame. We will come with you and see you comfortably installed."

Mrs. Hubbard was escorted by the three men to her new home. She looked round her happily.

"This is fine."

"It suits you, Madame? It is, you see, exactly like the compartment you have left."

"That's so—only it faces the other way. But that doesn't matter, for these trains go first one way and then the other. I said to my daughter, 'I want a carriage facing the engine,' and she said, 'Why, Momma, that'll be no good to you, for if you go to sleep one way, when you wake up the train's going the other.' And it was quite true what she said. Why, last evening we went into Belgrade one way and out the other."

"At any rate, Madame, you are quite happy and contented now?"

"Well, no, I wouldn't say that. Here we are stuck in a snowdrift and nobody doing anything about it, and my boat sailing the day after tomorrow."

"Madame," said M. Bouc, "we are all in the same case—every one of us."

"Well, that's true," admitted Mrs. Hubbard. "But nobody else has had a murderer walking right through their compartment in the middle of the night."

"What still puzzles me, Madame," said Poirot, "is how the man got into your compartment if the communicating door was bolted as you say. You are sure that it *was* bolted?"

"Why, the Swedish lady tried it before my eyes."

"Let us just reconstruct that little scene. You were lying in your bunk—so—and you could not see for yourself, you say?"

"No, because of the sponge bag. Oh, my, I shall have to get a new sponge bag. It makes me feel sick in my stomach to look at this one."

Poirot picked up the sponge bag and hung it on the handle of the communicating door into the next carriage.

"*Précisément*—I see," he said. "The bolt is just underneath the handle—the sponge bag masks it. You could not see from where you were lying whether the bolt were turned or not."

"Why, that's just what I've been telling you!"

"And the Swedish lady, Miss Ohlsson, stood so, between you and the door. She tried it and told you it was bolted."

"That's so."

"All the same, Madame, she may have made an error. You see what I mean." Poirot seemed anxious to explain. "The bolt is just a projection of metal—so. Turned to the right the door is locked, left straight, it is not. Possibly she merely tried the door, and as it was locked on the other side she may have assumed that it was locked on your side."

"Well I guess that would be rather stupid of her."

"Madame, the most kind, the most amiable are not always the cleverest."

"That's so, of course."

"By the way, Madame, did you travel out to Smyrna this way?"

"No. I sailed right to Stamboul, and a friend of my daughter's—Mr. Johnson (a perfectly lovely man; I'd like to have you know him)—met me and showed me all round Stamboul, which I found a very disappointing city—all tumbling down. And as for those mosques and putting on those great shuffling things over your shoes—where was I?"

"You were saying that Mr. Johnson met you."

"That's so, and he saw me on board a French Messagerie boat for Smyrna, and my daughter's husband was waiting right on the quay. What he'll say when he hears about all this! My daughter said this would be just the safest, easiest way imaginable. 'You just sit in your carriage,' she said, 'and you get right to Parrus and there the American Express will meet you.' And, oh dear, what am I to do about cancelling my steamship passage? I ought to let them know. I can't possibly make it now. This is just too terrible—"

Mrs. Hubbard showed signs of tears once more.

Poirot, who had been fidgeting slightly, seized his opportunity.

"You have had a shock, Madame. The restaurant attendant shall be instructed to bring you along some tea and some biscuits."

"I don't know that I'm so set on tea," said Mrs. Hubbard tearfully. "That's more an English habit."

"Coffee, then, Madame. You need some stimulant."

"That cognac's made my head feel mighty funny. I think I would like some coffee."

"Excellent. You must revive your forces."

"My, what a funny expression."

"But first, Madame, a little matter of routine. You permit that I make a search of your baggage?"

"Whatever for?"

"We are about to commence a search of all the passengers' luggage. I do not want to remind you of an unpleasant experience, but your sponge bag—remember."

"Mercy! Perhaps you'd better! I just couldn't bear to get any more surprises of that kind."

The examination was quickly over. Mrs. Hubbard was travelling with the minimum of luggage—a hat box, a cheap suitcase, and a well-burdened travelling bag. The contents of all three were simple and straightforward, and the examination would not have taken more than a couple of minutes had not Mrs. Hubbard delayed matters by insisting on due attention being paid to photographs of "My daughter" and two rather ugly children—"My daughter's children. Aren't they cunning?"

Fifteen

The Evidence of the Passengers' Luggage

Having delivered himself of various polite insincerities, and having told Mrs. Hubbard that he would order coffee to be brought to her, Poirot was able to take his leave accompanied by his two friends.

"Well, we have made a start and drawn a blank," observed M. Bouc. "Whom shall we tackle next?"

"It would be simplest, I think, just to proceed along the train carriage by carriage. That means that we start with No. 16—the amiable M. Hardman."

Mr. Hardman, who was smoking a cigar, welcomed them affably.

"Come right in, gentlemen—that is, if it's humanly possible. It's just a mite cramped in here for a party."

M. Bouc explained the object of their visit, and the big detective nodded comprehendingly.

"That's O.K. To tell the truth, I've been wondering you didn't get down to it sooner. Here are my keys, gentlemen and if you like to search my pockets too, why, you're welcome. Shall I reach the grips down for you?"

"The conductor will do that. Michel!"

The contents of Mr. Hardman's two "grips" were soon examined and passed. They contained perhaps an undue proportion of spirituous liquor. Mr. Hardman winked.

"It's not often they search your grips at the frontiers—not if you fix the conductor. I handed out a wad of Turkish notes right away, and there's been no trouble so far."

"And at Paris?"

Mr. Hardman winked again.

"By the time I get to Paris," he said, "what's left over of this little lot will go into a bottle labelled hairwash."

"You are not a believer in Prohibition, Monsieur Hardman," said M. Bouc with a smile.

"Well," said Hardman. "I can't say Prohibition has ever worried me any."

"Ah!" said M. Bouc. "The speakeasy." He pronounced the word with care, savouring it.

"Your American terms are so quaint, so expressive," he said.

"Me, I would much like to go to America," said Poirot.

"You'd learn a few go-ahead methods over there," said Hardman. "Europe wants waking up. She's half asleep."

"It is true that America is the country of progress," agreed Poirot. "There is much that I admire about Americans. Only—I am perhaps old-fashioned—but me, I find the American woman less charming than my own countrywomen. The French or Belgian girl, coquettish, charming—I think there is no one to touch her."

Hardman turned away to peer out at the snow for a minute.

"Perhaps you're right, M. Poirot," he said. "But I guess every nation likes its own girls best."

He blinked as though the snow hurt his eyes.

"Kind of dazzling, isn't it?" he remarked. "Say, gentlemen, this business is getting on my nerves. Murder and the snow and all, and nothing *doing*. Just hanging about and killing time. I'd like to get busy after someone or something."

"The true Western spirit of hustle," said Poirot with a smile.

The conductor replaced the bags and they moved on to the next compartment. Colonel Arbuthnot was sitting in a corner smoking a pipe and reading a magazine.

Poirot explained their errand. The Colonel made no demur. He had two heavy leather suitcases.

"The rest of my kit has gone by long sea," he explained.

Like most Army men, the Colonel was a neat packer. The examination of his baggage took only a few minutes. Poirot noted a packet of pipe cleaners.

"You always use the same kind?" he asked.

"Usually. If I can get 'em."

"Ah!" Poirot nodded.

These pipe cleaners were identical with the one he had found on the floor of the dead man's compartment.

Dr. Constantine remarked as much when they were out in the corridor again.

"*Tout de même,*" murmured Poirot, "I can hardly believe it. It is not *dans son caractère,* and when you have said that you have said everything."

The door of the next compartment was closed. It was that occupied by Princess Dragomiroff. They knocked on the door and the Princess's deep voice called, *"Entrez."*

M. Bouc was spokesman. He was very deferential and polite as he explained their errand.

The Princess listened to him in silence, her small toad-like face quite impassive.

"If it is necessary, Messieurs," she said quietly when he had finished, "that is all there is to it. My maid has the keys. She will attend to it with you."

"Does your maid always carry your keys, Madame?" asked Poirot.

"Certainly, Monsieur."

"And if during the night at one of the frontiers the Customs officials should require a piece of luggage to be opened?"

The old lady shrugged her shoulders.

"It is very unlikely. But in such a case this conductor would fetch her."

"You trust her, then, implicitly, Madame?"

"I have told you so already," said the Princess quietly. "I do not employ people whom I do not trust."

"Yes," said Poirot thoughtfully. "Trust is indeed something in these days. It is, perhaps, better to have a homely woman whom one can trust than a more *chic* maid—for example, some smart Parisienne."

He saw the dark intelligent eyes come slowly round and fasten themselves upon his face.

"What exactly are you implying, M. Poirot?"

"Nothing, Madame. I? Nothing."

"But yes. You think, do you not, that I should have a smart Frenchwoman to attend to my toilet?"

"It would be, perhaps, more usual, Madame."

She shook her head.

"Schmidt is devoted to me." Her voice dwelt lingeringly on the words. "Devotion—*c'est impayable.*"

The German woman had arrived with the keys. The Princess spoke to her in her own language, telling her to open the valises and help the gentlemen in their search. She herself remained in the corridor looking out at the snow and Poirot remained with her, leaving M. Bouc to the task of searching the luggage.

She regarded him with a grim smile.

"Well, Monsieur, do you not wish to see what my valises contain?"

He shook his head.

"Madame, it is a formality, that is all."

"Are you so sure?"

"In your case, yes."

"And yet I knew and loved Sonia Armstrong. What do you think, then? That I would not soil my hands with killing such *canaille* as that man Cassetti? Well, perhaps you are right."

She was silent a minute or two, then she said:

"With such a man as that, do you know what I should have liked to have done? I should have liked to call to my servants: "Flog this man to death and fling him out on the rubbish heap." That is the way things were done when I was young. Monsieur."

Still he did not speak, just listened attentively.

She looked at him with a sudden impetuosity.

"You do not say anything, M. Poirot. What is it that you are thinking, I wonder?"

He looked at her with a very direct glance.

"I think, Madame, that your strength is in your will—not in your arm."

She glanced down at her thin, black-clad arms ending in those claw-like yellow hands with the rings on the fingers.

"It is true," she said. "I have no strength in these—none. I do not know if I am sorry or glad."

Then she turned abruptly back towards her carriage, where the maid was busily packing up the cases.

The Princess cut short M. Bouc's apologies.

"There is not need for you to apologize, Monsieur," she said. "A murder has been committed. Certain actions have to be performed. That is all there is to it."

"Vous êtes bien amiable, Madame."

She inclined her head slightly as they departed.

The doors of the next two carriages were shut. M. Bouc paused and scratched his head.

"Diable!" he said. "This may be awkward. These are diplomatic passports. Their baggage is exempt."

"From Customs examination, yes. But a murder is different."

"I know. All the same—we do not want to have complications—"

"Do not distress yourself, my friend. The Count and Countess will be reasonable. See how amiable Princess Dragomiroff was about it."

"She is truly *grande dame*. These two are also of the same position, but the Count impressed me as a man of somewhat truculent disposition. He was not pleased when you insisted on questioning his wife. And this will annoy him still further. Suppose—eh—we omit them. After all, they can have nothing to do with the matter. Why should I stir up needless trouble for myself."

"I do not agree with you," said Poirot. "I feel sure that Count Andrenyi will be reasonable. At any rate, let us make the attempt."

And, before M. Bouc could reply, he rapped sharply on the door of No. 13.

A voice from within cried, *"Entrez."*

The Count was sitting in the corner near the door reading a newspaper. The

Countess was curled up in the opposite corner near the window. There was a pillow behind her head, and she seemed to have been asleep.

"Pardon, Monsieur le Comte," began Poirot. "Pray forgive this intrusion. It is that we are making a search of all the baggage on the train. In most cases a mere formality. But it has to be done. M. Bouc suggests that, as you have a diplomatic passport, you might reasonably claim to be exempt from such a search."

The Count considered for a moment.

"Thank you," he said. "But I do not think that I care for an exception to be made in my case. I should prefer that our baggage should be examined like that of the other passengers."

He turned to his wife.

"You do not object, I hope, Elena?"

"Not at all," said the Countess without hesitation.

A rapid and somewhat perfunctory search followed. Poirot seemed to be trying to mask an embarrassment in making various small pointless remarks, such as:

"Here is a label all wet on your suitcase, Madame," as he lifted down a blue morocco case with initials on it and a coronet.

The Countess did not reply to this observation. She seemed, indeed, rather bored by the whole proceeding, remaining curled up in her corner, staring dreamily out through the window whilst the men searched her luggage in the compartment next door.

Poirot finished his search by opening the little cupboard above the washbasin and taking a rapid glance at its contents—a sponge, face cream, powder and a small bottle labelled trional.

Then, with polite remarks on either side, the search party withdrew.

Mrs. Hubbard's compartment, that of the dead man, and Poirot's own came next.

They now came to the second-class carriages. The first one, Nos. 10, 11, was occupied by Mary Debenham, who was reading a book, and Greta Ohlsson, who was fast asleep but woke with a start at their entrance.

Poirot repeated his formula. The Swedish lady seemed agitated, Mary Debenham calmly indifferent.

Poirot addressed himself to the Swedish lady.

"If you permit, Mademoiselle, we will examine your baggage first, and then perhaps you would be so good as to see how the American lady is getting on. We have moved her into one of the carriages in the next coach, but she is still very upset as the result of her discovery. I have ordered coffee to be sent to her, but I think she is of those to whom someone to talk to is a necessity of the first water."

The good lady was instantly sympathetic. She would go immediately. It must have been indeed a terrible shock to the nerves, and already the poor lady was upset by the journey and leaving her daughter. Ah, yes, certainly she would go at once—her case was not locked—and she would take with her some sal ammoniac.

She bustled off. Her possessions were soon examined. They were meagre in the extreme. She had evidently not noticed the missing wires from the hat box.

Miss Debenham had put her book down. She was watching Poirot. When he asked her, she handed over her keys. Then, as he lifted down a case and opened it, she said:

"Why did you send her away, M. Poirot?"

"I, Mademoiselle? Why, to minister to the American lady."

"An excellent pretext—but a pretext all the same."

"I don't understand you, Mademoiselle."

"I think you understand me very well."

She smiled.

"You wanted to get me alone. Wasn't that it?"

"You are putting words into my mouth, Mademoiselle."

"And ideas into your head? No, I don't think so. The ideas are already there. That is right, isn't it?"

"Mademoiselle, we have a proverb—"

"*Que s'excuse s'accuse;* is that what you were going to say? You must give me the credit for a certain amount of observation and common sense. For some reason or other you have got it into your head that I know something about this sordid business—this murder of a man I never saw before."

"You are imagining things, Mademoiselle."

"No, I am not imagining things at all. But it seems to me that a lot of time is wasted by not speaking the truth—by beating about the bush instead of coming straight out with things."

"And you do not like the waste of time. No, you like to come straight to the point. You like the direct method. *Eh bien,* I will give it to you, the direct method. I will ask you the meaning of certain words that I overheard on the journey from Syria. I had got out of the train to do what the English call 'stretch the legs' at the station of Konya. Your voice and the Colonel's, Mademoiselle, they came to me out of the night. You said to him, *'Not now. Not now. When it's all over. When it's behind us.'* What did you mean by those words. Mademoiselle?"

She said very quietly:

"Do you think I meant—murder?"

"It is I who am asking you, Mademoiselle."

She sighed—was lost a minute in thought. Then, as though rousing herself, she said:

"Those words had a meaning, Monsieur, but not one that I can tell you. I can only give you my solemn word of honour that I had never set eyes on this man Ratchett in my life until I saw him on this train."

"And—you refuse to explain those words?"

"Yes—if you like to put it that way—I refuse. They had to do with—with a task I had undertaken."

"A task that is now ended?"

"What do you mean?"

"It is ended, is it not?"

"Why should you think so?"

"Listen, Mademoiselle, I will recall to you another incident. There was a delay to the train on the day we were to reach Stamboul. You were very agitated, Mademoiselle. You, so calm, so self-controlled. You lost that calm."

"I did not want to miss my connection."

"So you said. But, Mademoiselle, the Orient Express leaves Stamboul every day of the week. Even if you had missed the connection it would only have been a matter of twenty-four hours' delay."

Miss Debenham for the first time showed signs of losing her temper.

"You do not seem to realize that one may have friends awaiting one's arrival in London, and that a day's delay upsets arrangements and causes a lot of annoyance."

"Ah, it is like that? There are friends awaiting your arrival? You do not want to cause them inconvenience?"

"Naturally."

"And yet—it is curious—"

"What is curious?"

"On this train—again we have a delay. And this time a more serious delay, since there is no possibility of sending a telegram to your friends or of getting them on the long—the long—"

"The long distance? The telephone, you mean."

"Ah, yes, the portmanteau call, as you say in England."

Mary Debenham smiled a little in spite of herself.

"Trunk call," she corrected. "Yes, as you say, it is extremely annoying not to be able to get any word through, either by telephone or telegraph."

"And yet, mademoiselle, *this* time your manner is quite different. You no longer betray the impatience. You are calm and philosophical."

Mary Debenham flushed and bit her lip. She no longer felt inclined to smile.

"You do not answer, Mademoiselle?"

"I am sorry. I did not know that there was anything to answer."

"The explanation of your change of attitude, Mademoiselle."

"Don't you think that you are making rather a fuss about nothing, M. Poirot?"

Poirot spread out his hands in an apologetic gesture.

"It is perhaps a fault with us detectives. We expect the behaviour to be always consistent. We do not allow for changes of mood."

Mary Debenham made no reply.

"You know Colonel Arbuthnot well, Mademoiselle?"

He fancied that she was relieved by the change of subject.

"I met him for the first time on this journey."

"Have you any reason to suspect that he may have known this man Ratchett?"

She shook her head decisively.

"I am quite sure he didn't."

"Why are you sure?"

"By the way he spoke."

"And yet, Mademoiselle, we found a pipe cleaner on the floor of the dead man's compartment. And Colonel Arbuthnot is the only man on the train who smokes a pipe?"

He watched her narrowly, but she displayed neither surprise nor emotion, merely said:

"Nonsense. It's absurd. Colonel Arbuthnot is the last man in the world to be mixed up in a crime—especially a theatrical kind of crime like this."

It was so much what Poirot himself thought that he found himself on the point of agreeing with her. He said instead:

"I must remind you that you do not know him very well, Mademoiselle."

She shrugged her shoulders.

"I know the type well enough."

He said very gently:

"You still refuse to tell me the meaning of those words—'When it's behind us?' "

She said coldly:

"I have nothing more to say."

"It does not matter," said Hercule Poirot. "I shall find out."

He bowed and left the compartment, closing the door after him.

"Was that wise, my friend?" asked M. Bouc. "You have put her on her guard—and through her you have put the Colonel on his guard also."

"*Mon ami,* if you wish to catch a rabbit you put a ferret into the hole, and if the rabbit is there he runs. That is all I have done."

They entered the compartment of Hildegarde Schmidt.

The woman was standing in readiness, her face respectful but unemotional.

Poirot took a quick glance through the contents of the small case on the seat. Then he motioned to the attendant to get down the bigger suitcase from the rack.

"The keys?" he said.

"It is not locked, Monsieur."

Poirot undid the hasps and lifted the lid.

"Aha!" he said, and turning to M. Bouc, "You remember what I said? Look here a little moment!"

On the top of the suitcase was a hastily rolled up brown Wagon Lit uniform.

The stolidity of the German woman underwent a sudden change.

"Ach!" she cried. "That is not mine. I did not put it there. I have never looked in that case since we left Stamboul. Indeed, indeed, it is true."

She looked from one to another pleadingly.

Poirot took her gently by the arm and soothed her.

"No, no all is well. We believe you. Do not be agitated. I am as sure you did not hide the uniform there as I am sure that you are a good cook. See. You are a good cook, are you not?"

Bewildered, the woman smiled in spite of herself.

"Yes, indeed, all my ladies have said so. I—"

She stopped, her mouth open, looking frightened again.

"No, no," said Poirot. "I assure you all is well. See, I will tell you how this happened. This man, the man you saw in Wagon Lit uniform, comes out of the dead man's compartment. He collides with you. That is bad luck for him. He has hoped that no one will see him. What to do next? He must get rid of his uniform. It is now not a safeguard, but a danger."

His glance went to M. Bouc and Dr. Constantine, who were listening attentively.

"There is the snow, you see. The snow which confuses all his plans. Where can he hide these clothes? All the compartments are full. No, he passes one where the door is open and shows it to be unoccupied. It must be the one belonging to the woman with whom he has just collided. He slips in, removes the uniform and jams it hurriedly into a suitcase on the rack. It may be some time before it is discovered."

"And then?" said M. Bouc.

"That we must discuss," said Poirot with a warning glance.

He held up the tunic. A button, the third down, was missing. Poirot slipped his hand into the pocket and took out a conductor's pass key, used to unlock the doors of the compartments.

"Here is the explanation of how our man was able to pass through locked doors," said M. Bouc. "Your questions to Mrs. Hubbard were unnecessary. Locked or not locked, the man could easily get through the communicating door. After all, if a Wagon Lit uniform, why not a Wagon Lit key?"

"Why not, indeed," said Poirot.

"We might have known it, really. You remember Michel said that the door into the corridor of Mrs. Hubbard's compartment was locked when he came in answer to her bell."

"That is so, Monsieur," said the conductor. "That is why I thought the lady must have been dreaming."

"But now it is easy," continued M. Bouc. "Doubtless he meant to relock the communicating door also, but perhaps he heard some movement from the bed and it startled him."

"We have now," said Poirot, "only to find the scarlet kimono."

"True. And these last two compartments are occupied by men."

"We will search all the same."

"Oh! assuredly. Besides, I remember what you said."

Hector MacQueen acquiesced willingly in the search.

"I'd just as soon you did," he said with a rueful smile. "I feel I'm just definitely the most suspicious character on the train. You've only got to find a will in which the old man left me all his money, and that'll just about fix things."

M. Bouc bent a suspicious glance upon him.

"That's just my fun," said MacQueen hastily. "He'd never have left me a cent, really. I was just useful to him—languages and so on. You're apt to be done down, you know, if you don't speak anything but good American. I'm no linguist myself, but I know what I call shopping and hotel snappy bits in French and German and Italian."

His voice was a little louder than usual. It was as though he was slightly uneasy at the search in spite of his willingness.

Poirot emerged.

"Nothing," he said. "Not even a compromising bequest!"

MacQueen sighed.

"Well, that's a load off my mind," he said humorously.

They moved on to the last compartment. The examination of the luggage of the big Italian and of the valet yielded no result.

The three men stood at the end of the coach looking at each other.

"What next?" asked M. Bouc.

"We will go back to the dining car," said Poirot. "We know now all that we can know. We have the evidence of the passengers, the evidence of their baggage, the evidence of our eyes. We can expect no further help. It must be our part now to use our brains."

He felt in his pocket for his cigarette case. It was empty.

"I will join you in a moment," he said. "I shall need the cigarettes. This is a very difficult, a very curious affair. Who wore that scarlet kimono? Where is it now? I wish I knew. There is something in this case—some factor—that escapes me! It is difficult because it has been made difficult. But we will discuss it. Pardon me a moment."

He went hurriedly along the corridor to his own compartment. He had, he knew, a further supply of cigarettes in one of his valises.

He got it down and snapped back the lock.

Then he sat back on his heels and stared.

Neatly folded on the top of the case was a thin scarlet silk kimono embroidered with dragons.

"So," he murmured. "It is like that. A defiance. Very well. I take it up."

Part Three
Hercule Poirot
Sits Back and Thinks

One

WHICH OF THEM?

M. Bouc and Dr. Constantine were talking together when Poirot entered the dining car. M. Bouc was looking depressed.

"Le voilà," said the latter when he saw Poirot.

Then he added as his friend sat down:

"If you solve this case, *mon cher,* I shall indeed believe in miracles!"

"It worries you, this case?"

"Naturally it worries me. I cannot make head or tail of it."

"I agree," said the doctor.

He looked at Poirot with interest.

"To be frank," he said, "I cannot see what you are going to do next."

"No?" said Poirot thoughtfully.

He took out his cigarette case and lit one of his tiny cigarettes. His eyes were dreamy.

"That, to me, is the interest of this case," he said. "We are cut off from all the normal routes of procedure. Are these people whose evidence we have taken speaking the truth or lying? We have no means of finding out—except such means as we can devise ourselves. It is an exercise, this, of the brain."

"That is all very fine," said M. Bouc. "But what have you to go upon?"

"I told you just now. We have the evidence of the passengers and the evidence of our own eyes."

"Pretty evidence—that of the passengers! It told us just nothing at all."

Poirot shook his head.

"I do not agree, my friend. The evidence of the passengers gave us several points of interest."

"Indeed," said M. Bouc sceptically. "I did not observe it."

"That is because you did not listen."

"Well, tell me—what did I miss?"

"I will just take one instance—the first evidence we heard—that of the young MacQueen. He uttered, to my mind, one very significant phrase."

"About the letters?"

"No, not about the letters. As far as I can remember, his words were: '*We travelled about. Mr. Ratchett wanted to see the world. He was hampered by knowing no languages. I acted more as a courier than a secretary.*'"

He looked from the doctor's face to that of M. Bouc.

"What? You still do not see? That is inexcusable—for you had a second chance again just now when he said, '*You're apt to be done down if you speak nothing but good American.*'"

"You mean—?" M. Bouc still looked puzzled.

"Ah, it is that you want it given to you in words of one syllable. Well, here it is! *M. Ratchett spoke no French.* Yet, when the conductor came in answer to his bell last night, it was a voice speaking in *French* that told him that it was a mistake and that he was not wanted. It was, moreover, a perfectly idiomatic phrase that was used, not one that a man knowing only a few words of French would have selected. '*Ce n'est rien. Je me suis trompé.*'"

"It is true," cried Constantine excitedly. "We should have seen that! I remember your laying stress on the words when you repeated them to us. Now I understand your reluctance to rely upon the evidence of the dented watch. Already, at twenty-three minutes to one, Ratchett was dead—"

"And it was his murderer speaking!" finished M. Bouc impressively.

Poirot raised a deprecating hand.

"Let us not go too fast. And do not let us assume more than we actually know. It is safe, I think, to say that at that time, twenty-three minutes to one, *some other person* was in Ratchett's compartment and that that person was either French, or could speak the French language fluently."

"You are very cautious, *mon vieux*."

"One should advance only a step at a time. We have no actual *evidence* that Ratchett was dead at that time."

"There is the cry that awakened you."

"Yes, that is true."

"In one way," said M. Bouc thoughtfully, "this discovery does not affect things very much. You heard someone moving about next door. That some-one was not Ratchett, but the other man. Doubtless he is washing blood from his hands, clearing up after the crime, burning the incriminating letter. Then he waits till all is still, and when he thinks it is safe and the coast is clear he locks and chains Ratchett's door on the inside, unlocks the communicating door through into Mrs. Hubbard's compartment and slips out that way. In fact it is exactly as we thought—*with the difference that Ratchett was killed about half an hour earlier,* and the watch put on to a quarter past one to create an alibi."

"Not such a famous alibi," said Poirot. "The hands of the watch pointed to 1:15—the exact time when the intruder actually left the scene of the crime."

"True," said M. Bouc, a little confused. "What, then, does the watch convey to you?"

"If the hands were altered—I say *if*—then the time at which they were set *must* have a significance. The natural reaction would be to suspect anyone who had a reliable alibi for the time indicated—in this case 1:15."

"Yes, Yes," said the doctor. "That reasoning is good."

"We must also pay a little attention to the time the intruder *entered* the com-partment. When had he an opportunity of doing so? Unless we are to assume the complicity of the real conductor, there was only one time when he could have done so—during the time the train stopped at Vincovci. After the train left Vincovci the conductor was sitting facing the corridor and whereas any one of the passengers would pay little attention to a Wagon Lit attendant, the *one* person who would notice an imposter would be the real conductor. But during the halt at Vincovci the conductor is out on the platform. The coast is clear."

"And, by our former reasoning, it *must* be one of the passengers," said M. Bouc. "We come back to where we were. Which of them?"

Poirot smiled.

"I have made a list," he said, "If you like to see it, it will, perhaps, refresh your memory."

The doctor and M. Bouc pored over the list together. It was written out neatly in a methodical manner in the order in which the passengers had been interviewed.

Hector MacQueen—American subject. Berth No. 6. Second Class.

Motive: Possibly arising out of association with dead man?

Alibi: From midnight to 2 a.m. (Midnight to 1:30 vouched for by Col. Arbuthnot and 1:15 to 2 vouched for by conductor.)

Evidence Against Him: None.

Suspicious Circumstances: None.

Conductor—Pierre Michel—French subject.

Motive: None.

Alibi: From midnight to 2 a.m. (Seen by H.P. in corridor at same time as voice spoke from Ratchett's compartment at 12:37. From 1 a.m. to 1:16 vouched for by other two conductors.)

Evidence Against Him: None.

Suspicious Circumstances: The Wagon Lit uniform found is a point in his favour since it seems to have been intended to throw suspicion on him.

Edward Masterman—English subject. Berth No. 4. Second Class.

Motive: Possibly arising out of connection with deceased, whose valet he was.

Alibi: From midnight to 2 a.m. (Vouched for by Antonio Foscarelli.)

Evidence Against Him or Suspicious Circumstances: None, except that he is the only man the right height or size to have worn the Wagon Lit uniform. On the other hand, it is unlikely that he speaks French well.

Mrs. Hubbard—American subject. Berth No. 3. First Class.

Motive: None.

Alibi: From midnight to 2 a.m.—None.

Evidence Against Her or Suspicious Circumstances: Story of man in her compartment is substantiated by the evidence of Hardman and that of the woman Schmidt.

Greta Ohlsson—Swedish subject. Berth No. 10. Second Class.
Motive: None.
Alibi: From midnight to 2 a.m. (Vouched for by Mary Debenham.) Note.— Was last to see Ratchett alive.

Princess Dragomiroff—Naturalized French subject. Berth No. 14. First Class.
Motive: Was intimately acquainted with Armstrong family, and godmother to Sonia Armstrong.
Alibi: From midnight to 2 a.m. (Vouched for by conductor and maid.)
Evidence Against Her or Suspicious Circumstances: None.

Count Andrenyi—Hungarian subject. Diplomatic passport. Berth No. 13. First Class.
Motive: None.
Alibi: Midnight to 2 a.m. (Vouched for by conductor—this does not cover period from 1 to 1:15.)

Countess Andrenyi—As above. Berth No. 12.
Motive: None.
Alibi: Midnight to 2 a.m. Took trional and slept. (Vouched for by husband. Trional bottle in her cupboard.)

Colonel Arbuthnot—British subject. Berth No. 15. First Class.
Motive: None.
Alibi: Midnight to 2 a.m. Talked with MacQueen till 1:30. Went to own compartment and did not leave it. (Substantiated by MacQueen and conductor.)
Evidence Against Him or Suspicious Circumstances: Pipe cleaner.

Cyrus Hardman—American subject. Berth No. 16. Second Class.

Motive: None known.

Alibi: Midnight to 2 a.m. Did not leave compartment. (Substantiated by MacQueen and conductor.)

Evidence Against Him or Suspicious Circumstances: None.

Antonio Foscarelli—American subject. (Italian birth.) Berth No. 5. Second Class.

Motive: None known.

Alibi: Midnight to 2 a.m. (Vouched for by Edward Masterman.)

Evidence Against Him or Suspicious Circumstances: None, except that weapon used might be said to suit his temperament. (Vide M. Bouc.)

Mary Debenham—British subject. Berth No. 11. Second Class.

Motive: None.

Alibi: Midnight to 2 a.m. (Vouched for by Greta Ohlsson.)

Evidence Against Her or Suspicious Circumstances: Conversation overheard by H.P. and her refusal to explain same.

Hildegarde Schmidt—German subject. Berth No. 8. Second Class.

Motive: None.

Alibi: Midnight to 2 a.m. (Vouched for by conductor and her mistress.) Went to bed. Was aroused by conductor at 12:38 approx. and went to mistress.

Note: The evidence of the passengers is supported by the statement of the conductor that no one entered or left Mr. Ratchett's compartment between the hours of midnight to 1 o'clock (when he himself went into the next coach) and from 1:15 to 2 o'clock.

"That document, you understand," said Poirot, "is a mere *précis* of the evidence we heard, arranged that way for convenience."

With a grimace M. Bouc handed it back.

"It is not illuminating," he said.

"Perhaps you may find this more to your taste," said Poirot with a slight smile as he handed him a second sheet of paper.

Two

Ten Questions

On the paper was written:

Things needing explanation.

1. The handkerchief marked with the initial H. Whose is it?
2. The pipe cleaner. Was it dropped by Colonel Arbuthnot? Or by someone else?
3. Who wore the scarlet kimono?
4. Who was the man or woman masquerading in Wagon Lit uniform?
5. Why do the hands of the watch point to 1:15?
6. Was the murder committed at that time?
7. Was it earlier?
8. Was it later?
9. Can we be sure that Ratchett was stabbed by more than one person?
10. What other explanation of his wounds can there be?

"Well, let us see what we can do," said M. Bouc, brightening a little at this challenge to his wits. "The handkerchief to begin with. Let us by all means be orderly and methodical."

"Assuredly," said Poirot, nodding his head in a satisfied fashion.

M. Bouc continued somewhat didactically.

"The initial H is connected with three people—Mrs. Hubbard, Miss Debenham, whose second name is Hermione, and the maid Hildegarde Schmidt."

"Ah! And of those three?"

"It is difficult to say. But I *think* I should vote for Miss Debenham. For all one knows, she may be called by her second name and not her first. Also there is already some suspicion attaching to her. That conversation you overheard, *mon cher,* was certainly a little curious, and so is her refusal to explain it."

"As for me, I plump for the American," said Dr. Constantine. "It is a very expensive handkerchief that, and Americans, as all the world knows, do not care what they pay."

"So you both eliminate the maid?" asked Poirot.

"Yes. As she herself said, it is the handkerchief of a member of the upper classes."

"And the second question—the pipe cleaner. Did Colonel Arbuthnot drop it, or somebody else?"

"That is more difficult. The English, they do not stab. You are right there. I incline to the view that someone else dropped the pipe cleaner—and did so to incriminate the long-legged Englishman."

"As you said, M. Poirot," put in the doctor, "*two* clues is too much carelessness. I agree with M. Bouc. The handkerchief was a genuine oversight—hence no one will admit that it is theirs. The pipe cleaner is a faked clue. In support of that theory, you notice that Colonel Arbuthnot shows no embarrassment and admits freely to smoking a pipe and using that type of cleaner."

"You reason well," said Poirot.

"Question No. 3—who wore the scarlet kimono?" went on M. Bouc. "As to that I will confess I have not the slightest idea. Have you any views on the subject, Dr. Constantine?"

"None."

"Then we confess ourselves beaten there. The next question has, at any rate, possibilities. Who was the man or woman masquerading in Wagon Lit uniform? Well, one can say with certainty a number of people whom it could *not* be. Hardman, Colonel Arbuthnot, Foscarelli, Count Andrenyi and Hector MacQueen are all too tall. Mrs. Hubbard, Hildegarde Schmidt and Greta Ohlsson are too broad. That leaves the valet, Miss Debenham, Princess Dragomiroff and Countess Andrenyi—and none of them sounds likely! Greta Ohlsson in one case and Antonio Foscarelli in the other both swear that Miss Debenham and the valet never left their compartments, Hildegarde Schmidt swears to the Princess being in hers, and Count Andrenyi has told us that his wife took a sleeping draught. Therefore it seems impossible that it can be anybody—which is absurd!"

"As our old friend Euclid says," murmured Poirot.

"It must be one of those four," said Dr. Constantine. "Unless it is someone from outside who has found a hiding place—and that, we agreed, was impossible."

M. Bouc had passed on to the next question on the list.

"No. 5—why do the hands of the broken watch point to 1:15? I can see two explanations of that. Either it was done by the murderer to establish an alibi and afterwards he was prevented from leaving the compartment when he meant to do so by hearing people moving about, or else—wait—I have an idea coming—"

The other two waited respectfully while M. Bouc struggled in mental agony.

"I have it," he said at last. "It was *not* the Wagon Lit murderer who tampered with the watch! It was the person we have called the Second Murderer—the left-handed person—in other words the woman in the scarlet kimono. She arrives later and moves back the hands of the watch in order to make an alibi for herself."

"Bravo," said Dr. Constantine. "It is well imagined, that."

"In fact," said Poirot, "she stabbed him in the dark, not realizing that he was dead already, but somehow deduced that he had a watch in his pyjama pocket, took it out, put back the hands blindly and gave it the requisite dent."

M. Bouc looked at him coldly.

"Have you anything better to suggest yourself?" he asked.

"At the moment—no," admitted Poirot.

"All the same," he went on, "I do not think you have either of you appreciated the most interesting point about that watch."

"Does question No. 6 deal with it?" asked the doctor. "To that question—was the murder committed at that time—1:15—I answer, 'No.' "

"I agree," said M. Bouc. " 'Was it earlier?' is the next question. I say yes. You, too, doctor?"

The doctor nodded.

"Yes, but the question 'Was it later?' can also be answered in the affirmative. I agree with your theory, M. Bouc, and so, I think, does M. Poirot, although he does not wish to commit himself. The First Murderer came earlier than 1:15, the Second Murderer came *after* 1:15. And as regards the question of left-handedness, ought we not to take steps to ascertain which of the passengers is left-handed?"

"I have not completely neglected that point," said Poirot. "You may have noticed that I made each passenger write either a signature or an address. That is not conclusive, because some people do certain actions with the right hand and others with the left. Some write right-handed, but play golf left-handed. Still it is something. Every person questioned took the pen in their right hand—with the exception of Princess Dragomiroff, who refused to write."

"Princess Dragomiroff, impossible," said M. Bouc.

"I doubt if she would have had the strength to inflict that particular left-handed blow," said Dr. Constantine dubiously. "That particular wound had been inflicted with considerable force."

"More force than a woman could use?"

"No, I would not say that. But I think more force than an elderly woman could display, and Princess Dragomiroff's physique is particularly frail."

"It might be a question of the influence of mind over body," said Poirot. "Princess Dragomiroff has great personality and immense will power. But let us pass from that for the moment."

"To questions Nos. 9 and 10. Can we be sure that Ratchett was stabbed by more than one person, and what other explanation of the wounds can there be? In my opinion, medically speaking, there can be *no other* explanation of those wounds. To suggest that one man struck first feebly and then with violence, first with the right hand and then with the left, and after an interval of perhaps half an hour inflicted fresh wounds on a dead body—well, it does not make sense."

"No," said Poirot. "It does not make sense. And you think that two murderers do make sense?"

"As you yourself have said, what other explanation can there be?"

Poirot stared straight ahead of him.

"That is what I ask myself," he said. "That is what I never cease to ask myself."

He leaned back in his seat.

"From now on, it is all here," he tapped himself on the forehead. "We have thrashed it all out. The facts are all in front of us—neatly arranged with order and method. The passengers have sat here, one by one, giving their evidence. We know all that can be known—*from outside.* . . ."

He gave an affectionate smile at M. Bouc.

"It has been a little joke between us, has it not—this business of sitting back and *thinking* out the truth? Well, I am about to put my theory into practice—here before your eyes. You two must do the same. Let us all three close our eyes and *think.* . . ."

"One or more of those passengers killed Ratchett. *Which of them?*"

Three

CERTAIN SUGGESTIVE POINTS

It was quite a quarter of an hour before anyone spoke.

M. Bouc and Dr. Constantine had started by trying to obey Poirot's instructions. They had endeavoured to see through the maze of conflicting particulars to a clear and outstanding solution.

M. Bouc's thoughts had run something as follows:

"Assuredly I must think. But as far as that goes I have already thought . . . Poirot obviously thinks this English girl is mixed up in the matter. I cannot help feeling that that is most unlikely . . . The English are extremely cold. Probably it is because they have no figures . . . But that is not the point. It seems that the Italian could not have done it—a pity. I suppose the English valet is not lying when he said the other never left the compartment? But why should he? It is not easy to bribe the English, they are so unapproachable. The whole thing is most unfortunate. I wonder when we shall get out of this. There must be *some* rescue work in progress. They are so slow in these countries . . . it is hours before anyone thinks of doing anything. And the police of these countries, they will be most trying to deal with—puffed up with importance, touchy, on their dignity. They will make a grand affair of all this. It is not often that such a chance comes their way. It will be in all the newspapers. . . ."

And from there on M. Bouc's thoughts went along a well-worn course which they had already traversed some hundred times.

Dr. Constantine's thoughts ran thus:

"He is queer, this little man. A genius? Or a crank? Will he solve this mystery? Impossible. I can see no way out of it. It is all too confusing . . . Everyone is lying, perhaps . . . But even then that does not help one. If they are all lying it is just as confusing as if they were speaking the truth. Odd about those wounds. I cannot understand it . . . It would be easier to understand if he had been shot— after all, the term gunman must mean that they shoot with a gun. A curious country, America. I should like to go there. It is so progressive. When I get home I must get hold of Demetrius Zagone—he has been to America, he has all the modern ideas . . . I wonder what Zia is doing at this moment. If my wife ever finds out—"

His thoughts went on to entirely private matters.

Hercule Poirot sat very still.

One might have thought he was asleep.

And then, suddenly, after a quarter of an hour's complete immobility, his eyebrows began to move slowly up his forehead. A little sigh escaped him. He murmured beneath his breath:

"But, after all, why not? And if so—why, if so, that would explain everything."

His eyes opened. They were green like a cat's. He said softly:

"*Eh bien.* I have thought. And you?"

Lost in their reflections, both men started violently.

"I have thought also," said M. Bouc just a shade guilty. "But I have arrived at no conclusion. The elucidation of crime is your *métier,* not mine, my friend."

"I, too, have reflected with great earnestness," said the doctor unblushingly, recalling his thoughts from certain pornographic details. "I have thought of many possible theories, but not one that really satisfies me."

Poirot nodded amiably. His nod seemed to say:

"Quite right. That is the proper thing to say. You have given me the cue I expected."

He sat very upright, threw out his chest, caressed his moustache and spoke in the manner of a practised speaker addressing a public meeting.

"My friends, I have reviewed the facts in my mind, and have also gone over to myself the evidence of the passengers—with this result. I see, nebulously as yet, a certain explanation that would cover the facts as we know them. It is a very curious explanation, and I cannot be sure as yet that it is the true one. To find out definitely, I shall have to make certain experiments.

"I would like first to mention certain points which appear to me suggestive. Let us start with a remark made to me by M. Bouc in this very place on the occasion of our first lunch together on the train. He commented on the fact that we were surrounded by people of all classes, of all ages, of all nationalities. That is a fact somewhat rare at this time of year. The Athens-Paris and the Bucharest-Paris coaches, for instance, are almost empty. Remember also one passenger who failed to turn up. It is, I think, significant. Then there are some minor points that strike me as suggestive—for instance, the position of Mrs. Hubbard's sponge bag, the name of Mrs. Armstrong's mother, the detective methods of M. Hardman, the suggestion of M. MacQueen that Ratchett himself destroyed the charred note we found, Princess Dragomiroff's Christian name, and a grease spot on a Hungarian passport."

The two men stared at him.

"Do they suggest anything to you, those points?" asked Poirot.

"Not a thing," said M. Bouc frankly.

"And M. le docteur?"

"I do not understand in the least of what you are talking."

M. Bouc, meanwhile, seizing upon the one tangible thing his friend had mentioned, was sorting through the passports. With a grunt he picked up that of Count and Countess Andrenyi and opened it.

"Is this what you mean? This dirty mark?"

"Yes. It is a fairly fresh grease spot. You notice where it occurs?"

"At the beginning of the description of the Count's wife—her Christian name, to be exact. But I confess that I still do not see the point."

"I am going to approach it from another angle. Let us go back to the handkerchief found at the scene of the crime. As we have stated not long ago—three people are associated with the letter H. Mrs. Hubbard, Miss Debenham and the maid, Hildegarde Schmidt. Now let us regard that handkerchief from another point of view. It is, my friends, an extremely expensive handkerchief—an *objet de luxe,* hand made, embroidered in Paris. Which of the passengers, apart from the initial, was likely to own such a handkerchief? Not Mrs. Hubbard, a worthy woman with no pretensions to reckless extravagance in dress. Not Miss Debenham; that class of Englishwoman has a dainty linen handkerchief, but not an expensive wisp of cambric costing perhaps two hundred francs. And certainly not the maid. But there *are* two women on the train who would be likely to own such a handkerchief. Let us see if we can connect them in any way with the letter H. The two women I refer to are Princess Dragomiroff—"

"Whose Christian name is Natalia," put in M. Bouc ironically.

"Exactly. And her Christian name, as I said just now, is decidedly suggestive. The other woman is Countess Andrenyi. And at once something strikes us—"

"*You!*"

"*Me,* then. Her Christian name on her passport is disfigured by a blob of grease. Just an accident, anyone would say. But consider that Christian name. Elena. Suppose that, instead of Elena, it were *Helena.* That capital H could be turned into a capital E and then run over the small e next to it quite easily—and then a spot of grease dropped to cover up the alteration."

"Helena," cried M. Bouc. "It is an idea, that."

"Certainly it is an idea! I look about for any confirmation, however slight, of my idea—and I find it. One of the luggage labels on the Countess's baggage is slightly damp. It is one that happens to run over the first initial on top of the case. That label has been soaked off and put on again in a different place."

"You begin to convince me," said M. Bouc, "But the Countess Andrenyi— surely—"

"Ah, now, *mon vieux,* you must turn yourself round and approach an entirely different angle of the case. How was this murder intended to appear to everybody? Do not forget that the snow has upset all the murderer's original plan. Let us imagine, for a little minute, that there is no snow, that the train proceeded on its normal course. What, then, would have happened?"

"The murder, let us say, would still have been discovered in all probability at the Italian frontier early this morning. Much of the same evidence would have been given to the Italian police. The threatening letters would have been produced by M. MacQueen, M. Hardman would have told his story, Mrs. Hubbard would have been eager to tell how a man passed through her compartment, the button would have been found. I imagine that two things only would have been different. The man would have passed through Mrs. Hubbard's compartment just before one o'clock—and the Wagon Lit uniform would have been found cast off in one of the toilets."

"You mean?"

"I mean that the murder was *planned to look like an outside job*. The assassin would have been presumed to have left the train at Brod, where the train is timed to arrive at 00:58. Somebody would probably have passed a strange Wagon Lit conductor in the corridor. The uniform would be left in a conspicuous place so as to show clearly just how the trick had been played. No suspicion would have been attached to the passengers. That, my friends, was how the affair was intended to appear to the outside world.

"But the accident to the train changes everything. Doubtless we have here the reason why the man remained in the compartment with his victim so long. He was waiting for the train to go on. But at last he realized *that the train was not going on*. Different plans would have to be made. The murderer would now be *known* to be still on the train."

"Yes, yes," said M. Bouc impatiently. "I see all that. But where does the handkerchief come in?"

"I am returning to it by a somewhat circuitous route. To begin with, you must realize that the threatening letters were in the nature of a blind. They might have been lifted bodily out of an indifferently written American crime novel. They are not *real*. They are, in fact, simply intended for the police. What we have to ask ourselves is, 'Did they deceive Ratchett?' On the face of it, the answer seems to be, 'No.' His instructions to Hardman seem to point to a definite 'private' enemy of the identity of whom he was well aware. That is if we accept Hardman's story as true. But Ratchett certainly received *one* letter of a very different character—the one containing a reference to the Armstrong baby, a fragment of which we found in his compartment. In case Ratchett had not realized it sooner, this was to make sure that he understood the reason of the threats against his life. That letter, as I have said all along, was *not* intended to be found. The murderer's first care was to destroy it. This, then, was the second hitch in his plans. The first was the snow, the second was our reconstruction of that fragment.

"That note being destroyed so carefully can only mean one thing. *There must be on the train someone so intimately connected with the Armstrong family that the finding of that note would immediately direct suspicion upon that person.*

"Now we come to the other two clues that we found. I pass over the pipe cleaner. We have already said a good deal about that. Let us pass on to the hand-kerchief. Taken at its simplest, it is a clue which directly incriminates someone whose initial is H, and it was dropped there unwittingly by that person."

"Exactly," said Dr. Constantine. "She finds out that she has dropped the handkerchief and immediately takes steps to conceal her Christian name."

"How fast you go. You arrive at a conclusion much sooner than I would permit myself to do."

"Is there any other alternative?"

"Certainly there is. Suppose, for instance, that you have committed a crime and wish to cast suspicion for it on someone else. Well, there is on the train a certain person connected intimately with the Armstrong family—a woman. Suppose, then, that you leave there a handkerchief belonging to that woman. She will be questioned, her connection with the Armstrong family will be brought out—*et voilà*. Motive—*and* an incriminating article of evidence."

"But in such a case," objected the doctor, "the person indicated being in-nocent, would not take steps to conceal her identity."

"Ah, really? That is what you think? That is truly the opinion of the police court. But I know human nature, my friend, and I tell you that, suddenly con-fronted with the possibility of being tried for murder, the most innocent person will lose their head and do the most absurd things. No, no, the grease spot and the changed label do not prove guilt—they only prove that the Countess An-drenyi is anxious for some reason to conceal her identity."

"What do you think her connection with the Armstrong family can be? She has never been in America, she says."

"Exactly, and she speaks broken English, and she has a very foreign appear-ance which she exaggerates. But it should not be difficult to guess who she is. I mentioned just now the name of Mrs. Armstrong's mother. It was Linda Arden, and she was a very celebrated actress—among other things a Shakespearean actress. Think of *As You Like It*—the Forest of Arden and Rosalind. It was there she got the inspiration for her acting name. Linda Arden, the name by which she was known all over the world, was not her real name. It may have been Goldenberg—she quite likely had central European blood in her veins—a strain of Jewish, perhaps. Many nationalities drift to America. I suggest to you, gentlemen, that that young sister of Mrs. Armstrong's, little more than a child at the time of the tragedy, was Helena Goldenberg the younger daughter of Linda Arden, and that she married Count Andrenyi when he was an attaché in Washington."

"But Princess Dragomiroff says that she married an Englishman."

"Whose name she cannot remember! I ask you, my friends—is that really likely? Princess Dragomiroff loved Linda Arden as great ladies do love great artists. She was godmother to one of her daughters. Would she forget so quickly the married name of the other daughter? It is not likely. No, I think we can safely say that Princess Dragomiroff was lying. She knew Helena was on the train, she had seen her. She realized at once, as soon as she heard who Ratchett really was, that Helena would be suspected. And so, when we question her as to the sister she promptly lies—is vague, cannot remember, but 'thinks Helena married an Englishman'—a suggestion as far away from the truth as possible."

One of the restaurant attendants came through the door at the end and approached them. He addressed M. Bouc.

"The dinner, Monsieur, shall I serve it? It is ready some little time."

M. Bouc looked at Poirot. The latter nodded.

"By all means, let dinner be served."

The attendant vanished through the doors at the other end. His bell could be heard ringing and his voice upraised:

"*Premier Service. Le dîner est servi. Premier dîner*—First Service."

Four

The Grease Spot on a Hungarian Passport

Poirot shared a table with M. Bouc and the doctor.

The company assembled in the restaurant car was a very subdued one. They spoke little. Even the loquacious Mrs. Hubbard was unnaturally quiet. She murmured as she sat:

"I don't feel as though I've got the heart to eat anything," and then partook of everything offered her, encouraged by the Swedish lady, who seemed to regard her as a special charge.

Before the meal was served Poirot had caught the chief attendant by the sleeve and murmured something to him. Constantine had a pretty good guess what the instructions had been, as he noticed that the Count and Countess Andrenyi were always served last and that at the end of the meal there was a delay in making out their bill. It therefore came about that the Count and Countess were the last left in the restaurant car.

When they rose at length and moved in the direction of the door, Poirot sprang up and followed them.

"Pardon, Madame, you have dropped your handkerchief."

He was holding out to her the tiny monogrammed square.

She took it, glanced at it, then handed it back to him.

"You are mistaken, Monsieur, that is not my handkerchief."

"Not your handkerchief? Are you sure?"

"Perfectly sure, Monsieur."

"And yet, Madame, it has your initial—the initial H."

The Count made a sudden movement. Poirot ignored him. His eyes were fixed on the Countess's face.

Looking steadily at him she replied:

"I do not understand, Monsieur. My initials are E.A."

"I think not. Your name is Helena—not Elena. Helena Goldenberg, the younger daughter of Linda Arden—Helena Goldenberg, the sister of Mrs. Armstrong."

There was a dead silence for a minute or two. Both the Count and Countess had gone deadly white. Poirot said in a gentler tone:

"It is of no use denying. That is the truth, is it not?"

The Count burst out furiously:

"I demand, Monsieur, by what right you—"

She interrupted him, putting up a small hand towards his mouth.

"No, Rudolph. Let me speak. It is useless to deny what this gentleman says. We had better sit down and talk the matter out."

Her voice had changed. It still had the southern richness of tone, but it had become suddenly more clear cut and incisive. It was, for the first time, a definitely American voice.

The Count was silenced. He obeyed the gesture of her hand and they both sat down opposite Poirot.

"Your statement, Monsieur, is quite true," said the Countess. "I am Helena Goldenberg, the younger sister of Mrs. Armstrong."

"You did not acquaint me with that fact this morning, Madame la Comtesse."

"No."

"In fact, all that your husband and you told me was a tissue of lies."

"Monsieur," cried the Count angrily.

"Do not be angry, Rudolph. M. Poirot puts the fact rather brutally, but what he says is undeniable."

"I am glad you admit the fact so freely, Madame. Will you now tell me your reasons for so doing and also for altering your Christian name on your passport."

"That was my doing entirely," put in the Count.

Helena said quietly:

"Surely, M. Poirot, you can guess my reason—our reason. This man who was killed is the man who murdered my baby niece, who killed my sister, who broke my brother-in-law's heart. Three of the people I loved best and who made up my home—my world!"

Her voice rang out passionately. She was a true daughter of that mother, the emotional force of whose acting had moved huge audiences to tears.

She went on more quietly.

"Of all the people on the train, I alone had probably the best motive for killing him."

"And you did not kill him, Madame?"

"I swear to you, M. Poirot, and my husband knows and will swear also—that, much as I may have been tempted to do so, I never lifted a hand against that man."

"I too, gentlemen," said the Count. "I give you my word of honour that last night Helena never left her compartment. She took a sleeping draught exactly as I said. She is utterly and entirely innocent."

Poirot looked from one to the other of them.

"On my word of honour," repeated the Count.

Poirot shook his head slightly.

"And yet you took it upon yourself to alter the name in the passport?"

"Monsieur Poirot," the Count spoke earnestly and passionately. "Consider my position. Do you think I could stand the thought of my wife dragged through a sordid police case. She was innocent, I knew it, but what she said was true—because of her connection with the Armstrong family she would have been immediately suspected. She would have been questioned—arrested, perhaps. Since some evil chance had taken us on the same train as this man Ratchett, there was, I felt sure, but one thing for it. I admit, Monsieur, that I lied to you—all, that is, save in one thing. My wife never left her compartment last night."

He spoke with an earnestness that it was hard to gainsay.

"I do not say that I disbelieve you, Monsieur," said Poirot slowly. "Your family is, I know, a proud and ancient one. It would be bitter indeed for you to have your wife dragged into an unpleasant police case. With that I can sympathize. But how, then, do you explain the presence of your wife's handkerchief actually in the dead man's compartment?"

"That handkerchief is not mine, Monsieur," said the Countess.

"In spite of the initial H?"

"In spite of the initial. I have handkerchiefs not unlike that, but not one that is exactly of that pattern. I know, of course that I cannot hope to make you believe me, but I assure you that it is so. That handkerchief is not mine."

"It may have been placed there by someone in order to incriminate you?"

She smiled a little.

"You are enticing me to admit that, after all, it is mine? But indeed, M. Poirot, it isn't."

She spoke with great earnestness.

"Then why, if the handkerchief was not yours, did you alter the name in the passport?"

The Count answered this.

"Because we heard that a handkerchief had been found with the initial H on it. We talked the matter over together before we came to be interviewed. I pointed out to Helena that if it were seen that her Christian name began with an H she would immediately be subjected to much more rigorous questioning. And the thing was so simple—to alter Helena to Elena was easily done."

"You have, M. le Comte, the makings of a very fine criminal," remarked Poirot dryly. "A great natural ingenuity, and an apparently remorseless determination to mislead justice."

"Oh, no, no," the girl leaned forward. "M. Poirot, he's explained to you how it was." She broke from French into English. "I was scared—absolutely dead scared, you understand. It had been so awful—that time—and to have it all raked up again. And to be suspected and perhaps thrown into prison. I was just scared stiff, M. Poirot. Can't you understand at all?"

Her voice was lovely—deep—rich—pleading, the voice of the daughter of Linda Arden the actress.

Poirot looked gravely at her.

"If I am to believe you, Madame—and I do not say that I will *not* believe you—then you must help me."

"Help you?"

"Yes. The reason for the murder lies in the past—in that tragedy which broke up your home and saddened your young life. Take me back into the past, Mademoiselle, that I may find there the link that explains the whole thing."

"What can there be to tell you? They are all dead." She repeated mournfully. "All dead—all dead—Robert, Sonia—darling, darling Daisy. She was so sweet—so happy—she had such lovely curls. We were all just crazy about her."

"There was another victim, Madame. An indirect victim, you might say."

"Poor Susanne? Yes, I had forgotten about her. The police questioned her. They were convinced she had something to do with it. Perhaps she had—but if so, only innocently. She had, I believe, chatted idly with someone, giving information as to the time of Daisy's outings. The poor thing got terribly wrought up—she thought she was being held responsible." She shuddered. "She threw herself out of the window. Oh it was horrible."

She buried her face in her hands.

"What nationality was she, Madame?"

"She was French."

"What was her last name?"

"It's absurd, but I can't remember—we all called her Susanne. A pretty laughing girl. She was devoted to Daisy."

"She was the nurserymaid, was she not?"

"Yes."

"Who was the nurse?"

"She was a trained hospital nurse. Stengelberg her name was. She, too, was devoted to Daisy—and to my sister."

"Now, Madame, I want you to think carefully before you answer this question. Have you, since you were on this train, seen anyone that you recognized?"

She stared at him.

"I? No, no one at all."

"What about Princess Dragomiroff?"

"Oh, her? I know her, of course. I thought you meant anyone—anyone from—from that time."

"So I did, Madame. Now think carefully. Some years have passed, remember. The person might have altered their appearance."

Helena pondered deeply. Then she said:

"No—I am sure—there is no one."

"You yourself—you were a young girl at the time—did you have no one to superintend your studies or to look after you?"

"Oh, yes, I had a dragon—a sort of governess to me and secretary to Sonia combined. She was English or rather Scotch—a big, red-haired woman."

"What was her name?"

"Miss Freebody."

"Young or old?"

"She seemed frightfully old to me. I suppose she couldn't have been more than forty. Susanne, of course, used to look after my clothes and maid me."

"And there were no other inmates of the house?"

"Only servants."

"And you are certain—quite certain, Madame—that you have recognized no one on the train?"

She replied earnestly:

"No one, Monsieur. No one at all."

Five

THE CHRISTIAN NAME OF PRINCESS DRAGOMIROFF

When the Count and Countess had departed, Poirot looked across at the other two.

"You see," he said, "we make progress."

"Excellent work," said M. Bouc cordially. "For my part, I should never have dreamed of suspecting Count and Countess Andrenyi. I will admit I thought them quite *hors de combat.* I suppose there is no doubt that she committed the crime? It is rather sad. Still, they will not guillotine her. There are extenuating circumstances. A few years' imprisonment—that will be all."

"In fact you are quite certain of her guilt."

"My dear friend, surely there is no doubt of it? I thought your reassuring manner was only to smooth things over till we are dug out of the snow and the police take charge."

"You do not believe the Count's positive assertion—on his word of honour—that his wife is innocent?"

"*Mon cher*—naturally—what else *could* he say? He adores his wife. He wants to save her! He tells his lie very well—quite in the grand Seigneur manner, but what else than a lie could it be?"

"Well, you know, I had the preposterous idea that it might be the truth."

"No, no. The handkerchief, remember. The handkerchief clinches the matter."

"Oh, I am not so sure about the handkerchief. You remember, I always told you that there were two possibilities as to the ownership of the handkerchief."

"All the same—"

M. Bouc broke off. The door at the end had opened, and Princess Drago-miroff entered the dining car. She came straight to them and all three men rose to their feet.

She spoke to Poirot, ignoring the others.

"I believe, Monsieur," she said, "that you have a handkerchief of mine."

Poirot shot a glance of triumph at the other two.

"Is this it, Madame?"

He produced the little square of fine cambric.

"That is it. It has my initial in the corner."

"But, Madame la Princesse, that is the letter H," said M. Bouc. "Your Christian name—pardon me—is Natalia."

She gave him a cold stare.

"That is correct, Monsieur. My handkerchiefs are always initialled in the Russian characters. H is N in Russian."

M. Bouc was somewhat taken aback. There was something about this in-domitable old lady which made him feel flustered and uncomfortable.

"You did not tell us that this handkerchief was yours at the inquiry this morning."

"You did not ask me," said the Princess dryly.

"Pray be seated, Madame," said Poirot.

She sighed.

"I may as well, I suppose."

She sat down.

"You need not make a long business of this, Messieurs. Your next question will be—how did my handkerchief come to be lying by a murdered man's body? My reply to that is that I have no idea."

"You have really no idea."

"None whatever."

"You will excuse me, Madame, but how much can we rely upon the truth-fulness of your replies?"

Poirot said the words very softly. Princess Dragomiroff answered contemp-tuously.

"I suppose you mean because I did not tell you that Helena Andrenyi was Mrs. Armstrong's sister?"

"In fact you deliberately lied to us in the matter."

"Certainly. I would do the same again. Her mother was my friend. I believe, Messieurs, in loyalty—to one's friends and one's family and one's caste."

"You do not believe in doing your utmost to further the ends of justice?"

"In this case I consider that justice—strict justice—has been done."

Poirot leaned forward.

"You see my difficulty, Madame. In this matter of the handkerchief, even, am I to believe you? Or are you shielding your friend's daughter?"

"Oh! I see what you mean." Her face broke into a grim smile. "Well, Messieurs, this statement of mine can be easily proved. I will give you the address of the people in Paris who make my handkerchiefs. You have only to show them the one in question and they will inform you that it was made to my order over a year ago. The handkerchief is mine, Messieurs."

She rose.

"Have you anything further you wish to ask me?"

"Your maid, Madame, did she recognize this handkerchief when we showed it to her this morning?"

"She must have done so. She saw it and said nothing? Ah, well, that shows that she too can be loyal."

With a slight inclination of her head she passed out of the dining car.

"So that was it," murmured Poirot softly. "I noticed just a trifling hesitation when I asked the maid if she knew to whom the handkerchief belonged. She was uncertain whether or not to admit that it was her mistress's. But how does that fit in with that strange central idea of mine? Yes, it might well be."

"Ah!" said M. Bouc with a characteristic gesture—"she is a terrible old lady, that!"

"Could she have murdered Ratchett?" asked Poirot of the doctor.

He shook his head.

"Those blows—the ones delivered with great force penetrating the muscle—never, never could anyone with so frail a physique inflict them."

"But the feebler ones?"

"The feebler ones, yes."

"I am thinking," said Poirot, "of the incident this morning when I said to her that the strength was in her will rather than in her arm. It was in the nature of a trap, that remark. I wanted to see if she would look down at her right or her left arm. She did neither. She looked at them both. But she made a strange reply. She said, 'No, I have no strength in these. I do not know whether to be sorry or glad.' A curious remark that. It confirms me in my belief about the crime."

"It did not settle the point about the left-handedness."

"No. By the way, did you notice that Count Andrenyi keeps his handkerchief in his right-hand breast pocket?"

M. Bouc shook his head. His mind reverted to the astonishing revelations of the last half hour. He murmured:

"Lies—and again lies—it amazes me, the amount of lies we had told to us this morning."

"There are more still to discover," said Poirot cheerfully.

"You think so?"

"I shall be very disappointed if it is not so."

"Such duplicity is terrible," said M. Bouc. "But it seems to please you," he added reproachfully.

"It has this advantage," said Poirot. "If you confront anyone who has lied with the truth, they usually admit it—often out of sheer surprise. It is only necessary to guess *right* to produce your effect.

"That is the only way to conduct this case. I select each passenger in turn, consider their evidence and say to myself, '*If* so and so is lying, on what point are they lying and what is the *reason* for the lie?' And I answer *if* they are lying—*if*, you mark—it could only be for such a reason and on such a point. We have done that once very successfully with Countess Andrenyi. We shall now proceed to try the same method on several other persons."

"And supposing, my friend, that your guess happens to be wrong?"

"Then one person, at any rate, will be completely freed from suspicion."

"Ah! A process of elimination."

"Exactly."

"And who do we tackle next?"

"We are going to tackle that *pukka sahib,* Colonel Arbuthnot."

Six

A Second Interview with
Colonel Arbuthnot

Colonel Arbuthnot was clearly annoyed at being summoned to the dining car for a second interview. His face wore a most forbidding expression as he sat down and said:

"Well?"

"All my apologies for troubling you a second time," said Poirot. "But there is still some information that I think you might be able to give us."

"Indeed? I hardly think so."

"To begin with, you see this pipe cleaner?"

"Yes."

"Is it one of yours?"

"Don't know. I don't put a private mark on them, you know."

"Are you aware, Colonel Arbuthnot, that you are the only man amongst the passengers in the Stamboul-Calais carriage who smokes a pipe?"

"In that case it probably is one of mine."

"Do you know where it was found?"

"Not the least idea."

"It was found by the body of the murdered man."

Colonel Arbuthnot raised his eyebrows.

"Can you tell us, Colonel Arbuthnot, how it is likely to have got there?"

"If you mean did I drop it there myself, no, I didn't."

"Did you go into Mr. Ratchett's compartment at any time?"

"I never even spoke to the man."

"You never spoke to him and you did not murder him?"

The Colonel's eyebrows went up again sardonically.

"If I had, I should hardly be likely to acquaint you with the fact. As a matter of fact I *didn't* murder the fellow."

"Ah, well," murmured Poirot. "It is of no consequence."

"I beg your pardon?"

"I said that it was of no consequence."

"Oh!" Arbuthnot looked taken aback. He eyed Poirot uneasily.

"Because, you see," continued the little man, "the pipe cleaner, it is of no importance. I can myself think of eleven other excellent explanations of its presence."

Arbuthnot stared at him.

"What I really wished to see you about was quite another matter," went on Poirot. "Miss Debenham may have told you, perhaps, that I overheard some words spoken to you at the station of Konya?"

Arbuthnot did not reply.

"She said, *'Not now. When it's all over. When it's behind us.'* Do you know to what those words referred?"

"I am sorry, M. Poirot, but I must refuse to answer that question."

"Pourquoi?"

The Colonel said stiffly:

"I suggest that you should ask Miss Debenham herself for the meaning of those words."

"I have done so."

"And she refused to tell you?"

"Yes."

"Then I should think it would have been perfectly plain—even to you—that my lips are sealed."

"You will not give away a lady's secret?"

"You can put it that way, if you like."

"Miss Debenham told me that they referred to a private matter of her own."

"Then why not accept her word for it?"

"Because, Colonel Arbuthnot, Miss Debenham is what one might call a highly suspicious character."

"Nonsense," said the Colonel with warmth.

"It is not nonsense."

"You have nothing whatever against her."

"Not the fact that Miss Debenham was companion governess in the Armstrong household at the time of the kidnapping of little Daisy Armstrong?"

There was a minute's dead silence.

Poirot nodded his head gently.

"You see," he said, "we know more than you think. If Miss Debenham is innocent, why did she conceal that fact? Why did she tell me that she had never been in America?"

The Colonel cleared his throat.

"Aren't you possibly making a mistake?"

"I am making no mistake. Why did Miss Debenham lie to me?"

Colonel Arbuthnot shrugged his shoulders.

"You had better ask her. I still think that you are wrong."

Poirot raised his voice and called. One of the restaurant attendants came from the far end of the car.

"Go and ask the English lady in No. 11 if she will be good enough to come here."

"Bien, Monsieur."

The man departed. The four men sat in silence. Colonel Arbuthnot's face looked as though it were carved out of wood, it was rigid and impassive.

The man returned.

"Thank you."

A minute or two later Mary Debenham entered the dining car.

Seven

THE IDENTITY OF MARY DEBENHAM

She wore no hat. Her head was thrown back as though in defiance. The sweep of her hair back from her face, the curve of her nostril suggested the figurehead of a ship plunging gallantly into a rough sea. In that moment she was beautiful.

Her eyes went to Arbuthnot for a minute—just a minute.

She said to Poirot:

"You wished to see me?"

"I wished to ask you, Mademoiselle, why you lied to us this morning?"

"Lied to you? I don't know what you mean."

"You concealed the fact that at the time of the Armstrong tragedy you were actually living in the house. You told me that you had never been in America."

He saw her flinch for a moment and then recover herself.

"Yes," she said. "That is true."

"No, Mademoiselle, it was false."

"You misunderstood me. I mean that it is true that I lied to you."

"Ah, you admit it?"

Her lips curved into a smile.

"Certainly. Since you have found me out."

"You are at least frank, Mademoiselle."

"There does not seem anything else for me to be."

"Well, of course, that is true. And now, Mademoiselle, may I ask you the reason for these evasions?"

"I should have thought the reason leapt to the eye, M. Poirot?"

"It does not leap to mine, Mademoiselle."

She said in a quiet, even voice with a trace of hardness in it:

"I have my living to get."

"You mean—?"

She raised her eyes and looked him full in the face.

"How much do you know, M. Poirot, of the fight to get and keep decent employment? Do you think that a girl who had been detained in connection with a murder case, whose name and perhaps photographs were reproduced in the English papers—do you think that any nice ordinary middle-class English-woman would want to engage that girl as governess to her daughters?"

"I do not see why not—if no blame attached to you."

"Oh, blame—it is not blame—it is publicity! So far, M. Poirot, I have suc-ceeded in life. I have had well-paid, pleasant posts. I was not going to risk the position I had attained when no good end could have been served."

"I will venture to suggest, Mademoiselle, that I would have been the best judge of that, not you."

She shrugged her shoulders.

"For instance, you could have helped me in the matter of identification."

"What do you mean?"

"Is it possible, Mademoiselle, that you did not recognize in the Countess Andrenyi Mrs. Armstrong's young sister whom you taught in New York?"

"Countess Andrenyi? No." She shook her head. "It may seem extraordinary to you, but I did not recognize her. She was not grown up, you see, when I knew her. That was over three years ago. It is true that the Countess reminded me of someone—it puzzled me. But she looks so foreign—I never connected her with the little American schoolgirl. It is true that I only glanced at her casually when coming into the restaurant car. I noticed her clothes more than her face—" she smiled faintly—"women do! And then—well, I had my own preoccupations."

"You will not tell me your secret, Mademoiselle?"

Poirot's voice was very gentle and persuasive.

She said in a low voice:

"I can't—I can't."

And suddenly, without warning she broke down, dropping her face down upon her outstretched arms and crying as though her heart would break.

The Colonel sprang up and stood awkwardly beside her.

"I—look here—"

He stopped and, turning round, scowled fiercely at Poirot.

"I'll break every bone in your damned body, you dirty little whippersnapper," he said.

"Monsieur," protested M. Bouc.

Arbuthnot had turned back to the girl.

"Mary—for God's sake—"

She sprang up.

"It's nothing. I'm all right. You don't need me any more, do you, M. Poirot? If you do, you must come and find me. Oh, what an idiot—what an idiot I'm making of myself!"

She hurried out of the car. Arbuthnot, before following her, turned once more on Poirot.

"Miss Debenham's got nothing to do with this business—nothing, do you hear? And if she's worried and interfered with, you'll have me to deal with."

He strode out.

"I like to see an angry Englishman," said Poirot. "They are very amusing. The more emotional they feel the less command they have of language."

But M. Bouc was not interested in the emotional reactions of Englishmen. He was overcome by admiration of his friend.

"*Mon cher, vous êtes épatant,*" he cried. "Another miraculous guess. *C'est formidable.*"

"It is incredible how you think of these things," said Dr. Constantine admiringly.

"Oh, I claim no credit this time. It was not a guess. Countess Andrenyi practically told me."

"*Comment?* Surely not?"

"You remember I asked her about her governess or companion? I had already decided in my mind that *if* Mary Debenham were mixed up in the matter, she must have figured in the household in some such capacity."

"Yes, but the Countess Andrenyi described a totally different person."

"Exactly. A tall, middle-aged woman with red hair—in fact, the exact opposite in every respect of Miss Debenham, so much so as to be quite remarkable. But then she had to invent a name quickly, and there it was that the unconscious association of ideas gave her away. She said Miss Freebody, you remember."

"Yes?"

"*Eh bien,* you may not know it, but there is a shop in London that was called, until recently, Debenham & Freebody. With the name Debenham running in her head, the Countess clutches at another name quickly, and the first that comes is Freebody. Naturally I understood immediately."

"That is yet another lie. Why did she do it?"

"Possibly more loyalty. It makes things a little difficult."

"*Ma foi,*" said M. Bouc with violence. "But does everybody on this train tell lies?"

"That," said Poirot, "is what we are about to find out."

Eight

FURTHER SURPRISING REVELATIONS

"Nothing would surprise me now," said M. Bouc. "Nothing! Even if everybody in the train proved to have been in the Armstrong household I should not express surprise."

"That is a very profound remark," said Poirot. "Would you like to see what your favourite suspect, the Italian, has to say for himself?"

"You are going to make another of these famous guesses of yours?"

"Precisely."

"It is really a *most* extraordinary case," said Constantine.

"No, it is most natural."

M. Bouc flung up his arms in comic despair.

"If this is what you call natural, *mom ami*—"

Words failed him.

Poirot had by this time requested the dining car attendant to fetch Antonio Foscarelli.

The big Italian had a wary look in his eye as he came in. He shot nervous glances from side to side like a trapped animal.

"What do you want?" he said. "I have nothing to tell you—nothing, do you hear! *Per Dio*—" He struck his hand on the table.

"Yes, you have something more to tell us," said Poirot firmly. "The truth!"

"The truth?" He shot an uneasy glance at Poirot. All the assurance and geniality had gone out of his manner.

"*Mais oui*. It may be that I know it already. But it will be a point in your favour if it comes from you spontaneously."

"You talk like the American police. 'Come clean,' that is what they say—'come clean.'"

"Ah! so you have had experience of the New York police?"

"No, no, never. They could not prove a thing against me—but it was not for want of trying."

Poirot said quietly:

"That was in the Armstrong case, was it not? You were the chauffeur?"

His eyes met those of the Italian. The bluster went out of the big man. He was like a pricked balloon.

"Since you know—why ask me?"

"Why did you lie this morning?"

"Business reasons. Besides, I do not trust the Yugo-Slav police. They hate the Italians. They would not have given me justice."

"Perhaps it is exactly justice that they *would* have given you!"

"No, no, I had nothing to do with this business last night. I never left my carriage. The long-faced Englishman, he can tell you so. It was not I who killed this pig—this Ratchett. You cannot prove anything against me."

Poirot was writing something on a sheet of paper. He looked up and said quietly:

"Very good. You can go."

Foscarelli lingered uneasily.

"You realize that it was not I—that I could have had nothing to do with it?"

"I said that you could go."

"It is a conspiracy. You are going to frame me? All for a pig of a man who should have gone to the chair! It was an infamy that he did not. If it had been me—if I had been arrested—"

"But it was not you. You had nothing to do with the kidnapping of the child."

"What is that you are saying? Why, that little one—she was the delight of the house. Tonio, she called me. And she would sit in the car and pretend to hold the wheel. All the household worshipped her! Even the police came to understand that. Ah, the beautiful little one."

His voice had softened. The tears came into his eyes. Then he wheeled round abruptly on his heel and strode out of the dining car.

"Pietro," called Poirot.

The dining car attendant came at a run.

"The No. 10—the Swedish lady."

"Bien, Monsieur."

"Another?" cried M. Bouc. "Ah, no—it is not possible. I tell you it is not possible."

"Mon cher, we have to *know.* Even if in the end everybody on the train proves to have a motive for killing Ratchett, we have to know. Once we know, we can settle once for all where the guilt lies."

"My head is spinning," groaned M. Bouc.

Greta Ohlsson was ushered in sympathetically by the attendant. She was weeping bitterly.

She collapsed on the seat facing Poirot and wept steadily into a large handkerchief.

"Now do not distress yourself, Mademoiselle. Do not distress yourself." Poirot patted her on the shoulder. "Just a few little words of truth, that is all. You were the nurse who was in charge of little Daisy Armstrong?"

"It is true—it is true," wept the wretched woman. "Ah, she was an angel—a little sweet, trustful angel. She knew nothing but kindness and love—and she was taken away by that wicked man—cruelly treated—and her poor mother—and the other little one who never lived at all. You cannot understand—you cannot know—if you had been there as I was—if you had seen the whole terrible tragedy—I ought to have told you the truth about myself this morning. But I was afraid—afraid. I did so rejoice that that evil man was dead—that he could not any more kill or torture little children. Ah! I cannot speak—I have no words. . . ."

She wept with more vehemence than ever.

Poirot continued to pat her gently on the shoulder.

"There—there—I comprehend—I comprehend everything—everything, I tell you. I will ask you no more questions. It is enough that you have admitted what I know to be the truth. I understand, I tell you."

By now inarticulate with sobs, Greta Ohlsson rose and groped her way blindly towards the door. As she reached it she collided with a man coming in.

It was the valet—Masterman.

He came straight up to Poirot and spoke in his usual, quiet, unemotional voice.

"I hope I'm not intruding, sir. I thought it best to come along at once, sir, and tell you the truth. I was Colonel Armstrong's batman in the war, sir, and afterwards I was his valet in New York. I'm afraid I concealed that fact this morning. It was very wrong of me, sir, and I thought I'd better come and make a clean breast of it. But I hope, sir, that you're not suspecting Tonio in any way. Old Tonio, sir, wouldn't hurt a fly. And I can swear positively that he never left the carriage all last night. So, you see, sir, he couldn't have done it. Tonio may be a foreigner, sir, but he's a very gentle creature—not like those nasty murdering Italians one reads about."

He stopped.

Poirot looked steadily at him.

"Is that all you have to say?"

"That is all, sir."

He paused, then, as Poirot did not speak, he made an apologetic little bow, and after a momentary hesitation left the dining car in the same quiet, unobtrusive fashion as he had come.

"This," said Dr. Constantine, "is more wildly improbable than any *roman policier* I have ever read."

"I agree," said M. Bouc. "Of the twelve passengers in that coach, nine have been proved to have had a connection with the Armstrong case. What next, I ask you? Or, should I say, who next?"

"I can almost give you the answer to your question," said Poirot. "Here comes our American sleuth, M. Hardman."

"Is he, too, coming to confess?"

Before Poirot could reply, the American had reached their table. He cocked an alert eye at them and, sitting down, he drawled out:

"Just exactly what's up on this train? It seems bughouse to me."

Poirot twinkled at him:

"Are you quite sure, Mr. Hardman, that you yourself were not the gardener at the Armstrong home?"

"They didn't have a garden," replied Mr. Hardman literally.

"Or the butler?"

"Haven't got the fancy manner for a place like that. No, I never had any connection with the Armstrong house—but I'm beginning to believe I'm about the only one on this train who hadn't! Can you beat it—that's what I say? Can you beat it?"

"It is certainly a little surprising," said Poirot mildly.

"*C'est rigolo,*" burst from M. Bouc.

"Have you any ideas of your own about the crime, M. Hardman?" inquired Poirot.

"No, sir. It's got me beat. I don't know how to figure it out. They can't all be in it; but which one is the guilty party is beyond me. How did you get wise to all this, that's what I want to know?"

"I just guessed."

"Then, believe me, you're a pretty slick guesser. Yes, I'll tell the world you're a slick guesser."

Mr. Hardman leaned back and looked at Poirot admiringly.

"You'll excuse me," he said, "but no one would believe it to look at you. I take off my hat to you. I do, indeed."

"You are too kind, M. Hardman."

"Not at all. I've got to hand it to you."

"All the same," said Poirot, "the problem is not yet quite solved. Can we say with authority that we know who killed M. Ratchett?"

"Count me out," said Mr. Hardman. "I'm not saying anything at all. I'm just full of natural admiration. What about the other two you've not had a guess at yet? The old American dame and the lady's maid? I suppose we can take it that they're the only innocent parties on the train?"

"Unless," said Poirot, smiling, "we can fit them into our little collection as—shall we say?—housekeeper and cook in the Armstrong household."

"Well, nothing in the world would surprise me now," said Mr. Hardman with quiet resignation. "Bughouse—that's what this business is—bughouse!"

"Ah, *mon cher,* that would be indeed stretching coincidence a little too far," said M. Bouc. "They cannot all be in it."

Poirot looked at him.

"You do not understand," he said. "You do not understand at all. Tell me," he said, "do you know who killed Ratchett?"

"Do you?" countered M. Bouc.

Poirot nodded.

"Oh, yes," he said. "I have known for some time. It is so clear that I wonder you have not seen it also." He looked at Hardman and asked, "And you?"

The detective shook his head. He stared at Poirot curiously.

"I don't know," he said. "I don't know at all. Which of them was it?"

Poirot was silent a minute. Then he said:

"If you will be so good, M. Hardman, assemble everyone here. There are two possible solutions of this case. I want to lay them both before you all."

Nine

Poirot Propounds Two Solutions

The passengers came crowding into the restaurant car and took their seats round the tables. They all bore more or less the same expression, one of expectancy mingled with apprehension. The Swedish lady was still weeping and Mrs. Hubbard was comforting her.

"Now you must just take a hold on yourself, my dear. Everything's going to be perfectly all right. You mustn't lose your grip on yourself. If one of us is a nasty murderer we know quite well it isn't you. Why, anyone would be crazy even to think of such a thing. You sit here and I'll stay right by you; and don't you worry any."

Her voice died away as Poirot stood up.

The Wagon Lit conductor was hovering in the doorway.

"You permit that I stay, Monsieur?"

"Certainly, Michel."

Poirot cleared his throat.

"Messieurs et Mesdames, I will speak in English, since I think all of you know a little of that language. We are here to investigate the death of Samuel Edward Ratchett—alias Cassetti. There are two possible solutions of the crime. I shall put them both before you, and I shall ask M. Bouc and Dr. Constantine here to judge which solution is the right one.

"Now you all know the facts of the case. Mr. Ratchett was found stabbed this morning. He was last known to be alive at 12:37 last night, when he spoke to the Wagon Lit conductor through the door. A watch in his pyjama pocket was found to be badly dented and it had stopped at a quarter past one. Dr. Constantine, who examined the body when found, puts the time of death as having occurred between midnight and two in the morning. At half an hour after midnight, as you all know, the train ran into a snowdrift. After that time it *was impossible for anyone to leave the train*.

"The evidence of Mr. Hardman, who is a member of a New York Detective Agency" (several heads turned to look at Mr. Hardman) "shows that no one could have passed his compartment (No. 16 at the extreme end) without being seen by him. We are therefore forced to the conclusion that the murderer is to be found among the occupants of one particular coach—the Stamboul-Calais coach.

"That, I will say, *was* our theory."

"*Comment?*" ejaculated M. Bouc, startled.

"But I will put before you an alternative theory. It is very simple. Mr. Ratchett had a certain enemy whom he feared. He gave Mr. Hardman a description of this enemy and told him that the attempt, if made at all, would most probably be made on the second night out from Stamboul."

"Now I put it to you, ladies and gentlemen, that Mr. Ratchett knew a good deal more than he told. The enemy as Mr. Ratchett expected, joined the train at *Belgrade, or possibly at Vincouci*, by the door left open by Colonel Arbuthnot and Mr. MacQueen who had just descended to the platform. He was provided with a suit of Wagon Lit uniform, which he wore over his ordinary clothes, and a pass key which enabled him to gain access to Mr. Ratchett's compartment in spite of the door being locked. Mr. Ratchett was under the influence of a sleeping draught. This man stabbed him with great ferocity and left the compartment through the communicating door leading to Mrs. Hubbard's compartment—"

"That's so," said Mrs. Hubbard, nodding her head.

"He thrust the dagger he had used into Mrs. Hubbard's sponge bag in passing. Without knowing it, he lost a button of his uniform. Then he slipped out of the compartment and along the corridor. He hastily thrust the uniform into a suitcase in an empty compartment, and a few minutes later, dressed in ordinary clothes, he left the train just before it started off. Again using the same means of egress—the door near the dining car."

Everybody gasped.

"What about that watch?" demanded Mr. Hardman.

"There you have the explanation of the whole thing. *Mr. Ratchett had ommitted to put his watch back an hour as he should have done* at Tzaribrod. His watch still registered Eastern European time, which is one hour *ahead* of Central European time. It was a quarter past *twelve* when Mr. Ratchett was stabbed—not a quarter past one."

"But it is absurd, that explanation," cried M. Bouc. "What of the voice that spoke from the compartment at twenty-three minutes to one. It was either the voice of Ratchett—or else of his murderer."

"Not necessarily. It might have been—well—a third person. One who had gone in to speak to Ratchett and found him dead. He rang the bell to summon the conductor, then, as you express it, the wind rose in him—he was afraid of being accused of the crime and he spoke pretending to be Ratchett."

"*C'est possible,*" admitted M. Bouc grudgingly.

Poirot looked at Mrs. Hubbard.

"Yes, Madame, you were going to say—?"

"Well, I don't quite know what I was going to say. Do you think I forgot to put my watch back too?"

"No, Madame. I think you heard the man pass through—but unconsciously; later you had a nightmare of a man being in your compartment and woke up with a start and rang for the conductor."

"Well, I suppose that's possible," admitted Mrs. Hubbard.

Princess Dragomiroff was looking at Poirot with a very direct glance.

"How do you explain the evidence of my maid, Monsieur?"

"Very simply, Madame. Your maid recognized the handkerchief I showed her as yours. She somewhat clumsily tried to shield you. She did encounter the man—but earlier—while the train was at Vincovci station. She pretended to have seen him at a later hour with a confused idea of giving you a watertight *alibi.*"

The Princess bowed her head.

"You have thought of everything, Monsieur. I—I admire you."

There was a silence.

Then everyone jumped as Dr. Constantine suddenly hit the table a blow with his fist.

"But no," he said. "No, no, and again no! That is an explanation that will not hold water. It is deficient in a dozen minor points. The crime was not committed so—M. Poirot must know that perfectly well."

Poirot turned a curious glance on him.

"I see," he said, "that I shall have to give my second solution. But do not abandon this one too abruptly. You may agree with it later."

He turned back again to face the others.

"There is another possible solution of the crime. This is how I arrived at it.

"When I had heard all the evidence, I leaned back and shut my eyes and began to *think*. Certain points presented themselves to me as worthy of attention. I enumerated these points to my two colleagues. Some I have already elucidated—such as a grease spot on a passport, etc. I will run over the points that remain. The first and most important is a remark made to me by M. Bouc in the restaurant car at lunch on the first day after leaving Stamboul—to the effect that the company assembled was interesting because it was so varied—representing as it did all classes and nationalities.

"I agreed with him, but when this particular point came into my mind, I tried to imagine whether such an assembly were ever likely to be collected under any other conditions. And the answer I made to myself was—only in America. In America there might be a household composed of just such varied nationalities—an Italian chauffeur, and English governess, a Swedish nurse, a French lady's maid and so on. That led me to my scheme of 'guessing'—that is, casting each person for a certain part in the Armstrong drama much as a producer casts a play. Well, that gave me an extremely interesting and satisfactory result.

"I had also examined in my own mind each separate person's evidence with some curious results. Take first the evidence of Mr. MacQueen. My first interview with him was entirely satisfactory. But in my second he made rather a curious remark. I had described to him the finding of a note mentioning the Armstrong case. He said, 'But surely—' and then paused and went on, 'I mean—that was rather careless of the old man.'

"Now I could feel that that was not what he had started out to say. *Supposing what he had meant to say was, 'But surely that was burnt!'* In which case, *MacQueen knew of the note and of its destruction*—in other words, he was either the murderer or an accomplice of the murderer. Very good.

"Then the valet. He said his master was in the habit of taking a sleeping draught when travelling by train. That might be true, but *would Ratchett have taken one last night?* The automatic under his pillow gave the lie to that statement. Ratchett intended to be on the alert last night. Whatever narcotic was administered to him must have been done so without his knowledge. By whom? Obviously by MacQueen or the valet.

"Now we come to the evidence of Mr. Hardman. I believed all that he told me about his own identity, but when it came to the actual methods he had employed to guard Mr. Ratchett, his story was neither more nor less than absurd. The only way effectively to have protected Ratchett was to have passed the night actually in his compartment or in some spot where he could watch the door. The only thing that his evidence *did* show plainly was that no one *in any other part of the train could possibly have murdered Ratchett*. It drew a clear circle round the Stamboul-Calais carriage. That seemed to me a rather curious and inexplicable fact, and I put it aside to think over.

"You probably have all heard by now of the few words I overheard between Miss Debenham and Colonel Arbuthnot. The interesting thing to my mind was the fact that Colonel Arbuthnot called her *Mary* and was clearly on terms of intimacy with her. But the Colonel was only supposed to have met her a few days previously—and I know Englishmen of the Colonel's type. Even if he had fallen in love with the young lady at first sight, he would have advanced slowly and with decorum—not rushing things. Therefore I concluded that Colonel Arbuthnot and Miss Debenham were in reality well acquainted, and were for some reason pretending to be strangers. Another small point was Miss Debenham's easy familiarity with the term 'long distance' for a telephone call. Yet Miss Debenham had told me that she had never been in the States.

"To pass to another witness. Mrs. Hubbard had told us that lying in bed she was unable to see whether the communicating door was bolted or not, and so asked Miss Ohlsson to see for her. Now, though her statement would have been perfectly true if she had been occupying compartments Nos. 2, 4, 12, or any *even* number—where the bolt is directly under the handle of the door—in the *uneven* numbers, such as compartment No. 3, the bolt is well *above* the handle and could not therefore be masked by the sponge bag in the least. I was forced to the conclusion that Mrs. Hubbard was inventing an incident that had never occurred.

"And here let me say just a word or two about *times*. To my mind, the really interesting point about the dented watch was the place where it was found—in Ratchett's pyjama pocket, a singularly uncomfortable and unlikely place to keep one's watch, especially as there is a watch 'hook' provided just by the head of the bed. I felt sure, therefore, that the watch had been deliberately placed in the pocket and faked. The crime, then, was not committed at a quarter past one.

"Was it, then, committed earlier? To be exact, at twenty-three minutes to one? My friend M. Bouc advanced as an argument in favour of it the loud cry which awoke me from sleep. But if Ratchett were heavily drugged *he could not have cried out*. If he had been capable of crying out he would have been capable of making some kind of a struggle to defend himself, and there were no signs of any such struggle.

"I remembered that MacQueen had called attention, not once but twice (and the second time in a very blatant manner), to the fact that Ratchett could speak no French. I came to the conclusion that the whole business at twenty-three minutes to one was a comedy played for my benefit! Anyone might see through the watch business—it is a common enough device in detective stories. They assumed that I *should* see through it and that, pluming myself on my own cleverness, I would go on to assume that since Ratchett spoke no French the voice I heard at twenty-three minutes to one could not be his, and that Ratchett must be already dead. But I am convinced that at twenty-three minutes to one Ratchett was still lying in his drugged sleep.

"But the device has succeeded! I have opened my door and looked out. I have actually heard the French phrase used. If I am so unbelievably dense as not to realize the significance of that phrase, it must be brought to my attention. If necessary MacQueen can come right out in the open. He can say, 'Excuse me, M. Poirot, *that can't have been Mr. Ratchett speaking.* He can't speak French.'

"Now when was the real time of the crime? And who killed him?

"In my opinion, and this is only an opinion, Ratchett was killed at some time very close upon two o'clock, the latest hour the doctor gives us as possible.

"As to who killed him—"

He paused, looking at his audience. He could not complain of any lack of attention. Every eye was fixed upon him. In the stillness you could have heard a pin drop.

He went on slowly:

"I was particularly struck by the extraordinary difficulty of proving a case against any one person on the train and on the rather curious coincidence that in each case the testimony giving an alibi came from what I might describe as an 'unlikely' person. Thus Mr. MacQueen and Colonel Arbuthnot provided alibis for each other—two persons between whom it seemed most unlikely there should be any prior acquaintanceship. The same thing happened with the English valet and the Italian, with the Swedish lady and the English girl. I said to myself, 'This is extraordinary—they cannot *all* be in it!'

"And then, Messieurs, I saw light. They were *all* in it. For so many people connected with the Armstrong case to be travelling by the same train by a coincidence was not only unlikely, it was *impossible*. It must be not chance, but *design*. I remembered a remark of Colonel Arbuthnot's about trial by jury. A jury is composed of twelve people—there were twelve passengers—Ratchett was stabbed twelve times. And the thing that had worried me all along—the extraordinary crowd travelling in the Stamboul-Calais coach at a slack time of year was explained.

"Ratchett had escaped justice in America. There was no question as to his guilt. I visualized a self-appointed jury of twelve people who condemned him to death and were forced by exigencies of the case to be their own executioners. And immediately, on that assumption, the whole case fell into beautiful shining order.

"I saw it as a perfect mosaic, each person playing his or her allotted part. It was so arranged that if suspicion should fall on any one person, the evidence of one or more of the others would clear the accused person and confuse the issue. Hardman's evidence was necessary in case some outsider should be suspected of the crime and be unable to prove an alibi. The passengers in the Stamboul carriage were in no danger. Every minute detail of their evidence was worked out beforehand. The whole thing was a very cleverly planned jig-saw puzzle, so arranged that every fresh piece of knowledge that came to light made the solution of the whole more difficult. As my friend M. Bouc remarked, the case seemed fantastically impossible! That was exactly the impression intended to be conveyed.

"Did this solution explain everything? Yes, it did. The nature of the wounds—each inflicted by a different person. The artificial threatening letters—artificial since they were unreal, written only to be produced as evidence. (Doubtless there were real letters, warning Ratchett of his fate, which MacQueen destroyed, substituting for them these others.) Then Hardman's story of being called in by Ratchett—a lie, of course, from beginning to end—the description of the mythical 'small dark man with a womanish voice,' a convenient description, since it had the merit of not incriminating any of the actual Wagon Lit conductors and would apply equally well to a man or a woman.

"The idea of stabbing is at first sight a curious one, but on reflection nothing would fit the circumstances so well. A dagger was a weapon that could be used by everyone—strong or weak—and it made no noise. I fancy, though I may be wrong, that each person in turn entered Ratchett's darkened compartment through that of Mrs. Hubbard—and struck! They themselves would never know which blow actually killed him.

"The final letter which Ratchett had probably found on his pillow was carefully burnt. With no clue pointing to the Armstrong case, there would be absolutely no reason for suspecting any of the passengers on the train. It would be put down as an outside job, and the 'small dark man with the womanish voice' would actually have been seen by one or more of the passengers leaving the train at Brod.

"I do not know exactly what happened when the conspirators discovered that that part of their plan was impossible owing to the accident to the train.

There was, I imagine, a hasty consultation, and then they decided to go through with it. It was true that now one and all of the passengers were bound to come under suspicion, but that possibility had already been foreseen and provided for. The only additional thing to be done was to confuse the issue even further. Two so-called 'clues' were dropped in the dead man's compartment—one incriminating Colonel Arbuthnot (who had the strongest alibi and whose connection with the Armstrong family was probably the hardest to prove) and the second clue, the handkerchief, incriminating Princess Dragomiroff, who by virtue of her social position, her particularly frail physique and the alibi given her by her maid and the conductor, was practically in an unassailable position. Further to confuse the issue, a 'red herring' was drawn across the trail—the mythical woman in the red kimono. Again I am to bear witness to this woman's existence. There is a heavy bang at my door. I get up and look out—and see the scarlet kimono disappearing in the distance. A judicious selection of people—the conductor, Miss Debenham and MacQueen—will also have seen her. It was, I think, someone with a sense of humour who thoughtfully placed the scarlet kimono on the top of my suitcase whilst I was interviewing people in the dining car. Where the garment came from in the first place I do not know. I suspect it is the property of Countess Andrenyi, since her luggage contained only a chiffon negligée so elaborate as to be more a tea gown than a dressing gown.

"When MacQueen first learned that the letter which had been so carefully burnt had in part escaped destruction, and that the word Armstrong was exactly the word remaining, he must at once have communicated his news to the others. It was at this minute that the position of Countess Andrenyi became acute and her husband immediately took steps to alter the passport. It was their second piece of bad luck!

"They one and all agreed to deny utterly any connection with the Armstrong family. They knew I had no immediate means of finding out the truth, and they did not believe that I should go into the matter unless my suspicions were aroused against one particular person.

"Now there was one further point to consider. Allowing that my theory of the crime was the correct one, and I believe that it *must* be the correct one, then obviously the Wagon Lit conductor himself must be privy to the plot. But if so, that gave us thirteen persons, not twelve. Instead of the usual formula, 'Of so many people one is guilty,' I was faced with the problem that of thirteen persons one and one only was innocent. Which was that person?

"I came to a very odd conclusion. I came to the conclusion that the person who had taken no part in the crime was the person who would be considered the most likely to do so. I refer to Countess Andrenyi. I was impressed by the earnestness of her husband when he swore to me solemnly on his honour that his wife never left her compartment that night. I decided that Count Andrenyi took, so to speak, his wife's place.

"If so, then Pierre Michel was definitely one of the twelve. But how could one explain his complicity? He was a decent man who had been many years in the employ of the Company—not the kind of man who could be bribed to assist in a crime. Then Pierre Michel must be involved in the Armstrong case. But that seemed very improbable. Then I remembered that the dead nurserymaid was French. Supposing that that unfortunate girl had been Pierre Michel's daughter. That would explain everything—it would also explain the place chosen for the staging of the crime. Were there any others whose part in the drama was not clear? Colonel Arbuthnot I put down as a friend of the Armstrongs. They had probably been through the war together. The maid, Hildegarde Schmidt, I could guess her place in the Armstrong household. I am, perhaps, overgreedy, but I sense a good cook instinctively. I laid a trap for her—she fell into it. I said I knew she was a good cook. She answered, 'Yes, indeed, all my ladies have said so.' But if you are employed as a *lady's maid* your employers seldom have a chance of learning whether or not you are a good cook.

"Then there was Hardman. He seemed quite definitely not to belong to the Armstrong household. I could only imagine that he had been in love with the French girl. I spoke to him of the charm of foreign women—and again I obtained the reaction I was looking for. Sudden tears came into his eyes, which he pretended were dazzled by the snow.

"There remains Mrs. Hubbard. Now Mrs. Hubbard, let me say, played the most important part in the drama. By occupying the compartment communicating with that of Ratchett she was more open to suspicion than anyone else. In the nature of things she could not have an alibi to fall back upon. To play the part she played—the perfectly natural, slightly ridiculous American fond mother—an artist was needed. But there *was* an artist connected with the Armstrong family—Mrs. Armstrong's mother—Linda Arden, the actress . . ."

He stopped.

Then, in a soft rich dreamy voice, quite unlike the one she had used all the journey, Mrs. Hubbard said:

"I always fancied myself in comedy parts."

She went on still dreamily:

"That slip about the sponge bag was silly. It shows you should always rehearse properly. We tried it on the way out—I was in an even number compartment then, I suppose. I never thought of the bolts being in different places."

She shifted her position a little and looked straight at Poirot.

"You know all about it, M. Poirot. You're a very wonderful man. But even you can't quite imagine what it was like—that awful day in New York. I was just crazy with grief—so were the servants—and Colonel Arbuthnot was there, too. He was John Armstrong's best friend."

"He saved my life in the war," said Arbuthnot.

"We decided then and there—perhaps we were mad—I don't know—that the sentence of death that Cassetti had escaped had got to be carried out. There were twelve of us—or rather eleven—Susanne's father was over in France, of course. First we thought we'd draw lots as to who should do it, but in the end we decided on this way. It was the chauffeur, Antonio, who suggested it. Mary worked out all the details later with Hector MacQueen. He'd always adored Sonia—my daughter—and it was he who explained to us exactly how Cassetti's money had managed to get him off.

"It took a long time to perfect our plan. We had first to track Ratchett down. Hardman managed that in the end. Then we had to try to get Masterman and Hector into his employment—or at any rate one of them. Well, we managed that. Then we had a consultation with Susanne's father. Colonel Arbuthnot was very keen on having twelve of us. He seemed to think it made it more in order. He didn't like the stabbing idea much, but he agreed that it did solve most of our difficulties. Well, Susanne's father was willing. Susanne was his only child. We knew from Hector that Ratchett would be coming back from the East sooner or later by the Orient Express. With Pierre Michel actually working on that train, the chance was too good to be missed. Besides, it would be a good way of not incriminating any outsiders.

"My daughter's husband had to know, of course, and he insisted on coming on the train with her. Hector wangled it so that Ratchett selected the right day for travelling when Michel would be on duty. We meant to engage every carriage in the Stamboul-Calais coach, but unfortunately there was one carriage we couldn't get. It was reserved long beforehand for a director of the company. Mr. Harris, of course, was a myth. But it would have been awkward to have any stranger in Hector's compartment. And then, at the last minute, *you* came. . . ."

She stopped.

"Well," she said. "You know everything now, M. Poirot. What are you going to do about it? If it must all come out, can't you lay the blame upon me and me only? I would have stabbed that man twelve times willingly. It wasn't only that he was responsible for my daughter's death and her child's, and that of the other child who might have been alive and happy now. It was more than that. There had been other children before Daisy—there might be others in the future. Society had condemned him; we were only carrying out the sentence. But it's unnecessary to bring all these others into it. All these good faithful souls—and poor Michel—and Mary and Colonel Arbuthnot—they love each other. . . ."

Her voice was wonderful echoing through the crowded space—that deep, emotional, heart-stirring voice that had thrilled many a New York audience.

Poirot looked at his friend.

"You are a director of the company, M. Bouc," he said, "What do you say?"

M. Bouc cleared his throat.

"In my opinion, M. Poirot," he said, "the first theory you put forward was the correct one—decidedly so. I suggest that that is the solution we offer to the Yugo-Slavian police when they arrive. You agree, Doctor?"

"Certainly I agree," said Dr. Constantine. "As regards the medical evidence, I think—er—that I made one or two fantastic suggestions."

"Then," said Poirot, "having placed my solution before you, I have the honour to retire from the case. . . ."

THE MURDER OF ROGER ACKROYD

To Punkie
who likes an orthodox detective story, murder,
inquest, and suspicion falling on everyone in turn!

Contents

1 Dr. Sheppard at the Breakfast Table   223

2 Who's Who in King's Abbot   228

3 The Man Who Grew Vegetable Marrows   235

4 Dinner at Fernly   245

5 Murder   258

6 The Tunisian Dagger   270

7 I Learn My Neighbour's Profession   278

8 Inspector Raglan Is Confident   290

9 The Goldfish Pond   300

10 The Parlourmaid   309

11 Poirot Pays a Call   322

12 Round the Table   329

13 The Goose Quill   337

14 Mrs. Ackroyd   343

15 Geoffrey Raymond   352

16 An Evening at Mah Jong   360

17 Parker   369

18 Charles Kent   380

19 Flora Ackroyd   386

20 Miss Russell   394

21 The Paragraph in the Paper   403

22 Ursula's Story   410

23 Poirot's Little Reunion   417

24 Ralph Paton's Story   427

25 The Whole Truth   431

26 And Nothing but the Truth   437

27 Apologia   440

One

DR. SHEPPARD AT THE
BREAKFAST TABLE

Mrs. Ferrars died on the night of the 16th–17th September—a Thursday. I was sent for at eight o'clock on the morning of Friday the 17th. There was nothing to be done. She had been dead some hours.

It was just a few minutes after nine when I reached home once more. I opened the front door with my latchkey, and purposely delayed a few moments in the hall, hanging up my hat and the light overcoat that I had deemed a wise precaution against the chill of an early autumn morning. To tell the truth, I was considerably upset and worried. I am not going to pretend that at that moment I foresaw the events of the next few weeks. I emphatically did not do so. But my instinct told me that there were stirring times ahead.

From the dining room on my left there came the rattle of tea-cups and the short, dry cough of my sister Caroline.

"Is that you, James?" she called.

An unnecessary question, since who else could it be? To tell the truth, it was precisely my sister Caroline who was the cause of my few minutes' delay. The motto of the mongoose family, so Mr. Kipling tells us, is: "Go and find out." If Caroline ever adopts a crest, I should certainly suggest a mongoose rampant. One might omit the first part of the motto. Caroline can do any amount of finding out by sitting placidly at home. I don't know how she manages it, but there it is. I suspect that the servants and the tradesmen constitute her Intelligence

Corps. When she goes out, it is not to gather in information, but to spread it. At that, too, she is amazingly expert.

It was really this last named trait of hers which was causing me these pangs of indecision. Whatever I told Caroline now concerning the demise of Mrs. Ferrars would be common knowledge all over the village within the space of an hour and a half. As a professional man, I naturally aim at discretion. Therefore I have got into the habit of continually withholding all information possible from my sister. She usually finds out just the same, but I have the moral satisfaction of knowing that I am in no way to blame.

Mrs. Ferrars' husband died just over a year ago, and Caroline has constantly asserted, without the least foundation for the assertion, that his wife poisoned him.

She scorns my invariable rejoinder that Mr. Ferrars died of acute gastritis, helped on by habitual overindulgence in alcoholic beverages. The symptoms of gastritis and arsenical poisoning are not, I agree, unlike, but Caroline bases her accusation on quite different lines.

"You've only got to look at her," I have heard her say.

Mrs. Ferrars, though not in her first youth, was a very attractive woman, and her clothes, though simple, always seemed to fit her very well, but all the same, lots of women buy their clothes in Paris, and have not, on that account, necessarily poisoned their husbands.

As I stood hesitating in the hall, with all this passing through my mind, Caroline's voice came again, with a sharper note in it.

"What on earth are you doing out there, James? Why don't you come and get your breakfast?"

"Just coming, my dear," I said hastily. "I've been hanging up my overcoat."

"You could have hung up half a dozen overcoats in this time."

She was quite right. I could have.

I walked into the dining room, gave Caroline the accustomed peck on the cheek, and sat down to eggs and bacon. The bacon was rather cold.

"You've had an early call," remarked Caroline.

"Yes," I said. "King's Paddock. Mrs. Ferrars."

"I know," said my sister.

"How did you know?"

"Annie told me."

Annie is the house parlourmaid. A nice girl, but an inveterate talker.

There was a pause. I continued to eat eggs and bacon. My sister's nose, which is long and thin, quivered a little at the tip, as it always does when she is interested or excited over anything.

"Well?" she demanded.

"A sad business. Nothing to be done. Must have died in her sleep."

"I know," said my sister again.

This time I was annoyed.

"You can't know," I snapped. "I didn't know myself until I got there, and haven't mentioned it to a soul yet. If that girl Annie knows, she must be a clairvoyant."

"It wasn't Annie who told me. It was the milkman. He had it from the Ferrarses' cook."

As I say, there is no need for Caroline to go out to get information. She sits at home and it comes to her.

My sister continued:

"What did she die of? Heart failure?"

"Didn't the milkman tell you that?" I inquired sarcastically.

Sarcasm is wasted on Caroline. She takes it seriously and answers accordingly.

"He didn't know," she explained.

After all, Caroline was bound to hear sooner or later. She might as well hear from me.

"She died of an overdose of Veronal. She's been taking it lately for sleeplessness. Must have taken too much."

"Nonsense," said Caroline immediately. "She took it on purpose. Don't tell me!"

It is odd, when you have a secret belief of your own which you do not wish to acknowledge, the voicing of it by someone else will rouse you to a fury of denial. I burst immediately into indignant speech.

"There you go again," I said. "Rushing along without rhyme or reason. Why on earth should Mrs. Ferrars wish to commit suicide? A widow, fairly young still, very well off, good health, and nothing to do but enjoy life. It's absurd."

"Not at all. Even you must have noticed how different she has been looking lately. It's been coming on for the last six months. She's looked positively hag-ridden. And you have just admitted that she hasn't been able to sleep."

"What is your diagnosis?" I demanded coldly. "An unfortunate love affair, I suppose?"

My sister shook her head.

"Remorse," she said, with great gusto.

"Remorse?"

"Yes. You never would believe me when I told you she poisoned her husband. I'm more than ever convinced of it now."

"I don't think you're very logical," I objected. "Surely if a woman committed a crime like murder, she'd be sufficiently cold-blooded to enjoy the fruits of it without any weak-minded sentimentality such as repentance."

Caroline shook her head.

"There probably are women like that—but Mrs. Ferrars wasn't one of them. She was a mass of nerves. An overmastering impulse drove her on to get rid of her husband because she was the sort of person who simply can't endure suffer-ing of any kind, and there's no doubt that the wife of a man like Ashley Ferrars must have had to suffer a good deal—"

I nodded.

"And ever since she's been haunted by what she did. I can't help feeling sorry for her."

I don't think Caroline ever felt sorry for Mrs. Ferrars whilst she was alive. Now that she has gone where (presumably) Paris frocks can no longer be worn, Caroline is prepared to indulge in the softer emotions of pity and comprehension.

I told her firmly that her whole idea was nonsense. I was all the more firm because I secretly agreed with some part, at least, of what she had said. But it is all wrong that Caroline should arrive at the truth simply by a kind of inspired guesswork. I wasn't going to encourage that sort of thing. She will go round the village airing her views, and everyone will think that she is doing so on medical data supplied by me. Life is very trying.

"Nonsense," said Caroline, in reply to my strictures. "You'll see. Ten to one she's left a letter confessing everything."

"She didn't leave a letter of any kind," I said sharply, and not seeing where the admission was going to land me.

"Oh!" said Caroline. "So you *did* inquire about that, did you? I believe, James, that in your heart of hearts, you think very much as I do. You're a precious old humbug."

"One always has to take the possibility of suicide into consideration," I said impressively.

"Will there be an inquest?"

"There may be. It all depends. If I am able to declare myself absolutely satisfied that the overdose was taken accidentally, an inquest might be dispensed with."

"And are you absolutely satisfied?" asked my sister shrewdly.

I did not answer, but got up from the table.

Two

Who's Who in King's Abbot

Before I proceed further with what I said to Caroline and what Caroline said to me, it might be as well to give some idea of what I should describe as our local geography. Our village, King's Abbot, is, I imagine, very much like any other village. Our big town is Cranchester, nine miles away. We have a large railway station, a small post office, and two rival "General Stores." Able-bodied men are apt to leave the place early in life, but we are rich in unmarried ladies and retired military officers. Our hobbies and recreations can be summed up in the one word, "gossip."

There are only two houses of any importance in King's Abbot. One is King's Paddock, left to Mrs. Ferrars by her late husband. The other, Fernly Park, is owned by Roger Ackroyd. Ackroyd has always interested me by being a man more impossibly like a country squire than any country squire could really be. He reminds one of the red-faced sportsmen who always appeared early in the first act of an old-fashioned musical comedy, the setting being the village green. They usually sang a song about going up to London. Nowadays we have revues, and the country squire has died out of musical fashion.

Of course, Ackroyd is not really a country squire. He is an immensely successful manufacturer of (I think) wagon wheels. He is a man of nearly fifty years of age, rubicund of face and genial of manner. He is hand and glove with the vicar, subscribes liberally to parish funds (though rumour has it that he is extremely mean in personal expenditure), encourages cricket matches, Lads'

Clubs, and Disabled Soldiers' Institutes. He is, in fact, the life and soul of our peaceful village of King's Abbot.

Now when Roger Ackroyd was a lad of twenty-one, he fell in love with, and married, a beautiful woman some five or six years his senior. Her name was Paton, and she was a widow with one child. The history of the marriage was short and painful. To put it bluntly, Mrs. Ackroyd was a dipsomaniac. She succeeded in drinking herself into her grave four years after her marriage.

In the years that followed, Ackroyd showed no disposition to make a second matrimonial adventure. His wife's child by her first marriage was only seven years old when his mother died. He is now twenty-five. Ackroyd has always regarded him as his own son, and has brought him up accordingly, but he has been a wild lad and a continual source of worry and trouble to his stepfather. Nevertheless we are all very fond of Ralph Paton in King's Abbot. He is such a good-looking youngster for one thing.

As I said before, we are ready enough to gossip in our village. Everybody noticed from the first that Ackroyd and Mrs. Ferrars got on very well together. After her husband's death, the intimacy became more marked. They were always seen about together, and it was freely conjectured that at the end of her period of mourning, Mrs. Ferrars would become Mrs. Roger Ackroyd. It was felt, indeed, that there was a certain fitness in the thing. Roger Ackroyd's wife had admittedly died of drink. Ashley Ferrars had been a drunkard for many years before his death. It was only fitting that these two victims of alcoholic excess should make up to each other for all that they had previously endured at the hands of their former spouses.

The Ferrars only came to live here just over a year ago, but a halo of gossip has surrounded Ackroyd for many years past. All the time that Ralph Paton was growing up to manhood a series of lady housekeepers presided over Ackroyd's establishment, and each in turn was regarded with lively suspicion by Caroline and her cronies. It is not too much to say that for at least fifteen years the whole village has confidently expected Ackroyd to marry one of his housekeepers. The last of them, a redoubtable lady called Miss Russell, has reigned undisputed for five years, twice as long as any of her predecessors. It is felt that but for the advent of Mrs. Ferrars, Ackroyd could hardly have escaped. That—and one other factor—the unexpected arrival of a widowed sister-in-law with her daughter from Canada. Mrs. Cecil Ackroyd, widow of Ackroyd's ne'er-do-well younger brother, has taken up her residence at Fernley Park, and has succeeded, according to Caroline, in putting Miss Russell in her proper place.

I don't know exactly what a "proper place" constitutes—it sounds chilly and unpleasant—but I know that Miss Russell goes about with pinched lips, and what I can only describe as an acid smile, and that she professes the utmost sympathy for "poor Mrs. Ackroyd—dependent on the charity of her husband's brother. The bread of charity is so bitter, is it not? *I* should be quite miserable if I did not work for my living."

I don't know what Mrs. Cecil Ackroyd thought of the Ferrars affair when it came on the tapis. It was clearly to her advantage that Ackroyd should remain unmarried. She was always very charming—not to say gushing—to Mrs. Ferrars when they met. Caroline says that proves less than nothing.

Such have been our preoccupations in King's Abbot for the last few years. We have discussed Ackroyd and his affairs from every standpoint. Mrs. Ferrars has fitted into her place in the scheme.

Now there has been a rearrangement of the kaleidoscope. From a mild discussion of probable wedding presents, we had been jerked into the midst of tragedy.

Revolving these and sundry other matters in my mind, I went mechanically on my round. I had no cases of special interest to attend, which was, perhaps, as well, for my thoughts returned again and again to the mystery of Mrs. Ferrars's death. Had she taken her own life? Surely, if she had done so, she would have left some word behind to say what she contemplated doing? Women, in my experience, if they once reach the determination to commit suicide, usually wish to reveal the state of mind that led to the fatal action. They covet the limelight.

When had I last seen her? Not for over a week. Her manner then had been normal enough considering—well—considering everything.

Then I suddenly remembered that I had seen her, though not to speak to, only yesterday. She had been walking with Ralph Paton, and I had been surprised because I had had no idea that he was likely to be in King's Abbot.

I thought, indeed, that he had quarrelled finally with his stepfather. Nothing had been seen of him down here for nearly six months. They had been walking along, side by side, their heads close together, and she had been talking very earnestly.

I think I can safely say that it was at this moment that a foreboding of the future first swept over me. Nothing tangible as yet—but a vague premonition of the way things were setting. That earnest *tête-à-tête* between Ralph Paton and Mrs. Ferrars the day before struck me disagreeably.

I was still thinking of it when I came face to face with Roger Ackroyd.

"Sheppard!" he exclaimed. "Just the man I wanted to get hold of. This is a terrible business."

"You've heard then?"

He nodded. He had felt the blow keenly, I could see. His big red cheeks seemed to have fallen in, and he looked a positive wreck of his usual jolly, healthy self.

"It's worse than you know," he said quietly. "Look here, Sheppard, I've got to talk to you. Can you come back with me now?"

"Hardly. I've got three patients to see still, and I must be back by twelve to see my surgery patients."

"Then this afternoon—no, better still, dine tonight. At 7:30. Will that suit you?"

"Yes, I can manage that all right. What's wrong? Is it Ralph?"

I hardly knew why I said that—except, perhaps, that it had so often been Ralph.

Ackroyd stared blankly at me as though he hardly understood. I began to realize that there must be something very wrong indeed somewhere. I had never seen Ackroyd so upset before.

"Ralph?" he said vaguely. "Oh! no, it's not Ralph. Ralph's in London— Damn! Here's old Miss Gannett coming. I don't want to have to talk to her about this ghastly business. See you tonight, Sheppard. Seven-thirty."

I nodded, and he hurried away, leaving me wondering. Ralph in London? But he had certainly been in King's Abbot the preceding afternoon. He must have gone back to town last night or early this morning, and yet Ackroyd's manner had conveyed quite a different impression. He had spoken as though Ralph had not been near the place for months.

I had no time to puzzle the matter out further. Miss Gannett was upon me, thirsting for information. Miss Gannett has all the characteristics of my sister Caroline, but she lacks that unerring aim in jumping to conclusions which lends a touch of greatness to Caroline's manoeuvres. Miss Gannett was breathless and interrogatory.

Wasn't it sad about poor dear Mrs. Ferrars? A lot of people were saying she had been a confirmed drug-taker for years. So wicked the way people went about saying things. And yet, the worst of it was, there was usually a grain of truth somewhere in these wild statements. No smoke without fire! They were saying too that Mr. Ackroyd had found out about it, and had broken off the engagement—because there *was* an engagement. She, Miss Gannett, had proof positive of that. Of course *I* must know all about it—doctors always did—but they never tell?

And all this with a sharp beady eye on me to see how I reacted to these suggestions. Fortunately, long association with Caroline has led me to preserve an impassive countenance, and to be ready with small noncommittal remarks.

On this occasion I congratulated Miss Gannett on not joining in ill-natured gossip. Rather a neat counterattack, I thought. It left her in difficulties, and before she could pull herself together, I had passed on.

I went home thoughtful, to find several patients waiting for me in the surgery.

I had dismissed the last of them, as I thought, and was just contemplating a few minutes in the garden before lunch when I perceived one more patient waiting for me. She rose and came towards me as I stood somewhat surprised.

I don't know why I should have been, except that there is a suggestion of cast iron about Miss Russell, a something that is above the ills of the flesh.

Ackroyd's housekeeper is a tall woman, handsome but forbidding in appearance. She has a stern eye, and lips that shut tightly, and I feel that if I were an under housemaid or a kitchenmaid I should run for my life whenever I heard her coming.

"Good morning, Dr. Sheppard," said Miss Russell. "I should be much obliged if you would take a look at my knee."

I took a look, but, truth to tell, I was very little wiser when I had done so. Miss Russell's account of vague pains was so unconvincing that with a woman of less integrity of character I should have suspected a trumped-up tale. It did cross my mind for one moment that Miss Russell might have deliberately invented this affection of the knee in order to pump me on the subject of Mrs. Ferrars's death, but I soon saw that there, at least, I had misjudged her. She made a brief reference to the tragedy, nothing more. Yet she certainly seemed disposed to linger and chat.

"Well, thank you very much for this bottle of liniment, doctor," she said at last. "Not that I believe it will do the least good."

I didn't think it would either, but I protested in duty bound. After all, it couldn't do any harm, and one must stick up for the tools of one's trade.

"I don't believe in all these drugs," said Miss Russell, her eyes sweeping over my array of bottles disparagingly. "Drugs do a lot of harm. Look at the cocaine habit."

"Well, as far as that goes—"

"It's very prevalent in high society."

I'm sure Miss Russell knows far more about high society than I do. I didn't attempt to argue with her.

"Just tell me this, doctor," said Miss Russell. "Suppose you are really a slave of the drug habit, is there any cure?"

One cannot answer a question like that off-hand. I gave her a short lecture on the subject, and she listened with close attention. I still suspected her of seeking information about Mrs. Ferrars.

"Now, Veronal, for instance—" I proceeded.

But, strangely enough, she didn't seem interested in Veronal. Instead she changed the subject, and asked me if it was true that there were certain poisons so rare as to baffle detection.

"Ah!" I said. "You've been reading detective stories."

She admitted that she had.

"The essence of a detective story," I said, "is to have a rare poison—if possible something from South America, that nobody has ever heard of—something that one obscure tribe of savages use to poison their arrows with. Death is instantaneous, and Western science is powerless to detect it. Is that the kind of thing you mean?"

"Yes. Is there really such a thing?"

I shook my head regretfully.

"I'm afraid there isn't. There's *curare,* of course."

I told her a good deal about curare, but she seemed to have lost interest once more. She asked me if I had any in my poison cupboard, and when I replied in the negative I fancy I fell in her estimation.

She said she must be getting back, and I saw her out at the surgery door just as the luncheon gong went.

I should never have suspected Miss Russell of a fondness for detective stories. It pleases me very much to think of her stepping out of the housekeeper's room to rebuke a delinquent housemaid, and then returning to a comfortable perusal of *The Mystery of the Seventh Death,* or something of the kind.

Three

THE MAN WHO GREW VEGETABLE MARROWS

I told Caroline at lunch that I should be dining at Fernly. She expressed no objection—on the contrary.

"Excellent," she said. "You'll hear all about it. By the way, what is the trouble with Ralph?"

"With Ralph?" I said, surprised; "there isn't any."

"Then why is he staying at the Three Boars instead of at Fernly Park?"

I did not for a minute question Caroline's statement that Ralph Paton was staying at the local inn. That Caroline said so was enough for me.

"Ackroyd told me he was in London," I said. In the surprise of the moment I departed from my valuable rule of never parting with information.

"Oh!" said Caroline. I could see her nose twitching as she worked on this.

"He arrived at the Three Boars yesterday morning," she said. "And he's still there. Last night he was out with a girl."

That did not surprise me in the least. Ralph, I should say, is out with a girl most nights of his life. But I did rather wonder that he chose to indulge in the pastime in King's Abbot instead of in the gay Metropolis.

"One of the barmaids?" I asked.

"No. That's just it. He went out to meet her. I don't know who she is."

(Bitter for Caroline to have to admit such a thing.)

"But I can guess," continued my indefatigable sister.

I waited patiently.

"His cousin."

"Flora Ackroyd?" I exclaimed in surprise.

Flora Ackroyd is, of course, no relation whatever really to Ralph Paton but Ralph has been looked upon for so long as practically Ackroyd's own son, that cousinship is taken for granted.

"Flora Ackroyd," said my sister.

"But why not go to Fernly if he wanted to see her?"

"Secretly engaged," said Caroline, with immense enjoyment. "Old Ackroyd won't hear of it, and they have to meet this way."

I saw a good many flaws in Caroline's theory, but I forebore to point them out to her. An innocent remark about our new neighbour created a diversion.

The house next door, The Larches, has recently been taken by a stranger. To Caroline's extreme annoyance, she has not been able to find out anything about him, except that he is a foreigner. The Intelligence Corps has proved a broken reed. Presumably the man has milk and vegetables and joints of meat and occasional whitings just like everybody else, but none of the people who make it their business to supply these things seem to have acquired any information. His name, apparently, is Mr. Porrott—a name which conveys an odd feeling of unreality. The one thing we do know about him is that he is interested in the growing of vegetable marrows.

But that is certainly not the sort of information that Caroline is after. She wants to know where he comes from, what he does, whether he is married, what his wife was, or is, like, whether he has children, what his mother's maiden name was—and so on. Somebody very like Caroline must have invented the questions on passports, I think.

"My dear Caroline," I said. "There's no doubt at all about what the man's profession has been. He's a retired hairdresser. Look at that moustache of his."

Caroline dissented. She said that if the man was a hairdresser, he would have wavy hair—not straight. All hairdressers did.

I cited several hairdressers personally known to me who had straight hair, but Caroline refused to be convinced.

"I can't make him out at all," she said in an aggrieved voice. "I borrowed some garden tools the other day, and he was most polite, but I couldn't get anything out of him. I asked him point blank at last whether he was a Frenchman, and he said he wasn't—and, somehow, I didn't like to ask him any more."

I began to be more interested in our mysterious neighbour. A man who is capable of shutting up Caroline and sending her, like the Queen of Sheba, empty away, must be something of a personality.

"I believe," said Caroline, "that he's got one of those new vacuum cleaners—"

I saw a meditated loan and the opportunity of further questioning gleaming from her eye. I saw the chance to escape into the garden. I am rather fond of gardening. I was busily exterminating dandelion roots when a shout of warning sounded from close by and a heavy body whizzed by my ears and fell at my feet with a repellent squelch. It was a vegetable marrow!

I looked up angrily. Over the wall, to my left, there appeared a face. An egg-shaped head, partially covered with suspiciously black hair, two immense moustaches, and a pair of watchful eyes. It was our mysterious neighbour, Mr. Porrott.

He broke at once into fluent apologies.

"I demand of you a thousand pardons, monsieur. I am without defence. For some months now I cultivate the marrows. This morning suddenly I enrage myself with these marrows. I send them to promenade themselves—alas! not only mentally but physically. I seize the biggest. I hurl him over the wall. Monsieur, I am ashamed. I prostrate myself."

Before such profuse apologies, my anger was forced to melt. After all, the wretched vegetable hadn't hit me. But I sincerely hoped that throwing large vegetables over walls was not our new friend's hobby. Such a habit could hardly endear him to us as a neighbour.

The strange little man seemed to read my thoughts.

"Ah! no," he exclaimed. "Do not disquiet yourself. It is not with me a habit. But you can figure to yourself, monsieur, that a man may work towards a certain object, may labour and toil to attain a certain kind of leisure and occupation, and then find that, after all, he yearns for the old busy days, and the old occupations that he thought himself so glad to leave?"

"Yes," I said slowly. "I fancy that that is a common enough occurrence. I myself am perhaps an instance. A year ago I came into a legacy—enough to enable me to realize a dream. I have always wanted to travel, to see the world. Well, that was a year ago, as I said, and—I am still here."

My little neighbour nodded.

"The chains of habit. We work to attain an object, and the object gained, we find that what we miss is the daily toil. And mark you, monsieur, my work was interesting work. The most interesting work there is in the world."

"Yes?" I said encouragingly. For the moment the spirit of Caroline was strong within me.

"The study of human nature, monsieur!"

"Just so," I said kindly.

Clearly a retired hairdresser. Who knows the secrets of human nature better than a hairdresser?

"Also, I had a friend—a friend who for many years never left my side. Occasionally of an imbecility to make one afraid, nevertheless he was very dear to me. Figure to yourself that I miss even his stupidity. His *naïveté,* his honest outlook, the pleasure of delighting and surprising him by my superior gifts—all these I miss more than I can tell you."

"He died?" I asked sympathetically.

"Not so. He lives and flourishes—but on the other side of the world. He is now in the Argentine."

"In the Argentine," I said enviously.

I have always wanted to go to South America. I sighed, and then looked up to find Mr. Porrott eyeing me sympathetically. He seemed an understanding little man.

"Will you go there, yes?" he asked.

I shook my head with a sigh.

"I could have gone," I said. "A year ago. But I was foolish—and worse than foolish—greedy. I risked the substance for the shadow."

"I comprehend," said Mr. Porrott. "You speculated?"

I nodded mournfully, but in spite of myself I felt secretly entertained. This ridiculous little man was so portentously solemn.

"Not the Porcupine Oilfields?" he asked suddenly.

I stared.

"I thought of them, as a matter of fact, but in the end I plumped for a gold mine in Western Australia."

My neighbour was regarding me with a strange expression which I could not fathom.

"It is Fate," he said at last.

"What is Fate?" I asked irritably.

"That I should live next to a man who seriously considers Porcupine Oil-fields, and also West Australian Gold Mines. Tell me, have you also a penchant for auburn hair?"

I stared at him openmouthed, and he burst out laughing.

"No, no, it is not the insanity that I suffer from. Make your mind easy. It was a foolish question that I put to you there, for, you see, my friend of whom I spoke was a young man, a man who thought all women good, and most of them beautiful. But you are a man of middle age, a doctor, a man who knows the folly and the vanity of most things in this life of ours. Well, well, we are neighbours. I beg of you to accept and present to your excellent sister my best marrow."

He stooped, and with a flourish produced an immense specimen of the tribe, which I duly accepted in the spirit in which it was offered.

"Indeed," said the little man cheerfully, "this has not been a wasted morning. I have made the acquaintance of a man who in some ways resembles my far-off friend. By the way, I should like to ask you a question. You doubtless know everyone in this tiny village. Who is the young man with the very dark hair and eyes, and the handsome face. He walks with his head flung back, and an easy smile on his lips?"

The description left me in no doubt.

"That must be Captain Ralph Paton," I said slowly.

"I have not seen him about here before?"

"No, he has not been here for some time. But he is the son—adopted son, rather—of Mr. Ackroyd of Fernly Park."

My neighbour made a slight gesture of impatience.

"Of course, I should have guessed. Mr. Ackroyd spoke of him many times."

"You know Mr. Ackroyd?" I said, slightly surprised.

"Mr. Ackroyd knew me in London—when I was at work there. I have asked him to say nothing of my profession down here."

"I see," I said, rather amused by this patent snobbery, as I thought it.

But the little man went on with an almost grandiloquent smirk.

"One prefers to remain incognito. I am not anxious for notoriety. I have not even troubled to correct the local version of my name."

"Indeed," I said, not knowing quite what to say.

"Captain Ralph Paton," mused Mr. Porrott. "And so he is engaged to Mr. Ackroyd's niece, the charming Miss Flora."

"Who told you so?" I asked, very much surprised.

"Mr. Ackroyd. About a week ago. He is very pleased about it—has long desired that such a thing should come to pass, or so I understood from him. I even believe that he brought some pressure to bear upon the young man. That is never wise. A young man should marry to please himself—not to please a stepfather from whom he has expectations."

My ideas were completely upset. I could not see Ackroyd taking a hairdresser into his confidence, and discussing the marriage of his niece and stepson with him. Ackroyd extends a genial patronage to the lower orders, but he has a very great sense of his own dignity. I began to think that Porrott couldn't be a hairdresser after all.

To hide my confusion, I said the first thing that came into my head.

"What made you notice Ralph Paton? His good looks?"

"No, not that alone—though he is unusually good-looking for an Englishman—what your lady novelists would call a Greek God. No, there was something about that young man that I did not understand."

He said the last sentence in a musing tone of voice which made an indefinable impression upon me. It was as though he was summing up the boy by the light of some inner knowledge that I did not share. It was that impression that was left with me, for at that moment my sister's voice called me from the house.

I went in. Caroline had her hat on, and had evidently just come in from the village. She began without preamble.

"I met Mr. Ackroyd."

"Yes?" I said.

"I stopped him, of course, but he seemed in a great hurry, and anxious to get away."

I have no doubt but that that was the case. He would feel towards Caroline much as he had felt towards Miss Gannett earlier in the day—perhaps more so. Caroline is less easy to shake off.

"I asked him at once about Ralph. He was absolutely astonished. Had no idea the boy was down here. He actually said he thought I must have made a mistake. I! A mistake!"

"Ridiculous," I said. "He ought to have known you better."

"Then he went on to tell me that Ralph and Flora are engaged."

"I knew that, too," I interrupted, with modest pride.

"Who told you?"

"Our new neighbour."

Caroline visibly wavered for a second or two, much as if a roulette ball might coyly hover between two numbers. Then she declined the tempting red herring.

"I told Mr. Ackroyd that Ralph was staying at the Three Boars."

"Caroline," I said, "do you never reflect that you might do a lot of harm with this habit of yours of repeating everything indiscriminately?"

"Nonsense," said my sister. "People ought to know things. I consider it my duty to tell them. Mr. Ackroyd was very grateful to me."

"Well," I said, for there was clearly more to come.

"I think he went straight off to the Three Boars, but if so he didn't find Ralph there."

"No?"

"No. Because as I was coming back through the wood—"

"Coming back through the wood?" I interrupted.

Caroline had the grace to blush.

"It was such a lovely day," she exclaimed. "I thought I would make a little round. The woods with their autumnal tints are so perfect at this time of year."

Caroline does not care a hang for woods at any time of year. Normally she regards them as places where you get your feet damp, and where all kinds of unpleasant things may drop on your head. No, it was good sound mongoose instinct which took her to our local wood. It is the only place adjacent to the village of King's Abbot where you can talk with a young woman unseen by the whole of the village. It adjoins the Park of Fernly.

"Well," I said, "go on."

"As I say, I was just coming back through the wood when I heard voices." Caroline paused.

"Yes?"

"One was Ralph Paton's—I knew it at once. The other was a girl's. Of course I didn't mean to listen—"

"Of course not," I interjected, with patent sarcasm—which was, however, wasted on Caroline.

"But I simply couldn't help overhearing. The girl said something—I didn't quite catch what it was, and Ralph answered. He sounded very angry. 'My dear girl,' he said. 'Don't you realize that it is quite on the cards the old man will cut me off with a shilling? He's been pretty fed up with me for the last few years. A little more would do it. And we need the dibs, my dear. I shall be a very rich man when the old fellow pops off. He's mean as they make 'em, but he's rolling in money really. I don't want him to go altering his will. You leave it to me, and don't worry.' Those were his exact words. I remember them perfectly. Unfortunately, just then I stepped on a dry twig or something, and they lowered their voices and moved away. I couldn't, of course, go rushing after them, so wasn't able to see who the girl was."

"That must have been most vexing," I said. "I suppose, though, you hurried on to the Three Boars, felt faint, and went into the bar for a glass of brandy, and so were able to see if both the barmaids were on duty?"

"It wasn't a barmaid," said Caroline unhesitatingly. "In fact, I'm almost sure that it was Flora Ackroyd, only—"

"Only it doesn't seem to make sense," I agreed.

"But if it wasn't Flora, who could it have been?"

Rapidly my sister ran over a list of maidens living in the neighbourhood, with profuse reasons for and against.

When she paused for breath, I murmured something about a patient, and slipped out.

I proposed to make my way to the Three Boars. It seemed likely that Ralph Paton would have returned there by now.

I knew Ralph very well—better, perhaps, than anyone else in King's Abbot, for I had known his mother before him, and therefore I understood much in him that puzzled others. He was, to a certain extent, the victim of heredity. He had not inherited his mother's fatal propensity for drink, but nevertheless he had in him a strain of weakness. As my new friend of this morning had declared, he was extraordinarily handsome. Just on six feet, perfectly proportioned, with the easy grace of an athlete, he was dark, like his mother, with a handsome, sunburnt face always ready to break into a smile. Ralph Paton was of those born to charm easily and without effort. He was self-indulgent and extravagant, with no veneration for anything on earth, but he was lovable nevertheless, and his friends were all devoted to him.

Could I do anything with the boy? I thought I could.

On inquiry at the Three Boars I found that Captain Paton had just come in. I went up to his room and entered unannounced.

For a moment, remembering what I had heard and seen, I was doubtful of my reception, but I need have had no misgivings.

"Why, it's Sheppard! Glad to see you."

He came forward to meet me, hand outstretched, a sunny smile lighting up his face.

"The one person I am glad to see in this infernal place."

I raised my eyebrows.

"What's the place been doing?"

He gave a vexed laugh.

"It's a long story. Things haven't been going well with me, doctor. But have a drink, won't you?"

"Thanks," I said, "I will."

He pressed the bell, then coming back threw himself into a chair.

"Not to mince matters," he said gloomily, "I'm in the devil of a mess. In fact, I haven't the least idea what to do next."

"What's the matter?" I asked sympathetically.

"It's my confounded stepfather."

"What has he done?"

"It isn't what he's done yet, but what he's likely to do."

The bell was answered, and Ralph ordered the drinks. When the man had gone again, he sat hunched in the armchair, frowning to himself.

"Is it really—serious?" I asked.

He nodded.

"I'm fairly up against it this time," he said soberly.

The unusual ring of gravity in his voice told me that he spoke the truth. It took a good deal to make Ralph grave.

"In fact," he continued, "I can't see my way ahead . . . I'm damned if I can."

"If I could help—" I suggested diffidently.

But he shook his head very decidedly.

"Good of you, doctor. But I can't let you in on this. I've got to play a lone hand."

He was silent a minute and then repeated in a slightly different tone of voice:

"Yes—I've got to play a lone hand. . . ."

Four

DINNER AT FERNLY

I

It was just a few minutes before half past seven when I rang the frontdoor bell of Fernly Park. The door was opened with admirable promptitude by Parker, the butler.

The night was such a fine one that I had preferred to come on foot. I stepped into the big square hall and Parker relieved me of my overcoat. Just then Ackroyd's secretary, a pleasant young fellow by the name of Raymond, passed through the hall on his way to Ackroyd's study, his hands full of papers.

"Good evening, doctor. Coming to dine? Or is this a professional call?"

The last was in allusion to my black bag which I had laid down on the oak chest.

I explained that I expected a summons to a confinement case at any moment, and so had come out prepared for an emergency call. Raymond nodded, and went on his way, calling over his shoulder:

"Go into the drawing room. You know the way. The ladies will be down in a minute. I must just take these papers to Mr. Ackroyd, and I'll tell him you're here."

On Raymond's appearance Parker had withdrawn, so I was alone in the hall. I settled my tie, glanced in a large mirror which hung there, and crossed to the door directly facing me, which was, as I knew, the door of the drawing room.

I noticed, just as I was turning the handle, a sound from within—the shutting down of a window, I took it to be. I noticed it, I may say, quite mechanically, without attaching any importance to it at the time.

I opened the door and walked in. As I did so I almost collided with Miss Russell who was just coming out. We both apologized.

For the first time I found myself appraising the housekeeper and thinking what a handsome woman she must once have been—indeed, as far as that goes, still was. Her dark hair was unstreaked with grey, and when she had a colour, as she had at this minute, the stern quality of her looks was not so apparent.

Quite subconsciously I wondered whether she had been out, for she was breathing hard, as though she had been running.

"I'm afraid I'm a few minutes early," I said.

"Oh! I don't think so. It's gone half past seven, Dr. Sheppard." She paused a minute before saying, "I—didn't know you were expected to dinner tonight. Mr. Ackroyd didn't mention it."

I received a vague impression that my dining there displeased her in some way, but I couldn't imagine why.

"How's the knee?" I inquired.

"Much the same, thank you, doctor. I must be going now. Mrs. Ackroyd will be down in a moment. I—I only came in here to see if the flowers were all right."

She passed quickly out of the room. I strolled to the window, wondering at her evident desire to justify her presence in the room. As I did so, I saw what, of course, I might have known all the time had I troubled to give my mind to it, namely, that the windows were long french ones opening on the terrace. The sound I had heard, therefore, could not have been that of a window being shut down.

Quite idly, and more to distract my mind from painful thoughts than for any other reason, I amused myself by trying to guess what could have caused the sound in question.

Coals on the fire? No, that was not the kind of noise at all. A drawer of a bureau pushed in? No, not that.

Then my eye was caught by what, I believe, is called a silver table, the lid of which lifts, and through the glass of which you can see the contents. I crossed over to it, studying the contents. There were one or two pieces of old silver, a baby shoe belonging to King Charles the First, some Chinese jade figures, and quite a number of African implements and curios. Wanting to examine one of the jade figures more closely, I lifted the lid. It slipped through my fingers and fell.

At once I recognized the sound I had heard. It was this same table lid being shut down gently and carefully. I repeated the action once or twice for my own satisfaction. Then I lifted the lid to scrutinize the contents more closely.

I was still bending over the open silver table when Flora Ackroyd came into the room.

Quite a lot of people do not like Flora Ackroyd, but nobody can help admiring her. And to her friends she can be very charming. The first thing that strikes you about her is her extraordinary fairness. She has the real Scandinavian pale gold hair. Her eyes are blue—blue as the waters of a Norwegian fiord, and her skin is cream and roses. She has square, boyish shoulders and slight hips. And to a jaded medical man it is very refreshing to come across such perfect health.

A simple straightforward English girl—I may be old-fashioned, but I think the genuine article takes a lot of beating.

Flora joined me by the silver table, and expressed heretical doubts as to King Charles I ever having worn the baby shoe.

"And anyway," continued Miss Flora, "all this making a fuss about things because someone wore or used them seems to me all nonsense. They're not wearing or using them now. That pen that George Eliot wrote *The Mill on the Floss* with—that sort of thing—well, it's only just a pen after all. If you're really keen on George Eliot, why not get *The Mill on the Floss* in a cheap edition and read it."

"I suppose you never read such old out-of-date stuff, Miss Flora?"

"You're wrong, Dr. Sheppard. I love *The Mill on the Floss*."

I was rather pleased to hear it. The things young women read nowadays and profess to enjoy positively frighten me.

"You haven't congratulated me yet, Dr. Sheppard," said Flora. "Haven't you heard?"

She held out her left hand. On the third finger of it was an exquisitely set single pearl.

"I'm going to marry Ralph, you know," she went on. "Uncle is very pleased. It keeps me in the family, you see."

I took both her hands in mine.

My dear," I said, "I hope you'll be very happy."

"We've been engaged for about a month," continued Flora in her cool voice, "but it was only announced yesterday. Uncle is going to do up Cross-stones, and give it to us to live in, and we're going to pretend to farm. Really, we shall hunt all the winter, town for the season, and then go yachting. I love the sea. And, of course, I shall take a great interest in the parish affairs, and attend all the Mothers' Meetings."

Just then Mrs. Ackroyd rustled in, full of apologies for being late.

I am sorry to say I detest Mrs. Ackroyd. She is all chains and teeth and bones. A most unpleasant woman. She has small pale flinty blue eyes, and how ever gushing her words may be, those eyes of hers always remain coldly speculative.

I went across to her, leaving Flora by the window. She gave me a handful of assorted knuckles and rings to squeeze, and began talking volubly.

Had I heard about Flora's engagement? So suitable in every way. The dear young things had fallen in love at first sight. Such a perfect pair, he so dark and she so fair.

"I can't tell you, my dear Dr. Sheppard, the relief to a mother's heart."

Mrs. Ackroyd sighed—a tribute to her mother's heart, whilst her eyes remained shrewdly observant of me.

"I was wondering. You are such an old friend of dear Roger's. We know how much he trusts to your judgment. So difficult for me—in my position as poor Cecil's widow. But there are so many tiresome things—settlements, you know—all that. I fully believe that Roger intends to make settlements upon dear Flora, but, as you know, he is just a *leetle* peculiar about money. Very usual, I've heard, amongst men who are captains of industry. I wondered, you know, if you could just *sound* him on the subject? Flora is so fond of you. We feel you are quite an old friend, although we have only really known you just over two years."

Mrs. Ackroyd's eloquence was cut short as the drawing room door opened once more. I was pleased at the interruption. I hate interfering in other people's affairs, and I had not the least intention of tackling Ackroyd on the subject of Flora's settlements. In another moment I should have been forced to tell Mrs. Ackroyd as much.

"You know Major Blunt, don't you, doctor?"

"Yes, indeed," I said.

A lot of people know Hector Blunt—at least by repute. He has shot more wild animals in unlikely places than any man living, I suppose. When you mention him, people say: "Blunt—you don't mean the big game man, do you?"

His friendship with Ackroyd has always puzzled me a little. The two men are so totally dissimilar. Hector Blunt is perhaps five years Ackroyd's junior. They made friends early in life, and though their ways have diverged, the friendship still holds. About once in two years Blunt spends a fortnight at Fernly, and an immense animal's head, with an amazing number of horns which fixes you with a glazed stare as soon as you come inside the front door, is a permanent reminder of the friendship.

Blunt had entered the room now with his own peculiar, deliberate, yet soft-footed tread. He is a man of medium height, sturdily and rather stockily built. His face is almost mahogany coloured, and is peculiarly expressionless. He has grey eyes that give the impression of always watching something that is happening very far away. He talks little, and what he does say is said jerkily, as though the words were forced out of him unwillingly.

He said now: "How are you, Sheppard?" in his usual abrupt fashion, and then stood squarely in front of the fireplace looking over our heads as though he saw something very interesting happening in Timbuctoo.

"Major Blunt," said Flora, "I wish you'd tell me about these African things. I'm sure you know what they all are."

I have heard Hector Blunt described as a woman hater, but I noticed that he joined Flora at the silver table with what might be described as alacrity. They bent over it together.

I was afraid Mrs. Ackroyd would begin talking about settlements again, so I made a few hurried remarks about the new sweet pea. I knew there was a new sweet pea because the *Daily Mail* had told me so that morning. Mrs. Ackroyd knows nothing about horticulture, but she is the kind of woman who likes to appear well-informed about the topics of the day, and she, too, reads the *Daily Mail.* We were able to converse quite intelligently until Ackroyd and his secretary joined us, and immediately afterwards Parker announced dinner.

My place at table was between Mrs. Ackroyd and Flora. Blunt was on Mrs. Ackroyd's other side, and Geoffrey Raymond next to him.

Dinner was not a cheerful affair. Ackroyd was visibly preoccupied. He looked wretched, and ate next to nothing. Mrs. Ackroyd, Raymond, and I kept the conversation going. Flora seemed affected by her uncle's depression, and Blunt relapsed into his usual taciturnity.

II

Immediately after dinner Ackroyd slipped his arm through mine and led me off to his study.

"Once we've had coffee, we shan't be disturbed again," he explained. "I told Raymond to see to it that we shouldn't be interrupted."

I studied him quietly without appearing to do so. He was clearly under the influence of some strong excitement. For a minute or two he paced up and down the room, then, as Parker entered with the coffee tray, he sank into an armchair in front of the fire.

The study was a comfortable apartment. Bookshelves lined one wall of it. The chairs were big and covered in dark blue leather. A large desk stood by the window and was covered with papers neatly docketed and filed. On a round table were various magazines and sporting papers.

"I've had a return of that pain after food lately," remarked Ackroyd calmly, as he helped himself to coffee. "You must give me some more of those tablets of yours."

It struck me that he was anxious to convey the impression that our conference was a medical one. I played up accordingly.

"I thought as much. I brought some up with me."

"Good man. Hand them over now."

"They're in my bag in the hall. I'll get them."

Ackroyd arrested me.

"Don't you trouble. Parker will get them. Bring in the doctor's bag, will you, Parker?"

"Very good, sir."

Parker withdrew. As I was about to speak, Ackroyd threw up his hand.

"Not yet. Wait. Don't you see I'm in such a state of nerves that I can hardly contain myself?"

I saw that plainly enough. And I was very uneasy. All sorts of forebodings assailed me.

Ackroyd spoke again almost immediately.

"Make certain that window's closed, will you," he asked.

Somewhat surprised, I got up and went to it. It was not a french window, but one of the ordinary sash type. The heavy blue velvet curtains were drawn in front of it, but the window itself was open at the top.

Parker reentered the room with my bag while I was still at the window.

"That's all right," I said, emerging again into the room.

"You've put the latch across?"

"Yes, yes. What's the matter with you, Ackroyd?"

The door had just closed behind Parker, or I would not have put the question. Ackroyd waited just a minute before replying.

"I'm in hell," he said slowly, after a minute. "No, don't bother with those damn tablets. I only said that for Parker. Servants are so curious. Come here and sit down. The door's closed too, isn't it?"

"Yes. Nobody can overhear; don't be uneasy."

"Sheppard, nobody knows what I've gone through in the last twenty-four hours. If a man's house ever fell in ruin about him, mine has about me. This business of Ralph's is the last straw. But we won't talk about that now. It's the other—the other—! I don't know what to do about it. And I've got to make up my mind soon."

"What's the trouble?"

Ackroyd remained silent for a minute or two. He seemed curiously averse to begin. When he did speak, the question he asked came as a complete surprise. It was the last thing I expected.

"Sheppard, you attended Ashley Ferrars in his last illness, didn't you?"

"Yes, I did."

He seemed to find even greater difficulty in framing his next question.

"Did you ever suspect—did it ever enter your head—that—well, that he might have been poisoned?"

I was silent for a minute or two. Then I made up my mind what to say. Roger Ackroyd was not Caroline.

"I'll tell you the truth," I said. "At the time I had no suspicion whatever, but since—well, it was mere idle talk on my sister's part that first put the idea into my head. Since then I haven't been able to get it out again. But, mind you, I've no foundation whatever for that suspicion."

"He *was* poisoned," said Ackroyd.

He spoke in a dull heavy voice.

"Who by?" I asked sharply.

"His wife."

"How do you know that?"

"She told me so herself."

"When?"

"Yesterday! My God! yesterday! It seems ten years ago."

I waited a minute, then he went on.

"You understand, Sheppard, I'm telling you this in confidence. It's to go no further. I want your advice—I can't carry the whole weight by myself. As I said just now, I don't know what to do."

"Can you tell me the whole story?" I said. "I'm still in the dark. How did Mrs. Ferrars come to make this confession to you?"

"It's like this. Three months ago I asked Mrs. Ferrars to marry me. She refused. I asked her again and she consented, but she refused to allow me to make the engagement public until her year of mourning was up. Yesterday I called upon her, pointed out that a year and three weeks had now elapsed since her husband's death, and that there could be no further objection to making the engagement public property. I had noticed that she had been very strange in her manner for some days. Now, suddenly, without the least warning, she broke down completely. She—she told me everything. Her hatred of her brute of a husband, her growing love for me, and the—the dreadful means she had taken. Poison! My God! It was murder in cold blood."

I saw the repulsion, the horror, in Ackroyd's face. So Mrs. Ferrars must have seen it. Ackroyd's is not the type of the great lover who can forgive all for love's sake. He is fundamentally a good citizen. All that was sound and wholesome and law-abiding in him must have turned from her utterly in that moment of revelation.

"Yes," he went on, in a low, monotonous voice, "she confessed everything. It seems that there is one person who has known all along—who has been black-mailing her for huge sums. It was the strain of that that drove her nearly mad."

"Who was the man?"

Suddenly before my eyes there arose the picture of Ralph Paton and Mrs. Ferrars side by side. Their heads so close together. I felt a momentary throb of anxiety. Supposing—oh! but surely that was impossible. I remembered the frankness of Ralph's greeting that very afternoon. Absurd!

"She wouldn't tell me his name," said Ackroyd slowly. "As a matter of fact, she didn't actually say that it was a man. But of course—"

"Of course," I agreed. "It must have been a man. And you've no suspicion at all?"

For answer Ackroyd groaned and dropped his head into his hands.

"It can't be," he said. "I'm mad even to think of such a thing. No, I won't even admit to you the wild suspicion that crossed my mind. I'll tell you this much, though. Something she said made me think that the person in question might be actually among my household—but that can't be so. I must have mis-understood her."

"What did you say to her?" I asked.

"What could I say? She saw, of course, the awful shock it had been to me. And then there was the question, what was my duty in the matter? She had made me, you see, an accessory after the fact. She saw all that, I think, quicker than I did. I was stunned, you know. She asked me for twenty-four hours—

made me promise to do nothing till the end of that time. And she steadfastly refused to give me the name of the scoundrel who had been blackmailing her. I suppose she was afraid that I might go straight off and hammer him, and then the fat would have been in the fire as far as she was concerned. She told me that I should hear from her before twenty-four hours had passed. My God! I swear to you, Sheppard, that it never entered my head what she meant to do. Suicide! And I drove her to it."

"No, no," I said. "Don't take an exaggerated view of things. The responsibility for her death doesn't lie at your door."

"The question is, what am I to do now? The poor lady is dead. Why rake up past trouble?"

"I rather agree with you," I said.

"But there's another point. How am I to get hold of that scoundrel who drove her to death as surely as if he'd killed her? He knew of the first crime, and he fastened on to it like some obscene vulture. She's paid the penalty. Is he to go scot free?"

"I see," I said slowly. "You want to hunt him down? It will mean a lot of publicity, you know."

"Yes, I've thought of that. I've zigzagged to and fro in my mind."

"I agree with you that the villain ought to be punished, but the cost has got to be reckoned."

Ackroyd rose and walked up and down. Presently he sank into the chair again.

"Look here, Sheppard, suppose we leave it like this. If no word comes from her, we'll let the dead things lie."

"What do you mean by word coming from her?" I asked curiously.

"I have the strongest impression that somewhere or somehow she must have left a message for me—before she went. I can't argue about it, but there it is."

I shook my head.

"She left no letter or word of any kind?" I asked.

"Sheppard, I'm convinced that she did. And more, I've a feeling that by deliberately choosing death, she wanted the whole thing to come out, if only to be revenged on the man who drove her to desperation. I believe that if I could have seen her then, she would have told me his name and bid me go for him for all I was worth."

He looked at me.

"You don't believe in impressions?"

"Oh, yes, I do, in a sense. If, as you put it, word should come from her—"

I broke off. The door opened noiselessly and Parker entered with a salver on which were some letters.

"The evening post, sir," he said, handing the salver to Ackroyd.

Then he collected the coffee cups and withdrew.

My attention, diverted for a moment, came back to Ackroyd. He was staring like a man turned to stone at a long blue envelope. The other letters he had let drop to the ground.

"Her writing," he said in a whisper. "She must have gone out and posted it last night, just before—before—"

He ripped open the envelope and drew out a thick enclosure. Then he looked up sharply.

"You're sure you shut the window?" he said.

"Quite sure," I said, surprised. "Why?"

"All this evening I've had a queer feeling of being watched, spied upon. What's that—"

He turned sharply. So did I. We both had the impression of hearing the latch of the door give ever so slightly. I went across to it and opened it. There was no one there.

"Nerves," murmured Ackroyd to himself.

He unfolded the thick sheets of paper, and read aloud in a low voice.

"My dear, my very dear Roger,—A life calls for a life. I see that—I saw it in your face this afternoon. So I am taking the only road open to me. I leave to you the punishment of the person who has made my life a hell upon earth for the last year. I would not tell you the name, this afternoon, but I propose to write it to you now. I have no children or near relations to be spared, so do not fear publicity. If you can, Roger, my very dear Roger, forgive me the wrong I meant to do you, since when the time came, I could not do it after all. . . ."

Ackroyd, his finger on the sheet to turn it over, paused.

"Sheppard, forgive me, but I must read this alone," he said unsteadily. "It was meant for my eyes, and my eyes only."

He put the letter in the envelope and laid it on the table.

"Later, when I am alone."

"No," I cried impulsively, "read it now."

Ackroyd stared at me in some surprise.

"I beg your pardon," I said, reddening. "I do not mean read it aloud to me. But read it through whilst I am still here."

Ackroyd shook his head.

"No, I'd rather wait."

But for some reason, obscure to myself, I continued to urge him.

"At least, read the name of the man," I said.

Now Ackroyd is essentially pigheaded. The more you urge him to do a thing, the more determined he is not to do it. All my arguments were in vain.

The letter had been brought in at twenty minutes to nine. It was just on ten minutes to nine when I left him, the letter still unread. I hesitated with my hand on the door handle, looking back and wondering if there was anything I had left undone. I could think of nothing. With a shake of the head I passed out and closed the door behind me.

I was startled by seeing the figure of Parker close at hand. He looked embarrassed, and it occurred to me that he might have been listening at the door.

What a fat, smug, oily face the man had, and surely there was something decidedly shifty in his eye.

"Mr. Ackroyd particularly does not want to be disturbed," I said coldly. "He told me to tell you so."

"Quite so, sir. I—I fancied I heard the bell ring."

This was such a palpable untruth that I did not trouble to reply. Preceding me to the hall, Parker helped me on with my overcoat, and I stepped out into the night. The moon was overcast, and everything seemed very dark and still.

The village church clock chimed nine o'clock as I passed through the lodge gates. I turned to the left towards the village, and almost cannoned into a man coming in the opposite direction.

"This the way to Fernly Park, mister?" asked the stranger in a hoarse voice.

I looked at him. He was wearing a hat pulled down over his eyes, and his coat collar turned up. I could see little or nothing of his face, but he seemed a young fellow. The voice was rough and uneducated.

"These are the lodge gates here," I said.

"Thank you, mister." He paused, and then added, quite unnecessarily, "I'm a stranger in these parts, you see."

He went on, passing through the gates as I turned to look after him.

The odd thing was that his voice reminded me of someone's voice that I knew, but whose it was I could not think.

Ten minutes later I was at home once more. Caroline was full of curiosity to know why I had returned so early. I had to make up a slightly fictitious account of the evening in order to satisfy her, and I had an uneasy feeling that she saw through the transparent device.

At ten o'clock I rose, yawned, and suggested bed. Caroline acquiesced.

It was Friday night, and on Friday night I wind the clocks. I did it as usual, whilst Caroline satisfied herself that the servants had locked up the kitchen properly.

It was a quarter past ten as we went up the stairs. I had just reached the top when the telephone rang in the hall below.

"Mrs. Bates," said Caroline immediately.

"I'm afraid so," I said ruefully.

I ran down the stairs and took up the receiver.

"What?" I said. "*What?* Certainly, I'll come at once."

I ran upstairs, caught up my bag, and stuffed a few extra dressings into it.

"Parker telephoning," I shouted to Caroline, "from Fernly. They've just found Roger Ackroyd murdered."

Five

MURDER

I got out the car in next to no time, and drove rapidly to Fernly. Jumping out, I pulled the bell impatiently. There was some delay in answering, and I rang again.

Then I heard the rattle of the chain and Parker, his impassivity of countenance quite unmoved, stood in the open doorway.

I pushed past him into the hall.

"Where is he?" I demanded sharply.

"I beg your pardon, sir?"

"Your master. Mr. Ackroyd. Don't stand there staring at me, man. Have you notified the police?"

"The police, sir? Did you say the police?" Parker stared at me as though I were a ghost.

"What's the matter with you, Parker? If, as you say, your master has been murdered—"

A gasp broke from Parker.

"The master? Murdered? Impossible, sir!"

It was my turn to stare.

"Didn't you telephone to me, not five minutes ago, and tell me that Mr. Ackroyd had been found murdered?"

"Me, sir? Oh! no indeed, sir. I wouldn't dream of doing such a thing."

"Do you mean to say it's all a hoax? That there's nothing the matter with Mr. Ackroyd?"

"Excuse me, sir, did the person telephoning use my name?"

"I'll give you the exact words I heard. '*Is that Dr. Sheppard? Parker, the butler at Fernly, speaking. Will you please come at once, sir. Mr. Ackroyd has been murdered.*'"

Parker and I stared at each other blankly.

"A very wicked joke to play, sir," he said at last, in a shocked tone. "Fancy saying a thing like that."

"Where is Mr. Ackroyd?" I asked suddenly.

"Still in the study, I fancy, sir. The ladies have gone to bed, and Major Blunt and Mr. Raymond are in the billiard room."

"I think I'll just look in and see him for a minute," I said. "I know he didn't want to be disturbed again, but this odd practical joke has made me uneasy. I'd just like to satisfy myself that he's all right."

"Quite so, sir. It makes me feel quite uneasy myself. If you don't object to my accompanying you as far as the door, sir—?"

"Not at all," I said. "Come along."

I passed through the door on the right, Parker on my heels, traversed the little lobby where a small flight of stairs led upstairs to Ackroyd's bedroom, and tapped on the study door.

There was no answer. I turned the handle, but the door was locked.

"Allow me, sir," said Parker.

Very nimbly, for a man of his build, he dropped on one knee and applied his eye to the keyhole.

"Key is in the lock all right, sir," he said, rising. "On the inside. Mr. Ackroyd must have locked himself in and possibly just dropped off to sleep."

I bent down and verified Parker's statement.

"It seems all right," I said, "but, all the same, Parker, I'm going to wake your master up. I shouldn't be satisfied to go home without hearing from his own lips that he's quite all right."

So saying, I rattled the handle and called out, "Ackroyd, Ackroyd, just a minute."

But still there was no answer. I glanced over my shoulder.

"I don't want to alarm the household," I said hesitatingly.

Parker went across and shut the door from the big hall through which we had come.

"I think that will be all right now, sir. The billiard room is at the other side of the house, and so are the kitchen quarters and the ladies' bedrooms."

I nodded comprehendingly. Then I banged once more frantically on the door, and stooping down, fairly bawled through the keyhole:

"Ackroyd, Ackroyd! It's Sheppard. Let me in."

And still—silence. Not a sign of life from within the locked room. Parker and I glanced at each other.

"Look here, Parker," I said, "I'm going to break this door in—or rather, we are. I'll take the responsibility."

"If you say so, sir," said Parker, rather doubtfully.

"I do say so. I'm seriously alarmed about Mr. Ackroyd."

I looked round the small lobby and picked up a heavy oak chair. Parker and I held it between us and advanced to the assault. Once, twice, and three times we hurled it against the lock. At the third blow it gave, and we staggered into the room.

Ackroyd was sitting as I had left him in the armchair before the fire. His head had fallen sideways, and clearly visible, just below the collar of his coat, was a shining piece of twisted metalwork.

Parker and I advanced till we stood over the recumbent figure. I heard the butler draw in his breath with a sharp hiss.

"Stabbed from be'ind," he murmured. "'Orrible!"

He wiped his moist brow with his handkerchief, then stretched out a gingerly hand towards the hilt of the dagger.

"You mustn't touch that," I said sharply. "Go at once to the telephone and ring up the police station. Inform them of what has happened. Then tell Mr. Raymond and Major Blunt."

"Very good, sir."

Parker hurried away, still wiping his perspiring brow.

I did what little had to be done. I was careful not to disturb the position of the body, and not to handle the dagger at all. No object was to be attained by moving it. Ackroyd had clearly been dead some little time.

Then I heard young Raymond's voice, horror-stricken and incredulous, outside.

"What do you say? Oh! impossible! Where's the doctor?"

He appeared impetuously in the doorway, then stopped dead, his face very white. A hand put him aside, and Hector Blunt came past him into the room.

"My God!" said Raymond from behind him; "it's true, then."

Blunt came straight on till he reached the chair. He bent over the body, and I thought that, like Parker, he was going to lay hold of the dagger hilt. I drew him back with one hand.

"Nothing must be moved," I explained. "The police must see him exactly as he is now."

Blunt nodded in instant comprehension. His face was expressionless as ever, but I thought I detected signs of emotion beneath the stolid mask. Geoffrey Raymond had joined us now, and stood peering over Blunt's shoulder at the body.

"This is terrible," he said in a low voice.

He had regained his composure, but as he took off the pince-nez he habitually wore and polished them I observed that his hand was shaking.

"Robbery, I suppose," he said. "How did the fellow get in? Through the window? Has anything been taken?"

He went towards the desk.

"You think it's burglary?" I said slowly.

"What else could it be? There's no question of suicide, I suppose?"

"No man could stab himself in such a way," I said confidently. "It's murder right enough. But with what motive?"

"Roger hadn't an enemy in the world," said Blunt quietly. "Must have been burglars. But what was the thief after? Nothing seems to be disarranged?"

He looked round the room. Raymond was still sorting the papers on the desk.

"There seems nothing missing, and none of the drawers show signs of having been tampered with," the secretary observed at last. "It's very mysterious."

Blunt made a slight motion with his head.

"There are some letters on the floor here," he said.

I looked down. Three or four letters still lay where Ackroyd had dropped them earlier in the evening.

But the blue envelope containing Mrs. Ferrar's letter had disappeared. I half opened my mouth to speak, but at that moment the sound of a bell pealed through the house. There was a confused murmur of voices in the hall, and then Parker appeared with our local inspector and a police constable.

"Good evening, gentlemen," said the inspector. "I'm terribly sorry for this! A good kind gentleman like Mr. Ackroyd. The butler says it's murder. No possibility of accident or suicide, doctor?"

"None whatever," I said.

"Ah! A bad business."

He came and stood over the body.

"Been moved at all?" he asked sharply.

"Beyond making certain that life was extinct—an easy matter—I have not disturbed the body in any way."

"Ah! And everything points to the murderer having got clear away—for the moment, that is. Now then, let me hear all about it. Who found the body?"

I explained the circumstances carefully.

"A telephone message, you say? From the butler?"

"A message that I never sent," declared Parker earnestly. "I've not been near the telephone the whole evening. The others can bear me out that I haven't."

"Very odd, that. Did it sound like Parker's voice, doctor?"

"Well—I can't say I noticed. I took it for granted, you see."

"Naturally. Well, you got up here, broke in the door, and found poor Mr. Ackroyd like this. How long should you say he had been dead, doctor?"

"Half an hour at least—perhaps longer," I said.

"The door was locked on the inside, you say? What about the window?"

"I myself closed and bolted it earlier in the evening at Mr. Ackroyd's request."

The inspector strode across to it and threw back the curtains.

"Well, it's open now, anyway," he remarked.

True enough, the window was open, the lower sash being raised to its fullest extent.

The inspector produced a pocket torch and flashed it along the sill outside.

"This is the way he went all right," he remarked, "*and* got in. See here."

In the light of the powerful torch, several clearly defined footmarks could be seen. They seemed to be those of shoes with rubber studs in the soles. One particularly clear one pointed inwards, another, slightly overlapping it, pointed outwards.

"Plain as a pikestaff," said the inspector. "Any valuables missing?"

Geoffrey Raymond shook his head.

"Not so far that we can discover. Mr. Ackroyd never kept anything of particular value in this room."

"H'm," said the inspector. "Man found an open window. Climbed in, saw Mr. Ackroyd sitting there—maybe he'd fallen asleep. Man stabbed him from behind, then lost his nerve and made off. But he's left his tracks pretty clearly. We ought to get hold of *him* without much difficulty. No suspicious strangers been hanging about anywhere?"

"Oh!" I said suddenly.

"What is it, doctor?"

"I met a man this evening—just as I was turning out of the gate. He asked me the way to Fernly Park."

"What time would that be?"

"Just nine o'clock. I heard it chime the hour as I was turning out of the gate."

"Can you describe him?"

I did so to the best of my ability.

The inspector turned to the butler.

"Anyone answering that description come to the front door?"

"No, sir. No one has been to the house at all this evening."

"What about the back?"

"I don't think so, sir, but I'll make inquiries."

He moved towards the door, but the inspector held up a large hand.

"No, thanks. I'll do my own inquiring. But first of all I want to fix the times a little more clearly. When was Mr. Ackroyd last seen alive?"

"Probably by me," I said, "when I left at—let me see—about ten minutes to nine. He told me that he didn't wish to be disturbed, and I repeated the order to Parker."

"Just so, sir," said Parker respectfully.

"Mr. Ackroyd was certainly alive at half past nine," put in Raymond, "for I heard his voice in here talking."

"Who was he talking to?"

"That I don't know. Of course, at the time I took it for granted that it was Dr. Sheppard who was with him. I wanted to ask him a question about some papers I was engaged upon, but when I heard the voices I remembered that he had said he wanted to talk to Dr. Sheppard without being disturbed, and I went away again. But now it seems that the doctor had already left?"

I nodded.

"I was at home by a quarter past nine," I said. "I didn't go out again until I received the telephone call."

"Who could have been with him at half past nine?" queried the inspector. "It wasn't you, Mr—er—"

"Major Blunt," I said.

"Major Hector Blunt?" asked the inspector, a respectful tone creeping into his voice.

Blunt merely jerked his head affirmatively.

"I think we've seen you down here before, sir," said the inspector. "I didn't recognize you for the moment, but you were staying with Mr. Ackroyd a year ago last May."

"June," corrected Blunt.

"Just so, June it was. Now, as I was saying, it wasn't you with Mr. Ackroyd at nine-thirty this evening?"

Blunt shook his head.

"Never saw him after dinner," he volunteered.

The inspector turned once more to Raymond.

"You didn't overhear any of the conversation going on, did you, sir?"

"I did catch just a fragment of it," said the secretary, "and, supposing as I did that it was Dr. Sheppard who was with Mr. Ackroyd, that fragment struck me as distinctly odd. As far as I can remember, the exact words were these. Mr. Ack-royd was speaking. 'The calls on my purse have been so frequent of late'—that is what he was saying—'of late, that I fear it is impossible for me to accede to your request . . .' I went away again at once, of course, so I did not hear any more. But I rather wondered because Dr. Sheppard—"

"—Does not ask for loans for himself or subscriptions for others," I finished.

"A demand for money," said the inspector musingly. "It may be that here we have a very important clue." He turned to the butler. "You say, Parker, that nobody was admitted by the front door this evening?"

"That's what I say, sir."

"Then it seems almost certain that Mr. Ackroyd himself must have admitted this stranger. But I don't quite see—"

The inspector went into a kind of daydream for some minutes.

"One thing's clear," he said at length, rousing himself from his absorption. "Mr. Ackroyd was alive and well at nine-thirty. That is the last moment at which he is known to have been alive."

Parker gave vent to an apologetic cough which brought the inspector's eyes on him at once.

"Well?" he said sharply.

"If you'll excuse me, sir, Miss Flora saw him after that."

"Miss Flora?"

"Yes, sir. About a quarter to ten that would be. It was after that that she told me Mr. Ackroyd wasn't to be disturbed again tonight."

"Did he send her to you with that message?"

"Not exactly, sir. I was bringing a tray with soda and whisky when Miss Flora, who was just coming out of this room, stopped me and said her uncle didn't want to be disturbed."

The inspector looked at the butler with rather closer attention than he had bestowed on him up to now.

"You'd already been told that Mr. Ackroyd didn't want to be disturbed, hadn't you?"

Parker began to stammer. His hands shook.

"Yes, sir. Yes, sir. Quite so, sir."

"And yet you were proposing to do so?"

"I'd forgotten, sir. At least I mean, I always bring the whisky and soda about that time, sir, and ask if there's anything more, and I thought—well, I was doing as usual without thinking."

It was at this moment that it began to dawn upon me that Parker was most suspiciously flustered. The man was shaking and twitching all over.

"H'm," said the inspector. "I must see Miss Ackroyd at once. For the moment we'll leave this room exactly as it is. I can return here after I've heard what Miss Ackroyd has to tell me. I shall just take the precaution of shutting and bolting the window."

This precaution accomplished, he led the way into the hall and we followed him. He paused a moment, as he glanced up at the little staircase, then spoke over his shoulder to the constable.

"Jones, you'd better stay here. Don't let anyone go into that room."

Parker interposed deferentially.

"If you'll excuse me, sir. If you were to lock the door into the main hall, nobody could gain access to this part. That staircase leads only to Mr. Ackroyd's bedroom and bathroom. There is no communication with the other part of the house. There once was a door through, but Mr. Ackroyd had it blocked up. He liked to feel that his suite was entirely private."

To make things clear and explain the position, I have appended a rough sketch of the right-hand wing of the house. The small staircase leads, as Parker explained, to a big bedroom made by two being knocked into one, and an adjoining bathroom and lavatory.

The inspector took in the position at a glance. We went through into the large hall and he locked the door behind him, slipping the key into his pocket. Then he gave the constable some low-voiced instructions, and the latter prepared to depart.

"We must get busy on those shoe tracks," explained the inspector. "But first of all, I must have a word with Miss Ackroyd. She was the last person to see her uncle alive. Does she know yet?"

Raymond shook his head.

"Well, no need to tell her for another five minutes. She can answer my questions better without being upset by knowing the truth about her uncle. Tell her there's been a burglary, and ask her if she would mind dressing and coming down to answer a few questions."

It was Raymond who went upstairs on this errand.

"Miss Ackroyd will be down in a minute," he said, when he returned. "I told her just what you suggested."

In less than five minutes Flora descended the staircase. She was wrapped in a pale pink silk kimono. She looked anxious and excited.

The inspector stepped forward.

"Good evening, Miss Ackroyd," he said civilly. "We're afraid there's been an attempt at robbery, and we want you to help us. What's this room—the billiard room? Come in here and sit down."

Flora sat down composedly on the wide divan which ran the length of the wall, and looked up at the inspector.

"I don't quite understand. What has been stolen? What do you want me to tell you?"

"It's just this, Miss Ackroyd. Parker here says you came out of your uncle's study at about a quarter to ten. Is that right?"

"Quite right. I had been to say good night to him."

"And the time is correct?"

"Well, it must have been about then. I can't say exactly. It might have been later."

"Was your uncle alone, or was there anyone with him?"

"He was alone. Dr. Sheppard had gone."

"Did you happen to notice whether the window was open or shut?"

Flora shook her head.

"I can't say. The curtains were drawn."

"Exactly. And your uncle seemed quite as usual?"

"I think so."

"Do you mind telling us exactly what passed between you?"

Flora paused a minute, as though to collect her recollections.

"I went in and said, 'Good night, Uncle, I'm going to bed now. I'm tired tonight.' He gave a sort of grunt, and—I went over and kissed him, and he said something about my looking nice in the frock I had on, and then he told me to run away as he was busy. So I went."

"Did he ask specially not to be disturbed?"

"Oh! yes, I forgot. He said: 'Tell Parker I don't want anything more tonight, and that he's not to disturb me.' I met Parker just outside the door and gave him Uncle's message."

"Just so," said the inspector.

"Won't you tell me what it is that has been stolen?"

"We're not quite—certain," said the inspector hesitatingly.

A wide look of alarm came into the girl's eyes. She started up.

"What is it? You're hiding something from me?"

Moving in his usual unobtrusive manner, Hector Blunt came between her and the inspector. She half stretched out her hand, and he took it in both of his, patting it as though she were a very small child, and she turned to him as though something in his stolid, rocklike demeanour promised comfort and safety.

"It's bad news, Flora," he said quietly. "Bad news for all of us. Your Uncle Roger—"

"Yes?"

"It will be a shock to you. Bound to be. Poor Roger's dead."

Flora drew away from him, her eyes dilating with horror.

"When?" she whispered. "When?"

"Very soon after you left him, I'm afraid," said Blunt gravely.

Flora raised her hand to her throat, gave a little cry, and I hurried to catch her as she fell. She had fainted, and Blunt and I carried her upstairs and laid her on her bed. Then I got him to wake Mrs. Ackroyd and tell her the news. Flora soon revived, and I brought her mother to her, telling her what to do for the girl. Then I hurried downstairs again.

Six

THE TUNISIAN DAGGER

I met the inspector just coming from the door which led into the kitchen quarters.

"How's the young lady, doctor?"

"Coming round nicely. Her mother's with her."

"That's good. I've been questioning the servants. They all declare that no one has been to the back door tonight. Your description of that stranger was rather vague. Can't you give us something more definite to go upon?"

"I'm afraid not," I said regretfully. "It was a dark night, you see, and the fellow had his coat collar well pulled up and his hat squashed down over his eyes."

"H'm," said the inspector. "Looked as though he wanted to conceal his face. Sure it was no one you know?"

I replied in the negative, but not as decidedly as I might have done. I remembered my impression that the stranger's voice was not unfamiliar to me. I explained this rather haltingly to the inspector.

"It was a rough, uneducated voice, you say?"

I agreed, but it occurred to me that the roughness had been of an almost exaggerated quality. If, as the inspector thought, the man had wished to hide his face, he might equally well have tried to disguise his voice.

"Do you mind coming into the study with me again, doctor? There are one or two things I want to ask you."

I acquiesced. Inspector Davis unlocked the door of the lobby, we passed through, and he locked the door again behind him.

"We don't want to be disturbed," he said grimly. "And we don't want any eavesdropping either. What's all this about blackmail?"

"Blackmail!" I exclaimed, very much startled.

"Is it an effort of Parker's imagination? Or is there something in it?"

"If Parker heard anything about blackmail," I said slowly, "he must have been listening outside this door with his ear glued against the keyhole."

Davis nodded.

"Nothing more likely. You see, I've been instituting a few inquiries as to what Parker has been doing with himself this evening. To tell the truth, I didn't like his manner. The man knows something. When I began to question him, he got the wind up, and plumped out some garbled story of blackmail."

I took an instant decision.

"I'm rather glad you've brought the matter up," I said. "I've been trying to decide whether to make a clean breast of things or not. I'd already practically decided to tell you everything, but I was going to wait for a favourable opportunity. You might as well have it now."

And then and there I narrated the whole events of the evening as I have set them down here. The inspector listened keenly, occasionally interjecting a question.

"Most extraordinary story I ever heard," he said, when I had finished. "And you say that letter has completely disappeared? It looks bad—it looks very bad indeed. It gives us what we've been looking for—a motive for the murder."

I nodded.

"I realize that."

"You say that Mr. Ackroyd hinted at a suspicion he had that some member of his household was involved? Household's rather an elastic term."

"You don't think that Parker himself might be the man we're after?" I suggested.

"It looks very like it. He was obviously listening at the door when you came out. Then Miss Ackroyd came across him later bent on entering the study. Say he tried again when she was safely out of the way. He stabbed Ackroyd, locked the door on the inside, opened the window, and got out that way, and went round to a side door which he had previously left open. How's that?"

"There's only one thing against it," I said slowly. "If Ackroyd went on reading that letter as soon as I left, as he intended to do, I don't see him continuing to sit on here and turn things over in his mind for another hour. He'd have had Parker in at once, accused him then and there, and there would have been a fine old uproar. Remember, Ackroyd was a man of choleric temper."

"Mightn't have had time to go on with the letter just then," suggested the inspector. "We know someone was with him at half past nine. If that visitor turned up as soon as you left, and after he went, Miss Ackroyd came in to say good night—well, he wouldn't be able to go on with the letter until close upon ten o'clock."

"And the telephone call?"

"Parker sent that all right—perhaps before he thought of the locked door and open window. Then he changed his mind—or got in a panic—and decided to deny all knowledge of it. That was it, depend upon it."

"Ye—es," I said rather doubtfully.

"Anyway, we can find out the truth about the telephone call from the exchange. If it was put through from here, I don't see how anyone else but Parker could have sent it. Depend upon it, he's our man. But keep it dark—we don't want to alarm him just yet, till we've got all the evidence. I'll see to it he doesn't give us the slip. To all appearances we'll be concentrating on your mysterious stranger."

He rose from where he had been sitting astride the chair belonging to the desk, and crossed over to the still form in the armchair.

"The weapon ought to give us a clue," he remarked, looking up. "It's something quite unique—a curio, I should think, by the look of it."

He bent down, surveying the handle attentively, and I heard him give a grunt of satisfaction. Then, very gingerly, he pressed his hands down below the hilt and drew the blade out from the wound. Still carrying it so as not to touch the handle, he placed it in a wide china mug which adorned the mantelpiece.

"Yes," he said, nodding at it. "Quite a work of art. There can't be many of them about."

It was indeed a beautiful object. A narrow, tapering blade, and a hilt of elaborately intertwined metals of curious and careful workmanship. He touched the blade gingerly with his finger, testing its sharpness, and made an appreciative grimace.

"Lord, what an edge," he exclaimed. "A child could drive that into a man—as easy as cutting butter. A dangerous sort of toy to have about."

"May I examine the body properly now?" I asked.

He nodded.

"Go ahead."

I made a thorough examination.

"Well?" said the inspector, when I had finished.

"I'll spare you the technical language," I said. "We'll keep that for the inquest. The blow was delivered by a right-handed man standing behind him, and death must have been instantaneous. By the expression on the dead man's face, I should say that the blow was quite unexpected. He may have died without knowing who his assailant was."

"Butlers can creep about as soft-footed as cats," said Inspector Davis. "There's not going to be much mystery about this crime. Take a look at the hilt of that dagger."

I took the look.

"I dare say they're not apparent to you, but *I* can see them clearly enough." He lowered his voice. *"Fingerprints!"*

He stood off a few steps to judge of his effect.

"Yes," I said mildly. "I guessed that."

I do not see why I should be supposed to be totally devoid of intelligence. After all, I read detective stories, and the newspapers, and am a man of quite average ability. If there had been toe marks on the dagger handle, now, that would have been quite a different thing. I would then have registered any amount of surprise and awe.

I think the inspector was annoyed with me for declining to get thrilled. He picked up the china mug and invited me to accompany him to the billiard room.

"I want to see if Mr. Raymond can tell us anything about this dagger," he explained.

Locking the outer door behind us again, we made our way to the billiard room, where we found Geoffrey Raymond. The inspector held up his exhibit.

"Ever seen this before, Mr. Raymond?"

"Why—I believe—I'm almost sure that is a curio given to Mr. Ackroyd by Major Blunt. It comes from Morocco—no, Tunis. So the crime was committed with that? What an extraordinary thing. It seems almost impossible, and yet there could hardly be two daggers the same. May I fetch Major Blunt?"

Without waiting for an answer, he hurried off.

"Nice young fellow that," said the inspector. "Something honest and ingenuous about him."

I agreed. In the two years that Geoffrey Raymond has been secretary to Ackroyd, I have never seen him ruffled or out of temper. And he has been, I know, a most efficient secretary.

In a minute or two Raymond returned, accompanied by Blunt.

"I was right," said Raymond excitedly. "It *is* the Tunisian dagger."

"Major Blunt hasn't looked at it yet," objected the inspector.

"Saw it the moment I came into the study," said the quiet man.

"You recognized it, then?"

Blunt nodded.

"You said nothing about it," said the inspector suspiciously.

"Wrong moment," said Blunt. "Lot of harm done by blurting out things at the wrong time."

He returned the inspector's stare placidly enough.

The latter grunted at last and turned away. He brought the dagger over to Blunt.

"You're quite sure about it, sir. You identify it positively?"

"Absolutely. No doubt whatever."

"Where was this—er—curio usually kept? Can you tell me that, sir?"

It was the secretary who answered.

"In the silver table in the drawing room."

"What?" I exclaimed.

The others looked at me.

"Yes, doctor?" said the inspector encouragingly.

"It's nothing," said the inspector again, still encouragingly.

"It's so trivial," I explained apologetically. "Only that when I arrived last night for dinner I heard the lid of the silver table being shut down in the drawing room."

I saw profound scepticism and a trace of suspicion on the inspector's countenance.

"How did you know it was the silver table lid?"

I was forced to explain in detail—a long, tedious explanation which I would infinitely rather not have had to make.

The inspector heard me to the end.

"Was the dagger in its place when you were looking over the contents?" he asked.

"I don't know," I said. "I can't say I remember noticing it—but, of course, it may have been there all the time."

"We'd better get hold of the housekeeper," remarked the inspector, and pulled the bell.

A few minutes later Miss Russell, summoned by Parker, entered the room.

"I don't think I went near the silver table," she said, when the inspector had posed his question. "I was looking to see that all the flowers were fresh. Oh! yes, I remember now. The silver table was open—which it had no business to be, and I shut the lid down as I passed."

She looked at him aggressively.

"I see," said the inspector. "Can you tell me if this dagger was in its place then?"

Miss Russell looked at the weapon composedly.

"I can't say I'm sure," she replied. "I didn't stop to look. I knew the family would be down any minute, and I wanted to get away."

"Thank you," said the inspector.

There was just a trace of hesitation in his manner, as though he would have liked to question her further, but Miss Russell clearly accepted the words as a dismissal, and glided from the room.

"Rather a Tartar, I should fancy, eh?" said the inspector, looking after her. "Let me see. This silver table is in front of one of the windows, I think you said, doctor?"

Raymond answered for me.

"Yes, the left-hand window."

"And the window was open?"

"They were both ajar."

"Well, I don't think we need go into the question much further. Somebody—I'll just say somebody—could get that dagger any time he liked, and exactly when he got it doesn't matter in the least. I'll be coming up in the morning with the chief constable, Mr. Raymond. Until then, I'll keep the key of that door. I want Colonel Melrose to see everything exactly as it is. I happen to know that he's dining out the other side of the county, and, I believe, staying the night. . . ."

We watched the inspector take up the jar.

"I shall have to pack this carefully," he observed. "It's going to be an important piece of evidence in more ways than one."

A few minutes later as I came out of the billiard room with Raymond, the latter gave a low chuckle of amusement.

I felt the pressure of his hand on my arm, and followed the direction of his eyes. Inspector Davis seemed to be inviting Parker's opinion of a small pocket diary.

"A little obvious," murmured my companion. "So Parker is the suspect, is he? Shall we oblige Inspector Davis with a set of our fingerprints also?"

He took two cards from the card tray, wiped them with his silk handkerchief, then handed one to me and took the other himself. Then, with a grin, he handed them to the police inspector.

"Souvenirs," he said. "No. 1. Dr. Sheppard; No. 2, my humble self. One from Major Blunt will be forthcoming in the morning."

Youth is very buoyant. Even the brutal murder of his friend and employer could not dim Geoffrey Raymond's spirits for long. Perhaps that is as it should be. I do not know. I have lost the quality of resilience long since myself.

It was very late when I got back, and I hoped that Caroline would have gone to bed. I might have known better.

She had hot cocoa waiting for me, and whilst I drank it, she extracted the whole history of the evening from me. I said nothing of the blackmailing business, but contented myself with giving her the facts of the murder.

"The police suspect Parker," I said, as I rose to my feet and prepared to ascend to bed. "There seems a fairly clear case against him."

"Parker!" said my sister. "Fiddlesticks! That inspector must be a perfect fool. Parker indeed! Don't tell me." With which obscure pronouncement we went up to bed.

Seven

I Learn My Neighbour's Profession

On the following morning I hurried unforgivably over my rounds. My excuse can be that I had no very serious cases to attend. On my return Caroline came into the hall to greet me.

"Flora Ackroyd is here," she announced in an excited whisper.

"What?"

I concealed my surprise as best as I could.

"She's very anxious to see you. She's been here half an hour."

Caroline led the way into our small sitting room, and I followed.

Flora was sitting on the sofa by the window. She was in black and she sat nervously twisting her hands together. I was shocked by the sight of her face. All the colour had faded away from it. But when she spoke her manner was as composed and resolute as possible.

"Dr. Sheppard, I have come to ask you to help me?"

"Of course he'll help you, my dear," said Caroline.

I don't think Flora really wished Caroline to be present at the interview. She would, I am sure, have infinitely preferred to speak to me privately. But she also wanted to waste no time, so she made the best of it.

"I want you to come to The Larches with me."

"The Larches?" I queried, surprised.

"To see that funny little man?" exclaimed Caroline.

"Yes. You know who he is, don't you?"

"We fancied," I said, "that he might be a retired hairdresser."

Flora's blue eyes opened very wide.

"Why, he's Hercule Poirot! You know who I mean—the private detective. They say he's done the most wonderful things—just like detectives do in books. A year ago he retired and came to live down here. Uncle knew who he was, but he promised not to tell anyone, because M. Poirot wanted to live quietly without being bothered by people."

"So that's who he is," I said slowly.

"You've heard of him, of course?"

"I'm rather an old fogey, as Caroline tells me," I said, "but I *have* just heard of him."

"Extraordinary!" commented Caroline.

I don't know what she was referring to—possibly her own failure to discover the truth.

"You want to go and see him?" I asked slowly. "Now why?"

"To get him to investigate this murder, of course," said Caroline sharply. "Don't be so stupid, James."

I was not really being stupid. Caroline does not always understand what I am driving at.

"You haven't got confidence in Inspector Davis?" I went on.

"Of course she hasn't," said Caroline. "I haven't either."

Anyone would have thought it was Caroline's uncle who had been murdered.

"And how do you know he would take up the case?" I asked. "Remember he has retired from active work."

"That's just it," said Flora simply. "I've got to persuade him."

"You are sure you are doing wisely?" I asked gravely.

"Of course she is," said Caroline. "I'll go with her myself if she likes."

"I'd rather the doctor came with me, if you don't mind, Miss Sheppard," said Flora.

She knows the value of being direct on certain occasions. Any hints would certainly have been wasted on Caroline.

"You see," she explained, following directness with tact, "Dr. Sheppard being the doctor, and having found the body, he would be able to give all the details to M. Poirot."

"Yes," said Caroline grudgingly, "I see that."

I took a turn or two up and down the room.

"Flora," I said gravely, "be guided by me. I advise you not to drag this detective into the case."

Flora sprang to her feet. The colour rushed into her cheeks.

"I know why you say that," she cried. "But it's exactly for that reason I'm so anxious to go. You're afraid! But I'm not. I know Ralph better than you do."

"Ralph!" said Caroline. "What has Ralph got to do with it?"

Neither of us heeded her.

"Ralph may be weak," continued Flora. "He may have done foolish things in the past—wicked things even—but he wouldn't murder anyone."

"No, no," I exclaimed. "I never thought it of him."

"Then why did you go to the Three Boars last night?" demanded Flora. "On your way home—after Uncle's body was found?"

I was momentarily silenced. I had hoped that that visit of mine would remain unnoticed.

"How did you know about that?" I countered.

"I went there this morning," said Flora. "I heard from the servants that Ralph was staying there—"

I interrupted her.

"You had no idea that he was in King's Abbot?"

"No. I was astounded. I couldn't understand it. I went there and asked for him. They told me, what I suppose they told you last night, that he went out at about nine o'clock yesterday evening—and—and never came back."

Her eyes met mine defiantly, and as though answering something in my look, she burst out:

"Well, why shouldn't he? He might have gone—anywhere. He may even have gone back to London."

"Leaving his luggage behind?" I asked gently.

Flora stamped her foot.

"I don't care. There must be a simple explanation."

"And that's why you want to go to Hercule Poirot? Isn't it better to leave things as they are? The police don't suspect Ralph in the least, remember. They're working on quite another tack."

"But that's just *it,*" cried the girl. "They *do* suspect him. A man from Cranchester turned up this morning—Inspector Raglan, a horrid, weaselly little man. I found he had been to the Three Boars this morning before me. They told me all about his having been there, and the questions he had asked. He must think Ralph did it."

"That's a change of mind from last night, if so," I said slowly. "He doesn't believe in Davis's theory that it was Parker then?"

"Parker indeed," said my sister, and snorted.

Flora came forward and laid her hand on my arm.

"Oh! Dr. Sheppard, let us go at once to this M. Poirot. He will find out the truth."

"My dear Flora," I said gently, laying my hand on hers. "Are you quite sure it is the truth we want?"

She looked at me, nodding her head gravely.

"You're not sure," she said. "I am. I know Ralph better than you do."

"Of course he didn't do it," said Caroline, who had been keeping silent with great difficulty. "Ralph may be extravagant, but he's a dear boy, and has the nicest manners."

I wanted to tell Caroline that large numbers of murderers have had nice manners, but the presence of Flora restrained me. Since the girl was determined, I was forced to give in to her and we started at once, getting away before my sister was able to fire off any more pronouncements beginning with her favourite words, "Of course."

An old woman with an immense Breton cap opened the door of The Larches to us. M. Poirot was at home, it seemed.

We were ushered into a little sitting room arranged with formal precision, and there, after a lapse of a minute or so, my friend of yesterday came to us.

"Monsieur le docteur," he said, smiling. "Mademoiselle."

He bowed to Flora.

"Perhaps," I began, "you have heard of the tragedy which occurred last night."

His face grew grave.

"But certainly I have heard. It is horrible. I offer mademoiselle all my sympathy. In what way can I serve you?"

"Miss Ackroyd," I said, "wants you to—to—"

"To find the murderer," said Flora in a clear voice.

"I see," said the little man. "But the police will do that, will they not?"

"They might make a mistake," said Flora. "They are on their way to make a mistake now, I think. Please, M. Poirot, won't you help us? If—if it is a question of money—"

Poirot held up his hand.

"Not that, I beg of you, mademoiselle. Not that I do not care for money." His eyes showed a momentary twinkle. "Money, it means much to me and always has done. No, if I go into this, you must understand one thing clearly. *I shall go through with it to the end*. The good dog, he does not leave the scent, remember! You may wish that, after all, you had left it to the local police."

"I want the truth," said Flora, looking him straight in the eyes.

"All the truth?"

"All the truth."

"Then I accept," said the little man quietly. "And I hope you will not regret those words. Now, tell me all the circumstances."

"Dr. Sheppard had better tell you," said Flora. "He knows more than I do."

Thus enjoined, I plunged into a careful narrative, embodying all the facts I have previously set down. Poirot listened carefully, inserting a question here and there, but for the most part sitting in silence, his eyes on the ceiling.

I brought my story to a close with the departure of the inspector and myself from Fernly Park the previous night.

"And now," said Flora, as I finished, "tell him all about Ralph."

I hesitated, but her imperious glance drove me on.

"You went to this inn—this Three Boars—last night on your way home?" asked Poirot, as I brought my tale to a close. "Now exactly why was that?"

I paused a moment to choose my words carefully.

"I thought someone ought to inform the young man of his uncle's death.

It occurred to me after I had left Fernly that possibly no one but myself and Mr. Ackroyd were aware that he was staying in the village."

Poirot nodded.

"Quite so. That was your only motive in going there, eh?"

"That was my only motive," I said stiffly.

"It was not to—shall we say—reassure yourself about *ce jeune homme?*"

"Reassure myself?"

"I think, M. le docteur, that you know very well what I mean, though you pretend not to do so. I suggest that it would have been a relief to you if you had found that Captain Paton had been at home all the evening."

"Not at all," I said sharply.

The little detective shook his head at me gravely.

"You have not the trust in me of Miss Flora," he said. "But no matter. What we have to look at is this—Captain Paton is missing, under circumstances which call for an explanation. I will not hide from you that the matter looks grave. Still, it may admit of a perfectly simple explanation."

"That's just what I keep saying," cried Flora eagerly.

Poirot touched no more upon that theme. Instead he suggested an immediate visit to the local police. He thought it better for Flora to return home, and for me to be the one to accompany him there and introduce him to the officer in charge of the case.

We carried out this plan forthwith. We found Inspector Davis outside the police station looking very glum indeed. With him was Colonel Melrose, the Chief Constable, and another man whom, from Flora's description of "weaselly," I had no difficulty in recognizing as Inspector Raglan from Cranchester.

I know Melrose fairly well, and I introduced Poirot to him and explained the situation. The chief constable was clearly vexed, and Inspector Raglan looked as black as thunder. Davis, however, seemed slightly exhilarated by the sight of his superior officer's annoyance.

"The case is going to be plain as a pikestaff," said Raglan. "Not the least need for amateurs to come butting in. You'd think any fool would have seen the way things were last night, and then we shouldn't have lost twelve hours."

He directed a vengeful glance at poor Davis, who received it with perfect stolidity.

"Mr. Ackroyd's family must, of course, do what they see fit," said Colonel Melrose. "But we cannot have the official investigation hampered in any way. I know M. Poirot's great reputation, of course," he added courteously.

"The police can't advertise themselves, worse luck," said Raglan.

It was Poirot who saved the situation.

"It is true that I have retired from the world," he said. "I never intended to take up a case again. Above all things, I have a horror of publicity. I must beg, that in the case of my being able to contribute something to the solution of the mystery, my name may not be mentioned."

Inspector Raglan's face lightened a little.

"I've heard of some very remarkable successes of yours," observed the colonel, thawing.

"I have had much experience," said Poirot quietly. "But most of my successes have been obtained by the aid of the police. I admire enormously your English police. If Inspector Raglan permits me to assist him, I shall be both honoured and flattered."

The inspector's countenance became still more gracious.

Colonel Melrose drew me aside.

"From all I hear, this little fellow's done some really remarkable things," he murmured. "We're naturally anxious not to have to call in Scotland Yard. Raglan seems very sure of himself, but I'm not quite certain that I agree with him. You see, I—er—know the parties concerned better than he does. This fellow doesn't seem out after kudos, does he? Would work in with us unobtrusively, eh?"

"To the greater glory of Inspector Raglan," I said solemnly.

"Well, well," said Colonel Melrose breezily in a louder voice, "we must put you wise to the latest developments, M. Poirot."

"I thank you," said Poirot. "My friend, Doctor Sheppard, said something of the butler being suspected?"

"That's all bunkum," said Raglan instantly. "These high-class servants get in such a funk that they act suspiciously for nothing at all."

"The fingerprints?" I hinted.

"Nothing like Parker's." He gave a faint smile, and added: "And yours and Mr. Raymond's don't fit either, doctor."

"What about those of Captain Ralph Paton?" asked Poirot quietly.

I felt a secret admiration of the way he took the bull by the horns. I saw a look of respect creep into the inspector's eye.

"I see you don't let the grass grow under your feet, Mr. Poirot. It will be a pleasure to work with you, I'm sure. We're going to take that young gentleman's fingerprints as soon as we can lay hands upon him."

"I can't help thinking you're mistaken, Inspector," said Colonel Melrose warmly. "I've known Ralph Paton from a boy upward. He'd never stoop to murder."

"Maybe not," said the inspector tonelessly.

"What have you got against him?" I asked.

"Went out just on nine o'clock last night. Was seen in the neighbourhood of Fernly Park somewhere about nine-thirty. Not been seen since. Believed to be in serious money difficulties. I've got a pair of his shoes here—shoes with rubber studs in them. He had two pairs, almost exactly alike. I'm going up now to compare them with those footmarks. The constable is up there seeing that no one tampers with them."

"We'll go at once," said Colonel Melrose. "You and M. Poirot will accompany us, will you not?"

We assented, and all drove up in the colonel's car. The inspector was anxious to get at once to the footmarks, and asked to be put down at the lodge. About halfway up the drive, on the right, a path branched off which led round to the terrace and the window of Ackroyd's study.

"Would you like to go with the inspector, M. Poirot," asked the chief constable, "or would you prefer to examine the study?"

Poirot chose the latter alternative. Parker opened the door to us. His manner was smug and deferential, and he seemed to have recovered from his panic of the night before.

Colonel Melrose took a key from his pocket, and unlocking the door which let into the lobby, he ushered us through into the study.

"Except for the removal of the body, M. Poirot, this room is exactly as it was last night."

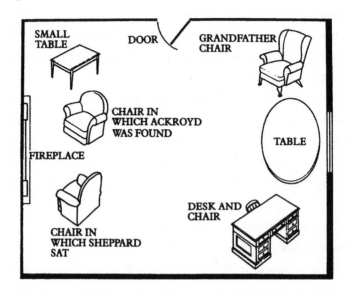

"And the body was found—where?"

As precisely as possible, I described Ackroyd's position. The armchair still stood in front of the fire.

Poirot went and sat down in it.

"The blue letter you speak of, where was it when you left the room?"

"Mr. Ackroyd had laid it down on this little table at his right hand."

Poirot nodded.

"Except for that, everything was in its place?"

"Yes, I think so."

"Colonel Melrose, would you be so extremely obliging as to sit down in this chair a minute. I thank you. Now M. le docteur, will you kindly indicate to me the exact position of the dagger?"

I did so, whilst the little man stood in the doorway.

"The hilt of the dagger was plainly visible from the door then. Both you and Parker could see it at once?"

"Yes."

Poirot went next to the window.

"The electric light was on, of course, when you discovered the body?" he asked over his shoulder.

I assented, and joined him where he was studying the marks on the windowsill.

"The rubber studs are the same pattern as those in Captain Paton's shoes," he said quietly.

Then he came back once more to the middle of the room. His eye travelled round, searching everything in the room with a quick, trained glance.

"Are you a man of good observation, Doctor Sheppard?" he asked at last.

"I think so," I said, surprised.

"There was a fire in the grate, I see. When you broke the door down and found Mr. Ackroyd dead, how was the fire? Was it low?"

I gave a vexed laugh.

"I—I really can't say. I didn't notice. Perhaps Mr. Raymond or Major Blunt—"

The little man opposite me shook his head with a faint smile.

"One must always proceed with method. I made an error of judgment in asking you that question. To each man his own knowledge. You could tell me the details of the patient's appearance—nothing there would escape you. If I wanted information about the papers on that desk, Mr. Raymond would have noticed anything there was to see. To find out about the fire, I must ask the man whose business it is to observe such things. You permit—"

He moved swiftly to the fireplace and rang the bell.

After a lapse of a minute or two Parker appeared.

"The bell rang, sir," he said hesitatingly.

"Come in, Parker," said Colonel Melrose. "This gentleman wants to ask you something."

Parker transferred a respectful attention to Poirot.

"Parker," said the little man, "when you broke down the door with Dr. Sheppard last night, and found your master dead, what was the state of the fire?"

Parker replied without a pause.

"It had burned very low, sir. It was almost out."

"Ah!" said Poirot. The exclamation sounded almost triumphant. He went on:

"Look round you, my good Parker. Is this room exactly as it was then?"

The butler's eye swept round. It came to rest on the windows.

"The curtains were drawn, sir, and the electric light was on."

Poirot nodded approval.

"Anything else?"

"Yes, sir, this chair was drawn out a little more."

He indicated a big grandfather chair to the left of the door between it and the window. I append a plan of the room with the chair in question marked with an X.

"Just show me," said Poirot.

The butler drew the chair in question out a good two feet from the wall, turning it so that the seat faced the door.

"*Voilà ce qui est curieux*," murmured Poirot. "No one would want to sit in a chair in such a position, I fancy. Now who pushed it back into place again, I wonder? Did you, my friend?"

"No, sir," said Parker. "I was too upset with seeing the master and all."

Poirot looked across at me.

"Did you, doctor?"

I shook my head.

"It was back in position when I arrived with the police, sir," put in Parker. "I'm sure of that."

"Curious," said Poirot again.

"Raymond or Blunt must have pushed it back," I suggested. "Surely it isn't important?"

"It is completely unimportant," said Poirot. "That is why it is so interesting," he added softly.

"Excuse me a minute," said Colonel Melrose. He left the room with Parker.

"Do you think Parker is speaking the truth?" I asked.

"About the chair, yes. Otherwise I do not know. You will find, M. le docteur, if you have much to do with cases of this kind, that they all resemble each other in one thing."

"What is that?" I asked curiously.

"Everyone concerned in them has something to hide."

"Have I?" I asked, smiling.

Poirot looked at me attentively.

"I think you have," he said quietly.

"But—"

"Have you told me everything known to you about this young man Paton?" He smiled as I grew red. "Oh! do not fear. I will not press you. I shall learn it in good time."

"I wish you'd tell me something of your methods," I said hastily, to cover my confusion. "The point about the fire, for instance?"

"Oh! that was very simple. You leave Mr. Ackroyd at—ten minutes to nine, was it not?"

"Yes, exactly, I should say."

"The window is then closed and bolted and the door unlocked. At a quarter past ten when the body is discovered, the door is locked and the window is open. Who opened it? Clearly only Mr. Ackroyd himself could have done so, and for one of two reasons. Either because the room became unbearably hot, but since the fire was nearly out and there was a sharp drop in temperature last night, that cannot be the reason, or because he admitted someone that way. And if he admitted someone that way, it must have been someone well known to him, since he had previously shown himself uneasy on the subject of that same window."

"It sounds very simple," I said.

"Everything is simple, if you arrange the facts methodically. We are concerned now with the personality of the person who was with him at nine-thirty last night. Everything goes to show that that was the individual admitted by the window, and though Mr. Ackroyd was seen alive later by Miss Flora, we cannot approach a solution of the mystery until we know who that visitor was. The window may have been left open after his departure and so afforded entrance to the murderer, or the same person may have returned a second time. Ah! here is the colonel who returns."

Colonel Melrose entered with an animated manner.

"That telephone call has been traced at last," he said. "It did not come from here. It was put through to Dr. Sheppard at 10:15 last night from a public call office at King's Abbot station. And at 10:23 the night mail leaves for Liverpool."

Eight

INSPECTOR RAGLAN IS CONFIDENT

We looked at each other.

"You'll have inquiries made at the station, of course?" I said.

"Naturally, but I'm not over sanguine as to the result. You know what that station is like."

I did. King's Abbot is a mere village, but its station happens to be an important junction. Most of the big expresses stop there, and trains are shunted, re-sorted, and made up. It has two or three public telephone boxes. At that time of night, three local trains come in close upon each other, to catch the connection with the express for the north which comes in at 10:19 and leaves at 10:23. The whole place is in a bustle, and the chances of one particular person being noticed telephoning or getting into the express are very small indeed.

"But why telephone at all?" demanded Melrose. "That is what I find so extraordinary. There seems no rhyme or reason in the thing."

Poirot carefully straightened a china ornament on one of the bookcases.

"Be sure there was a reason," he said over his shoulder.

"But what reason could it be?"

"When we know that, we shall know everything. This case is very curious and very interesting."

There was something almost indescribable in the way he said those last words. I felt that he was looking at the case from some peculiar angle of his own, and what he saw I could not tell.

He went to the window and stood there, looking out.

"You say it was nine o'clock, Dr. Sheppard, when you met this stranger outside the gate?"

He asked the question without turning round.

"Yes," I replied. "I heard the church clock chime the hour."

"How long would it take him to reach the house—to reach this window, for instance?"

"Five minutes at the outside. Two or three minutes only if he took the path at the right of the drive and came straight here."

"But to do that he would have to know the way. How can I explain myself?—it would mean that he had been here before—that he knew his surroundings."

"That is true," replied Colonel Melrose.

"We could find out, doubtless, if Mr. Ackroyd had received any strangers during the past week?"

"Young Raymond could tell us that," I said.

"Or Parker," suggested Colonel Melrose.

"*Ou tous les deux,*" suggested Poirot, smiling.

Colonel Melrose went in search of Raymond, and I rang the bell once more for Parker.

Colonel Melrose returned almost immediately, accompanied by the young secretary, whom he introduced to Poirot. Geoffrey Raymond was fresh and debonair as ever. He seemed surprised and delighted to make Poirot's acquaintance.

"No idea you'd been living among us incognito, M. Poirot," he said. "It will be a great privilege to watch you at work—Hallo, what's this?"

Poirot had been standing just to the left of the door. Now he moved aside suddenly, and I saw that while my back was turned he must have swiftly drawn out the armchair till it stood in the position Parker had indicated.

"Want me to sit in the chair whilst you take a blood test?" asked Raymond good-humouredly. "What's the idea?"

"M. Raymond, this chair was pulled out—so—last night when Mr. Ackroyd was found killed. Someone moved it back again into place. Did you do so?"

The secretary's reply came without a second's hesitation.

"No, indeed I didn't. I don't even remember that it was in that position, but it must have been if you say so. Anyway, somebody else must have moved it back to its proper place. Have they destroyed a clue in doing so? Too bad!"

"It is of no consequence," said the detective. "Of no consequence whatever. What I really want to ask you is this, M. Raymond: Did any stranger come to see Mr. Ackroyd during this past week?"

The secretary reflected for a minute or two, knitting his brows, and during the pause Parker appeared in answer to the bell.

"No," said Raymond at last. "I can't remember anyone. Can you, Parker?"

"I beg your pardon, sir?"

"Any stranger coming to see Mr. Ackroyd this week?"

The butler reflected for a minute or two.

"There was the young man who came on Wednesday, sir," he said at last. "From Curtis and Troute, I understood he was."

Raymond moved this aside with an impatient hand.

"Oh! yes, I remember, but that is not the kind of stranger this gentleman means." He turned to Poirot. "Mr. Ackroyd had some idea of purchasing a dictaphone," he explained. "It would have enabled us to get through a lot more work in a limited time. The firm in question sent down their representative, but nothing came of it. Mr. Ackroyd did not make up his mind to purchase."

Poirot turned to the butler.

"Can you describe this young man to me, my good Parker?"

"He was fair-haired, sir, and short. Very neatly dressed in a blue serge suit. A very presentable young man, sir, for his station in life."

Poirot turned to me.

"The man you met outside the gate, doctor, was tall, was he not?"

"Yes," I said. "Somewhere about six feet, I should say."

"There is nothing in that, then," declared the Belgian. "I thank you, Parker."

The butler spoke to Raymond.

"Mr. Hammond has just arrived, sir," he said. "He is anxious to know if he can be of any service, and he would be glad to have a word with you."

"I'll come at once," said the young man. He hurried out. Poirot looked inquiringly at the chief constable.

"The family solicitor, M. Poirot," said the latter.

"It is a busy time for this young M. Raymond," murmured M. Poirot. "He has the air efficient, that one."

"I believe Mr. Ackroyd considered him a most able secretary."

"He has been here—how long?"

"Just on two years, I fancy."

"His duties he fulfils punctiliously. Of that I am sure. In what manner does he amuse himself? Does he go in for *le sport?*"

"Private secretaries haven't much time for that sort of thing," said Colonel Melrose, smiling. "Raymond plays golf, I believe. And tennis in the summer time."

"He does not attend the courses—I should say the running of the horses?"

"Race meetings? No, I don't think he's interested in racing."

Poirot nodded and seemed to lose interest. He glanced slowly round the study.

"I have seen, I think, all that there is to be seen here."

I, too, looked round.

"If those walls could speak," I murmured.

Poirot shook his head.

"A tongue is not enough," he said. "They would have to have also eyes and ears. But do not be too sure that these dead things"—he touched the top of the bookcase as he spoke—"are always dumb. To me they speak sometimes—chairs, tables—they have their message!"

He turned away towards the door.

"What message?" I cried. "What have they said to you today?"

He looked over his shoulder and raised one eyebrow quizzically.

"An opened window," he said. "A locked door. A chair that apparently moved itself. To all three I say 'Why?' and I find no answer."

He shook his head, puffed out his chest, and stood blinking at us. He looked ridiculously full of his own importance. It crossed my mind to wonder whether he was really any good as a detective. Had his big reputation been built up on a series of lucky chances?

I think the same thought must have occurred to Colonel Melrose, for he frowned.

"Anything more you want to see, M. Poirot?" he inquired brusquely.

"You would perhaps be so kind as to show me the silver table from which the weapon was taken? After that, I will trespass on your kindness no longer."

We went to the drawing room, but on the way the constable waylaid the colonel, and after a muttered conversation the latter excused himself and left us together. I showed Poirot the silver table, and after raising the lid once or twice and letting it fall, he pushed open the window and stepped out on the terrace. I followed him.

Inspector Raglan had just turned the corner of the house, and was coming towards us. His face looked grim and satisfied.

"So there you are, M. Poirot," he said. "Well, this isn't going to be much of a case. I'm sorry, too. A nice enough young fellow gone wrong."

Poirot's face fell, and he spoke very mildly.

"I'm afraid I shall not be able to be of much aid to you, then?"

"Next time, perhaps," said the inspector soothingly. "Though we don't have murders every day in this quiet little corner of the world."

Poirot's gaze took on an admiring quality.

"You have been of a marvellous promptness," he observed. "How exactly did you go to work, if I may ask?"

"Certainly," said the inspector. "To begin with—method. That's what I always say—method!"

"Ah!" cried the other. "That, too, is my watchword. Method, order, and the little grey cells."

"The cells?" said the inspector, staring.

"The little grey cells of the brain," explained the Belgian.

"Oh, of course; well, we all use them, I suppose."

"In a greater or lesser degree," murmured Poirot. "And there are, too, differences in quality. Then there is the psychology of a crime. One must study that."

"Ah!" said the inspector, "you've been bitten with all this psycho-analysis stuff? Now, I'm a plain man—"

"Mrs. Raglan would not agree, I am sure, to that," said Poirot, making him a little bow.

Inspector Raglan, a little taken aback, bowed.

"You don't understand," he said, grinning broadly. "Lord, what a lot of difference language makes. I'm telling you how I set to work. First of all, method. Mr. Ackroyd was last seen alive at a quarter to ten by his niece, Miss Flora Ackroyd. That's fact number one, isn't it?"

"If you say so."

"Well, it is. At half past ten, the doctor here says that Mr. Ackroyd had been dead at least half an hour. You stick to that, doctor?"

"Certainly," I said. "Half an hour or longer."

"Very good. That gives us exactly a quarter of an hour in which the crime must have been committed. I make a list of everyone in the house, and work through it, setting down opposite their names where they were and what they were doing between the hour of 9:45 and 10 p.m."

He handed a sheet of paper to Poirot. I read it over his shoulder. It ran as follows, written in a neat script:

Major Blunt   In billiard room with Mr. Raymond. (Latter confirms.)

Mr. Raymond   Billiard room. (See above.)

Mrs. Ackroyd   9:45 watching billiard match. Went up to bed 9:55. (Raymond and Blunt watched her up staircase.)

Miss Ackroyd   Went straight from her uncle's room upstairs. (Confirmed by Parker, also housemaid, Elsie Dale.)

Servants:

Parker   Went straight to butler's pantry. (Confirmed by housekeeper, Miss Russell, who came down to speak to him about something at 9:47, and remained at least ten minutes.)

Miss Russell   As above. Spoke to housemaid, Elsie Dale, upstairs at 9:45.

Ursula Bourne (parlourmaid)   In her own room until 9:55. Then in Servants' Hall.

Mrs. Cooper (cook)   In Servants' Hall.

Gladys Jones (second housemaid)   In Servants' Hall.

Elsie Dale   Upstairs in bedroom. Seen there by Miss Russell and Miss Flora Ackroyd.

Mary Thripp (kitchenmaid)   Servants' Hall.

"The cook has been here seven years, the parlourmaid eighteen months, and Parker just over a year. The others are new. Except for something fishy about Parker, they all seem quite all right."

"A very complete list," said Poirot, handing it back to him. "I am quite sure that Parker did not do the murder," he added gravely.

"So is my sister," I struck in. "And she's usually right." Nobody paid any attention to my interpolation.

"That disposes pretty effectually of the household," continued the inspector. "Now we come to a very grave point. The woman at the lodge—Mary Black—was pulling the curtains last night when she saw Ralph Paton turn in at the gate and go up towards the house."

"She is sure of that?" I asked sharply.

"Quite sure. She knows him well by sight. He went past very quickly and turned off by the path to the right, which is a short cut to the terrace."

"And what time was that?" asked Poirot, who had sat with an immovable face.

"Exactly twenty-five minutes past nine," said the inspector gravely.

There was a silence. Then the inspector spoke again.

"It's all clear enough. It fits in without a flaw. At twenty-five minutes past nine, Captain Paton is seen passing the lodge; at nine-thirty or thereabouts, Mr. Geoffrey Raymond hears someone in here asking for money and Mr. Ackroyd refusing. What happens next? Captain Paton leaves the same way—through the window. He walks along the terrace, angry and baffled. He comes to the open drawing room window. Say it's now a quarter to ten. Miss Flora Ackroyd is saying goodnight to her uncle. Major Blunt, Mr. Raymond, and Mrs. Ackroyd are in the billiard room. The drawing room is empty. He steals in, takes the dagger from the silver table, and returns to the study window. He slips off his shoes, climbs in, and—well, I don't need to go into details. Then he slips out again and goes off. Hadn't the nerve to go back to the inn. He makes for the station, rings up from there—"

"Why?" said Poirot softly.

I jumped at the interruption. The little man was leaning forward. His eyes shone with a queer green light.

For a moment Inspector Raglan was taken aback by the question.

"It's difficult to say exactly why he did that," he said at last. "But murderers do funny things. You'd know that if you were in the police force. The cleverest of them make stupid mistakes sometimes. But come along and I'll show you those footprints."

We followed him round the corner of the terrace to the study window. At a word from Raglan a police constable produced the shoes which had been obtained from the local inn.

The inspector laid them over the marks.

"They're the same," he said confidently. "That is to say, they're not the same pair that actually made these prints. He went away in those. This is a pair just like them, but older—see how the studs are worn down?"

"Surely a great many people wear shoes with rubber studs in them?" asked Poirot.

"That's so, of course," said the inspector. "I shouldn't put so much stress on the footmarks if it wasn't for everything else."

"A very foolish young man, Captain Ralph Paton," said Poirot thoughtfully. "To leave so much evidence of his presence."

"Ah! well," said the inspector, "it was a dry, fine night, you know. He left no prints on the terrace or on the gravelled path. But, unluckily for him, a spring must have welled up just lately at the end of the path from the drive. See here."

A small gravelled path joined the terrace a few feet away. In one spot, a few yards from its termination, the ground was wet and boggy. Crossing this wet place there were again the marks of footsteps, and amongst them the shoes with rubber studs.

Poirot followed the path on a little way, the inspector by his side.

"You noticed the women's footprints?" he said suddenly.

The inspector laughed.

"Naturally. But several different women have walked this way—and men as well. It's a regular short cut to the house, you see. It would be impossible to sort out all the footsteps. After all, it's the ones on the windowsill that are really important."

Poirot nodded.

"It's no good going farther," said the inspector, as we came in view of the drive. "It's all gravelled again here, and hard as it can be."

Again Poirot nodded, but his eyes were fixed on a small garden house—a kind of superior summerhouse. It was a little to the left of the path ahead of us, and a gravelled walk ran up to it.

Poirot lingered about until the inspector had gone back towards the house. Then he looked at me.

"You must have indeed been sent from the good God to replace my friend Hastings," he said, with a twinkle. "I observe that you do not quit my side. How say you, Doctor Sheppard, shall we investigate that summerhouse? It interests me."

He went up to the door and opened it. Inside, the place was almost dark. There were one or two rustic seats, a croquet set, and some folded deck chairs.

I was startled to observe my new friend. He had dropped to his hands and knees and was crawling about the floor. Every now and then he shook his head as though not satisfied. Finally, he sat back on his heels.

"Nothing," he murmured. "Well, perhaps it was not to be expected. But it would have meant so much—"

He broke off, stiffening all over. Then he stretched out his hand to one of the rustic chairs. He detached something from one side of it.

"What is it?" I cried. "What have you found?"

He smiled, unclosing his hand so that I should see what lay in the palm of it. A scrap of stiff white cambric.

I took it from him, looked at it curiously, and then handed it back.

"What do you make of it, eh, my friend?" he asked, eyeing me keenly.

"A scrap torn from a handkerchief," I suggested, shrugging my shoulders.

He made another dart and picked up a small quill—a goose quill by the look of it.

"And that?" he cried triumphantly. "What do you make of that?"

I only stared.

He slipped the quill into his pocket, and looked again at the scrap of white stuff.

"A fragment of a handkerchief?" he mused. "Perhaps you are right. But remember this—*a good laundry does not starch a handkerchief.*"

He nodded at me triumphantly, then he put away the scrap carefully in his pocketbook.

Nine

THE GOLDFISH POND

We walked back to the house together. There was no sign of the inspector. Poirot paused on the terrace and stood with his back to the house, slowly turning his head from side to side.

"*Une belle propriété,*" he said at last appreciatively. "Who inherits it?"

His words gave me almost a shock. It is an odd thing, but until that moment the question of inheritance had never come into my head. Poirot watched me keenly.

"It is a new idea to you, that," he said at last. "You had not thought of it before—eh?"

"No," I said truthfully. "I wish I had."

He looked at me again curiously.

"I wonder just what you mean by that," he said thoughtfully. "Oh! no," as I was about to speak. "*Inutile!* You would not tell me your real thought."

"Everyone has something to hide," I quoted, smiling.

"Exactly."

"You still believe that?"

"More than ever, my friend. But it is not easy to hide things from Hercule Poirot. He has a knack of finding out."

He descended the steps of the Dutch garden as he spoke.

"Let us walk a little," he said over his shoulder. "The air is pleasant today."

I followed him. He led me down a path to the left enclosed in yew hedges.

A walk led down the middle, bordered each side with formal flower beds, and at the end was a round paved recess with a seat and a pond of goldfish. Instead of pursuing the path to the end, Poirot took another which wound up the side of a wooded slope. In one spot the trees had been cleared away, and a seat had been put. Sitting there one had a splendid view over the countryside, and one looked right down on the paved recess and the goldfish pond.

"England is very beautiful," said Poirot, his eyes straying over the prospect. Then he smiled. "And so are English girls," he said in a lower voice. "Hush, my friend, and look at the pretty picture below us."

It was then that I saw Flora. She was moving along the path we had just left and she was humming a little snatch of song. Her step was more dancing than walking, and, in spite of her black dress, there was nothing but joy in her whole attitude. She gave a sudden pirouette on her toes, and her black draperies swung out. At the same time she flung her head back and laughed outright.

As she did so a man stepped out from the trees. It was Hector Blunt.

The girl started. Her expression changed a little.

"How you startled me—I didn't see you."

Blunt said nothing, but stood looking at her for a minute or two in silence.

"What I like about you," said Flora, with a touch of malice, "is your cheery conversation."

I fancy that at that Blunt reddened under his tan. His voice, when he spoke, sounded different—it had a curious sort of humility in it.

"Never was much of a fellow for talking. Not even when I was young."

"That was a very long time ago, I suppose," said Flora gravely.

I caught the undercurrent of laughter in her voice, but I don't think Blunt did.

"Yes," he said simply, "it was."

"How does it feel to be Methuselah?" asked Flora.

This time the laughter was more apparent, but Blunt was following out an idea of his own.

"Remember the johnny who sold his soul to the devil? In return for being made young again? There's an opera about it."

"Faust, you mean?"

"That's the beggar. Rum story. Some of us would do it if we could."

"Anyone would think you were creaking at the joints to hear you talk," cried Flora, half vexed, half amused.

Blunt said nothing for a minute or two. Then he looked away from Flora into the middle distance and observed to an adjacent tree trunk that it was about time he got back to Africa.

"Are you going on another expedition—shooting things?"

"Expect so. Usually do, you know—shoot things, I mean."

"You shot that head in the hall, didn't you?"

Blunt nodded. Then he jerked out, going rather red as he did so:

"Care for some decent skins any time? If so, I could get 'em for you."

"Oh! please do," cried Flora. "Will you really? You won't forget?"

"I shan't forget," said Hector Blunt.

He added, in a sudden burst of communicativeness:

"Time I went. I'm no good in this sort of life. Haven't got the manners for it. I'm a rough fellow, no use in society. Never remember the things one's expected to say. Yes, time I went."

"But you're not going at once," cried Flora. "No—not while we're in all this trouble. Oh! please. If you go—"

She turned away a little.

"You want me to stay?" asked Blunt.

He spoke deliberately but quite simply.

"We all—"

"I meant you personally," said Blunt, with directness.

Flora turned slowly back again and met his eyes.

"I want you to stay," she said, "if—if that makes any difference."

"It makes all the difference," said Blunt.

There was a moment's silence. They sat down on the stone seat by the goldfish pond. It seemed as though neither of them knew quite what to say next.

"It—it's such a lovely morning," said Flora at last. "You know, I can't help feeling happy, in spite—in spite of everything. That's awful, I suppose?"

"Quite natural," said Blunt. "Never saw your uncle until two years ago, did you? Can't be expected to grieve very much. Much better to have no humbug about it."

"There's something awfully consoling about you," said Flora. "You make things seem so simple."

"Things are simple as a rule," said the big-game hunter.

"Not always," said Flora.

Her voice had lowered itself, and I saw Blunt turn and look at her, bringing his eyes back from (apparently) the coast of Africa to do so. He evidently put his own construction on her change of tone, for he said, after a minute or two, in rather an abrupt manner:

"I say, you know, you mustn't worry. About that young chap, I mean. Inspector's an ass. Everybody knows—utterly absurd to think he could have done it. Man from outside. Burglar chap. That's the only possible solution."

Flora turned to look at him.

"You really think so?"

"Don't you?" said Blunt quickly.

"I—oh, yes, of course."

Another silence, and then Flora burst out:

"I'm—I'll tell you why I felt so happy this morning. However heartless you think me, I'd rather tell you. It's because the lawyer has been—Mr. Hammond. He told us about the will. Uncle Roger has left me twenty thousand pounds. Think of it—twenty thousand beautiful pounds."

Blunt looked surprised.

"Does it mean so much to you?"

"Mean much to me? Why, it's everything. Freedom—life—no more scheming and scraping and lying—"

"Lying?" said Blunt, sharply interrupting.

Flora seemed taken aback for a minute.

"You know what I mean," she said uncertainly. "Pretending to be thankful for all the nasty cast-off things rich relations give you. Last year's coat and skirts and hats."

"Don't know much about ladies' clothes; should have said you were always very well turned out."

"It cost me something, though," said Flora in a low voice. "Don't let's talk of horrid things. I'm so happy. I'm free. Free to do what I like. Free not to—"

She stopped suddenly.

"Not to what?" asked Blunt quickly.

"I forget now. Nothing important."

Blunt had a stick in his hand, and he thrust it into the pond, poking at something.

"What are you doing, Major Blunt?"

"There's something bright down there. Wondered what it was—looks like a gold brooch. Now I've stirred up the mud and it's gone."

"Perhaps it's a crown," suggested Flora. "Like the one Melisande saw in the water."

"Melisande," said Blunt reflectively—"she's in an opera, isn't she?"

"Yes, you seem to know a lot about operas."

"People take me sometimes," said Blunt sadly. "Funny idea of pleasure—worse racket than the natives make with their tom-toms."

Flora laughed.

"I remember Melisande," continued Blunt, "married an old chap old enough to be her father."

He threw a small piece of flint into the goldfish pond. Then, with a change of manner, he turned to Flora.

"Miss Ackroyd, can I do anything? About Paton, I mean. I know how dreadfully anxious you must be."

"Thank you," said Flora in a cold voice. "There is really nothing to be done. Ralph will be all right. I've got hold of the most wonderful detective in the world, and he's going to find out all about it."

For some time I had felt uneasy as to our position. We were not exactly eavesdropping, since the two in the garden below had only to lift their heads to see us. Nevertheless, I should have drawn attention to our presence before now, had not my companion put a warning pressure on my arm. Clearly he wished me to remain silent. Now, however, he acted briskly.

He rose quickly to his feet, clearing his throat.

"I demand pardon," he cried. "I cannot allow mademoiselle thus extravagantly to compliment me, and not draw attention to my presence. They say the listener hears no good of himself, but that is not the case this time. To spare my blushes, I must join you and apologize."

He hurried down the path with me close behind him, and joined the others by the pond.

"This is M. Hercule Poirot," said Flora. "I expect you've heard of him."

Poirot bowed.

"I know Major Blunt by reputation," he said politely. "I am glad to have encountered you, monsieur. I am in need of some information that you can give me."

Blunt looked at him inquiringly.

"When did you last see M. Ackroyd alive?"

"At dinner."

"And you neither saw nor heard anything of him after that?"

"Didn't see him. Heard his voice."

"How was that?"

"I strolled out on the terrace—"

"Pardon me, what time was that?"

"About half past nine. I was walking up and down smoking in front of the drawing room window. I heard Ackroyd talking in his study—"

Poirot stopped and removed a microscopic weed.

"Surely you couldn't hear voices in the study from that part of the terrace," he murmured.

He was not looking at Blunt, but I was, and to my intense surprise, I saw the latter flush.

"Went as far as the corner," he explained unwillingly.

"Ah! indeed?" said Poirot.

In the mildest manner he conveyed an impression that more was wanted.

"Thought I saw—a woman disappearing into the bushes. Just a gleam of white, you know. Must have been mistaken. It was while I was standing at the corner of the terrace that I heard Ackroyd's voice speaking to that secretary of his."

"Speaking to Mr. Geoffrey Raymond?"

"Yes—that's what I supposed at the time. Seems I was wrong."

"Mr. Ackroyd didn't address him by name?"

"Oh, no."

"Then, if I may ask, why did you think—?"

Blunt explained laboriously.

"Took it for granted that it *would* be Raymond, because he had said just before I came out that he was taking some papers to Ackroyd. Never thought of it being anybody else."

"Can you remember what the words you heard were?"

"Afraid I can't. Something quite ordinary and unimportant. Only caught a scrap of it. I was thinking of something else at the time."

"It is of no importance," murmured Poirot. "Did you move a chair back against the wall when you went into the study after the body was discovered?"

"Chair? No, why should I?"

Poirot shrugged his shoulders but did not answer. He turned to Flora.

"There is one thing I should like to know from you, mademoiselle. When you were examining the things in the silver table with Dr. Sheppard, was the dagger in its place, or was it not?"

Flora's chin shot up.

"Inspector Raglan has been asking me that," she said resentfully. "I've told him, and I'll tell you. I'm perfectly certain the dagger was *not* there. He thinks it was and that Ralph sneaked it later in the evening. And—and he doesn't believe me. He thinks I'm saying it so—to shield Ralph."

"And aren't you?" I asked gravely.

Flora stamped her foot.

"You, too, Dr. Sheppard! Oh! it's too bad."

Poirot tactfully made a diversion.

"It is true what I heard you say, Major Blunt. There is something that glitters in this pond. Let us see if I can reach it."

He knelt down by the pond, baring his arm to the elbow, and lowered it in very slowly, so as not to disturb the bottom of the pond. But in spite of all his precautions the mud eddied and swirled, and he was forced to draw his arm out again empty-handed.

He gazed ruefully at the mud upon his arm. I offered him my handkerchief, which he accepted with fervent protestations of thanks. Blunt looked at his watch.

"Nearly lunch time," he said. "We'd better be getting back to the house."

"You will lunch with us, M. Poirot?" asked Flora. "I should like you to meet my mother. She is—very fond of Ralph."

The little man bowed.

"I shall be delighted, mademoiselle."

"And you will stay, too, won't you, Dr. Sheppard?"

I hesitated.

"Oh, do!"

I wanted to, so I accepted the invitation without further ceremony.

We set out towards the house, Flora and Blunt walking ahead.

"What hair," said Poirot to me in a low tone, nodding towards Flora. "The real gold! They will make a pretty couple. She and the dark, handsome Captain Paton. Will they not?"

I looked at him inquiringly, but he began to fuss about a few microscopic drops of water on his coat sleeve. The man reminded me in some ways of a cat. His green eyes and his finicking habits.

"And all for nothing, too," I said sympathetically. "I wonder what it was in the pond?"

"Would you like to see?" asked Poirot.

I stared at him. He nodded.

"My good friend," he said gently and reproachfully, "Hercule Poirot does not run the risk of disarranging his costume without being sure of attaining his object. To do so would be ridiculous and absurd. I am never ridiculous."

"But you brought your hand out empty," I objected.

"There are times when it is necessary to have discretion. Do you tell your patients everything—but everything, doctor? I think not. Nor do you tell your excellent sister everything either, is it not so? Before showing my empty hand, I dropped what it contained into my other hand. You shall see what that was."

He held out his left hand, palm open. On it lay a little circlet of gold. A woman's wedding ring.

I took it from him.

"Look inside," commanded Poirot.

I did so. Inside was an inscription in fine writing:

From R., March 13th.

I looked at Poirot, but he was busy inspecting his appearance in a tiny pocket glass. He paid particular attention to his moustaches, and none at all to me. I saw that he did not intend to be communicative.

Ten

THE PARLOURMAID

We found Mrs. Ackroyd in the hall. With her was a small dried-up little man, with an aggressive chin and sharp grey eyes, and "lawyer" written all over him.

"Mr. Hammond is staying to lunch with us," said Mrs. Ackroyd. "You know Major Blunt, Mr. Hammond? And dear Doctor Sheppard—also a close friend of poor Roger's. And, let me see—"

She paused, surveying Hercule Poirot in some perplexity.

"This is M. Poirot, Mother," said Flora. "I told you about him this morning."

"Oh! yes," said Mrs. Ackroyd vaguely. "Of course, my dear, of course. He is to find Ralph, is he not?"

"He is to find out who killed Uncle," said Flora.

"Oh! my dear," cried her mother. "Please! My poor nerves. I am a wreck this morning, a positive wreck. Such a dreadful thing to happen. I can't help feeling that it must have been an accident of some kind. Roger was so fond of handling queer curios. His hand must have slipped, or something."

This theory was received in polite silence. I saw Poirot edge up to the lawyer, and speak to him in a confidential undertone. They moved aside into the embrasure of the window. I joined them—then hesitated.

"Perhaps I'm intruding," I said.

"Not at all," cried Poirot heartily. "You and I, M. le docteur, we investigate this affair side by side. Without you I should be lost. I desire a little information from the good Mr. Hammond."

"You are acting on behalf of Captain Ralph Paton, I understand," said the lawyer cautiously.

Poirot shook his head.

"Not so. I am acting in the interests of justice. Miss Ackroyd has asked me to investigate the death of her uncle."

Mr. Hammond seemed slightly taken aback.

"I cannot seriously believe that Captain Paton can be concerned in this crime," he said, "however strong the circumstantial evidence against him may be. The mere fact that he was hard pressed for money—"

"Was he hard pressed for money?" interpolated Poirot quickly.

The lawyer shrugged his shoulders.

"It was a chronic condition with Ralph Paton," he said drily. "Money went through his hands like water. He was always applying to his stepfather."

"Had he done so of late? During the last year, for instance?"

"I cannot say. Mr. Ackroyd did not mention the fact to me."

"I comprehend. Mr. Hammond, I take it that you are acquainted with the provisions of Mr. Ackroyd's will?"

"Certainly. That is my principal business here today."

"Then, seeing that I am acting for Miss Ackroyd, you will not object to telling me the terms of that will?"

"They are quite simple. Shorn of legal phraseology, and after paying certain legacies and bequests—"

"Such as—?" interrupted Poirot.

Mr. Hammond seemed a little surprised.

"A thousand pounds to his housekeeper, Miss Russell; fifty pounds to the cook, Emma Cooper; five hundred pounds to his secretary, Mr. Geoffrey Raymond. Then to various hospitals—"

Poirot held up his hand.

"Ah! the charitable bequests, they interest me not."

"Quite so. The income on ten thousand pounds' worth of shares to be paid to Mrs. Cecil Ackroyd during her lifetime. Miss Flora Ackroyd inherits twenty thousand pounds outright. The residue—including this property, and the shares in Ackroyd and Son—to his adopted son, Ralph Paton."

"Mr. Ackroyd possessed a large fortune?"

"A very large fortune. Captain Paton will be an exceedingly wealthy young man."

There was a silence. Poirot and the lawyer looked at each other.

"Mr. Hammond," came Mrs. Ackroyd's voice plaintively from the fireplace.

The lawyer answered the summons. Poirot took my arm and drew me right into the window.

"Regard the irises," he remarked in a rather loud voice. "Magnificent, are they not? A straight and pleasing effect."

At the same time I felt the pressure of his hand on my arm, and he added in a low tone:

"Do you really wish to aid me? To take part in this investigation?"

"Yes, indeed," I said eagerly. "There's nothing I should like better. You don't know what a dull old fogey's life I lead. Never anything out of the ordinary."

"Good, we will be colleagues then. In a minute or two I fancy Major Blunt will join us. He is not happy with the good mamma. Now there are some things I want to know—but I do not wish to seem to want to know them. You comprehend? So it will be your part to ask the questions."

"What questions do you want me to ask?" I asked apprehensively.

"I want you to introduce the name of Mrs. Ferrars."

"Yes?"

"Speak of her in a natural fashion. Ask him if he was down here when her husband died. You understand the kind of thing I mean. And while he replies, watch his face without seeming to watch it. *C'est compris?*"

There was no time for more, for at that minute, as Poirot had prophesied, Blunt left the others in his abrupt fashion and came over to us.

I suggested strolling on the terrace, and he acquiesced. Poirot stayed behind.

I stopped to examine a late rose.

"How things change in the course of a day or two," I observed. "I was up here last Wednesday, I remember, walking up and down this same terrace. Ackroyd was with me—full of spirits. And now—three days later—Ackroyd's dead, poor fellow. Mrs. Ferrars dead—you knew her, didn't you? But of course you did."

Blunt nodded his head.

"Had you seen her since you'd been down this time?"

"Went with Ackroyd to call. Last Tuesday, think it was. Fascinating woman—but something queer about her. Deep—one would never know what she was up to."

I looked into his steady grey eyes. Nothing there surely. I went on:

"I suppose you'd met her before?"

"Last time I was here—she and her husband had just come here to live." He paused a minute and then added: "Rum thing, she had changed a lot between then and now."

"How—changed?" I asked.

"Looked ten years older."

"Were you down here when her husband died?" I asked, trying to make the question sound as casual as possible.

"No. From all I heard it would be good riddance. Uncharitable, perhaps, but the truth."

I agreed.

"Ashley Ferrars was by no means a pattern husband," I said cautiously.

"Blackguard, I thought," said Blunt.

"No," I said, "only a man with more money than was good for him."

"Oh! money! All the troubles in the world can be put down to money—or the lack of it."

"Which has been your particular trouble?" I asked.

"Enough for what I want. I'm one of the lucky ones."

"Indeed."

"I'm not too flush just now, as a matter of fact. Came into a legacy a year ago, and like a fool let myself be persuaded into putting it into some wild-cat scheme."

I sympathized, and narrated my own similar trouble.

Then the gong pealed out, and we all went in to lunch. Poirot drew me back a little.

"Eh bien?"

"He's all right," I said. "I'm sure of it."

"Nothing—disturbing?"

"He had a legacy just a year ago," I said. "But why not? Why shouldn't he? I'll swear the man is perfectly square and above board."

"Without doubt, without doubt," said Poirot soothingly. "Do not upset yourself."

He spoke as though to a fractious child.

We all trooped into the dining room. It seemed incredible that less than twenty-four hours had passed since I last sat at that table.

Afterwards, Mrs. Ackroyd took me aside and sat down with me on a sofa.

"I can't help feeling a little hurt," she murmured, producing a handkerchief of the kind obviously not meant to be cried into. "Hurt, I mean, by Roger's lack of confidence in me. That twenty thousand pounds ought to have been left to *me*—not to Flora. A mother could be trusted to safeguard the interests of her child. A lack of trust, I call it."

"You forget, Mrs. Ackroyd," I said, "Flora was Ackroyd's own niece, a blood relation. It would have been different had you been his sister instead of his sister-in-law."

"As poor Cecil's widow, I think my feelings ought to have been considered," said the lady, touching her eyelashes gingerly with the handkerchief. "But Roger was always most peculiar—not to say *mean*—about money matters. It has been a most difficult position for both Flora and myself. He did not even give the poor child an allowance. He would pay her bills, you know, and even that with a good deal of reluctance and asking what she wanted all those fal-lals for—so like a man—but—now I've forgotten what it was I was going to say! Oh, yes, not a penny we could call our own, you know. Flora resented it—yes, I must say she resented it—very strongly. Though devoted to her uncle, of course. But any girl would have resented it. Yes, I must say Roger had very strange ideas about money. He wouldn't even buy new face towels, though I told him the old ones were in holes. And then," proceeded Mrs. Ackroyd, with a sudden leap highly characteristic of her conversation, "to leave all that money—a thousand pounds, fancy, a thousand pounds!—to that woman."

"What woman?"

"That Russell woman. Something very queer about her, and so I've always said. But Roger wouldn't hear a word against her. Said she was a woman of great force of character, and that he admired and respected her. He was always going on about her rectitude and independence and moral worth. *I* think there's something fishy about her. She was certainly doing her best to marry Roger. But I soon put a stop to that. She always hated me. Naturally. *I* saw through her."

I began to wonder if there was any chance of stemming Mrs. Ackroyd's eloquence, and getting away.

Mr. Hammond provided the necessary diversion by coming up to say good-bye. I seized my chance and rose also.

"About the inquest," I said. "Where would you prefer it to be held? Here, or at the Three Boars?"

Mrs. Ackroyd stared at me with a dropped jaw.

"The inquest?" she asked, the picture of consternation. "But surely there won't have to be an inquest?"

Mr. Hammond gave a dry little cough and murmured, "Inevitable. Under the circumstances," in two short little barks.

"But surely Dr. Sheppard can arrange—"

"There are limits to my powers of arrangement," I said drily.

"If his death was an accident—"

"He was murdered, Mrs. Ackroyd," I said brutally.

She gave a little cry.

"No theory of accident will hold water for a minute."

Mrs. Ackroyd looked at me in distress. I had no patience with what I thought was her silly fear of unpleasantness.

"If there's an inquest, I—I shan't have to answer questions and all that, shall I?" she asked.

"I don't know what will be necessary," I answered. "I imagine Mr. Raymond will take the brunt of it off you. He knows all the circumstances, and can give formal evidence of identification."

The lawyer assented with a little bow.

"I really don't think there is anything to dread, Mrs. Ackroyd," he said. "You will be spared all the unpleasantness. Now, as to the question of money, have you all you need for the present? I mean," he added, as she looked at him inquiringly, "ready money. Cash, you know. If not, I can arrange to let you have whatever you require."

"That ought to be all right," said Raymond, who was standing by. "Mr. Ackroyd cashed a cheque for a hundred pounds yesterday."

"A hundred pounds?"

"Yes. For wages and other expenses due today. At the moment it is still intact."

"Where is this money? In his desk?"

"No, he always kept his cash in his bedroom. In an old collar box, to be accurate. Funny idea, wasn't it?"

"I think," said the lawyer, "we ought to make sure the money is there before I leave."

"Certainly," agreed the secretary. "I'll take you up now . . . Oh! I forgot. The door's locked."

Inquiry from Parker elicited the information that Inspector Raglan was in the housekeeper's room asking a few supplementary questions. A few minutes later the inspector joined the party in the hall, bringing the key with him. He unlocked the door and we passed into the lobby and up the small staircase. At the top of the stairs the door into Ackroyd's bedroom stood open. Inside the room it was dark, the curtains were drawn, and the bed was turned down just as it had been last night. The inspector drew the curtains, letting in the sunlight, and Geoffrey Raymond went to the top drawer of a rosewood bureau.

"He kept his money like that, in an unlocked drawer. Just fancy," commented the inspector.

The secretary flushed a little.

"Mr. Ackroyd had perfect faith in the honesty of all the servants," he said hotly.

"Oh! quite so," said the inspector hastily.

Raymond opened the drawer, took out a round leather collar box from the back of it, and opening it, drew out a thick wallet.

"Here is the money," he said, taking out a fat roll of notes. "You will find

the hundred intact, I know, for Mr. Ackroyd put it in the collar box in my presence last night when he was dressing for dinner, and of course it has not been
touched since."

Mr. Hammond took the roll from him and counted it. He looked up
sharply.

"A hundred pounds, you said. But there is only sixty here."

Raymond stared at him.

"Impossible," he cried, springing forward. Taking the notes from the other's
hand, he counted them aloud.

Mr. Hammond had been right. The total amounted to sixty pounds.

"But—I can't understand it," cried the secretary, bewildered.

Poirot asked a question.

"You saw Mr. Ackroyd put this money away last night when he was dressing
for dinner? You are sure he had not paid away any of it already?"

"I'm sure he hadn't. He even said, 'I don't want to take a hundred pounds
down to dinner with me. Too bulgy.' "

"Then the affair is very simple," remarked Poirot. "Either he paid out that
forty pounds some time last evening, or else it has been stolen."

"That's the matter in a nutshell," agreed the inspector. He turned to
Mrs. Ackroyd. "Which of the servants would come in here yesterday evening?"

"I suppose the housemaid would turn down the bed."

"Who is she? What do you know about her?"

"She's not been here very long," said Mrs. Ackroyd. "But she's a nice ordinary country girl."

"I think we ought to clear this matter up," said the inspector. "If Mr. Ackroyd paid that money away himself, it may have a bearing on the mystery of the
crime. The other servants all right, as far as you know?"

"Oh, I think so."

"Not missed anything before?"

"No."

"None of them leaving, or anything like that?"

"The parlourmaid is leaving."

"When?"

"She gave notice yesterday, I believe."

"To you?"

"Oh, no. *I* have nothing to do with the servants. Miss Russell attends to the household matters."

The inspector remained lost in thought for a minute or two. Then he nodded his head and remarked, "I think I'd better have a word with Miss Russell, and I'll see the girl Dale as well."

Poirot and I accompanied him to the housekeeper's room. Miss Russell received us with her usual sangfroid.

Elsie Dale had been at Fernly five months. A nice girl, quick at her duties, and most respectable. Good references. The last girl in the world to take anything not belonging to her.

What about the parlourmaid?

"She, too, was a most superior girl. Very quiet and ladylike. An excellent worker."

"Then why is she leaving?" asked the inspector.

Miss Russell pursed up her lips.

"It was none of my doing. I understand Mr. Ackroyd found fault with her yesterday afternoon. It was her duty to do the study, and she disarranged some of the papers on his desk, I believe. He was very annoyed about it, and she gave notice. At least, that is what I understood from her, but perhaps you'd like to see her yourselves?"

The inspector assented. I had already noticed the girl when she was waiting on us at lunch. A tall girl, with a lot of brown hair rolled tightly away at the back of her neck, and very steady grey eyes. She came in answer to the housekeeper's summons, and stood very straight with those same grey eyes fixed on us.

"You are Ursula Bourne?" asked the inspector.

"Yes, sir."

"I understand you are leaving?"

"Yes, sir."

"Why is that?"

"I disarranged some papers on Mr. Ackroyd's desk. He was very angry about it, and I said I had better leave. He told me to go as soon as possible."

"Were you in Mr. Ackroyd's bedroom at all last night? Tidying up or anything?"

"No, sir. That is Elsie's work. I never went near that part of the house."

"I must tell you, my girl, that a large sum of money is missing from Mr. Ackroyd's room."

At last I saw her roused. A wave of colour swept over her face.

"I know nothing about any money. If you think I took it, and that that is why Mr. Ackroyd dismissed me, you are wrong."

"I'm not accusing you of taking it, my girl," said the inspector. "Don't flare up so."

The girl looked at him coldly.

"You can search my things if you like," she said disdainfully. "But you won't find anything."

Poirot suddenly interposed.

"It was yesterday afternoon that Mr. Ackroyd dismissed you—or you dismissed yourself, was it not?" he asked.

The girl nodded.

"How long did the interview last?"

"The interview?"

"Yes, the interview between you and Mr. Ackroyd in the study?"

"I—I don't know."

"Twenty minutes? Half an hour?"

"Something like that."

"Not longer?"

"Not longer than half an hour, certainly."

"Thank you, mademoiselle."

I looked curiously at him. He was rearranging a few objects on the table, setting them straight with precise fingers. His eyes were shining.

"That'll do," said the inspector.

Ursula Bourne disappeared. The inspector turned to Miss Russell.

"How long has she been here? Have you got a copy of the reference you had with her?"

Without answering the first question, Miss Russell moved to an adjacent bureau, opened one of the drawers, and took out a handful of letters clipped together with a patent fastener. She selected one and handed it to the inspector.

"H'm," said he. "Reads all right. Mrs. Richard Folliott, Marby Grange, Marby. Who's this woman?"

"Quite good country people," said Miss Russell.

"Well," said the inspector, handing it back, "let's have a look at the other one, Elsie Dale."

Elsie Dale was a big fair girl, with a pleasant but slightly stupid face. She answered our questions readily enough, and showed much distress and concern at the loss of the money.

"I don't think there's anything wrong with her," observed the inspector, after he had dismissed her. "What about Parker?"

Miss Russell pursed her lips together and made no reply.

"I've a feeling there's something wrong about that man," the inspector continued thoughtfully. "The trouble is that I don't quite see when he got his opportunity. He'd be busy with his duties immediately after dinner, and he'd got a pretty good alibi all through the evening. I know, for I've been devoting particular attention to it. Well, thank you very much, Miss Russell. We'll leave things as they are for the present. It's highly probable Mr. Ackroyd paid that money away himself."

The housekeeper bade us a dry good afternoon, and we took our leave.

I left the house with Poirot.

"I wonder," I said, breaking the silence, "what the papers the girl disarranged could have been for Ackroyd to have got into such a state about them? I wonder if there is any clue there to the mystery."

"The secretary said there were no papers of particular importance on the desk," said Poirot quietly.

"Yes, but—" I paused.

"It strikes you as odd that Ackroyd should have flown into a rage about so trivial a matter?"

"Yes, it does rather."

"But was it a trivial matter?"

"Of course," I admitted, "we don't know what those papers may have been. But Raymond certainly said—"

"Leave M. Raymond out of it for a minute. What did you think of that girl?"

"Which girl? The parlourmaid?"

"Yes, the parlourmaid. Ursula Bourne."

"She seemed a nice girl," I said hesitatingly.

Poirot repeated my words, but whereas I had laid a slight stress on the fourth word, he put it on the second.

"She *seemed* a nice girl—yes."

Then, after a minute's silence, he took something from his pocket and handed it to me.

"See, my friend, I will show you something. Look there."

The paper he had handed me was that compiled by the inspector and given by him to Poirot that morning. Following the pointing finger, I saw a small cross marked in pencil opposite the name Ursula Bourne.

"You may not have noticed it at the time, my good friend, but there was one person on this list whose alibi had no kind of confirmation. Ursula Bourne."

"You don't think—?"

"Dr. Sheppard, I dare to think anything. Ursula Bourne may have killed Mr. Ackroyd, but I confess I can see no motive for her doing so. Can you?"

He looked at me very hard—so hard that I felt uncomfortable.

"Can you?" he repeated.

"No motive whatsoever," I said firmly.

His gaze relaxed. He frowned and murmured to himself:

"Since the blackmailer was a man, it follows that she cannot be the blackmailer, then—"

I coughed.

"As far as that goes—" I began doubtfully.

He spun round on me.

"What? What are you going to say?"

"Nothing, Nothing. Only that, strictly speaking, Mrs. Ferrars in her letter mentioned a *person*—she didn't actually specify a man. But we took it for granted, Ackroyd and I, that it *was* a man."

Poirot did not seem to be listening to me. He was muttering to himself again.

"But then it is possible after all—yes, certainly it is possible—but then—ah! I must rearrange my ideas. Method, order, never have I needed them more. Everything must fit in—in its appointed place—otherwise I am on the wrong track."

He broke off, and whirled round upon me again.

"Where is Marby?"

"It's on the other side of Cranchester."

"How far away?"

"Oh!—fourteen miles, perhaps."

"Would it be possible for you to go there? Tomorrow, say?"

"Tomorrow? Let me see, that's Sunday. Yes, I could arrange it. What do you want me to do there?"

"See this Mrs. Folliott. Find out all you can about Ursula Bourne."

"Very well. But—I don't much care for the job."

"It is not the time to make difficulties. A man's life may hang on this."

"Poor Ralph," I said with a sigh. "You believe him to be innocent, though?"

Poirot looked at me very gravely.

"Do you want to know the truth?"

"Of course."

"Then you shall have it. My friend, everything points to the assumption that he is guilty."

"What!" I exclaimed.

Poirot nodded.

"Yes, that stupid inspector—for he is stupid—has everything pointing his way. I seek for the truth—and the truth leads me every time to Ralph Paton. Motive, opportunity, means. But I will leave no stone unturned. I promised Mademoiselle Flora. And she was very sure, that little one. But very sure indeed."

Eleven

POIROT PAYS A CALL

I was slightly nervous when I rang the bell at Marby Grange the following afternoon. I wondered very much what Poirot expected to find out. He had entrusted the job to me. Why? Was it because, as in the case of questioning Major Blunt, he wished to remain in the background? The wish, intelligible in the first case, seemed to me quite meaningless here.

My meditations were interrupted by the advent of a smart parlourmaid.

Yes, Mrs. Folliott was at home. I was ushered into a big drawing room, and looked round me curiously as I waited for the mistress of the house. A large bare room, some good bits of old china, and some beautiful etchings, shabby covers and curtains. A lady's room in every sense of the term.

I turned from the inspection of a Bartolozzi on the wall as Mrs. Folliott came into the room. She was a tall woman, with untidy brown hair, and a very winning smile.

"Dr. Sheppard," she said hesitatingly.

"That is my name," I replied. "I must apologize for calling upon you like this, but I wanted some information about a parlourmaid previously employed by you, Ursula Bourne."

With the utterance of the name the smile vanished from her face, and all the cordiality froze out of her manner. She looked uncomfortable and ill at ease.

"Ursula Bourne?" she said hesitatingly.

"Yes," I said. "Perhaps you don't remember the name?"

"Oh, yes, of course. I—I remember perfectly."

"She left you just over a year ago, I understand?"

"Yes. Yes, she did. That is quite right."

"And you were satisfied with her whilst she was with you? How long was she with you, by the way?"

"Oh! a year or two—I can't remember exactly how long. She—she is very capable. I'm sure you will find her quite satisfactory. I didn't know she was leaving Fernly. I hadn't the least idea of it."

"Can you tell me anything about her?" I asked.

"Anything about her?"

"Yes, where she comes from, who her people are—that sort of thing?"

Mrs. Folliott's face wore more than ever its frozen look.

"I don't know at all."

"Who was she with before she came to you?"

"I'm afraid I don't remember."

There was a spark of anger now underlying her nervousness. She flung up her head in a gesture that was vaguely familiar.

"Is it really necessary to ask all these questions?"

"Not at all," I said, with an air of surprise and a tinge of apology in my manner. "I had no idea you would mind answering them. I am very sorry."

Her anger left her and she became confused again.

"Oh! I don't mind answering them. I assure you I don't. Why should I? It—it just seemed a little odd, you know. That's all. A little odd."

One advantage of being a medical practitioner is that you can usually tell when people are lying to you. I should have known from Mrs. Folliott's manner, if from nothing else, that she did mind answering my questions—minded intensely. She was thoroughly uncomfortable and upset, and there was plainly some mystery in the background. I judged her to be a woman quite unused to deception of any kind, and consequently rendered acutely uneasy when forced to practise it. A child could have seen through her.

But it was also clear the she had no intention of telling me anything further. Whatever the mystery centring round Ursula Bourne might be, I was not going to learn it through Mrs. Folliott.

Defeated, I apologized once more for disturbing her, took my hat and departed.

I went to see a couple of patients and arrived home about six o'clock. Caroline was sitting beside the wreck of tea things. She had that look of suppressed exultation on her face which I know only too well. It is a sure sign with her of either the getting or the giving of information. I wondered which it had been.

"I've had a very interesting afternoon," began Caroline, as I dropped into my own particular easy chair and stretched out my feet to the inviting blaze in the fireplace.

"Have you?" I said. "Miss Gannett drop in to tea?"

Miss Gannett is one of the chief of our newsmongers.

"Guess again," said Caroline, with intense complacency.

I guessed several times, working slowly through all the members of Caroline's Intelligence Corps. My sister received each guess with a triumphant shake of the head. In the end she volunteered the information herself.

"M. Poirot!" she said. "Now, what do you think of that?"

I thought a good many things of it, but I was careful not to say them to Caroline.

"Why did he come?" I asked.

"To see me, of course. He said that, knowing my brother so well, he hoped he might be permitted to make the acquaintance of his charming sister—your charming sister, I've got mixed up—but you know what I mean."

"What did he talk about?" I asked.

"He told me a lot about himself and his cases. You know that Prince Paul of Mauretania—the one who's just married a dancer?"

"Yes?"

"I saw a most intriguing paragraph about her in *Society Snippets* the other day, hinting that she was really a Russian Grand Duchess—one of the Czar's daughters who managed to escape from the Bolsheviks. Well, it seems that M. Poirot solved a baffling murder mystery that threatened to involve them both. Prince Paul was beside himself with gratitude."

"Did he give him an emerald tie pin the size of a plover's egg?" I inquired sarcastically.

"He didn't mention it. Why?"

"Nothing," I said. "I thought it was always done. It is in detective fiction anyway. The super-detective always has his rooms littered with rubies and pearls and emeralds from grateful Royal clients."

"It's very interesting to hear about these things from the inside," said my sister complacently.

It would be—to Caroline. I could not but admire the ingenuity of M. Hercule Poirot, who had selected unerringly the case of all others that would most appeal to an elderly lady living in a small village.

"Did he tell you if the dancer was really a Grand Duchess?" I inquired.

"He was not at liberty to speak," said Caroline importantly.

I wondered how far Poirot had strained the truth in talking to Caroline—probably not at all. He had conveyed his innuendoes by means of his eyebrows and his shoulders.

"And after all this," I remarked, "I suppose you were ready to eat out of his hand?"

"Don't be coarse, James. I don't know where you get these vulgar expressions from."

"Probably from my only link with the outside world—my patients. Unfortunately, my practice does not lie amongst Royal princes and interesting Russian *émigrés*."

Caroline pushed her spectacles up and looked at me.

"You seem very grumpy, James. It must be your liver. A blue pill, I think, tonight."

To see me in my own home, you would never imagine that I was a doctor of medicine. Caroline does the home prescribing both for herself and me.

"Damn my liver," I said irritably. "Did you talk about the murder at all?"

"Well, naturally, James. What else is there to talk about locally? I was able to set M. Poirot straight upon several points. He was very grateful to me. He said I had the makings of a born detective in me—and a wonderful psychological insight into human nature."

Caroline was exactly like a cat that is full to overflowing with rich cream. She was positively purring.

"He talked a lot about the little grey cells of the brain, and of their functions. His own, he says, are of the first quality."

"He would say so," I remarked bitterly. "Modesty is certainly not his middle name."

"I wish you wouldn't be so horribly American, James. He thought it very important that Ralph should be found as soon as possible, and induced to come forward and give an account of himself. He says that his disappearance will produce a very unfortunate impression at the inquest."

"And what did you say to that?"

"I agreed with him," said Caroline importantly. "And I was able to tell him the way people were talking already about it."

"Caroline," I said sharply, "did you tell M. Poirot what you overheard in the wood that day?"

"I did," said Caroline complacently.

I got up and began to walk about.

"You realize what you're doing, I hope," I jerked out. "You're putting a halter round Ralph Paton's neck as surely as you're sitting in that chair."

"Not at all," said Caroline, quite unruffled. "I was surprised *you* hadn't told him."

"I took very good care not to," I said. "I'm fond of that boy."

"So am I. That's why I say you're talking nonsense. I don't believe Ralph did it, and so the truth can't hurt him, and we ought to give M. Poirot all the help we can. Why, think, very likely Ralph was out with that identical girl on the night of the murder, and if so, he's got a perfect alibi."

"If he's got a perfect alibi," I retorted, "why doesn't he come forward and say so?"

"Might get the girl into trouble," said Caroline sapiently. "But if M. Poirot gets hold of her, and puts it to her as her duty, she'll come forward of her own accord and clear Ralph."

"You seem to have invented a romantic fairy story of your own," I said. "You read too many trashy novels, Caroline. I've always told you so."

I dropped into my chair again.

"Did Poirot ask you any more questions?" I inquired.

"Only about the patients you had that morning."

"The patients?" I demanded, unbelievingly.

"Yes, your surgery patients. How many and who they were."

"Do you mean to say you were able to tell him that?" I demanded.

Caroline is really amazing.

"Why not?" asked my sister triumphantly. "I can see the path up to the surgery door perfectly from this window. And I've got an excellent memory, James. Much better than yours, let me tell you."

"I'm sure you have," I murmured mechanically.

My sister went on, checking the names on her fingers.

"There was old Mrs. Bennett, and that boy from the farm with the bad finger, Dolly Grice to have a needle out of her finger; that American steward off the liner. Let me see—that's four. Yes, and old George Evans with his ulcer. And lastly—"

She paused significantly.

"Well?"

Caroline brought out her climax triumphantly. She hissed it in the most approved style—aided by the fortunate number of s's at her disposal.

"Miss Russell!"

She sat back in her chair and looked at me meaningly, and when Caroline looks at you meaningly, it is impossible to miss it.

"I don't know what you mean," I said, quite untruthfully. "Why shouldn't Miss Russell consult me about her bad knee?"

"Bad knee," said Caroline. "Fiddlesticks! No more bad knee than you and I. She was after something else."

"What?" I asked.

Caroline had to admit that she didn't know.

"But depend upon it, that was what he was trying to get at—M. Poirot, I mean. There's something fishy about that woman, and he knows it."

"Precisely the remark Mrs. Ackroyd made to me yesterday," I said. "That there was something fishy about Miss Russell."

"Ah!" said Caroline darkly, "Mrs. Ackroyd! There's another!"

"Another what?"

Caroline refused to explain her remarks. She merely nodded her head several times, rolling up her knitting, and went upstairs to don the high mauve silk blouse and the gold locket which she calls dressing for dinner.

I stayed there staring into the fire and thinking over Caroline's words. Had Poirot really come to gain information about Miss Russell, or was it only Caroline's tortuous mind that interpreted everything according to her own ideas?

There had certainly been nothing in Miss Russell's manner that morning to arouse suspicion. At least—

I remembered her persistent conversation on the subject of drug-taking—and from that she had led the conversation to poisons and poisoning. But there was nothing in that. Ackroyd had not been poisoned. Still, it was odd. . . .

I heard Caroline's voice, rather acid in tone, calling from the top of the stairs.

"James, you will be late for dinner."

I put some coal on the fire and went upstairs obediently.

It is well at any price to have peace in the home.

Twelve

ROUND THE TABLE

A joint inquest was held on Monday.

I do not propose to give the proceedings in detail. To do so would only be to go over the same ground again and again. By arrangement with the police, very little was allowed to come out. I gave evidence as to the cause of Ackroyd's death and the probable time. The absence of Ralph Paton was commented on by the coroner, but not unduly stressed.

Afterwards, Poirot and I had a few words with Inspector Raglan. The inspector was very grave.

"It looks bad, M. Poirot," he said. "I'm trying to judge the thing fair and square. I'm a local man, and I've seen Captain Paton many times in Cranchester. I'm not wanting him to be the guilty one—but it's bad whichever way you look at it. If he's innocent, why doesn't he come forward? We've got evidence against him, but it's just possible that the evidence could be explained away. Then why doesn't he give an explanation?"

A lot more lay behind the inspector's words than I knew at the time. Ralph's description had been wired to every port and railway station in England. The police everywhere were on the alert. His rooms in town were watched, and any houses he had been known to be in the habit of frequenting. With such a *cordon* it seemed impossible that Ralph should be able to evade detection. He had no luggage, and, as far as anyone knew, no money.

"I can't find anyone who saw him at the station that night," continued the inspector. "And yet he's well known down here, and you'd think somebody would have noticed him. There's no news from Liverpool either."

"You think he went to Liverpool?" queried Poirot.

"Well, it's on the cards. That telephone message from the station, just three minutes before the Liverpool express left—there ought to be something in that."

"Unless it was deliberately intended to throw you off the scent. That might just possibly be the point of the telephone message."

"That's an idea," said the inspector eagerly. "Do you really think that's the explanation of the telephone call?"

"My friend," said Poirot gravely, "I do not know. But I will tell you this: I believe that when we find the explanation of that telephone call we shall find the explanation of the murder."

"You said something like that before, I remember," I observed, looking at him curiously.

Poirot nodded.

"I always come back to it," he said seriously.

"It seems to me utterly irrelevant," I declared.

"I wouldn't say that," demurred the inspector. "But I must confess I think Mr. Poirot here harps on it a little too much. We've better clues than that. The fingerprints on the dagger, for instance."

Poirot became suddenly very foreign in manner, as he often did when excited over anything.

"M. l'Inspecteur," he said, "beware of the blind—the blind—*comment dire?*—the little street that has no end to it."

Inspector Raglan stared, but I was quicker.

"You mean a blind alley?" I said.

"That is it—the blind street that leads nowhere. So it may be with those fingerprints—they may lead you nowhere."

"I don't see how that can well be," said the police officer. "I suppose you're hinting that they're faked? I've read of such things being done, though I can't say I've ever come across it in my experience. But fake or true—they're bound to lead *somewhere.*"

Poirot merely shrugged his shoulders, flinging out his arms wide.

The inspector then showed us various enlarged photographs of the finger-prints, and proceeded to become technical on the subject of loops and whorls.

"Come now," he said at last, annoyed by Poirot's detached manner, "you've got to admit that those prints were made by someone who was in the house that night?"

"*Bien entendu,*" said Poirot, nodding his head.

"Well, I've taken the prints of every member of the household, everyone, mind you, from the old lady down to the kitchen maid."

I don't think Mrs. Ackroyd would enjoy being referred to as the old lady. She must spend a considerable amount on cosmetics.

"Everyone's," repeated the inspector fussily.

"Including mine," I said drily.

"Very well. None of them correspond. That leaves us two alternatives. Ralph Paton, or the mysterious stranger the doctor here tells us about. When we get hold of those two—"

"Much valuable time may have been lost," broke in Poirot.

"I don't quite get you, Mr. Poirot."

"You have taken the prints of everyone in the house, you say," murmured Poirot. "Is that the exact truth you are telling me there, M. l'Inspecteur?"

"Certainly."

"Without overlooking anyone?"

"Without overlooking anyone."

"The quick or the dead?"

For a moment the inspector looked bewildered at what he took to be a re-ligious observation. Then he reacted slowly.

"You mean—?"

"The dead, M. l'Inspecteur."

The inspector still took a minute or two to understand.

"I am suggesting," said Poirot placidly, "that the fingerprints on the dagger handle are those of Mr. Ackroyd himself. It is an easy matter to verify. His body is still available."

"But why? What would be the point of it? You're surely not suggesting suicide, Mr. Poirot?"

"Ah! no. My theory is that the murderer wore gloves or wrapped something round his hand. After the blow was struck, he picked up the victim's hand and closed it round the dagger handle."

"But why?"

Poirot shrugged his shoulders again.

"To make a confusing case even more confusing."

"Well," said the inspector. "I'll look into it. What gave you the idea in the first place?"

"When you were so kind as to show me the dagger and draw attention to the fingerprints. I know very little of loops and whorls—see, I confess my ignorance frankly. But it did occur to me that the position of the prints was somewhat awkward. Not so would I have held a dagger in order to strike. Naturally, with the right hand brought up over the shoulder backwards, it would have been difficult to put it in exactly the right position."

Inspector Raglan stared at the little man. Poirot, with an air of great unconcern, flecked a speck of dust from his coat sleeve.

"Well," said the inspector. "It's an idea. I'll look into it all right, but don't you be disappointed if nothing comes of it."

He endeavoured to make his tone kindly and patronising. Poirot watched him go off. Then he turned to me with twinkling eyes.

"Another time," he observed, "I must be more careful of his *amour propre*. And now that we are left to our own devices, what do you think, my good friend, of a little reunion of the family?"

The "little reunion," as Poirot called it, took place about half an hour later. We sat round the table in the dining room at Fernly. Poirot at the head of the table, like the chairman of some ghastly board meeting. The servants were not present, so we were six in all. Mrs. Ackroyd, Flora, Major Blunt, young Raymond, Poirot and myself.

When everyone was assembled, Poirot rose and bowed.

"Messieurs, mesdames, I have called you together for a certain purpose." He paused. "To begin with, I want to make a very special plea to mademoiselle."

"To me?" said Flora.

"Mademoiselle, you are engaged to Captain Ralph Paton. If anyone is in his confidence, you are. I beg you, most earnestly, if you know of his whereabouts, to persuade him to come forward. One little minute"—as Flora raised her head to speak—"say nothing till you have well reflected. Mademoiselle, his position grows daily more dangerous. If he had come forward at once, no matter how damning the facts, he might have had a chance of explaining them away. But this silence—this flight—what can it mean? Surely only one thing, knowledge of guilt. Mademoiselle, if you really believe in his innocence, persuade him to come forward before it is too late."

Flora's face had gone very white.

"Too late!" she repeated, very low.

Poirot leant forward, looking at her.

"See now, mademoiselle," he said very gently, "it is Papa Poirot who asks you this. The old Papa Poirot who has much knowledge and much experience. I would not seek to entrap you, mademoiselle. Will you not trust me—and tell me where Ralph Paton is hiding?"

The girl rose and stood facing him.

"M. Poirot," she said in a clear voice, "I swear to you—swear solemnly—that I have no idea where Ralph is, and that I have neither seen him nor heard from him either on the day of—of the murder, or since."

She sat down again. Poirot gazed at her in silence for a minute or two, then he brought his hand down on the table with a sharp rap.

"*Bien!* That is that," he said. His face hardened. "Now I appeal to these others who sit round this table, Mrs. Ackroyd, Major Blunt, Dr. Sheppard, Mr. Raymond. You are all friends and intimates of the missing man. If you know where Ralph Paton is hiding, speak out."

There was a long silence. Poirot looked to each in turn.

"I beg of you," he said in a low voice, "speak out."

But still there was silence, broken at last by Mrs. Ackroyd.

"I must say," she observed in a plaintive voice, "that Ralph's absence is most peculiar—most peculiar indeed. Not to come forward at such a time. It looks, you know, as though there were something *behind* it. I can't help thinking, Flora dear, that it was a very fortunate thing your engagement was never formally announced."

"Mother!" cried Flora angrily.

"Providence," declared Mrs. Ackroyd. "I have a devout belief in Providence—a divinity that shapes our ends, as Shakespeare's beautiful line runs."

"Surely you don't make the Almighty directly responsible for thick ankles, Mrs. Ackroyd, do you?" asked Geoffrey Raymond, his irresponsible laugh ringing out.

His idea was, I think, to loosen the tension, but Mrs. Ackroyd threw him a glance of reproach and took out her handkerchief.

"Flora has been saved a terrible amount of notoriety and unpleasantness. Not for a moment that I think dear Ralph had anything to do with poor Roger's death. I *don't* think so. But then I have a trusting heart—I always have had, ever since a child. I am loath to believe the worst of anyone. But, of course, one must remember that Ralph was in several air raids as a young boy. The results are apparent long after, sometimes, they say. People are not responsible for their actions in the least. They lose control, you know, without being able to help it."

"Mother," cried Flora, "you don't think Ralph did it?"

"Come, Mrs. Ackroyd," said Blunt.

"I don't know what to think," said Mrs. Ackroyd tearfully. "It's all very upsetting. What would happen to the estate, I wonder, if Ralph were found guilty?"

Raymond pushed his chair away from the table violently. Major Blunt remained very quiet, looking thoughtfully at her.

"Like shell shock, you know," said Mrs. Ackroyd obstinately, "and I dare say Roger kept him very short of money—with the best intentions, of course. I can see you are all against me, but I do think it is very odd that Ralph has not come forward, and I must say I am thankful Flora's engagement was never announced formally."

"It will be tomorrow," said Flora in a clear voice.

"Flora!" cried her mother, aghast.

Flora had turned to the secretary.

"Will you send the announcement to the *Morning Post*. And *The Times*, please, Mr. Raymond."

"If you are sure that it is wise, Miss Ackroyd," he replied gravely.

She turned impulsively to Blunt.

"You understand," she said. "What else can I do? As things are, I must stand by Ralph. Don't you see that I must?"

She looked very searchingly at him, and after a long pause he nodded abruptly.

Mrs. Ackroyd burst out into shrill protests. Flora remained unmoved. Then Raymond spoke.

"I appreciate your motives, Miss Ackroyd. But don't you think you're being rather precipitate? Wait a day or two."

"Tomorrow," said Flora in a clear voice. "It's no good, Mother, going on like this. Whatever else I am, I'm not disloyal to my friends."

"M. Poirot," Mrs. Ackroyd appealed tearfully. "Can't you say anything at all?"

"Nothing to be said," interpolated Blunt. "She's doing the right thing. I'll stand by her through thick and thin."

Flora held out her hand to him.

"Thank you, Major Blunt," she said.

"Mademoiselle," said Poirot, "will you let an old man congratulate you on your courage and your loyalty? And will you not misunderstand me if I ask you—ask you most solemnly—to postpone the announcement you speak of for at least two days more?"

Flora hesitated.

"I ask it in Ralph Paton's interests as much as in yours, mademoiselle. You frown. You do not see how that can be. But I assure you that it is so. *Pas de blagues.* You put the case into my hands—you must not hamper me now."

Flora paused a few minutes before replying.

"I do not like it," she said at last, "but I will do what you say."

She sat down again at the table.

"And now, messieurs et mesdames," said Poirot rapidly, "I will continue with what I was about to say. Understand this, I mean to arrive at the truth. The truth, however ugly in itself, is always curious and beautiful to the seeker after it. I am much aged, my powers may not be what they were." Here he clearly expected a contradiction. "In all probability this is the last case I shall ever investigate. But Hercule Poirot does not end with a failure. Messieurs et mesdames, I tell you, I mean to *know*. And I shall know—in spite of you all."

He brought out the last words provocatively, hurling them in our face as it were. I think we all flinched back a little, excepting Geoffrey Raymond, who remained good-humoured and imperturbable as usual.

"How do you mean—in spite of us all?" he asked, with slightly raised eyebrows.

"But—just that, monsieur. Every one of you in this room is concealing something from me." He raised his hand as a faint murmur of protest arose. "Yes, yes, I know what I am saying. It may be something unimportant— trivial—which is supposed to have no bearing on the case, but there it is. *Each one of you has something to hide.* Come now, am I right?"

His glance, challenging and accusing, swept round the table. And every pair of eyes dropped before his. Yes, mine as well.

"I am answered," said Poirot, with a curious laugh. He got up from his seat. "I appeal to you all. Tell me the truth—the whole truth." There was a silence. "Will no one speak?"

He gave the same short laugh again.

"*C'est dommage,*" he said, and went out.

Thirteen

The Goose Quill

That evening, at Poirot's request, I went over to his house after dinner. Caroline saw me depart with visible reluctance. I think she would have liked to have accompanied me.

Poirot greeted me hospitably. He had placed a bottle of Irish whiskey (which I detest) on a small table, with a soda water siphon and a glass. He himself was engaged in brewing hot chocolate. It was a favourite beverage of his, I discovered later.

He inquired politely after my sister, whom he declared to be a most interesting woman.

"I'm afraid you've been giving her a swelled head," I said drily. "What about Sunday afternoon?"

He laughed and twinkled.

"I always like to employ the expert," he remarked obscurely, but he refused to explain the remark.

"You got all the local gossip anyway," I remarked. "True, and untrue."

"And a great deal of valuable information," he added quietly.

"Such as—"

He shook his head.

"Why not have told me the truth?" he countered. "In a place like this, all Ralph Paton's doings were bound to be known. If your sister had not happened to pass through the wood that day somebody else would have done so."

"I suppose they would," I said grumpily. "What about this interest of yours in my patients?"

Again he twinkled.

"Only one of them, doctor. Only one of them."

"The last?" I hazarded.

"I find Miss Russell a study of the most interesting," he said evasively.

"Do you agree with my sister and Mrs. Ackroyd that there is something fishy about her?" I asked.

"Eh? What do you say—fishy?"

I explained to the best of my ability.

"And they say that, do they?"

"Didn't my sister convey as much to you yesterday afternoon?"

"*C'est possible.*"

"For no reason whatever," I declared.

"*Les femmes,*" generalized Poirot. "They are marvellous! They invent haphazard—and by miracle they are right. Not that it is that, really. Women observe subconsciously a thousand little details, without knowing that they are doing so. Their subconscious mind adds these little things together—and they call the result intuition. Me, I am very skilled in psychology. I know these things."

He swelled his chest out importantly, looking so ridiculous that I found it difficult not to burst out laughing. Then he took a small sip of his chocolate, and carefully wiped his moustache.

"I wish you'd tell me," I burst out, "what you really think of it all?"

He put down his cup.

"You wish that?"

"I do."

"You have seen what I have seen. Should not our ideas be the same?"

"I'm afraid you're laughing at me," I said stiffly. "Of course, I've no experience of matters of this kind."

Poirot smiled at me indulgently.

"You are like the little child who wants to know the way the engine works. You wish to see the affair, not as the family doctor sees it, but with the eye of a detective who knows and cares for no one—to whom they are all strangers and all equally liable to suspicion."

"You put it very well," I said.

"So I give you, then, a little lecture. The first thing is to get a clear history of what happened that evening—always bearing in mind that the person who speaks may be lying."

I raised my eyebrows.

"Rather a suspicious attitude."

"But necessary—I assure you, necessary. Now first—Dr. Sheppard leaves the house at ten minutes to nine. How do I know that?"

"Because I told you so."

"But you might not be speaking the truth—or the watch you went by might be wrong. But Parker also says that you left the house at ten minutes to nine. So we accept that statement and pass on. At nine o'clock you run into a man—and here we come to what we will call the Romance of the Mysterious Stranger—just outside the Park gates. How do I know that that is so?"

"I told you so," I began again, but Poirot interrupted me with a gesture of impatience.

"Ah! but it is that you are a little stupid tonight, my friend. *You* know that it is so—but how am *I* to know? *Eh bien,* I am able to tell you that the Mysterious Stranger was not a hallucination on your part, because the maid of a Miss Gannett met him a few minutes before you did, and of her too he inquired the way to Fernly Park. We accept his presence, therefore, and we can be fairly sure of two things about him—that he was a stranger to the neighbourhood, and that whatever his object in going to Fernly, there was no great secrecy about it, since he twice asked the way there."

"Yes," I said, "I see that."

"Now I have made it my business to find out more about this man. He had a drink at the Three Boars, I learn, and the barmaid there says that he spoke with an American accent and mentioned having just come over from the States. Did it strike you that he had an American accent?"

"Yes, I think he had," I said, after a minute or two, during which I cast my mind back; "but a very slight one."

"*Précisément.* There is also this, which, you will remember, I picked up in the summerhouse."

He held out to me the little quill. I looked at it curiously. Then a memory of something I had read stirred in me.

Poirot, who had been watching my face, nodded.

"Yes, heroin, 'snow.' Drug-takers carry it like this, and sniff it up the nose."

"Diamorphine hydrochloride," I murmured mechanically.

"This method of taking the drug is very common on the other side. Another proof, if we wanted one, that the man came from Canada or the States."

"What first attracted your attention to that summerhouse?" I asked curiously.

"My friend the inspector took it for granted that anyone using that path did so as a short cut to the house, but as soon as I saw the summerhouse, I realized that the same path would be taken by anyone using the summerhouse as a rendezvous. Now it seems fairly certain that the stranger came neither to the front nor to the back door. Then did someone from the house go out and meet him? If so, what could be a more convenient place than that little summerhouse? I searched it with the hope that I might find some clue inside. I found two, the scrap of cambric and the quill."

"And the scrap of cambric?" I asked curiously. "What about that?"

Poirot raised his eyebrows.

"You do not use your little grey cells," he remarked drily. "The scrap of starched cambric should be obvious."

"Not very obvious to me." I changed the subject. "Anyway," I said, "this man went to the summerhouse to meet somebody. Who was that somebody?"

"Exactly the question," said Poirot. "You will remember that Mrs. Ackroyd and her daughter came over from Canada to live here?"

"Is that what you meant today when you accused them of hiding the truth?"

"Perhaps. Now another point. What did you think of the parlourmaid's story?"

"What story?"

"The story of her dismissal. Does it take half an hour to dismiss a servant? Was the story of those important papers a likely one? And remember, though she says she was in her bedroom from nine-thirty until ten o'clock, there is no one to confirm her statement."

"You bewilder me," I said.

"To me it grows clearer. But tell me now your own ideas and theories."

I drew a piece of paper from my pocket.

"I just scribbled down a few suggestions," I said apologetically.

"But excellent—you have method. Let us hear them."

I read out in a somewhat embarrassed voice.

"To begin with, one must look at the thing logically—"

"Just what my poor Hastings used to say," interrupted Poirot, "but alas! he never did so."

"*Point No. 1.*—Mr. Ackroyd was heard talking to someone at half past nine.

"*Point No. 2.*—At some time during the evening Ralph Paton must have come in through the window, as evidenced by the prints of his shoes.

"*Point No. 3.*—Mr. Ackroyd was nervous that evening, and would only have admitted someone he knew.

"*Point No. 4.*—The person with Mr. Ackroyd at nine-thirty was asking for money. We know Ralph Paton was in a scrape.

"*These four points go to show that the person with Mr. Ackroyd at nine-thirty was Ralph Paton. But we know that Mr. Ackroyd was alive at a quarter to ten, therefore it was not Ralph who killed him. Ralph left the window open. Afterwards the murderer came in that way.*"

"And who was the murderer?" inquired Poirot.

"The American stranger. He may have been in league with Parker, and possibly in Parker we have the man who blackmailed Mrs. Ferrars. If so, Parker may have heard enough to realize the game was up, have told his accomplice so, and the latter did the crime with the dagger which Parker gave him."

"It is a theory that," admitted Poirot. "Decidedly you have cells of a kind. But it leaves a good deal unaccounted for."

"Such as—"

"The telephone call, the pushed-out chair—"

"Do you really think that latter important?" I interrupted.

"Perhaps not," admitted my friend. "It may have been pulled out by accident, and Raymond or Blunt may have shoved it into place unconsciously under the stress of emotion. Then there is the missing forty pounds."

"Given by Ackroyd to Ralph," I suggested. "He may have reconsidered his first refusal."

"That still leaves one thing unexplained."

"What?"

"Why was Blunt so certain in his own mind that it was Raymond with Mr. Ackroyd at nine-thirty?"

"He explained that," I said.

"You think so? I will not press the point. Tell me, instead, what were Ralph Paton's reasons for disappearing?"

"That's rather more difficult," I said slowly. "I shall have to speak as a medical man. Ralph's nerves must have gone phut! If he suddenly found out that his uncle had been murdered within a few minutes of his leaving him—after, perhaps, a rather stormy interview—well, he might get the wind up and clear right out. Men have been known to do that—act guiltily when they're perfectly innocent."

"Yes, that is true," said Poirot. "But we must not lose sight of one thing."

"I know what you're going to say," I remarked: "motive. Ralph Paton inherits a great fortune by his uncle's death."

"That is one motive," agreed Poirot.

"One?"

"Mais oui. Do you realize that there are three separate motives staring us in the face. Somebody certainly stole the blue envelope and its contents. That is one motive. Blackmail! Ralph Paton may have been the man who blackmailed Mrs. Ferrars. Remember, as far as Hammond knew, Ralph Paton had not applied to his uncle for help of late. That looks as though he were being supplied with money elsewhere. Then there is the fact that he was in some—how do you say—scrape?—which he feared might get to his uncle's ears. And finally there is the one you have just mentioned."

"Dear me," I said, rather taken aback. "The case does seem black against him."

"Does it?" said Poirot. "That is where we disagree, you and I. Three motives—it is almost too much. I am inclined to believe that, after all, Ralph Paton is innocent."

Fourteen

MRS. ACKROYD

After the evening talk I have just chronicled, the affair seemed to me to enter on a different phase. The whole thing can be divided into two parts, each clear and distinct from the other. Part I ranges from Ackroyd's death on the Friday evening to the following Monday night. It is the straightforward narrative of what occurred, as presented to Hercule Poirot. I was at Poirot's elbow the whole time. I saw what he saw. I tried my best to read his mind. As I know now, I failed in this latter task. Though Poirot showed me all his discoveries—as, for instance, the gold wedding-ring—he held back the vital and yet logical impressions that he formed. As I came to know later, this secrecy was characteristic of him. He would throw out hints and suggestions, but beyond that he would not go.

As I say, up till the Monday evening, my narrative might have been that of Poirot himself. I played Watson to his Sherlock. But after Monday our ways diverged. Poirot was busy on his own account. I got to hear of what he was doing, because in King's Abbot you get to hear of everything, but he did not take me into his confidence beforehand. And I, too, had my own preoccupations.

On looking back, the thing that strikes me most is the piecemeal character of this period. Everyone had a hand in the elucidation of the mystery. It was rather like a jig-saw puzzle to which everyone contributed their own little piece of knowledge or discovery. But their task ended there. To Poirot alone belongs the renown of fitting those pieces into their correct place.

Some of the incidents seemed at the time irrelevant and unmeaning. There was, for instance, the question of the black boots. But that comes later. . . . To take things strictly in chronological order, I must begin with the summons from Mrs. Ackroyd.

She sent for me early on Tuesday morning, and since the summons sounded an urgent one, I hastened there, expecting to find her *in extremis.*

The lady was in bed. So much did she concede to the etiquette of the situation. She gave me her bony hand, and indicated a chair drawn up to the bedside.

"Well, Mrs. Ackroyd," I said, "and what's the matter with you?"

I spoke with that kind of spurious geniality which seems to be expected of general practitioners.

"I'm prostrated," said Mrs. Ackroyd in a faint voice. "Absolutely prostrated. It's the shock of poor Roger's death. They say these things often aren't felt at the *time,* you know. It's the reaction afterwards."

It is a pity that a doctor is precluded by his profession from being able sometimes to say what he really thinks.

I would have given anything to be able to answer "Bunkum!"

Instead, I suggested a tonic. Mrs. Ackroyd accepted the tonic. One move in the game seemed now to be concluded. Not for a moment did I imagine that I had been sent for because of the shock occasioned by Ackroyd's death. But Mrs. Ackroyd is totally incapable of pursuing a straightforward course on any subject. She always approaches her object by tortuous means. I wondered very much why it was she had sent for me.

"And then that scene—yesterday," continued my patient.

She paused as though expecting me to take up a cue.

"What scene?"

"Doctor, how can you? Have you forgotten? That dreadful little Frenchman—or Belgian—or whatever he is. Bullying us all like he did. It has quite upset me. Coming on the top of Roger's death."

"I'm very sorry, Mrs. Ackroyd," I said.

"I don't know what he meant—shouting at us like he did. I should hope I know my duty too well to *dream* of concealing anything. I have given the police *every* assistance in my power."

Mrs. Ackroyd paused, and I said, "Quite so." I was beginning to have a glimmering of what all the trouble was about.

"No one can say that I have failed in my duty," continued Mrs. Ackroyd. "I am sure Inspector Raglan is perfectly satisfied. Why should this little upstart of a foreigner make a fuss? A most ridiculous-looking creature he is too—just like a comic Frenchman in a revue. I can't think why Flora insisted on bringing him into the case. She never said a word to me about it. Just went off and did it on her own. Flora is too independent. I am a woman of the world and her mother. She should have come to me for advice first."

I listened to all this in silence.

"What does he think? That's what I want to know. Does he actually imagine I'm hiding something? He—he—positively *accused* me yesterday."

I shrugged my shoulders.

"It is surely of no consequence, Mrs. Ackroyd," I said. "Since you are not concealing anything, any remarks he may have made do not apply to you."

Mrs. Ackroyd went off at a tangent, after her usual fashion.

"Servants are so tiresome," she said. "They gossip, and talk amongst themselves. And then it gets round—and all the time there's probably nothing in it at all."

"Have the servants been talking?" I asked. "What about?"

Mrs. Ackroyd cast a very shrewd glance at me. It quite threw me off my balance.

"I was sure *you'd* know, doctor, if anyone did. You were with M. Poirot all the time, weren't you?"

"I was."

"Then of course you know. It was that girl, Ursula Bourne, wasn't it? Naturally—she's leaving. She *would* want to make all the trouble she could. Spiteful, that's what they are. They're all alike. Now, you being there, doctor, you must know exactly what she did say? I'm most anxious that no wrong impression should get about. After all, you don't repeat every little detail to the police, do you? There are family matters sometimes—nothing to do with the question of the murder. But if the girl was spiteful, she may have made out all sorts of things."

I was shrewd enough to see that a very real anxiety lay behind these outpourings. Poirot had been justified in his premises. Of the six people round the table yesterday, Mrs. Ackroyd at least had had something to hide. It was for me to discover what that something might be.

"If I were you, Mrs. Ackroyd," I said brusquely, "I should make a clean breast of things."

She gave a little scream.

"Oh! doctor, how can you be so abrupt. It sounds as though—as though— And I can explain everything so simply."

"Then why not do so?" I suggested.

Mrs. Ackroyd took out a frilled handkerchief, and became tearful.

"I thought, doctor, that you might put it to M. Poirot—explain it, you know—because it's so difficult for a foreigner to see our point of view. And you don't know—nobody could know—what I've had to contend with. A martyrdom—a long martyrdom. That's what my life has been. I don't like to speak ill of the dead—but there it is. Not the smallest bill but it had all to be gone over—just as though Roger had had a few miserly hundreds a year instead of being (as Mr. Hammond told me yesterday) one of the wealthiest men in these parts."

Mrs. Ackroyd paused to dab her eyes with the frilled handkerchief.

"Yes," I said encouragingly. "You were talking about bills?"

"Those dreadful bills. And some I didn't like to show Roger at all. They were things a man wouldn't understand. He would have said the things weren't necessary. And of course they mounted up, you know, and they kept coming in—"

She looked at me appealingly, as though asking me to condole with her on this striking peculiarity.

"It's a habit they have," I agreed.

And the tone altered—became quite abusive. "I assure you, doctor, I was becoming a nervous wreck. I couldn't sleep at nights. And a dreadful fluttering round the heart. And then I got a letter from a Scotch gentleman—as a matter of fact there were two letters—both Scotch gentlemen. Mr. Bruce MacPherson was one, and the other was Colin MacDonald. Quite a coincidence."

"Hardly that," I said drily. "They are usually Scotch gentlemen, but I suspect a Semitic strain in their ancestry."

"Ten pounds to ten thousand on note of hand alone," murmured Mrs. Ackroyd reminiscently. "I wrote to one of them, but it seemed there were difficulties."

She paused.

I gathered that we were just coming to delicate ground. I have never known anyone more difficult to bring to the point.

"You see," murmured Mrs. Ackroyd, "it's all a question of expectations, isn't it? Testamentary expectations. And though, of course, I expected that Roger would provide for me, I didn't *know.* I thought that if only I could glance over a copy of his will—not in any sense of vulgar prying—but just so that I could make my own arrangements."

She glanced sideways at me. The position was now very delicate indeed. Fortunately words, ingeniously used, will serve to mask the ugliness of naked facts.

"I could only tell this to you, dear Doctor Sheppard," said Mrs. Ackroyd rapidly. "I can trust you not to misjudge me, and to represent the matter in the right light to M. Poirot. It was on Friday afternoon—"

She came to a stop and swallowed uncertainly.

"Yes," I repeated encouragingly. "On Friday afternoon. Well?"

"Everyone was out, or so I thought. And I went into Roger's study—I had some real reason for going there—I mean, there was nothing underhand about it. And as I saw all the papers heaped on the desk, it just came to me, like a flash: 'I wonder if Roger keeps his will in one of the drawers of the desk.' I'm so impulsive, always was, from a child. I do things on the spur of the moment. He'd left his keys—very careless of him—in the lock of the top drawer."

"I see," I said helpfully. "So you searched the desk. Did you find the will?"

Mrs. Ackroyd gave a little scream, and I realized that I had not been sufficiently diplomatic.

"How dreadful it sounds. But it wasn't at all like that really."

"Of course it wasn't," I said hastily. "You must forgive my unfortunate way of putting things."

"Of course, men are so peculiar. In dear Roger's place, I should have not objected to revealing the provisions of my will. But men are so secretive. One is forced to adopt little subterfuges in self-defence."

"And the result of the little subterfuge?" I asked.

"That's just what I'm telling you. As I got to the bottom drawer, Bourne came in. Most awkward. Of course I shut the drawer and stood up, and I called her attention to a few specks of dust on the surface. But I didn't like the way she looked—quite respectful in manner, but a very nasty light in her eyes. Almost contemptuous, if you know what I mean. I never have liked that girl very much. She's a good servant, and she says Ma'am, and doesn't object to wearing caps and aprons (which I declare to you a lot of them do nowadays), and she can say 'Not at home' without scruples if she has to answer the door instead of Parker, and she doesn't have those peculiar gurgling noises inside which so many parlourmaids seem to have when they wait at table—Let me see, where was I?"

"You were saying, that in spite of several valuable qualities, you never liked Bourne."

"No more I do. She's—odd. There's something different about her from the others. Too well educated, that's my opinion. You can't tell who are ladies and who aren't nowadays."

"And what happened next?" I asked.

"Nothing. At last, Roger came in. And I thought he was out for a walk. And he said: 'What's all this?' and I said, 'Nothing. I just came in to fetch *Punch*.' And I took *Punch* and went out with it. Bourne stayed behind. I heard her asking Roger if she could speak to him for a minute. I went straight up to my room, to lie down. I was very upset."

There was a pause.

"You will explain to M. Poirot, won't you? You can see for yourself what a trivial matter the whole thing was. But, of course, when he was so stern about concealing things, I thought of this at once. Bourne may have made some extraordinary story out of it, but you can explain, can't you?"

"That is all?" I said. "You have told me everything?"

"Ye-es," said Mrs. Ackroyd. "Oh! yes," she added firmly.

But I had noted the momentary hesitation, and I knew that there was still something she was keeping back. It was nothing less than a flash of sheer genius that prompted me to ask the question I did.

"Mrs. Ackroyd," I said, "was it you who left the silver table open?"

I had my answer in the blush of guilt that even rouge and powder could not conceal.

"How did you know?" she whispered.

"It was you, then?"

"Yes—I—you see—there were one or two pieces of old silver—very interesting. I had been reading up the subject and there was an illustration of quite a small piece which had fetched an immense sum at Christy's. It looked to be just the same as the one in the silver table. I thought I would take it up to London with me when I went—and—and have it valued. Then if it really was a valuable piece, just think what a charming surprise it would have been for Roger."

I refrained from comments, accepting Mrs. Ackroyd's story on its merits. I even forbore to ask her why it was necessary to abstract what she wanted in such a surreptitious manner.

"Why did you leave the lid open?" I asked. "Did you forget?"

"I was startled," said Mrs. Ackroyd. "I heard footsteps coming along the terrace outside. I hastened out of the room and just got up the stairs before Parker opened the front door to you."

"That must have been Miss Russell," I said thoughtfully. Mrs. Ackroyd had revealed to me one fact that was extremely interesting. Whether her designs upon Ackroyd's silver had been strictly honourable I neither knew nor cared. What did interest me was the fact that Miss Russell must have entered the drawing room by the window, and that I had not been wrong when I judged her to be out of breath with running. Where had she been? I thought of the summerhouse and the scrap of cambric.

"I wonder if Miss Russell has had her handkerchiefs starched!" I exclaimed on the spur of the moment.

Mrs. Ackroyd's start recalled me to myself, and I rose.

"You think you can explain to M. Poirot?" she asked anxiously.

"Oh, certainly. Absolutely."

I got away at last, after being forced to listen to more justifications of her conduct.

The parlourmaid was in the hall, and it was she who helped me on with my overcoat. I observed her more closely than I had done heretofore. It was clear that she had been crying.

"How is it," I asked, "that you told us that Mr. Ackroyd sent for you on Friday to his study? I hear now that it was *you* who asked to speak to *him*."

For a minute the girl's eyes dropped before mine.

Then she spoke.

"I meant to leave in any case," she said uncertainly.

I said no more. She opened the front door for me. Just as I was passing out, she said suddenly in a low voice:

"Excuse me, sir, is there any news of Captain Paton?"

I shook my head, looking at her inquiringly.

"He ought to come back," she said. "Indeed—indeed he ought to come back."

She was looking at me with appealing eyes.

"Does no one know where he is?" she asked.

"Do you?" I said sharply.

She shook her head.

"No, indeed. I know nothing. But anyone who was a friend to him would tell him this: he ought to come back."

I lingered, thinking that perhaps the girl would say more. Her next question surprised me.

"When do they think the murder was done? Just before ten o'clock?"

"That is the idea," I said. "Between a quarter to ten and the hour."

"Not earlier? Not before a quarter to ten?"

I looked at her attentively. She was so clearly eager for a reply in the affirmative.

"That's out of the question," I said. "Miss Ackroyd saw her uncle alive at a quarter to ten."

She turned away, and her whole figure seemed to droop.

"A handsome girl," I said to myself as I drove off. "An exceedingly handsome girl."

Caroline was at home. She had had a visit from Poirot and was very pleased and important about it.

"I am helping him with the case," she explained.

I felt rather uneasy. Caroline is bad enough as it is. What will she be like with her detective instincts encouraged?

"Are you going round the neighbourhood looking for Ralph Paton's mysterious girl?" I inquired.

"I might do that on my own account," said Caroline. "No, this is a special thing M. Poirot wants me to find out for him."

"What is it?" I asked.

"He wants to know whether Ralph Paton's boots were black or brown," said Caroline with tremendous solemnity.

I stared at her. I see now that I was unbelievably stupid about these boots. I failed altogether to grasp the point.

"They were brown shoes," I said. "I saw them."

"Not shoes, James, boots. M. Poirot wants to know whether a pair of boots Ralph had with him at the hotel were brown or black. A lot hangs on it."

Call me dense if you like. I didn't see.

"And how are you going to find out?" I asked.

Caroline said there would be no difficulty about that. Our Annie's dearest friend was Miss Gannett's maid, Clara. And Clara was walking out with the Boots at the Three Boars. The whole thing was simplicity itself, and by the aid of Miss Gannett, who cooperated loyally, at once giving Clara leave of absence, the matter was rushed through at express speed.

It was when we were sitting down to lunch that Caroline remarked, with would-be unconcern:

"About those boots of Ralph Paton's."

"Well," I said, "what about them?"

"M. Poirot thought they were probably brown. He was wrong. They're black."

And Caroline nodded her head several times. She evidently felt that she had scored a point over Poirot.

I did not answer. I was puzzling over what the colour of a pair of Ralph Paton's boots had to do with the case.

Fifteen

GEOFFREY RAYMOND

I was to have a further proof that day of the success of Poirot's tactics. That challenge of his had been a subtle touch born of his knowledge of human nature. A mixture of fear and guilt had wrung the truth from Mrs. Ackroyd. She was the first to react.

That afternoon when I returned from seeing my patients, Caroline told me that Geoffrey Raymond had just left.

"Did he want to see me?" I asked, as I hung up my coat in the hall.

Caroline was hovering by my elbow.

"It was M. Poirot he wanted to see," she said. "He'd just come from The Larches. M. Poirot was out. Mr. Raymond thought that he might be here, or that you might know where he was."

"I haven't the least idea."

"I tried to make him wait," said Caroline, "but he said he would call back at The Larches in half an hour, and went away down the village. A great pity, because M. Poirot came in practically the minute after he left."

"Came in here?"

"No, to his own house."

"How do you know?"

"The side window," said Caroline briefly.

It seemed to me that we had now exhausted the topic. Caroline thought otherwise.

"Aren't you going across?"

"Across where?"

"To The Larches, of course."

"My dear Caroline," I said, "what for?"

"Mr. Raymond wanted to see him very particularly," said Caroline. "You might hear what it's all about."

I raised my eyebrows.

"Curiosity is not my besetting sin," I remarked coldly. "I can exist comfortably without knowing exactly what my neighbours are doing and thinking."

"Stuff and nonsense, James," said my sister. "You want to know just as much as I do. You're not so honest, that's all. You always have to pretend."

"Really, Caroline," I said, and retired into my surgery.

Ten minutes later Caroline tapped at the door and entered. In her hand she held what seemed to be a pot of jam.

"I wonder, James," she said, "if you would mind taking this pot of medlar jelly across to M. Poirot? I promised it to him. He has never tasted any home-made medlar jelly."

"Why can't Annie go?" I asked coldly.

"She's doing some mending. I can't spare her."

Caroline and I looked at each other.

"Very well," I said, rising. "But if I take the beastly thing, I shall just leave it at the door. You understand that?"

My sister raised her eyebrows.

"Naturally," she said. "Who suggested you should do anything else?"

The honours were with Caroline.

"If you *do* happen to see M. Poirot," she said, as I opened the front door, "you might tell him about the boots."

It was a most subtle parting shot. I wanted dreadfully to understand the enigma of the boots. When the old lady with the Breton cap opened the door to me, I found myself asking if M. Poirot was in, quite automatically.

Poirot sprang up to meet me, with every appearance of pleasure.

"Sit down, my good friend," he said. "The big chair? This small one? The room is not too hot, no?"

I thought it was stifling, but refrained from saying so. The windows were closed, and a large fire burned in the grate.

"The English people, they have a mania for the fresh air," declared Poirot. "The big air, it is all very well outside, where it belongs. Why admit it to the house? But let us not discuss such banalities. You have something for me, yes?"

"Two things," I said. "First—this—from my sister."

I handed over the pot of medlar jelly.

"How kind of Mademoiselle Caroline. She has remembered her promise. And the second thing?"

"Information—of a kind."

And I told him of my interview with Mrs. Ackroyd. He listened with interest, but not much excitement.

"It clears the ground," he said thoughtfully. "And it has a certain value as confirming the evidence of the housekeeper. She said, you remember, that she found the silver table lid open and closed it down in passing."

"What about her statement that she went into the drawing room to see if the flowers were fresh?"

"Ah! we never took that very seriously, did we, my friend? It was patently an excuse, trumped up in a hurry, by a woman who felt it urgent to explain her presence—which, by the way, you would probably never have thought of questioning. I considered it possible that her agitation might arise from the fact that she had been tampering with the silver table, but I think now that we must look for another cause."

"Yes," I said. "Whom did she go out to meet? And why?"

"You think she went to meet someone?"

"I do."

Poirot nodded.

"So do I," he said thoughtfully.

There was a pause.

"By the way," I said, "I've got a message for you from my sister. Ralph Paton's boots were black, not brown."

I was watching him closely as I gave the message, and I fancied that I saw a momentary flicker of discomposure. If so, it passed almost immediately.

"She is absolutely positive they are not brown?"

"Absolutely."

"Ah!" said Poirot regretfully. "That is a pity."

And he seemed quite crestfallen.

He entered into no explanations, but at once started a new subject of conversation.

"The housekeeper, Miss Russell, who came to consult you on that Friday morning—is it indiscreet to ask what passed at the interview—apart from the medical details, I mean?"

"Not at all," I said. "When the professional part of the conversation was over, we talked for a few minutes about poisons, and the ease or difficulty of detecting them, and about drug-taking and drug-takers."

"With special reference to cocaine?" asked Poirot.

"How did you know?" I asked, somewhat surprised.

For answer, the little man rose and crossed the room to where newspapers were filed. He brought me a copy of the *Daily Budget,* dated Friday, 16th September, and showed me an article dealing with the smuggling of cocaine. It was a somewhat lurid article, written with an eye to picturesque effect.

"That is what put cocaine into her head, my friend," he said.

I would have catechized him further, for I did not quite understand his meaning, but at that moment the door opened and Geoffrey Raymond was announced.

He came in fresh and debonair as ever, and greeted us both.

"How are you, doctor? M. Poirot, this is the second time I've been here this morning. I was anxious to catch you."

"Perhaps I'd better be off," I suggested rather awkwardly.

"Not on my account, doctor. No, it's just this," he went on, seating himself at a wave of invitation from Poirot, "I've got a confession to make."

"*En verité?*" said Poirot, with an air of polite interest.

"Oh, it's of no consequence, really. But, as a matter of fact, my conscience has been pricking me ever since yesterday afternoon. You accused us all of keeping back something, M. Poirot. I plead guilty. I've had something up my sleeve."

"And what is that, M. Raymond?"

"As I say, it's nothing of consequence—just this. I was in debt—badly, and that legacy came in the nick of time. Five hundred pounds puts me on my feet again with a little to spare."

He smiled at us both with that engaging frankness that made him such a likeable youngster.

"You know how it is. Suspicious-looking policemen—don't like to admit you were hard up for money—think it will look bad to them. But I was a fool, really, because Blunt and I were in the billiard room from a quarter to ten onwards, so I've got a watertight alibi and nothing to fear. Still, when you thundered out that stuff about concealing things, I felt a nasty prick of conscience, and I thought I'd like to get it off my mind."

He got up again and stood smiling at us.

"You are a very wise young man," said Poirot, nodding at him with approval. "See you, when I know that anyone is hiding things from me, I suspect that the thing hidden may be something very bad indeed. You have done well."

"I'm glad I'm cleared from suspicion," laughed Raymond. "I'll be off now."

"So that is that," I remarked, as the door closed behind the young secretary.

"Yes," agreed Poirot. "A mere bagatelle—but if he had not been in the billiard room—who knows? After all, many crimes have been committed for the sake of less than five hundred pounds. It all depends on what sum is sufficient to break a man. A question of relativity, is it not? Have you reflected, my friend, that many people in that house stood to benefit by Mr. Ackroyd's death? Mrs. Ackroyd, Miss Flora, young Mr. Raymond, the housekeeper, Miss Russell. Only one, in fact, does not, Major Blunt."

His tone in uttering that name was so peculiar that I looked up, puzzled.

"I don't understand you," I said.

"Two of the people I accused have given me the truth."

"You think Major Blunt has something to conceal also?"

"As for that," remarked Poirot nonchalantly, "there is a saying, is there not, that Englishmen conceal only one thing—their love? And Major Blunt, I should say, is not good at concealments."

"Sometimes," I said, "I wonder if we haven't rather jumped to conclusions on one point."

"What is that?"

"We've assumed that the blackmailer of Mrs. Ferrars is necessarily the murderer of Mr. Ackroyd. Mightn't we be mistaken?"

Poirot nodded energetically.

"Very good. Very good indeed. I wondered if that idea would come to you. Of course it is possible. But we must remember one point. The letter disappeared. Still, that, as you say, may not necessarily mean that the murderer took it. When you first found the body, Parker may have abstracted the letter unnoticed by you."

"Parker?"

"Yes, Parker. I always come back to Parker—not as the murderer—no, he did not commit the murder; but who is more suitable than he as the mysterious scoundrel who terrorized Mrs. Ferrars? He may have got his information about Mr. Ferrars's death from one of the King's Paddock servants. At any rate, he is more likely to have come upon it than a casual guest such as Blunt, for instance."

"Parker might have taken the letter," I admitted. "It wasn't till later that I noticed it was gone."

"How much later? After Blunt and Raymond were in the room, or before?"

"I can't remember," I said slowly. "I think it was before—no, afterwards. Yes, I'm almost sure it was afterwards."

"That widens the field to three," said Poirot thoughtfully. "But Parker is the most likely. It is in my mind to try a little experiment with Parker. How say you, my friend, will you accompany me to Fernly?"

I acquiesced, and we set out at once. Poirot asked to see Miss Ackroyd, and presently Flora came to us.

"Mademoiselle Flora," said Poirot, "I have to confide in you a little secret. I am not yet satisfied of the innocence of Parker. I propose to make a little experiment with your assistance. I want to reconstruct some of his actions on that night. But we must think of something to tell him—ah! I have it. I wish to satisfy myself as to whether voices in the little lobby could have been heard outside on the terrace. Now, ring for Parker, if you will be so good."

I did so, and presently the butler appeared, suave as ever.

"You rang, sir?"

"Yes, my good Parker. I have in mind a little experiment. I have placed Major Blunt on the terrace outside the study window. I want to see if anyone there could have heard the voices of Miss Ackroyd and yourself in the lobby that night. I want to enact that little scene over again. Perhaps you would fetch the tray or whatever it was you were carrying?"

Parker vanished, and we repaired to the lobby outside the study door. Presently we heard a chink in the outer hall, and Parker appeared in the doorway carrying a tray with a siphon, a decanter of whisky, and two glasses on it.

"One moment," cried Poirot, raising his hand and seemingly very excited. "We must have everything in order. Just as it occurred. It is a little method of mine."

"A foreign custom, sir," said Parker. "Reconstruction of the crime they call it, do they not?"

He was quite imperturbable as he stood there politely waiting on Poirot's orders.

"Ah! he knows something, the good Parker," cried Poirot. "He has read of these things. Now, I beg you, let us have everything of the most exact. You came from the outer hall—so. Mademoiselle was—where?"

"Here," said Flora, taking up her stand just outside the study door.

"Quite right, sir," said Parker.

"I had just closed the door," continued Flora.

"Yes, miss," agreed Parker. "Your hand was still on the handle as it is now."

"Then *allez*," said Poirot. "Play me the little comedy."

Flora stood with her hand on the door handle, and Parker came stepping through the door from the hall, bearing the tray.

He stopped just inside the door. Flora spoke.

"Oh! Parker. Mr. Ackroyd doesn't want to be disturbed again tonight."

"Is that right?" she added in an undertone.

"To the best of my recollection, Miss Flora," said Parker, "but I fancy you used the word evening instead of night." Then, raising his voice in a somewhat theatrical fashion: "Very good, miss. Shall I lock up as usual?"

"Yes, please."

Parker retired through the door, Flora followed him, and started to ascend the main staircase.

"Is that enough?" she asked over her shoulder.

"Admirable," declared the little man, rubbing his hands. "By the way, Parker, are you sure there were two glasses on the tray that evening? Who was the second one for?"

"I always bring two glasses, sir," said Parker. "Is there anything further?"

"Nothing. I thank you."

Parker withdrew, dignified to the last.

Poirot stood in the middle of the hall frowning. Flora came down and joined us.

"Has your experiment been successful?" she asked. "I don't quite understand, you know—"

Poirot smiled admiringly at her.

"It is not necessary that you should," he said. "But tell me, were there indeed two glasses on Parker's tray that night?"

Flora wrinkled her brows a minute.

"I really can't remember," she said. "I think there were. Is—is that the object of your experiment?"

Poirot took her hand and patted it.

"Put it this way," he said. "I am always interested to see if people will speak the truth."

"And did Parker speak the truth?"

"I rather think he did," said Poirot thoughtfully.

A few minutes later saw us retracing our steps to the village.

"What was the point of that question about the glasses?" I asked curiously.

Poirot shrugged his shoulders.

"One must say something," he remarked. "That particular question did as well as any other."

I stared at him.

"At any rate, my friend," he said seriously, "I know now something I wanted to know. Let us leave it at that."

Sixteen

An Evening at Mah Jong

That night we had a little Mah Jong party. This kind of simple entertainment is very popular in King's Abbot. The guests arrive in galoshes and waterproofs after dinner. They partake of coffee and later of cake, sandwiches and tea.

On this particular night our guests were Miss Gannett and Colonel Carter, who lives near the church. A good deal of gossip is handed round at these evenings, sometimes seriously interfering with the game in progress. We used to play bridge—chatty bridge of the worst description. We find Mah Jong much more peaceful. The irritated demand as to why on earth your partner did not lead a certain card is entirely done away with, and though we still express criticisms frankly, there is not the same acrimonious spirit.

"Very cold evening, eh, Sheppard?" said Colonel Carter, standing with his back to the fire. Caroline had taken Miss Gannett to her own room, and was there assisting her to disentangle herself from her many wraps. "Reminds me of the Afghan passes."

"Indeed?" I said politely.

"Very mysterious business this about poor Ackroyd," continued the colonel, accepting a cup of coffee. "A deuce of a lot behind it—that's what I say. Between you and me, Sheppard, I've heard the word blackmail mentioned!"

The colonel gave me the look which might be tabulated "one man of the world to another."

"A woman in it, no doubt," he said. "Depend upon it, a woman in it."

Caroline and Miss Gannett joined us at this minute. Miss Gannett drank coffee whilst Caroline got out the Mah Jong box and poured out the tiles upon the table.

"Washing the tiles," said the colonel facetiously. "That's right—washing the tiles, as we used to say in the Shanghai Club."

It is the private opinion of both Caroline and myself that Colonel Carter has never been in the Shanghai Club in his life. More, that he has never been farther east than India, where he juggled with tins of bully beef and plum and apple jam during the Great War. But the colonel is determinedly military, and in King's Abbot we permit people to indulge their little idiosyncrasies freely.

"Shall we begin?" said Caroline.

We sat round the table. For some five minutes there was complete silence, owing to the fact that there is tremendous secret competition amongst us as to who can build their wall quickest.

"Go on, James," said Caroline at last. "You're East Wind."

I discarded a tile. A round or two proceeded, broken by the monotonous remarks of "Three Bamboos," "Two Circles," "Pung," and frequently from Miss Gannett "Unpung," owing to that lady's habit of too hastily claiming tiles to which she had no right.

"I saw Flora Ackroyd this morning," said Miss Gannett. "Pung—no—Unpung. I made a mistake."

"Four Circles," said Caroline. "Where did you see her?"

"She didn't see *me,*" said Miss Gannett, with that tremendous significance only to be met with in small villages.

"Ah!" said Caroline interestedly. "Chow."

"I believe," said Miss Gannett, temporarily diverted, "that it's the right thing nowadays to say 'Chee' not 'Chow.' "

"Nonsense," said Caroline. "I have always said '*Chow.*' "

"In the Shanghai Club," said Colonel Carter, "they say '*Chow.*' "

Miss Gannett retired, crushed.

"What were you saying about Flora Ackroyd?" asked Caroline, after a moment or two devoted to the game. "Was she with anyone?"

"Very much so," said Miss Gannett.

The eyes of the two ladies met, and seemed to exchange information.

"Really," said Caroline interestedly. "Is that it? Well, it doesn't surprise me in the least."

"We're waiting for you to discard, Miss Caroline," said the colonel. He sometimes affects the pose of the bluff male, intent on the game and indifferent to gossip. But nobody is deceived.

"If you ask me," said Miss Gannett. ("Was that a Bamboo you discarded, dear? Oh! no, I see now—it was a Circle.) As I was saying, if you ask me, Flora's been exceedingly lucky. Exceedingly lucky she's been."

"How's that, Miss Gannett?" asked the colonel. "I'll Pung that Green Dragon. How do you make out that Miss Flora's been lucky? Very charming girl and all that, I know."

"I mayn't know very much about crime," said Miss Gannett, with the air of one who knows everything there is to know, "but I can tell you one thing. The first question that's always asked is 'Who last saw the deceased alive?' And the person who did is regarded with suspicion. Now, Flora Ackroyd last saw her uncle alive. It might have looked very nasty for her—very nasty indeed. It's my opinion—and I give it for what it's worth, that Ralph Paton is staying away on her account, to draw suspicion away from her."

"Come, now," I protested mildly, "you surely can't suggest that a young girl like Flora Ackroyd is capable of stabbing her uncle in cold blood?"

"Well, I don't know," said Miss Gannett. "I've just been reading a book from the library about the underworld of Paris, and it says that some of the worst women criminals are young girls with the faces of angels."

"That's in France," said Caroline instantly.

"Just so," said the colonel. "Now, I'll tell you a very curious thing—a story that was going round the Bazaars in India. . . ."

The colonel's story was one of interminable length, and of curiously little interest. A thing that happened in India many years ago cannot compare for a moment with an event that took place in King's Abbot the day before yesterday.

It was Caroline who brought the colonel's story to a close by fortunately going Mah Jong. After the slight unpleasantness always caused by my corrections of Caroline's somewhat faulty arithmetic, we started a new hand.

"East Wind passes," said Caroline. "I've got an idea of my own about Ralph Paton. Three Characters. But I'm keeping it to myself for the present."

"Are you, dear?" said Miss Gannett. "Chow—I mean Pung."

"Yes," said Caroline firmly.

"Was it all right about the boots?" asked Miss Gannett. "Their being black, I mean?"

"Quite all right," said Caroline.

"What was the point, do you think?" asked Miss Gannett.

Caroline pursed up her lips, and shook her head with an air of knowing all about it.

"Pung," said Miss Gannett. "No—Unpung. I suppose that now the doctor's in with M. Poirot he knows all the secrets?"

"Far from it," I said.

"James is so modest," said Caroline. "Ah! A concealed Kong."

The colonel gave vent to a whistle. For the moment gossip was forgotten.

"Your own wind, too," he said. "*And* you've got two Pungs of Dragons. We must be careful. Miss Caroline's out for a big hand."

We played for some minutes with no irrelevant conversation.

"This M. Poirot now," said Colonel Carter, "is he really such a great detective?"

"The greatest the world has ever known," said Caroline solemnly. "He has to come here incognito to avoid publicity."

"Chow," said Miss Gannett. "Quite wonderful for our little village, I'm sure. By the way, Clara—my maid, you know—is great friends with Elsie, the housemaid at Fernly, and what do you think Elsie told her? That there's been a lot of money stolen, and it's her opinion—Elsie's, I mean—that the parlourmaid had something to do with it. She's leaving at the month, and she's crying a good deal at night. If you ask me, the girl is very likely in league with a *gang*. She's always been a queer girl—she's not friends with any of the girls round here. She goes off by herself on her days out—very unnatural, I call it, and most suspicious. I asked her once to come to our Friendly Girls' Evenings, but she refused, and then I asked her a few questions about her home and her family—all that sort of thing, and I'm bound to say I considered her manner most impertinent. Outwardly very respectful—but she shut me up in the most barefaced way."

Miss Gannett stopped for breath, and the colonel, who was totally uninterested in the servant question, remarked that in the Shanghai Club brisk play was the invariable rule.

We had a round of brisk play.

"That Miss Russell," said Caroline. "She came here pretending to consult James on Friday morning. It's my opinion she wanted to see where the poisons were kept. Five Characters."

"Chow," said Miss Gannett. "What an extraordinary idea! I wonder if you can be right."

"Talking of poisons," said the colonel. "Eh—what? Haven't I discarded? Oh! Eight Bamboos."

"Mah Jong!" said Miss Gannett.

Caroline was very much annoyed.

"One Red Dragon," she said regretfully, "and I should have had a hand of three doubles."

"I've had two Red Dragons all the time," I mentioned.

"So exactly like you, James," said Caroline reproachfully. "You've no conception of the spirit of the game."

I myself thought I had played rather cleverly. I should have had to pay Caroline an enormous amount if she had gone Mah Jong. Miss Gannett's Mah Jong was of the poorest variety possible, as Caroline did not fail to point out to her.

East Wind passed, and we started a new hand in silence.

"What I was going to tell you just now was this," said Caroline.

"Yes?" said Miss Gannett encouragingly.

"My idea about Ralph Paton, I mean."

"Yes, dear," said Miss Gannett, still more encouragingly. "Chow!"

"It's a sign of weakness to Chow so early," said Caroline severely. "You should go for a big hand."

"I know," said Miss Gannett. "You were saying—about Ralph Paton, you know?"

"Yes. Well, I've a pretty shrewd idea where he is."

We all stopped to stare at her.

"This is very interesting, Miss Caroline," said Colonel Carter. "All your own idea, eh?"

"Well, not exactly. I'll tell you about it. You know that big map of the county we have in the hall?"

We all said Yes.

"As M. Poirot was going out the other day, he stopped and looked at it, and he made some remark—I can't remember exactly what it was. Something about Cranchester being the only big town anywhere near us—which is true, of course. But after he had gone—it came to me suddenly."

"What came to you?"

"His meaning. Of course Ralph is in Cranchester."

It was at that moment that I knocked down the rack that held my pieces. My sister immediately reproved me for clumsiness, but half-heartedly. She was intent on her theory.

"Cranchester, Miss Caroline?" said Colonel Carter. "Surely not Cranchester! It's so near."

"That's exactly it," cried Caroline triumphantly. "It seems quite clear by now that he didn't get away from here by train. He must simply have walked into Cranchester. And I believe he's there still. No one would dream of his being so near at hand."

I pointed out several objections to the theory, but when once Caroline has got something firmly into her head, nothing dislodges it.

"And you think M. Poirot has the same idea," said Miss Gannett thoughtfully. "It's a curious coincidence, but I was out for a walk this afternoon on the Cranchester road, and he passed me in a car coming from that direction."

We all looked at each other.

"Why, dear me," said Miss Gannett suddenly, "I'm Mah Jong all the time, and I never noticed it."

Caroline's attention was distracted from her own inventive exercises. She pointed out to Miss Gannett that a hand consisting of mixed suits and too many Chows was hardly worth going Mah Jong on. Miss Gannett listened imperturbably and collected her counters.

"Yes, dear, I know what you mean," she said. "But it rather depends on what kind of a hand you have to start with, doesn't it?"

"You'll never get the big hands if you don't go for them," urged Caroline.

"Well, we must all play our own way, mustn't we?" said Miss Gannett. She looked down at her counters. "After all, I'm up, so far."

Caroline, who was considerably down, said nothing.

East Wind passed, and we set to once more. Annie brought in the tea things. Caroline and Miss Gannett were both slightly ruffled as is often the case during one of these festive evenings.

"If you would only play a leetle quicker, dear," said Caroline, as Miss Gannett hesitated over her discard. "The Chinese put down the tiles so quickly it sounds like little birds pattering."

For some minutes we played like the Chinese.

"You haven't contributed much to the sum of information, Sheppard," said Colonel Carter genially. "You're a sly dog. Hand in glove with the great detective, and not a hint as to the way things are going."

"James is an extraordinary creature," said Caroline. "He can *not* bring himself to part with information."

She looked at me with some disfavour.

"I assure you," I said, "that I don't know anything. Poirot keeps his own counsel."

"Wise man," said the colonel with a chuckle. "He doesn't give himself away. But they're wonderful fellows, these foreign detectives. Up to all sorts of dodges, I believe."

"Pung," said Miss Gannett, in a tone of quiet triumph. "And Mah Jong."

The situation became more strained. It was annoyance at Miss Gannett's going Mah Jong for the third time running which prompted Caroline to say to me as we built a fresh wall:

"You are too tiresome, James. You sit there like a deadhead, and say nothing at all!"

"But, my dear," I protested, "I have really nothing to say—that is, of the kind you mean."

"Nonsense," said Caroline, as she sorted her hand. "You *must* know something interesting."

I did not answer for a moment. I was overwhelmed and intoxicated. I had read of there being such a thing as The Perfect Winning—going Mah Jong on one's original hand. I had never hoped to hold the hand myself.

With suppressed triumph I laid my hand face upwards on the table.

"As they say in the Shanghai Club," I remarked—"Tin-ho—the Perfect Winning!"

The colonel's eyes nearly bulged out of his head.

"Upon my soul," he said. "what an extraordinary thing. I never saw that happen before!"

It was then that I went on, goaded by Caroline's gibes, and rendered reckless by my triumph.

"And as to anything interesting," I said. "What about a gold wedding ring with a date and 'From R.' inside."

I pass over the scene that followed. I was made to say exactly where this treasure was found. I was made to reveal the date.

"March 13th," said Caroline. "Just six months ago. Ah!"

Out of a babel of excited suggestions and suppositions three theories were evolved:

1. That of Colonel Carter: that Ralph was secretly married to Flora. The first or most simple solution.

2. That of Miss Gannett: that Roger Ackroyd had been secretly married to Mrs. Ferrars.

3. That of my sister: that Roger Ackroyd had married his housekeeper, Miss Russell.

A fourth or super theory was propounded by Caroline later as we went up to bed.

"Mark my words," she said suddenly, "I shouldn't be at all surprised if Geoffrey Raymond and Flora weren't married."

"Surely it would be 'From G.,' not 'From R.' then," I suggested.

"You never know. Some girls call men by their surnames. And you heard what Miss Gannett said this evening—about Flora's carryings on."

Strictly speaking, I had not heard Miss Gannett say anything of the kind, but I respected Caroline's knowledge of innuendoes.

"How about Hector Blunt?" I hinted. "If it's anybody—"

"Nonsense," said Caroline. "I dare say he admires her—may even be in love with her. But depend upon it a girl isn't going to fall in love with a man old enough to be her father when there's a good-looking secretary about. She may encourage Major Blunt just as a blind. Girls are very artful. But there's one thing I *do* tell you, James Sheppard. Flora Ackroyd does not care a penny piece for Ralph Paton, and never has. You can take it from me."

I took it from her meekly.

Seventeen

PARKER

It occurred to me the next morning that under the exhilaration produced by Tin-ho or the Perfect Winning, I might have been slightly indiscreet. True, Poirot had not asked me to keep the discovery of the ring to myself. On the other hand, he had said nothing about it whilst at Fernly, and as far as I knew, I was the only person aware that it had been found. I felt distinctly guilty. The fact was by now spreading through King's Abbot like wildfire. I was expecting wholesale reproaches from Poirot any minute.

The joint funeral of Mrs. Ferrars and Roger Ackroyd was fixed for eleven o'clock. It was a melancholy and impressive ceremony. All the party from Fernly were there.

After it was over, Poirot, who had also been present, took me by the arm, and invited me to accompany him back to The Larches. He was looking very grave, and I feared that my indiscretion of the night before had got round to his ears. But it soon transpired that his thoughts were occupied by something of a totally different nature.

"See you," he said. "We must act. With your help I propose to examine a witness. We will question him, we will put such fear into him that the truth is bound to come out."

"What witness are you talking about?" I asked, very much surprised.

"Parker!" said Poirot. "I asked him to be at my house this morning at twelve o'clock. He should await us there at this very minute."

"What do you think?" I ventured, glancing sideways at his face.

"I know this—that I am not satisfied."

"You think that it was he who blackmailed Mrs. Ferrars?"

"Either that, or—"

"Well?" I said, after waiting a minute or two.

"My friend, I will say this to you—I hope it was he."

The gravity of his manner, and something indefinable that tinged it, reduced me to silence.

On arrival at The Larches, we were informed that Parker was already there awaiting our return. As we entered the room, the butler rose respectfully.

"Good morning, Parker," said Poirot pleasantly. "One instant, I pray of you."

He removed his overcoat and gloves.

"Allow me, sir," said Parker, and sprang forward to assist him. He deposited the articles neatly on a chair by the door. Poirot watched him with approval.

"Thank you, my good Parker," he said. "Take a seat, will you not? What I have to say may take some time."

Parker seated himself with an apologetic bend of the head.

"Now what do you think I asked you to come here for this morning—eh?"

Parker coughed.

"I understood, sir, that you wished to ask me a few questions about my late master—private like."

"*Précisément,*" said Poirot, beaming. "Have you made many experiments in blackmail?"

"Sir!"

The butler sprang to his feet.

"Do not excite yourself," said Poirot placidly. "Do not play the farce of the honest, injured man. You know all there is to know about the blackmail, is it not so?"

"Sir, I—I've never—never been—"

"Insulted," suggested Poirot, "in such a way before. Then why, my excellent Parker, were you so anxious to overhear the conversation in Mr. Ackroyd's study the other evening, after you had caught the word blackmail?"

"I wasn't—I—"

"Who was your last master?" rapped out Poirot suddenly.

"My last master?"

"Yes, the master you were with before you came to Mr. Ackroyd."

"A Major Ellerby, sir—"

Poirot took the words out of his mouth.

"Just so, Major Ellerby. Major Ellerby was addicted to drugs, was he not? You travelled about with him. When he was in Bermuda there was some trouble—a man was killed. Major Ellerby was partly responsible. It was hushed up. But you knew about it. How much did Major Ellerby pay you to keep your mouth shut?"

Parker was staring at him openmouthed. The man had gone to pieces, his cheeks shook flabbily.

"You see, me, I have made inquiries," said Poirot pleasantly. "It is as I say. You got a good sum then as blackmail, and Major Ellerby went on paying you until he died. Now I want to hear about your latest experiment."

Parker still stared.

"It is useless to deny. Hercule Poirot *knows*. It is so, what I have said about Major Ellerby, is it not?"

As though against his will, Parker nodded reluctantly once. His face was ashen pale.

"But I never hurt a hair of Mr. Ackroyd's head," he moaned. "Honest to God, sir, I didn't. I've been afraid of this coming all the time. And I tell you I didn't—I didn't kill him."

His voice rose almost to a scream.

"I am inclined to believe you, my friend," said Poirot. "You have not the nerve—the courage. But I must have the truth."

"I'll tell you anything, sir, anything you want to know. It's true that I tried to listen that night. A word or two I heard made me curious. And Mr. Ackroyd's wanting not to be disturbed, and shutting himself up with the doctor the way he did. It's God's own truth what I told the police. I heard the word blackmail, sir, and well—"

He paused.

"You thought there might be something in it for you?" suggested Poirot smoothly.

"Well—well, yes, I did, sir. I thought that if Mr. Ackroyd was being blackmailed, why shouldn't I have a share of the pickings?"

A very curious expression passed over Poirot's face. He leaned forward.

"Had you any reason to suppose before that night that Mr. Ackroyd was being blackmailed?"

"No, indeed, sir. It was a great surprise to me. Such a regular gentleman in all his habits."

"How much did you overhear?"

"Not very much, sir. There seemed what I might call a spite against me. Of course I had to attend to my duties in the pantry. And when I did creep along once or twice to the study it was no use. The first time Dr. Sheppard came out and almost caught me in the act, and another time Mr. Raymond passed me in the big hall and went that way, so I knew it was no use; and when I went with the tray, Miss Flora headed me off."

Poirot stared for a long time at the man, as if to test his sincerity. Parker returned his gaze earnestly.

"I hope you believe me, sir. I've been afraid all along the police would rake up that old business with Major Ellerby and be suspicious of me in consequence."

"*Eh bien,*" said Poirot at last. "I am disposed to believe you. But there is one thing I must request of you—to show me your bankbook. You have a bankbook, I presume?"

"Yes, sir, as a matter of fact, I have it with me now."

With no sign of confusion, he produced it from his pocket. Poirot took the slim, green-covered book and perused the entries.

"Ah! I perceive you have purchased £500 worth of National Savings Certificates this year?"

"Yes, sir. I have already over a thousand pounds saved—the result of my connection with—er—my late master, Major Ellerby. And I have had quite a little flutter on some horses this year—very successful. If you remember, sir, a rank outsider won the Jubilee. I was fortunate enough to back it—£20."

Poirot handed him back the book.

"I will wish you good morning. I believe that you have told me the truth. If you have not—so much the worse for you, my friend."

When Parker had departed, Poirot picked up his overcoat once more.

"Going out again?" I asked.

"Yes, we will pay a little visit to the good M. Hammond."

"You believe Parker's story?"

"It is credible enough on the face of it. It seems clear that—unless he is a very good actor indeed—he genuinely believes it was Ackroyd himself who was the victim of blackmail. If so, he knows nothing at all about the Mrs. Ferrars business."

"Then in that case—who—?"

"*Précisément!* Who? But our visit to M. Hammond will accomplish one purpose. It will either clear Parker completely or else—"

"Well?"

"I fall into the bad habit of leaving my sentences unfinished this morning," said Poirot apologetically. "You must bear with me."

"By the way," I said, rather sheepishly, "I've got a confession to make. I'm afraid I have inadvertently let out something about that ring."

"What ring?"

"The ring you found in the goldfish pond."

"Ah! yes," said Poirot, smiling broadly.

"I hope you're not annoyed? It was very careless of me."

"But not at all, my good friend, not at all. I laid no commands upon you. You were at liberty to speak of it if you so wished. She was interested, your sister?"

"She was indeed. It created a sensation. All sorts of theories are flying about."

"Ah! And yet it is so simple. The true explanation leapt to the eye, did it not?"

"Did it?" I said drily.

Poirot laughed.

"The wise man does not commit himself," he observed. "Is not that so? But here we are at Mr. Hammond's."

The lawyer was in his office, and we were ushered in without any delay. He rose and greeted us in his dry, precise manner.

Poirot came at once to the point.

"Monsieur, I desire from you certain information, that is, if you will be so good as to give it to me. You acted, I understand, for the late Mrs. Ferrars of King's Paddock?"

I noticed the swift gleam of surprise which showed in the lawyer's eyes, before his professional reserve came down once more like a mask over his face.

"Certainly. All her affairs passed through our hands."

"Very good. Now, before I ask you to tell me anything, I should like you to listen to the story Dr. Sheppard will relate to you. You have no objection, have you, my friend, to repeating the conversation you had with Mr. Ackroyd last Friday night?"

"Not in the least," I said, and straightway began the recital of that strange evening.

Hammond listened with close attention.

"That is all," I said, when I had finished.

"Blackmail," said the lawyer thoughtfully.

"You are surprised?" asked Poirot.

The lawyer took off his pince-nez and polished them with his handkerchief.

"No," he replied, "I can hardly say that I am surprised. I have suspected something of the kind for some time."

"That brings us," said Poirot, "to the information for which I am asking. If anyone can give us an idea of the actual sums paid, you are the man, monsieur."

"I see no object in withholding the information," said Hammond, after a moment or two. "During the past year, Mrs. Ferrars has sold out certain securities, and the money for them was paid into her account and not reinvested. As her income was a large one, and she lived very quietly after her husband's death, it seems certain that these sums of money were paid away for some special purpose. I once sounded her on the subject, and she said that she was obliged to support several of her husband's poor relations. I let the matter drop, of course. Until now, I have always imagined that the money was paid to some woman who had had a claim on Ashley Ferrars. I never dreamed that Mrs. Ferrars herself was involved."

"And the amount?" asked Poirot.

"In all, I should say the various sums totalled at least twenty thousand pounds."

"Twenty thousand pounds!" I exclaimed. "In one year!"

"Mrs. Ferrars was a very wealthy woman," said Poirot drily. "And the penalty for murder is not a pleasant one."

"Is there anything else that I can tell you?" inquired Mr. Hammond.

"I thank you, no," said Poirot, rising. "All my excuses for having deranged you."

"Not at all, not at all."

"The word derange," I remarked, when we were outside again, "is applicable to mental disorder only."

"Ah!" cried Poirot. "Never will my English be quite perfect. A curious language. I should then have said disarranged, *n'est-ce pas?*"

"Disturbed is the word you had in mind."

"I thank you, my friend. The word exact, you are zealous for it. *Eh bien,* what about our friend Parker now? With twenty thousand pounds in hand, would he have continued being a butler? *Je ne pense pas.* It is, of course, possible that he banked the money under another name, but I am disposed to believe he spoke the truth to us. If he is a scoundrel, he is a scoundrel on a mean scale. He has not the big ideas. That leaves us as a possibility, Raymond, or—well—Major Blunt."

"Surely not Raymond," I objected. "Since we know that he was desperately hard up for a matter of five hundred pounds."

"That is what he says, yes."

"And as to Hector Blunt—"

"I will tell you something as to the good Major Blunt," interrupted Poirot. "It is my business to make inquiries. I make them. *Eh bien*—that legacy of which he speaks, I have discovered that the amount of it was close upon twenty thousand pounds. What do you think of that?"

I was so taken aback that I could hardly speak.

"It's impossible," I said at last. "A well-known man like Hector Blunt."

Poirot shrugged his shoulders.

"Who knows? At least he is a man with big ideas. I confess that I hardly see him as a blackmailer, but there is another possibility that you have not even considered."

"What is that?"

"The fire, my friend. Ackroyd himself may have destroyed that letter, blue envelope and all, after you left him."

"I hardly think that likely," I said slowly. "And yet—of course, it may be so. He might have changed his mind."

We had just arrived at my house, and on the spur of the moment I invited Poirot to come in and take pot luck.

I thought Caroline would be pleased with me, but it is hard to satisfy one's womenfolk. It appears that we were eating chops for lunch—the kitchen staff being regaled on tripe and onions. And two chops set before three people are productive of embarrassment.

But Caroline is seldom daunted for long. With magnificent mendacity, she explained to Poirot that although James laughed at her for doing so, she adhered strictly to a vegetarian diet. She descanted ecstatically on the delights of nut cutlets (which I am quite sure she has never tasted) and ate a Welsh rarebit with gusto and frequent cutting remarks as to the dangers of "flesh" foods.

Afterwards, when we were sitting in front of the fire and smoking, Caroline attacked Poirot directly.

"Not found Ralph Paton yet?" she asked.

"Where should I find him, mademoiselle?"

"I thought, perhaps, you'd found him in Cranchester," said Caroline, with intense meaning in her tone.

Poirot looked merely bewildered.

"In Cranchester? But why in Cranchester?"

I enlightened him with a touch of malice.

"One of our ample staff of private detectives happened to see you in a car on the Cranchester road yesterday," I explained.

Poirot's bewilderment vanished. He laughed heartily.

"Ah, that! A simple visit to the dentist, *c'est tout*. My tooth, it aches. I go there. My tooth, it is at once better. I think to return quickly. The dentist, he says No. Better to have it out. I argue. He insists. He has his way! That particular tooth, it will never ache again."

Caroline collapsed rather like a pricked balloon.

We fell to discussing Ralph Paton.

"A weak nature," I insisted. "But not a vicious one."

"Ah!" said Poirot. "But weakness, where does it end?"

"Exactly," said Caroline. "Take James here—weak as water, if I weren't about to look after him."

"My dear Caroline," I said irritably, "can't you talk without dragging in personalities?"

"You *are* weak, James," said Caroline, quite unmoved. "I'm eight years older than you are—oh! I don't mind M. Poirot knowing that—"

"I should never have guessed it, mademoiselle," said Poirot, with a gallant little bow.

"Eight years older. And I've always considered it my duty to look after you. With a bad bringing up, Heaven knows what mischief you might have got into by now."

"I might have married a beautiful adventuress," I murmured, gazing at the ceiling, and blowing smoke rings.

"Adventuress!" said Caroline, with a snort. "If we're talking of adventuresses—"

She left the sentence unfinished.

"Well?" I said, with some curiosity.

"Nothing. But I can think of someone not a hundred miles away."

Then she turned to Poirot suddenly.

"James sticks to it that you believe someone in the house committed the murder. All I can say is, you're wrong."

"I should not like to be wrong," said Poirot. "It is not—how do you say—my *métier*?"

"I've got the facts pretty clearly," continued Caroline, taking no notice of Poirot's remark, "from James and others. As far as I can see, of the people in the house, only two *could* have had the chance of doing it. Ralph Paton and Flora Ackroyd."

"My dear Caroline—"

"Now, James, don't interrupt me. I know what I'm talking about. Parker met her *outside* the door, didn't he? He didn't hear her uncle saying good night to her. She could have killed him then and there."

"Caroline!"

"I'm not saying she *did,* James. I'm saying she *could* have done. As a matter of fact, though, Flora is like all these young girls nowadays, with no veneration for their betters and thinking they know best on every subject under the sun, I don't for a minute believe she'd kill even a chicken. But there it is. Mr. Raymond and Major Blunt have alibis. Mrs. Ackroyd's got an alibi. Even that Russell woman seems to have one—and a good job for her it is she has. Who is left? Only Ralph and Flora! And say what you will, I don't believe Ralph Paton is a murderer. A boy we've known all our lives."

Poirot was silent for a minute, watching the curling smoke rise from his cigarette. When at last he spoke, it was in a gentle far-away voice that produced a curious impression. It was totally unlike his usual manner.

"Let us take a man—a very ordinary man. A man with no idea of murder in his heart. There is in him somewhere a strain of weakness—deep down. It has so far never been called into play. Perhaps it never will be—and if so he will go to his grave honoured and respected by everyone. But let us suppose that something occurs. He is in difficulties—or perhaps not that even. He may stumble by accident on a secret—a secret involving life or death to someone. And his first impulse will be to speak out—to do his duty as an honest citizen. And then the strain of weakness tells. Here is a chance of money—a great amount of money. He wants money—he desires it—and it is so easy. He has to do nothing for it— just keep silence. That is the beginning. The desire for money grows. He must have more—and more! He is intoxicated by the gold mine which has opened at his feet. He becomes greedy. And in his greed he overreaches himself. One can press a man as far as one likes—but with a woman one must not press too far. For a woman has at heart a great desire to speak the truth. How many husbands who have deceived their wives go comfortably to their graves, carrying their secret with them! How many wives who have deceived their husbands wreck their lives by throwing the fact in those same husbands' teeth! They have been pressed too far. In a reckless moment (which they will afterwards regret, *bien entendu*) they fling safety to the winds and turn at bay, proclaiming the truth with great momentary satisfaction to themselves. So it was, I think, in this case. The strain was too great. And so there came your proverb, the death of the goose that laid the golden eggs. But that is not the end. Exposure faced the man of whom we are speaking. And he is not the same man he was—say, a year ago. His moral fibre is blunted. He is desperate. He is fighting a losing battle, and he is prepared to take any means that come to his hand, for exposure means ruin to him. And so—the dagger strikes!"

He was silent for a moment. It was as though he had laid a spell upon the room. I cannot try to describe the impression his words produced. There was something in the merciless analysis, and the ruthless power of vision which struck fear into both of us.

"Afterwards," he went on softly, "the dagger removed, he will be himself again, normal, kindly. But if the need again arises, then once more he will strike."

Caroline roused herself at last.

"You are speaking of Ralph Paton," she said. "You may be right, you may not, but you have no business to condemn a man unheard."

The telephone bell rang sharply. I went out into the hall, and took off the receiver.

"What?" I said. "Yes. Dr. Sheppard speaking."

I listened for a minute or two, then replied briefly. Replacing the receiver, I went back into the drawing room.

"Poirot," I said, "they have detained a man at Liverpool. His name is Charles Kent, and he is believed to be the stranger who visited Fernly that night. They want me to go to Liverpool at once and identify him."

Eighteen

CHARLES KENT

Half an hour later saw Poirot, myself, and Inspector Raglan in the train on the way to Liverpool. The inspector was clearly very excited.

"We may get a line on the blackmailing part of the business, if on nothing else," he declared jubilantly. "He's a rough customer, this fellow, by what I heard over the phone. Takes dope, too. We ought to find it easy to get what we want out of him. If there was the shadow of a motive, nothing's more likely than that he killed Mr. Ackroyd. But in that case, why is young Paton keeping out of the way. The whole thing's a muddle—that's what it is. By the way, M. Poirot, you were quite right about those fingerprints. They were Mr. Ackroyd's own. I had rather the same idea myself, but I dismissed it as hardly feasible."

I smiled to myself. Inspector Raglan was so very plainly saving his face.

"As regard this man," said Poirot, "he is not yet arrested, eh?"

"No, detained under suspicion."

"And what account does he give of himself?"

"Precious little," said the inspector, with a grin. "He's a wary bird, I gather. A lot of abuse, but very little more."

On arrival at Liverpool I was surprised to find that Poirot was welcomed with acclamation. Superintendent Hayes, who met us, had worked with Poirot over some case long ago, and had evidently an exaggerated opinion of his powers.

"Now we've got M. Poirot here we shan't be long," he said cheerfully. "I thought you'd retired, moosior?"

"So I had, my good Hayes, so I had. But how tedious is retirement! You cannot imagine to yourself the monotony with which day comes after day."

"Very likely. So you've come to have a look at our own particular find? Is this Dr. Sheppard? Think you'll be able to identify him, sir?"

"I'm not very sure," I said doubtfully.

"How did you get hold of him?" inquired Poirot.

"Description was circulated, as you know. In the press and privately. Not much to go on, I admit. This fellow has an American accent all right, and he doesn't deny that he was near King's Abbot that night. Just asks what the hell it is to do with us, and that he'll see us in—before he answers any questions."

"Is it permitted that I, too, see him?" asked Poirot.

The superintendent closed one eye knowingly.

"Very glad to have you, sir. You've got permission to do anything you please. Inspector Japp of Scotland Yard was asking after you the other day. Said he'd heard you were connected unofficially with this case. Where's Captain Paton hiding, sir, can you tell me that?"

"I doubt if it would be wise at the present juncture," said Poirot primly, and I bit my lips to prevent a smile.

The little man really did it very well.

After some further parley, we were taken to interview the prisoner.

He was a young fellow, I should say not more than twenty-two or three. Tall, thin, with slightly shaking hands, and the evidences of considerable physical strength somewhat run to seed. His hair was dark, but his eyes were blue and shifty, seldom meeting a glance squarely. I had all along cherished the illusion that there was something familiar about the figure I had met that night, but if this were indeed he, I was completely mistaken. He did not remind me in the least of anyone I knew.

"Now then, Kent," said the superintendent. "Stand up. Here are some visitors come to see you. Recognize any of them?"

Kent glared at us sullenly, but did not reply. I saw his glance waver over the three of us, and come back to rest on me.

"Well, sir," said the superintendent to me, "what do you say?"

"The height's the same," I said, "and as far as general appearance goes it might well be the man in question. Beyond that, I couldn't go."

"What the hell's the meaning of all this?" asked Kent. "What have you got against me? Come on, out with it! What am I supposed to have done?"

I nodded my head.

"It's the man," I said. "I recognize the voice."

"Recognize my voice, do you? Where do you think you heard it before?"

"On Friday evening last, outside the gates of Fernly Park. You asked me the way there."

"I did, did I?"

"Do you admit it?" asked the inspector.

"I don't admit anything. Not till I know what you've got on me."

"Have you not read the papers in the last few days?" asked Poirot, speaking for the first time.

The man's eyes narrowed.

"So that's it, is it? I saw an old gent had been croaked at Fernly. Trying to make out I did the job, are you?"

"You were there that night," said Poirot quietly.

"How do you know, mister?"

"By this." Poirot took something from his pocket and held it out.

It was the goose quill we had found in the summer house.

At the sight of it the man's face changed. He half held out his hand.

"Snow," said Poirot thoughtfully. "No, my friend, it is empty. It lay where you dropped it in the summer house that night."

Charles Kent looked at him uncertainly.

"You seem to know a hell of a lot about everything, you little foreign cock duck. Perhaps you remember this: the papers say that the old gent was croaked between a quarter to ten and ten o'clock?"

"That is so," agreed Poirot.

"Yes, but is it really so? That's what I'm getting at."

"This gentleman will tell you," said Poirot.

He indicated Inspector Raglan. The latter hesitated, glanced at Superintendent Hayes, then at Poirot, and finally, as though receiving sanction, he said:

"That's right. Between a quarter to ten and ten o'clock."

"Then you've nothing to keep me here for," said Kent. "I was away from Fernly Park by twenty-five minutes past nine. You can ask at the Dog and Whistle. That's a saloon about a mile out of Fernly on the road to Cranchester. I kicked up a bit of a row there, I remember. As near as nothing to quarter to ten, it was. How about that?"

Inspector Raglan wrote down something in his notebook.

"Well?" demanded Kent.

"Inquiries will be made," said the inspector. "If you've spoken the truth, you won't have anything to complain about. What were you doing at Fernly Park anyway?"

"Went there to meet someone."

"Who?"

"That's none of your business."

"You'd better keep a civil tongue in your head, my man," the superintendent warned him.

"To hell with a civil tongue. I went there on my own business, and that's all there is to it. If I was clear away before the murder was done, that's all that concerns the cops."

"Your name, it is Charles Kent," said Poirot. "Where were you born?"

The man stared at him, then he grinned.

"I'm a full-blown Britisher all right," he said.

"Yes," said Poirot meditatively. "I think you are. I fancy you were born in Kent."

The man stared.

"Why's that? Because of my name? What's that to do with it? Is a man whose name is Kent bound to be born in that particular county?"

"Under certain circumstances, I can imagine he might be," said Poirot very deliberately. "Under certain circumstances, you comprehend."

There was so much meaning in his voice as to surprise the two police officers. As for Charles Kent, he flushed a brick red, and for a moment I thought he was going to spring at Poirot. He thought better of it, however, and turned away with a kind of laugh.

Poirot nodded as though satisfied, and made his way out through the door. He was joined presently by the two officers.

"We'll verify that statement," remarked Raglan. "I don't think he's lying, though. But he's got to come clean with a statement as to what he was doing at Fernly. It looks to me as though we'd got our blackmailer all right. On the other hand, granted his story's correct, he couldn't have had anything to do with the actual murder. He'd got ten pounds on him when he was arrested—rather a large sum. I fancy that forty pounds went to him—the numbers of the notes didn't correspond, but of course he'd have changed them first thing. Mr. Ackroyd must have given him the money, and he made off with it as fast as possible. What was that about Kent being his birthplace? What's that got to do with it?"

"Nothing whatever," said Poirot mildly. "A little idea of mine, that was all. Me, I am famous for my little ideas."

"Are you really?" said Raglan, studying him with a puzzled expression.

The superintendent went into a roar of laughter.

"Many's the time I've heard Inspector Japp say that. M. Poirot and his little ideas! Too fanciful for me, he'd say, but always something in them."

"You mock yourself at me," said Poirot, smiling; "but never mind. The old ones they laugh last sometimes, when the young, clever ones do not laugh at all."

And nodding his head at them in a sage manner he walked out into the street.

He and I lunched together at an hotel. I know now that the whole thing lay clearly unravelled before him. He had got the last thread he needed to lead him to the truth.

But at the time I had no suspicion of the fact. I overestimated his general self-confidence, and I took it for granted that the things which puzzled me must be equally puzzling to him.

My chief puzzle was what the man Charles Kent could have been doing at Fernly. Again and again I put the question to myself and could get no satisfactory reply. At last I ventured a tentative query to Poirot. His reply was immediate.

"*Mon ami, I* do not think, I know."

"Really?" I said incredulously.

"Yes, indeed. I suppose now that to you it would not make sense if I said that he went to Fernly that night because he was born in Kent?"

I stared at him.

"It certainly doesn't seem to make sense to me," I said drily.

"Ah!" said Poirot pityingly. "Well, no matter. I have still my little idea."

Nineteen

FLORA ACKROYD

As I was returning from my round the following morning, I was hailed by Inspector Raglan. I pulled up, and the inspector mounted on the step.

"Good morning, Dr. Sheppard," he said. "Well, that alibi is all right enough."

"Charles Kent's?"

"Charles Kent's. The barmaid at the Dog and Whistle, Sally Jones, she remembers him perfectly. Picked out his photograph from among five others. It was just a quarter to ten when he came into the bar, and the Dog and Whistle is well over a mile from Fernly Park. The girl mentions that he had a lot of money on him—she saw him take a handful of notes out of his pocket. Rather surprised her, it did, seeing the class of fellow he was, with a pair of boots clean dropping off him. That's where that forty pounds went right enough."

"The man still refuses to give an account of his visit to Fernly?"

"Obstinate as a mule he is. I had a chat with Hayes at Liverpool over the wire this morning."

"Hercule Poirot says he knows the reason the man went there that night," I observed.

"Does he?" cried the inspector eagerly.

"Yes," I said maliciously. "He says he went there because he was born in Kent."

I felt a distinct pleasure in passing on my own discomfiture.

Raglan stared at me for a moment or two uncomprehendingly. Then a grin overspread his weasely countenance and he tapped his forehead significantly.

"But gone here," he said. "I've thought so for some time. Poor old chap, so that's why he had to give up and come down here. In the family, very likely. He's got a nephew who's quite off his crumpet."

"Poirot has?" I said, very surprised.

"Yes. Hasn't he ever mentioned him to you? Quite docile, I believe, and all that, but mad as a hatter, poor lad."

"Who told you that?"

Again a grin showed itself on Inspector Raglan's face.

"Your sister, Miss Sheppard, she told me all about it."

Really, Caroline is amazing. She never rests until she knows the last details of everybody's family secrets. Unfortunately, I have never been able to instil into her the decency of keeping them to herself.

"Jump in, Inspector," I said, opening the door of the car. "We'll go up to The Larches together, and acquaint our Belgian friend with the latest news."

"Might as well, I suppose. After all, even if he is a bit barmy, it was a useful tip he gave me about those fingerprints. He's got a bee in his bonnet about the man Kent, but who knows—there may be something useful behind it."

Poirot received us with his usual smiling courtesy.

He listened to the information we had brought him, nodding his head now and then.

"Seems quite O.K., doesn't it?" said the inspector rather gloomily. "A chap can't be murdering someone in one place when he's drinking in the bar in another place a mile away."

"Are you going to release him?"

"Don't see what else we can do. We can't very well hold him for obtaining money on false pretences. Can't prove a ruddy thing."

The inspector tossed a match into the grate in a disgruntled fashion. Poirot retrieved it and put it neatly in a little receptacle designed for the purpose. His action was purely mechanical. I could see that his thoughts were on something very different.

"If I were you," he said at last, "I should not release the man Charles Kent yet."

"What do you mean?"

Raglan stared at him.

"What I say. I should not release him yet."

"You don't think he can have had anything to do with the murder, do you?"

"I think probably not—but one cannot be certain yet."

"But haven't I just told you—?"

Poirot raised a hand protestingly.

"*Mais oui, mais oui.* I heard. I am not deaf—or stupid, thank the good God! But you see, you approach the matter from the wrong—the wrong—premises, is not that the word?"

The inspector stared at him heavily.

"I don't see how you make that out. Look here, we know Mr. Ackroyd was alive at a quarter to ten. You admit that, don't you?"

Poirot looked at him for a moment, then shook his head with a quick smile.

"I admit nothing that is not—*proved!*"

"Well, we've got proof enough of that. We've got Miss Flora Ackroyd's evidence."

"That she said good night to her uncle? But me—I do not always believe what a young lady tells me—no, not even when she is charming and beautiful."

"But hang it all, man, Parker saw her coming out of the door."

"No." Poirot's voice rang out with sudden sharpness. "That is just what he did not see. I satisfied myself of that by a little experiment the other day—you remember, doctor? Parker saw her *outside* the door, with her hand on the handle. He did not see her come out of the room."

"But—where else could she have been?"

"Perhaps on the stairs."

"The stairs?"

"That is my little idea—yes."

"But those stairs only lead to Mr. Ackroyd's bedroom."

"Precisely."

And still the inspector stared.

"You think she'd been up to her uncle's bedroom? Well, why not? Why should she lie about it?"

"Ah! that is just the question. It depends on what she was doing there, does it not?"

"You mean—the money? Hang it all, you don't suggest that it was Miss Ackroyd who took that forty pounds?"

"I suggest nothing," said Poirot. "But I will remind you of this. Life was not very easy for that mother and daughter. There were bills—there was constant trouble over small sums of money. Roger Ackroyd was a peculiar man over money matters. The girl might be at her wits' end for a comparatively small sum. Figure to yourself then what happens. She has taken the money, she descends the little staircase. When she is halfway down she hears the chink of glass from the hall. She has not a doubt of what it is—Parker coming to the study. At all costs she must not be found on the stairs—Parker will not forget it, he will think it odd. If the money is missed, Parker is sure to remember having seen her come down those stairs. She has just time to rush down to the study door—with her hand on the handle to show that she has just come out, when Parker appears in the doorway. She says the first thing that comes into her head, a repetition of Roger Ackroyd's orders earlier in the evening, and then goes upstairs to her own room."

"Yes, but later," persisted the inspector, "she must have realized the vital importance of speaking the truth? Why, the whole case hinges on it!"

"Afterwards," said Poirot drily, "it was a little difficult for Mademoiselle Flora. She is told simply that the police are here and that there has been a robbery. Naturally she jumps to the conclusion that the theft of the money has been discovered. Her one idea is to stick to her story. When she learns that her uncle is dead she is panic-stricken. Young women do not faint nowadays, monsieur, without considerable provocation. *Eh bien!* There it is. She is bound to stick to her story, or else confess everything. And a young and pretty girl does not like to admit that she is a thief—especially before those whose esteem she is anxious to retain."

Raglan brought his fist down with a thump on the table.

"I'll not believe it," he said. "It's—it's not credible. And you—you've known this all along?"

"The possibility has been in my mind from the first," admitted Poirot. "I was always convinced that Mademoiselle Flora was hiding something from us. To satisfy myself, I made the little experiment I told you of. Dr. Sheppard accompanied me."

"A test for Parker, you said it was," I remarked bitterly.

"Mon ami," said Poirot apologetically, "as I told you at the time, one must say something."

The inspector rose.

"There's only one thing for it," he declared. "We must tackle the young lady right away. You'll come up to Fernly with me, M. Poirot?"

"Certainly. Dr. Sheppard will drive us up in his car."

I acquiesced willingly.

On inquiry for Miss Ackroyd, we were shown into the billiard room. Flora and Major Hector Blunt were sitting on the long window seat.

"Good morning, Miss Ackroyd," said the inspector. "Can we have a word or two alone with you?"

Blunt got up at once and moved to the door.

"What is it?" asked Flora nervously. "Don't go, Major Blunt. He can stay, can't he?" she asked, turning to the inspector.

"That's as you like," said the inspector drily. "There's a question or two it's my duty to put to you, miss, but I'd prefer to do so privately, and I dare say you'd prefer it also."

Flora looked keenly at him. I saw her face grow whiter. Then she turned and spoke to Blunt.

"I want you to stay—please—yes, I mean it. Whatever the inspector has to say to me, I'd rather you heard it."

Raglan shrugged his shoulders.

"Well, if you will have it so, that's all there is to it. Now, Miss Ackroyd, M. Poirot here has made a certain suggestion to me. He suggests that you weren't in the study at all last Friday night, that you never saw Mr. Ackroyd to say goodnight to him, that instead of being in the study you were on the stairs leading down from your uncle's bedroom when you heard Parker coming across the hall."

Flora's gaze shifted to Poirot. He nodded back at her.

"Mademoiselle, the other day, when we sat round the table, I implored you to be frank with me. What one does not tell to Papa Poirot he finds out. It was that, was it not? See, I will make it easy for you. You took the money, did you not?"

"The money?" said Blunt sharply.

There was a silence which lasted for at least a minute.

Then Flora drew herself up and spoke.

"M. Poirot is right. I took that money. I stole. I am a thief—yes, a common, vulgar little thief. Now you know! I am glad it has come out. It's been a nightmare, these last few days!" She sat down suddenly and buried her face in her hands. She spoke huskily through her fingers. "You don't know what my life has been since I came here. Wanting things, scheming for them, lying, cheating, running up bills, promising to pay—oh! I hate myself when I think of it all! That's what brought us together, Ralph and I. We were both weak! I understood him, and I was sorry—because I'm the same underneath. We're not strong enough to stand alone, either of us. We're weak, miserable, despicable things."

She looked at Blunt and suddenly stamped her foot.

"Why do you look at me like that—as though you couldn't believe? I may be a thief—but at any rate I'm real now. I'm not lying any more. I'm not pretending to be the kind of girl you like, young and innocent and simple. I don't care if you never want to see me again. I hate myself, despise myself—but you've got to believe one thing, if speaking the truth would have made things better for Ralph, I would have spoken out. But I've seen all along that it wouldn't be better for Ralph—it makes the case against him blacker than ever. I was not doing him any harm by sticking to my lie."

"Ralph," said Blunt. "I see—always Ralph."

"You don't understand," said Flora hopelessly. "You never will."

She turned to the inspector.

"I admit everything; I was at my wits' end for money. I never saw my uncle that evening after he left the dinner table. As to the money, you can take what steps you please. Nothing could be worse than it is now!"

Suddenly she broke down again, hid her face in her hands, and rushed from the room.

"Well," said the inspector in a flat tone, "so that's that."

He seemed rather at a loss what to do next.

Blunt came forward.

"Inspector Raglan," he said quietly, "that money was given to me by Mr. Ackroyd for a special purpose. Miss Ackroyd never touched it. When she says she did, she is lying with the idea of shielding Captain Paton. The truth is as I said, and I am prepared to go into the witness-box and swear to it."

He made a kind of jerky bow, then turning abruptly he left the room.

Poirot was after him in a flash. He caught the other up in the hall.

"Monsieur—a moment, I beg of you, if you will be so good."

"Well, sir?"

Blunt was obviously impatient. He stood frowning down on Poirot.

"It is this," said Poirot rapidly: "I am not deceived by your little fantasy. No, indeed. It was truly Miss Flora who took the money. All the same it is well imagined what you say—it pleases me. It is very good what you have done there. You are a man quick to think and to act."

"I'm not in the least anxious for your opinion, thank you," said Blunt coldly.

He made once more as though to pass on, but Poirot, not at all offended, laid a detaining hand on his arm.

"Ah! but you are to listen to me. I have more to say. The other day I spoke of concealments. Very well, all along I have seen what you are concealing. Mademoiselle Flora, you love her with all your heart. From the first moment you saw her, is it not so? Oh! let us not mind saying these things—why must one in England think it necessary to mention love as though it were some disgraceful secret? You love Mademoiselle Flora. You seek to conceal that fact from all the world. That is very good—that is as it should be. But take the advice of Hercule Poirot—do not conceal it from mademoiselle herself."

Blunt had shown several signs of restlessness whilst Poirot was speaking, but the closing words seemed to rivet his attention.

"What d'you mean by that?" he said sharply.

"You think that she loves the Capitaine Ralph Paton—but I, Hercule Poirot, tell you that that is not so. Mademoiselle Flora accepted Captain Paton to please her uncle, and because she saw in the marriage a way of escape from her life here which was becoming frankly insupportable to her. She liked him, and there was much sympathy and understanding between them. But love—no! It is not Captain Paton Mademoiselle Flora loves."

"What the devil do you mean?" asked Blunt.

I saw the dark flush under his tan.

"You have been blind, monsieur. Blind! She is loyal, the little one. Ralph Paton is under a cloud, she is bound in honour to stick by him."

I felt it was time I put in a word to help on the good work.

"My sister told me the other night," I said encouragingly, "that Flora had never cared a penny piece for Ralph Paton, and never would. My sister is always right about these things."

Blunt ignored my well-meant offers. He spoke to Poirot.

"D'you really think—" he began, and stopped.

He is one of those inarticulate men who find it hard to put things into words.

Poirot knows no such disability.

"If you doubt me, ask her yourself, monsieur. But perhaps you no longer care to—the affair of the money—"

Blunt gave a sound like an angry laugh.

"Think I'd hold that against her? Roger was always a queer chap about money. She got in a mess and didn't dare tell him. Poor kid. Poor lonely kid."

Poirot looked thoughtfully at the side door.

"Mademoiselle Flora went into the garden, I think," he murmured.

"I've been every kind of a fool," said Blunt abruptly. "Rum conversation we've been having. Like one of those Danish plays. But you're a sound fellow, M. Poirot. Thank you."

He took Poirot's hand and gave it a grip which caused the other to wince in anguish. Then he strode to the side door and passed out into the garden.

"Not every kind of a fool," murmured Poirot, tenderly nursing the injured member. "Only one kind—the fool in love."

Twenty

Miss Russell

Inspector Raglan had received a bad jolt. He was not deceived by Blunt's valiant lie any more than we had been. Our way back to the village was punctuated by his complaints.

"This alters everything, this does. I don't know whether you've realized it, Monsieur Poirot?"

"I think so, yes, I think so," said Poirot. "You see, me, I have been familiar with the idea for some time."

Inspector Raglan, who had only had the idea presented to him a short half hour ago, looked at Poirot unhappily, and went on with his discoveries.

"Those alibis now. Worthless! Absolutely worthless. Got to start again. Find out what everyone was doing from nine-thirty onwards. Nine-thirty—that's the time we've got to hang on to. You were quite right about the man Kent—we don't release *him* yet awhile. Let me see now—nine-forty-five at the Dog and Whistle. He might have got there in a quarter of an hour if he ran. It's just possible that it was *his* voice Mr. Raymond heard talking to Mr. Ackroyd—asking for money which Mr. Ackroyd refused. But one thing's clear—it wasn't he who sent the telephone message. The station is half a mile in the other direction—over a mile and a half from the Dog and Whistle, and he was at the Dog and Whistle until about ten minutes past ten. Dang that telephone call! We always come up against it."

"We do indeed," agreed Poirot. "It is curious."

"It's just possible that if Captain Paton climbed into his uncle's room and found him there murdered, *he* may have sent it. Got the wind up, thought he'd be accused, and cleared out. That's possible, isn't it?"

"Why should he have telephoned?"

"May have had doubts if the old man was really dead. Thought he'd get the doctor up there as soon as possible, but didn't want to give himself away. Yes, I say now, how's that for a theory? Something in that, I should say."

The inspector swelled his chest out importantly. He was so plainly delighted with himself that any words of ours would have been quite superfluous.

We arrived back at my house at this minute, and I hurried in to my surgery patients, who had all been waiting a considerable time, leaving Poirot to walk to the police station with the inspector.

Having dismissed the last patient, I strolled into the little room at the back of the house which I call my workshop—I am rather proud of the home-made wireless set I turned out. Caroline hates my workroom. I have kept my tools there, and Annie is not allowed to wreak havoc with a dustpan and brush. I was just adjusting the interior of an alarm clock which had been denounced as wholly unreliable by the household, when the door opened and Caroline put her head in.

"Oh! there you are, James," she said, with deep disapproval. "M. Poirot wants to see you."

"Well," I said, rather irritably, for her sudden entrance had startled me and I had let go of a piece of delicate mechanism. "If he wants to see me, he can come in here."

"In here?" said Caroline.

"That's what I said—in here."

Caroline gave a sniff of disapproval and retired. She returned in a moment or two, ushering in Poirot, and then retired again, shutting the door with a bang.

"Aha! my friend," said Poirot, coming forward and rubbing his hands. "You have not got rid of me so easily, you see!"

"Finished with the inspector?" I asked.

"For the moment, yes. And you, you have seen all the patients?"

"Yes."

Poirot sat down and looked at me, tilting his egg-shaped head on one side, with the air of one who savours a very delicious joke.

"You are in error," he said at last. "You have still one patient to see."

"Not you?" I exclaimed in surprise.

"Ah, not me, *bien entendu*. Me, I have the health magnificent. No, to tell you the truth, it is a little *complot* of mine. There is someone I wish to see, you understand—and at the same time it is not necessary that the whole village should intrigue itself about the matter—which is what would happen if the lady were seen to come to my house—for it is a lady. But to you she has already come as a patient before."

"Miss Russell!" I exclaimed.

"*Précisément*. I wish much to speak with her, so I send her the little note and make the appointment in your surgery. You are not annoyed with me?"

"On the contrary," I said. "That is, presuming I am allowed to be present at the interview?"

"But naturally! In your own surgery!"

"You know," I said, throwing down the pincers I was holding, "it's extraordinarily intriguing, the whole thing. Every new development that arises is like the shake you give to a kaleidoscope—the thing changes entirely in aspect. Now, why are you so anxious to see Miss Russell?"

Poirot raised his eyebrows.

"Surely it is obvious?" he murmured.

"There you go again," I grumbled. "According to you everything is obvious. But you leave me walking about in a fog."

Poirot shook his head genially to me.

"You mock yourself at me. Take the matter of Mademoiselle Flora. The inspector was surprised—but you—you were not."

"I never dreamed of her being the thief," I expostulated.

"That—perhaps no. But I was watching your face and you were not—like Inspector Raglan—startled and incredulous."

I thought for a minute or two.

"Perhaps you are right," I said at last. "All along I've felt that Flora was keeping back something—so the truth, when it came, was subconsciously expected. It upset Inspector Raglan very much indeed, poor man."

"Ah! *pour ça oui!* The poor man must rearrange all his ideas. I profited by his state of mental chaos to induce him to grant me a little favour."

"What was that?"

Poirot took a sheet of notepaper from his pocket. Some words were written on it, and he read them aloud.

"The police have, for some days, been seeking for Captain Ralph Paton, the nephew of Mr. Ackroyd of Fernly Park, whose death occurred under such tragic circumstances last Friday. Captain Paton has been found at Liverpool, where he was on the point of embarking for America."

He folded up the piece of paper again.

"That, my friend, will be in the newspapers tomorrow morning."

I stared at him, dumbfounded.

"But—but it isn't true! He's not at Liverpool!"

Poirot beamed on me.

"You have the intelligence so quick! No, he has not been found at Liverpool. Inspector Raglan was very loath to let me send this paragraph to the press, especially as I could not take him into my confidence. But I assured him most solemnly that very interesting results would follow its appearance in print, so he gave in, after stipulating that he was, on no account, to bear the responsibility."

I stared at Poirot. He smiled back at me.

"It beats me," I said at last, "what you expect to get out of that."

"You should employ your little grey cells," said Poirot gravely.

He rose and came across to the bench.

"It is that you have really the love of the machinery," he said, after inspecting the débris of my labours.

Every man has his hobby. I immediately drew Poirot's attention to my home-made wireless. Finding him sympathetic, I showed him one or two little inventions of my own—trifling things, but useful in the house.

"Decidedly," said Poirot, "you should be an inventor by trade, not a doctor. But I hear the bell—that is your patient. Let us go into the surgery."

Once before I had been struck by the remnants of beauty in the house-keeper's face. This morning I was struck anew. Very simply dressed in black, tall, upright and independent as ever, with her big dark eyes and an unwonted flush of colour in her usually pale cheeks, I realized that as a girl she must have been startlingly handsome.

"Good morning, mademoiselle," said Poirot. "Will you be seated? Dr. Sheppard is so kind as to permit me the use of his surgery for a little conversation I am anxious to have with you."

Miss Russell sat down with her usual composure. If she felt any inward agitation, it did not display itself in any outward manifestation.

"It seems a queer way of doing things, if you'll allow me to say so," she remarked.

"Miss Russell—I have news to give you."

"Indeed!"

"Charles Kent has been arrested at Liverpool."

Not a muscle of her face moved. She merely opened her eyes a trifle wider, and asked, with a tinge of defiance:

"Well, what of it?"

But at that moment it came to me—the resemblance that had haunted me all along, something familiar in the defiance of Charles Kent's manner. The two voices, one rough and coarse, the other painfully ladylike—were strangely the same in timbre. It was of Miss Russell that I had been reminded that night outside the gates of Fernly Park.

I looked at Poirot, full of my discovery, and he gave me an imperceptible nod.

In answer to Miss Russell's question, he threw out his hands in a thoroughly French gesture.

"I thought you might be interested, that is all," he said mildly.

"Well, I'm not particularly," said Miss Russell. "Who is this Charles Kent anyway?"

"He is a man, mademoiselle, who was at Fernly on the night of the murder."

"Really?"

"Fortunately for him, he has an alibi. At a quarter to ten he was at a public-house a mile from here."

"Lucky for him," commented Miss Russell.

"But we still do not know what he was doing at Fernly—who it was he went to meet, for instance."

"I'm afraid I can't help you at all," said the housekeeper politely. "Nothing came to *my* ears. If that is all—"

She made a tentative movement as though to rise. Poirot stopped her.

"It is not quite all," he said smoothly. "This morning fresh developments have arisen. It seems now that Mr. Ackroyd was murdered, not at a quarter to ten, but *before*. Between ten minutes to nine, when Dr. Sheppard left, and a quarter to ten."

I saw the colour drain from the housekeeper's face, leaving it dead white. She leaned forward, her figure swaying.

"But Miss Ackroyd said—Miss Ackroyd said—"

"Miss Ackroyd has admitted that she was lying. She was never in the study at all that evening."

"Then—"

"Then it would seem that in this Charles Kent we have the man we are looking for. He came to Fernly, can give no account of what he was doing there—"

"I can tell you what he was doing there. He never touched a hair of old Ackroyd's head—he never went near the study. He didn't do it, I tell you."

She was leaning forward. That iron self-control was broken through at last. Terror and desperation was in her face.

"M. Poirot! M. Poirot! Oh, do believe me."

Poirot got up and came to her. He patted her reassuringly on the shoulder.

"But yes—but yes, I will believe. I had to make you speak, you know."

For an instant suspicion flared up in her.

"Is what you said true?"

"That Charles Kent is suspected of the crime? Yes, that is true. You alone can save him, by telling the reason for his being at Fernly."

"He came to see me." She spoke in a low, hurried voice. "I went out to meet him—"

"In the summerhouse, yes, I know."

"How do you know?"

"Mademoiselle, it is the business of Hercule Poirot to know things. I know that you went out earlier in the evening, that you left a message in the summerhouse to say what time you would be there."

"Yes, I did. I had heard from him—saying he was coming. I dared not let him come to the house. I wrote to the address he gave me and said I would meet him in the summerhouse, and described it to him so that he would be able to find it. Then I was afraid he might not wait there patiently, and I ran out and left a piece of paper to say I would be there about ten minutes past nine. I didn't want the servants to see me, so I slipped out through the drawing room window. As I came back, I met Dr. Sheppard, and I fancied that he would think it queer. I was out of breath, for I had been running. I had no idea that he was expected to dinner that night."

She paused.

"Go on," said Poirot. "You went out to meet him at ten minutes past nine. What did you say to each other?"

"It's difficult. You see—"

"Mademoiselle," said Poirot, interrupting her, "in this matter I must have the whole truth. What you tell us need never go beyond these four walls. Dr. Sheppard will be discreet, and so shall I. See, I will help you. This Charles Kent, he is your son, is he not?"

She nodded. The colour had flamed into her cheeks.

"No one has ever known. It was long ago—long ago—down in Kent. I was not married. . . ."

"So you took the name of the county as a surname for him. I understand."

"I got work. I managed to pay for his board and lodging. I never told him that I was his mother. But he turned out badly, he drank, then took to drugs. I managed to pay his passage out to Canada. I didn't hear of him for a year or two. Then, somehow or other, he found out that I was his mother. He wrote asking me for money. Finally, I heard from him back in this country again.

He was coming to see me at Fernly, he said. I dared not let him come to the house. I have always been considered so—so very respectable. If anyone got an inkling—it would have been all up with my post as housekeeper. So I wrote to him in the way I have just told you."

"And in the morning you came to see Dr. Sheppard?"

"Yes. I wondered if something could be done. He was not a bad boy—before he took to drugs."

"I see," said Poirot. "Now let us go on with the story. He came that night to the summerhouse?"

"Yes, he was waiting for me when I got there. He was very rough and abusive. I had brought with me all the money I had, and I gave it to him. We talked a little, and then he went away."

"What time was that?"

"It must have been between twenty and twenty-five minutes past nine. It was not yet half past when I got back to the house."

"Which way did he go?"

"Straight out the same way he came, by the path that joined the drive just inside the lodge gates."

Poirot nodded.

"And you, what did you do?"

"I went back to the house. Major Blunt was walking up and down the terrace smoking, so I made a detour to get round to the side door. It was just then on half past nine, as I tell you."

Poirot nodded again. He made a note or two in a microscopic pocketbook.

"I think that is all," he said thoughtfully.

"Ought I—?" she hesitated. "Ought I to tell all this to Inspector Raglan?"

"It may come to that. But let us not be in a hurry. Let us proceed slowly, with due order and method. Charles Kent is not yet formally charged with murder. Circumstances may arise which will render your story unnecessary."

Miss Russell rose.

"Thank you very much, M. Poirot," she said. "You have been very kind—very kind indeed. You—you do believe me, don't you? That Charles had nothing to do with this wicked murder!"

"There seems no doubt that the man who was talking to Mr. Ackroyd in the library at nine-thirty could not possibly have been your son. Be of good courage, mademoiselle. All will yet be well."

Miss Russell departed. Poirot and I were left together.

"So that's that," I said. "Every time we come back to Ralph Paton. How did you manage to spot Miss Russell as the person Charles Kent came to meet? Did you notice the resemblance?"

"I had connected her with the unknown man long before we actually came face to face with him. As soon as we found that quill. The quill suggested dope, and I remembered your account of Miss Russell's visit to you. Then I found the article on cocaine in that morning's paper. It all seemed very clear. She had heard from someone that morning—someone addicted to drugs, she read the article in the paper, and she came to ask you a few tentative questions. She mentioned cocaine, since the article in question was on cocaine. Then, when you seemed too interested, she switched hurriedly to the subject of detective stories and untraceable poisons. I suspected a son or a brother, or some other undesirable male relation. Ah! but I must go. It is the time of the lunch."

"Stay and lunch with us," I suggested.

Poirot shook his head. A faint twinkle came into his eye.

"Not again today. I should not like to force Mademoiselle Caroline to adopt a vegetarian diet two days in succession."

It occurred to me that there was not much which escaped Hercule Poirot.

Twenty-one

The Paragraph in the Paper

Caroline, of course, had not failed to see Miss Russell come to the surgery door. I had anticipated this, and had ready an elaborate account of the lady's bad knee. But Caroline was not in a cross-questioning mood. Her point of view was that she knew what Miss Russell had really come for and that *I* didn't.

"Pumping you, James," said Caroline. "Pumping you in the most shameless manner, I've no doubt. It's no good interrupting. I dare say you hadn't the least idea she was doing it even. Men *are* so simple. She knows that you are in M. Poirot's confidence, and she wants to find out things. Do you know what I think, James?"

"I couldn't begin to imagine. You think so many extraordinary things."

"It's no good being sarcastic. I think Miss Russell knows more about Mr. Ackroyd's death than she is prepared to admit."

Caroline leaned back triumphantly in her chair.

"Do you really think so?" I said absently.

"You are very dull today, James. No animation about you. It's that liver of yours."

Our conversation then dealt with purely personal matters.

The paragraph inspired by Poirot duly appeared in our daily paper the next morning. I was in the dark as to its purpose, but its effect on Caroline was immense.

She began by stating, most untruly, that she had said as much all along. I raised my eyebrows, but did not argue. Caroline, however, must have felt a prick of conscience, for she went on:

"I mayn't have actually mentioned Liverpool, but I knew he'd try to get away to America. That's what Crippen did."

"Without much success," I reminded her.

"Poor boy, and so they've caught him. I consider, James, that it's your duty to see that he isn't hung."

"What do you expect me to do?"

"Why, you're a medical man, aren't you? You've known him from a boy upwards. Not mentally responsible. That's the line to take, clearly. I read only the other day that they're very happy in Broadmoor—it's quite like a high-class club."

But Caroline's words had reminded me of something.

"I never knew that Poirot had an imbecile nephew?" I said curiously.

"Didn't you? Oh, he told me all about it. Poor lad. It's a great grief to all the family. They've kept him at home so far, but it's getting to such a pitch that they're afraid he'll have to go into some kind of institution."

"I suppose you know pretty well everything there is to know about Poirot's family by this time," I said, exasperated.

"Pretty well," said Caroline complacently. "It's a great relief to people to be able to tell all their troubles to someone."

"It might be," I said, "if they were ever allowed to do so spontaneously. Whether they enjoy having confidences screwed out of them by force is another matter."

Caroline merely looked at me with an air of a Christian martyr enjoying martyrdom.

"You are so self-contained, James," she said. "You hate speaking out, or parting with any information yourself, and you think everybody else must be just like you. I should hope that I never screw confidences out of anybody. For instance, if M. Poirot comes in this afternoon, as he said he might do, I shall not dream of asking him who it was arrived at his house early this morning."

"Early this morning?" I queried.

"Very early," said Caroline. "Before the milk came. I just happened to be looking out of the window—the blind was flapping. It was a man. He came in a closed car, and he was all muffled up. I couldn't get a glimpse of his face. But I will tell you *my* idea, and you'll see that I'm right."

"What's your idea?"

Caroline dropped her voice mysteriously.

"A Home Office expert," she breathed.

"A Home Office expert," I said, amazed. "My dear Caroline!"

"Mark my words, James, you'll see that I'm right. That Russell woman was here that morning after your poisons. Roger Ackroyd might easily have been poisoned in his food that night."

I laughed out loud.

"Nonsense," I cried. "He was stabbed in the neck. You know that as well as I do."

"After death, James," said Caroline; "to make a false clue."

"My good woman," I said, "I examined the body, and I know what I'm talking about. That wound wasn't inflicted after death—it was the cause of death, and you need make no mistake about it."

Caroline merely continued to look omniscient, which so annoyed me that I went on:

"Perhaps you will tell me, Caroline, if I have a medical degree or if I have not?"

"You have the medical degree, I dare say, James—at least, I mean I know you have. But you've no imagination whatever."

"Having endowed you with a treble portion, there was none left over for me," I said drily.

I was amused to see Caroline's manoeuvres that afternoon when Poirot duly arrived. My sister, without asking a direct question, skirted the subject of the mysterious guest in every way imaginable. By the twinkle in Poirot's eyes, I saw that he realized her object. He remained blandly impervious, and blocked her bowling so successfully that she herself was at a loss how to proceed.

Having, I suspect, enjoyed the little game, he rose to his feet and suggested a walk.

"It is that I need to reduce the figure a little," he explained. "You will come with me, doctor? And perhaps later, Miss Caroline will give us some tea."

"Delighted," said Caroline. "Won't your—er—guest come in also?"

"You are too kind," said Poirot. "But no, my friend reposes himself. Soon you must make his acquaintance."

"Quite an old friend of yours, so somebody told me," said Caroline, making one last valiant effort.

"Did they?" murmured Poirot. "Well, we must start."

Our tramp took us in the direction of Fernly. I had guessed beforehand that it might do so. I was beginning to understand Poirot's methods. Every little irrelevancy had a bearing upon the whole.

"I have a commission for you, my friend," he said at last. "Tonight, at my house. I desire to have a little conference. You will attend, will you not?"

"Certainly," I said.

"Good. I need also those in the house—that is to say: Mrs. Ackroyd, Mademoiselle Flora, Major Blunt, Mr. Raymond. I want you to be my ambassador. This little reunion is fixed for nine o'clock. You will ask them—yes?"

"With pleasure; but why not ask them yourself?"

"Because they will then put the questions: Why? What for? They will demand what my idea is. And, as you know, my friend, I much dislike to have to explain my little ideas until the time comes."

I smiled a little.

"My friend Hastings, he of whom I told you, used to say of me that I was the human oyster. But he was unjust. Of facts, I keep nothing to myself. But to everyone his own interpretation of them."

"When do you want me to do this?"

"Now, if you will. We are close to the house."

"Aren't you coming in?"

"No, me, I will promenade myself in the grounds. I will rejoin you by the lodge gates in a quarter of an hour's time."

I nodded, and set off on my task. The only member of the family at home proved to be Mrs. Ackroyd, who was sipping an early cup of tea. She received me very graciously.

"So grateful to you, doctor," she murmured, "for clearing up that little matter with M. Poirot. But life is one trouble after another. You have heard about Flora, of course?"

"What exactly?" I asked cautiously.

"This new engagement. Flora and Hector Blunt. Of course not such a good match as Ralph would have been. But after all, happiness comes first. What dear Flora needs is an older man—someone steady and reliable, and then Hector is really a very distinguished man in his way. You saw the news of Ralph's arrest in the paper this morning?"

"Yes," I said, "I did."

"Horrible." Mrs. Ackroyd closed her eyes and shuddered. "Geoffrey Raymond was in a terrible way. Rang up Liverpool. But they wouldn't tell him anything at the police station there. In fact, they said they hadn't arrested Ralph at all. Mr. Raymond insists that it's all a mistake—a—what do they call it?—*canard* of the newspaper's. I've forbidden it to be mentioned before the servants. Such a terrible disgrace. Fancy if Flora had actually been married to him."

Mrs. Ackroyd shut her eyes in anguish. I began to wonder how soon I should be able to deliver Poirot's invitation.

Before I had time to speak, Mrs. Ackroyd was off again.

"You were here yesterday, weren't you, with that dreadful Inspector Raglan? Brute of a man—he terrified Flora into saying she took that money from poor Roger's room. And the matter was so simple, really. The dear child wanted to borrow a few pounds, didn't like to disturb her uncle since he'd given strict orders against it. But knowing where he kept his notes she went there and took what she needed."

"Is that Flora's account of the matter?" I asked.

"My dear doctor, you know what girls are nowadays. So easily acted on by suggestion. You, of course, know all about hypnosis and that sort of thing. The inspector shouts at her, says the word 'steal' over and over again, until the poor child gets an inhibition—or is it a complex?—I always mix up those two words—and actually thinks herself that she has stolen the money. I saw at once how it was. But I can't be too thankful for the whole misunderstanding in one way—it seems to have brought those two together—Hector and Flora, I mean.

And I assure you that I have been very much worried about Flora in the past: why, at one time I actually thought there was going to be some kind of understanding between her and young Raymond. Just think of it!" Mrs. Ackroyd's voice rose in shrill horror. "A private secretary—with practically no means of his own."

"It would have been a severe blow to you," I said. "Now, Mrs. Ackroyd, I've got a message for you from M. Hercule Poirot."

"For me?"

Mrs. Ackroyd looked quite alarmed.

I hastened to reassure her, and I explained what Poirot wanted.

"Certainly," said Mrs. Ackroyd rather doubtfully. "I suppose we must come if M. Poirot says so. But what is it all about? I like to know beforehand."

I assured the lady truthfully that I myself did not know any more than she did.

"Very well," said Mrs. Ackroyd at last, rather grudgingly, "I will tell the others, and we will be there at nine o'clock."

Thereupon I took my leave, and joined Poirot at the agreed meeting-place.

"I've been longer than a quarter of an hour, I'm afraid," I remarked. "But once that good lady starts talking it's a matter of the utmost difficulty to get a word in edgeways."

"It is of no matter," said Poirot. "Me, I have been well amused. This park is magnificent."

We set off homewards. When we arrived, to our great surprise Caroline, who had evidently been watching for us, herself opened the door.

She put her finger to her lips. Her face was full of importance and excitement.

"Ursula Bourne," she said, "the parlourmaid from Fernly. She's here! I've put her in the dining room. She's in a terrible way, poor thing. Says she must see M. Poirot at once. I've done all I could. Taken her a cup of hot tea. It really goes to one's heart to see anyone in such a state."

"In the dining room?" asked Poirot.

"This way," I said, and flung open the door.

Ursula Bourne was sitting by the table. Her arms were spread out in front of her, and she had evidently just lifted her head from where it had been buried. Her eyes were red with weeping.

"Ursula Bourne," I murmured.

But Poirot went past me with outstretched hands.

"No," he said, "that is not quite right, I think. It is not Ursula Bourne, is it, my child—but Ursula Paton? Mrs. Ralph Paton."

Twenty-two

Ursula's Story

For a moment or two the girl looked mutely at Poirot. Then, her reserve breaking down completely, she nodded her head once, and burst into an outburst of sobs.

Caroline pushed past me, and putting her arm round the girl, patted her on the shoulder.

"There, there, my dear," she said soothingly, "it will be all right. You'll see—everything will be all right."

Buried under curiosity and scandal-mongering there is a lot of kindness in Caroline. For the moment, even the interest of Poirot's revelation was lost in the sight of the girl's distress.

Presently Ursula sat up and wiped her eyes.

"This is very weak and silly of me," she said.

"No, no, my child," said Poirot kindly. "We can all realize the strain of this last week."

"It must have been a terrible ordeal," I said.

"And then to find that you knew," continued Ursula. "How did you know? Was it Ralph who told you?"

Poirot shook his head.

"You know what brought me to you tonight," went on the girl. *"This—"*

She held out a crumpled piece of newspaper, and I recognized the paragraph that Poirot had had inserted.

"It says that Ralph has been arrested. So everything is useless. I need not pretend any longer."

"Newspaper paragraphs are not always true, mademoiselle," murmured Poirot, having the grace to look ashamed of himself. "All the same, I think you will do well to make a clean breast of things. The truth is what we need now."

The girl hesitated, looking at him doubtfully.

"You do not trust me," said Poirot gently. "Yet all the same you came here to find me, did you not? Why was that?"

"Because I don't believe that Ralph did it," said the girl in a very low voice. "And I think that you are clever, and will find out the truth. And also—"

"Yes?"

"I think you are kind."

Poirot nodded his head several times.

"It is very good that—yes, it is very good. Listen, I do in verity believe that this husband of yours is innocent—but the affair marches badly. If I am to save him, I must know all there is to know—even if it should seem to make the case against him blacker than before."

"How well you understand," said Ursula.

"So you will tell me the whole story, will you not? From the beginning."

"You're not going to send *me* away, I hope," said Caroline, settling herself comfortably in an armchair. "What I want to know," she continued, "is why this child was masquerading as a parlourmaid?"

"Masquerading?" I queried.

"That's what I said. Why did you do it, child? For a wager?"

"For a living," said Ursula drily.

And encouraged, she began the story which I reproduce here in my own words.

Ursula Bourne, it seemed, was one of a family of seven—impoverished Irish gentlefolk. On the death of her father, most of the girls were cast out into the world to earn their own living. Ursula's eldest sister was married to Captain Folliott. It was she whom I had seen that Sunday, and the cause of her embarrassment was clear enough now. Determined to earn her living and not attracted to the idea of being a nursery governess—the one profession open to an untrained girl—Ursula preferred the job of parlourmaid. She scorned to label herself a "lady parlourmaid." She would be the real thing, her reference being supplied by her sister. At Fernly, despite an aloofness which, as has been seen, caused some comment, she was a success at her job—quick, competent and thorough.

"I enjoyed the work," she explained. "And I had plenty of time to myself."

And then came her meeting with Ralph Paton, and the love affair which culminated in a secret marriage. Ralph had persuaded her into that, somewhat against her will. He had declared that his stepfather would not hear of his marrying a penniless girl. Better to be married secretly, and break the news to him at some later and more favourable minute.

And so the deed was done, and Ursula Bourne became Ursula Paton. Ralph had declared that he meant to pay off his debts, find a job, and then, when he was in a position to support her, and independent of his adopted father, they would break the news to him.

But to people like Ralph Paton, turning over a new leaf is easier in theory than in practice. He hoped that his stepfather, whilst still in ignorance of the marriage, might be persuaded to pay his debts and put him on his feet again. But the revelation of the amount of Ralph's liabilities merely enraged Roger Ackroyd, and he refused to do anything at all. Some months passed, and then Ralph was bidden once more to Fernly. Roger Ackroyd did not beat about the bush. It was the desire of his heart that Ralph should marry Flora, and he put the matter plainly before the young man.

And here it was that the innate weakness of Ralph Paton showed itself. As always, he grasped at the easy, the immediate solution. As far as I could make out, neither Flora nor Ralph made any pretence of love. It was, on both sides, a business arrangement. Roger Ackroyd dictated his wishes—they agreed to them. Flora accepted a chance of liberty, money and an enlarged horizon, Ralph, of course, was playing a different game. But he was in a very awkward hole financially. He seized at the chance. His debts would be paid. He could start again with a clean sheet. His was not a nature to envisage the future, but I gather that he saw vaguely the engagement with Flora being broken off after a decent interval had elapsed. Both Flora and he stipulated that it should be kept a secret for the present. He was anxious to conceal it from Ursula. He felt instinctively that her nature, strong and resolute, with an inherent distaste for duplicity, was not one to welcome such a course.

Then came the crucial moment when Roger Ackroyd, always high-handed, decided to announce the engagement. He said no word of his intention to Ralph—only to Flora, and Flora, apathetic, raised no objection. On Ursula, the news fell like a bombshell. Summoned by her, Ralph came hurriedly down from town. They met in the wood, where part of their conversation was overheard by my sister. Ralph implored her to keep silent for a little while longer, Ursula was equally determined to have done with concealments. She would tell Mr. Ackroyd the truth without any further delay. Husband and wife parted acrimoniously.

Ursula, steadfast in her purpose, sought an interview with Roger Ackroyd that very afternoon, and revealed the truth to him. Their interview was a stormy one—it might have been even more stormy had not Roger Ackroyd been already obsessed with his own troubles. It was bad enough, however. Ackroyd was not the kind of man to forgive the deceit that had been practised upon him. His rancour was mainly directed to Ralph, but Ursula came in for her share, since he regarded her as a girl who had deliberately tried to "entrap" the adopted son of a very wealthy man. Unforgivable things were said on both sides.

That same evening Ursula met Ralph by appointment in the small summerhouse, stealing out from the house by the side door in order to do so. Their interview was made up of reproaches on both sides. Ralph charged Ursula with having irretrievably ruined his prospects by her ill-timed revelation. Ursula reproached Ralph with his duplicity.

They parted at last. A little over half an hour later came the discovery of Roger Ackroyd's body. Since that night Ursula had neither seen nor heard from Ralph.

As the story unfolded itself, I realized more and more what a damning series of facts it was. Alive, Ackroyd could hardly have failed to alter his will—I knew him well enough to realize that to do so would be his first thought. His death came in the nick of time for Ralph and Ursula Paton. Small wonder the girl had held her tongue, and played her part so consistently.

My meditations were interrupted. It was Poirot's voice speaking, and I knew from the gravity of his tone that he, too, was fully alive to the implications of the position.

"Mademoiselle, I must ask you one question, and you must answer it truthfully, for on it everything may hang: What time was it when you parted from Captain Ralph Paton in the summerhouse? Now, take a little minute so that your answer may be very exact."

The girl gave a half laugh, bitter enough in all conscience.

"Do you think I haven't gone over that again and again in my own mind? It was just half past nine when I went out to meet him. Major Blunt was walking up and down the terrace, so I had to go round through the bushes to avoid him. It must have been about twenty-seven minutes to ten when I reached the summerhouse. Ralph was waiting for me. I was with him ten minutes—not longer, for it was just a quarter to ten when I got back to the house."

I saw now the insistence of her question the other day. If only Ackroyd could have been proved to have been killed before a quarter to ten, and not after.

I saw the reflection of that thought in Poirot's next question.

"Who left the summerhouse first?"

"I did."

"Leaving Ralph Paton in the summerhouse?"

"Yes—but you don't think—"

"Mademoiselle, it is of no importance what I think. What did you do when you got back to the house?"

"I went up to my room."

"And stayed there until when?"

"Until about ten o'clock."

"Is there anyone who can prove that?"

"Prove? That I was in my room, you mean? Oh! no. But surely—oh! I see, they might think—they might think—"

I saw the dawning horror in her eyes.

Poirot finished the sentence for her.

"That it was *you* who entered by the window and stabbed Mr. Ackroyd as he sat in his chair? Yes, they might think just that."

"Nobody but a fool would think any such thing," said Caroline indignantly.

She patted Ursula on the shoulder.

The girl had her face hidden in her hands.

"Horrible," she was murmuring. "Horrible."

Caroline gave her a friendly shake.

"Don't worry, my dear," she said. "M. Poirot doesn't think that really. As for that husband of yours, I don't think much of him, and I tell you so candidly. Running away and leaving you to face the music."

But Ursula shook her head energetically.

"Oh, no," she cried. "It wasn't like that at all. Ralph would not run away on his own account. I see now. If he heard of his stepfather's murder, he might think himself that I had done it."

"He wouldn't think any such thing," said Caroline.

"I was so cruel to him that night—so hard and bitter. I wouldn't listen to what he was trying to say—wouldn't believe that he really cared. I just stood there telling him what I thought of him, and saying the coldest, cruellest things that came into my mind—trying my best to hurt him."

"Do him no harm," said Caroline. "Never worry about what you say to a man. They're so conceited that they never believe you mean it if it's unflattering."

Ursula went on nervously twisting and untwisting her hands.

"When the murder was discovered and he didn't come forward, I was terribly upset. Just for a moment I wondered—but then I knew he couldn't—he couldn't . . . But I wished he would come forward and say openly that he'd had nothing to do with it. I knew that he was fond of Dr. Sheppard, and I fancied that perhaps Dr. Sheppard might know where he was hiding."

She turned to me.

"That's why I said what I did to you that day. I thought, if you knew where he was, you might pass on the message to him."

"I?" I exclaimed.

"Why should James know where he was?" demanded Caroline sharply.

"It was very unlikely, I know," admitted Ursula, "but Ralph had often spoken of Dr. Sheppard, and I knew that he would be likely to consider him as his best friend in King's Abbot."

"My dear child," I said, "I have not the least idea where Ralph Paton is at the present moment."

"That is true enough," said Poirot.

"But—" Ursula held out the newspaper cutting in a puzzled fashion.

"Ah! that," said Poirot, slightly embarrassed; "a *bagatelle,* mademoiselle. A *rien du tout.* Not for a moment do I believe that Ralph Paton has been arrested."

"But then—" began the girl slowly.

Poirot went on quickly:

"There is one thing I should like to know—did Captain Paton wear shoes or boots that night?"

Ursula shook her head.

"I can't remember."

"A pity! But how should you? Now, madame," he smiled at her, his head on one side, his forefinger wagging eloquently, "no questions. And do not torment yourself. Be of good courage, and place your faith in Hercule Poirot."

Twenty-three

Poirot's Little Reunion

"And now," said Caroline, rising, "that child is coming upstairs to lie down. Don't you worry, my dear. M. Poirot will do everything he can for you—be sure of that."

"I ought to go back to Fernly," said Ursula uncertainly.

But Caroline silenced her protests with a firm hand.

"Nonsense. You're in my hands for the time being. You'll stay here for the present, anyway—eh, M. Poirot?"

"It will be the best plan," agreed the little Belgian. "This evening I shall want mademoiselle—I beg her pardon, madame—to attend my little reunion. Nine o'clock at my house. It is most necessary that she should be there."

Caroline nodded, and went with Ursula out of the room. The door shut behind them. Poirot dropped down into a chair again.

"So far, so good," he said. "Things are straightening themselves out."

"They're getting to look blacker and blacker against Ralph Paton," I observed gloomily.

Poirot nodded.

"Yes, that is so. But it was to be expected, was it not?"

I looked at him, slightly puzzled by the remark. He was leaning back in the chair, his eyes half closed, the tips of his fingers just touching each other. Suddenly he sighed and shook his head.

"What is it?" I asked.

"It is that there are moments when a great longing for my friend Hastings comes over me. That is the friend of whom I spoke to you—the one who resides now in the Argentine. Always, when I have had a big case, he has been by my side. And he has helped me—yes, often he has helped me. For he had a knack, that one, of stumbling over the truth unawares—without noticing it himself, *bien entendu*. At times, he has said something particularly foolish, and behold that foolish remark has revealed the truth to me! And then, too, it was his practice to keep a written record of the cases that proved interesting."

I gave a slightly embarrassed cough.

"As far as that goes," I began, and then stopped.

Poirot sat upright in his chair. His eyes sparkled.

"But yes? What is it that you would say?"

"Well, as a matter of fact, I've read some of Captain Hasting's narratives, and I thought, why not try my hand at something of the same kind. Seemed a pity not to—unique opportunity—probably the only time I'll be mixed up with anything of this kind."

I felt myself getting hotter and hotter, and more and more incoherent, as I floundered through the above speech.

Poirot sprang from his chair. I had a moment's terror that he was going to embrace me French fashion, but mercifully he refrained.

"But this is magnificent—you have then written down your impressions of the case as you went along?"

I nodded.

"*Epatant!*" cried Poirot. "Let me see them—this instant."

I was not quite prepared for such a sudden demand. I racked my brains to remember certain details.

"I hope you won't mind," I stammered. "I may have been a little—er— *personal* now and then."

"Oh! I comprehend perfectly; you have referred to me as comic—as, perhaps, ridiculous now and then? It matters not at all. Hastings, he also was not always polite. Me, I have the mind above such trivialities."

Still somewhat doubtful, I rummaged in the drawers of my desk and produced an untidy pile of manuscript which I handed over to him. With an eye on possible publication in the future, I had divided the work into chapters, and the night before I had brought it up to date with an account of Miss Russell's visit. Poirot had therefore twenty chapters.

I left him with them.

I was obliged to go out to a case at some distance away, and it was past eight o'clock when I got back, to be greeted with a plate of hot dinner on a tray, and the announcement that Poirot and my sister had supped together at half past seven, and that the former had then gone to my workshop to finish his reading of the manuscript.

"I hope, James," said my sister, "that you've been careful in what you say about me in it?"

My jaw dropped. I had not been careful at all.

"Not that it matters very much," said Caroline, reading my expression correctly. "M. Poirot will know what to think. He understands me much better than you do."

I went into the workshop. Poirot was sitting by the window. The manuscript lay neatly piled on a chair beside him. He laid his hand on it and spoke.

"*Eh bien,*" he said, "I congratulate you—on your modesty!"

"Oh!" I said, rather taken aback.

"And on your reticence," he added.

I said "Oh!" again.

"Not so did Hastings write," continued my friend. "On every page, many, many times was the word 'I'. What *he* thought—what *he* did. But you—you have kept your personality in the background; only once or twice does it obtrude—in scenes of home life, shall we say?"

I blushed a little before the twinkle of his eye.

"What do you really think of the stuff?" I asked nervously.

"You want my candid opinion?"

"Yes."

Poirot laid his jesting manner aside.

"A very meticulous and accurate account," he said kindly. "You have recorded all the facts faithfully and exactly—though you have shown yourself becomingly reticent as to your own share in them."

"And it has helped you?"

"Yes. I may say that it has helped me considerably. Come, we must go over to my house and set the stage for my little performance."

Caroline was in the hall. I think she hoped that she might be invited to accompany us. Poirot dealt with the situation tactfully.

"I should much like to have had you present, mademoiselle," he said regretfully, "but at this juncture it would not be wise. See you, all these people tonight are suspects. Amongst them, I shall find the person who killed Mr. Ackroyd."

"You really believe that?" I said incredulously.

"I see that you do not," said Poirot drily. "Not yet do you appreciate Hercule Poirot at his true worth."

At that minute Ursula came down the staircase.

"You are ready, my child?" said Poirot. "That is good. We will go to my house together. Mademoiselle Caroline, believe me, I do everything possible to render you service. Good evening."

We went off, leaving Caroline rather like a dog who has been refused a walk, standing on the front door step gazing after us.

The sitting room at The Larches had been got ready. On the table were various *siropes* and glasses. Also a plate of biscuits. Several chairs had been brought in from the other room.

Poirot ran to and fro rearranging things. Pulling out a chair here, altering the position of a lamp there, occasionally stooping to straighten one of the mats that covered the floor. He was specially fussing over the lighting. The lamps were arranged in such a way as to throw a clear light on the side of the room where the chairs were grouped, at the same time leaving the other end of the room, where I presumed Poirot himself would sit, in a dim twilight.

Ursula and I watched him. Presently a bell was heard.

"They arrive," said Poirot. "Good, all is in readiness."

The door opened and the party from Fernly filed in. Poirot went forward and greeted Mrs. Ackroyd and Flora.

"It is most good of you to come," he said. "And Major Blunt and Mr. Raymond."

The secretary was debonair as ever.

"What's the great idea?" he said, laughing. "Some scientific machine? Do we have bands round our wrists which register guilty heart-beats? There is such an invention, isn't there?"

"I have read of it, yes," admitted Poirot. "But me, I am old-fashioned. I use the old methods. I work only with the little grey cells. Now let us begin—but first I have an announcement to make to you all."

He took Ursula's hand and drew her forward.

"This lady is Mrs. Ralph Paton. She was married to Captain Paton last March."

A little shriek burst from Mrs. Ackroyd.

"Ralph! Married! Last March! Oh! but it's absurd. How could he be?"

She stared at Ursula as though she had never seen her before.

"Married to Bourne?" she said. "Really, M. Poirot, I don't believe you."

Ursula flushed and began to speak, but Flora forestalled her.

Going quickly to the other girl's side, she passed her hand through her arm.

"You must not mind our being surprised," she said. "You see, we had no idea of such a thing. You and Ralph have kept your secret very well. I am—very glad about it."

"You are very kind, Miss Ackroyd," said Ursula in a low voice, "and you have every right to be exceedingly angry. Ralph behaved very badly—especially to you."

"You needn't worry about that," said Flora, giving her arm a consoling little pat. "Ralph was in a corner and took the only way out. I should probably have done the same in his place. I do think he might have trusted me with the secret, though. I wouldn't have let him down."

Poirot rapped gently on a table and cleared his throat significantly.

"The board meeting's going to begin," said Flora. "M. Poirot hints that we mustn't talk. But just tell me one thing. Where is Ralph? You must know if anyone does."

"But I don't," cried Ursula, almost in a wail. "That's just it, I don't."

"Isn't he detained at Liverpool?" asked Raymond. "It said so in the paper."

"He is not at Liverpool," said Poirot shortly.

"In fact," I remarked, "no one knows where he is."

"Except Hercule Poirot, eh?" said Raymond.

Poirot replied seriously to the other's banter.

"Me, I know everything. Remember that."

Geoffrey Raymond lifted his eyebrows.

"Everything?" He whistled. "Whew! that's a tall order."

"Do you mean to say you can really guess where Ralph Paton is hiding?" I asked incredulously.

"You call it guessing. I call it knowing, my friend."

"In Cranchester?" I hazarded.

"No," replied Poirot gravely, "not in Cranchester."

He said no more, but at a gesture from him the assembled party took their seats. As they did so, the door opened once more and two other people came in and sat down near the door. They were Parker and the housekeeper.

"The number is complete," said Poirot. "Everyone is here."

There was a ring of satisfaction in his tone. And with the sound of it I saw a ripple of something like uneasiness pass over all those faces grouped at the other end of the room. There was a suggestion in all this as of a trap—a trap that had closed.

Poirot read from a list in an important manner.

"Mrs. Ackroyd, Miss Flora Ackroyd, Major Blunt, Mr. Geoffrey Raymond, Mrs. Ralph Paton, John Parker, Elizabeth Russell."

He laid the paper down on the table.

"What's the meaning of all this?" began Raymond.

"The list I have just read," said Poirot, "is a list of suspected persons. Every one of you present had the opportunity to kill Mr. Ackroyd—"

With a cry Mrs. Ackroyd sprang up, her throat working.

"I don't like it," she wailed. "I don't like it. I would much prefer to go home."

"You cannot go home, madame," said Poirot sternly, "until you have heard what I have to say."

He paused a moment, then cleared his throat.

"I will start at the beginning. When Miss Ackroyd asked me to investigate the case, I went up to Fernly Park with the good Doctor Sheppard. I walked with him along the terrace, where I was shown the footprints on the window-sill. From there Inspector Raglan took me along the path which leads to the drive. My eye was caught by a little summerhouse, and I searched it thoroughly. I found two things—a scrap of starched cambric and an empty goose quill. The scrap of cambric immediately suggested to me a maid's apron. When Inspector Raglan showed me his list of the people in the house, I noticed at once that one of the maids—Ursula Bourne, the parlourmaid—had no real alibi. According to her own story, she was in her bedroom from nine-thirty until ten. But supposing that instead she was in the summerhouse? If so, she must have gone there to meet someone. Now we know from Dr. Sheppard that someone from outside *did* come to the house that night—the stranger whom he met just by the gate. At first glance it would seem that our problem was solved, and that the stranger went to the summerhouse to meet Ursula Bourne. It was fairly certain that he *did* go to the summerhouse because of the goose quill. That suggested at once to my mind a taker of drugs—and one who had acquired the habit on the other side of the Atlantic where sniffing 'snow' is more common than in this country. The man whom Dr. Sheppard met had an American accent, which fitted in with that supposition.

"But I was held up by one point. *The times did not fit.* Ursula Bourne could certainly not have gone to the summerhouse before nine-thirty, whereas the man must have got there by a few minutes past nine. I could, of course, assume that he waited there for half an hour. The only alternative supposition was that there had been two separate meetings in the summerhouse that night. *Eh bien,* as soon as I went into that alternative I found several significant facts. I discovered that Miss Russell, the housekeeper, had visited Dr. Sheppard that morning, and had displayed a good deal of interest in cures for victims of the drug habit. Taking that in conjunction with the goose quill, I assumed that the man in question came to Fernly to meet the housekeeper, and not Ursula Bourne. Who, then, did Ursula Bourne come to the rendezvous to meet? I was not long in doubt. First I found a ring—a wedding ring—with 'From R.' and a date inside it. Then I learnt that Ralph Paton had been seen coming up the path which led to the summerhouse at twenty-five minutes past nine, and I also heard of a certain conversation which had taken place in the wood near the village that very afternoon—a conversation between Ralph Paton and some unknown girl. So I had my facts succeeding each other in a neat and orderly manner. A secret marriage, an engagement announced on the day of the tragedy, the stormy interview in the wood, and the meeting arranged for the summerhouse that night.

"Incidentally this proved to me one thing, that both Ralph Paton and Ursula Bourne (or Paton) had the strongest motives for wishing Mr. Ackroyd out of the way. And it also made one other point unexpectedly clear. It could not have been Ralph Paton who was with Mr. Ackroyd in the study at nine-thirty.

"So we come to another and most interesting aspect of the crime. Who was it in the room with Mr. Ackroyd at nine-thirty? Not Ralph Paton, who was in the summerhouse with his wife. Not Charles Kent, who had already left. Who, then? I posed my cleverest—my most audacious question: *Was anyone with him?*"

Poirot leaned forward and shot the last words triumphantly at us, drawing back afterwards with the air of one who has made a decided hit.

Raymond, however, did not seem impressed, and lodged a mild protest.

"I don't know if you're trying to make me out a liar, M. Poirot, but the matter does not rest on my evidence alone—except perhaps as to the exact words used. Remember, Major Blunt also heard Mr. Ackroyd talking to someone. He was on the terrace outside, and couldn't catch the words clearly, but he distinctly heard the voices."

Poirot nodded.

"I have not forgotten," he said quietly. "But Major Blunt was under the impression that it was *you* to whom Mr. Ackroyd was speaking."

For a moment Raymond seemed taken aback. Then he recovered himself.

"Blunt knows now that he was mistaken," he said.

"Exactly," agreed the other man.

"Yet there must have been some reason for his thinking so," mused Poirot. "Oh! no," he held up his hand in protest, "I know the reason you will give—but it is not enough. We must seek elsewhere. I will put it this way. From the beginning of the case I have been struck by one thing—the nature of those words which Mr. Raymond overheard. It has been amazing to me that no one has commented on them—has seen anything odd about them."

He paused a minute, and then quoted softly:

"*. . . the calls on my purse have been so frequent of late that I fear it is impossible for me to accede to your request.* Does nothing strike you as odd about that?"

"I don't think so," said Raymond. "He has frequently dictated letters to me, using almost exactly those same words."

"Exactly," cried Poirot. "That is what I seek to arrive at. Would any man use such a phrase in *talking* to another? Impossible that that should be part of a real conversation. Now, if he had been dictating a letter—"

"You mean he was reading a letter aloud," said Raymond slowly. "Even so, he must have been reading to someone."

"But why? We have no evidence that there was anyone else in the room. No other voice but Mr. Ackroyd's was heard, remember."

"Surely a man wouldn't read letters of that type aloud to himself—not unless he was—well—going barmy."

"You have all forgotten one thing," said Poirot softly: "the stranger who called at the house the preceding Wednesday."

They all stared at him.

"But yes," said Poirot, nodding encouragingly, "on Wednesday. The young man was not of himself important. But the firm he represented interested me very much."

. "The Dictaphone Company," gasped Raymond. "I see it now. A dictaphone. That's what you think?"

Poirot nodded.

"Mr. Ackroyd had promised to invest in a dictaphone, you remember. Me, I had the curiosity to inquire of the company in question. Their reply is that Mr. Ackroyd *did* purchase a dictaphone from their representative. Why he concealed the matter from you, I do not know."

"He must have meant to surprise me with it," murmured Raymond. "He had quite a childish love of surprising people. Meant to keep it up his sleeve for a day or so. Probably was playing with it like a new toy. Yes, it fits in. You're quite right—no one would use quite those words in casual conversation."

"It explains, too," said Poirot, "why Major Blunt thought it was you who were in the study. Such scraps as came to him were fragments of dictation, and so his subconscious mind deduced that you were with him. His conscious mind was occupied with something quite different—the white figure he had caught a glimpse of. He fancied it was Miss Ackroyd. Really, of course, it was Ursula Bourne's white apron he saw as she was stealing down to the summerhouse."

Raymond had recovered from his first surprise.

"All the same," he remarked, "this discovery of yours, brilliant though it is (I'm quite sure I should never have thought of it), leaves the essential position unchanged. Mr. Ackroyd was alive at nine-thirty, since he was speaking into the dictaphone. It seems clear that the man Charles Kent was really off the premises by then. As to Ralph Paton—?"

He hesitated, glancing at Ursula.

Her colour flared up, but she answered steadily enough.

"Ralph and I parted just before a quarter to ten. He never went near the house, I am sure of that. He had no intention of doing so. The last thing on earth he wanted was to face his stepfather. He would have funked it badly."

"It isn't that I doubt your story for a moment," explained Raymond. "I've always been quite sure Captain Paton was innocent. But one has to think of a court of law—and the questions that would be asked. He is in a most unfortunate position, but if he were to come forward—"

Poirot interrupted.

"That is your advice, yes? That he should come forward?"

"Certainly. If you know where he is—"

"I perceive that you do not believe that I do know. And yet I have told you just now that I know everything. The truth of the telephone call, of the footprints on the windowsill, of the hiding place of Ralph Paton—"

"Where is he?" said Blunt sharply.

"Not very far away," said Poirot, smiling.

"In Cranchester?" I asked.

Poirot turned towards me.

"Always you ask me that. The idea of Cranchester, it is with you an *idée fixe*. No, he is not in Cranchester. He is—*there!*"

He pointed a dramatic forefinger. Everyone's head turned.

Ralph Paton was standing in the doorway.

Twenty-four

RALPH PATON'S STORY

It was a very uncomfortable minute for *me*. I hardly took in what happened next, but there were exclamations and cries of surprise! When I was sufficiently master of myself to be able to realize what was going on, Ralph Paton was standing by his wife, her hand in his, and he was smiling across the room at me.

Poirot, too, was smiling, and at the same time shaking an eloquent finger at me.

"Have I not told you at least thirty-six times that it is useless to conceal things from Hercule Poirot?" he demanded. "That in such a case he finds out?"

He turned to the others.

"One day, you remember, we held a little séance about a table—just the six of us. I accused the other five persons present of concealing something from me. Four of them gave up their secret. Dr. Sheppard did not give up his. But all along I have had my suspicions. Dr. Sheppard went to the Three Boars that night hoping to find Ralph. He did not find him there; but supposing, I said to myself, that he met him in the street on his way home? Dr. Sheppard was a friend of Captain Paton's, and he had come straight from the scene of the crime. He must know that things looked very black against him. Perhaps he knew more than the general public did—"

"I did," I said ruefully. "I suppose I might as well make a clean breast of things now. I went to see Ralph that afternoon. At first he refused to take me into his confidence, but later he told me about his marriage, and the hole he was in. As soon as the murder was discovered, I realized that once the facts were known, suspicion could not fail to attach to Ralph—or, if not to him, to the girl he loved. That night I put the facts plainly before him. The thought of having possibly to give evidence which might incriminate his wife made him resolve at all costs to—to—"

I hesitated, and Ralph filled up the gap.

"To do a bunk," he said graphically. "You see, Ursula left me to go back to the house. I thought it possible that she might have attempted to have another interview with my stepfather. He had already been very rude to her that afternoon. It occurred to me that he might have so insulted her—in such an unforgivable manner—that without knowing what she was doing—"

He stopped. Ursula released her hand from his, and stepped back.

"You thought that, Ralph! You actually thought that I might have done it?"

"Let us get back to the culpable conduct of Dr. Sheppard," said Poirot drily. "Dr. Sheppard consented to do what he could to help him. He was successful in hiding Captain Paton from the police."

"Where?" asked Raymond. "In his own house?"

"Ah, no, indeed," said Poirot. "You should ask yourself the question that I did. If the good doctor is concealing the young man, what place would he choose? It must necessarily be somewhere near at hand. I think of Cranchester. A hotel? No. Lodgings? Even more emphatically, no. Where, then? Ah! I have it. A nursing home. A home for the mentally unfit. I test my theory. I invent a nephew with mental trouble. I consult Mademoiselle Sheppard as to suitable homes. She gives me the names of two near Cranchester to which her brother has sent patients. I make inquiries. Yes, at one of them a patient was brought there by the doctor himself early on Saturday morning. That patient, though known by another name, I had no difficulty in identifying as Captain Paton. After certain necessary formalities, I was allowed to bring him away. He arrived at my house in the early hours of yesterday morning."

I looked at him ruefully.

"Caroline's Home Office expert," I murmured. "And to think I never guessed!"

"You see now why I drew attention to the reticence of your manuscript," murmured Poirot. "It was strictly truthful as far as it went—but it did not go very far, eh, my friend?"

I was too abashed to argue.

"Dr. Sheppard has been very loyal," said Ralph. "He has stood by me through thick and thin. He did what he thought was best. I see now, from what M. Poirot has told me, that it was not really the best. I should have come forward and faced the music. You see, in the home, we never saw a newspaper. I knew nothing of what was going on."

"Dr. Sheppard has been a model of discretion," said Poirot drily. "But me, I discover all the little secrets. It is my business."

"Now we can have your story of what happened that night," said Raymond impatiently.

"You know it already," said Ralph. "There's very little for me to tell. I left the summerhouse about nine forty-five, and tramped about the lanes, trying to make up my mind as to what to do next—what line to take. I'm bound to admit that I've not the shadow of an alibi, but I give you my solemn word that I never went to the study, that I never saw my stepfather alive—or dead. Whatever the world thinks, I'd like all of you to believe me."

"No alibi," murmured Raymond. "That's bad. I believe you, of course, but—it's a bad business."

"It makes things very simple, though," said Poirot, in a cheerful voice. "Very simple indeed."

We all stared at him.

"You see what I mean? No? Just this—to save Captain Paton the real criminal must confess."

He beamed round at us all.

"But yes—I mean what I say. See now, I did not invite Inspector Raglan to be present. That was for a reason. I did not want to tell him all that I knew—at least I did not want to tell him tonight."

He leaned forward, and suddenly his voice and his whole personality changed. He suddenly became dangerous.

"I who speak to you—I know the murderer of Mr. Ackroyd is in this room now. It is to the murderer I speak. *Tomorrow the truth goes to Inspector Raglan.* You understand?"

There was a tense silence. Into the midst of it came the old Breton woman with a telegram on a salver. Poirot tore it open.

Blunt's voice rose abrupt and resonant.

"The murderer is amongst us, you say? You know—which?"

Poirot had read the message. He crumpled it up in his hand.

"I know—now."

He tapped the crumpled ball of paper.

"What is that?" said Raymond sharply.

"A wireless message—from a steamer now on her way to the United States."

There was a dead silence. Poirot rose to his feet bowing.

"Messieurs et Mesdames, this reunion of mine is at an end. Remember—*the truth goes to Inspector Raglan in the morning.*"

Twenty-five

The Whole Truth

A slight gesture from Poirot enjoined me to stay behind the rest. I obeyed, going over to the fire and thoughtfully stirring the big logs on it with the toe of my boot.

I was puzzled. For the first time I was absolutely at sea as to Poirot's meaning. For a moment I was inclined to think that the scene I had just witnessed was a gigantic piece of bombast—that he had been what he called "playing the comedy" with a view to making himself interesting and important. But, in spite of myself, I was forced to believe in an underlying reality. There had been real menace in his words—a certain indisputable sincerity. But I still believed him to be on entirely the wrong tack.

When the door shut behind the last of the party he came over to the fire.

"Well, my friend," he said quietly, "and what do you think of it all?"

"I don't know what to think," I said frankly. "What was the point? Why not go straight to Inspector Raglan with the truth instead of giving the guilty person this elaborate warning?"

Poirot sat down and drew out his case of tiny Russian cigarettes. He smoked for a minute or two in silence. Then:

"Use your little grey cells," he said. "There is always a reason behind my actions."

I hesitated for a moment, and then I said slowly:

"The first one that occurs to me is that you yourself do not know who the guilty person is, but that you are sure that he is to be found amongst the people here tonight. Therefore your words were intended to force a confession from the unknown murderer?"

Poirot nodded approvingly.

"A clever idea, but not the truth."

"I thought, perhaps, that by making him believe you knew, you might force him out into the open—not necessarily by confession. He might try to silence you as he formerly silenced Mr. Ackroyd—before you could act tomorrow morning."

"A trap with myself as the bait! *Merci, mon ami,* but I am not sufficiently heroic for that."

"Then I fail to understand you. Surely you are running the risk of letting the murderer escape by thus putting him on his guard?"

Poirot shook his head.

"He cannot escape," he said gravely. "There is only one way out—and that way does not lead to freedom."

"You really believe that one of those people here tonight committed the murder?" I asked incredulously.

"Yes, my friend."

"Which one?"

There was a silence for some minutes. Then Poirot tossed the stump of his cigarette into the grate and began to speak in a quiet, reflective tone.

"I will take you the way that I have travelled myself. Step by step you shall accompany me, and see for yourself that all the facts point indisputably to one person. Now, to begin with, there were two facts and a little discrepancy in time which especially attracted my attention. The first fact was the telephone call. If Ralph Paton were indeed the murderer, the telephone call became meaningless and absurd. Therefore, I said to myself, Ralph Paton is not the murderer.

"I satisfied myself that the call could not have been sent by anyone in the house, yet I was convinced that it was amongst those present on the fatal evening that I had to look for my criminal. Therefore I concluded that the telephone call must have been sent by an accomplice. I was not quite pleased with that deduction, but I let it stand for the minute.

"I next examined the *motive* for the call. That was difficult. I could only get at it by judging its *result*. Which was—that the murder was discovered that night instead of—in all probability—the following morning. You agree with that?"

"Ye-es," I admitted. "Yes. As you say, Mr. Ackroyd, having given orders that he was not to be disturbed, nobody would have been likely to go to the study that night."

"*Très bien*. The affair marches, does it not? But matters were still obscure. What was the advantage of having the crime discovered that night in preference to the following morning? The only idea I could get hold of was that the murderer, knowing the crime was to be discovered at a certain time, could make sure of being present when the door was broken in—or at any rate immediately afterwards. And now we come to the second fact—the chair pulled out from the wall. Inspector Raglan dismissed that as of no importance. I, on the contrary, have always regarded it as of supreme importance.

"In your manuscript you have drawn a neat little plan of the study. If you had it with you this minute you would see that—the chair being drawn out in the position indicated by Parker—it would stand in a direct line between the door and the window."

"The window!" I said quickly.

"You, too, have my first idea. I imagined that the chair was drawn out so that something connected with the window should not be seen by anyone entering through the door. But I soon abandoned that supposition, for though the chair was a grandfather with a high back, it obscured very little of the window—only the part between the sash and the ground. No, *mon ami*—but remember that just in front of the window there stood a table with books and magazines upon it. Now that table *was* completely hidden by the drawn-out chair—and immediately I had my first shadowy suspicion of the truth.

"Supposing that there had been something on that table not intended to be seen? Something placed there by the murderer? As yet I had no inkling of what that something might be. But I knew certain very interesting facts about it. For instance, it was something that the murderer had not been able to take away with him at the time that he committed the crime. At the same time it was vital that it should be removed as soon as possible after the crime had been discovered. And so—the telephone message, and the opportunity for the murderer to be on the spot when the body was discovered.

"Now four people were on the scene before the police arrived. Yourself, Parker, Major Blunt, and Mr. Raymond. Parker I eliminated at once, since at whatever time the crime was discovered, he was the one person certain to be on the spot. Also it was he who told me of the pulled-out chair. Parker, then, was cleared (of the murder, that is. I still thought it possible that he had been blackmailing Mrs. Ferrars). Raymond and Blunt, however, remained under suspicion since, if the crime had been discovered in the early hours of the morning, it was quite possible that they might have arrived on the scene too late to prevent the object on the round table being discovered.

"Now what was that object? You heard my arguments tonight in reference to the scrap of conversation overheard? As soon as I learned that a representative of a dictaphone company had called, the idea of a dictaphone took root in my mind. You heard what I said in this room not half an hour ago? They all agreed with my theory—but one vital fact seems to have escaped them. Granted that a dictaphone was being used by Mr. Ackroyd that night—why was no dictaphone found?"

"I never thought of that," I said.

"We know that a dictaphone was supplied to Mr. Ackroyd. But no dictaphone has been found amongst his effects. So, if something was taken from the table—why should not that something be the dictaphone? But there were certain difficulties in the way. The attention of everyone was, of course, focused on the murdered man. I think anyone could have gone to the table unnoticed by the other people in the room. But a dictaphone has a certain bulk—it cannot be slipped casually into a pocket. There must have been a receptacle of some kind capable of holding it.

"You see where I am arriving? The figure of the murderer is taking shape. A person who was on the scene straightaway, but who might not have been if the crime had been discovered the following morning. A person carrying a receptacle into which the dictaphone might be fitted—"

I interrupted.

"But why remove the dictaphone? What was the point?"

"You are like Mr. Raymond. You take it for granted that what was heard at nine-thirty was Mr. Ackroyd's voice speaking into a dictaphone. But consider this useful invention for a little minute. You dictate into it, do you not? And at some later time a secretary or a typist turns it on, and the voice speaks again."

"You mean—?" I gasped.

Poirot nodded.

"Yes, I meant that. *At nine-thirty Mr. Ackroyd was already dead.* It was the dictaphone speaking—not the man."

"And the murderer switched it on. Then he must have been in the room at that minute?"

"Possibly. But we must not exclude the likelihood of some mechanical device having been applied—something after the nature of a time lock, or even of a simple alarm clock. But in that case we must add two qualifications to our imaginary portrait of the murderer. It must be someone who knew of Mr. Ackroyd's purchase of the dictaphone and also someone with the necessary mechanical knowledge.

"I had got thus far in my own mind when we came to the footprints on the window ledge. Here there were three conclusions open to me. (1) They might really have been made by Ralph Paton. He had been at Fernly that night, and might have climbed into the study and found his uncle dead there. That was one hypothesis. (2) There was the possibility that the footmarks might have been made by somebody else who happened to have the same kind of studs in his shoes. But the inmates of the house had shoes soled with crêpe rubber, and I declined to believe in the coincidence of someone from outside having the same kind of shoes as Ralph Paton wore. Charles Kent, as we know from the barmaid of the Dog and Whistle, had on a pair of boots 'clean dropping off him.' (3) Those prints were made by someone deliberately trying to throw suspicion on Ralph Paton. To test this last conclusion, it was necessary to ascertain certain facts. One pair of Ralph's shoes had been obtained from the Three Boars by the police. Neither Ralph nor anyone else could have worn them that evening, since they were downstairs being cleaned. According to the police theory,

Ralph was wearing another pair of the same kind, and I found out that it was true that he had two pairs. Now for my theory to be proved correct it was necessary for the murderer to have worn Ralph's shoes that evening—in which case Ralph must have been wearing yet a *third* pair of footwear of some kind. I could hardly suppose that he would bring three pairs of shoes all alike—the third pair of footwear were more likely to be boots. I got your sister to make inquiries on this point—laying some stress on the colour, in order—I admit it frankly—to obscure the real reason for my asking.

"You know the result of her investigations. Ralph Paton *had* had a pair of boots with him. The first question I asked him when he came to my house yesterday morning was what he was wearing on his feet on the fatal night. He replied at once that he had worn *boots*—he was still wearing them, in fact—having nothing else to put on.

"So we get a step further in our description of the murderer—a person who had the opportunity to take these shoes of Ralph Paton's from the Three Boars that day."

He paused, and then said, with a slightly raised voice:

"There is one further point. The murderer must have been a person who had the opportunity to purloin that dagger from the silver table. You might argue that anyone in the house might have done so, but I will recall to you that Flora Ackroyd was very positive that the dagger was not there when she examined the silver table."

He paused again.

"Let us recapitulate—now that all is clear. A person who was at the Three Boars earlier that day, a person who knew Ackroyd well enough to know that he had purchased a dictaphone, a person who was of a mechanical turn of mind, who had the opportunity to take the dagger from the silver table before Miss Flora arrived, who had with him a receptacle suitable for hiding the dictaphone—such as a black bag—and who had the study to himself for a few minutes after the crime was discovered while Parker was telephoning for the police. In fact—*Dr. Sheppard!*"

Twenty-six

AND NOTHING BUT THE TRUTH

There was a dead silence for a minute and a half.

Then I laughed.

"You're mad," I said.

"No," said Poirot placidly. "I am not mad. It was the little discrepancy in time that first drew my attention to you—right at the beginning."

"Discrepancy in time?" I queried, puzzled.

"But yes. You will remember that everyone agreed—you yourself included—that it took five minutes to walk from the lodge to the house—less if you took the short cut to the terrace. But you left the house at ten minutes to nine—both by your own statement and that of Parker, and yet it was nine o'clock when you passed through the lodge gates. It was a chilly night—not an evening a man would be inclined to dawdle; why had you taken ten minutes to do a five minutes' walk? All along I realized that we had only your statement for it that the study window was ever fastened. Ackroyd asked you if you had done so—he never looked to see. Supposing, then, that the study window was unfastened? Would there be time in that ten minutes for you to run round the outside of the house, change your shoes, climb in through the window, kill Ackroyd, and get to the gate by nine o'clock? I decided against that theory since in all probability a man as nervous as Ackroyd was that night would hear you climbing in, and then there would have been a struggle. But supposing that you killed Ackroyd *before* you left—as you were standing beside his chair? Then you go out of the front door, run round to the summerhouse, take Ralph Paton's shoes out of the bag you brought up with you that night, slip them on, walk through the mud in them, and leave prints on the window ledge, you climb in, lock the study door on the inside, run back to the summerhouse, change back into your own shoes, and race down to the gate. (I went through similar actions the other day, when you were with Mrs. Ackroyd—it took ten minutes exactly.) Then home—and an alibi—since you had timed the dictaphone for half past nine."

"My dear Poirot," I said in a voice that sounded strange and forced to my own ears, "you've been brooding over this case too long. What on earth had I to gain by murdering Ackroyd?"

"Safety. It was you who blackmailed Mrs. Ferrars. Who could have had a better knowledge of what killed Mr. Ferrars than the doctor who was attending him? When you spoke to me that first day in the garden, you mentioned a legacy received about a year ago. I have been unable to discover any trace of a legacy. You had to invent some way of accounting for Mrs. Ferrars's twenty thousand pounds. It has not done you much good. You lost most of it in speculation— then you put the screw on too hard, and Mrs. Ferrars took a way out that you had not expected. If Ackroyd had learnt the truth he would have had no mercy on you—you were ruined forever."

"And the telephone call?" I asked, trying to rally. "You have a plausible explanation of that also, I suppose?"

"I will confess to you that it was my greatest stumbling block when I found that a call had actually been put through to you from King's Abbot station. I at first believed that you had simply invented the story. It was a very clever touch, that. You must have some excuse for arriving at Fernly, finding the body, and so getting the chance to remove the dictaphone on which your alibi depended. I had a very vague notion of how it was worked when I came to see your sister that first day and inquired as to what patients you had seen on Friday morning. I had no thought of Miss Russell in my mind at that time. Her visit was a lucky coincidence, since it distracted your mind from the real object of my questions. I found what I was looking for. Among your patients that morning was the steward of an American liner. Who more suitable than he to be leaving for Liverpool by the train that evening? And afterwards he would be on the high seas, well out of the way. I noted that the *Orion* sailed on Saturday, and having obtained the name of the steward I sent him a wireless message asking a certain question. This is his reply you saw me receive just now."

He held out the message to me. It ran as follows:

"Quite correct. Dr. Sheppard asked me to leave a note at a patient's house. I was to ring him up from the station with the reply. Reply was 'No answer.' "

"It was a clever idea," said Poirot. "The call was genuine. Your sister saw you take it. But there was only one man's word as to what was actually said—your own!"

I yawned.

"All this," I said, "is very interesting—but hardly in the sphere of practical politics."

"You think not? Remember what I said—the truth goes to Inspector Raglan in the morning. But, for the sake of your good sister, I am willing to give you the chance of another way out. There might be, for instance, an over-dose of a sleeping draught. You comprehend me? But Captain Ralph Paton must be cleared—*ça va sans dire*. I should suggest that you finish that very interesting manuscript of yours—but abandoning your former reticence."

"You seem to be very prolific of suggestions," I remarked. "Are you sure you've quite finished?"

"Now that you remind me of the fact, it is true that there is one thing more. It would be most unwise on your part to attempt to silence me as you silenced M. Ackroyd. That kind of business does not succeed against Hercule Poirot, you understand."

"My dear Poirot," I said, smiling a little, "whatever else I may be, I am not a fool."

I rose to my feet.

"Well, well," I said, with a slight yawn, "I must be off home. Thank you for a most interesting and instructive evening."

Poirot also rose and bowed with his accustomed politeness as I passed out of the room.

Twenty-seven

Apologia

Five a.m. I am very tired—but I have finished my task. My arm aches from writing.

A strange end to my manuscript. I meant it to be published some day as the history of one of Poirot's failures! Odd, how things pan out.

All along I've had a premonition of disaster, from the moment I saw Ralph Paton and Mrs. Ferrars with their heads together. I thought then that she was confiding in him; as it happened I was quite wrong there, but the idea persisted even after I went into the study with Ackroyd that night, until he told me the truth.

Poor old Ackroyd. I'm always glad that I gave him a chance. I urged him to read that letter before it was too late. Or let me be honest—didn't I subconsciously realize that with a pigheaded chap like him, it was my best chance of getting him *not* to read it? His nervousness that night was interesting psychologically. He knew danger was close at hand. And yet he never suspected *me*.

The dagger was an afterthought. I'd brought up a very handy little weapon of my own, but when I saw the dagger lying in the silver table, it occurred to me at once how much better it would be to use a weapon that couldn't be traced to me.

I suppose I must have meant to murder him all along. As soon as I heard of Mrs. Ferrars's death, I felt convinced that she would have told him everything before she died. When I met him and he seemed so agitated, I thought that perhaps he knew the truth, but that he couldn't bring himself to believe it, and was going to give me the chance of refuting it.

So I went home and took my precautions. If the trouble were after all only something to do with Ralph—well, no harm would have been done. The dictaphone he had given me two days ago to adjust. Something had gone a little wrong with it, and I persuaded him to let me have a go at it, instead of sending it back. I did what I wanted to, and took it up with me in my bag that evening.

I am rather pleased with myself as a writer. What could be neater, for instance, than the following:

"The letters were brought in at twenty minutes to nine. It was just on ten minutes to nine when I left him, the letter still unread. I hesitated with my hand on the door handle, looking back and wondering if there was anything I had left undone."

All true, you see. But suppose I had put a row of stars after the first sentence! Would somebody then have wondered what exactly happened in that blank ten minutes?

When I looked round the room from the door, I was quite satisfied. Nothing had been left undone. The dictaphone was on the table by the window, timed to go off at nine-thirty (the mechanism of that little device was rather clever—based on the principle of an alarm clock), and the armchair was pulled out so as to hide it from the door.

I must admit that it gave me rather a shock to run into Parker just outside the door. I have faithfully recorded that fact.

Then later, when the body was discovered, and I sent Parker to telephone for the police, what a judicious use of words: *"I did what little had to be done!"* It was quite little—just to shove the dictaphone into my bag and push back the chair against the wall in its proper place. I never dreamed that Parker would have noticed that chair. Logically, he ought to have been so agog over the body as to be blind to everything else. But I hadn't reckoned with the trained servant complex.

I wish I could have known beforehand that Flora was going to say she'd seen her uncle alive at a quarter to ten. That puzzled me more than I can say. In fact, all through the case there have been things that puzzled me hopelessly. Everyone seems to have taken a hand.

My greatest fear all through has been Caroline. I have fancied she might guess. Curious the way she spoke that day of my "strain of weakness."

Well, she will never know the truth. There is, as Poirot said, one way out. . . .

I can trust him. He and Inspector Raglan will manage it between them. I should not like Caroline to know. She is fond of me, and then, too, she is proud . . . My death will be a grief to her, but grief passes. . . .

When I have finished writing, I shall enclose this whole manuscript in an envelope and address it to Poirot.

And then—what shall it be? Veronal? There would be a kind of poetic justice. Not that I take any responsibility for Mrs. Ferrars's death. It was the direct consequence of her own actions. I feel no pity for her.

I have no pity for myself either.

So let it be Veronal.

But I wish Hercule Poirot had never retired from work and come here to grow vegetable marrows.

CURTAIN: POIROT'S
LAST CASE

One

I

Who is there who has not felt a sudden startled pang at reliving an old experience, or feeling an old emotion?

"I have done this before. . . ."

Why do those words always move one so profoundly?

That was the question I asked myself as I sat in the train watching the flat Essex landscape outside.

How long ago was it that I had taken this selfsame journey? Had felt (ridiculously) that the best of life was over for me! Wounded in that war that for me would always be *the* war—the war that was wiped out now by a second and a more desperate war.

It had seemed in 1916 to young Arthur Hastings that he was already old and mature. How little had I realized that, for me, life was only then beginning.

I had been journeying, though I did not know it, to meet the man whose influence over me was to shape and mould my life. Actually, I had been going to stay with my old friend, John Cavendish, whose mother, recently remarried, had a country house named Styles. A pleasant renewing of old acquaintanceships, that was all I had thought it, not foreseeing that I was shortly to plunge into all the dark embroilments of a mysterious murder.

It was at Styles that I had met again that strange little man, Hercule Poirot, whom I had first come across in Belgium.

How well I remembered my amazement when I had seen the limping figure with the large moustache coming up the village street.

Hercule Poirot! Since those days he had been my dearest friend, his influence had moulded my life. In company with him, in the hunting down of yet another murderer, I had met my wife, the truest and sweetest companion any man could have had.

She lay now in Argentine soil, having died as she would have wished, with no long drawn out suffering, or feebleness of old age. But she had left a very lonely and unhappy man behind her.

Ah! If I could go back—live life all over again. If this could have been that day in 1916 when I first travelled to Styles . . . What changes had taken place since then! What gaps amongst the familiar faces! Styles itself had been sold by the Cavendishes. John Cavendish was dead, though his wife, Mary (that fascinating enigmatical creature), was still alive, living in Devonshire. Laurence was living with his wife and children in South Africa. Changes—changes everywhere.

But *one* thing, strangely enough, was the same. I was going to Styles to meet Hercule Poirot.

How stupefied I had been to receive his letter, with its heading Styles Court, Styles, Essex.

I had not seen my old friend for nearly a year. The last time I had seen him I had been shocked and saddened. He was now a very old man, and almost crippled with arthritis. He had gone to Egypt in the hopes of improving his health, but had returned, so his letter told me, rather worse than better. Nevertheless, he wrote cheerfully. . . .

II

And does it not intrigue you, my friend, to see the address from which I write? It recalls old memories, does it not? Yes, I am here, at Styles. Figure to yourself, it is now what they call a guest house. Run by one of your so British old Colonels— very "old school tie" and "Poonar." It is his wife, bien entendu, *who makes it pay. She is a good manage, that one, but the tongue like vinegar, and the poor Colonel, he suffers much from it. If it were me I would take a hatchet to her!*

I saw their advertisement in the paper, and the fancy took me to go once again to the place which first was my home in this country. At my age one enjoys reliving the past.

Then figure to yourself, I find here a gentleman, a baronet who is a friend of the employer of your daughter. (That phrase it sounds a little like the French exercise, does it not?)

Immediately I conceive a plan. He wishes to induce the Franklins to come here for the summer. I in my turn will persuade you and we shall be all together, en famille. *It will be most agreeable. Therefore, mon cher Hastings,* dépêchez-vous, *arrive with the utmost celerity. I have commanded for you a room with bath (it is modernized now, you comprehend, the dear old Styles) and disputed the price with Mrs. Colonel Luttrell until I have made an arrangement* très bon marché.

The Franklins and your charming Judith have been here for some days. It is all arranged, so make no histories.

A bientôt,

Yours always, Hercule Poirot

The prospect was alluring, and I fell in with my old friend's wishes without demur. I had no ties and no settled home. Of my children, one boy was in the Navy, the other married and running the ranch in the Argentine. My daughter Grace was married to a soldier and was at present in India. My remaining child, Judith, was the one whom secretly I had always loved best, although I had never for one moment understood her. A queer, dark, secretive child, with a passion for keeping her own counsel, which had sometimes affronted and distressed me. My wife had been more understanding. It was, she assured me, no lack of trust or confidence on Judith's part, but a kind of fierce compulsion. But she, like myself, was sometimes worried about the child. Judith's feelings, she said, were too intense, too concentrated, and her instinctive reserve deprived her of any safety valve. She had queer fits of brooding silence and a fierce, almost bitter power of partisanship. Her brains were the best of the family and we gladly fell in with her wish for a university education. She had taken her B.Sc. about a year ago, and had then taken the post of secretary to a doctor who was engaged in research work connected with tropical disease. His wife was somewhat of an invalid.

I had occasionally had qualms as to whether Judith's absorption in her work, and devotion to her employer, were not signs that she might be losing her heart, but the businesslike footing of their relationship assured me.

Judith was, I believed, fond of me, but she was very undemonstrative by nature, and she was often scornful and impatient of what she called my sentimental and outworn ideas. I was, frankly, a little nervous of my daughter!

At this point my meditations were interrupted by the train drawing up at the station of Styles St. Mary. That at least had not changed. Time had passed it by. It was still perched up in the midst of fields, with apparently no reason for existence.

As my taxi passed through the village, though, I realized the passage of years. Styles St. Mary was altered out of all recognition. Petrol stations, a cinema, two more inns and rows of council houses.

Presently we turned in at the gate of Styles. Here we seemed to recede again from modern times. The park was much as I remembered it, but the drive was badly kept and much overgrown with weeds growing up over the gravel. We turned a corner and came in view of the house. It was unaltered from the outside and badly needed a coat of paint.

As on my arrival all those years ago, there was a woman's figure stooping over one of the garden beds. My heart missed a beat. Then the figure straightened up and came towards me, and I laughed at myself. No greater contrast to the robust Evelyn Howard could have been imagined.

This was a frail elderly lady, with an abundance of curly white hair, pink cheeks, and a pair of cold pale blue eyes that were widely at variance with the easy geniality of her manner, which was frankly a shade too gushing for my taste.

"It'll be Captain Hastings now, won't it?" she demanded. "And me with my hands all over dirt and not able to shake hands. We're delighted to see you here—the amount we've heard about you! I must introduce myself. I'm Mrs. Luttrell. My husband and I bought this place in a fit of madness and have been trying to make a paying concern of it. I never thought the day would come when I'd be a hotel keeper! But I'll warn you, Captain Hastings, I'm a very businesslike woman. I pile up the extras all I know how."

We both laughed as though at an excellent joke, but it occurred to me that what Mrs. Luttrell had just said was in all probability the literal truth. Behind the veneer of her charming old lady manner, I caught a glimpse of flint-like hardness.

Although Mrs. Luttrell occasionally affected a faint brogue, she had no Irish blood. It was a mere affectation.

I enquired after my friend.

"Ah, poor little M. Poirot. The way he's been looking forward to your coming. It would melt a heart of stone. Terribly sorry I am for him, suffering the way he does."

We were walking towards the house and she was peeling off her gardening gloves.

"And your pretty daughter, too," she went on. "What a lovely girl she is. We all admire her tremendously. But I'm old-fashioned, you know, and it seems to me a shame and a sin that a girl like that, that ought to be going to parties and dancing with young men, should spend her time cutting up rabbits and bending over a microscope all day. Leave that sort of thing to the frumps, I say."

"Where is Judith?" I asked. "Is she somewhere about?"

Mrs. Luttrell made what children call "a face."

"Ah, the poor girl. She's cooped up in that studio place down at the bottom of the garden. Dr. Franklin rents it from me and he's had it all fitted up. Hutches of guinea pigs he's got there, the poor creatures, and mice and rabbits. I'm not sure that I like all this science, Captain Hastings. Ah, here's my husband."

Colonel Luttrell had just come round the corner of the house. He was a very tall, attenuated old man, with a cadaverous face, mild blue eyes and a habit of irresolutely tugging at his little white moustache.

He had a vague, rather nervous manner.

"Ah, George, here's Captain Hastings arrived."

Colonel Luttrell shook hands. "You came by the five—er—forty, eh?"

"What else should he have come by?" said Mrs. Luttrell sharply. "And what does it matter anyway? Take him up and show him his room, George. And then maybe he'd like to go straight to M. Poirot—or would you rather have tea first?"

I assured her that I did not want tea and would prefer to go and greet my friend.

Colonel Luttrell said, "Right. Come along. I expect—er—they'll have taken your things up already—eh, Daisy?"

Mrs. Luttrell said tartly, "That's your business, George. I've been gardening. I can't see to everything."

"No, no, of course not. I—I'll see to it, my dear."

I followed him up the front steps. In the doorway we encountered a grey-haired man, slightly built, who was hurrying out with a pair of field glasses. He limped, and had a boyish eager face. He said, stammering slightly: "There's a pair of n-nesting blackcaps down by the sycamore."

As we went into the hall, Luttrell said, "That's Norton. Nice fellow. Crazy about birds."

In the hall itself, a very big man was standing by the table. He had obviously just finished telephoning. Looking up he said, "I'd like to hang, draw and quarter all contractors and builders. Never get anything done right, curse 'em."

His wrath was so comical and so rueful, that we both laughed. I felt very attracted at once towards the man. He was very good-looking, though a man well over fifty, with a deeply tanned face. He looked as though he had led an out-of-doors life, and he looked, too, the type of man that is becoming more and more rare, an Englishman of the old school, straightforward, fond of out-of-doors life, and the kind of man who can command.

I was hardly surprised when Colonel Luttrell introduced him as Sir William Boyd Carrington. He had been, I knew, Governor of a province in India, where he had been a signal success. He was also renowned as a first-class shot and big game hunter. The sort of man, I reflected sadly, that we no longer seemed to breed in these degenerate days.

"Aha," he said. "I'm glad to meet in the flesh that famous personage *mon ami* Hastings." He laughed. "The dear old Belgian fellow talks about you a lot, you know. And then, of course, we've got your daughter here. She's a fine girl."

"I don't suppose Judith talks about me much," I said, smiling.

"No, no, far too modern. These girls nowadays always seem embarrassed at having to admit to a father or mother at all."

"Parents," I said, "are practically a disgrace."

He laughed. "Oh, well—I don't suffer that way. I've no children, worse luck. Your Judith is a very good-looking wench, but terribly highbrow. I find it rather alarming." He picked up the telephone receiver again. "Hope you don't mind, Luttrell, if I start damning your exchange to hell. I'm not a patient man."

"Do 'em good," said Luttrell.

He led the way upstairs and I followed him. He took me along the left wing of the house to a door at the end, and I realized that Poirot had chosen for me the room I had occupied before.

There were changes here. As I walked along the corridor some of the doors were open and I saw that the old-fashioned large bedrooms had been partitioned off so as to make several smaller ones.

My own room, which had not been large, was unaltered save for the installation of hot and cold water, and part of it had been partitioned off to make a small bathroom. It was furnished in a cheap modern style which rather disappointed me. I should have preferred a style more nearly approximating to the architecture of the house itself.

My luggage was in my room and the Colonel explained that Poirot's room was exactly opposite. He was about to take me there when a sharp cry of "George" echoed up from the hall below.

Colonel Luttrell started like a nervous horse. His hand went to his lips.

"I—I—sure you're all right? Ring for what you want—"

"*George.*"

"Coming, my dear, coming."

He hurried off down the corridor. I stood for a moment looking after him. Then, with my heart beating slightly faster, I crossed the corridor and rapped on the door of Poirot's room.

Two

Nothing is so sad, in my opinion, as the devastation wrought by age.

My poor friend. I have described him many times. Now to convey to you the difference. Crippled with arthritis, he propelled himself about in a wheeled chair. His once plump frame had fallen in. He was a thin little man now. His face was lined and wrinkled. His moustache and hair, it is true, were still of a jet black colour, but candidly, though I would not for the world have hurt his feelings by saying so to him, this was a mistake. There comes a moment when hair dye is only too painfully obvious. There had been a time when I had been surprised to learn that the blackness of Poirot's hair came out of a bottle. But now the theatricality was apparent and merely created the impression that he wore a wig and had adorned his upper lip to amuse the children!

Only his eyes were the same as ever, shrewd and twinkling, and now—yes, undoubtedly—softened with emotion.

"Ah, *mon ami* Hastings—*mon ami* Hastings. . . ."

I bent my head and, as was his custom, he embraced me warmly.

"*Mon ami* Hastings!"

He leaned back, surveying me with his head a little to one side.

"Yes, just the same—the straight back, the broad shoulders, the grey of the hair—*très distingué.* You know, my friend, you have worn well. *Les femmes,* they still take an interest in you? Yes?"

"Really, Poirot," I protested. "Must you—"

"But I assure you, my friend, it is a test—it is the test. When the very young girls come and talk to you kindly, oh so kindly—it is the end! 'The poor old man,' they say, 'we must be nice to him. It must be so awful to be like that.' But you, Hastings—*vous êtes encore jeune.* For you there are still possibilities. That is right, twist your moustache, hunch your shoulders—I see it is as I say—you would not look so self-conscious otherwise."

I burst out laughing. "You really are the limit, Poirot. And how are you yourself?"

"Me," said Poirot with a grimace. "I am a wreck. I am a ruin. I cannot walk. I am crippled and twisted. Mercifully I can still feed myself, but otherwise I have to be attended to like a baby. Put to bed, washed and dressed. *Enfin,* it is not amusing that. Mercifully, though the outside decays, the core is still sound."

"Yes, indeed. The best heart in the world."

"The heart? Perhaps. I was not referring to the heart. The brain, *mon cher,* is what I mean by the core. My brain, it still functions magnificently."

I could at least perceive clearly that no deterioration of the brain in the direction of modesty had taken place.

"And you like it here?" I asked.

Poirot shrugged his shoulders. "It suffices. It is not, you comprehend, the Ritz. No, indeed. The room I was in when I first came here was both small and inadequately furnished. I moved to this one with no increase of price. Then, the cooking, it is English at its worst. Those Brussels sprouts so enormous, so hard, that the English like so much. The potatoes boiled and either hard or falling to pieces. The vegetables that taste of water, water, and again water. The complete absence of the salt and pepper in any dish—" he paused expressively.

"It sounds terrible," I said.

"I do not complain," said Poirot, and proceeded to do so. "And there is also the modernization, so called. The bathrooms, the taps everywhere and what comes out of them? Lukewarm water, *mon ami,* at most hours of the day. And the towels, so thin, so meagre!"

"There is something to be said for the old days," I said thoughtfully. I remembered the clouds of steam which had gushed from the hot tap of the one bathroom Styles had originally possessed, one of those bathrooms in which an immense bath with mahogany sides had reposed proudly in the middle of the bathroom floor. Remembered, too, the immense bath towels, and the frequent shining brass cans of boiling hot water that stood in one's old-fashioned basin.

"But one must not complain," said Poirot again. "I am content to suffer— for a good cause."

A sudden thought struck me.

"I say, Poirot, you're not—er—hard up, are you? I know the war hit investments very badly—"

Poirot reassured me quickly.

"No, no, my friend. I am in most comfortable circumstances. Indeed, I am rich. It is not the economy that brings me here."

"Then that's all right," I said. I went on: "I think I can understand your feeling. As one gets on, one tends more and more to revert to the old days. One tries to recapture old emotions. I find it painful to be here, in a way, and yet it brings back to me a hundred old thoughts and emotions that I'd quite forgotten I ever felt. I daresay you feel the same."

"Not in the least. I do not feel like that at all."

"They were good days," I said sadly.

"You may speak for yourself, Hastings. For me, my arrival at Styles St. Mary was a sad and painful time. I was a refugee, wounded, exiled from home and country, existing by charity in a foreign land. No, it was not gay. I did not know then that England would come to be my home and that I should find happiness here."

"I had forgotten that," I admitted.

"Precisely. You attribute always to others the sentiments that you yourself experience. Hastings was happy—everybody was happy!"

"No, no," I protested, laughing.

"And in any case it is not true," continued Poirot. "You look back, you say, the tears rising in your eyes, 'Oh, the happy days. Then I was young.' But indeed, my friend, you were not so happy as you think. You had recently been severely wounded, you were fretting at being no longer fit for active service, you had just been depressed beyond words by your sojourn in a dreary convalescent home and, as far as I remember, you proceeded to complicate matters by falling in love with two women at the same time."

I laughed and flushed.

"What a memory you have, Poirot."

"Ta ta ta—I remember now the melancholy sigh you heaved as you murmured fatuities about two lovely women."

"Do you remember what you said? You said, 'And neither of them for you! But *courage, mon ami.* We may hunt together again and then perhaps—' "

I stopped. For Poirot and I had gone hunting again to France and it was there that I had met the one woman. . . .

Gently my friend patted my arm.

"I know, Hastings, I know. The wound is still fresh. But do not dwell on it, do not look back. Instead look forward."

I made a gesture of disgust.

"Look forward? What is there to look forward to?"

"*Eh bien,* my friend, there is work to be done."

"Work? Where?"

"Here."

I stared at him.

"Just now," said Poirot, "you asked me why I had come here. You may not have observed that I gave you no answer. I will give the answer now. I am here to hunt down a murderer."

I stared at him with even more astonishment. For a moment I thought he was rambling.

"You really mean that?"

"But certainly I mean it. For what other reason did I urge you to join me? My limbs, they are no longer active, but my brain, as I told you, is unimpaired. My rule, remember, has been always the same—sit back and think. That I still can do—in fact it is the only thing possible for me. For the more active side of the campaign I shall have with me my invaluable Hastings."

"You really mean it?" I gasped.

"Of course I mean it. You and I, Hastings, *are going hunting once again.*"

It took some minutes to grasp that Poirot was really in earnest.

Fantastic though his statement sounded, I had no reason to doubt his judgement.

With a slight smile he said, "At last you are convinced. At first you imagined, did you not, that I had the softening of the brain?"

"No, no," I said hastily. "Only this seems such an unlikely place."

"Ah, you think so?"

"Of course I haven't seen all the people yet—"

"Whom have you seen?"

"Just the Luttrells, and a man called Norton, seems an inoffensive chap, and Boyd Carrington—I must say I took the greatest fancy to him."

Poirot nodded. "Well, Hastings, I will tell you this, when you have seen the rest of the household, my statement will seem to you just as improbable as it is now."

"Who else is there?"

"The Franklins—Doctor and Mrs., the hospital nurse who attends to Mrs. Franklin, your daughter Judith. Then there is a man called Allerton, something of a lady-killer, and a Miss Cole, a woman in her thirties. They are all, let me tell you, very nice people."

"And one of them is a murderer?"

"And one of them is a murderer."

"But why—how—why should you think—?"

I found it hard to frame my questions, they tumbled over each other.

"Calm yourself, Hastings. Let us begin from the beginning. Reach me, I pray you, that small box from the bureau. *Bien.* And now the key—so—"

Unlocking the despatch case, he took from it a mass of typescript and newspaper clippings.

"You can study these at your leisure, Hastings. For the moment I should not bother with the newspaper cuttings. They are merely the press accounts of various tragedies, occasionally inaccurate, sometimes suggestive. To give you an idea of the cases I suggest that you should read through the précis I have made."

Deeply interested, I started reading.

CASE A. ETHERINGTON

Leonard Etherington. Unpleasant habits—took drugs and also drank. A peculiar and sadistic character. Wife young and attractive. Desperately unhappy with him. Etherington died, apparently of food poisoning. Doctor not satisfied. As a result of autopsy, death discovered to be due to arsenical poisoning. Supply of weed killer in the house, but ordered a long time previously. Mrs. Etherington arrested and charged with murder. She had recently been friends with a man in Civil Service returning to India. No suggestion of actual infidelity, but evidence of deep sympathy between them. Young man had since become engaged to be married to girl he met on voyage out. Some doubt as to whether letter telling Mrs. Etherington of this fact was received by her after or before her husband's death. She herself says before. Evidence against her mainly circumstantial, absence of another likely suspect and accident highly unlikely. Great sympathy felt with her at trial owing to husband's character and the bad treatment she had received from him. Judge's summing up was in her favour stressing that verdict must be beyond any reasonable doubt.

Mrs. Etherington was acquitted. General opinion, however, was that she was guilty. Her life afterwards very difficult owing to friends, etc., cold-shouldering her. She died as a result of taking an overdose of sleeping draught two years after the trial. Verdict of accidental death returned at inquest.

CASE B. MISS SHARPLES

Elderly spinster. An invalid. Difficult, suffering much pain. She was looked after by her niece, Freda Clay. Miss Sharples died as a result of an overdose of morphia. Freda Clay admitted an error, saying that her aunt's sufferings were so bad that she could not stand it and gave her more morphia to ease the pain. Opinion of police that act was deliberate, not a mistake, but they considered evidence insufficient on which to prosecute.

CASE C. EDWARD RIGGS

Agricultural labourer. Suspected his wife of infidelity with their lodger, Ben Craig. Craig and Mrs. Riggs found shot. Shots proved to be from Riggs's gun. Riggs gave himself up to the police, said he supposed he must have done it, but couldn't remember. His mind went blank, he said. Riggs sentenced to death, sentence afterwards commuted to penal servitude for life.

CASE D. DEREK BRADLEY

Was carrying on an intrigue with a girl. His wife discovered this, she threatened to kill him. Bradley died of potassium cyanide administered in his beer. Mrs. Bradley arrested and tried for murder. Broke down under cross-examination. Convicted and hanged.

CASE E. MATTHEW LITCHFIELD

Elderly tyrant. Four daughters at home, not allowed any pleasures or money to spend. One evening on returning home, he was attacked outside his side door and killed by a blow on the head. Later, after police investigation, his eldest daughter, Margaret, walked into the police station and gave herself up for her father's murder. She did it, she said, in order that her younger sisters might be able to have a life of their own before it was too late. Litchfield left a large fortune. Margaret Litchfield was adjudged insane and committed to Broadmoor, but died shortly afterwards.

I read carefully, but with a growing bewilderment. Finally I put the paper down and looked enquiringly at Poirot.

"Well, *mon ami?*"

"I remember the Bradley case," I said slowly, "I read about it at the time. She was a very good-looking woman."

Poirot nodded.

"But you must enlighten me. What is all this about?"

"Tell me first what it amounts to in your eyes."

I was rather puzzled.

"What you gave me was an account of five different murders. They all occurred in different places and amongst different classes of people. Moreover there seems no superficial resemblance between them. That is to say, one was a case of jealousy, one was an unhappy wife seeking to get rid of her husband, another had money for a motive, another was, you might say, unselfish in aim since the murderer did not try to escape punishment, and the fifth was frankly brutal, probably committed under the influence of drink." I paused and said doubtfully: "Is there something in common between them all that I have missed?"

"No, no, you have been very accurate in your summing up. The only point that you might have mentioned, but did not, was the fact that in none of those cases did any real *doubt* exist."

"I don't think I understand."

"Mrs. Etherington, for instance, was acquitted. But everybody, nevertheless, was quite certain that she did it. Freda Clay was not openly accused, but no one thought of any alternative solution to the crime. Riggs stated that he did not remember killing his wife and her lover, but there was never any question of anybody else having done so. Margaret Litchfield confessed. In each case, you see, Hastings, there was one clear suspect and no other."

I wrinkled my brow. "Yes, that is true—but I don't see what particular inferences you draw from that."

"Ah, but you see, I am coming to a fact that you do not know as yet. Supposing, Hastings, that in each of these cases that I have outlined, there was one alien note common to them all?"

"What do you mean?"

Poirot said slowly: "I intend, Hastings, to be very careful in what I say. Let me put it this way. There is a certain person—X. In none of these cases did X (apparently) have any motive in doing away with the victim. In one case, as far as I have been able to find out, X was actually two hundred miles away when the crime was committed. Nevertheless I will tell you this. X was on intimate terms with Etherington, X lived for a time in the same village as Riggs, X was acquainted with Mrs. Bradley. I have a snap of X and Freda Clay walking together in the street, and X was near the house when old Matthew Litchfield died. What do you say to that?"

I stared at him. I said slowly: "Yes, it's a bit too much. Coincidence might account for two cases, or even three, but five is a bit too thick. There must, unlikely as it seems, be some connection between these different murders."

"You assume, then, what I have assumed?"

"That X is the murderer? Yes."

"In that case, Hastings, you will be willing to go with me one step farther. Let me tell you this. *X is in this house.*"

"Here? At Styles?"

"At Styles. What is the logical inference to be drawn from that?"

I knew what was coming as I said: "Go on—say it."

Hercule Poirot said gravely: "A murder will shortly be committed here—*here.*"

Three

For a moment or two I stared at Poirot in dismay, then I reacted.

"No, it won't," I said. "You'll prevent that."

Poirot threw me an affectionate glance.

"My loyal friend. How much I appreciate your faith in me. *Tout de même,* I am not sure if it is justified in this case."

"Nonsense. Of course you can stop it."

Poirot's voice was grave as he said: "Reflect a minute, Hastings. One can catch a murderer, yes. But how does one proceed to stop a murder?"

"Well, you—you—well, I mean—if you know beforehand—"

I paused rather feebly—for suddenly I saw the difficulties.

Poirot said: "You see? It is not so simple. There are, in fact, only three methods. The first is to warn the victim. To put the victim on his or her guard. That does not always succeed, for it is unbelievably difficult to convince some people that they are in grave danger—possibly from someone near and dear to them. They are indignant and refuse to believe. The second course is to warn the murderer. To say, in language that is only slightly veiled, '*I know your intentions.* If so-and-so dies, my friend, *you* will most surely hang.' That succeeds more often than the first method, but even there it is likely to fail. For a murderer, my friend, is more conceited than any creature on this earth. A murderer is always more clever than anyone else—no one will ever suspect him or her—

the police will be utterly baffled, etc. Therefore he (or she) goes ahead just the same, and all you can have is the satisfaction of hanging them afterwards." He paused and said thoughtfully: "Twice in my life I have warned a murderer— once in Egypt, once elsewhere. In each case, the criminal was determined to kill . . . It may be so here."

"You said there was a third method," I reminded him.

"Ah yes. For that one needs the utmost ingenuity. You have to guess exactly how and when the blow is timed to fall and you have to be ready to step in at the exact psychological moment. You have to catch the murderer, if not quite red-handed, then guilty of the intention beyond any possible doubt.

"And that, my friend," went on Poirot, "is, I can assure you, a matter of great difficulty and delicacy, and I would not for a moment guarantee its success! I may be conceited, but I am not so conceited as *that*."

"Which method do you propose to try here?"

"Possibly all three. The first is the most difficult."

"Why? I should have thought it the easiest."

"Yes, if you know the intended victim. But do you not realize, Hastings, that here I do not know the victim?"

"What?"

I gave vent to the exclamation without reflecting. Then the difficulties of the position began to draw on me. There was, there must be, some link connecting this series of crimes, but we did not know what that link was. The motive, the vitally important motive, was missing. And without knowing that, we could not tell who was threatened.

Poirot nodded as he saw by my face that I was realizing the difficulties of the situation.

"You see, my friend, it is not so easy."

"No," I said. "I see that. You have so far been able to find no connection between these varying cases?"

Poirot shook his head. "Nothing."

I reflected again. In the ABC crimes, we had to deal with what purported to be an alphabetical series, though in actuality it had turned out to be something very different.

I asked: "There is, you are quite sure, no far-fetched financial motive—nothing, for instance, like you found in the case of Evelyn Carlisle?"

"No. You may be quite sure, my dear Hastings, that financial gain is the first thing for which I look."

That was true enough. Poirot had always been completely cynical about money.

I thought again. A vendetta of some kind? That was more in accordance with the facts. But even there, there seemed a lack of any connecting link. I recalled a story I had read of a series of purposeless murders—the clue being that the victims had happened to serve as members of a jury, and the crimes had been committed by a man whom they had condemned. It struck me that something of that kind would meet this case. I am ashamed to say that I kept the idea to myself. It would have been such a feather in my cap if I could go to Poirot with the solution.

Instead I asked: "And now tell me, who is X?"

To my intense annoyance Poirot shook his head very decidedly. "That, my friend, I do not tell."

"Nonsense. Why not?"

Poirot's eyes twinkled. "Because, *mon cher,* you are still the same old Hastings. You have still the speaking countenance. I do not wish, you see, that you should sit staring at X with your mouth hanging open, your face saying plainly: 'This—this that I am looking at—is a murderer.'"

"You might give me credit for a little dissimulation at need."

"When you try to dissimulate, it is worse. No, no, *mon ami,* we must be very incognito, you and I. Then, when we pounce, we pounce."

"You obstinate old devil," I said. "I've a good mind to—"

I broke off as there was a tap on the door. Poirot called, "Come in," and my daughter Judith entered.

I should like to describe Judith, but I've always been a poor hand at descriptions.

Judith is tall, she holds her head high, she has level dark brows, and a very lovely line of cheek and jaw, severe in its austerity. She is grave and slightly scornful, and to my mind there has always hung about her a suggestion of tragedy.

Judith didn't come and kiss me—she is not that kind. She just smiled at me and said, "Hullo, Father."

Her smile was shy and a little embarrassed, but it made me feel that in spite of her undemonstrativeness she was pleased to see me.

"Well," I said, feeling foolish as I so often do with the younger generation, "I've got here."

"Very clever of you, darling," said Judith.

"I describe to him," said Poirot, "the cooking."

"Is it very bad?" asked Judith.

"You should not have to ask that, my child. Is it that you think of nothing but the test tubes and the microscopes? Your middle finger it is stained with methylene blue. It is not a good thing for your husband if you take no interest in his stomach."

"I daresay I shan't have a husband."

"Certainly you will have a husband. What did the *bon Dieu* create you for?"

"Many things, I hope," said Judith.

"*Le mariage* first of all."

"Very well," said Judith. "You will find me a nice husband and I will look after his stomach very carefully."

"She laughs at me," said Poirot. "Some day she will know how wise old men are."

There was another tap on the door and Dr. Franklin entered. He was a tall, angular young man of thirty-five, with a decided jaw, reddish hair, and bright blue eyes. He was the most ungainly man I had ever known, and was always knocking into things in an absentminded way.

He cannoned into the screen round Poirot's chair, and half turning his head murmured "I beg your pardon" to it automatically.

I wanted to laugh, but Judith, I noted, remained quite grave. I suppose she was quite used to that sort of thing.

"You remember my father," said Judith.

Dr. Franklin started, shied nervously, screwed up his eyes and peered at me, then stuck out a hand, saying awkwardly: "Of course, of course, how are you? I heard you were coming down." He turned to Judith. "I say, do you think we need change? If not we might go on a bit after dinner. If we got a few more of those slides prepared—"

"No," said Judith. "I want to talk to my father."

"Oh, yes. Oh, of course." Suddenly he smiled, an apologetic, boyish smile. "I am sorry—I get so awfully wrapped up in a thing. It's quite unpardonable— makes me so selfish. Do forgive me."

The clock struck and Franklin glanced at it hurriedly.

"Good Lord, is it as late as that? I shall get into trouble. Promised Barbara I'd read to her before dinner."

He grinned at us both and hurried out, colliding with the door post as he went.

"How is Mrs. Franklin?" I asked.

"The same and rather more so," said Judith.

"It's very sad her being such an invalid," I said.

"It's maddening for a doctor," said Judith. "Doctors like healthy people."

"How hard you young people are!" I exclaimed.

Judith said coldly: "I was just stating a fact."

"Nevertheless," said Poirot, "the good doctor hurries to read to her."

"Very stupid," said Judith. "That nurse of hers can read to her perfectly well if she wants to be read to. Personally I should loathe anyone reading aloud to *me*."

"Well, well, tastes differ," I said.

"She's a very stupid woman," said Judith.

"Now there, *mon enfant,*" said Poirot, "I do not agree with you."

"She never reads anything but the cheapest kind of novel. She takes no interest in his work. She doesn't keep abreast of current thought. She just talks about her health to everyone who will listen."

"I still maintain, said Poirot, "that she uses her grey cells in ways that you, my child, know nothing about."

"She's a very feminine sort of woman," said Judith. "She coos and purrs. I expect you like 'em like that, Uncle Hercule."

"Not at all," I said. "He likes them large and flamboyant and Russian for choice."

"So that is how you give me away, Hastings? Your father, Judith, has always had a penchant for auburn hair. It has landed him in trouble many a time."

Judith smiled at us both indulgently. She said: "What a funny couple you are."

She turned away and I rose.

"I must get unpacked, and I might have a bath before dinner."

Poirot pressed a little bell within reach of his hand and a minute or two later his valet attendant entered. I was surprised to find that the man was a stranger.

"Why! Where's George?"

Poirot's valet George had been with him for many years.

"George has returned to his family. His father is ill. I hope he will come back to me some time. In the meantime—" he smiled at the new valet—"Curtiss looks after me."

Curtiss smiled back respectfully. He was a big man with a bovine, rather stupid, face.

As I went out of the door I noted that Poirot was carefully locking up the despatch case with the papers inside it.

My mind in a whirl I crossed the passage to my own room.

Four

I went down to dinner that night feeling that the whole of life had become suddenly unreal.

Once or twice, while dressing, I had asked myself if possibly Poirot had imagined the whole thing. After all, the dear old chap *was* an old man now and sadly broken in health. He himself might declare his brain was as sound as ever—but in point of fact, *was* it? His whole life had been spent in tracking down crime. Would it really be surprising if, in the end, he was to fancy crimes where no crimes were? His enforced inaction must have fretted him sorely. What more likely than that he should invent for himself a new manhunt? Wishful thinking—a perfectly reasonable neurosis. He had selected a number of publicly reported happenings, and had read into them something that was not there—a shadowy figure behind them, a mad mass murderer. In all probability Mrs. Etherington had really killed her husband, the labourer had shot his wife, a young woman had given her old aunt an overdose of morphia, a jealous wife had polished off her husband as she had threatened to do, and a crazy spinster had really committed the murder for which she had subsequently given herself up. In fact these crimes were exactly what they seemed!

Against that view (surely the commonsense one) I could only set my own inherent belief in Poirot's acumen.

Poirot said that a murder had been arranged. For the second time Styles was to house a crime.

Time would prove or disprove that assertion, but if it were true, it behoved us to forestall that happening.

And Poirot knew the identity of the murderer which I did not.

The more I thought about that, the more annoyed I became! Really, frankly, it was damned cheek of Poirot! He wanted my cooperation and yet he refused to take me into his confidence!

Why? There was the reason he gave—surely a most inadequate one! I was tired of this silly joking about my "speaking countenance." I could keep a secret as well as anyone. Poirot had always persisted in the humiliating belief that I am a transparent character and that anyone can read what is passing in my mind. He tries to soften the blow sometimes by attributing it to my beautiful and honest character which abhors all form of deceit!

Of course, I reflected, if the whole thing was a chimera of Poirot's imagination, his reticence was easily explained.

I had come to no conclusion by the time the gong sounded, and I went down to dinner with an open mind, but with an alert eye, for the detection of Poirot's mythical X.

For the moment I would accept everything that Poirot had said as gospel truth. There *was* a person under this roof who had already killed five times and who was preparing to kill again. *Who was it?*

In the drawing room before we went in to dinner I was introduced to Miss Cole and Major Allerton. The former was a tall, still handsome woman of thirty-three or four. Major Allerton I instinctively disliked. He was a good-looking man in the early forties, broad-shouldered, bronzed of face, with an easy way of talking, most of what he said holding a double implication. He had the pouches under his eyes that come with a dissipated way of life. I suspected him of racketing around, of gambling, of drinking hard, and of being first and last a womanizer.

Old Colonel Luttrell, I saw, did not much like him either, and Boyd Carrington was also rather stiff in his manner towards him. Allerton's success was with the women of the party. Mrs. Luttrell twittered to him delightedly, whilst he flattered her lazily and with a hardly concealed impertinence. I was also annoyed to see that Judith, too, seemed to enjoy his company and was exerting herself far more than usual to talk to him. Why the worst type of man can always be relied upon to please and interest the nicest of women has long been a problem beyond me. I knew instinctively that Allerton was a rotter—and nine men out of ten would have agreed with me. Whereas nine women or possibly the whole ten would have fallen for him immediately.

As we sat down at the dinner table and plates of white gluey liquid were set before us, I let my eyes rove round the table whilst I summed up the possibilities.

If Poirot were right, and retained his clearness of brain unimpaired, one of these people was a dangerous murderer—and probably a lunatic as well.

Poirot had not actually said so, but I presumed that X was probably a man. Which of these men was it likely to be?

Surely not old Colonel Luttrell, with his indecision, and his general air of feebleness. Norton, the man I had met rushing out of the house with field glasses? It seemed unlikely. He appeared to be a pleasant fellow, rather ineffective and lacking in vitality. Of course, I told myself, many murderers have been small insignificant men—driven to assert themselves by crime for that very reason. They resented being passed over and ignored. Norton might be a murderer of this type. But there was his fondness for birds. I have always believed that a love of nature was essentially a healthy sign in a man.

Boyd Carrington? Out of the question. A man with a name known all over the world. A fine sportsman, an administrator, a man universally liked and looked up to. Franklin I also dismissed. I knew how Judith respected and admired him.

Major Allerton now. I dwelt on him appraisingly. A nasty fellow if I ever saw one! The sort of fellow who would skin his grandmother. And all glossed over with this superficial charm of manner. He was talking now—telling a story of his own discomfiture and making everybody laugh with his rueful appreciation of a joke at his expense.

If Allerton was X, I decided, his crimes had been committed for profit in some way.

It was true that Poirot had not definitely said that X was a man. I considered Miss Cole as a possibility. Her movements were restless and jerky—obviously a woman of nerves. Handsome in a hag-ridden kind of way. Still, she looked normal enough. She, Mrs. Luttrell and Judith were the only women at the dinner table. Mrs. Franklin was having dinner upstairs in her room, and the nurse who attended to her had her meals after us.

After dinner I was standing by the drawing room window looking out into the garden and thinking back to the time when I had seen Cynthia Murdoch, a young girl with auburn hair, run across that lawn. How charming she had looked in her white overall. . . .

Lost in thoughts of the past, I started when Judith passed her arm through mine and led me with her out of the window on to the terrace.

She said abruptly: "What's the matter?"

I was startled. "The matter? What do you mean?"

"You've been so queer all through the evening. Why were you staring at everyone at dinner?"

I was annoyed. I had had no idea I had allowed my thoughts so much sway over me.

"Was I? I suppose I was thinking of the past. Seeing ghosts perhaps."

"Oh, yes, of course you stayed here, didn't you, when you were a young man? An old lady was murdered here, or something?"

"Poisoned with strychnine."

"What was she like? Nice or nasty?"

I considered the question.

"She was a very kind woman," I said slowly. "Generous. Gave a lot to charity."

"Oh, *that* kind of generosity."

Judith's voice sounded faintly scornful. Then she asked a curious question: "Were people—happy here?"

No, they had not been happy. That, at least, I knew. I said slowly: "No."

"Why not?"

"Because they felt like prisoners. Mrs. Inglethorp, you see, had all the money—and—doled it out. Her stepchildren could have no life of their own."

I heard Judith take a sharp breath. The hand on my arm tightened.

"That's wicked—wicked. An abuse of power. It shouldn't be allowed. Old people, sick people, they shouldn't have the power to hold up the lives of the young and strong. To keep them tied down, fretting, wasting their power and energy that could be used—that's needed. It's just selfishness."

"The old," I said drily, "have not got a monopoly of that quality."

"Oh, I know, Father, you think the young are selfish. So we are, perhaps, but it's a *clean* selfishness. At least we only want to do what we want ourselves, we don't want everybody else to do what we want, we don't want to make slaves of other people."

"No, you just trample them down if they happen to be in your way."

Judith squeezed my arm. She said: "Don't be so bitter! I don't really do much trampling—and you've never tried to dictate our lives to any of us. We are grateful for that."

"I'm afraid," I said honestly, "that I'd have liked to, though. It was your mother who insisted *you* should be allowed to make your own mistakes."

Judith gave my arm another quick squeeze. She said: "I know. You'd have liked to fuss over us like a hen! I do hate fuss. I won't stand it. But you do agree with me, don't you, about useful lives being sacrificed to useless ones?"

"It does sometimes happen," I admitted. "But there's no need for drastic measures . . . It's up to anybody just to walk out, you know."

"Yes, but is it? *Is* it?"

Her tone was so vehement that I looked at her in some astonishment. It was too dark to see her face clearly. She went on, her voice low and troubled: "There's so much—it's difficult—financial considerations, a sense of responsibility, reluctance to hurt someone you've been fond of—all those things, and some people are so unscrupulous—they know just how to play on all those feelings. Some people—some people are like *leeches!*"

"My dear Judith," I exclaimed, taken aback by the positive fury of her tone.

She seemed to realize that she had been overvehement, for she laughed, and withdrew her arm from mine.

"Was I sounding very intense? It's a matter I feel rather hotly about. You see, I've known a case . . . An old brute. And when someone was brave enough to—to cut the knot and set the people she loved free, they called her mad. Mad? It was the sanest thing anyone could do—*and* the bravest!"

A horrible qualm passed over me. Where, not long ago, had I heard something like that?

"Judith," I said sharply. "Of what case are you talking?"

"Oh, nobody you know. Some friends of the Franklins. Old man called Litchfield. He was quite rich and practically starved his wretched daughters—never let them see anyone, or go out. He was mad really, but not sufficiently so in the medical sense."

"And the eldest daughter murdered him," I said.

"Oh, I expect you read about it? I suppose you would call it murder—but it wasn't done from personal motives. Margaret Litchfield went straight to the police and gave herself up. I think she was very brave. I wouldn't have had the courage."

"The courage to give yourself up or the courage to commit murder?"

"Both."

"I'm very glad to hear it," I said severely, "and I don't like to hear you talking of murder as justified in certain cases." I paused, and added: "What did Dr. Franklin think?"

"Thought it served him right," said Judith. "You know, Father, some people really *ask* to be murdered."

"I won't have you talking like this, Judith. Who's been putting these ideas into your head?"

"Nobody."

"Well, let me tell you that it's all pernicious nonsense."

"I see. We'll leave it at that." She paused. "I came really to give you a message from Mrs. Franklin. She'd like to see you if you don't mind coming up to her bedroom."

"I shall be delighted. I'm so sorry she was feeling too ill to come down to dinner."

"She's all right," said Judith unfeelingly. "She just likes making a fuss."

The young are very unsympathetic.

Five

I had only met Mrs. Franklin once before. She was a woman about thirty—of what I should describe as the madonna type. Big brown eyes, hair parted in the centre, and a long gentle face. She was very slender and her skin had a transparent fragility.

She was lying on a day bed, propped up with pillows, and wearing a very dainty negligee of white and pale blue.

Franklin and Boyd Carrington were there drinking coffee. Mrs. Franklin welcomed me with an outstretched hand and a smile.

"How glad I am you've come, Captain Hastings. It will be so nice for Judith. The child has really been working far too hard."

"She looks very well on it," I said as I took the fragile little hand in mine.

Barbara Franklin sighed. "Yes, she's lucky. How I envy her. I don't believe really that she knows what ill health is. What do you think, Nurse? Oh! Let me introduce you. This is Nurse Craven who's so terribly, terribly good to me. I don't know what I should *do* without her. She treats me just like a baby."

Nurse Craven was a tall, good-looking young woman with a fine colour and a handsome head of auburn hair. I noticed her hands which were long and white—very different from the hands of so many hospital nurses. She was in some respects a taciturn girl, and sometimes did not answer. She did not now, merely inclined her head.

"But really," went on Mrs. Franklin, "John has been working that wretched girl of yours too hard. He's such a slave driver. You are a slave driver, aren't you, John?"

Her husband was standing looking out of the window. He was whistling to himself and jingling some loose change in his pocket. He started slightly at his wife's question.

"What's that, Barbara?"

"I was saying that you overwork poor Judith Hastings shamefully. Now Captain Hastings is here, he and I are going to put our heads together and we're not going to allow it."

Persiflage was not Dr. Franklin's strong point. He looked vaguely worried and turned to Judith enquiringly. He mumbled: "You must let me know if I overdo it."

Judith said: "They're just trying to be funny. Talking of work, I wanted to ask you about that stain for the second slide—you know, the one that—"

He turned to her eagerly and broke in. "Yes, yes. I say, if you don't mind, let's go down to the lab. I'd like to be quite sure—"

Still talking, they went out of the room together.

Barbara Franklin lay back on her pillows. She sighed. Nurse Craven said suddenly and rather disagreeably: "It's Miss Hastings who's the slave driver, I think!"

Again Mrs. Franklin sighed. She murmured: "I feel so *inadequate*. I ought, I know, to take more interest in John's work, but I just can't do it. I daresay it's something wrong in me, but—"

She was interrupted by a snort from Boyd Carrington who was standing by the fireplace.

"Nonsense, Babs," he said. "*You're* all right. Don't worry yourself."

"Oh but, Bill, dear, I *do* worry. I get so discouraged about myself. It's all—I can't help feeling it—it's all so *nasty*. The guinea pigs and the rats and everything. Ugh!" She shuddered. "I know it's stupid, but I'm such a fool. It makes me feel quite sick. I just want to think of all the lovely happy things—birds and flowers and children playing. *You* know, Bill."

He came over and took the hand she held out to him so pleadingly. His face as he looked down at her was changed, as gentle as any woman's. It was, some-how, impressive—for Boyd Carrington was so essentially a manly man.

"You've not changed much since you were seventeen, Babs," he said. "Do you remember that garden house of yours and the bird bath and the coconuts?"

He turned his head to me. "Barbara and I are old playmates," he said.

"Old playmates!" she protested.

"Oh, I'm not denying that you're over fifteen years younger than I am. But I played with you as a tiny tot when I was a young man. Gave you pick-a-backs, my dear. And then later I came home to find you a beautiful young lady—just on the point of making your début in the world—and I did my share by taking you out on the golf links and teaching you to play golf. Do you remember?"

"Oh, Bill, do you think I'd forget?"

"My people used to live in this part of the world," she explained to me. "And Bill used to come and stay with his old uncle, Sir Everard, at Knatton."

"And what a mausoleum it was—and is," said Boyd Carrington. "Some-times I despair of getting the place liveable."

"Oh, Bill, it could be made marvellous—quite marvellous!"

"Yes, Babs, but the trouble is I've got no ideas. Baths and some really com-fortable chairs—that's all I can think of. It needs a woman."

"I've told you I'll come and help. I mean it. Really."

Sir William looked doubtfully towards Nurse Craven.

"If you're strong enough, I could drive you over. What do you think, Nurse?"

"Oh yes, Sir William. I really think it would do Mrs. Franklin good—if she's careful not to overtire herself, of course."

"That's a date, then," said Boyd Carrington. "And now you have a good night's sleep. Get into good fettle for tomorrow."

We both wished Mrs. Franklin good night and went out together. As we went down the stairs, Boyd Carrington said gruffly: "You've no idea what a lovely creature she was at seventeen. I was home from Burma—my wife died out there, you know. Don't mind telling you I completely lost my heart to her. She married Franklin three or four years afterwards. Don't think it's been a happy marriage. It's my idea that that's what lies at the bottom of her ill health. Fellow doesn't understand her or appreciate her. And she's the sensitive kind.

I've an idea that this delicacy of hers is partly nervous. Take her out of herself, amuse her, interest her, and she looks a different creature! But that damned saw-bones only takes an interest in test tubes and West African natives and cultures." He snorted angrily.

I thought that there was, perhaps, something in what he said. Yet it surprised me that Boyd Carrington should be attracted by Mrs. Franklin who, when all was said and done, was a sickly creature, though pretty in a frail, chocolate-box way. But Boyd Carrington himself was so full of vitality and life that I should have thought he would merely have been impatient with the neurotic type of invalid. However, Barbara Franklin must have been quite lovely as a girl, and with many men, especially those of the idealistic type such as I judged Boyd Carrington to be, early impressions die hard.

Downstairs, Mrs. Luttrell pounced upon us and suggested bridge. I excused myself on the plea of wanting to join Poirot.

I found my friend in bed. Curtiss was moving around the room tidying up, but he presently went out, shutting the door behind him.

"Confound you, Poirot," I said. "You and your infernal habit of keeping things up your sleeve. I've spent the whole evening trying to spot X."

"That must have made you somewhat *distrait*," observed my friend. "Did nobody comment on your abstraction and ask you what was the matter?"

I reddened slightly, remembering Judith's questions. Poirot, I think, observed my discomfiture. I noticed a small malicious smile on his lips. He merely said, however: "And what conclusion have you come to on that point?"

"Would you tell me if I was right?"

"Certainly not."

I watched his face closely.

"I had considered Norton—"

Poirot's face did not change.

"Not," I said, "that I've anything to go upon. He just struck me as perhaps less unlikely than anyone else. And then he's—well—inconspicuous. I should imagine the kind of murderer we're after would have to be inconspicuous."

"That is true. But there are more ways than you think of being incon-spicuous."

"What do you mean?"

"Supposing, to take a hypothetical case, that if a sinister stranger arrives there some weeks before the murder, for no apparent reason, he will be noticeable. It would be better, would it not, if the stranger were to be a negligible personality, engaged in some harmless sport like fishing."

"Or watching birds," I agreed. "Yes, but that's just what I was saying."

"On the other hand," said Poirot, "it might be better still if the murderer were already a prominent personality—that is to say, he might be the butcher. That would have the further advantage that no one notices bloodstains on a butcher!"

"You're just being ridiculous. Everybody would know if the butcher had quarrelled with the baker."

"Not if the butcher had become a butcher *simply in order to have a chance of murdering the baker.* One must always look one step behind, my friend."

I looked at him closely, trying to decide if a hint lay concealed in those words. If they meant anything definite, they would seem to point to Colonel Luttrell. Had he deliberately opened a guest house in order to have an opportunity of murdering one of the guests?

Poirot very gently shook his head. He said: "It is not from my face that you will get the answer."

"You really are a maddening fellow, Poirot," I said with a sigh. "Anyway, Norton isn't my only suspect. What about this fellow Allerton?"

Poirot, his face still impassive, enquired: "You do not like him?"

"No, I don't."

"Ah. What you call the nasty bit of goods. That is right, is it not?"

"Definitely. Don't you think so?"

"Certainly. He is a man," said Poirot slowly, "very attractive to women."

I made an exclamation of contempt. "How women can be so foolish. What do they see in a fellow like that?"

"Who can say? But it is always so. The *mauvais sujet*—always women are attracted to him."

"But why?"

Poirot shrugged his shoulders. "They see something, perhaps, that we do not."

"But what?"

"Danger, possibly . . . Everyone, my friend, demands a spice of danger in their lives. Some get it vicariously—as in bullfights. Some read about it. Some find it at the cinema. But I am sure of this—too much safety is abhorrent to the nature of a human being. Men find danger in many ways—women are reduced to finding their danger mostly in affairs of sex. That is why, perhaps, they welcome the hint of the tiger—the sheathed claws, the treacherous spring. The excellent fellow who will make a good and kind husband—they pass him by."

I considered this gloomily in silence for some minutes. Then I reverted to the previous theme.

"You know, Poirot," I said. "It will be easy enough really for me to find out who X is. I've only got to poke about and find who was acquainted with all the people. I mean the people of your five cases."

I brought this out triumphantly, but Poirot merely gave me a look of scorn.

"I have not demanded your presence here, Hastings, in order to watch you clumsily and laboriously following the way I have already trodden. And let me tell you it is not quite so simple as you think. Four of those cases took place in this county. The people assembled under this roof are not a collection of strangers who have arrived here independently. This is not a hotel in the usual sense of the word. The Luttrells come from this part of the world; they were badly off and bought this place and started it as a venture. The people who come here are their friends, or friends recommended by their friends. Sir William persuaded the Franklins to come. They in turn suggested it to Norton, and, I believe, to Miss Cole—and so on. Which is to say that there is a very fair chance of a certain person who is known to one of these people being known to all of these people. It is also open to X to lie wherever the facts are best known. Take the case of the labourer Riggs. The village where that tragedy occurred is not far from the house of Boyd Carrington's uncle. Mrs. Franklin's people, also, lived near. The inn in the village is much frequented by tourists. Some of Mrs. Franklin's family friends used to put up there. Franklin himself has stayed there. Norton and Miss Cole may have stayed there and probably have.

"No, no, my friend. I beg that you will not make these clumsy attempts to unravel a secret that I refuse to reveal to you."

"It's so damned silly. As though I should be likely to give it away. I tell you, Poirot, I'm tired of these jokes about my speaking countenance. It's not funny."

Poirot said quietly: "Are you so sure that is the only reason? Do you not realize, my friend, that such knowledge may be dangerous? Do you not see that I concern myself with your safety?"

I stared at him openmouthed. Up till that minute I had not appreciated that aspect of the matter. But it was, of course, true enough. If a clever and resourceful murderer who had already got away with five crimes—unsuspected as he thought—once awoke to the fact that someone was on his trail, then indeed there was danger for those on his track.

I said sharply: "But then you—you yourself are in danger, Poirot?"

Poirot, as far as he was able to in his crippled state, made a gesture of supreme disdain.

"I am accustomed to that; I can protect myself. And see, have I not here my faithful dog to protect me also? My excellent and loyal Hastings!"

Six

Poirot was supposed to keep early hours. I left him therefore to go to sleep and went downstairs, pausing to have a few words with the attendant Curtiss on the way.

I found him a stolid individual, slow in the uptake, but trustworthy and competent. He had been with Poirot since the latter's return from Egypt. His master's health, he told me, was fairly good, but he occasionally had alarming heart attacks, and his heart was much weakened in the last few months. It was a case of the engine slowly failing.

Oh well, it had been a good life. Nevertheless my heart was wrung for my old friend who was fighting so gallantly every step of the downward way. Even now, crippled and weak, his indomitable spirit was still leading him to ply the craft at which he was so expert.

I went downstairs sad at heart. I could hardly imagine life without Poirot. . . .

A rubber was just finished in the drawing room, and I was invited to cut in. I thought it might serve to distract my mind and I accepted. Boyd Carrington was the one to cut out, and I sat down with Norton and Colonel and Mrs. Luttrell.

"What do you say now, Mr. Norton," said Mrs. Luttrell. "Shall you and I take the other two on? Our late partnership's been very successful."

Norton smiled pleasantly, but murmured that perhaps, really, they ought to cut—what?

Mrs. Luttrell assented, but with rather an ill-grace, I thought.

Norton and I cut together against the Luttrells. I noticed that Mrs. Luttrell was definitely displeased by this. She bit her lip and her charm and Irish brogue disappeared completely for the moment.

I soon found out why. I played on many future occasions with Colonel Luttrell, and he was not really such a bad player. He was what I should describe as a moderate player, but inclined to be forgetful. Every now and then he would make some really bad mistake owing to this. But playing with his wife he made mistake after mistake without ceasing. He was obviously nervous of her, and this caused him to play about three times as badly as was normal. Mrs. Luttrell was a very good player indeed, though a rather unpleasant one to play with. She snatched every conceivable advantage, ignored the rules if her adversary was unaware of them, and enforced them immediately when they served her. She was also extremely adept at a quick sideways glance into her opponent's hands. In other words, she played to win.

And I understood soon enough what Poirot had meant by vinegar. At cards her self-restraint failed, and her tongue lashed every mistake her wretched husband made. It was really most uncomfortable for both Norton and myself, and I was thankful when the rubber came to an end.

We both excused ourselves from playing another on the score of the lateness of the hour.

As we moved away, Norton rather incautiously gave way to his feelings.

"I say, Hastings, that was pretty ghastly. It gets my back up to see that poor old boy bullied like that. And the meek way he takes it! Poor chap. Not much of the peppery-tongued Indian Colonel about him."

"Ssh," I warned him, for Norton's voice had been incautiously raised and I was afraid old Colonel Luttrell would overhear.

"No, but it is too bad."

I said with feeling: "I shall understand it if he ever takes a hatchet to her."

Norton shook his head. "He won't. The iron's entered his soul. He'll go on:

'Yes, m'dear, no, m'dear, sorry, m'dear', pulling at his moustache and bleating meekly until he's put in his coffin. *He* couldn't assert himself if he tried!"

I shook my head sadly, for I was afraid Norton was right.

We paused in the hall and I noticed that the side door to the garden was open and the wind blowing in.

"Ought we to shut that?" I asked.

Norton hesitated a minute before saying: "Well—er—I don't think every-body's in yet."

A sudden suspicion darted through my mind.

"Who's out?"

"Your daughter, I think—and—er—Allerton."

He tried to make his voice extra casual, but the information coming on top of my conversation with Poirot made me feel suddenly uneasy.

Judith—and Allerton. Surely Judith, my clever, cool Judith, would not be taken in by a man of that type? Surely she would see through him?

I told myself that repeatedly as I undressed, but the vague uneasiness per-sisted. I could not sleep and lay tossing from side to side.

As is the way with night worries, everything gets exaggerated. A fresh sense of despair and loss swept over me. If only my dear wife were alive. She on whose judgement I had relied for so many years. She had always been wise and under-standing about the children.

Without her I felt miserably inadequate. The responsibility for their safety and happiness was mine. Would I be equal to that task? I was not, Heaven help me, a clever man. I blundered—made mistakes. If Judith was to ruin her chances of happiness, if she were to suffer—

Desperately I switched the light on and sat up.

It was no good going on like this. I must get some sleep. Getting out of bed I walked over to the washbasin and looked doubtfully at a bottle of aspirin tablets.

No, I needed something stronger than aspirin. I reflected that Poirot, prob-ably, would have some sleeping stuff of some kind. I crossed the passage to his room and stood hesitating a minute outside the door. Rather a shame to wake the old boy up.

As I hesitated I heard a footfall and looked round. Allerton was coming along the corridor towards me. It was dimly lit, and until he came near I could not see his face, and wondered for a minute who it was. Then I saw, and stiffened all over. For the man was smiling to himself, and I disliked that smile very much.

He looked up and raised his eyebrows. "Hullo, Hastings, still about?"

"I couldn't sleep," I said shortly.

"Is that all? I'll soon fix you up. Come with me."

I followed him into his room, which was the next one to mine. A strange fascination drove me to study this man as closely as I could.

"You keep late hours yourself," I remarked.

"I've never been an early bed-goer. Not when there's sport abroad. These fine evenings aren't made to be wasted."

He laughed—and I disliked the laugh.

I followed him into the bathroom. He opened a little cupboard and took out a bottle of tablets.

"Here you are. This is the real dope. You'll sleep like a log—and have pleasant dreams too. Wonderful stuff Slumberyl—that's the patent name for it."

The enthusiasm in his voice gave me a slight shock. Was he a drugtaker as well? I said doubtfully: "It isn't—dangerous?"

"It is if you take too much of it. It's one of the barbiturates—whose toxic dose is very near the effective one." He smiled, the corners of his mouth sliding up his face in an unpleasant way.

"I shouldn't have thought you could get it without a doctor's prescription," I said.

"You can't, old boy. Anyway, quite literally, *you* can't. I've got a pull in that line."

I suppose it was foolish of me, but I get these impulses. I said: "You knew Etherington, I think?"

At once I knew that it had struck a note of some kind. His eyes grew hard and wary. He said—and his voice had changed—it was light and artificial: "Oh yes—I knew Etherington. Poor chap." Then, as I did not speak, he went on: "Etherington took drugs—of course—but he overdid it. One's got to know when to stop. He didn't. Bad business. That wife of his was lucky. If the sympathy of the jury hadn't been with her, she'd have hanged."

He passed me over a couple of the tablets. Then he said casually: "Did you know Etherington as well?"

I answered with the truth. "No."

He seemed for a moment at a loss how to proceed. Then he turned it off with a light laugh.

"Funny chap. Not exactly a Sunday school character but he was good company sometimes."

I thanked him for the tablets and went back to my room.

As I lay down again and turned off the lights I wondered if I had been foolish.

For it came to me very strongly that Allerton was almost certainly X. And I had let him see that I suspected the fact.

Seven

I

My narrative of the days spent at Styles must necessarily be somewhat rambling. In my recollection of it, it presents itself to me as a series of conversations—of suggestive words and phrases that etched themselves into my consciousness.

First of all, and very early on, there came the realization of Hercule Poirot's infirmity and helplessness. I did believe, as he had said, that his brain still functioned with all its old keenness, but the physical envelope had worn so thin that I realized at once that my part was destined to be a far more active one than usual. I had to be, as it were, Poirot's eyes and ears.

True, every fine day Curtiss would pick up his master and carry him carefully downstairs to where his chair had been carried down beforehand and was awaiting him. Then he would wheel Poirot out into the garden and select a spot that was free of draughts. On other days, when the weather was not propitious, he would be carried to the drawing room.

Wherever he might be, someone or other was sure to come and sit with him and talk, but this was not the same thing as if Poirot could have selected for himself his partner in the tête-à-tête. He could no longer single out the person he wanted to talk to.

On the day after my arrival I was taken by Franklin to an old studio in the garden which had been fitted up in a rough and ready fashion for scientific purposes.

Let me make clear here and now that I myself have not got the scientific mind. In my account of Dr. Franklin's work I shall probably use all the wrong terms and arouse the scorn of those properly instructed in such matters.

As far as I, a mere layman, could make out, Franklin was experimenting with various alkaloids derived from the Calabar bean, *Physostigma venenosum.* I understood more after a conversation which took place one day between Franklin and Poirot. Judith, who tried to instruct me, was, as is customary with the earnest young, almost impossibly technical. She referred learnedly to the alkaloids physostigmine, eserine, physoveine and geneserine, and then proceeded to a most impossible sounding substance, prostigmin or the demethylcarbonic ester of 3 hydroxypheyl trimethyl lammonum, etc. etc., and a good deal more which, it appeared, was the same thing, only differently arrived at! It was all, at any rate, double Dutch to me, and I aroused Judith's contempt by asking what *good* all this was likely to do mankind? There is no question that annoys your true scientist more. Judith at once threw me a scornful glance and embarked on another lengthy and learned explanation. The upshot of it was, so I gathered, that certain obscure tribes of West African natives had shown a remarkable immunity to an equally obscure, though deadly disease called, as far as I remember, Jordanitis—a certain enthusiastic Dr. Jordan having originally tracked it down. It was an extremely rare tropical ailment, which had been, on one or two occasions, contracted by white people, with fatal results.

I risked inflaming Judith's rage by remarking that it would be more sensible to find some drug that would counteract the after-effects of measles!

With pity and scorn Judith made it clear to me that it was not the benefaction of the human race, but the enlargement of human *knowledge,* that was the only goal worthy of attainment.

I looked at some slides through the microscope, studied some photographs of West African natives (really quite entertaining!), caught the eye of a soporific rat in a cage and hurried out again into the air.

As I say, any interest I could feel was kindled by Franklin's conversation with Poirot.

He said: "You know, Poirot, the stuff's really more up your street than mine. It's the ordeal bean—supposed to prove innocence or guilt. These West

African tribes believe it implicitly—or did do so—they're getting sophisticated nowadays. They'll solemnly chew it up quite confident that it will kill them if they're guilty and not harm them if they're innocent."

"And so, alas, they die?"

"No, they don't all die. That's what has always been overlooked up to now. There's a lot behind the whole thing—a medicine man ramp, I rather fancy. There are two distinct species of this bean—only they look so much alike that you can hardly spot the difference. But there *is* a difference. They both contain physostigmine and geneserine and the rest of it, but in the second species you can isolate, or I think I can, yet another alkaloid—and the action of that alkaloid neutralizes the effect of the others. What's more that second species is regularly eaten by a kind of inner ring in a secret ritual—and the people who eat it never go down with Jordanitis. This third substance has a remarkable effect on the muscular system—without deleterious effects. It's damned interesting. Unfortunately the pure alkaloid is very unstable. Still, I'm getting results. But what's wanted is a lot more research out there *on the spot*. It's work that *ought* to be done! Yes, by heck it is . . . I'd sell my soul to—" He broke off abruptly. The grin came again. "Forgive the shop. I get too het up over these things!"

"As you say," said Poirot placidly, "it would certainly make my profession much easier if I could test guilt and innocence so easily. Ah, if there were a substance that could do what is claimed for the Calabar bean."

Franklin said: "Ah, but your troubles wouldn't end there. After all, what *is* guilt or innocence?"

"I shouldn't think there could be any doubt about *that*," I remarked.

He turned to me. "What is evil? What is good? Ideas on them vary from century to century. What you would be testing would probably be a *sense* of guilt or a sense of innocence. In fact no value as a test at all."

"I don't see how you make that out."

"My dear fellow, suppose a man thinks he has a divine right to kill a dictator or a moneylender or a pimp or whatever arouses his moral indignation. He commits what *you* consider a guilty deed—but what *he* considers is an innocent one. What is your poor ordeal bean to do about it?"

"Surely," I said, "there must always be a feeling of guilt with murder?"

"Lots of people *I'd* like to kill," said Dr. Franklin cheerfully. "Don't believe my conscience would keep me awake at night afterwards. It's an idea of mine, you know, that about eighty percent of the human race *ought* to be eliminated. We'd get on much better without them."

He got up and strolled away, whistling cheerfully to himself.

I looked after him doubtfully. A low chuckle from Poirot recalled me.

"You look, my friend, like one who has envisaged a nest of serpents. Let us hope that our friend the doctor does not practise what he preaches."

"Ah," I said. "But supposing he does?"

II

After some hesitations I decided that I ought to sound Judith on the subject of Allerton. I felt that I must know what her reactions were. She was, I knew, a levelheaded girl, well able to take care of herself, and I did not think that she would really be taken in by the cheap attraction of a man like Allerton. I suppose, actually, that I tackled her on the subject because I wanted to be reassured on that point.

Unfortunately, I did not get what I wanted . . . I went about it clumsily, I daresay. There is nothing that young people resent so much as advice from their elders. I tried to make my words quite careless and debonair. I suppose that I failed.

Judith bristled at once.

"What's this?" she said. "A paternal warning against the big bad wolf?"

"No, no, Judith, of course not."

"I gather you don't like Major Allerton?"

"Frankly, I don't. Actually, I don't suppose you do either."

"Why not?"

"Well—er—he isn't your type, is he?"

"What do you consider is my type, Father?"

Judith can always flurry me. I boggled rather badly. She stood looking at me, her mouth curving upwards in a slightly scornful smile.

"Of course *you* don't like him," she said. "I do. I think he's very amusing."

"Oh, amusing—perhaps." I endeavoured to pass it off.

Judith said deliberately: "He's very attractive. Any woman would think so. Men, of course, wouldn't see it."

"They certainly wouldn't." I went on, rather clumsily: "You were out with him very late the other night—"

I was not allowed to finish. The storm broke.

"Really, Father, you're being too idiotic. Don't you realize that at my age I'm capable of managing my own affairs? You've no earthly right to control what I do or whom I choose to make a friend of. It's this senseless interfering in their children's lives that is so infuriating about fathers and mothers. I'm very fond of you—but I'm an adult woman and my life is my own. Don't start making a Mr. Barrett of yourself."

I was so hurt by this extremely unkind remark that I was quite incapable of replying, and Judith went quickly away.

I was left with the dismayed feeling that I had done more harm than good.

I was standing lost in my thoughts when I was roused by the voice of Mrs. Franklin's nurse exclaiming archly: "A penny for your thoughts, Captain Hastings!"

I turned gladly to welcome the interruption.

Nurse Craven was really a very good-looking young woman. Her manner was, perhaps, a little on the arch and sprightly side, but she was pleasant and intelligent.

She had just come from establishing her patient in a sunny spot not far from the improvised laboratory.

"Is Mrs. Franklin interested in her husband's work?" I asked.

Nurse Craven tossed her head contemptuously. "Oh, it's a good deal too technical for *her*. She's not at all a clever woman, you know, Captain Hastings."

"No, I suppose not."

"Dr. Franklin's work, of course, can only be appreciated by someone who knows something about medicine. He's a very clever man indeed, you know. Brilliant. Poor man, I feel so sorry for him."

"Sorry for him?"

"Yes. I've seen it happen so often. Marrying the wrong type of woman, I mean."

"You think she's the wrong type for him?"

"Well, don't you? They've nothing at all in common."

"He seems very fond of her," I said. "Very attentive to her wishes and all that."

Nurse Craven laughed rather disagreeably. "She sees to that all right!"

"You think she trades on her—on her ill health?" I asked doubtfully.

Nurse Craven laughed. "There isn't much you could teach her about getting her own way. Whatever her ladyship wants happens. Some women are like that—clever as a barrelful of monkeys. If anyone opposes them they just lie back and shut their eyes and look ill and pathetic, or else they have a nerve storm—but Mrs. Franklin's the pathetic type. Doesn't sleep all night and is all white and exhausted in the morning."

"But she is really an invalid, isn't she?" I asked, rather startled.

Nurse Craven gave me a rather peculiar glance. She said drily: "Oh, of course," and then turned the subject rather abruptly.

She asked me if it was true that I had been here long ago, in the first war.

"Yes, that's quite true."

She lowered her voice. "There was a murder here, wasn't there? So one of the maids was telling me. An old lady?"

"Yes."

"And you were here at the time?"

"I was."

She gave a slight shiver. She said: "That explains it, doesn't it?"

"Explains what?"

She gave me a quick sideways glance. "The—the atmosphere of the place. Don't you feel it? I do. Something *wrong*, if you know what I mean?"

I was silent a moment considering. Was it true what she had just said? Did the fact that death by violence—by malice aforethought—had taken place in a certain spot leave its impression on that spot so strongly that it was perceptible after many years? Psychic people said so. Did Styles definitely bear traces of that event that had occurred so long ago? Here, within these walls, in these gardens, thoughts of murder had lingered and grown stronger and had at last come to fruition in the final act. Did they still taint the air?

Nurse Craven broke in on my thoughts by saying abruptly: "I was in a house where there was a murder case once. I've never forgotten it. One doesn't, you know. One of my patients. I had to give evidence and everything. Made me feel quite queer. It's a nasty experience for a girl."

"It must be. I know myself—"

I broke off as Boyd Carrington came striding round the corner of the house.

As usual, his big, buoyant personality seemed to sweep away shadows and intangible worries. He was so large, so sane, so out-of-doors—one of those lovable, forceful personalities that radiate cheerfulness and common sense.

"Morning, Hastings, morning, Nurse. Where's Mrs. Franklin?"

"Good morning, Sir William. Mrs. Franklin's down at the bottom of the garden under the beech tree near the laboratory."

"And Franklin, I suppose, is *inside* the laboratory?"

"Yes, Sir William—with Miss Hastings."

"Wretched girl. Fancy being cooped up doing stinks on a morning like this! You ought to protest, Hastings."

Nurse Craven said quickly: "Oh, Miss Hastings is *quite* happy. She likes it, you know, and the doctor couldn't do without her, I'm sure."

"Miserable fellow," said Boyd Carrington. "If I had a pretty girl like your Judith as a secretary, I'd be looking at *her* instead of at guinea pigs, eh, what?"

It was the kind of joke that Judith would particularly have disliked but it went down quite well with Nurse Craven who laughed a good deal.

"Oh, Sir William," she exclaimed. "You really mustn't say things like that. I'm sure we all know what *you'd* be like! But poor Dr. Franklin is so serious—quite wrapped up in his work."

Boyd Carrington said cheerfully: "Well, his wife seems to have taken up her position where she can keep her eye on her husband. I believe she's jealous."

"You know far too much, Sir William!"

Nurse Craven seemed delighted with this *badinage*. She said reluctantly: "Well, I suppose I ought to be going to see about Mrs. Franklin's malted milk."

She moved away slowly and Boyd Carrington stood looking after her.

"Good-looking girl," he remarked. "Lovely hair and teeth. Fine specimen of womanhood. Must be a dull life on the whole always looking after sick people. A girl like that deserves a better fate."

"Oh, well," I said. "I suppose she'll marry one day."

"I expect so."

He sighed—and it occurred to me that he was thinking of his dead wife. Then he said: "Like to come over with me to Knatton and see the place?"

"Rather. I'd like to. I'll just see first if Poirot needs me."

I found Poirot sitting on the veranda, well muffled up. He encouraged me to go.

"But certainly go, Hastings, go. It is, I believe, a most handsome property. You should certainly see it."

"I'd like to. But I didn't want to desert you."

"My faithful friend! No, no, go with Sir William. A charming man, is he not?"

"First-class," I said with enthusiasm.

Poirot smiled. "Ah yes. I thought he was your type."

III

I enjoyed my expedition enormously.

Not only was the weather fine—a really lovely summer's day—but I enjoyed the companionship of the man.

Boyd Carrington had that personal magnetism, that wide experience of life and of places that made him excellent company. He told me stories of his administrative days in India, some intriguing details of East African tribal lore, and was altogether so interesting that I was quite taken out of myself and forgot my worries about Judith and the deep anxieties that Poirot's revelations had given me.

I liked, too, the way Boyd Carrington spoke of my friend. He had a deep respect for him—both for his work and his character. Sad though his present condition of ill health was, Boyd Carrington uttered no facile words of pity. He seemed to think that a lifetime spent as Poirot's had been was in itself a rich reward and that in his memories my friend could find satisfaction and self-respect.

"Moreover," he said, "I'd wager his brain is as keen as ever it was."

"It is, indeed it is," I assented eagerly.

"No greater mistake than to think that because a man's tied by the leg it affects his brain pan. Not a bit of it. Anno Domini affects head work much less than you'd think. By Jove, I wouldn't care to undertake to commit a murder under Hercule Poirot's nose—even at this time of day."

"He'd get you if you did," I said grinning.

"I bet he would. Not," he added ruefully, "that I should be much good at doing a murder anyway. I can't plan things, you know. Too impatient. If I did a murder it would be done on the spur of the moment."

"That might be the most difficult crime to spot."

"I hardly think so. I'd probably leave clues trailing along behind me in every direction. Well, it's lucky I haven't got a criminal mind. Only kind of man I can imagine myself killing is a blackmailer. That is a foul thing if you like. I've always thought a blackmailer ought to be shot. What do you say?"

I confessed to some sympathy with his point of view.

Then we passed on to an examination of the work done on the house as a young architect came forward to meet us.

Knatton was mainly of Tudor date with a wing added later. It had not been modernized or altered since the installation of two primitive bathrooms in the eighteen forties or thereabouts.

Boyd Carrington explained that his uncle had been more or less of a hermit, disliking people and living in a corner of the vast house. Boyd Carrington and his brother had been tolerated, and had spent their holidays there as schoolboys before Sir Everard had become as much of a recluse as he afterwards became.

The old man had never married, and had spent only a tenth of his large income, so that even after death duties had been paid, the present baronet had found himself a very rich man.

"But a very lonely one," he said sighing.

I was silent. My sympathy was too acute to be put into words. For I, too, was a lonely man. Since Cinders had died, I felt myself to be only half a human being.

Presently, a little haltingly, I expressed a little of what I felt.

"Ah yes, Hastings, but you've had something I never had."

He paused a moment and then—rather jerkily—he gave me an outline of his own tragedy.

Of the beautiful young wife, a lovely creature full of charm and accomplishments but with a tainted heritage. Her family had nearly all died of drink, and she herself fell victim to the same curse. Barely a year after their marriage she had succumbed and had died a dipsomaniac's death. He did not blame her. He realized that heredity had been too strong for her.

After her death he had settled down to lead a lonely life. He had determined, saddened by his experience, not to marry again.

"One feels," he said simply, "safer alone."

"Yes, I can understand your feeling like that—at any rate at first."

"The whole thing was such a tragedy. It left me prematurely aged and embittered." He paused. "It's true—I was once very much tempted. But she was so young—I didn't feel it would be fair to tie her to a disillusioned man. I was too old for her—she was such a child—so pretty—so completely untouched."

He broke off, shaking his head.

"Wasn't that for her to judge?"

"I don't know, Hastings. I thought not. She—she seemed to like me. But then, as I say, she was so young. I shall always remember her as I saw her the last day of that leave. Her head a little on one side—that slightly bewildered look—her little hand—"

He stopped. The words conjured up a picture that seemed vaguely familiar, though I could not think why.

Boyd Carrington's voice, suddenly harsh, broke into my thoughts.

"I was a fool," he said. "Any man is a fool who lets opportunity slip by him. Anyway, here I am, with a great mansion of a house far too big for me, and no gracious presence to sit at the head of my table."

To me there was a charm in his slightly old-fashioned way of putting things. It conjured up a picture of old world charm and ease.

"Where is the lady now?" I asked.

"Oh—married." He turned it off briefly. "Fact is, Hastings, I'm cut out now for a bachelor existence. I've got my little ways. Come and look at the gardens. They've been badly neglected, but they're very fine in their way."

We walked round the place and I was much impressed with all I saw. Knatton was undoubtedly a very fine estate and I did not wonder that Boyd Carrington was proud of it. He knew the neighbourhood well and most of the people round about, though of course there had been newcomers since his time.

He had known Colonel Luttrell in the old days and expressed his earnest hope that the Styles venture was going to pay.

"Poor old Toby Luttrell's very hard up, you know," he said. "Nice fellow. Good soldier, too, and a very fine shot. Went on safari with him in Africa once. Ah, those were the days! He was married then, of course, but his missus didn't come along, thank goodness. Pretty woman she was—but always a bit of a Tartar. Funny the things a man will stand from a woman. Old Toby Luttrell who used to make subalterns shake in their shoes, he was such a stern martinet! And there he is, henpecked and bullied and meek as they make 'em! No doubt about it, that woman's got a tongue like vinegar. Still, she's got a head on her. If anyone can make the place pay, she will. Luttrell never had much of a head for business—but Mrs. Toby would skin her grandmother!"

"She's so gushing with it all," I complained.

Boyd Carrington looked amused. "I know. All sweetness. But have you played bridge with them?"

I replied feelingly that I had.

"On the whole I steer clear of women bridge players," said Boyd Carrington. "And if you take my tip you'll do the same."

I told him how uncomfortable Norton and myself had felt on the first evening of my arrival.

"Exactly. One doesn't know where to look!" He added: "Nice fellow, Norton. Very quiet, though. Always looking at birds and things. Doesn't care for shooting them, he told me. Extraordinary! No feeling for sport. I told him he missed a lot. Can't see myself what excitement there can be stalking about through cold woods peering at birds through glasses."

How little we realized that Norton's hobby might have an important part to play in the events that were to come.

Eight

I

The days passed. It was an unsatisfactory time, with its uneasy feeling of waiting for something.

Nothing, if I may put it in such a way, actually *happened*. Yet there were incidents, scraps of odd conversations, sidelights upon the various inmates of Styles, elucidating remarks. They all mounted up and, if properly pieced together, could have done a lot towards enlightening me.

It was Poirot who, with a few forceful words, showed me something to which I had been criminally blind.

I was complaining, for the umpteenth time, of his wilful refusal to admit me to his confidence. It was not fair, I told him. Always he and I had had equal knowledge—even if I had been dense and he had been astute in drawing the right conclusions from that knowledge.

He waved an impatient hand. "Quite so, my friend. It is not fair! It is not sporting! It is not playing the game! Admit all that and pass from it. This is *not* a game—it is not *le sport*. For you, you occupy yourself in guessing wildly at the identity of X. It is not for that that I asked you to come here. Unnecessary for you to occupy yourself with that. *I* know the answer to that question. But what I do not know and what I must know is this: 'Who is going to die—very soon?' It is a question, *mon vieux*, not of you playing a guessing game, but of preventing a human being from dying."

I was startled. "Of course," I said slowly. "I—well, I did know that you practically said so once, but I haven't quite realized it."

"Then realize it now—immediately."

"Yes, yes, I will—I mean, I do."

"*Bien!* Then tell me, Hastings, who is it who is going to die?"

I stared at him blankly. "I have really no idea!"

"Then you should have an idea! What else are you here for?"

"Surely," I said, going back over my meditations on the subject, "there must be a connection between the victim and X so that if you told me who X was—"

Poirot shook his head with so much vigour that it was quite painful to watch.

"Have I not told you that that is the essence of X's technique? There will be nothing connecting X with the death. That is certain."

"The connection will be hidden, you mean?"

"It will be so well hidden that neither you nor I will find it."

"But surely by studying X's past—"

"I tell you, no. Certainly not in the *time*. Murder may happen any moment, you comprehend?"

"To someone in this house?"

"To someone in this house."

"And you really do not know who, or how?"

"Ah! If I did, I should not be urging you to find out for me."

"You simply base your assumption on the presence of X?"

I sounded a little doubtful. Poirot, whose self-control had lessened as his limbs were perforce immobile, fairly howled at me.

"Ah, *ma foi,* how many times am I to go over all this? If a lot of war correspondents arrive suddenly in a certain spot of Europe, it means what? It means war! If doctors come from all over the world to a certain city, it shows what? That there is to be there a medical conference. Where you see a vulture hovering, there will be a carcass. If you see beaters walking up a moor, there will be a shoot. If you see a man stop suddenly, tear off his coat and plunge into the sea, it means that there, there will be a rescue from drowning.

"If you see ladies of middle age and respectable appearance peering through a hedge, you may deduce that there is there an impropriety of some kind! And finally, if you smell a succulent smell and observe several people all walking along a corridor in the same direction you may safely assume that a meal is about to be served!"

I considered these analogies for a minute or two, then I said, taking the first one: "All the same, one war correspondent does not make a war!"

"Certainly not. And one swallow does not make a summer. But one murderer, Hastings, does make a murder."

That, of course, was undeniable. But it still occurred to me, as it did not seem to have occurred to Poirot, that even a murderer has his off times. X might be at Styles simply for a holiday with no lethal intent. Poirot was so worked up, however, that I dared not propound this suggestion. I merely said that the whole thing seemed to me hopeless. We must wait—

"And see," finished Poirot. "Like your Mr. Asquith in the last war. That, *mon cher,* is just what we must not do. I do not say, mark you, that we shall succeed, for as I have told you before, when a killer has determined to kill, it is not easy to circumvent him. But we can at least try. Figure to yourself, Hastings, that you have here the bridge problem in the paper. You can see all the cards. What you are asked to do is 'Forecast the result of the deal.' "

I shook my head. "It's no good, Poirot, I haven't the least idea. If I knew who X was—"

Poirot howled at me again. He howled so loud that Curtiss came running in from the next room looking quite frightened. Poirot waved him away and when he had gone out again, my friend spoke in a more controlled manner.

"Come, Hastings, you are not so stupid as you like to pretend. You have studied those cases I gave you to read. You may not know who X is, but you know X's technique for committing a crime."

"Oh," I said. "I see."

"Of course you see. The trouble with you is that you are mentally lazy. You like to play games and guess. You do not like to work with your head. What is the essential element of X's technique? Is it not that the crime, when committed, is *complete?* That is to say, there is a motive for the crime, there is an opportunity, there is means and there is, last and most important, the guilty person all ready for the dock."

At once I grasped the essential point and realized what a fool I had been not to see it sooner.

"I see," I said. "I've got to look round for somebody who—who answers to those requirements—the potential victim."

Poirot leaned back with a sigh. "*Enfin!* I am very tired. Send Curtiss to me. You understand your job now. You are active, you can get about, you can follow people about, talk to them, spy upon them unobserved—" (I nearly uttered an indignant protest, but quelled it. It was too old an argument)—"You can listen to conversations, you have knees that will bend and permit you to kneel and look through keyholes—"

"I will not look through keyholes," I interrupted hotly.

Poirot closed his eyes. "Very well, then. You will not look through keyholes. You will remain the English gentleman and someone will be killed. It does not matter, that. Honour comes first with an Englishman. Your honour is more important than somebody else's life. *Bien!* It is understood."

"No, but dash it all, Poirot—"

Poirot said coldly: "Send Curtiss to me. Go away. You are obstinate and extremely stupid and I wish that there were someone else whom I could trust, but I suppose I shall have to put up with you and your absurd ideas of fair play. Since you cannot use your grey cells as you do not possess them, at any rate use your eyes, your ears and your nose if need be in so far as the dictates of honour allow."

II

It was on the following day that I ventured to broach an idea which had come into my mind more than once. I did so a little dubiously, for one never knows how Poirot may react!

I said: "I've been thinking, Poirot, I know I'm not much of a fellow. You've said I'm stupid—well, in a way it's true. And I'm only half the man I was. Since Cinders's death—"

I stopped. Poirot made a gruff noise indicative of sympathy.

I went on: "But there is a man here who could help us—just the kind of man we need. Brains, imagination, resource—used to taking decisions and a man of wide experience. I'm talking of Boyd Carrington. He's the man we want, Poirot. Take him into your confidence. Put the whole thing before him."

Poirot opened his eyes and said with immense decision: "Certainly not."

"But why not? You can't deny that he's clever—a good deal cleverer than I am."

"THAT," said Poirot with biting sarcasm, "would be easy. But dismiss the idea from your mind, Hastings. We take *no one* into our confidence. That is understood—*hein?* You comprehend, I forbid you to speak of this matter."

"All right, if you say so, but really Boyd Carrington—"

"Ah, ta ta! Boyd Carrington. Why are you so obsessed with Boyd Carrington? What is he, after all? A big man who is pompous and pleased with himself because people have called him 'Your Excellency.' A man with—yes, a certain amount of tact and charm of manner. But he is not so wonderful, your Boyd Carrington. He repeats himself, he tells the same story twice—and what is more, his memory is so bad that he tells back to you the story that you have told to him! A man of outstanding ability? Not at all. An old bore, a windbag—*enfin*—the stuffed shirt!"

"Oh," I said as enlightenment came to me.

It was quite true that Boyd Carrington's memory was not good. And he had actually been guilty of a gaffe which I now saw had annoyed Poirot a good deal. Poirot had told him a story of his police days in Belgium, and only a couple of days afterwards, when several of us were assembled in the garden, Boyd Carrington had in bland forgetfulness told the same story back again to Poirot, prefacing it with the remark: "I remember the Chef de la Sûreté in Paris telling me...."

I now perceived that this had rankled!

Tactfully, I said no more, and withdrew.

III

I wandered downstairs and out into the garden. There was no one about and I strolled through a grove of trees and up to a grassy knoll which was surmounted by a somewhat earwiggy summerhouse in an advanced stage of decrepitude. Here I sat down, lit my pipe, and settled to think things out.

Who was there at Styles who had a fairly definite motive for murdering somebody else—or who might be made out to have one?

Putting aside the somewhat obvious case of Colonel Luttrell, who, I was afraid, was hardly likely to take a hatchet to his wife in the middle of a rubber, justifiable though that course might be, I could not at first think of anyone.

The trouble was that I did not really know enough about these people. Norton, for instance, and Miss Cole? What were the usual motives for murder? Money? Boyd Carrington was, I fancied, the only rich man of the party. If he died, who would inherit that money? Anyone at present in the house? I hardly thought so, but it was a point that might bear enquiry. He might, for instance, have left his money to research, making Franklin a trustee. That, with the doctor's rather injudicious remarks on the subject of eliminating eighty percent of the human race, might make out a fairly damning case against the red-haired doctor. Or possibly Norton or Miss Cole might be a distant relative and would inherit automatically. Far-fetched but possible. Would Colonel Luttrell, who was an old friend, benefit under Boyd Carrington's will? These possibilities seemed to exhaust the money angle. I turned to more romantic possibilities. The Franklins. Mrs. Franklin was an invalid. Was it possible that she was being slowly poisoned—and would the responsibility for her death be laid at her husband's door? He was a doctor, he had opportunity and means, no doubt. What about motive? An unpleasant qualm shot across my mind as it occurred to me that Judith might be involved. I had good reason to know how businesslike their relations were—but would the general public believe that? Would a cynical police officer believe it? Judith was a very beautiful young woman. An attractive secretary or assistant had been the motive for many crimes. The possibility dismayed me.

I considered Allerton next. Could there be any reason for doing away with Allerton? If we had to have a murder I would prefer to see Allerton the victim! One ought to be able to find motives easily for doing away with him. Miss Cole, though not young, was still a good-looking woman. She might, conceivably, be actuated by jealousy if she and Allerton had ever been on intimate terms, though I had no reason to believe that that was the case. Besides, if Allerton was X—

I shook my head impatiently. All this was getting me nowhere. A footstep on the gravel below attracted my attention. It was Franklin walking rapidly towards the house, his hands in his pockets, his head thrust forward. His whole attitude was one of dejection. Seeing him thus, off guard, I was struck by the fact that he looked a thoroughly unhappy man.

I was so busy staring at him that I did not hear a footfall nearer at hand, and turned with a start when Miss Cole spoke to me.

"I didn't hear you coming," I explained apologetically as I sprang up.

She was examining the summerhouse.

"What a Victorian relic!"

"Isn't it? It's rather spidery, I'm afraid. Do sit down. I'll dust the seat for you."

For it occurred to me that here was a chance to get to know one of my fellow guests a little better. I studied Miss Cole covertly as I brushed away cobwebs.

She was a woman of between thirty and forty, slightly haggard, with a clear-cut profile and really very beautiful eyes. There was about her an air of reserve, more—of suspicion. It came to me suddenly that this was a woman who had suffered and who was, in consequence, deeply distrustful of life. I felt that I would like to know more about Elizabeth Cole.

"There," I said with a final flick of the handkerchief, "that's the best I can do."

"Thank you." She smiled and sat down. I sat down beside her. The seat creaked ominously but no catastrophe occurred.

Miss Cole said: "Do tell me, what were you thinking about when I came up to you? You seemed quite sunk in thought."

I said slowly: "I was watching Dr. Franklin."

"Yes?"

I saw no reason for not repeating what had been in my mind.

"It struck me that he looked a very unhappy man."

The woman beside me said quietly: "But of course he is. You must have realized that."

I think I showed my surprise. I said, stammering slightly: "No—no—I haven't. I've always thought of him as absolutely wrapped up in his work."

"So he is."

"Do you call that unhappiness? I should have said it was the happiest state imaginable."

"Oh yes, I'm not disputing it—but not if you're hampered from doing what you feel it's in you to do. If you can't, that is to say, produce your best."

I looked at her, feeling rather puzzled. She went on to explain: "Last autumn Dr. Franklin was offered the chance of going out to Africa and continuing his research work there. He's tremendously keen, as you know, and has really done first-class work already in the realm of tropical medicine."

"And he didn't go?"

"No. His wife protested. She herself wasn't well enough to stand the climate and she kicked against the idea of being left behind, especially as it would have meant very economical living for her. The pay offered was not high."

"Oh," I said. I went on slowly: "I suppose he felt that in her state of health he couldn't leave her."

"Do you know much about her state of health, Captain Hastings?"

"Well, I—no—But she is an invalid, isn't she?"

"She certainly enjoys bad health," said Miss Cole drily. I looked at her doubtfully. It was easy to see that her sympathies were entirely with the husband.

"I suppose," I said slowly, "that women who are—delicate are apt to be selfish?"

"Yes, I think invalids—chronic invalids—usually are very selfish. One can't blame them perhaps. It's so easy."

"You don't think that there's really very much the matter with Mrs. Franklin?"

"Oh, I shouldn't like to say that. It's just a suspicion. She always seems able to do anything she wants to do."

I reflected in silence for a minute or two. It struck me that Miss Cole seemed very well acquainted with the ramifications of the Franklin ménage. I asked with some curiosity: "You know Dr. Franklin well, I suppose?"

She shook her head. "Oh, no. I had only met them once or twice before we met here."

"But he has talked to you about himself, I suppose?"

Again she shook her head. "No, what I have just told you I learnt from your daughter Judith."

Judith, I reflected, with a moment's bitterness, talked to everyone except me.

Miss Cole went on: "Judith is terrifically loyal to her employer and very much up in arms on his behalf. Her condemnation of Mrs. Franklin's selfishness is sweeping."

"You, too, think she is selfish?"

"Yes, but I can see her point of view. I—I understand invalids. I can understand, too, Dr. Franklin's giving way to her. Judith, of course, thinks he should park his wife anywhere and get on with the job. Your daughter's a very enthusiastic scientific worker."

"I know," I said rather disconsolately. "It worries me sometimes. It doesn't seem natural, if you know what I mean. I feel she ought to be—more human—more keen on having a good time. Amuse herself—fall in love with a nice boy or two. After all, youth is the time to have one's fling—not to sit poring over test tubes. It isn't natural. In our young days we were having fun—flirting—enjoying ourselves—*you* know."

There was a moment's silence. Then Miss Cole said in a queer cold voice: "I don't know."

I was instantly horrified. Unconsciously I had spoken as though she and I were contemporaries—but I realized suddenly that she was well over ten years my junior and that I had been unwittingly extremely tactless.

I apologized as best I could. She cut into my stammering phrases.

"No, no, I didn't mean that. Please don't apologize. I meant just simply what I said. *I don't know.* I was never what you meant by 'young.' I never had what is called 'a good time.'"

Something in her voice, a bitterness, a deep resentment, left me at a loss. I said, rather lamely, but with sincerity: "I'm sorry."

She smiled. "Oh, well, it doesn't matter. Don't look so upset. Let's talk about something else."

I obeyed. "Tell me something about the other people here," I said. "Unless they're all strangers to you."

"I've known the Luttrells all my life. It's rather sad that they should have to do this—especially for him. He's rather a dear. And she's nicer than you'd think. It's having had to pinch and scrape all her life that has made her rather—well—predatory. If you're always on the make, it does tell in the end. The only thing I do rather dislike about her is that gushing manner."

"Tell me something about Mr. Norton."

"There isn't really much to tell. He's very nice—rather shy—just a little stupid, perhaps. He's always been rather delicate. He's lived with his mother—rather a peevish, stupid woman. She bossed him a good deal, I think. She died a few years ago. He's keen on birds and flowers and things like that. He's a very kind person—and he's the sort of person who sees a lot."

"Through his glasses, you mean?"

Miss Cole smiled. "Well, I wasn't meaning it quite so literally as that. I meant more that he *notices* a good deal. Those quiet people often do. He's unselfish—and very considerate for a man, but he's rather—*ineffectual,* if you know what I mean."

I nodded. "Oh, yes, I know."

Elizabeth Cole said suddenly, and once more the deep bitter note was in her voice: "That's the depressing part of places like this. Guest houses run by broken-down gentlepeople. They're full of failures—of people who have never got anywhere and never will get anywhere, of people who—who have been defeated and broken by life, of people who are old and tired and finished."

Her voice died away. A deep and spreading sadness permeated me. How true it was! Here we were, a collection of twilit people. *Grey heads, grey hearts, grey dreams.* Myself, sad and lonely, the woman beside me also a bitter and disillusioned creature. Dr. Franklin, eager, ambitious, curbed and thwarted, his wife a prey to ill health. Quiet little Norton limping about looking at birds. Even Poirot, the once brilliant Poirot, now a broken, crippled old man.

How different it had been in the old days—the days when I had first come to Styles. The thought was too much for me—a stifled exclamation of pain and regret came to my lips.

My companion said quickly: "What is it?"

"Nothing. I was just struck by the contrast—I was here, you know, many years ago, as a young man. I was thinking of the difference between then and now."

"I see. It was a happy house then? Everyone was happy here?"

Curious, sometimes, how one's thoughts seemed to swing in a kaleidoscope. It happened to me now. A bewildering shuffling and reshuffling of memories, of events. Then the mosaic settled into its true pattern.

My regret had been for the past as the past, not for the reality. For even then, in that far-off time, there had been no happiness at Styles. I remembered dispassionately the real facts. My friend John and his wife, both unhappy and chafing at the life they were forced to lead. Laurence Cavendish, sunk in melancholy. Cynthia, her girlish brightness damped by her dependent position. Inglethorp married to a rich woman for her money. No, none of them had been happy. And now, again, no one here was happy. Styles was not a lucky house.

I said to Miss Cole: "I've been indulging in false sentiment. This was never a happy house. It isn't now. Everyone here is unhappy."

"No, no. Your daughter—"

"Judith's not happy."

I said it with the certainty of sudden knowledge. No, Judith wasn't happy.

"Boyd Carrington," I said doubtfully. "He was saying the other day that he was lonely—but for all that I think he's enjoying himself quite a good deal—what with his house and one thing and another."

Miss Cole said sharply: "Oh yes, but then Sir William is different. He doesn't belong here like the rest of us do. He's from the outside world—the world of success and independence. He's made a success of his life and he knows it. He's not one of—of the maimed."

It was a curious word to choose. I turned and stared at her.

"Will you tell me," I asked, "why you used that particular expression?"

"Because," she said with a sudden fierce energy, "it's the truth. The truth about me, at any rate. I am maimed."

"I can see," I said gently, "that you have been very unhappy."

She said quietly: "You don't know who I am, do you?"

"Er—I know your name—"

"Cole isn't my name—that is to say, it was my mother's name. I took it—afterwards."

"After?"

"My real name is Litchfield."

For a minute or two it didn't sink in—it was just a name vaguely familiar. Then I remembered.

"Matthew Litchfield."

She nodded. "I see you know about it. That was what I meant just now. My father was an invalid and a tyrant. He forbade us any kind of normal life. We couldn't ask friends to the house. He kept us short of money. We were—in prison."

She paused, her eyes, those beautiful eyes, wide and dark.

"And then my sister—my sister—"

She stopped.

"Please don't—don't go on. It is too painful for you. I know about it. There is no need to tell me."

"But you don't know. You can't. Maggie. It's inconceivable—unbelievable. I know that she went to the police, that she gave herself up, that she confessed. But I still sometimes can't believe it! I feel somehow that it wasn't true—that it didn't—that it couldn't have happened like she said it did."

"You mean—" I hesitated—"that the facts were at—at variance—"

She cut me short. "No, no. Not that. No, it's Maggie herself. It wasn't like her. It wasn't—it wasn't *Maggie!*"

Words trembled on my lips, but I did not say them. The time had not yet come when I could say to her: "You are right. *It wasn't Maggie. . . .*"

Nine

It must have been about six o'clock when Colonel Luttrell came along the path. He had a rook rifle with him and was carrying a couple of dead wood pigeons.

He started when I hailed him and seemed surprised to see us.

"Hullo, what are you two doing here? That tumbledown old place isn't very safe, you know. It's falling to pieces. Probably break up about your ears. Afraid you'll get dirty there, Elizabeth."

"Oh, that's all right. Captain Hastings has sacrificed a pocket handkerchief in the good cause of keeping my dress clean."

The Colonel murmured vaguely: "Oh really? Oh well, that's all right."

He stood there pulling at his lip and we got up and joined him.

His mind seemed far away this evening. He roused himself to say: "Been trying to get some of these cursed wood pigeons. Do a lot of damage, you know."

"You're a very fine shot, I hear," I told him.

"Eh? Who told you that? Oh, Boyd Carrington. Used to be—used to be. Bit rusty nowadays. Age will tell."

"Eyesight," I suggested.

He negatived the suggestion immediately. "Nonsense. Eyesight's as good as ever it was. That is—have to wear glasses for reading, of course. But far sight's all right."

He repeated a minute or two later: "Yes—all right. Not that it matters . . ." His voice trailed off into an absentminded mutter.

Miss Cole said, looking round: "What a beautiful evening it is."

She was quite right. The sun was drawing to the west and the light was a rich golden, bringing out the deeper shades of green in the trees in a deep glowing effect. It was an evening, still and calm, and very English, such as one remembers when in far-off tropical countries. I said as much.

Colonel Luttrell agreed eagerly. "Yes, yes, often used to think of evenings like this—out in India, you know. Makes you look forward to retiring and settling down, what?"

I nodded. He went on, his voice changing: "Yes, settling down, coming home—nothing's ever quite what you picture it—no—no."

I thought that that was probably particularly true in his case. He had not pictured himself running a guest house, trying to make it pay, with a nagging wife forever snapping at him and complaining.

We walked slowly towards the house. Norton and Boyd Carrington were sitting on the veranda and the Colonel and I joined them whilst Miss Cole went on into the house.

We chatted for a few minutes. Colonel Luttrell seemed to have brightened up. He made a joke or two and seemed far more cheerful and wide awake than usual.

"Been a hot day," said Norton. "I'm thirsty."

"Have a drink, you fellows. On the house, what?" The Colonel sounded eager and happy.

We thanked him and accepted. He got up and went in.

The part of the terrace where we were sitting was just outside the dining room window, and that window was open.

We heard the Colonel inside opening a cupboard, then heard the squeak of a corkscrew and the subdued pop as the cork of the bottle came out.

And then, sharp and high, came the unofficial voice of Mrs. Colonel Luttrell!

"What are you doing, George?"

The Colonel's voice was subdued to a mutter. We only heard a mumbled word here and there—"fellows outside"—"drink"—

The sharp, irritating voice burst out indignantly: "You'll do no such thing, George. The idea now. How do you think we'll ever make this place pay if you go round standing everybody drinks? Drinks here will be paid for. *I've* got a business-head if you haven't. Why, you'd be bankrupt tomorrow if it wasn't for me! I've got to look after you like a child. Yes, just like a child. You've got no sense at all. Give me that bottle. Give it to me, I say."

Again there was an agonized low protesting mumble.

Mrs. Luttrell answered snappishly: "I don't care whether they do or they don't. The bottle's going back in the cupboard, and I'm going to lock the cupboard too."

There was the sound of a key being turned in the lock.

"There now. That's the way of it."

This time the Colonel's voice came more clearly: "You're going too far, Daisy. I won't have it."

"*You* won't have it? And who are you I'd like to know? Who runs this house? I do. And don't you forget it."

There was a faint swish of draperies and Mrs. Luttrell evidently flounced out of the room.

It was some few moments before the Colonel reappeared. He looked in those few moments to have grown much older and feebler.

There was not one of us who did not feel deeply sorry for him and who would not willingly have murdered Mrs. Luttrell.

"Awfully sorry, you chaps," he said, his voice sounding stiff and unnatural. "Seem to have run out of whisky."

He must have realized that we could not have helped overhearing what had passed. If he had not realized it, our manner would soon have told him. We were all miserably uncomfortable, and Norton quite lost his head, hurriedly saying first that he didn't really want a drink—too near dinner, wasn't it—and then elaborately changing the subject and making a series of the most unconnected remarks. It was indeed a bad moment. I myself felt paralysed and Boyd

Carrington, who was the only one of us who might conceivably have managed to pass it off, got no opportunity with Norton's babble.

Out of the tail of my eye I saw Mrs. Luttrell stalking away down one of the paths equipped with gardening gloves and a dandelion weeder. She was certainly an efficient woman, but I felt bitterly towards her just then. No human being has a right to humiliate another human being.

Norton was still talking feverishly. He had picked up a wood pigeon, and from first telling us how he had been laughed at at his prep school for being sick when he saw a rabbit killed, had gone on to the subject of grouse moors, telling a long and rather pointless story of an accident that had occurred in Scotland when a beater had been shot. We talked of various shooting accidents we had known, and then Boyd Carrington cleared his throat and said:

"Rather an amusing thing happened once with a batman of mine. Irish chap. He had a holiday and went off to Ireland for it. When he came back I asked him if he had had a good holiday.

" 'Ah shure, your Honour, best holiday I've ever had in my life!'

" 'I'm glad of that,' I said, rather surprised at his enthusiasm.

" 'Ah yes, shure, it was a grand holiday! I shot my brother.'

" 'You shot your brother!' I exclaimed.

" 'Ah yes, indade. It's years now that I've been wanting to do it. And there I was on a roof in Dublin and who should I see coming down the street but my brother and I there with a rifle in my hand. A lovely shot it was, though I say it myself. Picked him off as clean as a bird. Ah, it was a foine moment, that, and I'll never forget it!' "

Boyd Carrington told a story well, with exaggerated dramatic emphasis, and we all laughed and felt easier. When he got up and strolled off, saying he must get a bath before dinner, Norton voiced our feeling by saying with enthusiasm: "What a splendid chap he is!"

I agreed and Luttrell said: "Yes, yes, a good fellow."

"Always been a success everywhere, so I understand," said Norton. "Everything he's turned his hand to has succeeded. Clear-headed, knows his own mind—essentially a man of action. The true successful man."

Luttrell said slowly: "Some men are like that. Everything they turn their hand to succeeds. They can't go wrong. Some people—have all the luck."

Norton gave a quick shake of the head. "No, no, sir. Not luck." He quoted with meaning: "*Not in our stars, dear Brutus—but in ourselves.*"

Luttrell said: "Perhaps you're right."

I said quickly: "At any rate he's lucky to have inherited Knatton. What a place! But he certainly ought to marry. He'll be lonely there by himself."

Norton laughed. "Marry and settle down? And suppose his wife bullies him—"

It was the purest bad luck. The sort of remark that anyone could make. But it was unfortunate in the circumstances, and Norton realized it just at the moment that the words came out. He tried to catch them back, hesitated, stammered, and stopped awkwardly. It made the whole thing worse.

Both he and I began to speak at once. I made some idiotic remark about the evening light. Norton said something about having some bridge after dinner.

Colonel Luttrell took no notice of either of us. He said in a queer, inexpressive voice: "No, Boyd Carrington won't get bullied by his wife. He's not the sort of man who *lets* himself get bullied. *He's* all right. He's a *man!*"

It was very awkward. Norton began babbling about bridge again. In the middle of it a large wood pigeon came flapping over our heads and settled on the branch of a tree not far away.

Colonel Luttrell picked up his gun. "There's one of the blighters," he said.

Before he could take aim the bird had flown off again through the trees where it was impossible to get a shot at it.

At the same moment, however, the Colonel's attention was diverted by a movement on the far slope.

"Damn, there's a rabbit nibbling the bark of those young fruit trees. Thought I'd wired the place."

He raised the rifle and fired, and as I saw—

There was a scream in a woman's voice. It died in a kind of horrible gurgle. The rifle fell from the Colonel's hand, his body sagged—he caught his lip.

"My God—it's Daisy."

I was already running across the lawn. Norton came behind me. I reached the spot and knelt down. It was Mrs. Luttrell. She had been kneeling, tying a stake against one of the small fruit trees. The grass was long there so that I realized how it was that the Colonel had not seen her clearly and had only distinguished movements in the grass. The light too was confusing. She had been shot through the shoulder and the blood was gushing out.

I bent to examine the wound and looked up at Norton. He was leaning against a tree and was looking green and as though he were going to be sick. He said apologetically: "I can't stand blood."

I said sharply: "Get hold of Franklin at once. Or the nurse."

He nodded and ran off.

It was Nurse Craven who appeared first upon the scene. She was there in an incredibly short time and at once set about in a businesslike way to stop the bleeding. Franklin arrived at a run soon afterwards. Between them they got her into the house and to bed: Franklin dressed and bandaged the wound and sent for her own doctor and Nurse Craven stayed with her.

I ran across Franklin just as he left the telephone.

"How is she?"

"Oh, she'll pull through all right. It missed any vital spot, luckily. How did it happen?"

I told him. He said: "I see. Where's the old boy? He'll be feeling knocked out, I shouldn't wonder. Probably needs attention more than she does. I shouldn't say his heart is any too good."

We found Colonel Luttrell in the smoking room. He was a blue colour round the mouth and looked completely dazed. He said brokenly: "Daisy? Is she—how is she?"

Franklin said quickly: "She'll be all right, sir. You needn't worry."

"I—thought—rabbit—nibbling the bark—don't know how I came to make such a mistake. Light in my eyes."

"These things happen," said Franklin drily. "I've seen one or two of them in my time. Look here, sir, you'd better let me give you a pick-me-up. You're not feeling too good."

"I'm all right. Can I—can I go to her?"

"Not just now. Nurse Craven is with her. But you don't need to worry. She's all right. Dr. Oliver will be here presently and he'll tell you the same."

I left the two of them together and went out into the evening sunshine. Judith and Allerton were coming along the path towards me. His head was bent to hers and they were both laughing.

Coming on top of the tragedy that had just happened, it made me feel very angry. I called sharply to Judith and she looked up, surprised. In a few words I told them what had occurred.

"What an extraordinary thing to happen," was my daughter's comment.

She did not seem nearly as perturbed as she should have been, I thought.

Allerton's manner was outrageous. He seemed to take the whole thing as a good joke.

"Serve the old harridan damn well right," he observed. "Think the old boy did it on purpose?"

"Certainly not," I said sharply. "It was an accident."

"Yes, but I know these accidents. Damned convenient sometimes. My word, if the old boy shot her deliberately I take off my hat to him."

"It was nothing of the kind," I said angrily.

"Don't be too sure. I've known two men who shot their wives. Cleaning his revolver one was. The other fired point-blank at her as a joke, he said. Didn't know the thing was loaded. Got away with it, both of them. Damned good release, I should say myself."

"Colonel Luttrell," I said coldly, "isn't that type of man."

"Well you couldn't say it wouldn't be a blessed release, could you?" demanded Allerton pertinently. "They hadn't just had a row or anything, had they?"

I turned away angrily, at the same time trying to hide a certain perturbation. Allerton had come a little too near the mark. For the first time a doubt crept into my mind.

It was not bettered by meeting Boyd Carrington. He had been for a stroll down towards the lake, he explained. When I told him the news he said at once: "You don't think he meant to shoot her, do you, Hastings?"

"My dear man."

"Sorry, sorry. I shouldn't have said that. It was only, for the moment, one wondered . . . She—she gave him a bit of provocation, you know."

We were both silent for a moment as we remembered the scene we had so unwillingly overheard.

I went upstairs feeling unhappy and worried, and rapped on Poirot's door.

He had already heard through Curtiss of what had occurred, but he was eager for full details. Since my arrival at Styles I had got into the way of reporting most of my daily encounters and conversations in full detail. In this way I felt that the dear old fellow felt less cut off. It gave him the illusion of actually participating in everything that went on. I have always had a good and accurate memory and found it a simple matter to repeat conversations verbatim.

Poirot listened very attentively. I was hoping that he would be able definitely to pooh-pooh the dreadful suggestion that had by now taken easy control of my mind, but before he had a chance of telling me what he thought, there came a light tap on the door.

It was Nurse Craven. She apologized for disturbing us.

"I'm sorry, but I thought Doctor was here. The old lady is conscious now and she's worrying about her husband. She'd like to see him. Do you know where he is, Captain Hastings? I don't want to leave my patient."

I volunteered to go and look for him. Poirot nodded approval and Nurse Craven thanked me warmly.

I found Colonel Luttrell in a little morning room that was seldom used. He was standing by the window looking out.

He turned sharply as I came in. His eyes asked a question. He looked, I thought, afraid.

"Your wife is conscious, Colonel Luttrell, and is asking for you."

"Oh." The colour surged up in his cheeks and I realized then how very white he had been before. He said slowly, fumblingly, like an old, old man: "She—she—is asking for me? I'll—I'll come—at once."

He was so unsteady as he began shuffling towards the door that I came and helped him. He leaned on me heavily as we went up the stairs. His breathing was coming with difficulty. The shock, as Franklin had prophesied, was severe.

We came to the door of the sickroom. I tapped and Nurse Craven's brisk, efficient voice called: "Come in."

Still supporting the old man, I went with him into the room. There was a screen round the bed. We came round the corner of it.

Mrs. Luttrell was looking very ill—white and frail, her eyes closed. She opened them as we came round the corner of the screen.

She said in a small, breathless voice: "George—George. . . ."

"Daisy—my dear. . . ."

One of her arms was bandaged and supported. The other, the free one, moved unsteadily towards him. He took a step forward and clasped her frail little hand in his. He said again: "Daisy . . ." And then, gruffly . . . "Thank God, you're all right."

And looking up at him, seeing his eyes slightly misty and the deep love and anxiety in them, I felt bitterly ashamed of all our ghoulish imaginings.

I crept quietly out of the room. Camouflaged accident indeed! There was no disguising that heartfelt note of thankfulness. I felt immeasurably relieved.

The sound of the gong startled me as I went along the passage. I had completely forgotten the passage of time. The accident had upset everything. Only the cook had gone on as usual and produced dinner at the usual time.

Most of us had not changed and Colonel Luttrell did not appear. But Mrs. Franklin, looking quite attractive in a pale pink evening dress, was downstairs for once and seemed in good health and spirits. Franklin, I thought, was moody and absorbed.

After dinner, to my annoyance, Allerton and Judith disappeared into the garden together. I sat around a while, listening to Franklin and Norton discussing tropical diseases. Norton was a sympathetic and interested listener, even if he knew little of the subject under discussion.

Mrs. Franklin and Boyd Carrington were talking at the other end of the room. He was showing her some patterns of curtains or cretonnes.

Elizabeth Cole had a book and seemed deeply absorbed in it. I fancied that she was slightly embarrassed and ill at ease with me. Perhaps not unnaturally so after the confidences of the afternoon. I was sorry about it, all the same, and hoped she did not regret all she had told me. I should have liked to have made it clear to her that I should respect her confidence and not repeat it. However she gave me no chance.

After a while I went up to Poirot.

I found Colonel Luttrell sitting in the circle of light thrown by the one small electric lamp that was turned on.

He was talking and Poirot was listening. I think the Colonel was speaking to himself rather than to his listener.

"I remember so well—yes, it was at a hunt ball. She wore white stuff, called tulle, I think it was. Floated all round her. Such a pretty girl—bowled me over then and there. I said to myself: 'That's the girl I'm going to marry.' And by Jove I brought it off. Awfully pretty way she had with her—saucy, you know, plenty of backchat. Always gave as good as she got, bless her."

He chuckled.

I saw the scene in my mind's eye. I could imagine Daisy Luttrell with a young saucy face and that smart tongue—so charming then, so apt to turn shrewish with the years.

But it was as that young girl, his first real love, that Colonel Luttrell was thinking of her tonight. His Daisy.

And again I felt ashamed of what we had said such a few hours previously.

Of course, when Colonel Luttrell had at last taken himself off to bed, I blurted out the whole thing to Poirot.

He listened very quietly. I could make nothing of the expression on his face.

"So that is what you thought, Hastings—that the shot was fired on purpose?"

"Yes. I feel ashamed now—"

Poirot waved aside my present feelings.

"Did the thought occur to you of your own accord, or did someone else suggest it to you?"

"Allerton said something of the kind," I said resentfully. "He would, of course."

"Anyone else?"

"Boyd Carrington suggested it."

"Ah! Boyd Carrington."

"And after all, he's a man of the world and has experience of these things."

"Oh, quite so, quite so. He did not see the thing happen, though?"

"No, he'd gone for a walk. Bit of exercise before changing for dinner."

"I see."

I said uneasily: "I don't think I really believed that theory. It was only—"

Poirot interrupted me. "You need not be so remorseful about your suspicions, Hastings. It was an idea quite likely to occur to anyone given the circumstances. Oh, yes, it was all quite natural."

There was something in Poirot's manner I did not quite understand. A reserve. His eyes were watching me with a curious expression.

I said slowly: "Perhaps. But seeing now how devoted he really is to her—"

Poirot nodded. "Exactly. That is often the case, remember. Underneath the quarrels, the misunderstandings, the apparent hostility of everyday life, a real and true affection can exist."

I agreed. I remembered the gentle affectionate look in little Mrs. Luttrell's eyes as she looked up at her husband stooping over her bed. No more vinegar, no impatience, no ill-temper.

Married life, I mused, as I went to bed, was a curious thing.

That something in Poirot's manner still worried me. That curious watchful look—as though he were waiting for me to see—what?

I was just getting into bed when it came to me. Hit me bang between the eyes.

If Mrs. Luttrell had been killed, it would have been a case *like those other cases*. Colonel Luttrell would, apparently, have killed his wife. It would have been accounted an accident, yet at the same time nobody would have been sure that it was an accident, or whether it had been done on purpose. Insufficient evidence to show it as murder, but quite enough evidence for murder to be suspected.

But that meant—that meant—

What did it mean?

It meant—if anything at all was to make sense—that it was *not* Colonel Luttrell who shot Mrs. Luttrell, but X.

And that was clearly impossible. I had seen the whole thing. It was Colonel Luttrell who had fired the shot. No other shot had been fired.

Unless—But surely that would be impossible. No, perhaps not *impossible*—merely highly improbable. But possible, yes . . . Supposing that someone else had waited his moment, and at the exact instant when Colonel Luttrell had fired (at a rabbit), this other person had fired at Mrs. Luttrell. Then only the one shot would have been heard. Or, even with a slight discrepancy, it would have been put down as an echo. (Now I come to think of it, there had been an echo, surely.)

But no, that was absurd. There were ways of deciding exactly what weapon a bullet had been fired from. The marks on the bullet must agree with the rifling of the barrel.

But that, I remembered, was only when the police were anxious to establish what weapon had fired the shot. There would have been no enquiry in this business. For Colonel Luttrell would have been quite as certain as everyone else that it was he who had fired the fatal shot. That fact would have been admitted, accepted without question; there would have been no question of tests. The only doubt would have been whether the shot was fired accidentally or with criminal intent—a question that could never be resolved.

And therefore the case fell into line exactly with those other cases—with the case of the labourer Riggs who didn't remember but supposed he must have done it, with Maggie Litchfield who went out of her mind and gave herself up—for a crime she had not committed.

Yes, this case fell into line with the rest and I knew now the meaning of Poirot's manner. He was waiting for me to appreciate the fact.

Ten

I

I opened the subject with Poirot the following morning. His face lighted up and he wagged his head appreciatively.

"Excellent, Hastings. I wondered if you would see the similarity. I did not want to prompt you, you understand."

"Then I am right. This is another X case?"

"Undeniably."

"But *why,* Poirot? What is the motive?"

Poirot shook his head.

"Don't you know? Haven't you any idea?"

Poirot said slowly: "I have an idea, yes."

"You've got the connection between all these different cases?"

"I think so."

"Well then."

I could hardly restrain my impatience.

"No, Hastings."

"But I've got to know."

"It is much better that you should not."

"Why?"

"You must take it from me that it is so."

"You are incorrigible," I said. "Twisted up with arthritis. Sitting here help-less. And still trying to play a lone hand."

"Do not figure to yourself that I am playing a lone hand. Not at all. You are, on the contrary, very much in the picture, Hastings. You are my eyes and ears. I only refuse to give you information that might be dangerous."

"To me?"

"To the murderer."

"You want him," I said slowly, "not to suspect that you are on his track? That is it, I suppose. Or else you think that I cannot take care of myself."

"You should at least know one thing, Hastings. A man who has killed once will kill again—and again and again and again."

"At any rate," I said grimly, "there hasn't been another murder this time. One bullet at least has gone wide."

"Yes, that was very fortunate—very fortunate indeed. As I told you, these things are difficult to foresee."

He sighed. His face took on a worried expression.

I went away quietly, realizing sadly how unfit Poirot was now for any sus-tained effort. His brain was still keen, but he was a sick and tired man.

Poirot had warned me not to try and penetrate the personality of X. In my own mind I still clung to my belief that I had penetrated that personality. There was only one person at Styles who struck me as definitely evil. By a simple ques-tion, however, I could make sure of one thing. The test would be a negative one, but would nevertheless have a certain value.

I tackled Judith after breakfast.

"Where had you been yesterday evening when I met you, you and Major Allerton?"

The trouble is that when you are intent on one aspect of a thing, you tend to ignore all other aspects. I was quite startled when Judith flared out at me.

"Really, Father, I don't see what business it is of yours."

I stared at her, rather taken aback. "I—I only asked."

"Yes, but *why?* Why do you have to be continually asking questions? What was I doing? Where did I go? Who was I with? It's really intolerable!"

The funny part of it was, of course, that this time I was not really asking at all where Judith was. It was Allerton I was interested in.

I tried to pacify her.

"Really, Judith, I don't see why I can't ask a simple question."

"I don't see why you want to know."

"I don't particularly. I mean, I just wondered why neither of you—er— seemed to know what had happened."

"About the accident, do you mean? I'd been down to the village, if you must know, to get some stamps."

I pounced on the personal pronoun.

"Allerton wasn't with you then?"

Judith gave an exasperated gasp.

"No, he was not," she said in tones of cold fury. "Actually, we'd met just near the house and only about two minutes before we met you. I hope you're satisfied now. But I'd just like to say that if I'd spent the whole day walking around with Major Allerton, it's really not your business. I'm twenty-one and earning my own living, and how I spend my time is entirely my own business."

"Entirely," I said, quickly trying to stem the tide.

"I'm glad you agree." Judith looked mollified. She gave a rueful half smile. "Oh, dearest, do try and not come the heavy father quite so much. You don't know how maddening it is. If you just wouldn't *fuss* so."

"I won't—I really won't in the future," I promised her.

Franklin came striding along at this minute.

"Hullo, Judith. Come along. We're later than usual."

His manner was curt and really hardly polite. In spite of myself I felt annoyed. I knew that Franklin was Judith's employer, that he had a call upon her time and that, since he paid for it, he was entitled to give her orders. Nevertheless, I did not see why he could not behave with common courtesy. His manners were not what one would call polished to anyone, but he did at least behave to most people with a certain amount of everyday politeness. But to Judith, especially of late, his manner was always curt and dictatorial in the extreme. He hardly looked at her when he spoke and merely barked out orders. Judith never appeared to resent this, but I did on her behalf. It crossed my mind that it was especially unfortunate since it contrasted in such a very marked way with Allerton's exaggerated attention. No doubt John Franklin was a ten times better man than Allerton, but he compared very badly with him from the point of view of attraction.

I watched Franklin as he strode along the path towards the laboratory, his ungainly walk, his angular build, the jutting bones of his face and head, his red hair and his freckles. An ugly man and an ungainly man. None of the more obvious qualities. A good brain, yes, but women seldom fall for brains alone. I reflected with dismay that Judith, owing to the circumstances of her job, practically never came into contact with other men. She had no opportunity of sizing up various attractive men. Compared with the gruff and unattractive Franklin, Allerton's meretricious charms stood out with all the force of contrast. My poor girl had no chance of appraising him at his true worth.

Supposing that she should come seriously to lose her heart to him? The irritability she had shown just now was a disquieting sign. Allerton, I knew, was a real bad lot. He was possibly something more. If Allerton were X—?

He could be. At the time that the shot was fired he had not been with Judith.

But what was the motive of all these seemingly purposeless crimes? There was, I felt sure, nothing of the madman about Allerton. He was sane—altogether sane—and utterly unprincipled.

And Judith—my Judith—was seeing altogether too much of him.

II

Up to this time, though I had been faintly worried about my daughter, my preoccupation over X and the possibility of a crime occurring at any moment had successfully driven more personal problems to the back of my mind.

Now that the blow had fallen, that a crime had been attempted and had mercifully failed, I was free to reflect on these things. And the more I did so, the more anxious I became. A chance word spoken one day revealed to me the fact that Allerton was a married man.

Boyd Carrington, who knew all about everyone, enlightened me further.

Allerton's wife was a devout Roman Catholic. She had left him a short time after their marriage. Owing to her religion there had never been any question of divorce.

"And if you ask me," said Boyd Carrington frankly, "it suits the blighter down to the ground. His intentions are always dishonourable, and a wife in the background suits the book very well."

Pleasant hearing for a father!

The days after the shooting accident passed uneventfully enough on the surface, but they accompanied a growing undercurrent of unrest on my part.

Colonel Luttrell spent much time in his wife's bedroom. A nurse had arrived to take charge of the patient and Nurse Craven was able to resume her ministrations to Mrs. Franklin.

Without wishing to be ill-natured, I must admit that I had observed signs on Mrs. Franklin's part of irritation at not being the invalid *en chef*. The fuss and attention that centred round Mrs. Luttrell was clearly very displeasing to the little lady who was accustomed to her own health being the main topic of the day.

She lay about in a hammock chair, her hand to her side, complaining of palpitation. No food that was served was suitable for her, and all her exactions were masked by a veneer of patient endurance.

"I do so hate making a fuss," she murmured plaintively to Poirot. "I feel so ashamed of my wretched health. It's so—so *humiliating* always to have to ask people to be doing things for me. I sometimes think ill health is really a crime. If one isn't healthy and insensitive one isn't fit for this world and one should just be put quietly away."

"Ah no, madame." Poirot, as always, was gallant. "The delicate exotic flower has to have the shelter of the greenhouse—it cannot endure the cold winds. It is the common weed that thrives in the wintry air, but it is not to be prized higher on that account. Consider my case—cramped, twisted, unable to move, but I—I do not think of quitting life. I enjoy still what I can—the food, the drink, the pleasures of the intellect."

Mrs. Franklin sighed and murmured: "Ah, but it's different for you. You have no one but yourself to consider. In my case, there is my poor John. I feel acutely what a burden I am to him. A sickly useless wife. A millstone hung round his neck."

"He has never said that you are that, I am sure."

"Oh, not *said* so. Of course not. But men are so transparent, poor dears. And John isn't any good at concealing his feelings. He doesn't mean, of course, to be unkind, but he's—well, mercifully for himself he's a very insensitive sort of person. He's no feelings and so he doesn't expect anyone else to have them. It's so terribly lucky to be born thick-skinned."

"I should not describe Dr. Franklin as thick-skinned."

"Wouldn't you? Oh, but you don't know him as well as I do. Of course I know that if it wasn't for me, he would be much freer. Sometimes, you know, I get so terribly depressed that I think what a relief it would be to end it all."

"Oh, come, madame."

"After all, what use am I to anybody? To go out of it all into the Great Unknown . . ." she shook her head. "And then John would be free."

"Great fiddlesticks," said Nurse Craven when I repeated this conversation to her. "She won't do anything of the kind. Don't you worry, Captain Hastings. These ones that talk about 'ending it all' in a dying-duck voice haven't the faintest intention of doing anything of the kind."

And I must say that once the excitement aroused by Mrs. Luttrell's injury had died down, and Nurse Craven was once more in attendance, Mrs. Franklin's spirits improved very much.

On a particularly fine morning Curtiss had taken Poirot down to the corner below the beech trees near the laboratory. This was a favourite spot of his. It was sheltered from any east wind and in fact hardly any breeze could ever be felt there. This suited Poirot, who abhorred draughts and was always suspicious of the fresh air. Actually, I think he much preferred to be indoors but had grown to tolerate the outer air when muffled in rugs.

I strolled down to join him and as I got there Mrs. Franklin came out of the laboratory.

She was most becomingly dressed and looked remarkably cheerful. She explained that she was driving over with Boyd Carrington to see the house and give expert advice in choosing cretonnes.

"I left my handbag in the lab yesterday when I was talking to John," she explained. "Poor John, he and Judith have driven into Tadcaster—they were short of some chemical reagent or other."

She sank down on a seat near Poirot and shook her head with a comical expression. "Poor dears—I'm so glad I haven't got the scientific mind. On a lovely day like this it all seems so puerile."

"You must not let scientists hear you say that, madame."

"No, of course not." Her face changed. It grew serious. She said quietly: "You mustn't think, M. Poirot, that I don't admire my husband. I do. I think the way he just lives for his work is really—tremendous."

There was a little tremor in her voice.

A suspicion crossed my mind that Mrs. Franklin rather liked playing different roles. At this moment she was being the loyal and hero-worshipping wife.

She leaned forward, placing an earnest hand on Poirot's knee. "John," she said, "is really a—a kind of *saint*. It makes me quite frightened sometimes."

To call Franklin a saint was somewhat overstating the case, I thought, but Barbara Franklin went on, her eyes shining.

"He'll do anything—take any risk—just to advance the sum of human knowledge. That is pretty fine, don't you think?"

"Assuredly, assuredly," said Poirot quickly.

"But sometimes, you know," went on Mrs. Franklin, "I'm really nervous about him. The lengths to which he'll go, I mean. This horrible bean thing he's experimenting with now. I'm so afraid he'll start experimenting on himself."

"He'd take every precaution, surely," I said.

She shook her head with a slight, rueful smile. "You don't know John. Did you never hear about what he did with that new gas?"

I shook my head.

"It was some new gas they wanted to find out about. John volunteered to test it. He was shut up in a tank for something like thirty-six hours, taking his pulse and temperature and respiration, to see what the aftereffects were and if they were the same for men as for animals. It was a frightful risk, so one of the professors told me afterwards. He might easily have passed out altogether. But that's the sort of person John is—absolutely oblivious of his own safety. I think it's rather wonderful, don't you, to be like that? *I* should never be brave enough."

"It needs, indeed, high courage," said Poirot, "to do these things in cold blood."

Barbara Franklin said: "Yes, it does. I'm awfully proud of him, you know, but at the same time it makes me rather nervous, too. Because, you see, guinea pigs and frogs are no good after a certain point. You want the human reaction. That's why I feel so terrified that John will go and dose himself with this nasty ordeal bean and that something awful might happen." She sighed and shook her head. "But he only laughs at my fears. He really *is* a sort of saint, you know."

At this moment Boyd Carrington came towards us.

"Hullo, Babs, ready?"

"Yes, Bill, waiting for you."

"I do hope it won't tire you too much."

"Of course it won't. I feel better today than I have for ages."

She got up, smiled prettily at us both, and walked up the lawn with her tall escort.

"Dr. Franklin, the modern saint—h'm," said Poirot.

"Rather a change of attitude," I said. "But I think the lady is like that."

"Like what?"

"Given to dramatizing herself in various roles. One day the misunderstood, neglected wife, then the self-sacrificing, suffering woman who hates to be a burden on the man she loves. Today it's the hero-worshipping helpmate. The trouble is that all the roles are slightly overdone."

Poirot said thoughtfully: "You think Mrs. Franklin, do you not, rather a fool?"

"Well, I wouldn't say that—yes, perhaps not a very brilliant intellect."

"Ah, she is not your type."

"Who is my type?" I snapped.

Poirot replied unexpectedly: "Open your mouth and shut your eyes and see what the fairies will send you—"

I was prevented from replying because Nurse Craven came tripping hastily across the grass. She gave us a smile with a brilliant flash of teeth, unlocked the door of the lab, passed inside and reappeared with a pair of gloves.

"First a hanky and now gloves, always *something* left behind," she observed as she sped back with them to where Barbara Franklin and Boyd Carrington were waiting.

Mrs. Franklin, I reflected, was that rather feckless type of woman who always did leave things behind, shedding her possessions and expecting everybody to retrieve them as a matter of course and even, I fancied, was rather proud of herself for so doing. I had heard her more than once murmur complacently: "Of course I've got a head like a *sieve*."

I sat looking after Nurse Craven as she ran across the lawn and out of sight. She ran well, her body was vigorous and well balanced. I said impulsively: "I should think a girl must get fed up with that sort of life. I mean when there isn't much nursing to be done—when it's just fetch and carry. I don't suppose Mrs. Franklin is particularly considerate or kindly."

Poirot's response was distinctly annoying. For no reason whatever, he closed his eyes and murmured: "Auburn hair."

Undoubtedly Nurse Craven had got auburn hair, but I did not see why Poirot should choose just this minute to comment upon it.

I made no reply.

Eleven

It was, I think, on the following morning before lunch that a conversation took place which left me vaguely disquieted.

There were four of us—Judith, myself, Boyd Carrington and Norton.

Exactly how the subject started, I am not sure, but we were talking of euthanasia—the case for and against it.

Boyd Carrington, as was natural, did most of the talking, Norton putting in a word or two here and there and Judith sitting silent but closely attentive.

I myself had confessed that though there seemed, on the face of it, every reason to support the practice, yet in actuality I felt a sentimental shrinking from it. Besides, I said, I thought it would put too much power in the hands of relatives.

Norton agreed with me. He added that he thought it should only be done by the wish and consent of the patient himself where death after prolonged suffering was certain.

Boyd Carrington said: "Ah, but that's the curious thing. Does the person most concerned ever wish to 'put himself out of his misery,' as we say?"

He then told a story which he said was authentic, of a man in terrible pain from inoperable cancer. This man had begged the doctor in attendance to "give him something that would finish it all." The doctor had replied: "I can't do that, old man. " Later, on leaving, he had placed by the patient some morphia tablets, telling him carefully how many he could safely take and what dose would be dangerous. Although these were left in the patient's charge and he could easily have taken a fatal quantity, he did not do so. "Thus proving," said Boyd Carrington, "that, in spite of his words, the man preferred his suffering to a swift and merciful release."

It was then that Judith spoke for the first time, spoke with vigour and abruptly. "Of course he would," she said. "It shouldn't have been left to him to decide."

Boyd Carrington asked what she meant.

"I mean that anyone who's weak—in pain and ill—hasn't got the strength to make a decision—they can't. It must be done for them. It's the duty of someone who loves them to take the decision."

"Duty?" I queried abruptly.

Judith turned on me. "Yes, *duty*. Someone whose mind is clear and who will take the responsibility."

Boyd Carrington shook his head. "And end up in the dock charged with murder?"

"Not necessarily. Anyway, if you love someone, you would take the risk."

"But look here, Judith," said Norton, "what you're suggesting is simply a terrific responsibility to take."

"I don't think it is. People are too afraid of responsibility. They'll take responsibility where a dog is concerned—why not with a human being?"

"Well—it's rather different, isn't it?"

Judith said: "Yes, it's more important."

Norton murmured: "You take my breath away."

Boyd Carrington asked curiously: "So *you'd* take the risk, would you?"

"I think so. I'm not afraid of taking risks."

Boyd Carrington shook his head. "It wouldn't do, you know. You can't have people here, there, and everywhere, taking the law into their own hands, deciding matters of life and death."

Norton said: "Actually, you know, Boyd Carrington, most people wouldn't have the *nerve* to take the responsibility." He smiled faintly as he looked at Judith. "Don't believe you would if it came to the point."

Judith said composedly: "One can't be sure, of course. I think I should."

Norton said with a slight twinkle: "Not unless you had an axe of your own to grind."

Judith flushed hotly. She said sharply: "That just shows you don't understand at all. If I had a—a personal motive, I couldn't do anything. Don't you see?" she appealed to us all. "It's got to be absolutely impersonal. You could only take the responsibility of—of ending a life if you were quite sure of your motive. It must be absolutely selfless."

"All the same," said Norton, "you wouldn't do it."

Judith insisted: "I would. To begin with I don't hold life as sacred as all you people do. Unfit lives, useless lives—they should be got out of the way. There's so much *mess* about. Only people who can make a decent contribution to the community ought to be allowed to live. The others ought to be put painlessly away."

She appealed suddenly to Boyd Carrington.

"You agree with me, don't you?"

He said slowly: "In principle, yes. Only the worthwhile should survive."

"Wouldn't you take the law into your own hands if it was necessary?"

Boyd Carrington said slowly: "Perhaps. I don't know. . . ."

Norton said quietly: "A lot of people would agree with you in theory. But practice is a different matter."

"That's not logical."

Norton said impatiently: "Of course it's not. It's really a question of *courage.* One just hasn't got the *guts,* to put it vulgarly."

Judith was silent. Norton went on.

"Frankly, you know, Judith, you'd be just the same yourself. You wouldn't have the courage when it came to it."

"Don't you think so?"

"I'm sure of it."

"I think you're wrong, Norton," said Boyd Carrington. "I think Judith has any amount of courage. Fortunately the issue doesn't present itself."

The gong sounded from the house.

Judith got up.

She said very distinctly to Norton: "You're wrong, you know. I've got more—more guts than you think."

She went swiftly towards the house. Boyd Carrington followed her saying, "Hey, wait for me, Judith."

I followed, feeling for some reason rather dismayed. Norton, who was always quick to sense a mood, endeavoured to console me.

"She doesn't mean it, you know," he said. "It's the sort of half-baked idea one has when one is young, but fortunately one doesn't carry it out. It remains just talk."

I think Judith overheard, for she cast a furious glance over her shoulder.

Norton dropped his voice. "Theories needn't worry anybody," he said. "But look here, Hastings—"

"Yes?"

Norton seemed rather embarrassed. He said: "I don't want to butt in, but what do you know of Allerton?"

"Of Allerton?"

"Yes, sorry if I'm being a Nosy Parker, but frankly if I were you I shouldn't let that girl of yours see too much of him. He's—well, his reputation isn't very good."

"I can see for myself the sort of rotter he is," I said bitterly. "But it's not so easy in these days."

"Oh, I know. Girls can look after themselves, as the saying goes. Most of them can, too. But—well—Allerton has rather a special technique in that line." He hesitated, then said: "Look here, I feel I ought to tell you. Don't let it go farther, of course—but I do happen to know something pretty foul about him."

He told it to me then and there—and I was able to verify it in every detail later. It was a revolting tale. The story of a girl, sure of herself, modern, independent. Allerton had brought all his technique to bear upon her. Later had come the other side of the picture—the story ended with a desperate girl taking her own life with an overdose of Veronal.

And the horrible part was that the girl in question had been much the same type as Judith—the independent, highbrow kind. The kind of girl who when she does lose her heart, loses it with a desperation and an abandonment that the silly little fluffy type can never know.

I went in to lunch with a horrible sense of foreboding.

Twelve

I

"Is anything worrying you, *mon ami?*" asked Poirot that afternoon.

I did not answer him, merely shook my head. I felt that I had no right to burden Poirot with this, my purely personal problem. It was not as though he could help in any way.

Judith would have treated any remonstrances on his part with the smiling detachment of the young towards the boring counsels of the old.

Judith, my Judith. . . .

It is hard now to describe just what I went through that day. Afterwards, thinking it over, I am inclined to put something down to the atmosphere of Styles itself. Evil imaginings came easily to the mind there. There was, too, not only the past, but a sinister present. The shadow of murder and a murderer haunted the house.

And to the best of my belief the murderer was Allerton and Judith was losing her heart to him! It was unbelievable—monstrous—and I didn't know what to do.

It was after lunch that Boyd Carrington drew me aside. He hemmed and hawed a bit before coming to the point. At last he said rather jerkily: "Don't think I'm interfering, but I think you ought to speak to that girl of yours. Give her a word of warning, eh? You know this fellow Allerton—reputation's pretty bad, and she—well, it looks rather like a case."

So easy for these men without children to speak like that! Give her a word of warning?

Would it be any use? Would it make things worse?

If only Cinders were here. She would know what to do, what to say.

I was tempted, I admit, to hold my peace and say nothing. But I reflected after a while that this was really only cowardice. I shrank from the unpleasant-ness of having things out with Judith. I was, you see, afraid of my tall, beautiful daughter.

I paced up and down the gardens in increasing agitation of mind. My foot-steps led me at last to the rose garden, and there, as it were, the decision was taken out of my hands, for Judith was sitting on a seat alone, and in all my life I have never seen an expression of greater unhappiness on any woman's face.

The mask was off. Indecision and deep unhappiness showed only too plainly.

I took my courage in my hands. I went to her. She did not hear me until I was beside her.

"Judith," I said. "For God's sake, Judith, don't mind so much."

She turned on me, startled. "Father? I didn't hear you."

I went on, knowing that it would be fatal if she managed to turn me back to normal everyday conversation.

"Oh, my dearest child, don't think I don't know, that I can't see. He isn't worth it—oh, do believe me, he isn't worth it."

Her face, troubled, alarmed, was turned towards me. She said quietly: "Do you think you really know what you are talking about?"

"I do know. You care about this man. But, my dear, it's no good."

She smiled sombrely. A heartbreaking smile.

"Perhaps I know that as well as you do."

"You don't. You can't. Oh, Judith, what can come of it all? He's a married man. There can be no future there for you—only sorrow and shame—and all ending in bitter self-loathing."

Her smile grew wider—even more sorrowful.

"How fluently you talk, don't you?"

"Give it up, Judith—give it all up."

"No!"

"He's not worth it, my dear."

She said very quietly and slowly: "He's worth everything in the world to me."

"No, no. Judith, I beg of you—"

The smile vanished. She turned on me like an avenging fury.

"How dare you? How dare you interfere? I won't stand it. You are never to speak to me of this again. I hate you, I hate you. It's no business of yours. It's *my* life—my own secret inside life!"

She got up. With one firm hand she pushed me aside and went past me. Like an avenging fury. I stared after her, dismayed.

II

I was still there, dazed and helpless, unable to think out my next course of action, some quarter of an hour later.

I was there when Elizabeth Cole and Norton found me.

They were, I realized later, very kind to me. They saw, they must have seen, that I was in a state of great mental perturbation. But tactfully enough they made no slightest allusion to my state of mind. Instead they took me with them on a rambling walk. They were both nature lovers. Elizabeth Cole pointed out wild flowers to me, Norton showed me birds through his field glasses.

Their talk was gentle, soothing, concerned only with feathered beings and with woodland flora. Little by little I came back to normal, although underneath I was still in a state of the utmost perturbation.

Moreover I was, as people are, convinced that any happening that occurred was connected with my own particular perplexity.

So, therefore, when Norton, his glasses to his eyes, exclaimed: "Hullo, if that isn't a speckled woodpecker. I never—" and then broke off suddenly, I immediately leapt to suspicion. I held out my hand for the glasses.

"Let me see." My voice was peremptory.

Norton fumbled with the glasses. He said, in a curious hesitating voice: "I—I—made a mistake. It's flown away—at least, as a matter of fact, it was quite a common bird."

His face was white and troubled, he avoided looking at us. He seemed both bewildered and distressed.

Even now I cannot think I was altogether unreasonable in jumping to the conclusion that he had seen through those glasses of his something that he was determined to prevent my seeing.

Whatever it was that he had seen, he was so thoroughly taken aback by it that it was noticeable to both of us.

His glasses had been trained on a distant belt of woodland. What had he seen there?

I said peremptorily: "Let me look."

I snatched at the glasses. I remember he tried to defend them from me, but he did it clumsily. I seized them roughly.

Norton said weakly: "It wasn't really—I mean, the bird's gone. I wish—"

My hands shaking a little, I adjusted the glasses to my eyes. They were powerful glasses. I trained them as nearly as I could on the spot where I thought Norton had been looking.

But I saw nothing—nothing but a gleam of white (a girl's white dress?) disappearing into the trees.

I lowered the glasses. Without a word I handed them back to Norton. He did not meet my eyes. He was looking worried and perplexed.

We walked back to the house together and I remember that Norton was very silent all the way.

III

Mrs. Franklin and Boyd Carrington came in shortly after we got back to the house. He had taken her in his car to Tadcaster because she wanted to do some shopping.

She had done it, I gather, pretty thoroughly. Lots of parcels came out of the car and she was looking quite animated, talking and laughing and with quite a colour in her cheeks.

She sent Boyd Carrington up with a particularly fragile purchase and I gallantly received a further consignment.

Her talk was quicker and more nervous than usual.

"Frightfully hot, isn't it? I think there's going to be a storm. This weather must break soon. They say, you know, there's quite a water shortage. The worst drought there's been for years."

She went on, turning to Elizabeth Cole: "What have you all been doing with yourselves? Where's John? He said he'd got a headache and was going to walk it off. Very unlike him to have a headache. I think, you know, he's worried about his experiments. They aren't going right or something. I wish he'd talk more about things."

She paused and then addressed Norton: "You're very silent, Mr. Norton. Is anything the matter? You look—you look scared. You haven't seen the ghost of old Mrs. Whoever-it-was?"

Norton started. "No, no. I haven't seen any ghosts. I—I was just thinking of something."

It was at that moment that Curtiss came through the doorway wheeling Poirot in his invalid chair.

He stopped with it in the hall, preparatory to taking his master out and carrying him up the stairs.

Poirot, his eyes suddenly alert, looked from one to the other of us.

He said sharply: "What is it? Is anything the matter?"

None of us answered for a minute, then Barbara Franklin said with a little artificial laugh: "No, of course not. What should be the matter? It's just—perhaps thunder coming? I—oh dear—I'm terribly tired. Bring those things up, will you, Captain Hastings? Thank you so much."

I followed her up the stairs and along the east wing. Her room was the end one on that side.

Mrs. Franklin opened the door. I was behind her, my arms full of parcels.

She stopped abruptly in the doorway. By the window Boyd Carrington was having his palm examined by Nurse Craven.

He looked up and laughed a little sheepishly. "Hullo, I'm having my fortune told. Nurse is no end of a hand reader."

"Really? I had no idea of that." Barbara Franklin's voice was sharp. I had an idea that she was annoyed with Nurse Craven. "Please take these things, Nurse, will you? And you might mix me an egg flip. I feel very tired. A hot-water bottle, too, please. I'll get to bed as soon as possible."

"Certainly, Mrs. Franklin."

Nurse Craven moved forward. She showed no signs of anything but professional concern.

Mrs. Franklin said: "Please go, Bill, I'm terribly tired."

Boyd Carrington looked very concerned. "Oh, I say, Babs, has it been too much for you? I *am* sorry. What a thoughtless fool I am. I shouldn't have let you overtire yourself."

Mrs. Franklin gave him her angelic martyr's smile. "I didn't want to say anything. I do hate being *tiresome*."

We two men went out of the room, somewhat abashed, and left the two women together.

Boyd Carrington said contritely: "What a damned fool I am. Barbara seemed so bright and gay I forgot all about tiring her. Hope she's not knocked herself up."

I said mechanically: "Oh, I expect she'll be all right after a night's rest."

He went down the stairs. I hesitated and then went along the other wing towards my own room, and Poirot's. The little man would be expecting me. For the first time I was reluctant to go to him. I had so much to occupy my thoughts, and I still had that dull sick feeling at the pit of my stomach.

I went slowly along the corridor.

From inside Allerton's room I heard voices. I don't think I meant consciously to listen though I stopped for a minute automatically outside his door. Then, suddenly, the door opened and my daughter Judith came out.

She stopped dead when she saw me. I caught her by the arm and hustled her along into my room. I was suddenly intensely angry.

"What do you mean by going to that fellow's room?"

She looked at me steadily. She showed no anger now, only complete coldness. For some few seconds she did not reply.

I shook her by the arm. "I won't have it, I tell you. You don't know what you are doing."

She said then, in a low biting voice: "I think you have a perfectly filthy mind."

I said: "I daresay I have. It's a reproach your generation is fond of levelling at mine. We have, at least, certain standards. Understand this, Judith, I forbid you absolutely to have anything more to do with that man."

She looked at me steadily. Then she said quietly: "I see. So that's it."

"Do you deny that you're in love with him?"

"No."

"But you don't know what he is. You can't know."

Deliberately, without mincing my language, I repeated to her the story I had heard about Allerton.

"You see," I said when I had finished. "That's the kind of foul brute he is."

She seemed quite annoyed. Her lips curled upwards scornfully.

"I never thought he was a saint, I can assure you."

"Doesn't this make any difference to you? Judith, you can't be utterly depraved."

"Call it that if you like."

"Judith, you haven't—you aren't—"

I could not put my meaning into words. She shook her arm free from my detaining hand.

"Now, listen, Father. I do what I choose. You can't bully me. And it's no good ranting. I shall do exactly as I please with my life, and you can't stop me."

In another instant she was out of the room.

I found my knees trembling.

I sank down on to a chair. It was worse—much worse than I thought. The child was utterly infatuated. There was no one to whom I could appeal. Her mother, the only person she might have listened to, was dead. It all depended on me.

I do not think that either before or since I have ever suffered as I suffered then. . . .

IV

Presently I roused myself. I washed and shaved and changed. I went down to dinner. I behaved, I fancy, in quite a normal manner. Nobody seemed to notice anything amiss.

Once or twice I saw Judith flash a curious glance at me. She must have been puzzled, I think, by the way I was able to appear quite like my usual self.

And all the time, underneath, I was growing more and more determined.

All that I needed was courage—courage and brains.

After dinner we went outside, looked up at the sky, commented on the closeness of the atmosphere, prophesied rain—thunder—a storm.

Out of the tail of my eye I saw Judith disappear round the corner of the house. Presently Allerton strolled in the same direction.

I finished what I was saying to Boyd Carrington and wandered that way myself.

Norton, I think, tried to stop me. He took my arm. He tried, I think, to suggest walking up to the rose garden. I took no notice.

He was still with me as I turned the corner of the house.

They were there. I saw Judith's upturned face, saw Allerton's bent down over it, saw how he took her in his arms and the kiss that followed.

Then they broke away quickly. I took a step forward. Almost by main force, Norton hauled me back and round the corner. He said: "Look here, you can't—"

I interrupted him. I said forcefully: "I can. And I will."

"It's no *good,* my dear fellow. It's all very distressing but all it comes to is that there's nothing you *can* do."

I was silent. He might think that that was so, but I knew better.

Norton went on: "I know how ineffectual and maddened one feels, but the only thing to do is to admit defeat. *Accept* it, man!"

I didn't contradict him. I waited, allowing him to talk. Then I went firmly round the corner of the house again.

The two of them had disappeared now, but I had a shrewd idea of where they might be. There was a summerhouse concealed in a grove of lilac trees not far away.

I went towards it. I think Norton was still with me, but I'm not sure.

As I got nearer I heard voices and stopped. It was Allerton's voice I heard.

"Well, then, my dear girl, that's settled. Don't make anymore objections. You go up to town tomorrow. I'll say I'm running over to Ipswich to stay with a pal for a night or two. You wire from London that you can't get back. And who's to know of that charming little dinner at my flat? You won't regret it, I can promise you."

I felt Norton tugging at me, and suddenly, meekly, I turned. I almost laughed at the sight of his worried anxious face. I let him drag me back to the house. I pretended to give in because I knew, at that moment, exactly what I was going to do. . . .

I said to him clearly and distinctly: "Don't worry, old chap. It's all no good—I see that now. You can't control your children's lives. I'm through."

He was ridiculously relieved.

Shortly afterwards, I told him I was going to bed early. I'd got a bit of a headache, I said.

He had no suspicions at all of what I was going to do.

V

I paused for a moment in the corridor. It was quite quiet. There was no one about. The beds had been all turned down ready for the night. Norton, who had a room on this side, I had left downstairs. Elizabeth Cole was playing bridge. Curtiss, I knew, would be downstairs having his supper. I had the place to myself.

I flatter myself that I have not worked with Poirot for so many years in vain. I knew just what precautions to take.

Allerton was *not* going to meet Judith in London tomorrow.

Allerton was not going anywhere tomorrow. . . .

The whole thing was really so ridiculously simple.

I went to my own room and picked up my bottle of aspirins. Then I went into Allerton's room and into the bathroom. The tablets of Slumberyl were in the cupboard. Eight, I considered, ought to do the trick. One or two was the stated dose. Eight, therefore, ought to be ample. Allerton himself had said the toxic dose was not high. I read the label. "It is dangerous to exceed the prescribed dose."

I smiled to myself.

I wrapped a silk handkerchief round my hand and unscrewed the bottle carefully. There must be no fingerprints on it.

I emptied out the tablets. Yes, they were almost exactly the same size as the aspirins. I put eight aspirins in the bottle, then filled up with the Slumberyls, leaving out eight of them. The bottle now looked exactly as it had before. Allerton would notice no difference.

I went back to my room. I had a bottle of whisky there—most of us had at Styles. I got out two glasses and a syphon. I'd never known Allerton refuse a drink yet. When he came up I'd ask him in for a nightcap.

I tried the tablets in a little of the spirit. They dissolved easily enough. I tasted the mixture gingerly. A shade bitter perhaps but hardly noticeable. I had my plan. I should be just pouring myself out a drink when Allerton came up. I would hand that to him and pour myself out another. All quite easy and natural.

He could have no idea of my feelings—unless of course Judith had told him. I considered this for a moment, but decided that I was quite safe here. Judith never told anyone anything.

He would probably believe me to be quite unsuspicious of their plan.

I had nothing to do but to wait. It would be a long time, probably an hour or two, before Allerton came up to bed. He was always a late bird.

I sat there quietly waiting.

A sudden knock on the door made me start. It was only Curtiss, however. Poirot was asking for me.

I came to myself with a shock. Poirot! I had never once thought of him all evening. He must have wondered what had become of me. It worried me a little. First of all because I was ashamed of never having been near him, and secondly I did not want him to suspect that anything out of the way had happened.

I followed Curtiss across the passage.

"*Eh bien!*" exclaimed Poirot. "So you desert me, *hein?*"

I forced a yawn and an apologetic smile. "Awfully sorry, old boy," I said. "But to tell the truth I've got such a blinding headache I can hardly see out of my eyes. It's the thunder in the air, I suppose. I really have been feeling quite muzzy with it—in fact, so much so I entirely forgot I hadn't been in to say good night to you."

As I had hoped, Poirot was immediately solicitous. He offered remedies. He fussed. He accused me of having sat about in the open air in a draught. (On the hottest day of the summer!) I refused aspirin on the grounds that I had already taken some, but I was not able to avoid being given a cup of sweet and wholly disgusting chocolate!

"It nourishes the nerves, you comprehend," Poirot explained.

I drank it to avoid argument and then, with Poirot's anxious and affectionate exclamations still ringing in my ears, I bade him good night.

I returned to my own room, and shut the door ostentatiously. Later, I opened it a crack with the utmost caution. I could not fail now to hear Allerton when he came. But it would be some time yet.

I sat there waiting. I thought of my dead wife. Once, under my breath, I murmured: "You understand, darling, I'm going to save her."

She had left Judith in my care, I was not going to fail her.

In the quiet and the stillness I suddenly felt that Cinders was very near to me.

I felt almost as though she were in the room.

And still I sat on grimly, waiting.

Thirteen

I

There is something about writing down an anticlimax in cold blood that is somewhat shattering to one's self-esteem.

For the truth of the matter is, you see, that I sat there waiting for Allerton and that I fell asleep!

Not so surprising really, I suppose. I had slept very badly the night before. I had been out in the air the whole day. I was worn out with worry and the strain of nerving myself for doing what I had decided to do. On top of all that was the heavy thundery weather. Possibly even the fierce effort of concentration I was making helped.

Anyway, it happened. I fell asleep there in my chair, and when I woke birds were twittering outside, the sun was up and there was I, cramped and uncomfortable, slipped down in my chair in my evening dress, with a foul taste in the mouth and a splitting head.

I was bewildered, incredulous, disgusted, and finally immeasurably and overwhelmingly relieved.

Who was it who wrote, "The darkest day, lived till tomorrow, will have passed away?" And how true it is. I saw now, clearly and sanely, how overwrought and wrongheaded I had been. Melodramatic, lost to all sense of proportion. I had actually made up my mind to kill another human being.

At this moment my eyes fell on the glass of whisky in front of me. With a shudder I got up, drew the curtains and poured it out of the window. I must have been mad last night!

I shaved, had a bath and dressed. Then, feeling very much better, I went across to Poirot. He always woke very early, I knew. I sat down and made a clean breast of the whole thing to him.

I may say it was a great relief.

He shook his head gently at me. "Ah, but what follies it is you contemplate. I am glad you came to confess your sins to me. But why, my dear friend, did you not come to me last night and tell me what was in your mind?"

I said shamefacedly: "I was afraid, I suppose, that you would have tried to stop me."

"Assuredly I would have stopped you. Ah that, certainly. Do you think I want to see you hanged by the neck, all on account of a very unpleasant scoundrel called Major Allerton?"

"I shouldn't have been caught," I said. "I'd taken every precaution."

"That is what all murderers think. You had the true mentality! But let me tell you, *mon ami,* you were not as clever as you thought yourself."

"I took every precaution. I wiped my fingerprints off the bottle."

"Exactly. You also wiped Allerton's fingerprints off. And when he is found dead, what happens? They perform the autopsy and it is established that he died of an overdose of Slumberyl. Did he take it by accident or intention? *Tiens,* his fingerprints are not on the bottle. But why not? Whether accident or suicide he would have no reason to wipe them off. And then they analyse the remaining tablets and find nearly half of them have been replaced by aspirin."

"Well, practically everyone has aspirin tablets," I murmured weakly.

"Yes, but it is not everyone who has a daughter whom Allerton is pursuing with dishonourable intentions—to use an old-fashioned dramatic phrase. And you have had a quarrel with your daughter on the subject the day before. Two people, Boyd Carrington and Norton, can swear to your violent feeling against the man. No, Hastings, it would not have looked too good. Attention would immediately have been focused upon you, and by that time you would probably have been in such a state of fear—or even remorse—that some good solid inspector of police would have made up his mind quite definitely that you were the guilty party. It is quite possible, even, that someone may have seen you tampering with the tablets."

"They couldn't. There was no one about."

"There is a balcony outside the window. Somebody might have been there, peeping in. Or, who knows, someone might have been looking through the keyhole."

"You've got keyholes on the brain, Poirot. People don't really spend their time looking through keyholes as much as you seem to think."

Poirot half-closed his eyes and remarked that I had always had too trusting a nature.

"And let me tell you, very funny things happen with keys in this house. Me, I like to feel that my door is locked on the inside, even if the good Curtiss is in the adjoining room. Soon after I am here, my key disappears—but entirely! I have to have another one made."

"Well, anyway," I said with a deep breath of relief, my mind still laden with my own troubles, "it didn't come off. It's awful to think one can get worked up like that." I lowered my voice. "Poirot, you don't think that because—because of that murder long ago there's a sort of infection in the air?"

"A virus of murder, you mean? Well, it is an interesting suggestion."

"Houses do have an atmosphere," I said thoughtfully. "This house has a bad history."

Poirot nodded. "Yes. There have been people here—several of them—who desired deeply that someone else should die. That is true enough."

"I believe it gets hold of one in some way. But now, Poirot, tell me, what am I to do about all this—Judith and Allerton, I mean. It's got to be stopped somehow. What do you think I'd better do?"

"Do nothing," said Poirot with emphasis.

"Oh, but—"

"Believe me, you will do least harm by not interfering."

"If I were to tackle Allerton—"

"What can you say or do? Judith is twenty-one and her own mistress."

"But I feel I ought to be able—"

Poirot interrupted me. "No, Hastings. Do not imagine that you are clever enough, forceful enough, or even cunning enough to impose your personality on either of those two people. Allerton is accustomed to dealing with angry and impotent fathers and probably enjoys it as a good joke. Judith is not the sort of creature who can be browbeaten. I would advise you—if I advised you at all—to do something very different. I would trust her if I were you."

I stared at him.

"Judith," said Hercule Poirot, "is made of very fine stuff. I admire her very much."

I said, my voice unsteady: "I admire her, too. But I'm afraid for her."

Poirot nodded his head with sudden energy. "I, too, am afraid for her," he said. "But not in the way you are. I am terribly afraid. And I am powerless—or nearly so. And the days go by. There is danger, Hastings, and it is very close."

II

I knew as well as Poirot that the danger was very close. I had more reason to know it than he had, because of what I had actually overheard the previous night.

Nevertheless I pondered on that phrase of Poirot's as I went down to breakfast. "I would trust her if I were you."

It had come unexpectedly, but it had given me an odd sense of comfort. And almost immediately, the truth of it was justified. For Judith had obviously changed her mind about going up to London that day.

Instead she went off with Franklin to the lab as usual directly after breakfast, and it was clear that they were to have an arduous and busy day there.

A feeling of intense thanksgiving rushed over me. How mad, how despairing I had been last night. I had assumed—assumed quite certainly—that Judith had yielded to Allerton's specious proposals. But it was true, I reflected now, that I had never heard her actually assent. No, she was too fine, too essentially good and true, to give in. She had refused the rendezvous.

Allerton had breakfasted early, I found, and gone off to Ipswich. He, then, had kept to the plan and must assume that Judith was going up to London as arranged.

"Well," I thought grimly, "he will get a disappointment."

Boyd Carrington came along and remarked rather grumpily that I looked very cheerful this morning.

"Yes," I said. "I've had some good news."

He said that it was more than he had. He'd had a tiresome telephone call from the architect, some building difficulty—a local surveyor cutting up rough. Also worrying letters. And he was afraid he'd let Mrs. Franklin overdo herself the day before.

Mrs. Franklin was certainly making up for her recent bout of good health and spirits. She was, so I gathered from Nurse Craven, making herself quite impossible.

Nurse Craven had had to give up her day off which had been promised her to go and meet some friends, and she was decidedly sour about it. Since early morning Mrs. Franklin had been calling for sal volatile, hot-water bottles, various patent food and drinks, and was unwilling to let Nurse leave the room. She had neuralgia, a pain round the heart, cramps in her feet and legs, cold shivers and I don't know what else.

I may say here and now that neither I, nor anyone else, was inclined to be really alarmed. We all put it down as part of Mrs. Franklin's hypochondriacal tendencies.

This was true of Nurse Craven and Dr. Franklin as well.

The latter was fetched from the laboratory; he listened to his wife's complaints, asked her if she would like the local doctor called in (violently negatived by Mrs. Franklin); he then mixed her a sedative, soothed her as best he could and went off back to work again.

Nurse Craven said to me: "He knows, of course, she's just playing up."

"You don't really think there's anything much the matter?"

"Her temperature is normal, and her pulse is perfectly good. Just fuss, if you ask me."

She was annoyed and spoke out more imprudently than usual.

"She likes to interfere with anyone else enjoying themselves. She'd like her husband all worked up, and me running round after her, and even Sir William has got to be made to feel like a brute because he 'overtired her yesterday.' She's one of that kind."

Nurse Craven was clearly finding her patient almost impossible today. I gathered that Mrs. Franklin had been really extremely rude to her. She was the kind of woman whom nurses and servants instinctively disliked, not only because of the trouble she gave, but because of her manner of doing so.

So, as I say, none of us took her indisposition seriously.

The only exception was Boyd Carrington, who wandered round looking rather pathetically like a small boy who has been scolded.

How many times since then have I not gone over and over the events of that day, trying to remember something so far unheeded—some tiny forgotten incident, striving to remember exactly the manner of everybody. How far they were normal, or showed excitement.

Let me, once more, put down exactly what I remember of everybody.

Boyd Carrington, as I have said, looked uncomfortable and rather guilty. He seemed to think that he had been rather over-exuberant the day before and had been selfish in not thinking more of the frail health of his companion. He had been up once or twice to enquire about Barbara Franklin, and Nurse Craven, herself not in the best of tempers, had been tart and snappish with him. He had even been to the village and purchased a box of chocolates. This had been sent down. "Mrs. Franklin couldn't bear chocolates."

Rather disconsolately, he opened the box in the smoking room and Norton and I and he all solemnly helped ourselves.

Norton, I now think, had definitely something on his mind that morning. He was abstracted, once or twice his brows drew together as though he were puzzling over something.

He was fond of chocolates, and ate a good many in an abstracted fashion.

Outside, the weather had broken. Since ten o'clock the rain had been pouring down.

It had not the melancholy that sometimes accompanies a wet day. Actually it was a relief to us all.

Poirot had been brought down by Curtiss about midday and ensconced in the drawing room. Here Elizabeth Cole had joined him and was playing the piano to him. She had a pleasant touch, and played Bach and Mozart, both favourite composers of my friend's.

Franklin and Judith came up from the garden about a quarter to one. Judith looked white and strained. She was very silent, looked vaguely about her as though lost in a dream and then went away. Franklin sat down with us. He, too, looked tired and absorbed, and he had, too, the air of a man very much on edge.

I said, I remember, something about the rain being a relief, and he said quickly: "Yes. There are times when *something's* got to break. . . ."

And somehow I got the impression that it was not merely of the weather that he spoke. Awkward as always in his movements, he jerked against the table and upset half the chocolates. With his usual startled air, he apologized—apparently to the box.

"Oh, sorry."

It ought to have been funny, but somehow it wasn't. He bent quickly and picked up the spilt chocolates.

Norton asked him if he had had a tiring morning.

His smile flashed out then—eager, boyish, very much alive.

"No—no—just realized, suddenly, I've been on the wrong track. Much simpler process altogether is what's needed. Can take a shortcut now."

He stood swaying slightly to and fro on his feet, his eyes absent yet resolved.

"Yes, shortcut. Much the best way."

III

If we were all nervy and aimless in the morning, the afternoon was unexpectedly pleasant. The sun came out, the temperature was cool and fresh. Mrs. Luttrell was brought down and sat on the veranda. She was in excellent form—exercising her charm and manner with less gush than usual, and with no latent hint of vinegar in reserve. She chaffed her husband, but gently and with a kind of affection, and he beamed at her. It was really delightful to see them on such good terms.

Poirot permitted himself to be wheeled out also, and he was in good spirits too. I think he liked seeing the Luttrells on such a friendly footing with each other. The Colonel was looking years younger. His manner seemed less vacillating, he tugged less at his moustache. He even suggested that there might be some bridge that evening.

"Daisy here misses her bridge."

"Indeed I do," said Mrs. Luttrell.

Norton suggested it would be tiring for her.

"I'll play one rubber," said Mrs. Luttrell, and added with a twinkle: "And I'll behave myself and not bite poor George's head off."

"My dear," protested her husband, "I know I'm a shocking player."

"And what of that?" said Mrs. Luttrell. "Doesn't it give me grand pleasure badgering and bullying you about it?"

It made us all laugh. Mrs. Luttrell went on: "Oh, I know my faults, but I'm not going to give them up at my time of life. George has just got to put up with me."

Colonel Luttrell looked at her quite fatuously.

I think it was seeing them both on such good terms that led to a discussion on marriage and divorce that took place later in the day.

Were men and women actually happier by reason of the greater facilities afforded for divorce, or was it often the case that a temporary period of irritation and estrangement—or trouble over a third person—gave way after a while to a resumption of affection and friendliness?

It is odd sometimes to see how much at variance people's ideas are with their own personal experiences.

My own marriage had been unbelievably happy and successful, and I am essentially an old-fashioned person, yet I was on the side of divorce—of cutting one's losses and starting afresh. Boyd Carrington, whose marriage had been unhappy, yet held for an indissoluble marriage bond. He had, he said, the utmost reverence for the institution of marriage. It was the foundation of the state.

Norton, with no ties and no personal angle, was of my way of thinking. Franklin, the modern scientific thinker, was, strangely enough, resolutely opposed to divorce. It offended, apparently, his ideal of clear-cut thinking and action. One assumed certain responsibilities. Those must be carried through and not shirked or set aside. A contract, he said, is a contract. One enters upon it of one's own free will, and must abide by it. Anything else resulted in what he called a mess. Loose ends, half-dissolved ties.

Leaning back in his chair, his long legs kicking vaguely at a table, he said: "A man chooses his wife. She's his responsibility until she dies—or he does."

Norton said rather comically: "And sometimes—Oh blessed death, eh?"

We laughed, and Boyd Carrington said: "You needn't talk, my lad, you've never been married."

Shaking his head, Norton said: "And now I've left it too late."

"Have you?" Boyd Carrington's glance was quizzical. "Sure of that?"

It was just at that moment that Elizabeth Cole joined us. She had been up with Mrs. Franklin.

I wondered if it was my fancy, or did Boyd Carrington look meaningly from her to Norton, and was it possible that Norton blushed?

It put a new idea into my head and I looked searchingly at Elizabeth Cole. It was true that she was still a comparatively young woman. Moreover she was quite a handsome one. In fact a very charming and sympathetic person who was capable of making any man happy. And she and Norton had spent a good deal of time together of late. In their hunts for wildflowers and birds, they had become friends; I remembered how she had spoken of Norton being such a kind person.

Well, if so, I was glad for her sake. Her starved and barren girlhood would not stand in the way of her ultimate happiness. The tragedy that had shattered her life would not have been enacted in vain. I thought, looking at her, that she certainly looked much happier and—yes, gayer, than when I had first come to Styles.

Elizabeth Cole and Norton—yes, it might be.

And suddenly, from nowhere, a vague feeling of uneasiness and disquiet assailed me. It was not safe—it was not right—to plan happiness here. There was something malignant about the air of Styles. I felt it now—this minute, felt suddenly old and tired—yes, and afraid.

A minute later the feeling passed. Nobody had noticed it, I think, except Boyd Carrington. He said to me in an undertone a few minutes later: "Anything the matter, Hastings?"

"No, why?"

"Well—you looked—I can't quite explain it."

"Just a feeling—apprehension."

"A premonition of evil?"

"Yes, if you like to put it that way. A feeling that—that something was going to happen."

"Funny. I've felt that once or twice. Any idea *what?*"

He was watching me narrowly.

I shook my head. For indeed I had had no definite apprehension of any particular thing. It had only been a wave of deep depression and fear.

Then Judith had come out of the house. She had come slowly, her head held high, her lips pressed together, her face grave and beautiful.

I thought how unlike she was to either me or Cinders. She looked like some young priestess. Norton felt something of that too. He said to her: "You look like your namesake might have looked before she cut off the head of Holofernes."

Judith smiled and raised her eyebrows a little. "I can't remember now why she wanted to."

"Oh, strictly on the highest moral grounds for the good of the community."

The light banter in his tone annoyed Judith. She flushed and went past him to sit by Franklin. She said: "Mrs. Franklin is feeling much better. She wants us all to come up and have coffee with her this evening."

IV

Mrs. Franklin was certainly a creature of moods, I thought, as we trooped upstairs after dinner. Having made everyone's life unbearable all day, she was now sweetness itself to everybody.

She was dressed in a negligee of pale eau-de-Nil and was lying on her chaise longue. Beside her was a small revolving bookcase-table with the coffee apparatus set out. Her fingers, deft and white, dealt with the ritual of coffee making, with some slight aid from Nurse Craven. We were all there with the exception of Poirot who always retired before dinner, Allerton who had not returned from Ipswich, and Mrs. and Colonel Luttrell who had remained downstairs.

The aroma of coffee came to our noses—a delicious smell. The coffee at Styles was an uninteresting muddy fluid, so we all looked forward to Mrs. Franklin's brew with freshly ground berries.

Franklin sat on the other side of the table handing the cups as she filled them. Boyd Carrington stood by the foot of the sofa, Elizabeth Cole and Norton were by the window. Nurse Craven had retired to the background by the head of the bed. I was sitting in an armchair wrestling with *The Times* crossword, and reading out the clues.

"Even love or third party risk?" I read out. "Eight letters."

"Probably an anagram," said Franklin.

We thought for a minute. I went on. "The chaps between the hills are unkind."

"Tormentor," said Boyd Carrington quickly.

"Quotation: 'And Echo whate'er is asked her answers'—blank. Tennyson. Five letters."

"Where," suggested Mrs. Franklin. "Surely that's right. 'And Echo answers where?' "

I was doubtful. "It would make a word end in 'W'."

"Well, lots of words end in 'W.' How and now and snow."

Elizabeth Cole said from the window: "The Tennyson quotation is: 'And Echo whate'er is asked her answers Death.' "

I heard a quick sharp intake of breath behind me. I looked up. It was Judith. She went past us to the window and out upon the balcony.

I said, as I wrote the last clue in: "Even love can't be an anagram. The second letter now is 'A.' "

"What's the clue again?"

"Even love or third party risk? Blank A and six blanks."

"Paramour," said Boyd Carrington.

I heard the teaspoon rattle on Barbara Franklin's saucer. I went on to the next clue.

" 'Jealousy is a green-eyed monster,' this person said."

"Shakespeare," said Boyd Carrington.

"Was it Othello or Emilia?" said Mrs. Franklin.

"All too long. The clue is only four letters."

"Iago."

"I'm *sure* it was Othello."

"It wasn't in *Othello* at all. Romeo said it to Juliet."

We all voiced our opinions. Suddenly from the balcony Judith cried out: "Look, a shooting star. Oh, there's another."

Boyd Carrington said: "Where? We must wish." He went out on the balcony, joining Elizabeth Cole, Norton and Judith. Nurse Craven went out too. Franklin got up and joined them. They stood there, exclaiming, gazing out into the night.

I remained with my head bent over the crossword. Why should *I* wish to see a falling star? I had nothing to wish for. . . .

Suddenly Boyd Carrington wheeled back into the room.

"Barbara, you must come out."

Mrs. Franklin said sharply: "No, I can't. I'm too tired."

"Nonsense, Babs. You must come and wish!" He laughed. "Now don't protest. I'll carry you."

And suddenly stooping he picked her up in his arms. She laughed and protested: "Bill, put me down—don't be so silly."

"Little girls have got to come out and wish." He carried her through the window and set her down on the balcony.

I bent closer over the paper. For I was remembering . . . A clear tropical night, frogs croaking . . . and a shooting star. I was standing there by the window, and I had turned and picked up Cinders and carried her out in my arms to see the stars and wish. . . .

The lines of my crossword ran and blurred before my eyes.

A figure detached itself from the balcony and came into the room—Judith.

Judith must never catch me with tears in my eyes. It would never do. Hastily I swung round the bookcase and pretended to be looking for a book. I remembered having seen an old edition of Shakespeare there. Yes, here it was. I looked through *Othello*.

"What are you doing, Father?"

I mumbled something about the clue, my fingers turning over the pages. Yes, it was Iago.

"O beware, my lord, of jealousy;
It is the green-eyed monster which doth mock
The meat it feeds on."

Judith went on with some other lines:

"Not poppy, nor mandragora, nor all the drowsy syrups of the world
Shall ever medicine thee to that sweet sleep which thouow'dst yesterday."

Her voice rang out, beautiful and deep.

The others were coming back, laughing and talking. Mrs. Franklin resumed her place on the chaise longue, Franklin came back to his seat and stirred his coffee. Norton and Elizabeth Cole finished drinking theirs and excused themselves as they had promised to play bridge with the Luttrells.

Mrs. Franklin drank her coffee and then demanded her "drops." Judith got them for her from the bathroom as Nurse Craven had just gone out.

Franklin was wandering aimlessly round the room. He stumbled over a small table. His wife said sharply:

"Don't be so clumsy, John."

"Sorry, Barbara. I was thinking of something."

Mrs. Franklin said rather affectedly: "Such a great bear, aren't you, darling?"

He looked at her rather abstractedly. Then he said: "Nice night, think I'll take a stroll."

He went out.

Mrs. Franklin said: "He *is* a genius, you know. You can tell it from his manner. I really do admire him terrifically. Such a passion for his work."

"Yes, yes, clever fellow," said Boyd Carrington rather perfunctorily.

Judith left the room abruptly, nearly colliding with Nurse Craven in the doorway.

Boyd Carrington said: "What about a game of picquet, Babs?"

"Oh, lovely. Can you get hold of some cards, Nurse?"

Nurse Craven went to get cards, and I wished Mrs. Franklin good night and thanked her for the coffee.

Outside I overtook Franklin and Judith. They were standing looking out of the passage window. They were not speaking, just standing side by side.

Franklin looked over his shoulder as I approached. He moved a step or two, hesitated and said: "Coming out for a stroll, Judith?"

My daughter shook her head. "Not tonight." She added abruptly: "I'm going to bed. Good night."

I went downstairs with Franklin. He was whistling softly to himself and smiling.

I remarked rather crossly, for I was feeling depressed myself: "You seem pleased with yourself tonight."

He admitted it.

"Yes. I've done something that I've been meaning to do for a long time. Very satisfactory, that."

I parted from him downstairs, and looked in on the bridge players for a minute. Norton winked at me when Mrs. Luttrell wasn't looking. The rubber seemed to be progressing with unusual harmony.

Allerton had still not come back. It seemed to me that the house was happier and less oppressive without him.

I went up to Poirot's room. I found Judith sitting with him. She smiled at me when I came in and did not speak.

"She has forgiven you, *mon ami,*" said Poirot—an outrageous remark.

"Really," I spluttered. "I hardly think—"

Judith got up. She put an arm round my neck and kissed me. She said: "Poor Father. Uncle Hercule shall *not* attack your dignity. *I* am the one to be forgiven. So forgive me and say good night."

I don't quite know why, but I said: "I'm sorry, Judith. I'm very sorry, I didn't mean—"

She stopped me. "That's all right. Let's forget it. Everything's all right now." She smiled a slow, faraway smile. She said again: "Everything's all right now . . ." and quietly left the room.

When she had gone Poirot looked at me.

"Well?" he demanded. "What has been happening this evening?"

I spread out my hands. "Nothing has happened, or is likely to happen," I told him.

Actually I was very wide of the mark. For something did happen that night. Mrs. Franklin was taken violently ill. Two more doctors were sent for, but in vain. She died the following morning.

It was not until twenty-four hours later that we learned that her death was due to poisoning by physostigmine.

Fourteen

I

The inquest took place two days later. It was the second time I had attended an inquest in this part of the world.

The coroner was an able middle-aged man with a shrewd glance and a dry manner of speech.

The medical evidence was taken first. It established the fact that death was the result of poisoning by physostigmine, and that other alkaloids of the Calabar bean were also present. The poison must have been taken some time on the preceding evening between seven o'clock and midnight. The police surgeon and his colleague refused to be more precise.

The next witness was Dr. Franklin. He created on the whole a good impression. His evidence was clear and simple. After his wife's death he had checked over his solutions in the laboratory. He had discovered that a certain bottle, which should have contained a strong solution of alkaloids of the Calabar bean with which he had been conducting experiments, had been filled up with ordinary water in which only a trace of the original contents was present. He could not say with certainty when this had been done as he had not used that particular preparation for some days.

The question of access to the laboratory was then gone into. Dr. Franklin agreed that the laboratory was usually kept locked and that he usually had the key in his pocket. His assistant, Miss Hastings, had a duplicate key. Anyone who wished to go into the studio had to get the key from her or from himself. His wife had borrowed it occasionally, when she had left things belonging to her in the laboratory. He himself had never brought a solution of physostigmine into the house or into his wife's room and he thought that by no possibility could she have taken it accidentally.

Questioned further by the coroner, he said that his wife had for some time been in a low and nervous state of health. There was no organic disease. She suffered from depression and from a rapid alteration of moods.

Of late, he said, she had been cheerful and he had considered her improved in health and spirits. There had been no quarrel between them and they had been on good terms. On the last evening his wife had seemed in good spirits and not melancholy.

He said that his wife had occasionally spoken of ending her life but that he had not taken her remarks seriously. Asked the question definitely, he replied that in his opinion his wife had not been a suicidal type. That was his medical opinion as well as his personal one.

He was followed by Nurse Craven. She looked smart and efficient in her trim uniform and her replies were crisp and professional. She had been in attendance on Mrs. Franklin for over two months. Mrs. Franklin suffered badly from depression. Witness had heard her say at least three times that she "wanted to end it all," that her life was useless and that she was a millstone round her husband's neck.

"Why did she say that? Had there been any altercation between them?"

"Oh no, but she was aware that her husband had recently been offered an appointment abroad. He had refused that in order not to leave her."

"And sometimes she felt morbidly about the fact?"

"Yes. She would blame her miserable health, and get all worked up."

"Did Dr. Franklin know about this?"

"I do not think she often said so to him."

"But she was subject to fits of depression."

"Oh, definitely."

"Did she ever specifically mention committing suicide?"

"I think 'I want to end it all' was the phrase she used."

"She never suggested any particular method of taking her own life?"

"No. She was quite vague."

"Had there been anything especially to depress her of late?"

"No. She had been in reasonably good spirits."

"Do you agree with Dr. Franklin that she was in good spirits on the night of her death?"

Nurse Craven hesitated. "Well—she was excited. She'd had a bad day—complained of pain and giddiness. She had seemed better in the evening, but her good spirits were a bit unnatural. She seemed feverish and rather artificial."

"Did you see anything of a bottle, or anything that might have contained the poison?"

"No."

"What did she eat and drink?"

"She had soup, a cutlet, green peas and mashed potatoes, and cherry tart. She had a glass of burgundy with it."

"Where did the burgundy come from?"

"There was a bottle in her room. There was some left afterwards but I believe it was examined and found to be quite all right."

"Could she have put the drug in her glass without you seeing?"

"Oh yes, easily. I was to and fro in the room, tidying up and arranging things. I was not watching her. She had a little despatch case beside her and also a handbag. She could have put anything in the burgundy, or later in the coffee, or in the hot milk she had last thing."

"Have you any idea as to what she could have done with the bottle or container if so?"

Nurse Craven considered. "Well, I suppose she could have thrown it out of the window later. Or put it in the wastepaper basket, or even washed it out in the bathroom and put it back in the medicine cupboard. There are several empty bottles there. I save them because they come in handy."

"When did you last see Mrs. Franklin?"

"At ten-thirty. I settled her for the night. She had hot milk and said she'd like an aspirin."

"How was she then?"

The witness considered a minute.

"Well, really, just as usual . . . No, I'd say she was perhaps just a bit over-excited."

"Not depressed?"

"Well, no, more strung up, so to speak. But if it's suicide you're thinking of, it might take her that way. She might feel noble or exalted about it."

"Do you consider she was a likely person to take her own life?"

There was a pause. Nurse Craven seemed to be struggling to make up her mind.

"Well," she said at last, "I do and I don't. I—yes, on the whole I do. She was very unbalanced."

Sir William Boyd Carrington came next. He seemed genuinely upset, but gave his evidence clearly.

He had played picquet with the deceased on the night of her death. He had not noticed any signs of depression then, but in a conversation some days previously Mrs. Franklin had mentioned the subject of taking her own life. She was a very unselfish woman, and deeply distressed at feeling that she was hampering her husband's career. She was devoted to her husband and very ambitious for him. She was sometimes very depressed about her own health.

Judith was called, but she had little to say.

She knew nothing about the removal of the physostigmine from the laboratory. On the night of the tragedy Mrs. Franklin had seemed to her much as usual, though perhaps overexcited. She had never heard Mrs. Franklin mention suicide.

The last witness was Hercule Poirot. His evidence was given with much emphasis and caused a considerable impression. He described a conversation he had had with Mrs. Franklin on the day previous to her decease. She had been very depressed and had expressed several times a wish to be out of it all. She was worried about her health and had confided in him that she had fits of deep melancholy when life did not seem worth living. She said that sometimes she felt it would be wonderful to go to sleep and never wake up.

His next reply caused an even greater sensation.

"On the morning of June 10th you were sitting outside the laboratory door?"

"Yes."

"Did you see Mrs. Franklin come out of the laboratory?"

"I did."

"Did she have anything in her hand?"

"She had a small bottle clasped in her right hand."

"You are quite sure of that?"

"Yes."

"Did she show any confusion at seeing you?"

"She looked startled, that is all."

The coroner proceeded to his summing up. They must make up their minds, he said, how the deceased came to her death. They would have no difficulty in assigning the cause of death, the medical evidence had told them that. Deceased was poisoned by physostigmine sulphate. All they had to decide was whether she took it accidentally or by intent, or if it was administered to her by some other person. They had heard that the deceased had fits of melancholy, that she was in poor health, and that while there was no organic disease, she was in a bad nervous condition. Mr. Hercule Poirot, a witness whose name must carry weight, had asserted positively that he had seen Mrs. Franklin come out of the laboratory with a small bottle in her hand and that she seemed startled to see him. They might come to the conclusion that she had taken the poison from the laboratory with the intention of doing away with herself. She seemed to be suffering from an obsession that she was standing in her husband's light and obstructing his career. It was only fair to Dr. Franklin to say that he seemed to have been a kind and affectionate husband, and that he had never expressed annoyance at her delicacy, or complained that she hindered his career. The idea seemed to be entirely her own. Women in a certain condition of nervous collapse did get these persistent ideas. There was no evidence to show at what time or in what vehicle the poison was taken. It was, perhaps, a little unusual that the bottle which originally contained the poison had not been found, but it was possible that, as Nurse Craven suggested, Mrs. Franklin had washed it and put it away in the bathroom cupboard from where she may have originally taken it. It was for the jury to make their own decision.

The verdict was arrived at after only a short delay.

The jury found that Mrs. Franklin took her own life while temporarily of unsound mind.

II

Half an hour later I was in Poirot's room. He was looking very exhausted. Curtiss had put him to bed and was reviving him with a stimulant.

I was dying to talk but I had to contain myself until the valet had finished and left the room.

Then I burst out. "Was that true, Poirot, what you said? That you saw a bottle in Mrs. Franklin's hand when she came out of the laboratory?"

A very faint smile crept over Poirot's bluish-tinged lips. He murmured: "Did not *you* see it, my friend?"

"No, I did not."

"But you might not have noticed, *hein?*"

"No, perhaps not. I certainly can't swear she didn't have it." I looked at him doubtfully. "The question is, are you speaking the truth?"

"Do you think I would lie, my friend?"

"I wouldn't put it past you."

"Hastings, you shock and surprise me. Where is now your simple faith?"

"Well," I conceded. "I don't suppose you would really commit perjury."

Poirot said mildly: "It would not be perjury. It was not on oath."

"Then it was a lie?"

Poirot waved his hand automatically. "What I have said, *mon ami,* is said. It is unnecessary to discuss it."

"I simply don't understand you!" I cried.

"What don't you understand?"

"Your evidence—all that about Mrs. Franklin's having talked about committing suicide, about her being depressed."

"*Enfin,* you heard her say such things yourself."

"Yes. But it was only one of many moods. You didn't make that clear."

"Perhaps I did not want to."

I stared at him. "You *wanted* the verdict to be suicide?"

Poirot paused before replying. Then he said: "I think, Hastings, that you do not appreciate the gravity of the situation. Yes, if you like, I wanted the verdict to be suicide. . . ."

I said: "But you didn't think—yourself—that she did commit suicide?"

Slowly Poirot shook his head.

I said: "You think—that she was murdered?"

"Yes, Hastings, she was murdered."

"Then why try to hush it up, to have it labelled and put aside as suicide? That stops all enquiry."

"Precisely."

"You want that?"

"Yes."

"But *why?*"

"Is it conceivable that you do not see? Never mind—let us not go into that. You must take my word for it that it *was* murder—deliberate preconceived murder. I told you, Hastings, that a crime would be committed here, and that it was unlikely we should be able to prevent it—for the killer is both ruthless and determined."

I shivered. I said: "And what happens next?"

Poirot smiled. "The case is solved—labelled and put away as suicide. But you and I, Hastings, go on working underground, like moles. And, sooner or later, *we get X.*"

I said: "And supposing that, meanwhile, someone else is killed?"

Poirot shook his head. "I do not think so. Unless, that is, somebody saw something or knows something, but if so, surely, they would have come forward to say so . . . ?"

Fifteen

I

My memory is a little vague about the events of the days immediately following the inquest on Mrs. Franklin. There was, of course, the funeral, which I may say was attended by a large number of the curious of Styles St. Mary. It was on that occasion that I was addressed by an old woman with rheumy eyes and an unpleasant ghoulish manner.

She accosted me just as we were filing out of the cemetery.

"Remember you, sir, don't I?"

"Well—er—possibly. . . ."

She went on, hardly listening to what I said.

"Twenty years ago and over. When the old lady died up at the Court. That was the first murder we had at Styles. Won't be the last, I say. Old Mrs. Inglethorp, her husband done her in so we all said. Sure of it we was." She leered at me cunningly. "Maybe it's the husband this time."

"What do you mean?" I said sharply. "Didn't you hear the verdict was suicide?"

"That's what Coroner said. But he might be wrong, don't you think?" She nudged me. "Doctors, they know how to do away with their wives. And she wasn't much good to him seemingly."

I turned on her angrily and she slunk away murmuring she hadn't meant anything, only it seemed odd like, didn't it, happening a second time. "And it's queer you should be there both times, sir, isn't it now?"

For one fantastic moment I wondered if she suspected me of having really committed both crimes. It was most disturbing. It certainly made me realize what a queer, haunting thing local suspicion is.

And it was not, after all, so far wrong. For somebody had killed Mrs. Franklin.

As I say I remember very little of those days. Poirot's health, for one thing, was giving me grave concern. Curtiss came to me with his wooden face slightly disturbed and reported that Poirot had had a somewhat alarming heart attack.

"Seems to me, sir, he ought to see a doctor."

I went posthaste to Poirot who negatived the suggestion most vigorously. It was, I thought, a little unlike him. He had always been, in my opinion, extremely fussy about his health. Distrusting draughts, wrapping up his neck in silk and wool, showing a horror of getting his feet damp, and taking his temperature and retiring to bed at the least suspicion of a chill—"For otherwise it may be for me a *fluxion de poitrine!*" In most little ailments, he had, I knew, always consulted a doctor immediately.

Now, when he was really ill, the position seemed reversed.

Yet perhaps that was the real reason. Those other ailments *had* been trifling. Now, when he was indeed a sick man, he feared, perhaps, admitting the reality of his illness. He made light of it because he was afraid.

He answered my protests with energy and bitterness.

"Ah, but I have consulted doctors! Not one but many. I have been to Blank and to Dash [he named two specialists] and they do what?—they send me to Egypt where immediately I am rendered much worse. I have been, too, to R. . . ."

R. was, I knew, a heart specialist. I asked quickly: "What did he say?"

Poirot gave me a sudden sidelong glance—and my heart gave an agonized leap.

He said quietly: "He has done for me all that can be done. I have my treatments, my remedies, all close at hand. Beyond that—there is nothing. So you see, Hastings, to call in more doctors would be of no avail. The machine, *mon ami,* wears out. One cannot, alas, install the new engine and continue to run as before like a motor car."

"But look here, Poirot, surely there's something. Curtiss—"

Poirot said sharply: "Curtiss?"

"Yes, he came to me. He was worried—You had an attack—"

Poirot nodded gently. "Yes, yes. They are sometimes, these attacks, painful to witness. Curtiss, I think, is not used to these attacks of the heart."

"Won't you really see a doctor?"

"It is of no avail, my friend."

He spoke very gently but with finality. And again my heart felt a painful constriction. Poirot smiled at me. He said: "This, Hastings, will be my last case. It will be, too, my most interesting case—and my most interesting criminal. For in X we have a technique superb, magnificent, that arouses admiration in spite of oneself. So far, *mon cher,* this X has operated with so much ability that he has defeated me, Hercule Poirot! He has developed the attack to which I can find no answer."

"If you had your health—" I began soothingly.

But apparently that was not the right thing to say. Hercule Poirot immediately flew into a rage.

"Ah! Have I got to tell you thirty-six times, and then again thirty-six, that there is no need of *physical* effort? One needs only—to think."

"Well—of course—yes, you can do that all right."

"All right? I can do it superlatively. My limbs they are paralysed, my heart, it plays me the tricks, but my brain, Hastings, my brain it functions without impairment of any kind. It is still of the first excellence my brain."

"That," I said soothingly, "is splendid."

But as I went slowly downstairs, I thought to myself that Poirot's brain was not getting on with things as fast as it might do. First the narrow escape of Mrs. Luttrell and now the death of Mrs. Franklin. And what were we doing about it? Practically nothing.

II

It was the following day that Poirot said to me: "You suggested, Hastings, that I should see a doctor."

"Yes," I said eagerly. "I'd feel much happier if you would."

"*Eh bien,* I will consent. I will see Franklin."

"Franklin?" I looked doubtful.

"Well, he is a doctor, is he not?"

"Yes, but—his main line is research, is it not?"

"Undoubtedly. He would not succeed, I fancy, as a general practitioner. He has not sufficiently what you call the 'side of the bed manner.' But he has the qualifications. In fact I should say that, as the films say, 'he knows his stuff better than most.'"

I was still not entirely satisfied. Although I did not doubt Franklin's ability, he had always struck me as a man who was impatient of and uninterested in human ailments. Possibly an admirable attitude for research work, but not so good for any sick persons he might attend.

However, for Poirot to go so far was a concession, and as Poirot had no local medical attendant, Franklin readily agreed to take a look at him. But he explained that if regular medical attendance was needed, a local practitioner must be called in. He could not attend the case.

Franklin spent a long time with him.

When he came out finally I was waiting for him. I drew him into my room and shut the door.

"Well?" I demanded anxiously.

Franklin said thoughtfully: "He's a very remarkable man."

"Oh, that. Yes—" I brushed aside this self-evident fact. "But his health?"

"Oh! His health?" Franklin seemed quite surprised—as though I had mentioned something of no importance at all. "Oh! His health's rotten, of course."

It was not, I felt, at all a professional way of putting it. And yet I had heard—from Judith—that Franklin had been one of the most brilliant students of his time.

"How bad is he?" I demanded anxiously.

He shot me a look. "D'you want to know?"

"Of course."

What did the fool think?

He almost immediately told me.

"Most people," he said, "don't want to know. They want soothing syrup.

They want hope. They want reassurance ladled out in driblets. And of course amazing recoveries *do* occur. But they won't in Poirot's case."

"Do you mean—" Again that cold hand closed round my heart.

Franklin nodded. "Oh yes, he's for it all right. And pretty soon, I should say. I shouldn't tell you so if he hadn't authorized me to do so."

"Then—he knows."

Franklin said: "He knows all right. That heart of his may go out—phut— any moment. One can't say, of course, exactly *when*."

He paused, then he said slowly: "From what he says, I gather he's worrying about getting something finished, something that, as he puts it, he's undertaken. D'you know about that?"

"Yes," I said. "I know."

Franklin shot me an interested glance.

"He wants to be sure of finishing off the job."

"I see."

I wondered if John Franklin had any idea of what that job was!

He said slowly: "I hope he'll manage it. From what he said it means a lot to him." He paused and added: "He's got a methodical mind."

I asked anxiously: "Isn't there something that can be done—something in the way of treatment—"

He shook his head. "Nothing doing. He's got ampoules of amyl nitrate to use when he feels an attack is coming on."

Then he said a rather curious thing.

"Got a very great respect for human life, hasn't he?"

"Yes, I suppose he has."

How often had I not heard Poirot say: "I do not approve of murder." That understatement, made so primly, had always tickled my fancy.

Franklin was going on. "That's the difference between us. *I* haven't . . . !"

I looked at him curiously. He inclined his head with a faint smile.

"Quite true," he said. "Since death comes anyway, what does it matter if it comes early or late? There's so little difference."

"Then what on earth made you become a doctor if you feel like that?" I demanded with some indignation.

"Oh, my dear fellow, doctoring isn't just a matter of dodging the ultimate end. It's a lot more—it's improving *living*. If a healthy man dies, it doesn't matter—much. If an imbecile—a cretin—dies, it's a good thing—but if by the discovery of administering the correct gland you turn your cretin into a healthy normal individual by correcting his thyroid deficiency, that, to my mind, matters a good deal."

I looked at him with more interest. I still felt that it would not be Dr. Franklin I should call in if I had influenza, but I had to pay tribute to a kind of white-hot sincerity and a very real force in the man. I had noticed a change in him since his wife's death. He had displayed few of the conventional signs of mourning. On the contrary he seemed more alive, less absentminded, and full of a new energy and fire.

He said abruptly, breaking into my thoughts: "You and Judith aren't much alike, are you?"

"No, I suppose we're not."

"Is she like her mother?"

I reflected, then slowly shook my head. "Not really. My wife was a merry, laughing creature. She wouldn't take anything seriously—and tried to make me the same, without much success I'm afraid."

He smiled faintly. "No, you're rather the heavy father, aren't you? So Judith says. Judith doesn't laugh much—serious young woman. Too much work, I expect. My fault."

He went into a brown study. I said conventionally: "Your work must be very interesting."

"Eh?"

"I said your work must be interesting."

"Only to about half a dozen people. To everybody else it's darned dull—and they're probably right. Anyway—" he flung his head back, his shoulders squared themselves, he suddenly looked what he was, a powerful and virile man—"I've got my chance now! God, I could shout out loud. The Minister Institute people let me know today. The job's still open and I've got it. I start in ten days' time."

"For Africa?"

"Yes. It's grand."

"So soon." I felt slightly shocked.

He stared at me. "What do you mean—*soon?* Oh." His brow cleared. "You mean after Barbara's death? Why on earth not? It's no good pretending, is it, that her death wasn't the greatest relief to me."

He seemed amused by the expression on my face.

"I've not time, I'm afraid, for conventional attitudes. I fell in love with Barbara—she was a very pretty girl—married her and fell out of love with her again in about a year. I don't think it lasted even as long as that with her. I was a disappointment to her, of course. She thought she could influence me. She couldn't. I'm a selfish, pigheaded sort of brute, and I do what I want to do."

"But you did refuse this job in Africa on her account," I reminded him.

"Yes. That was purely financial, though. I'd undertaken to support Barbara in the way of life she was accustomed to. If I'd gone it would have meant leaving her very short. But now—" he smiled, a completely frank, boyish smile—"it's turned out amazingly lucky for me."

I was revolted. It is true, I suppose, that many men whose wives die are not precisely heartbroken and everyone more or less knows the fact. But this was so blatant.

He saw my face, but did not seem put out.

"Truth," he said, "is seldom appreciated. And yet it saves a lot of time and a lot of inaccurate speech."

I said sharply: "And it doesn't worry you at all that your wife committed suicide?"

He said thoughtfully: "I don't really believe she did commit suicide. Most unlikely—"

"But, then, what do you think happened?"

He caught me up: "I don't know. I don't think I—want to know. Understand?"

I stared at him. His eyes were hard and cold.

He said again: "I don't want to know. I'm not—interested. See?"

I did see—but I didn't like it.

III

I don't know when it was that I noticed that Stephen Norton had something on his mind. He had been very silent after the inquest, and after that and the funeral were over he still walked about, his eyes on the ground and his forehead puckered. He had a habit of running his hands through his short grey hair until it stuck up on end like Struwwelpeter. It was comical but quite unconscious and denoted some perplexity of his mind. He returned absentminded answers when you spoke to him, and it did at last dawn upon me that he was definitely worried about something. I asked him tentatively if he had had bad news of any kind, which he promptly negatived. That closed the subject for the time being.

But a little later he seemed to be trying to get an opinion from me on some matter in a clumsy, roundabout way.

Stammering a little, as he always did when he was serious about a thing, he embarked on an involved story centring about a point of ethics.

"You know, Hastings, it should be awfully simple to say when a thing's right or wrong—but really when it comes to it, it isn't quite such plain sailing. I mean, one may come across something—the kind of thing, you see, that isn't meant for you—it's all a kind of accident, and it's the sort of thing you couldn't take advantage of, and yet it might be most frightfully important. Do you see what I mean?"

"Not very well, I'm afraid," I confessed.

Norton's brow furrowed again. He ran his hands up through his hair again so that it stood upright in its usual comical manner.

"It's so hard to explain. What I mean is, suppose you just happened to see something in a private letter—one opened by mistake, that sort of thing—a letter meant for someone else and you began reading it because you thought it was written to you and so you actually read something you weren't meant to before you realized. That could happen, you know."

"Oh yes, of course it could."

"Well, I mean, what would one do?"

"Well—" I gave my mind to the problem. "I suppose you'd go to the person and say, 'I'm awfully sorry but I opened this by mistake.' "

Norton sighed. He said it wasn't quite so simple as that.

"You see, you might have read something rather embarrassing, Hastings."

"That would embarrass the other person, you mean? I suppose you'd have to pretend you hadn't actually read anything—that you'd discovered your mistake in time."

"Yes." Norton said it after a moment's pause, and he did not seem to feel that he had yet arrived at a satisfactory solution.

He said rather wistfully: "I wish I did know what I ought to do."

I said that I couldn't see that there was anything else he could do.

Norton said, the perplexed frown still on his forehead: "You see, Hastings, there's rather more to it than that. Supposing that what you read was—well, rather important, to someone else again, I mean."

I lost patience. "Really, Norton, I don't see what you do mean. You can't go about reading other people's private letters, can you?"

"No, no, of course not. I didn't mean that. And anyway, it wasn't a letter at all. I only said that to try and explain the sort of thing. Naturally anything you saw or heard or read—by accident—you'd keep to yourself, unless—"

"Unless what?"

Norton said slowly: "Unless it was something you *ought* to speak about."

I looked at him with suddenly awakened interest. He went on: "Look here, think of it this way, supposing you saw something through a—a keyhole—"

Keyholes made me think of Poirot! Norton was stumbling on:

"What I mean is, you'd got a perfectly good reason for looking through the keyhole—the key might have stuck and you just looked to see if it was clear—or—or some quite good reason—and you never for one minute expected to see what you did see. . . ."

For a moment or two I lost thread of his stumbling sentences, for enlightenment had come to me. I remembered a day on a grassy knoll and Norton swinging up his glasses to see a speckled woodpecker. I remembered his immediate distress and embarrassment, his endeavours to prevent me from looking through the glasses in my turn. At the moment I had leaped to the conclusion that what he had seen was something to do with *me*—in fact that it was Allerton and Judith. But supposing that that was not the case? That he had seen something quite different? I had assumed that it was something to do with Allerton and Judith because I was so obsessed by them at that time that I could think of nothing else.

I said abruptly: "Was it something you saw through those glasses of yours?"

Norton was both startled and relieved.

"I say, Hastings, how did you guess?"

"It was that day when you and I and Elizabeth Cole were up on that knoll, wasn't it?"

"Yes, that's right."

"And you didn't want me to see?"

"No. It wasn't—well, I mean it wasn't meant for any of us to see."

"What was it?"

Norton frowned again. "That's just it. Ought I to say? I mean it was—well, it was spying. I saw something I wasn't meant to see. I wasn't looking for it—there really was a speckled woodpecker—a lovely fellow, and then I saw the other thing."

He stopped. I was curious, intensely curious, yet I respected his scruples.

I asked: "Was it—something that mattered?"

He said slowly: "It might matter. That's just it. I don't know."

I asked then: "Has it something to do with Mrs. Franklin's death?"

He started. "It's queer you should say that."

"Then it has?"

"No—no, not directly. But it might have." He said slowly: "It would throw a different light on certain things. It would mean that—Oh, damn it all, *I* don't know what to do!"

I was in a dilemma. I was agog with curiosity, yet I felt that Norton was very reluctant to say what he had seen. I could understand that. I should have felt the same myself. It is always unpleasant to come into possession of a piece of information that has been acquired in what the outside world would consider a dubious manner.

Then an idea struck me.

"Why not consult Poirot?"

"Poirot?" Norton seemed a little doubtful.

"Yes, ask his advice."

"Well," said Norton slowly, "it's an idea. Only, of course, he's a foreigner—" he stopped, rather embarrassed.

I knew what he meant. Poirot's scathing remarks on the subject of "playing the game" were only too familiar to me. I only wondered that Poirot had never thought of taking to bird glasses himself! He would have done it if he had thought of it.

"He'd respect your confidence," I urged. "And you needn't act upon his advice if you don't like it."

"That's true," said Norton, his brow clearing. "You know, Hastings, I think that's just what I will do."

IV

I was astonished at Poirot's instant reaction to my piece of information.

"What is that you say, Hastings?"

He dropped the piece of thin toast he had been raising to his lips. He poked his head forward.

"Tell me. Tell me quickly."

I repeated the story.

"He saw something through the glasses that day," repeated Poirot thoughtfully. "Something that he will not tell you." His hand shot out and gripped my arm. "He has not told anyone else of this?"

"I don't think so. No, I'm sure he hasn't."

"Be very careful, Hastings. It is urgent that he should not tell anyone—he must not even hint. To do so might be dangerous."

"Dangerous?"

"Very dangerous."

Poirot's face was grave. "Arrange with him, *mon ami,* to come up and see me this evening. Just an ordinary friendly little visit, you understand. Do not let anyone else suspect that there is any special reason for his coming. And be careful, Hastings, be very, very careful. Who else did you say was with you at the time?"

"Elizabeth Cole."

"Did she notice anything odd about his manner?"

I tried to recollect. "I don't know. She may have. Shall I ask her if—?"

"You will say nothing, Hastings—absolutely nothing."

Sixteen

I

I gave Norton Poirot's message.

"I'll go up and see him, certainly. I'd like to. But you know, Hastings, I'm rather sorry I mentioned the matter even to you."

"By the way," I said, "you haven't said anything to anyone else about it, have you?"

"No—at least—no, of course not."

"You're quite sure?"

"No, no, I haven't said anything."

"Well, don't. Not until after you've seen Poirot."

I had noticed the slight hesitation in his tone when he first answered, but his second assurance was quite firm. I was to remember that slight hesitation afterwards, though.

II

I went up again to the grassy knoll where we had been on that day. Someone else was there already. Elizabeth Cole. She turned her head as I came up the slope.

She said: "You look very excited, Captain Hastings. Is anything the matter?"

I tried to calm myself.

"No, no, nothing at all. I'm just out of breath with walking fast." I added in an everyday, commonplace voice: "It's going to rain."

She looked up at the sky. "Yes, I think it is."

We stood there silent for a minute or two. There was something about this woman that I found very sympathetic. Ever since she had told me who she really was, and the tragedy that had ruined her life, I had taken an interest in her. Two people who have suffered unhappiness have a great bond in common. Yet for her there was, or so I suspected, a second spring. I said now impulsively: "Far from being excited, I'm depressed today. I've had bad news about my dear old friend."

"About M. Poirot?"

Her sympathetic interest led me to unburden myself.

When I had finished she said softly: "I see. So—the end might come at any time?"

I nodded, unable to speak.

After a minute or two I said: "When he's gone I shall indeed be alone in the world."

"Oh, no, you've got Judith—and your other children."

"They're scattered over the world, and Judith—well, she's got her work, she doesn't need me."

"I suspect that children don't ever need their parents until they are in trouble of some kind. I should make up your mind to that as to some fundamental law. I'm far more lonely than you are. My two sisters are far away, one in America and one in Italy."

"My dear girl," I said. "You're life's beginning."

"At thirty-five?"

"What's thirty-five? I wish I were thirty-five." I added maliciously: "I'm not quite blind, you know."

She turned an enquiring glance on me, then blushed.

"You don't think—oh! Stephen Norton and I are only friends. We've got a good deal in common—"

"All the better."

"He's—he's just awfully kind."

"Oh, my dear," I said. "Don't believe it's all kindness. We men aren't made that way."

But Elizabeth Cole had turned suddenly white. She said in a low, strained voice: "You're cruel—blind! How can I ever think of—of marriage? With my history. With my sister a murderess—or if not that, insane. I don't know which is worse."

I said strongly: "Don't let that prey on your mind. Remember, it may not be true."

"What do you mean? It is true."

"Don't you remember saying to me once, 'That wasn't Maggie?' "

She caught her breath. "One feels like that."

"What one feels is often—true."

She stared at me. "What do you mean?"

"Your sister," I said, "did not kill her father."

Her hand crept up to her mouth. Her eyes, wide and scared, looked into mine.

"You're mad," she said. "You must be mad. Who told you that?"

"Never mind," I said. "It's true. Some day I'll prove it to you."

III

Near the house I ran into Boyd Carrington.

"This is my last evening," he told me. "I move out tomorrow."

"To Knatton?"

"Yes."

"That's very exciting for you."

"Is it? I suppose it is." He gave a sigh. "Anyway, Hastings, I don't mind telling you, I shall be glad to leave here."

"The food is certainly pretty bad and the service isn't good."

"I don't mean that. After all, it's cheap, and you can't expect much from these paying-guest places. No, Hastings, I mean more than discomfort. I don't like this house—there's some malign influence about it. Things happen here."

"They certainly do."

"I don't know what it is. Perhaps a house that has once had a murder in it is never quite the same afterwards . . . But I don't like it. First there was that accident to Mrs. Luttrell—a damned unlucky thing to happen. And then there was poor little Barbara." He paused. "The most unlikely person in the world to have committed suicide *I* should have said."

I hesitated. "Well, I don't know that I'd go as far as that—"

He interrupted me. "Well, I would. Hang it all, I was with her most of the day before. She was in good spirits—enjoyed our outing. The only thing she was worrying about was whether John wasn't getting too much wrapped up in his experiments and might overdo things, or try some of his messes upon himself. Do you know what I think, Hastings?"

"No."

"That husband of hers is the one who's responsible for her death. Nagged at her, I expect. She was always happy enough when she was with me. He let her see that she handicapped his precious career (I'd give him a career!) and it broke her up. Damned callous, that fellow, hasn't turned a hair. Told me as cool as anything he was off to Africa now. Really, you know, Hastings, I shouldn't be surprised if he'd actually murdered her."

"You don't mean that," I said sharply.

"No—no, I don't really. Though, mind you, mainly because I can see that if he murdered her, he wouldn't do it that way. I mean, he was known to be working on this stuff physostigmine, so it stands to reason if he'd done her in, he wouldn't have used that. But all the same, Hastings, I'm not the only one to think that Franklin's a suspicious character. I had the tip from someone who ought to know."

"Who was that?" I asked sharply.

Boyd Carrington lowered his voice. "Nurse Craven."

"What?" I was intensely surprised.

"Hush. Don't shout. Yes, Nurse Craven put the idea into my head. She's a smart girl, you know, got her wits about her. She doesn't like Franklin—hasn't liked him all along."

I wondered. I should have said that it was her own patient whom Nurse

Craven had disliked. It occurred to me suddenly that Nurse Craven must know a good deal about the Franklin ménage.

"She's staying here tonight," said Boyd Carrington.

"What?" I was rather startled. Nurse Craven had left immediately after the funeral.

"Just for a night between cases," explained Boyd Carrington.

"I see."

I was vaguely disquieted by Nurse Craven's return, yet I could hardly have said why. Was there, I wondered, any reason for her coming back? She didn't like Franklin, Boyd Carrington had said. . . .

Reassuring myself I said with sudden vehemence: "She's no right to hint things about Franklin. After all, it was her evidence that helped to establish suicide. That, and Poirot's seeing Mrs. Franklin coming out of the studio with a bottle in her hand."

Boyd Carrington snapped: "What's a bottle? Women are always carrying bottles—scent bottles, hair lotion, nail polish. That wench of yours was running about with a bottle in her hand that evening—it doesn't mean *she* was thinking of suicide, does it? Nonsense!"

He broke off as Allerton came up to us. Most appropriately, in melodramatic fashion, there was a low rumble of thunder in the distance. I reflected, as I had reflected before, that Allerton was certainly cast for the part of the villain.

But he had been away from the house on the night of Barbara Franklin's death. And besides, what possible motive could he have had?

But then, I reflected, X never had a motive. That was the strength of his position. It was that, and that only, that was holding us up. And yet, at any minute, that tiny flash of illumination might come.

IV

I think that here and now I should like to place on record that I had never, all through, considered for one moment that Poirot might fail. In the conflict between Poirot and X I had never contemplated the possibility that X might come out victor. In spite of Poirot's feebleness and ill health, I had faith in him as potentially the stronger of the two. I was used, you see, to Poirot's succeeding.

It was Poirot himself who first put a doubt into my head.

I went in to see him on my way down to dinner. I forget now exactly what led to it, but he suddenly used the phrase "if anything happens to me."

I protested immediately and loudly. Nothing would happen—nothing could happen.

"*Eh bien,* then you have not listened carefully to what Dr. Franklin told you."

"Franklin doesn't know. You're good for many a long year yet, Poirot."

"It is possible, my friend, though extremely unlikely. But I speak now in the particular and not the general sense. Though I may die very soon, it may still be not soon enough to suit our friend X."

"What?" My face showed my shocked reaction.

Poirot nodded. "But yes, Hastings. X is, after all, intelligent. In fact, most intelligent. And X cannot fail to perceive that my elimination, even if it were only to precede natural decease by a few days, might be of inestimable advantage."

"But then—but then—what would happen?" I was bewildered.

"When the Colonel falls, *mon ami,* the second in command takes over. You will continue."

"How can I? I'm entirely in the dark."

"I have arranged for that. If anything happens to me, my friend, you will find here—" he patted the locked despatch case by his side—"all the clues you need. I have arranged, you see, for every eventuality."

"There is really no need to be clever. Just tell me now everything there is to know."

"No, my friend. The fact that you do not know what I know is a valuable asset."

"You have left me a clearly written account of things?"

"Certainly not. X might get hold of it."

"Then what have you left?"

"Indications in kind. They will mean nothing to X—be assured of that— but they will lead you to the discovery of the truth."

"I'm not so sure of that. Why must you have such a tortuous mind, Poirot? You always like making everything difficult. You always have!"

"And it is now with me a passion? Is that what you would say? Perhaps. But rest assured, my indications will lead you to the truth." He paused. Then he said: "And perhaps, then, you would wish that they had not led you so far. You would say instead: 'Ring down the curtain.' "

Something in his voice started again that vague unformulated dread that I had once or twice felt spasms of already. It was as though somewhere, just out of sight, was a fact that I did not want to see—that I could not bear to acknowledge. Something that already, deep down, *I knew.* . . .

I shook the feeling off and went down to dinner.

Seventeen

I

Dinner was a reasonably cheerful meal. Mrs. Luttrell was down again and in her best vein of artificial Irish gaiety. Franklin was more animated and cheerful than I had yet seen him. Nurse Craven I saw for the first time in mufti instead of her nurse's uniform. She was certainly a very attractive young woman now that she had cast off her professional reserve.

After dinner Mrs. Luttrell suggested bridge, but in the end some round games were started. About half past nine Norton declared his intention of going up to see Poirot.

"Good idea," said Boyd Carrington. "Sorry he's been under the weather lately. I'll come up too."

I had to act quickly.

"Look here," I said, "do you mind—it really tires him too much to talk to more than one person at a time."

Norton took the cue and said quickly: "I promised to lend him a book on birds."

Boyd Carrington said: "All right. You coming back again, Hastings?"

"Yes."

I went up with Norton. Poirot was waiting. After a word or two I came down again. We began playing rummy.

Boyd Carrington, I think, resented the carefree atmosphere of Styles tonight. He thought, perhaps, that it was too soon after the tragedy for everyone to forget. He was absentminded, forgot frequently what he was doing, and at last excused himself from further play.

He went to the window and opened it. The sound of thunder could be heard in the distance. There was a storm about although it had not yet reached us. He closed the window again and came back. He stood for a minute or two watching us play. Then he went out of the room.

I went up to bed at a quarter to eleven. I did not go in to Poirot. He might be asleep. Moreover I felt a reluctance to think anymore about Styles and its problems. I wanted to sleep—to sleep and forget.

I was just dropping off when a sound wakened me. I thought it might have been a tap on my door. I called "Come in," but as there was no response, I switched the light on and, getting up, looked out into the corridor.

I saw Norton just coming from the bathroom and going into his own room. He wore a checked dressing gown of particularly hideous colouring and his hair was sticking up on end as usual. He went into his room and shut the door, and immediately afterwards I heard him turn the key in the lock.

Overhead there was a low rumbling of thunder. The storm was coming nearer.

I went back to bed with a slightly uneasy feeling induced by the sound of that turning key.

It suggested, very faintly, sinister possibilities. Did Norton usually lock his door at night, I wondered? Had Poirot warned him to do so? I remembered with sudden uneasiness how Poirot's door key had mysteriously disappeared.

I lay in bed and my uneasiness grew whilst the storm overhead added to my feeling of nerviness. I got up at last and locked my own door. Then I went back to bed and slept.

II

I went in to Poirot before going down to breakfast.

He was in bed and I was struck again by how ill he looked. Deep lines of weariness and fatigue were on his face.

"How are you, old boy?"

He smiled patiently at me. "I exist, my friend. I still exist."

"Not in pain?"

"No—just tired—" he sighed—"very tired."

I nodded. "What about last night? Did Norton tell you what he saw that day?"

"He told me, yes."

"What was it?"

Poirot looked at me long and thoughtfully before he replied: "I am not sure, Hastings, that I had better tell you. You might misunderstand."

"What are you talking about?"

"Norton," said Poirot, "tells me he saw two people—"

"Judith and Allerton," I cried. "I thought so at the time."

"*Eh bien, non.* Not Judith and Allerton. Did I not tell you you would misunderstand? You are a man of one idea!"

"Sorry," I said, a little abashed. "Tell me."

"I will tell you tomorrow. I have much on which I wish to reflect."

"Does it—does it help with the case?"

Poirot nodded. He closed his eyes, leaning back in his pillows.

"The case is ended. Yes, it is ended. There are only some loose ends to be tied. Go down to breakfast, my friend. And as you go, send Curtiss to me."

I did so and went downstairs. I wanted to see Norton. I was deeply curious to know what it was that he had told Poirot.

Subconsciously I was still not happy. The lack of elation in Poirot's manner struck me disagreeably. Why this persistent secrecy? Why that deep inexplicable sadness? What was the *truth* of all this?

Norton was not at breakfast.

I strolled out into the garden afterwards. The air was fresh and cool after the storm. I noticed that it had rained heavily. Boyd Carrington was on the lawn. I felt pleased to see him and wished that I could take him into my confidence. I had wanted to all along. I was very tempted to do so now. Poirot was really unfit to carry on by himself.

This morning Boyd Carrington looked so vital, so sure of himself, that I felt a wave of warmth and reassurance.

"You're late up this morning," he said.

I nodded. "I slept late."

"Bit of a thunderstorm last night. Hear it?"

I remembered now that I had been conscious of the rolling of thunder through my sleep.

"I felt a bit under the weather last night," said Boyd Carrington. "I feel a lot better today." He stretched his arms out and yawned.

"Where's Norton?" I asked.

"Don't think he's up yet. Lazy devil."

With common accord we raised our eyes. Where we were standing the windows of Norton's room were just above us. I started. For alone in the façade of windows Norton's were still shuttered.

I said: "That's odd. Do you think they've forgotten to call him?"

"Funny. Hope he's not ill. Let's go up and see."

We went up together. The housemaid, a rather stupid-looking girl, was in the passage. In answer to a question she replied that Mr. Norton hadn't answered when she knocked. She'd knocked once or twice but he hadn't seemed to hear. His door was locked.

A nasty foreboding swept over me. I rapped loudly on the door, calling as I did so: "Norton—Norton. Wake up!"

And again with growing uneasiness: "Wake up. . . ."

III

When it was apparent that there was going to be no answer we went and found Colonel Luttrell. He listened to us with a vague alarm showing in his faded blue eyes. He pulled uncertainly at his moustache.

Mrs. Luttrell, always the one for prompt decisions, made no bones about it.

"You'll have to get that door open somehow. There's nothing else for it."

For the second time in my life, I saw a door broken open at Styles. Behind that door was what had been behind a locked door on the first occasion. *Death by violence.*

Norton was lying on his bed in his dressing gown. The key of the door was in the pocket. In his hand was a small pistol, a mere toy, but capable of doing its work. There was a small hole in the exact centre of his forehead.

For a moment or two I could not think of what I was reminded. Something, surely very old. . . .

I was too tired to remember.

As I came into Poirot's room he saw my face.

He said quickly: "What has happened? Norton?"

"Dead!"

"How? When?"

Briefly I told him.

I ended wearily: "They say it's suicide. What else can they say? The door was locked. The windows were shuttered. The key was in his pocket. Why! I actually saw him go in and heard him lock the door."

"You saw him, Hastings?"

"Yes, last night."

I explained.

"You're sure it was Norton?"

"Of course. I'd know that awful old dressing gown anywhere."

For a moment Poirot became his old self.

"Ah, but it is a *man* you are identifying, not a *dressing gown. Ma foi!* Anyone can wear a dressing gown."

"It's true," I said slowly, "that I didn't see his face. But it was his hair all right, and that slight limp—"

"Anyone could limp, *mon Dieu!*"

I looked at him, startled. "Do you mean to suggest, Poirot, that it *wasn't* Norton that I saw?"

"I am not suggesting anything of the kind. I am merely annoyed by the unscientific reasons you give for saying it was Norton. No, no, I do not for one minute suggest that it was *not* Norton. It would be difficult for it to be anyone else, for every man here is tall—very much taller than he was—and *enfin* you cannot disguise height—that, no. Norton was only five foot five, I should say. *Tout de même,* it is like a conjuring trick, is it not? He goes into his room, locks the door, puts the key in his pocket, and is found shot with the pistol in his hand and the key still in his pocket."

"Then you don't believe," I said, "that he shot himself?"

Slowly Poirot shook his head. "No," he said. "Norton did not shoot himself. He was deliberately killed."

IV

I went downstairs in a daze. The thing was so inexplicable I may be forgiven, I hope, for not seeing the next inevitable step. I was dazed. My mind was not working properly.

And yet it was so logical. Norton had been killed—why? To prevent, or so I believed, his telling what he had seen.

But he had confided that knowledge to one other person.

So that person, too, was in danger. . . .

And was not only in danger, but was helpless.

I *should* have known.

I *should* have foreseen. . . .

"*Cher ami!*" Poirot had said to me as I left the room.

They were the last words I was ever to hear him say. For when Curtiss came to attend to his master he found that master dead. . . .

Eighteen

I

I don't want to write about it at all.

I want, you see, to think about it as little as possible. Hercule Poirot was dead—and with him died a good part of Arthur Hastings.

I will give you the bare facts without embroidery. It is all I can bear to do.

He died, they said, of natural causes. That is to say he died of a heart attack. It was the way, so Franklin said, that he had expected him to go. Doubtless the shock of Norton's death brought one on. By some oversight, it seems, the amyl nitrate ampoules were not by his bed.

Was it an oversight? Did someone deliberately remove them? No, it must have been something more than that. X could not count on Poirot's having a heart attack.

For, you see, I refuse to believe that Poirot's death was natural. He was killed, as Norton was killed, as Barbara Franklin was killed. And I don't know *why* they were killed—and I don't know who killed them!

There was an inquest on Norton and a verdict of suicide. The only point of doubt was raised by the surgeon who said it was unusual for a man to shoot himself in the exact centre of his forehead. But that was the only shadow of doubt. The whole thing was so plain. The door locked on the inside, the key in the dead man's pocket, the windows closely shuttered, the pistol in his hand. Norton had complained of headaches, it seemed, and some of his investments had been doing badly lately. Hardly reasons for suicide, but they had to put forward something.

The pistol was apparently his own. It had been seen lying on his dressing-table twice by the housemaid during his stay at Styles. So that was that. Another crime beautifully stage-managed and as usual with no alternative solution.

In the duel between Poirot and X, X had won.

It was now up to me.

I went to Poirot's room and took away the despatch box.

I knew that he had made me his executor, so I had a perfect right to do so. The key was round his neck.

In my own room I opened the box.

And at once I had a shock. *The dossiers of X's cases were gone.* I had seen them there only a day or two previously when Poirot unlocked it. That was proof, if I had been needing it, that X had been at work. Either Poirot had destroyed those papers himself (most unlikely) or else X had done so.

X. X. That damned fiend X.

But the case was not empty. I remembered Poirot's promise that I should find other indications which X would not know about.

Were these the indications?

There was a copy of one of Shakespeare's plays, *Othello,* in a small cheap edition. The other book was the play *John Fergueson* by St. John Ervine. There was a marker in it at the third act.

I stared at the two books blankly.

Here were the clues that Poirot had left for me—and they meant nothing to me at all!

What *could* they mean?

The only thing I could think of was a *code* of some kind. A word code based on the plays.

But if so, how was I to get at it?

There were no words, no letters, underlined anywhere. I tried gentle heat with no result.

I read the third act of *John Fergueson* carefully through. A most admirable and thrilling scene where the "wanting" Clutie John sits and talks, and which ends with the younger Fergueson going out to seek for the man who has wronged his sister. Masterly character drawing—but I could hardly think that Poirot had left them to improve my taste in literature!

And then, as I turned the leaves of the book over, a slip of paper fell out. It bore a phrase in Poirot's handwriting.

"*Talk to my valet George.*"

Well, here was something. Possibly the key to the code—if code it was—had been left with George. I must get hold of his address and go to see him.

But first there was the sad business of burying my dear friend.

Here was the spot where he had lived when he first came to this country. He was to lie here at the last.

Judith was very kind to me in these days.

She spent a lot of time with me and helped to make all the arrangements. She was gentle and sympathetic. Elizabeth Cole and Boyd Carrington were very kind too.

Elizabeth Cole was less affected by Norton's death than I should have thought. If she felt any deep grief she kept it to herself.

And so it was all ended. . . .

II

Yes, I must put it down.

It must be said.

The funeral was over. I was sitting with Judith, trying to make a few sketchy plans for the future.

She said then: "But you see, dear, *I shan't be here.*"

"Not here?"

"*I shan't be in England.*"

I stared at her.

"I haven't liked to tell you before, Father. I didn't want to make things worse for you. But you've got to know now. I hope you won't mind too much. I'm going to Africa, you see, with Dr. Franklin."

I burst out at that. It was impossible. She couldn't do a thing like that.

Everyone would be bound to talk. To be an assistant to him in England and especially when his wife was alive was one thing, but to go abroad with him to Africa was another. It was impossible and I was going to forbid it absolutely. Judith must not do such a thing!

She didn't interrupt. She let me finish. She smiled very faintly.

"But, dearest," she said, "I'm not going as his assistant. I'm going as his wife."

It hit me between the eyes.

I said—or rather stammered: "Al—Allerton?"

She looked faintly amused. "There was never anything in that. I would have told you so if you hadn't made me so angry. Besides, I wanted you to think, well—what you did think. I didn't want you to know it was—John."

"But I saw him kiss you one night—on the terrace."

She said impatiently: "Oh, I daresay. I was miserable that night. These things happen. Surely you know that?"

I said: "You can't marry Franklin yet—so soon."

"Yes, I can. I want to go out with him, and you've just said yourself it's easier. We've nothing to wait for—now."

Judith and Franklin. Franklin and Judith.

Do you understand the thoughts that came into my mind—the thoughts that had lain under the surface for some time?

Judith with a bottle in her hand, Judith with her young passionate voice declaring that useless lives should go to make way for useful ones—Judith whom I loved and whom Poirot also had loved. Those two people that Norton had seen—had they been Judith and *Franklin?* But if so—if so—no, that couldn't be true. Not Judith. Franklin, perhaps—a strange man, a ruthless man, a man who if he made up his mind to murder, might murder again and again.

Poirot had been willing to consult Franklin.

Why? What had he said to him that morning?

But not Judith. Not my lovely grave young Judith.

And yet how strange Poirot had looked. How those words had rung out: "You may prefer to say 'Ring down the curtain . . . ' "

And suddenly a fresh idea struck me. Monstrous! Impossible! Was the whole story of X a fabrication? Had Poirot come to Styles because he feared a tragedy in the Franklin ménage? Had he come to watch over Judith? Was *that* why he had resolutely told me nothing? Because the whole story of X was a fabrication, a smoke screen?

Was the whole heart of the tragedy Judith, my daughter?

Othello! It was *Othello* I had taken from the bookcase that night when Mrs. Franklin had died. Was that the clue?

Judith that night looking, so someone had said, like her namesake before she cut off the head of Holofernes. Judith—with death in her heart?

Nineteen

I am writing this in Eastbourne.

I came to Eastbourne to see George, formerly Poirot's valet.

George had been with Poirot many years. He was a competent matter-of-fact man, with absolutely no imagination. He always stated things literally and took them at their face value.

Well, I went to see him. I told him about Poirot's death and George reacted as George would react. He was distressed and grieved and managed very nearly to conceal the fact.

Then I said: "He left you, did he not, a message for me?"

George said at once: "For you, sir? No, not that I am aware of."

I was surprised. I pressed him, but he was quite definite.

I said at last: "My mistake, I suppose. Well, that's that. I wish you had been with him at the end."

"I wish so, too, sir."

"Still I suppose if your father was ill you had to come to him."

George looked at me in a very curious manner. He said: "I beg your pardon, sir, I don't quite understand you."

"You had to leave in order to look after your father, isn't that right?"

"I didn't wish to leave, sir. M. Poirot sent me away."

"Sent you away?" I stared.

"I don't mean, sir, that he discharged me. The understanding was that I was to return to his service later. But I left by his wish, and he arranged for suitable remuneration whilst I was here with my old father."

"But why, George, why?"

"I really couldn't say, sir."

"Didn't you ask?"

"No, sir. I didn't think it was my place to do so. M. Poirot always had his ideas, sir. A very clever gentleman, I always understood, sir, and very much respected."

"Yes, yes," I murmured abstractedly.

"Very particular about his clothes, he was—though given to having them rather foreign and fancy if you know what I mean. But that, of course, is understandable as he was a foreign gentleman. His hair, too, and his moustache."

"Ah, those famous moustaches." I felt a twinge of pain as I remembered his pride in them.

"Very particular about his moustache, he was," went on George. "Not very fashionable the way he wore it, but it suited *him,* sir, if you know what I mean."

I said I did know. Then I murmured delicately: "I suppose he dyed it as well as his hair?"

"He did—er—touch up his moustache a little—but not his hair—not of late years."

"Nonsense," I said. "It was as black as a raven—looked quite like a wig it was so unnatural."

George coughed apologetically. "Excuse me, sir, it was a wig. M. Poirot's hair came out a good deal lately, so he took to a wig."

I thought how odd it was that a valet knew more about a man than his closest friend did.

I went back to the question that puzzled me.

"But have you really no idea why M. Poirot sent you away as he did? Think, man, *think.*"

George endeavoured to do so, but he was clearly not very good at thinking.

"I can only suggest, sir," he said at last, "that he discharged me because he wanted to engage Curtiss."

"Curtiss? Why should he want to engage Curtiss?"

George coughed again. "Well, sir, I really cannot say. He did not seem to me, when I saw him, as a—excuse me—particularly bright specimen, sir. He was strong physically, of course, but I should hardly have thought that he was quite the class M. Poirot would have liked. He'd been assistant in a mental home at one time, I believe."

I stared at George.

Curtiss!

Was that the reason why Poirot had insisted on telling me so little? Curtiss, the one man I had never considered! Yes, and Poirot was content to have it so, to have me combing the guests at Styles for the mysterious X. But X was *not* a guest.

Curtiss!

One-time assistant in a mental home. And hadn't I read somewhere that people who have been patients in mental homes and asylums sometimes remain or go back there as assistants?

A queer, dumb, stupid-looking man—a man who might kill for some strange warped reason of his own. . . .

And if so—if so. . . .

Why, then a great cloud would roll away from me!

Curtiss . . . ?

Postscript

Note by Captain Arthur Hastings: The following manuscript came into my possession four months after the death of my friend Hercule Poirot. I received a communication from a firm of lawyers asking me to call at their office. There "in accordance with the instructions of their client, the late M. Hercule Poirot," they handed me a sealed packet. I reproduce its contents here.

Manuscript written by Hercule Poirot:

"Mon cher ami,

"*I shall have been dead four months when you read these words. I have debated long whether or not to write down what is written here, and I have decided that it is necessary for someone to know the truth about the second 'Affaire Styles.' Also I hazard a conjecture that by the time you read this you will have evolved the most preposterous theories—and possibly may be giving pain to yourself.*

"*But let me say this: You should, mon ami, have easily been able to arrive at the truth. I saw to it that you had every indication. If you have not, it is because, as always, you have far too beautiful and trusting a nature. A la fin comme au commencement.*

"*But you should know, at least, who killed Norton—even if you are still in the dark as to who killed Barbara Franklin. The latter may be a shock to you.*

"To begin with, as you know, I sent for you. I told you that I needed you. That was true. I told you that I wanted you to be my ears and my eyes. That again was true, very true—if not in the sense that you understood it! You were to see what I wanted you to see and hear what I wanted you to hear.

"You complained, cher ami, that I was 'unfair' in my presentation of this case. I withheld from you knowledge that I had myself. That is to say, I refused to tell you the identity of X. That is quite true. I had to do so—though not for the reasons that I advanced. You will see the reason presently.

"And now let us examine this matter of X. I showed you the résumé of the various cases. I pointed out to you that in each separate case it seemed quite clear that the person accused, or suspected, had actually committed the crimes in question, that there was no alternate solution. And I then proceeded to the second important fact—that in each case X had been either on the scene or closely involved. You then jumped to a deduction that was, paradoxically, both true and false. You said that X had committed all the murders.

"But, my friend, the circumstances were such that in each case (or very nearly) only the accused person could have done the crime. On the other hand, if so, how account for X? Apart from a person connected with the police force or with, say, a firm of criminal lawyers, it is not reasonable for any man or woman to be involved in five murder cases. It does not, you comprehend, happen! Never, never does it occur that someone says confidentially: 'Well, as a matter of fact, I've actually known five murderers!' No, no, mon ami, it is not possible, that. So we get the curious result that we have here a case of catalysis—a reaction between two substances that takes place only in the presence of a third substance, that third substance apparently taking no part in the reaction and remaining unchanged. That is the position. It means that where X was present, crimes took place—but X did not actively take part in these crimes.

"An extraordinary, an abnormal situation! And I saw that I had come across at last, at the end of my career, the perfect criminal, the criminal who had invented such a technique that he could never be convicted of crime.

"It was amazing. But it was not new. There were parallels. And here comes in the first of the 'clues' I left you. The play of Othello. For there, magnificently delineated, we have the original X. Iago is the perfect murderer. The deaths of Desdemona, of Cassio—indeed of Othello himself—are all Iago's crimes, planned by him, carried out by him. *And* he *remains outside the circle, untouched by suspicion—or could have done so. For your great Shakespeare, my friend, had to deal with the dilemma that his own art had brought about. To unmask Iago he had to resort to the clumsiest of devices—the handkerchief—a piece of work not at all in keeping with Iago's general technique and a blunder of which one feels certain he would not have been guilty.*

"*Yes, there is there the perfection of the art of murder. Not even a word of direct suggestion. He is always holding back others from violence, refuting with horror suspicions that have not been entertained until he mentions them!*

"*And the same technique is seen in the brilliant third act of* John Fergueson, *where the 'half-witted' Clutie John induces others to kill the man that he himself hates. It is a wonderful piece of psychological suggestion.*

"*Now you must realize this, Hastings. Everyone is a potential murderer. In everyone there arises from time to time the* wish *to kill—though not the* will *to kill. How often have you not felt or heard others say: 'She made me so furious I felt I could have killed her!' 'I could have killed B. for saying so and so!' 'I was so angry I could have murdered him!' And all those statements are literally true. Your mind at such moments is quite clear. You would like to kill so and so. But you do not do it. Your will has to assent to your desire. In young children, the brake is as yet acting imperfectly. I have known a child, annoyed by its kitten, say 'Keep still or I'll hit you on the head and kill you' and actually do so—to be stunned and horrified a moment later when it realizes that the kitten's life will not return—because, you see, really the child loves that kitten dearly. So then, we are all potential murderers. And the art of X was this, not to suggest the* desire, *but to break down the normal decent resistance. It was an art perfected by long practice. X knew the exact word, the exact phrase, the intonation even to suggest and to bring cumulative pressure on a weak spot! It could be done. It was done without the victim ever suspecting. It was not hypnotism—hypnotism would not have been successful. It was something more insidious, more deadly. It was a marshalling of the forces of a human being to widen a breach instead of repairing it. It called on the best in a man and set it in alliance with the worst.*

"You *should know, Hastings—for it happened to you . . .*

"*So now, perhaps, you begin to see what some of my remarks, that annoyed and confused you, really meant. When I spoke of a crime to be committed, I was not always referring to the same crime. I told you that I was at Styles for a purpose. I was there, I said, because a crime was going to be committed. You were surprised at my certainty on that point. But I was able to be certain—for the crime, you see, was to be committed by myself. . . .*

"*Yes, my friend—it is odd—and laughable—and terrible! I, who do not approve of murder—I, who value human life—have ended my career by committing murder. Perhaps it is because I have been too self-righteous, too conscious of rectitude, that this terrible dilemma had to come to me. For you see, Hastings, there are two sides to it. It is my work in life to save the innocent—to prevent murder—and this— this is the only way I can do it! Make no mistake, X could not be touched by the law. He was safe. By no ingenuity that I could think of could he be defeated any other way.*

"*And yet, my friend, I was reluctant. I saw what had to be done—but I could not bring myself to do it. I was like Hamlet—eternally putting off the evil day . . . And then the next attempt happened—the attempt on Mrs. Luttrell.*

"*I had been curious, Hastings, to see if your well-known flair for the obvious would work. It did. Your very first reaction was a mild suspicion of Norton. And you were quite right. Norton was the man. You had no reason for your belief—except the perfectly sound if slightly halfhearted suggestion that he was insignificant. There, I think, you came very close to the truth.*

"*I have considered his life history with some care. He was the only son of a masterful and bossy woman. He seems to have had at no time any gift for asserting himself or for impressing his personality on other people. He has always been slightly lame and was unable to take part in games at school.*

"*One of the most significant things you told me was a remark about him having been laughed at at school for nearly being sick when seeing a dead rabbit. There, I think, was an incident that may have left a deep impression on him. He disliked blood and violence and his prestige suffered in consequence. Subconsciously, I should say, he has waited to redeem himself by being bold and ruthless.*

"*I should imagine that he began to discover quite young his own power for influencing people. He was a good listener, he had a quiet sympathetic personality. People liked him without, at the same time, noticing him very much. He resented this—and then made use of it. He discovered how ridiculously easy it was, by using the correct words and supplying the correct stimuli, to influence his fellow creatures. The only thing necessary was to understand them—to penetrate their thoughts, their secret reactions and wishes.*

"Can you realize, Hastings, that such a discovery might feed a sense of power? Here was he, Stephen Norton whom everyone liked and despised, and he would make people do things they didn't want to do—or (mark this) thought they did not want to do.

"I can visualize him, developing this hobby of his . . . And little by little developing a morbid taste for violence at secondhand. The violence for which he lacked physical stamina and for the lack of which he had been derided.

"Yes, his hobby grows and grows until it comes to be a passion, a necessity! It was a drug, Hastings—a drug that induced craving as surely as opium or cocaine might have done.

"Norton, the gentle-hearted, loving man, was a secret sadist. He was an addict of pain, of mental torture. There has been an epidemic of that in the world of late years—L'appétit vient en mangeant.

"It fed two lusts, the lust of the sadist and the lust of power. He, Norton, had the keys of life and of death.

"Like any other drug slave, he had to have his supply of the drug. He found victim after victim. I have no doubt there have been more cases than the five I actually tracked down. In each of those he played the same part. He knew Etherington, he stayed one summer in the village where Riggs lived and drank with Riggs in the local pub. On a cruise he met the girl Freda Clay and encouraged and played upon her half-formed conviction that if her old aunt died it would be really a good thing—a release for Auntie and a life of financial ease and pleasure for herself. He was a friend of the Litchfields, and when talking to him, Margaret Litchfield saw herself in the light of a heroine delivering her sisters from their life sentence of imprisonment. But I do not believe, Hastings, that any of these people would have done what they did—but for Norton's influence.

"And now we come to the events at Styles. I had been on Norton's tracks for some time. He became acquainted with the Franklins and at once I scented danger. You must understand that even Norton has to have a nucleus on which to work. You can only develop a thing of which the seed is already present. In Othello, for *instance, I have always been of the belief that already present in Othello's mind was the conviction (possibly correct) that Desdemona's love for him was the passionate unbalanced hero-worship of a young girl for a famous warrior and not the balanced love of a woman for Othello the man. He may have realized that Cassio was her true mate and that in time she would come to realize the fact.*

"The Franklins presented a most agreeable prospect to our Norton. All kinds of possibilities! You have doubtless realized by now, Hastings, (what anyone of sense could have seen perfectly plainly all along) that Franklin was in love with Judith and she with him. His brusqueness, his habit of never looking at her, of forsaking any attempt at courtesy, ought to have told you that the man was head over ears in love with her. But Franklin is a man of great strength of character and also of great rectitude. His speech is brutally unsentimental, but he is a man of very definite standards. In his code a man sticks to the wife he has chosen.

"Judith, as I should have thought even you could have seen, was deeply and unhappily in love with him. She thought you had grasped the fact that day you found her in the rose garden. Hence her furious outburst. Characters like hers cannot stand any expression of pity or sympathy. It was like touching a raw wound.

"Then she discovered that you thought it was Allerton she cared for. She let you think so, thereby shielding herself from clumsy sympathy and from a further probing of the wound. She flirted with Allerton as a kind of desperate solace. She knew exactly the type of man he was. He amused her and distracted her, but she never had the least feeling for him.

"Norton, of course, knew exactly how the wind lay. He saw possibilities in the Franklin trio. I may say that he started first on Franklin, but drew a complete blank. Franklin is the one type of man who is quite immune from Norton's type of insidious suggestion. Franklin has a clear-cut, black and white mind, with an exact knowledge of his own feeling—and a complete disregard for outside pressure. Moreover the great passion of his life is his work. His absorption in it makes him far less vulnerable.

"With Judith, Norton was far more successful. He played very cleverly on the theme of useless lives. It was an article of faith with Judith—and the fact that her secret desires were in accordance with it was a fact that she ignored stridently whilst Norton knew it to be an ally. He was very clever about it—taking himself the opposite point of view, gently ridiculing the idea that she would ever have the nerve to do such

a decisive action. 'It is the kind of thing that all young people say—but never do!' Such an old cheap jibe—and how often it works, Hastings! So vulnerable they are, these children! So ready, though they do not recognize it that way, to take a dare!

"And with the useless Barbara out of the way, then the road is clear *for Franklin and Judith. That was never said—that was never allowed to come into the open. It was stressed that the* personal *angle had nothing to do with it—nothing at all. For if Judith once recognized that it had, she would have reacted violently. But with a murder addict so far advanced as Norton, one iron in the fire is not enough. He sees opportunities for pleasure everywhere. He found one in the Luttrells.*

"Cast your mind back, Hastings. Remember the very first evening you played *bridge. Norton's remarks to you afterwards, uttered so loud that you were afraid Colonel Luttrell would hear. Of course! Norton meant* him *to hear! He never lost an opportunity of underlining it, rubbing it in—And finally his efforts culminated in success. It happened under your nose, Hastings, and you never saw how it was done. The foundations were already laid—the increasing sense of a burden borne, of shame at the figure he cut in front of other men, in a deep growing resentment against his wife.*

"Remember exactly what happened. Norton says he is thirsty. (Did he know *Mrs. Luttrell is in the house and will come upon the scene?) The Colonel reacts immediately as the openhanded host which he is by nature. He offers drinks. He goes to get them. You are all sitting outside the window. His wife arrives—there is the inevitable scene, which he knows is being overheard. He comes out. It might have been glossed over by a good pretence—Boyd Carrington could have done it well. (He has a certain amount of worldly wisdom and a tactful manner, though otherwise he is one of the most pompous and boring individuals that I have ever come across! Just the sort of man you* would admire!) You yourself could have acquitted yourself not *too badly. But Norton rushes into speech, heavily, fatuously, underlining tact until it screams to Heaven and makes things much worse. He babbles of bridge (more recalled humiliations), talks aimlessly of shooting incidents. And prompt on his cue, just as Norton intended, that old woolly-headed ass Boyd Carrington comes out with his story of an Irish batman who shot his brother—a story, Hastings, that* Norton told to Boyd Carrington, *knowing quite well that the old fool would bring it out as his own whenever suitably prompted. You see, the supreme suggestion will* not *come from* Norton. *Mon Dieu, non!*

"It is all set, then. The cumulative effect. The breaking point. Affronted in his instincts as a host, shamed before his fellow men, writhing under the knowledge that they are quite convinced he has not got the guts to do anything but submit meekly to bullying—and then the key words of escape. The rook rifle, accidents—man who shot his brother—and suddenly, bobbing up, his wife's head . . . 'quite safe—an accident . . . I'll show them . . . I'll show* her *. . . damn her! I wish she was dead . . . she* shall *be dead!'*

"He did not kill her, Hastings. Myself, I think that, even as he *fired, instinc-tively he missed* because he wanted to miss. *And afterwards—afterwards the evil spell was broken. She was his wife, the woman he loved in spite of everything.*

"One of Norton's crimes that did not quite come off.

"Ah, but his next attempt! Do you realize, Hastings, that it was you who came next? Throw your mind back—recall everything. You, my honest, kindly Hastings! He found every weak spot in your mind—yes, and every decent and conscientious one, too.*

"Allerton is the type of man you instinctively dislike and fear. He is the type of man that you think* ought *to be abolished. And everything you heard about him and thought about him was true. Norton tells you a certain story about him—an entirely true story as far as the facts go. (Though actually the girl concerned was a neurotic type and came of poor stock.)*

"It appeals to your conventional and somewhat old-fashioned instincts. This man is the villain, the seducer, the man who ruins girls and drives them to suicide! Norton induces Boyd Carrington to tackle you also. You are impelled to 'speak to Judith.' Judith, as could be predicted, immediately responds by saying she will do as she chooses with her life. That makes you believe the worst.*

"See now the different stops on which Norton plays. Your love for your child. The intense old-fashioned sense of responsibility that a man like you feels for his chil-dren. The slight self-importance of your nature: 'I must do something. It all depends on me.' Your feeling of helplessness owing to the lack of your wife's wise judgement. Your loyalty—I must not fail her. And, on the baser side, your vanity—through as-*

sociation with me you have learned all the tricks of the trade! And lastly, that inner feeling which most men have about their daughters—the unreasoning jealousy and dislike for the man who takes her away from him. Norton played, Hastings, like a virtuoso on all these themes. And you responded.

"You accept things too easily at their face value. You always have done. You accepted quite easily the fact that it was Judith to whom Allerton was talking in the summerhouse. Yet you did not see her, you did not even hear her speak. And incredibly, even the next morning, you still thought it was Judith. You rejoiced because she had 'changed her mind.'

"But if you had taken the trouble to examine the facts you would have discovered at once that there had never been any question of Judith going up to London that day! And you failed to make another most obvious inference. There was someone who was going off for the day—and who was furious at not being able to do so. Nurse Craven. Allerton is not a man who confines himself to the pursuit of one woman! His affair with Nurse Craven had progressed much farther than the mere flirtation he was having with Judith.

"No, stage management again by Norton.

"You saw Allerton and Judith kiss. Then Norton shoves you back round the corner. He doubtless knows quite well that Allerton is going to meet Nurse Craven in the summerhouse. After a little argument he lets you go but still accompanies you. The sentence you overhear Allerton speaking is magnificent for his purpose and he swiftly drags you away before you have a chance to discover that the woman is not Judith!

"Yes, the virtuoso! And your reaction is immediate, complete on all those themes! You responded. You made up your mind to do murder.

"But fortunately, Hastings, you had a friend whose brain still functioned. And not only his brain!

"I said at the beginning of this that if you have not arrived at the truth it is because you have too trusting a nature. You believe what is said to you. You believed what I said to you. . . .

"Yet it was all very easy for you to discover the truth. I had sent George away— why? I had replaced him with a less experienced and clearly much less intelligent *man—why? I was not being attended by a doctor—I who have always been careful about my health—I would not hear of seeing one—why?*

"Do you see now why you were necessary to me at Styles? *I had to have someone who* accepted what I said without question. *You accepted my statement that I came back from Egypt much worse than when I went. I did not. I came back very much better! You could have found out the fact if you had taken the trouble. But no, you* believed. *I sent away George because I could not have succeeded in making him think that I had suddenly lost all power in my limbs. George is extremely intelligent about what he sees. He would have known that I was shamming.*

"Do you understand, Hastings? *All the time that I was pretending to be helpless, and deceiving Curtiss,* I was not helpless at all. *I could walk—with a limp.*

"I heard you come up that evening. I heard you hesitate and then go into Allerton's room. And at once I was on the alert. I was already much exercised about your state of mind.

"I did not delay. I was alone. Curtiss had gone down to supper. I slipped out of my room and across the passage. I heard you in Allerton's bathroom. And promptly, my friend, in the manner you so much deplore, I dropped to my knees and looked through the keyhole of the bathroom door. One could see through it, fortunately, as there is a bolt and not a key on the inside.

"I perceived your manipulations with the sleeping tablets. I realized what your idea was.

"And so, my friend, I acted. I went back to my room. I made my preparations. When Curtiss came up I sent him to fetch you. You came, yawning and explaining that you had a headache. I made at once the big fuss—urged remedies on you. For the sake of peace you consented to drink a cup of chocolate. You gulped it down quickly so as to get away quicker.* But I, too, my friend, have some sleeping tablets.

"And so, you slept—slept until morning when you awoke your own sane self and were horrified at what you had so nearly done.

"You were safe now—one does not attempt these things twice—not when one has relapsed into sanity.

"But it decided me, Hastings! *For whatever I might not know about other people did not apply to you. You are not a murderer, Hastings! But you might have been hanged for one—for a murder committed by another man who in the eyes of the law would be guiltless.*

"*You, my good, my honest, my oh so honourable Hastings—so kindly, so conscientious—so innocent!*

"*Yes, I must act. I knew that my time was short—and for that I was glad. For the worst part of murder, Hastings, is its effect on the murderer. I, Hercule Poirot, might come to believe myself divinely appointed to deal out death to all and sundry . . . But mercifully there would not be time for that to happen. The end would come soon. And I was afraid that Norton might succeed with someone who was unutterably dear to both of us. I am talking of your daughter. . . .*

"*And now we come to the death of Barbara Franklin. Whatever your ideas may be on the subject, Hastings, I do not think you have once suspected the truth.*

"*For you see, Hastings, you killed Barbara Franklin.*

"Mais oui, *you did!*

"*There was, you see, yet another angle to the triangle. One that I did not fully take into account. As it happened, Norton's tactics there were unseen and unheard by either of us. But I have no doubt that he employed them. . . .*

"*Did it ever enter your mind to wonder, Hastings, why Mrs. Franklin was willing to come to Styles? It is not, when you think of it, at all her line of country. She likes comfort, good food and above all social contacts. Styles is not gay; it is not well-run; it is in the dead country. And yet it was Mrs. Franklin who insisted on spending the summer there.*

"*Yes, there was a third angle. Boyd Carrington. Mrs. Franklin was a disappointed woman. That was at the root of her neurotic illness. She was ambitious both socially and financially. She married Franklin because she expected him to have a brilliant career.*

"*He was brilliant but not in her way. His brilliance would never bring him newspaper notoriety, or a Harley Street reputation. He would be known to half a dozen men of his own profession and would publish articles in learned journals. The outside world would not hear of him—and he would certainly not make money.*

"*And here is Boyd Carrington—home from the East—just come into a baronetcy and money, and Boyd Carrington has always felt tenderly sentimental towards the pretty seventeen-year-old girl he nearly asked to marry him. He is going to Styles, he suggests the Franklins come too—and Barbara comes.*

"How maddening it is for her! Obviously she has lost none of her old charm for this rich attractive man, but he is old-fashioned—not the type of man to suggest divorce. And John Franklin, too, has no use for divorce. If John Franklin were to die, then she could be Lady Boyd Carrington—and oh what a wonderful life that would be!

"Norton, I think, found her only too ready a tool.

"It was all too obvious, Hastings, when you come to think of it. Those first few tentative attempts at establishing how fond she was of her husband. She overdid it a little—murmuring about 'ending it all' because she was a drag on him.

"And then an entirely new line. Her fears that Franklin might experiment upon himself.

"It ought to have been so obvious to us, Hastings! She was preparing us for John Franklin to die of physostigmine poisoning. No question, you see, of anyone trying to poison him—oh no—just pure scientific research. He takes the harmless alkaloid, and it turns out to be harmful after all.

"The only thing was it was a little too swift. You told me that she was not pleased to find Boyd Carrington having his fortune told by Nurse Craven. Nurse Craven was an attractive young woman with a keen eye for men. She had had a try at Dr. Franklin and had not met with success. (Hence her dislike for Judith.) She is carrying on with Allerton, but she knows quite well he is not serious. Inevitable that she should cast her eye on the rich and still attractive Sir William—and Sir William was, perhaps, only too ready to be attracted. He had already noticed Nurse Craven as a healthy, good-looking girl.

"Barbara Franklin has a fright and decides to act quickly. The sooner she is a pathetic, charming and not inconsolable widow the better.

"And so, after a morning of nerves, she sets the scene.

"Do you know, mon ami, I have some respect for the Calabar bean. This time, you see, it worked. It spared the innocent and slew the guilty.

"Mrs. Franklin asks you all up to her room. She makes coffee with much fuss and display. As you tell me, her own coffee is beside her, her husband's on the other side of the bookcase-table.

"And then there are the shooting stars and everyone goes out and only you, my friend, are left, you and your crossword puzzle and your memories—and to hide emotion you swing round the bookcase to find a quotation in Shakespeare.

"And so they come back and Mrs. Franklin drinks the coffee full of the Calabar bean alkaloids that were meant for dear scientific John, and John Franklin drinks the nice plain cup of coffee that was meant for clever Mrs. Franklin.

"But you will see, Hastings, if you think a minute, that although I realized what had happened, I saw that there was only one thing to be done. I could not prove what had happened. And if Mrs. Franklin's death was thought to be anything but suicide suspicion would inevitably fall on either Franklin or Judith. On two people who were utterly and completely innocent. So I did what I had a perfect right to do, laid stress on and put conviction into, my repetition of Mrs. Franklin's extremely unconvincing remarks on the subject of putting an end to herself.

"I could do it—and I was probably the only person who could. For you see my statement carried weight. I am a man experienced in the matter of committing murder—if I am convinced it is suicide, well, then, it will be accepted as suicide.

"It puzzled you, I could see, and you were not pleased. But mercifully you did not suspect the true danger.

"But will you think of it after I am gone? Will it come into your mind, lying there like some dark serpent that now and then raises its head and says: 'Suppose Judith . . . ?'

"It may do. And therefore I am writing this. You must know the truth.

"There was one person whom the verdict of suicide did not satisfy. Norton. He was balked, you see, of his pound of flesh. As I say, he is a sadist. He wants the whole gamut of emotion, suspicion, fear, the coils of the law. He was deprived of all that. The murder he had arranged had gone awry.

"But presently he saw what one may call a way of recouping himself. He began to throw out hints. Earlier on he had pretended to see something through his glasses. Actually he intended to convey the exact impression that he did convey—namely that he saw Allerton and Judith in some compromising attitude. But not having said anything definite, he could use that incident in a different way.

"Supposing, for instance, that he says he saw Franklin and Judith. That will open up an interesting new angle of the suicide case! It may, perhaps, throw doubts on whether it was suicide. . . .

"So, mon ami, I decided that what had to be done must be done at once. I arranged that you should bring him to my room that night. . . .

"I will tell you exactly what happened. Norton, no doubt, would have been delighted to tell me his arranged story. I gave him no time. I told him, clearly and definitely, all that I knew about him.

"He did not deny it. No, mon ami, he sat back in his chair and smirked. Mais oui, there is no other word for it, he smirked. He asked me what I thought I was going to do about this amusing idea of mine. I told him that I proposed to execute him.

" 'Ah,' he said, 'I see. The dagger or the cup of poison?'

"We were about to have chocolate together at the time. He has a sweet tooth, M. Norton.

" 'The simplest,' I said, 'would be the cup of poison.'

"And I handed him the cup of chocolate I had just poured out.

" 'In that case,' he said, 'would you mind my drinking from your cup instead of from mine?'

"I said, 'Not at all.' In effect, it was quite immaterial. As I have said, I, too, take the sleeping tablets. The only thing is that since I have been taking them every night for a considerable period, I have acquired a certain tolerance, and a dose that would send M. Norton to sleep would have very little effect upon me. The dose was in the chocolate itself. We both had the same. His portion took effect in due course, mine had little effect upon me, especially when counteracted with a dose of my strychnine tonic.

"And so to the last chapter. When Norton was asleep I got him into my wheeled chair—fairly easy, it has many types of mechanism—and wheeled him back in it to its usual place in the window embrasure behind the curtains.

"Curtiss then 'put me to bed.' When everything was quiet I wheeled Norton to his room. It remained, then, to avail myself of the eyes and ears of my excellent friend Hastings.

"You may not have realized it, but I wear a wig, Hastings. You will realize even less that I wear a false moustache. (Even George does not know that!) I pretended *to burn it by accident soon after Curtiss came, and at once had my hairdresser make me a replica.*

"*I put on Norton's dressing gown, ruffled up my grey hair on end, and came down the passage and rapped on your door. Presently you came and looked with sleepy eyes into the passage. You saw Norton leave the bathroom and limp across the passage into his own room. You heard him turn the key in the lock on the inside.*

"*I then replaced the dressing gown on Norton, laid him on his bed, and shot him with a small pistol that I acquired abroad and which I have kept carefully locked up except for two occasions when (nobody being about) I have put it ostentatiously on Norton's dressing table, he himself being well away somewhere that morning.*

"*Then I left the room after putting the key in Norton's pocket. I myself locked the door from the outside with the duplicate key which I have possessed for some time. I wheeled the chair back to my room.*

"*Since then I have been writing this explanation.*

"*I am very tired—and the exertions I have been through have strained me a good deal. It will not, I think, be long before. . . .*

"*There are one or two things I would like to stress.*

"*Norton's were the perfect crimes.*

"*Mine was not. It was not intended to be.*

"*The easiest way and the best way for me to have killed him was to have done so quite openly—to have had, shall we say, an accident with my little pistol. I should have professed dismay, regret—a most unfortunate accident. They would have said, 'Old ga ga, didn't realize it was loaded—ce pauvre vieux.'*

"*I did not choose to do that.*

"*I will tell you why.*

"*It is because, Hastings, I chose to be 'sporting.'*

"*Mais oui, sporting! I am doing all the things that so often you have reproached me with not doing. I am playing fair with you. I am giving you a run for your money. I am playing the game. You have every chance to discover the truth.*

"*In case you disbelieve me let me enumerate all the clues.*

"*The keys.*

"*You know, for I have told you so, that Norton arrived here after I did. You know, for you have been told, that I changed my room after I got here. You know,* for again it has been told to you, *that since I have been at Styles the key of my room disappeared and I had another made.*

"*Therefore when you ask yourself who could have killed Norton? Who could have shot and still have left the room (apparently) locked on the inside since the key is in Norton's pocket?*—

"*The answer is 'Hercule Poirot, who since he has been here has possessed duplicate keys of one of the rooms.'*

"*The man you saw in the passage.*

"*I myself asked you if you were sure the man you saw in the passage was Norton. You were startled. You asked me if I intended to suggest it was* not *Norton. I replied, truthfully, that I did not at all intend to suggest it was not Norton. (Naturally, since I had taken a good deal of trouble to suggest it* was *Norton.) I then brought up the question of height. All the men, I said, were much taller than Norton. But there was a man who was shorter than Norton—Hercule Poirot. And it is comparatively easy with raised heels or elevators in the shoes to add to one's height.*

"*You were under the impression that I was a helpless invalid. But why? Only because I said so. And I had sent away George. That was my last indication to you, 'Go and talk to George.'*

"*Othello and Clutie John show you that X was Norton.*

"*Then who could have killed Norton?*

"*Only Hercule Poirot.*

"*And once you suspected that, everything would have fallen into place, the things I had said and done, my inexplicable reticence. Evidence from the doctors in Egypt, from my own doctor in London, that I was not incapable of walking about. The evidence of George as to my wearing a wig. The fact which I was unable to disguise, and which you ought to have noticed, that I limp much more than Norton does.*

"*And last of all, the pistol shot. My one weakness. I should, I am aware, have shot him through the temple. I could not bring myself to produce an effect so lopsided, so haphazard. No, I shot him symmetrically, in the exact centre of the forehead. . . .*

"*Oh, Hastings, Hastings, that* should *have told you the truth.*

"*But perhaps, after all, you* have *suspected the truth? Perhaps when you read this, you already* know.

"*But somehow I do not think so. . . .*

"No, you are too trusting. . . .

"You have too beautiful a nature. . . .

"What shall I say more to you? Both Franklin and Judith, I think you will find, knew the truth although they will not have told it to you. They will be happy together, those two. They will be poor and innumerable tropical insects will bite them and strange fevers will attack them—but we all have our own ideas of the perfect life, have we not?

"And you, my poor lonely Hastings? Ah, my heart bleeds for you, dear friend. Will you, for the last time, take the advice of your old Poirot?

"After you have read this, take a train or a car or a series of buses and go to find Elizabeth Cole who is also Elizabeth Litchfield. Let her read this, or tell her what is in it. Tell her that you, too, might have done what her sister Margaret did—only for Margaret Litchfield there was no watchful Poirot at hand. Take the nightmare away from her, show her that her father was killed, not by his daughter, but by that kind sympathetic family friend, that 'honest Iago' Stephen Norton.

"For it is not right, my friend, that a woman like that, still young, still attractive, should refuse life because she believes herself to be tainted. No, it is not right. Tell her so, you, my friend, who are yourself still not unattractive to women. . . .

"Eh bien, I have no more now to say. I do not know, Hastings, if what I have done is justified or not justified. No—I do not know. I do not believe that a man should take the law into his own hands. . . .

"But on the other hand, I am the law! As a young man in the Belgian police force I shot down a desperate criminal who sat on a roof and fired at people below. In a state of emergency martial law is proclaimed.

"By taking Norton's life, I have saved other lives—innocent lives. But still I do not know . . . It is perhaps right that I should not know. I have always been so sure—too sure. . . .

"But now I am very humble and I say like a little child 'I do not know . . .'

"Good-bye, cher ami. I have moved the amyl nitrate ampoules away from beside my bed. I prefer to leave myself in the hands of the bon Dieu. May his punishment, or his mercy, be swift!

"We shall not hunt together again, my friend. Our first hunt was here—and our last. . . .

"They were good days.

"Yes, they have been good days. . . ."

(End of Hercule Poirot's manuscript.)

Final note by Captain Arthur Hastings: I have finished reading . . . cannot believe it all yet . . . But he is right. I should have known. I should have known when I saw the bullet hole so symmetrically in the middle of the forehead.

Queer—it's just come to me—the thought in the back of my mind that morning.

The mark on Norton's forehead—it was like the brand of Cain. . . .